BLOOD SUN IN JERUSALEM

BLOOD SUN
IN
JERUSALEM

A Historical Novel by

HerBert G. Wittels

An Exposition-Banner Book

Exposition Press   *Smithtown, New York*

First Edition

©1984 by Herbert G. Wittels

Herbert G. Wittels
RD 9, Box 315
Hopewell Jct., NY 12533

Library of Congress Catalog Card Number: 84-90322

ISBN 0-682-40180-3

Printed in the United States of America

Dedicated

to the memory of all the thousands who suffered and died during this epochal period of history; to all those millions still embroiled in the conflicts of the area today; to all the individuals who helped me do the research and were constructively critical—with special thanks to the late Dr. Samuel Moses, professor of English, University of Hartford, for his unflagging aid and encouragement; and a special dedication to Beatrice, my wife, who endured all the pains of my writing and bore the burden of the editing to the last page

Some Thoughts and a Disclaimer

When the idea for this work germinated I felt that I had to find and incorporate each detail of the period involved. Soon I became painfully aware that the job was impossible. One inquiry led only to another, then a third, and so on. To search did not necessarily mean to find, and to find did not necessarily mean to be completely informed. Like the pot at the end of the rainbow, the gold eluded me.

I decided, therefore, to shrink my vista and use that which I could find. At least that way I could begin to write.

In a perfect (sic!) sense this is not a historical novel as much as it is a story built around a period of great historical significance. The historical characters are kept as close to fact as possible—even to the words history records they uttered—while other characters have been contrived by my imagination.

This is not an academic, scholarly work but one where research was done and embroidered. The source material is available to everyone who seeks it, but I have placed my own interpretation and subjective judgments upon it. Therefore, this "history" is my attempt to portray the human condition as I saw it as I read. I have attempted to keep the "facts" as I found them, highlighting the foibles, frustrations, human qualities, morals, dreams and contradictions, and value judgments.

History students may take some small comfort that the basic events are as correct as I could make them.

Herbert G. Wittels

Main Characters of Historical Record

From the Church:
    Emperor Alexius: First Apostle of God; of Byzantium
    Pope Clement III: chosen by Emperor Henry IV of Germany
    Pope Urban II: chosen at the Synod at Cluny
    Abbot Hugh of Cluny Abbey
    Bishop Adhemar of Monteil: vassal of Count Raymond

The Knights:
    Lord Baldwin: younger brother of Duke Godfrey
    Lord Bohemund of Taranto
    Count Eustace of Bologna: older brother of Godfrey
    Duke Godfrey of Lorraine
    Count Hugh of Vermandois: younger brother of King Philip
    Count Raymond of Toulouse: St. Gillis
    Count Robert of Flanders
    Duke Robert of Normandy
    Lord Tancred of Apulia: Bohemund's nephew

The Byzantine Nobles:
    Admiral Butumites: First Admiral of the Byzantine Navy
    Baron John Ducas: brother-in-law of Emperor Alexius
    General Phoacus: Byzantine Army
    General Taticius: Engineer of Bombardment

The Pilgrims:
    Peter Bartholomew: a serf with visions
    Geoffrey Burel: a pilgrim soldier
    Sir Walter Gautier (Walter the Penniless): a vagrant knight
    Peter the Hermit: a visionary itinerant monk
    Tafur: a ribald from Paris

The Moslems:
    Kilij Arslan (the Red Lion): a Seljuk prince
    Firouz: the Moslem traitor in Antioch
    Iftikhar ad-Daulah: Egyptian commander of Jerusalem

Captain Ilkhan: of Arslan's army
Kerbogha, the Terrible: Moslem emir who attacks at Antioch
Yaghi Siyan: Moslem commander of Antioch

ROUTES of the CRUSADE

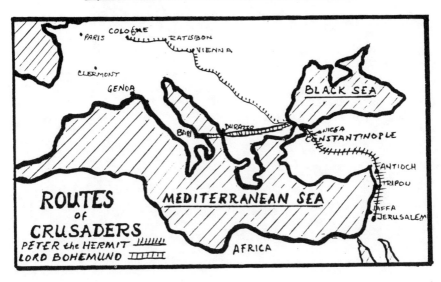

PARIS • COLOGNE RATISBON VIENNA CLERMONT GENOA BLACK SEA BARI DURAZZO NICEA CONSTANTINOPLE MEDITERRANEAN SEA ANTIOCH TRIPOLI JAFFA JERUSALEM AFRICA

ROUTES of CRUSADERS
PETER the HERMIT
LORD BOHEMUND

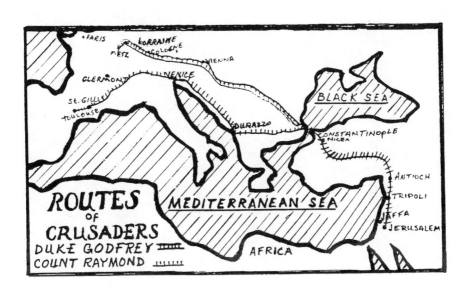

PARIS LORRAINE METZ COLOGNE VIENNA CLERMONT VENICE ST. GILLES TOULOUSE DURAZZO BLACK SEA CONSTANTINOPLE NICEA ANTIOCH TRIPOLI JAFFA JERUSALEM MEDITERRANEAN SEA AFRICA

ROUTES of CRUSADERS
DUKE GODFREY
COUNT RAYMOND

Prelude, Prologue, and Preface

A RECOUNTING OF PRIOR EVENTS
SPECIAL FOR HISTORY BUFFS

It was December, in the year of Our Lord, 1088, and there were three popes in the Catholic Church. Two vied for power in Europe while the third, who called himself Emperor of the Romans and the First Chosen of God, sat in Constantinople and ruled the Greek Church of Byzantium and the Byzantium Empire.

In Europe, King Henry IV of the Germanic States, an elected king, was determined to consummate his authority and make himself emperor over a resurrected Holy Roman Empire. To accomplish this he felt he had to be crowned by the pope, as had Charlemagne, and he marched on Rome and ousted Pope Gregory, an old enemy who had excommunicated him, driving the pope into exile and death. He then convoked a special synod of his own appointed bishops and picked his own pope—Clement III—who dutifully placed Charlemagne's crown on his head.

The great Cluny Abbey in France would not stand for this and subsequently elected its own pope—Urban II. The abbey was the strongest church in Europe, with threads reaching all the principalities, and it was soon locked in a fierce struggle against Henry.

Charlemagne the Great, after his coronation in A.D. 800, had taken unto himself the power to appoint clerics, and the kings of Europe had followed suit ever since, expanding and enlarging the practice enormously. Henry, always needing money, sold bishoprics and other clerical positions for gold. The higher prelates held fiefdoms, controlled land which they bought and sold, controlled serfs and peasants, and had special taxing privileges. They were the vassals of the king and subject to his commands, and they became sovereigns in their own right, living openly in sinful marriages and buying church positions for their children.

The sale of bishoprics—lay investiture—diluted the control the church prelates exercised, and the rivalry between the kings' clerics and those appointed by the churchmen became a war for power and gold as well as religious doctrine.

Clement III, requiring money, offered to sell the Lateran, the traditional home of the pope, to Cluny, and Pope Urban purchased it and moved into Rome.

Proud and autocratic Rome. Once the Queen City of the world and declaimer of the fate of nations and men; conqueror, builder, and ruler of man's universe; destroyed by the barbarian hordes, rebuilt and then conquered again by the Christian martyrs it had thrown to the lions for amusement; the city lay like a drunken sot in filth and ruins.

The nobles raged their wars and feuds in a sporting fashion, and the battles moved from hill to hill in rotation. More mercenaries would be hired each time the fighting flared, and the lords were not too fussy how the men were procured. Impressment gangs roamed the countryside, picking up able-bodied men and boys and selling them to the highest bidder.

Beggars infested the alleys and plied their trade in the squares under the shadows of the dirt-streaked marble of the palace walls. Garbage was piled against the buildings, the rats running bold, and the flies swarming like a black flowing mesh over the feculence.

Thieves haunted the damp cellars of the old Forum, drinking watered wine, shooting craps, and quarreling among themselves. Here and there, old, haggard females, with wild, dirty hair and misshapen bodies, huddled in their ragged dresses or danced a drunken song for the price of a copper. For a few pennies they would strip and jiggle.

The killers were the army deserters who had pawned their last piece of loot and were seeking wine money. They worked eagerly and cheaply, as competition was fierce, and they sneered at the beggars.

Nunneries were whore infested, and enough coppers in the hands of the Mother Superiors would open any nun's door for any man—or woman. Prostitutes crowded the inns or walked the streets complaining about the nuns, flaunting their youth (for they started when they were ten), and pandering for the boys in the taverns for an extra copper. Brother-sister teams could be hired by the hour or day, and they worked with the specially trained animals in the ''barns'' in the narrow, back alleys, the delight of many voyeurs and participants.

The priests sold ecclesiastical rights to any bidder; the merchants and peddlers sold shoddy goods for the highest prices; the artisans—carpenters, masons, bootmakers, tanners, weavers—lived on the edge of poverty and starvation, eking out a miserable existence and fighting one another for crumbs.

Standing guard at the Lateran were Urban's men, grim-faced and seemingly impervious to the vermin and putrescence oozing around them, the armed priests, determined to keep the pope's home uncontaminated; and they were failing.

Rome was an open sewer, a degraded abomination, and its squalor was flowing over the countryside, defiling everything it touched. The city sank in decadence and decay; and no one cared.

Five years had passed since Urban had become pope, and the Christmas of the year 1093 was one of weeping, spilling into the new year. In Constantinople, the third pope, Alexius Comnenus, Beloved of Jesus, Basileus, First Apostle of God, Emperor of all Byzantium, sat solitary—huddled morosely in his chair.

He was a small man, and he pulled his azure mantle close, wrapping it about his thin shoulders to keep out the January chill. It had rained that afternoon, and the wind coming off the Marmora Sea had an edge. Through the clearing clouds were the outlines of the far gray hills of Asia, silhouetted against the sky. The setting sun had touched the waters with fiery fingers, and the spray of the breaking waves were dancing sparks, flickering for a moment with life, then diving to death in the pink, choppy water.

He stirred impatiently, for it was growing late and he was expecting someone. He brooded over his empire. At one time it had reached from Gibraltar's Gate to the dense forests of the Caucasus. Now, the diamond cities of Antioch and Alexandria were gone, swept away by the Moslem hordes. Only the stonebare hills of Greece remained—and Athens.

In the north, the Scythians and other barbarians had seized beautiful Adrianople and roamed its countryside with no one to stop them. Byzantium had become a withdrawn, self-centered, old woman still holding, with her girdle strings, the southern coastline of the Black Sea, the Straits, and the inner Sea of Marmora. The rich city of Smyrna was still under her mantle, but Byzantium was a widow. The Seljuk Turk—wild and filled with the religious fanaticism of the newly converted Mohammedan—had sheared off Nicea, not more than a day's ride to the Bosporus.

He remembered grimly how hard he had fought as a general of the army to hold the empire together. Becoming emperor he had stopped at nothing. By guile, by trickery, by gold, by flattery, by fraud, by brutality, by corruption, stooping to anything, be it perjury, betrayal, intrigue, poison, or the cold steel of the assassin's knife—it was all calculated to mold and shape his power, to confound his enemies, and to save his throne.

He shifted uncomfortably in his seat. His eunuch guard pounded twice on the marble floor, heralding the arrival of two men. They strode rapidly toward him and bowed ceremoniously.

"You are late, John," murmured the emperor to the older man.

"I had to await your amanuensis. He had difficulty transcribing your exact meaning. We embark for Genoa at dawn," said his brother-in-law.

Alexius nodded. "Do you think it will be enough?"

The diplomat shrugged. "We have had promises before and we can but ask again. As always, I am optimistic. We will reach out to Urban and the tidings may be good this time. He will listen."

"He has troubles enough of his own." Alexius was moody. "We will pray for you. A favorable wind, and may the Spirit of Jesus protect and aid you. Good-bye, John; good-bye, captain." He nodded to the younger man.

The men bowed and withdrew.

Alexius sighed. It was the hour of the candles, and his personal servants would be waiting impatiently in his chambers, for the hour to darkness was running short. Already the sun had set, leaving a bloody sky. He wondered. Was it an omen?

They dressed him in his new, white robe and fastened his girdle; they fussed over the fall of his golden mantle and the curl of its ruffle; and at last he was ready. Alexius the Emperor had become Alexius, First Father of the Order of St. Basil, Basileus; First Vicar of the Apostles, Pope.

He entered the Sancta Sophia, the most beautiful church in all Byzantium, and was ushered to his high throne by the bearded priests, bowing in syco-phantic reverence. A thousand candles burned as sparkling jewels in the dark-ened areas, and incense poured from the hanging censers, rising like a heavy, gray mist, gyrating in the upper air currents. The haze obscured the red mot-tling of the polished marble columns, and it billowed like a massive, flowing curtain in the gentle breezes around the columns' white capitals.

He lifted his eyes, barely seeing the stylized figures of the Apostles in the mosaic, and his eyes clouded for he began to believe he could distinguish the gesticulating apparitions of his predecessors. He averted his eyes quickly as the low chant of the priests reverberated from the great dome and permeated his inner being.

"*Kyrie eleison miserere Domino . . . kyrie eleison . . .*"

His head bowed slowly, his eyes closed, and his thoughts became unsub-stanial and vague; his mind dulled into oblivion.

"*Washed in the Blood of the Lamb . . . Beloved Son . . .*"

His spirit wavered before his inner eye, turning a reddish blur as a slowly sinking inner sun poured blood-red light over his darkened, shrinking soul.

"*Kyrie eleison . . . eleison . . .*"

It was late January, in the year of Our Lord, 1094, and Urban II was struggling with the anti-pope, Clement III.

The Faithful were being torn between the conflicts of the two popes, and the Faith was being shattered. Urban fretted as it wrung his soul, and he closeted himself with Abbot Hugh, his mentor at Cluny.

"We are losing our Lambs to the heresies," he cried bitterly. "Demonology is flourishing again. The lesser lords are ready for peace, but they need a rallying point; the burghers are sick of the constant warfare which destroys their trade and commerce; the peasants are bewildered and frightened. They starve and they resort to murder and looting to remain alive. The Truce of God does not maintain the peace and we must find something new. But what? Each day I pray for the Lord to enlighten me."

"Urban, listen to me," said Hugh. "The two parts of the Mother Church must be united into one body, and the disease which Clement has brought must be cauterized. There is no other way."

"It is Emperor Henry who gives Clement his strength. It is his ability to appoint bishops which divides the Church. We must deal with Henry, and the other kings who follow his example," said Urban.

"He should be forced to stand barefoot and undressed in the snows of Canossa, just as he did once before, for Gregory. There are those of us who believe Father Gregory, may his soul rest in peace, was wrong to forgive him so lightly last time."

"He is too strong for that now." Urban shook his head and added grimly, "I intend to excommunicate him again, but I believe it will have more form than substance. His vassals will not leave him this time."

There was silence between them and Urban began to think aloud. "The lesser lords fight each other . . . for land and serfs, for power, for food . . . one takes from the other, hoping, meanwhile, to protect what he owns. They all squeeze taxes out of the poor. The barons and kings fight for wealth— and power—to control more wealth . . . and they sell bishoprics for the money to fight for more wealth. The Church cannot dissuade them from this—and it certainly cannot bless them. We must divert them . . . show them a new source to be exploited, steer them away from the Church body less they chew and shred her, and then control her remains." He sighed. "Another source? We must find one."

Hugh leaned forward. "You must not fail, Urban. First, there is Henry; then there will be Philip in France; and William of England is not far behind. They will all make the Church a golden cow, milking her for their personal grandeur and ambitions. You cannot fail."

"You are right, my friend." Urban nodded his head in agreement. "First Henry, then Philip, then William. Let us pray."

He met that month with his Council of Advisors, and they listened to his plans, his doubts, and his questions. Some did not agree with his plans to excommunicate Henry, urging caution.

"We deepen the schism by this. Let us wait."

"If we wait he expands his power. So does Philip, in his adultery. Some of his vassals will help us now."

"We have heard that before." There was ironic laughter.

"Can we depend on Norman Italy and Lower France?"

"To what use? They will stay home to fight their own wars."

Urban listened and fretted. Brushing all disputations aside, he told them, "The Synod will meet in the spring at Piacenza at Bobbio. The date and time will be forthcoming." Then he sent them home.

Henry had more spears, but God, Urban was sure, was on his side.

BLOOD SUN IN JERUSALEM

1

It was late in the morning, and the sky, with its heavy, dark-gray clouds, cast a dreary, gun-metal sheen on the water near the harbor. Two young boys stood near a large stone of the jetty, idly tossing pebbles into the murkish water and watching the strange ship riding at anchor.

"It's a Dromond. Look at the length of those oars," said Leo, the older boy. He was dark skinned, with a thin, long face, dark hair, intense eyes, and a thin-lipped mouth.

"A Dromond?" questioned his companion. "I never heard of a ship like that." There was doubt in his voice.

Leo shook his head. "Comes from the East, Con . . . Constan . . . tinople," he finished triumphantly. "See that high dragon head on the prow and the square sail? That's a Dromond all right. A warship, too. And fast. I wonder what it's doing here."

"Where'd you ever hear about a ship like that?" Pietro was still dubious. He had heard Leo's boastful lies before.

"From my papa, and I listen a lot to the sailors at the inn."

"How'd your papa know? He's no sailor." Pietro was unconvinced.

"No, but he's been all over. He says that once—years ago—maybe ten, maybe more, some of those ships came here to help us fight the Normans. He says that those dragon heads spit out real fire and burn up any ship that comes near them. It's Devil's fire and water can't put it out."

Pietro laughed. "Water puts out any fire."

"Not Devil's fire," Leo insisted. "That fire comes straight from Hell. The Devil carries it around with him all the time, and he uses it on the souls he catches. It laughs at water because water can't put it out."

Pietro sniggered, unimpressed. "Only devils carry Devil's fire. If it burns everything, why doesn't it burn the dragon head? Answer me that!" he challenged.

"They've got ways." Leo was mysterious. "That fire shoots out like lightning, my papa says. It's like the fire in the mountain after an explosion. It burned my papa's arm. You've seen it."

Pietro had, and belief began to gnaw at him. "If they're devils, let's go." Fear made him uneasy.

"They're Christians," Leo placated him. "They pray to Our Lord Jesus, but they have strange ways." His knowledge made him important. "My papa used to fight for them. They're rich—richer even than Count Fienzo."

1

"That's plenty rich." Pietro was finally impressed.

"They have silk coats with gold threads," Leo went on. "And they wear gold shoes during the day and silver ones at night. They even put gold on the roofs of their houses and rubies and diamonds in the walls. They eat on gold plates, with silver spoons, and they have thick rugs, higher than grass."

This was too much for Pietro. "You're making that all up," he protested. "Only the duke is that rich . . . and maybe the bishop."

"It's all true. You just wait and see when they come ashore. Their armor will flash like silver, and their sword scabbards will have rubies and diamonds, just like my papa's. You'll see."

A dray, pulled by a lame horse, was rumbling over the cobbled street toward them. Leo recognized the square-set, muscular, old man in the driver's seat. The cart carried barrels of wine.

"You there . . . you . . ." The man pointed to Leo with a whip. "You're Cannelli's boy? From the Good Sailor's Inn?"

Leo's head bobbed. "Yes, Mr. Toon."

"You know me?" There was suspicion in the voice.

"Of course," Leo shrugged. "You and Michael deliver the wine."

"Oh . . ." The man pinched his nose at the obvious. "Tell your papa I'll be late with the delivery. The mare dropped a shoe. You remember all that?"

"Sure, Mr. Toon. I'll tell him."

"Good. It'll be a while before I'll come by." He slapped the croup of the horse with the whip and the dray moved on.

"They're coming ashore!" Pietro called excitedly. "Look!"

A boat had left the ship's side and was moving toward the quay. Two men sat in the rear. They wore long, deep-blue coats, with white fur running down the front and around their wide collars. Their headcap lappets had pearls hanging in small circlets on either side. And they sat beneath a broad, white canopy.

Sitting in front of them were two men with bright steel, conical helms, which were topped with stringy plumes hanging downward in graceful sweeps. Their long, blond hair was free and loose under the helm and fell in waves over their shoulders. Thin, blond whiskers drooped on either side of their clean-shaven chins, and the hair swung freely each time they moved their heads. Their chests were encased in shirts of ring-mail, and the steel sparkled like mirrors when it caught the sun. They were two yellow-haired giants from the North, and two others like them were seated in the rear of the boat.

Four oarsmen rowed, keeping firm, steady strokes to the beat of a coxswain drum at the bow, and the sailors knew their work, for the long boat skimmed smoothly over the choppy waters. These were no ordinary travelers.

As the boat neared, the boys could see a row of emeralds sewn along the front of the older gentleman's coat and the three rings, with huge stones, on his hand resting easily on a walking stick.

"Look at those rings," whispered Pietro. "Did you ever see any so big? Even the king can't have anything like that."

"I told you," said Leo smugly.

The boat docked and two of the sailors jumped to the pier, holding the craft fast. The soldiers came out first, then helped the two gentlemen climb out. Leo whistled. These soldiers were giants, bigger than his father, and despite their size they were lithe and agile. He wondered if he could outrun them.

The older gentleman noticed the boys and said something to the tallest of the giants, who glanced their way and started toward them. They turned and fled.

"Boy!" boomed the deep, basso of the soldier. "Be not afraid! We only seek directions!" The words rumbled from his huge chest.

Leo stopped and looked back; Pietro disappeared down an alley.

The giant advanced slowly. "Do you know the way to the Good Sailor's Inn?" There was no language accent.

On Leo's nod, he asked, "Can you lead me there?"

Leo nodded again. His mind turned rapidly. "I . . . I will show you . . . "—he looked at the gentlemen— ". . . for five coppers."

The eyes of the blond giant opened in surprise, then his head snapped back in a loud guffaw. "Five coppers? Spoken like a true Genoan! Everything has a price! I should have remembered!"

He is not from Genoa, Leo told himself. His ear was fine tuned to different languages; he had heard travelers and seamen from far places at the inn, and the big soldiers were Vikings, either Normans or Celts, the highest-paid mercenaries in the world.

"All right, boy; five coppers it is. But mark . . ." the Viking's face grew stern and his hand stiffened on his sword. "No back alleys and a straight road. Otherwise . . ." he showed his teeth and drew his left thumb across his throat with a quick motion while his lips sputtered with a finality which left no avenue of misunderstanding. His eyes were hard.

Leo suppressed a shiver. "It isn't far." The soldier's face was ferocious. Pietro was gone and he was all alone; and he wondered if he had been too clever, asking for money, but when he glanced at the man again, he was relieved to see the soldier smiling. His courage returned. "You will pay me first?" he asked timidly.

The Viking, surprised, raised an eyebrow. "I pay when we arrive."

"When we get there you will forget," Leo demurred. "It is better you pay me first. Then I won't have to bother you."

The soldier chuckled. "Your father must be a trader. All right, come with me."

They walked back to the waiting group, and the Viking, with laughter, explained in a strange language what had occurred. All the men laughed. The Viking gave an order and another soldier went to the boat and came back with a rope. The Viking held out a coin. "Your pay as a guide, so lead true."

Leo sucked in his breath. Silver! He had only asked for five coppers. Never had he been given silver. He took it carefully, turning it over in his hand and fondling it. He was so enthralled by his good fortune he hardly felt the rope encircling his waist.

"All right, boy, lead on." The giant held the other end of the rope in his huge hand. "And no tricks," he said grimly.

With his eyes starry, the coin grasped firmly in his fist, Leo set out for his father's inn. The big soldier walked at his side, the rope dangling between them. A single soldier followed, then the two smiling gentlemen, then the other two tall soldiers as a rear guard.

The inn was an old building of solid stone, two stories high, with a frontage on the street facing a dip in the harbor. Its outer, weather-beaten walls were gray-black and salt-encrusted, and the stones of the inner courtyard were grimed and dirty. A roofed balustrade ran completely around the second story and provided an open-air hallway for the entrances of the many rooms. Despite its decrepit appearance, it was the center for many gay parties, with wining, dining, and whoring being the chief activities inside its begrimed walls.

Most of its trade came from the harbor. Sailors, and others who used the sea for travel, rented its rooms. Passengers awaiting the arrival or departure of their ships would beguile their lonely hours with the host's entertainment. Some of the lower citizenry would drop in once in a while, but the host quickly discouraged their stay. But the visits of the young gentlemen, the lesser noblemen of the city, were welcomed, and they were provided ample company for the evening. Special private rooms upstairs were kept for their incognito visits.

Favio Cannelli, a large man with a sagging stomach, stood in the kitchen doorway and surveyed the littered courtyard with a scowl on his face. He squinted at the rain clouds and frowned.

"Infernal rain," he muttered and spat. "Where's old man Toon?" he asked himself in disgust. He noticed the droppings of a horse and grimaced. Turning inside he yelled, "Maria! Where's Leo? The yard is full of dung." He watched some chickens' desultory peckings at the manure. "Maria! The yard needs cleaning!"

"Get Nicholas," came back. "You pay him good money."

"Get Nicholas . . ." He imitated his wife's high-pitched voice. "That's all you say when I want Leo."

"Get Nicholas. Leo isn't here."

"Nicholas has only two hands and one ass," he yelled back. "He's grooming the horses. Leo's old enough . . . and strong enough to help. You make a woman out of him." He spat in disgust.

He knew his wife wasn't listening, and if she did hear him at all, his arguments would have no effect. He was simply venting his spleen in an ongoing, useless debate.

A short, squat, rotund woman, her dark hair curled into a bun and pinned to the top of her head, came out of the inn. She was carrying a basket of broken bread in the crook of her arm, and she glanced about the yard with a critical eye.

"Nicholas should have slopped the yard early this morning," she said with finality. "The rain will make a mess of that." She pointed.

"Thank you for telling me," her husband retorted. "I would have never known."

She ignored his sarcasm and called the chickens, tossing the bread in a small arc.

"I haven't seen Leo in two days," Favio said. "Where is he?"

"I sent him to confession."

"What does he do that he has to confess so much? It's like every other day you send him to the priest. Does he consort with the Devil?"

"Bite your tongue. It wouldn't hurt if you went once in a while yourself. The priest asks for you."

"So let him ask. I ask for Leo and you send *me* to a priest. What is this with you? There is work around here for him."

"A young boy needs time for himself." She had said this many times, and it was an unwritten law in her arguments. "Do you want him to grow up looking like you? Mercy Mother of Jesus! You are like a pig! The priest says Leo has a good head, and maybe he can push him into a monastery, maybe even into the clergy. Who knows what could happen after that."

"And how much gold do you think I have, woman? It costs money every time you talk like that. We don't have it."

His wife parked herself in front of him and grasped the basket firmly in her hands. "You have more now than when you came here! Have you forgotten, Cannelli? You were a beggar! My father took pity on you." She spat.

"I was no beggar, woman," he retorted. "And your father was happy I agreed to marry you. So were you, if I remember right." The argument was old. "I was a soldier coming home. Was I supposed to be as rich as the count?"

"Rich? Huh! All you had was a sword, a few coppers, and a big mouth." She brushed the front of her dress.

"Big enough to close yours . . . like this!" He reached out suddenly and pinched her cheeks between his fingers, making her mouth pucker. Then, he kissed her.

"Paughhhh!" she sputtered. "Act your age."

She knew she had won the argument; she always did when it came to Leo, but she knew Favio was right. Leo troubled her. He had been a weak, sickly child despite all of her novenas and prayers to the Virgin Mother, and she continued to overprotect him as he grew older. He should be working more at the inn and acting more like a man. His peers were already moving in men's circles. He played with younger boys, like Pietro.

Maybe it was all her fault. It could be the Lord's punishment for her sins. No; she rejected the blame. Her father, on the demand of the younger brother of the count, had delivered her at age fourteen to the upper bedroom. The young gentleman had become interested when her father, in an odd moment, had boasted that his daughter was the only virgin on the premises, and Lord Eurde, half-drunk, had proclaimed that he would be the judge and verifier of that truth. He offered a toast to all virgins and to the men who deflowered them, then ordered the host to bring his daughter aloft for the testing.

The other lords cheered. Her father, suddenly realizing what he had started, tried to back away, but spurred on by his friends, the young lord was obdurate, and the innkeeper lapsed into silence when a dagger was placed at his throat.

The merriment continued for the week's end, and Maria was delivered three times to the bedroom of the lord. After each encounter he would stagger to the head of the balcony and announce that there were problems: she bled too much; he couldn't be sure he had penetrated deeply enough. Finally, after the third attempt, he proclaimed victory. His cheering friends argued over their bets and decided that payment toward the girl's dowry would be an act of kindness. She was so ugly, they said, it would be difficult to secure a husband, and they were glad to help.

Maria's father snatched the gold they offered. The public news of the breaking of her maidenhead would spread rapidly, and he began the search for a husband immediately. But the story outran him everywhere. Some suitors were attracted by the exaggerated tales of much gold; others whom he approached just laughed. Then Favio walked into the inn.

It took only a few minutes of conversation and the innkeeper knew he had his man. Negotiations began and after two days of carefree drinking and trading, an agreement was reached. Each, delighted with their arrangement, drank himself insensible, and Maria somehow managed to put both of them to bed. She was married the next week, a proper amount of time spent for her father to introduce his prospective son-in-law to his friends and patrons.

Favio had been told the story of his bride's nights and days with the young Eurde, and the drinkers of the inn alluded to it with leers, smirks, and winks. At first he dismissed it as "noisy chatter," but one man finally nettled him, and the jeerer's broken nose and misplaced teeth convinced the others that it was time to forget. Maria, however, discovered she was pregnant and trembled at the discovery. She told no one, except her confessor, and he died before the child was born.

To Maria, it became a lonely secret and her conscience was troubled. She cringed inwardly at any mention of Leo's dark skin and puny growth, for Eurde was dark and small. Favio could not understand how such a puny child could spring from his loins, but Maria's midwife would count off eight months from the marriage to the birth and informed him that it was only natural for Leo to be adversely affected by his premature entrance into the world. Leo, she advised with great authority, would have his full development later. And had not the Lord favored him by allowing him to live?

In time even Maria's doubts weakened. Who knew God's Will? Young girls change their bleeding time after their first encounters with men. Her midwife had told her so. Lord Eurde had had a difficult time with her; she had bled heavily. And her bleeding times had been irregular before the young lord had touched her. Her midwife repeated the reasons incessantly, and Maria was assured that Leo was Favio's son. What was most important, Favio believed her.

Maria became convinced that the Holy Virgin, to whom she made special novenas on her wedding night, had worked a miracle. Favio believed as he was told: it was due to his hot blood and virility on that night. The boy resembled no one, but he had a quick mind. To Maria, Mother Mary had interceded for her with the Lord, and Leo had become Favio's son. She was content.

Leo was ten years old when a monk in a black habit, his cowl over his head despite the heat, his face hidden in the shadowy folds of the cloth, came into the inn and seated himself in a dark corner. Lydia, Maria's scullery maid, bustled in with a pot of hot, soapy water and began her regular chore of swabbing and scouring the tables to remove the glutinous residues of the spills of the previous evening. She approached the monk's table without seeing him and splashed the water carelessly. When he moved, she gasped in consternation. "Forgive me, Father! I didn't see you!"

"Is your mistress here?" came from the recesses of the cowl.

He turned as he spoke, and she could see the emaciated, skull face, and the small, purply rash-scabs on his skin. She shuddered as she recognized the symptoms of the dreaded French disease, a common complaint of the sailors.

"She's busy in the kitchen, Father." She was frightened and sidled away.

"Please get her for me." It was a cold voice and flat.

"Yes, Father." She flew from the barroom.

Maria lumbered in, annoyed and disturbed. She had been busy and did not like the interruption. "Can I be of service, Brother?" She was brusque and had no awe of the cloak; a monk was not a priest.

He did not answer but turned so she could see his face. She gasped, her hands flying to her ample bosom.

"Lord Eurde!" She strangled on his name.

"I see you recognize me," he said. "I had thought . . . perhaps my face . . . the change . . ." he faltered.

She remained in petrified shock, then suddenly collapsed inwardly. "Why have you come?" she whispered.

"I do penance." There was a crying supplication in his voice. "I must seek out all those I have wronged and beseech their forgiveness. Only then can my soul find peace. I implore your pardon." He fell to his knees. "Forgive me, for I have sinned against you. My soul and body have both been damned, and from my wrong to you I know there has been a child."

"Who . . . who told you that?" she whispered.

"Your confessor, before he died. He wanted me to expiate my sin. How little I understood his words then."

"No . . . no! Leo is not yours! He belongs to Favio! Go away! *GO AWAY!*" She was hoarse with fear. "*Get thee behind me, Satan!*" she hissed. "You come to tempt me! To test me! *You cannot have him! He is Favio's!*"

She was panting in fear and resolution at the same time. "*Out! Out!*" She pointed toward the door.

Eurde pulled himself erect. "Will it or not, woman, you know he is mine. But he is not the reason for my coming." He propped himself against the table and leaned forward. "It is for *my* soul that I plead. The boy is yours and stays with you. I ask only that you forgive me, and I will go in peace. I journey to the Holy Land to seek my ultimate release, and you will see no more of me."

"You swear that on the Cross?" She was trembling.

"I swear to Our Lord Jesus. If I fail to keep it, I shall die a thousand deaths in Hell. The torment here on earth has already begun, and the sickness is eating the skin. They say it will start on the bone next. Only penance and absolution at the Holy Sepulchre can save me, but first I must have the forgiveness of all I have wronged. Have mercy on me; forgive me, I beg of you." Tears flowed from his eyes.

A welling of tenderness and pity rose within her. No man had cried before her; no man had pleaded with her. She could not turn him away. "Go with God," she whispered. "I forgive you. You were but a man doing what many men do without thinking. May the Lord have mercy on your soul."

His face lit with joy. "May the Lord's blessing be upon you for the kindness of your heart. I can now leave in peace." He bowed to her and was gone.

Maria drew a deep breath, a sigh in sorrow and in contentment. It was now over; her secret was safe; the Virgin Mother had protected her to the end. Suddenly her hand flew to her mouth. "His brother! The count! Had he been told?"

Leo led the soldiers and the gentlemen into the courtyard of the inn. His mother, still busy with the chickens, quickly evaluated the lordly status of the group. Never had she seen such huge men, nor gentlemen in such rich garments, and her eye was trained to calculate the level of charges for services quickly. Then she noticed the rope around Leo's waist.

"Mother of Mercy!" she shrieked. "What has he done?" The basket flew from her hands, and the chickens exploded in a cloud of feathers as she ran toward her son.

The large Viking holding the rope attached to Leo let out a whoop which halted her in her tracks in fright. Never had she heard such a sound from any human being; the stones seemed to rattle at the noise and her ears deafened. But he was not looking at her. He dropped the rope and strode toward Favio, who was standing in the kitchen doorway.

"*BY MY SAINTS!*" he shouted. "*FAVIO! FAVIO CANNELLI!*"

Favio wrinkled his brow. "Skora?" he fumbled. "Skora?"

The huge soldier let out another whoop. "YES! SKORA! SKORA!" And he enclosed the innkeeper in a bear's embrace.

Favio pushed him away. "The mail," he protested. "I'm not in iron."

Skora laughed boisterously. "Only in fat, I see. What do you here?" He poked at the heavy stomach. "The Lord has been good to you."

"I live here. This is my inn," said Favio. He was unsure how to handle the situation.

Skora was astonished. "The Lord has really been good to you; an innkeeper, no less."

"What have you done to my son?"

Skora's eyes widened. He grinned. "Your son? This is your . . ." Then he roared with laughter. "You must have conceived him on your side," he gasped. "Your son?" He clapped his huge hands. "I should have known. He has your fist for pay." He roared again.

There was a cough from the older gentleman and Skora stiffened immediately. "I forget myself," said the soldier, standing straight. "I seek the innkeeper, but you are he!" He motioned to the two gentlemen. "They would have a few private words with you." He led Favio to the two men. "My lords, this is the man you seek. I know him well, from Constantinople."

Favio bowed. "My humble inn is at your service, my lords. How can I serve you?"

The older man rattled something in a foreign tongue. Skora smiled; Favio grinned.

"Honorable," said Skora. "Favio was a mercenary for more than twelve years, and he was on the Golden Gate for more than three. He was in my regiment, and he understands Greek. He was a good fighter and well trusted. His Holiness knew his man when he sent us here."

"It is true, my lords," Favio added. "I was not so big then." He patted his stomach. "The emperor always paid me well, but I decided to come home. But I do not understand. Why have you come here, to me?"

"A room, good innkeeper," said the older man in Greek, "and we will clear your understanding."

Favio bowed. "Yes, my lords. Come this way." He led them to the covered stairwell of the balustrade, then called to his wife. "Quickly, Maria. Food and wine for their lordships." The group followed him up the stairs and they disappeared into a room.

Maria was busy with Leo, stripping the rope from his body and muttering imprecations upon whoever came to mind. She paid no heed to her husband nor the soldiers or their gentlemen, and Leo was trying to stop the hurricane of invective coming from her lips. He was finally successful when he laid the silver coin across her mouth. She drew in her breath sharply and grabbed the coin.

"Where did you steal this?" she demanded shrilly.

Leo protested. "The big soldier gave it to me, for bringing him here." He reached for it. "It's mine. Give it back."

She slapped his hand away. "I'll keep it for you. Tell Lydia to prepare some cheese and wine for the gentlemen."

Leo pouted but did as he was told, and soon food and drink were brought to the new guests. Leo haunted the yard, waiting for the long meeting to end. Perhaps, he thought, he could do another errand and receive another silver coin. And if he did, he would not tell his mother. Restless, walking the cobbles, finally running up the steps, he tried to listen through the door of the conference room. He heard only the murmur of voices.

He began to fantasize about the mysterious men. Someday he would sail to the East, just as his father had done, and he would return rich. The East was full of riches—so everyone said—and he wondered why his father had come home poor.

Unexpectedly, the door of the room opened and he jumped.

"Get Nicholas up here right away," said his father.

He took the steps down two at a time and ran to the stables. Soon, he and Nicholas, a gangling, flat-footed youth of twenty, with unkempt hair and smelly clothes, were hustling up the stairs, Leo in front, urging the other to move faster. When they entered the room Leo expected that the soldiers would give orders, but it was his father who took command.

Nicholas was sent to a nearby stable to get horses and saddles and Leo accompanied him. Leo was disappointed. There would be no silver for this trip. They rode the horses back, Leo bubbling and talking. Maybe, if they hurried, they would get a coin. He was entranced with their secret mission and could not keep still.

"I wonder where they are going?"

Nicholas shrugged. "What's the difference?" The affairs of the inn's customers did not concern him. "They come. They go. The world goes on. Nothing changes except we die. Maybe we go to Heaven; maybe to Hell. I'm not even sure about that."

"Don't you care? These men came all the way from the East to see my papa. It must be important."

"So why should I care? They ride out and we won't see them anymore. I wonder how we're going to get the horses back."

"They're coming back." Leo was smug in his knowledge. "Their ship's in the the harbor. A Dromond. A warship. It must be important. My papa is giving them six horses."

"Maybe he does it because they have enough silver," Nicholas said dryly. "Your papa gives nothing away for nothing."

Nicholas lapsed into silence, wondering whether he had talked too much. Leo wanted to tell the hosteler about his silver coin but decided against it. He could not understand the groom's lack of curiosity and lapsed into an irritated unrest at the slow pace.

Reaching the courtyard, the groom tied the horses to the hitching post and went back into the stable to saddle the other two horses there. Leo, still dreaming of another coin, mounted the steps in a rush to inform his father and the others that the horses were ready, sure of an offering. But he was disappointed. Skora praised him but gave him nothing, and he stayed in the background pouting.

The four soldiers and two gentlemen mounted the horses and waved as they rode out of the yard. Favio, his hands on his hips, was deep in thought as he watched them go. Leo stood beside him.

Suddenly the innkeeper roused himself. "Nicholas!" he roared.

Nicholas poked his head out of the stable door, his face blank.

"Clean up the yard," yelled Favio. "If the rain comes we'll be sliding in dung!"

Nicholas nodded and disappeared just as the wine dray, driven by Matthieu Toon, the wine peasant, turned into the yard.

"You're late," said Favio.

"I told your boy, there." He indicated Leo. "The mare dropped a shoe. Didn't he tell you?"

"I forgot," said Leo and he quickly disappeared into the inn.

Favio scratched his head. "I need a good port; the gentlemen complain. You have one?"

"I have one, but you'll have to pay. Count Fienzo likes it."

"So let him swill in it." Favio turned away. "How much?" he called over his shoulder.

"For you?" Toon was in thought. "We'll work it out. Michael can bring some in tomorrow."

2

Favio, his business with Toon completed, reentered the inn and automatically glanced toward the bay window where a dark-skinned monk sat, staring out into the courtyard. The innkeeper had little trust for any man of the cloth, but this skinny cleric irritated him. The man rarely moved from his observation seat; he had a lean, hungry face, which, to Favio, was malevolent. He spoke little, and if it were not for giving the inn a bad name, Favio would have been rid of him. He was bad for business.

"Every monk has a fat pouch," he growled at Maria. "Except him."

"What kind of Christian are you?" she retorted. "Have you no respect for the cloth? You refuse to attend church, and you never go to confession. At least leave God's workers alone."

"What work does he do? He sits; he eats; he drinks wine. That's God's work?" He spat.

"So be a heathen!" And she spat, too. "What do you know what God wants of him? Go! Throw him out! See how Jesus will punish you!"

"Aurrgh!" he threw at her in disgust. "Who but you believes all that? Jesus has enough to do without watching me."

"Heathen! Pagan!" she hissed at him. "God will curse you for that! My father should hear you now!"

His face contorted. "What kind of woman brings curses on her husband? You are a makebate!"

"I look after my own," she shot back. "I say he stays! You bring enough of God's wrath upon us!"

"All right! All right! He stays! But no true monk has a flat stomach. He is up to mischief!" He felt he had warned her.

The cleric was different from most other churchmen. He did not beg, and he paid for his food and drink in silver, not coppers, a detail which only made Favio more suspicious. Who had ever heard of an ordinary monk having so much silver? Each week the bill was settled in full and there was no argument on prices. Favio collected his money and shook his head. Questions, relative to a departure date, only elicited smiles, but the monk did promise to give the innkeeper a day's notice before leaving. Attempts at conversation only brought weak smiles, and it was this closed-mouthedness which made Favio so unhappy. The monk was too secretive.

There was another cause for the innkeeper's concern. Leo fussed too much over the man, with Maria's benign agreement.

"No good will come of it," he growled at Maria.

She hushed him. "Maybe he'll open a door for Leo into the church," she dreamed.

"So he can become a thief like the rest of them?"

"God will have your tongue when you talk like that."

"My tongue doesn't make them thieves. It only speaks the truth."

"It will speak the truth when you come to church, to confession."

"Woman, there is a devil in you! I talk of the monk; you talk of God! I talk of Leo; you talk of God! If I talked of a horse, would you still talk of God? There are other things to talk about besides God!" With that pronouncement, he stormed into the inn.

The day the soldiers arrived, Brother Parenti, the monk, was in his usual seat, and he watched the scene in the courtyard closely, his dark, ferretlike eyes darting over the rich garments of the gentlemen and their escorts. He was one of many monks under the orders of the anti-pope, Clement, seeking the contacts between Pope Urban and Emperor Alexius, for the church was rife with the rumors of an impending alliance between the Roman and Eastern popes. If it happened, Clement, as the Germanic pope, would be in trouble. Parenti watched the northern ports, and when he heard Skora speak Greek he knew he had found his quarry. He called Leo, and the boy came running.

"Who were those men?" he asked.

"I don't know but the big soldier gave me a silver coin to bring him here. They talk a funny language. Do you know it?"

"Yes, it's Greek. Do you have the coin?" Byzantine silver would be proof.

"Mama took it. Maybe I'll get another when they return to their ship in the harbor. You should see it! A Dromond! A warship!"

Parenti nodded in satisfaction. He was right. The destination of the Greeks was obvious—they were headed for Piacenza, north of Genoa, to see Urban. Everyone knew Urban had convened a Synod at the abbey there. If he followed them and learned the details of the negotiations, he would have a prize. Clement's reward would be handsome enough for him to live at ease for at least a year. He smiled, contemplating a year of luxury, and sent Leo for wine.

By the time Leo returned, Parenti's thoughts had taken another turn. The pictures of wealth and ease had conjured up from the submerged mists of the past a new being, a shape and figure with whom he had struggled so often, which always merged into his inner core each time he sought to cast it aside, which always returned in satanic triumph. He struggled with his repressed consciousness, but the form was solidifying into the shape of a boy very much like Leo, and while his spirit urged suppression, it was beaten back and imprisoned in a corner of his mind. A shiver ran through him.

With sudden clarity he realized that he had been watching the boy for some time, and the resurgence of his inner fires was not an abrupt flaming but a burning he had thought he had thoroughly extinguished. It had been so long . . . he made an impulsive decision . . . he would take the boy with him when he left in the morning. Leo could be useful . . . in many ways.

"Would you like to become my disciple, Leo?"

"Huh?" Leo did not understand.

"My disciple. A novice; to enter the Mother Church and serve her forever. I have been watching you, and I think you may have the call. Tell me, do you love Our Lord?"

"Yes, always. And the Holy Virgin, too! With all my soul."

"That is a beginning. But you should know that the life of a novice is not easy. There will be hard times."

"I'm not afraid!" Leo was caught up in his mother's oft-spoken dream for him to enter the Church. "I will study night and day! You'll see! I'll do everything you say! And Mama will be so happy! Talk to her! Talk to Mama!"

"Very well, I'll take care of it." He became mysterious suddenly. "But I must warn you. You cannot tell this to anyone. It is between you, me . . . and God. You talk to no one." His head nodded knowingly.

Leo felt an elation he had never experienced before. Mama had always said he was destined for the Church; now it was coming true. The monk had picked him! He could hardly contain himself. "Leo!" He came out of his cloud.

"Listen carefully and do exactly what I tell you. It will be a test of your faith, so remember, there can be no mistakes."

"I will be perfect. What shall I do?" Leo's eyes were bright.

"First," Parenti raised a finger, "you . . . will . . . not . . . tell . . . anyone . . . of . . . this. Do you understand?"

"Not even Mama?"

"I will talk to her; you say nothing to her, nor to your papa. You say nothing to Lydia; nothing to Nicholas. Not even to your confessor. Nobody!"

"All right," Leo shook his head in agreement. "Nobody."

"We will start tomorrow at dawn. From the Corda Pier. You know where it is."

"I know. Where are we going?"

"Be there at dawn, before sunup. I will not wait long. If you are not there I will go on without you. We are going on a secret trip, to an abbey, so we will need food while we are on the road. Get a table covering; put in two or three roasted chickens or meat, some bread, and cheese. Also a bottle of my favorite wine. Do all this late at night so no one sees you. *No one must see you! Do you understand?*"

Leo, caught up in the mystery, shook his head. "Can I say good-bye to my friend, Pietro?"

"You already forget what I told you! I said *NOBODY!* Would you open the door to the Devil?"

"No! No! I wouldn't do that!" Leo cringed.

Parenti leaned forward. "If you are not careful," he whispered hoarsely, "dreadful things will happen. When we bring a new soul to Jesus, the Devil rages. We must be sure he doesn't see us or hear us, because if he finds out . . ." his face became grim, "he will take you straight to hell."

Leo tightened in fear.

"Be not afraid," comforted Parenti. "We can stop him." He winked knowingly. "We will outsmart him; fool him. You must remember he is everywhere, always watching, always sneaking around corners, and standing in dark places. He listens to everything so he can learn when a soul is approaching God. *If you say one thing about going with me he will hear it . . . and take your soul!"*

Leo was terrified. "Doesn't he hear us now?" he quavered.

Parenti's eyes grew wary. "His imps are all around us, sending him messages all the time. *But they can't hear us!"* He was whispering hoarsely. "My cross . . ." He held up the large silver cross dangling from his neck. "This keeps them from coming too close, and when we talk we are surrounded by a shield of silence put there by God. Only a priest's or monk's cross has that power. When you become a monk your cross will have that power, too. So remember, you talk to no one! They are listening." He placed his finger on his lips.

"I'll be quiet," Leo promised. "He won't find me."

"You are a bright boy. Remember, I won't wait long at the pier."

Leo, his mouth open, shook his head in understanding and hurried off while Parenti, satisfied, watched him go. He will make a good novice, he told himself, obedient; a little dull but eager to please; just the right combination for a road companion. He was well pleased with his luck and his choice.

At nightfall, Leo could not sleep, seized with the excitement of all the things which had happened that day. It was the most wonderful day of his life. He carried out the orders of the monk after the inn became still for the night, raiding the kitchen for food and even braving the darkness of the wine cellar for Parenti's favorite wine. He had spoken to no one, avoiding his mother for fear she might worm something out of him, but he consoled himself with the feeling that she must know of his good fortune, for the monk had promised to talk to her. She seemed very happy that evening, and he knew it was due to his being chosen.

Before the false dawn grayed the sky, he seated himself on the lowest step of the courtyard stairway, his sleepy head resting aginst the newel post, and it was there that Parenti found him.

"I said to meet me at the pier," the monk hissed. "Someone could have seen you here."

"There was no-body," Leo said timidly. "I was afraid I would miss you. Look, I remembered everything," he said proudly.

Parenti was angry but there was nothing he could do, he realized. "Pick up the bundle," he ordered. "We must leave quickly."

They walked rapidly, the boy a few paces behind the man. As they left the courtyard Leo looked back, instinctively feeling he might never see it again.

The yard was dark although the sky was lightening, and he felt a wrenching fear of the unknown.

They came to a small chapel of the Madonna and the monk stopped. He had Leo kneel before the image of the Virgin Mother while he prayed. When he was done, he said, "Clasp your hands and bow your head." He placed his hands upon the boy's shoulders and addressed himself to the Madonna:

"Dear Lord, we stand before Your Blessed Mother and we pray for guidance and counsel. I offer You this youth for the salvation of his soul. He will follow the monastic life and enter into Thy service for the deliverance of his soul. He does this with a full heart and of free will, and he promises to stay with Thee forever; and he will not be tempted by the forces of evil, nor will he leave Thee because the way becomes difficult. He pledges Thee his life, his labor, his love, and his everlasting soul, and he begs Thee to accept him for what he is, in Thy everlasting Love and Mercy. Amen." He prodded Leo.

"Amen," said the boy, quickly.

"Get up. From this point forward, for the rest of your life, and even into your death, you will serve the Lord. You must never forget. From now on you are to call me Brother Parenti."

"Yes, Brother," Leo said happily, his face radiant. He was sure he had ascended to glory and that the Madonna had acknowledged and accepted him, for he had seen Her nod just as he had lifted his head to say "Amen."

Parenti produced a folded garment from beneath his habit and ordered the boy to strip and put it on. It was large and the monk rolled up the sleeves, pulled up the waist, and folded it over the tying cord. "It will have to do," he told the boy, "until we can get another. We have lost enough time. Take the bundle and let us go. Leave your clothes there; your mother will find them." He strode off quickly, not looking to see whether Leo obeyed him.

Leo scooped up the bundle of provisions and hurried after him. They walked for three hours into the morning without another word.

3

The grapes were not good that year and the wine of 1095 would not be kept in the wine cellars too long. First, the clouds had been sparse and the rain did not fall; the ground had baked to dust and even the grass had withered. When the rains finally came, the waters poured from the heavens seven days and nights, and the streams from the mountains flooded the lower areas. God, said the cynics, had just cause, for the people were evil, but the world was to have ended in the year 1000. The reason for the delay was disconcerting.

The wine peasants would squeeze some grapes between the palms of their hands and suck the juice, spit it out, and mutter their despair. Their prayers to the saints were loud, and the women wept, for it was that kind of year when everyone would be hungry, the vegetables rotting in the ground, and the unripe fruit falling from the trees.

Mary's father, Matthieu Toon, was a wine peasant, a son of a wine peasant, and his eldest son would be a wine peasant. Each year he tended his vines diligently, and in the fall he watched his developing grapes more closely than he watched his wife. He delivered wines to some inns in Genoa, to the castle of Count Fienzo, to some wealthy burghers of the city, and to some of the churches. It was his wines which brightened the Feast of October One, and he was very proud that his wines were often the first choice of the deacons.

As in the tradition, only the eldest son inherited the eight hectares of vines, and the other sons would leave the farm on the death of their father, seeking their fortunes elsewhere.

The men of the family tended toward the dark side, with black silky hair, dark eyes which sometimes slanted, and high cheekbones. Their swarthy skin was pulled tightly over their long faces and sharp noses, revealing the blood of the Magyar, that fearful conqueror from Hungary who had ravaged through Europe many years gone by and had come to Genoa through Giovi Pass.

The women, however, were fair, even to the red, showing the legacy of the Frank and the Vandal. Tall, slender, graceful, their pale-skinned comeliness made them attractive targets of the nobles, but not as wives.

Master Toon was close to fifty when Mary was born, and her tired, unhappy mother was thirty-five. Only three of her twelve previous pregnancies had lived, and the worn woman clutched convulsively at her goose-down coverlet as the midwife guided the new infant into the world. She never opened her eyes, but with a deep sigh expelled her soul and last breath. Mary, however, was lusty.

17

"The baby needs milk," said the midwife after she had informed Toon of the death of his wife.

"So? Get her a she-goat. The mare hasn't foaled yet."

The woman's lip curled. "You want her dead, too? For money I can get her a wet nurse. You need a woman in the house."

Toon had little use for a new daughter, but the loss of his wife created a problem. He needed someone to cook, sew, and take care of the children, and he was in a quandary. He was surly and angry; his wife had died at the wrong time and he was inconvenienced.

"So get," he snapped at the woman. "Don't bother me, I have work to do."

The woman ground her teeth in anger as he slammed the door. She knew a young, unmarried girl who just had a stillborn child, and whose milk had not been dried up as yet, and who would be very willing, for a small fee, to nurse the baby.

That night Mary suckled some warm-watered goat's milk and cried herself to sleep. The next morning, the midwife ushered a shy, young girl into the kitchen where Michael, aged seven, Andre, five, and Ruth, four, were attempting to get breakfast. Toon entered with a small pitcher of milk, and his eyes roved over the girl, making her fidget. "This the one?" he finally said.

"You see anyone else?" the midwife snapped at him. "Her name's Jeanne, and she can cook and take care of the others, too."

"How old are you?" he fired at the girl.

"Fifteen—old enough," said the midwife.

"Let her talk," Toon barked. "Well, can you take care of the house? Clothes? Everything?"

She nodded. "Ye-es, Master Toon."

He turned to the woman. "She's got a husband?"

"No, but no need to worry. Her father's agreeable if you make it permanent."

"Oh, he is." The thought of marriage had not entered his mind. He would need a woman, but a young one would mean more children, and an old one wouldn't last too long. He looked at the girl again. The baby had stopped whimpering. The girl had seated herself in a corner, opened her gunnysack jacket, releasing her breast to nurse. He stared and scratched his ear, then he barked, "Call me when breakfast is ready," and stomped out.

"You've got the job," said the midwife with a chuckle.

Later, alone with the girl, Toon made it very clear that he did not expect to remarry. If she did her work well, she could remain on the farm—he would supply all her needs—but there would be no wages; she would be like one of the family as long as she was to remain. She accepted his offer immediately but pointed out there might be some talk about the arrangement.

"So?" Toon raised a shaggy eyebrow.

She had no further comment; she had nowhere else to go.

Michael and Andre were completely indifferent to their new sister, but Ruth would coo and play with her for hours, helping Jeanne. This child was different from the other Toon females. She was small; she had dark hair and eyes—like the boys—and she acted more like a boy than a girl as she grew. She liked boys' games and irritated her brothers when she interfered with them. They scolded and tried beating her to drive her away, but they found sand in their food and fleas in their clothes in retaliation. She knew every thicket, every hiding place in the barn and outbuildings, and she delved into everything, learning every secret.

When she was ten, Ruth suddenly disappeared.

Mary was puzzled. After two days she asked her brothers, but they were ignorant, too, so she turned toward Jeanne. The woman's face clouded and she became agitated. "Ask your papa," she said.

"You know!" Mary stamped her foot. "Tell me!"

Jeanne stopped her work, an inner conflict boiling up inside her. Mary was close enough to be her daughter. She had nursed her, cleaned her, hovered over her bed as though she had carried and given birth to her. She loved her very much, but . . . did she dare? Ruth had run away with an old bawd who had tried to buy her from Toon. When Ruth had heard him tell the old woman that he had promised the girl to the nunnery and that the priest was coming for her, Ruth left in the middle of the night.

Mary did not understand. Didn't papa love her anymore? Why would the old woman take her? Where did they go? She was full of questions.

Jeanne bit her lip in agitation. Master Toon had kept a sharp line between his family and his relationship with her, and her continued life on the farm was all in his hands. He could throw her out at anytime. Mary was reaching the age of understanding. Was she going too far explaining what had happened? The girl was alone; someone had to explain to her—just as she had explained to Ruth—what would probably happen in a few years.

"These bawds come to find pretty girls to take them and train them . . . to live in the houses of the lords . . . to be like servants . . . or to be . . . well, the girls live in fancy houses, and they are paid for what they do . . . with men. They are called harlots. It's a sin," she finished rapidly.

"What's a harlot?"

"It's a sin . . . I'll tell you some other time. I have work to do." She put away her sewing.

"Maybe Michael knows," mused Mary.

"No! Don't ask him!" Jeanne felt herself cornered. "I'll tell you but you must promise never to tell anyone else."

Mary shook her head vigorously. "I promise! I promise!"

"It's . . . it's when an unmarried girl . . . takes money, or jewelry, for sleeping with a man, in the same bed." She breathed deeply, glad to have finally said it. "It's very sinful."

Mary screwed up her face. "But why? I've seen you sleeping with papa . . ." Jeanne gasped ". . . and you're not married."

"*Oh!*" Jeanne ran from the room.

Mary, much perplexed, sat and thought; then her face lit up; she would ask Michael. He would know.

Mary had discovered a new game. A few years had made her more understanding to the ways of adults, and she was privy to many of the secrets of the family, many more than the others knew. A natural curiosity, and the awakening of new and strange emotions which she could not explain, drove her to seek erotic scenes among the animals and a compulsive voyeurism in the family.

Many times, after leaving Papa Toon in the barn, Michael would come back to the house. At those times, Jeanne would give Mary some chore outside. Papa couldn't sleep some nights and would go to the kitchen and drink wine until he fell asleep in a chair. Mary, if awake, would hear boards creak and doors close. Jeanne was very fond of Michael and fussed over his clothes. And one day, after Jeanne gave her a chore to pluck some chickens outside, she sneaked back and saw Michael and Jeanne holding each other fast and kissing. Once, when Papa was asleep downstairs, she crept to Jeanne's door and she could hear noises and talking inside.

After that she smiled knowingly at Jeanne. The woman became self-conscious under the girl's stare and their relationship cooled. Despite all her efforts, Mary could not catch Michael and Jeanne again. She wondered whether to talk to Andre but decided against it. After all, it was her secret.

It was early next summer that she noticed Andre loitering about the house, and her suspicions were immediately aroused. She began to watch. Andre did his household chores after lunch, instead of after dinner when Papa and Michael were usually in the vineyards. One morning, when Papa Toon announced that he and Michael were going into Genoa, seeing customers and checking the needs of the churches and Count Fienzo, Andre made no protest when he was ordered to load some barrels onto the dray by himself.

After their departure, Mary busied herself in the kitchen. She caught a knowing glance between Jeanne and Andre. Impulsively, she announced that she was going to the barn to check the newborn kid, and when she arrived there she quickly placed her eye at the jamb crack behind the door from where she could see the kitchen doorway. Andre was standing there, watching the barn. Suddenly he disappeared.

She crept back to the house cautiously. The kitchen was empty. Listening intently, she mounted the steps. They were in the big bedroom, Papa's room, and she stood outside the door, fearful of opening it but filled with the overwhelming desire to see what was happening. Suddenly the sounds stopped and Jeanne's voice, angry, came through.

"I said it was enough! We'll have more time later!"

"Mary will be in the way." It was Andre's whine.

"I'll take care of Mary. Get dressed and go down to the barn so she can see you."

Quickly, Mary headed down the steps and out to the barn, giggling all the way. In her mind's eye she saw Jeanne and Michael together; then Michael was replaced by Andre; then Papa. She found it difficult to restrain her laughter . . . first Michael, then Andre, then Papa, then Michael, then . . . She plopped down beside the goat and shook. It would have to be a secret; Papa would not understand.

Papa Toon began to notice a notable change in Mary's behavior, but he blamed it on her growth. She was more reserved, more thoughtful; her wild exuberances were disappearing; and she spoke less. He knew her bleeding period had begun early last year, and her breasts were beginning to fill out, and she was beginning to pad in the right places. Soon, the boys would notice.

"Keep a sharp eye on that girl," he said to Jeanne. "She's changing, growing up." He scratched his ear. "She'll become a breeding mare, so I'd better do something before she goes looking for a stallion by herself." He was quiet for a moment. "Maybe she could take Ruth's place in the nunnery; I owe them that."

Mary did not hear him, but Andre, now eighteen and smart with the girls at Cannelli's inn, looked at her closely. For years she had simply existed under his feet and he had taken her growth for granted. Now, he saw something else.

The sharp nose and angular cheekbones of Mary's face had filled and softened, and her slightly pear-shaped face, with her slanted, dark, long-lashed sloe eyes, set off by a short haircut, gave her an impish appearance. She cut her hair herself, although Jeanne wanted her to keep it long, an idea Mary dismissed as too impractical. A mischievous smile flitted easily around her full, red lips and her eyes twinkled with laughter. Her thin arms and knobby-kneed legs had somehow straightened, becoming symmetrical, and she looked taller as she walked erectly, thrusting her bud breasts forward. Andre could see the entire form of the nipple area as they strained against her tight shift, and his eyes grew dark as he felt his arousal. His tongue wet his drying lips; his loins tensed. He rose abruptly from his chair and left the kitchen.

That night Mary was awakened by a hand over her mouth, and when she tried to struggle she found herself in a tight grip.

"*Sh-h-h! It's me! Andre! Keep quiet!*" His breath was in her ear and when she stopped struggling, he released her.

"What's wrong?" she hissed, a thousand calamities invading her.

"It's all right," he whispered back, "but be quiet. You'll wake everybody up."

"But what's wrong?" She was still half-asleep and bewildered.

"Everything is all right, little sister. I just wanted to talk."

"In the middle of the night?" She rubbed her neck. "You almost strangled me. What's so important?"

"You're growing up, my little Mary." He still held her and she became conscious of his hands. "Yes, you are growing up." A hand ran lightly over her bosom and down her side, toward her rear.

"Do you have to rub me like a cow to know that?"

He pressed her buttock. "It's time for you to be with a man. A girl must learn early. A man knows these things."

Her laugh, although soft, had a slight edge. "And you are a man?"

"Of course. I've had many girls in town."

"Where did you get the money? I know about Cannelli's inn."

"I manage. I know a lot." He was boastful and moved closer to her. His hand had come across her thigh, pressing, caressing, moving over the soft, firm flesh of the inner muscle, persistently separating her legs. She found she liked the sensation and relaxed, and his hand crept further in, reaching for her softness. His breath became shorter, and she moved against his hand, accommodating herself to the new sensations. Suddenly, he touched something and she jumped. "Don't do that," she said weakly.

"It's all right," he whispered. "I know how."

"Jeanne was a good teacher."

He froze. There was a sharp intake of his breath, and he drew his hand back as though it had touched a hot stove. "What do you mean by that?" There was fear and belligerence in his voice.

"Oh, I know all about you and her." She was offhand.

"*What do you know?*" He grabbed her by the arms and pulled her straight up in bed. "*What?*"

"*Let go of me or I'll scream,*" she said hoarsely.

He released her. "*If you mean Jeanne and me . . . it's a lie!*"

She took a deep breath and giggled. "You don't fool me with all your big airs. I know all about you and Jeanne . . . and all the times you stayed when Michael and Papa were racking the wine."

"*You little bitch.*" He struck her and she fell over with a cry, more surprised than hurt.

"Don't ever do that again," she threatened, "or I'll tell Papa all about you and Jeanne."

He collapsed like a falling tree. "I'm sorry. I'm sorry. It wasn't my fault . . ." he was stammering and pleading. "She began it with me . . . when I was sick, last winter. She . . . came into bed, to warm me . . . she said I was old enough to learn . . . and . . . and she began showing me. She did it. You won't tell Papa, will you? He'll kill me."

She sat up, tucking her feet under her, lotus fashion. She was all excited and wanted to hear more. "What happened then?"

"Well, you know. You've seen what happens when we bring a bull to a cow." An odd mixture of sexual excitement and fear was coursing through him, spreading through his pores, and heating the blood in his veins. He saw how eager she was and it excited him.

"After the first time," he began speaking softly, sensing that she wanted to hear all the details, "we got together often. She would show me what to do, and I learned fast. After a while, she wanted me with her often. I can show you . . .'' Fear still nagged at him. "But you must promise not to tell anyone.''

She drew back, confused by conflicting emotions. This was the closest she had ever been, and, in a way, she relished her obvious power over Andre. Any threat to tell Papa would have him groveling. But not now. A different idea was forming in her mind. For the first time, she noticed that he was naked and she alternately bit and licked her upper lip. She felt so *warm*.

"If I promise not tell Papa . . .'' she began.

"I'll do anything you say . . . anything, little sister. I'll never bother you again.'' He was kneeling and sobbing. "I beg you! He'll whip me and drive me off the farm. Where would I go? Michael has promised I can stay after Papa dies. Please, Mary . . . anything.''

She leaned forward and straightened the coverlet. "Aren't you cold, standing naked like that?''

He shuddered convulsively. "I am, now.''

"Come on, get into bed. We'll talk.''

Gratefully, he obeyed her, slipping under the warm quilt. The chill of the night and the coldness of his predicament had entered his bones. He huddled, fetus fashion, tense and trembling.

Mary reached out and touched him. "You are cold. Let's talk about the girls. What do you do first?''

The sudden twist of her thinking had an immediate effect on him. He relaxed, straightening his body, and timidly reached out to touch her. He was surprised to feel her cool skin instead of her cloth nightgown. "Well, I . . .'' His hand moved slowly. She was lying on her side, facing him. Suddenly, she was astraddle him, her thighs pressing him fast, her naked body pushing against his.

"Now, *I'll* keep you warm,'' she hissed into his ear, her arms holding him tightly against her. "*Show me!*'' she demanded, her nakedness sliding over him as she writhed, a sleek smoothness. "Show me what you do with Jeanne. Like she showed you!''

She was hoarse with passion, her breath short, her whole body hot and demanding as she moved against him.

He recovered quickly from his surprise and tightened his arms around her, stopping her movement. His passion flared; his face contorted as he bared his teeth. His hand slid between them, seeking her pubic area, seeking her moistness and finding it dry. His fingers moved about and she became wet as she twisted with them. Suddenly, he withdrew them and thrust upward savagely. *He'd show her!*

She gasped as he entered. They thrashed about in their wildness. Suddenly, her whole being exploded with the light of a thousand suns.

After that, their trysts became a nightly affair and the rings under their eyes deepened. The others noticed their lassitude and rising irritability and commented upon it. Andre shrugged; Mary held her tongue.

Master Toon studied his daughter and said to Jeanne, "I talked to the priest yesterday, and he's ready to take Mary in Ruth's place. At least she can help me that way. I'll take her on the next trip to Genoa."

Mary heard him and that evening, after a brief lovemaking, she curled her feet under her buttocks and declared she wanted to talk. "Papa told Jeanne he's going to take me to Genoa, to the nunnery. I won't go. We're going to run away, to Paris. Just like Ruth did."

He was alert immediately. "We can't!" burst from him.

"I'm not going to be some stinking nunner," she snapped at him. "If I'm not on my back with some old priest, I'll be singin' 'Hail Marys' with some Mother Superior all day. I won't do it! I won't."

"We can't go," he insisted. His mouth was dry as chaff. "We have no money . . . we've never traveled so far . . . winter is coming . . . Papa needs me . . ."

"And you don't want to go," she finished bitterly. "Well, brother," she warned, "I need you. I can't walk the roads alone. And if you don't come I can always tell Papa how you came to my bed that night, and how you and Jeanne . . ."

"Mary, please. I didn't say I didn't *want* to go with you. But it's going to be hard. It's a big trip."

"After we find Ruth, you can go back home, if you want to. We won't need you. Just think, you'll be rid of me."

She was right, he thought. It would solve his problem . . . everyone's problem. When Papa died, and Michael had the farm, Michael would keep Jeanne and marry someone else. He and Jeanne could . . . and there were always the girls at the inn . . . he wouldn't marry anyway. His life would be set. His dark clouds disappeared. He smiled. "All right, Mary, I'll take you to Paris."

She was puzzled by his sudden change. "What are you scheming?"

"Nothing," he said blandly. "I just think I should help you."

"I think you're lying." She stopped his protest. "It doesn't matter. Papa and Michael go to Genoa the day after tomorrow. I'll put up a basket. We'll leave right after they go."

Suddenly, he hated her. "What if it rains?"

"We go anyway. We won't melt." She was afraid she had waited too long; she should have left sooner. Andre had served his purpose, and she would be rid of him in Paris after they found Ruth. Ruth . . . Ruth was the only one who could save her now.

He rose from the bed. "Since you have it all arranged, I'm going to bed. I'm tired." He left, escaping her.

There was a grimace on her face as he closed the door. He could become spiteful and tell everything . . . no, he couldn't, he would be in too much trouble himself, she consoled herself. She would pray to the Virgin Mary to help her. The Mother of Jesus would understand. The next time she went to church she would light a candle. Her promise soothed her and she tried to sleep.

4

Pope Urban was not happy, for there had been much more disagreement in his council than he had anticipated, and his displeasure grew as the disputes intensified. Otto, of Bavaria, was urging flexibility, compromise. The man, Urban thought, could not comprehend that the Pontifex Maximus, the Pope, could not compromise on fundamental tenets of the Doctrine. He decided to interrupt.

"The Truce of God is sworn," he said sternly, "and it shall be enforced. We must deal firmly with our enemies. We must enforce the peace; and peace there must be."

"Peace, yes," said Otto, "but we all know that peace takes many different forms."

"It has been made distinctive," said Urban with finality. "Any man or woman who assaults or slays another; who attacks and seizes a castle or monastery; who uses craft or violence for personal gain, must—I repeat—must suffer the Will of the Church. Father Gregory consecrated his life to this end and we shall not fail him."

"But, your Holiness," interjected a cardinal, "to be exiled for thirty years? To make full compensation and do penance?" He threw up his hands. "Too long! Too harsh! Otto has a point."

Otto could cause many troubles and others would follow his lead. The cardinal returned to the attack. "And what if one claims innocence and denies all charges, claiming defense? What if proof is slender and witnesses are vague? Every charged man cannot undergo the Ordeal of the Hot Iron, nor stand excommunicate on unproven, unsubstantiated charges." He shook his head. "Too rigid!"

Urban's lips thinned in scorn. Otto was not known for his kindnesses, and pleas for mercy from him were ironic. King Henry and his anti-pope, Clement, were bending pillars of the Church to their will. Those men must be rooted out: trunk, branch, leaf, and fingerling.

Otto was pushing his argument further. "Think, Holy Father, thirty years of exile. It is a lifetime! How can we win adherents when we threaten Christians for every flash of anger? A starving peasant steals a crust, a serf hides a lamb from the tax collector, a housewife steals a little extra milk for her children. All these can lead to blows and the peace is broken."

Another cardinal took up the argument, echoing Otto's thoughts. "One man can slay another in anger; in rape, a man can kill the woman, and the kin can kill the raper; even a hoyden, when she is rude, can be attacked . . .''

"Enough! Enough!" cried Urban. "You have made your point. But your point is not the main point of the problem. You cry for the poor and the weak, but you use them to confuse the issue. The clerics settle these disputes every day. We talk of major crimes, of premeditated slaughter of men. You try to weaken the Truce of God by examples of personal injuries of the poor. We would strengthen it by dealing with crimes against the peace by the strong— wars, feuds, castle burnings, the destruction of monasteries. You can see the difference, I think. Reaffirm the Truce!''

But Otto was not finished. "Push people too harshly and you lose them," he warned. "It makes little difference if he be serf or noble. What knight will come to us after this when he can go to Clement and buy forgiveness?"

"His name is still Guibert, Bishop of Ravenna," warned Urban. "We recognize no Clement the Third."

"Very right, your Holiness," said Otto smoothly, "but we must still be realistic. Guibert gathers sinners every day because *they say* he understands mercy. Lord Jesus was always merciful."

"We need no lecture on mercy," said Urban, restraining his temper. "Guibert's mercy is tempered by the feel of gold in his palm." His hands tightened on his robes. "Let me ask once more. Shall we have mercy on abbots who buy their salvation with gold while the slaves they buy, Christian slaves, work their fields? Does gold, secured by the sale of church positions, bless the Name of the Lord? Shall we have mercy for monks who use swords—not to defend the poor and the weak, as they should do—but for the extortion of exorbitant tithes? Shall we have mercy for clerics who pander for nunneries in the name of Our Holy Christ?"

"No! No!" A cry arose from his listeners.

"No!" echoed Urban, his teeth clenched. "Christ weeps at these defilements! It is an oozing slime and it is spreading and covering the Church. It becomes more foul every day. Hear me well! There can be no compromise with the Devil's abominations! The Church will be cleansed and shine clean as a bright star, and Godly!"

He was breathing hard when he finished, his eyes wide as though he was seeing a vision, and the men seated before him swore afterward that he was looking at them but seeing Heaven. Moments passed in silence. None dared to speak. Urban's head suddenly lifted and his eyes focused. His face was granite. He had decided to take an immediate vote. "I ask confirmation," he said, and his stern glance fell on each cardinal-bishop in turn. They nodded their agreement, some quickly, others more slowly, and when Otto's turn came, his head, too, finally dropped in submission. Emperor Henry of Germany stood triple excommunicate. Hearing of it, Henry laughed.

Urban rose. "It is well, and now the matter of King Philip. He lives in open sin with a brazen woman, ignoring his queen. He sells bishoprics and collects tithes. We must consider excommunication for him also.''

Heads nodded and Urban was pleased, but he knew that the opposition had been silenced, not eradicated, for the gold of the Church offered endless treasure to the greed of the kings. The lifeblood of the Church was at stake.

''There will be many knights in France to convince,'' said one cardinal dryly. ''To act against Philip will stir many clerics.''

''More in France than in Germany?'' asked Otto, sarcastically. ''We took no heed before.''

''There are always knights to convince,'' said a third. ''Do we listen to knights or to the Lord?''

''Truly said,'' answered Urban. His eyes roved over the group and many squirmed uneasily in their chairs. ''King Henry repented his sins standing in ashes and sackcloth in the snows of Canossa, and he shall do so again. King Philip may join him this time.''

''Perhaps . . .'' Otto offered, ''one strong antagonist at a time.''

Urban considered Otto's suggestion. The Church could not err, but it could take well-tendered advice. Philip could wait. He nodded his agreement. ''Very well, we will wait with Philip until we meet at Cluny in November. Better to confer there, in France.''

There was relieved affirmation, and during the momentary lull, there was a furtive knock upon the door. A black-robed monk put his head through and glanced at Urban, who motioned him to come forth. The monk approached and whispered into his ear. Urban, surprised, nodded; the monk bowed and withdrew.

''Brothers,'' Urban addressed the Synod, ''an extraordinary event has been brought before me. Two couriers from Alexius from Constantinople have just arrived and crave audience.''

There was a startled intake of breath.

''They carry an urgent message,'' Urban went on. ''I suggest we suspend for a noon meal and confer again in two hours. If there is no objection . . .'' he glanced about. ''Seeing none, so be it.'' He strode from the room, leaving a hubbub of questioning voices.

Two hours later the Synod reconvened. Silencing the noisy talk, Urban said, ''Thank you for your prompt attendance. I will come to the point. The couriers bring a message from our brother prelate from Byzantium. Alexius makes a request.''

There was a sharp intake of breath, for a great deal of animosity existed between the two centers of the Church. But Urban ignored the reaction.

''One courier is John Ducas, a nobleman by birth and influence, a diplomat and soldier, with the title of Baron.'' Urban smiled. ''He is also the brother-in-law of Alexius.'' His last words were a reference to the marriage of the man calling himself a pope. ''Shall we invite the gentleman to our deliberations?''

The cardinal-bishops acclaimed the affirmative, and Urban nodded to the black-robed monk waiting at the door. He returned immediately, leading the Byzantines down the center aisle, toward the dais. Urban held out his right hand, and each gentleman kneeled and kissed his ring, and Urban blessed them with the sign of the Cross.

"The council bids you welcome, gentlemen, and trusts your journey was pleasant. Permit me to introduce you: Baron John Ducas . . ." The baron bowed . . . "And his aide, Capt. Bardas Anatol." The captain bowed. "They bring personal greetings from *Emperor* Alexius." He stressed the lay title. There was a polite clapping of palms striking against robed thighs, a courtesy recognition.

Urban indicated two chairs which had been placed beside the dais, and the Byzantines were seated. Urban continued. "Baron Ducas has requested that he be permitted to read the message from *Emperor* Alexius. Permission has been granted."

To Ducas, Urban's continued stress of Alexius' lay title was acerbic. Alexius was the Basileus, First in service to the Apostles of Christ, designated as such by Constantine, the Proto-Apostolos in the holy city of Constantinople. Alexius, to Ducas, stood above Urban in Christ's Church, and the slight in protocol was unforgiving. Only his mission and diplomatic training kept him quiet, and he masked his anger as he rose. He bowed to Urban and to the council and rolled the document handed to him by his aide. A stillness settled over the room as everyone but Urban, who knew the content of the message, grew tense with expectancy.

"To my Highly Esteemed and Beloved Brother Prelate of Rome:

"Greetings: May the Blessings of Our Lord Jesus Christ be always upon thee; and it is our heartfelt wish and prayers that the Thoughts of Our Beloved Holy Mother Mary be ever present in thy soul.

"It is my everlasting prayer that all goes well with thee and that the Lord smiles with favor upon all thy undertakings.

"It is with great sorrow and much melancholy that I find I must convey an unhappy situation and condition of Our Mother Church to your awareness. My heart is heavy because of it.

"The Christian lands of the East have been outraged and mutilated by a barbarous people, heathens from the Kingdom of Persia who are estranged from God. With fire and steel they have ravaged the Sacred Land and killed our Christian brothers. These devilish Turks and Arabs have advanced to the Mediterranean Sea, conquering our armies and leading thousands of Christians into slavery. They have destroyed the churches of Christ everywhere and, worse yet, they defile them with their pagan rites, befouling the altars with their filth and excrement from their bodies, and pouring Christian blood into the stoups and baptismal fonts.

"They torture Christian prisoners by using them as practice targets for games, teaching their young soldiers to shoot arrows at the living, writhing bodies. They amuse themselves with their saber practices, cutting the skin so fine that it will not bleed but sensitizes the feelings. They will slice off noses, ears, breasts of women with a swing of their scimitars, or decapitate prisoners who kneel bound before them.

"What shall I tell you of the bestial performances compelled on our women? Or the use put to our young Christian daughters as well as their mothers? Or of the perversions of our young sons? Mother Mary weeps tears of blood for the children, and the chorus of woe from the mothers is heard over the stricken land.

"I find it difficult to go on, yet I must.

"We need and plead for your help. We need and plead for cavalry and men-at-arms. Our soldiers are brave, and they are true Christian fighters, but our enemies are devils, and there are too many of them.

"Well do we remember the knights of the West and their noble destriers, those stalwart stallions who fight with their hooves and teeth beside their masters. If some of your knights are willing to take service with our Christian armies, they will be serving the Lord and they will be well paid, in gold and prayer. Christ, I am sure, will look upon them with great favor, and, if they so desire, they may bring their own priests with them.

"We both know the deep and difficult disputes which have long separated Rome and Constantinople, and they hang heavy on my heart, but we are One in Jesus Christ. I cannot order my people to yield to Rome any more than you can order yours to do the reverse, but there is a mutual understanding, a certainty which arises from a mutual defense of the Faith which binds us together. Possibly, a healing could be affected much easier after a victory of our defenders over the murderous Arabs.

"The heathens are gathered, and if Constantinople should fall, they will be camped on the borders of the West. We are the Eastern Bastion of the Cross, in dire need of our Western Brethren.

"Hear us, in the Name of Our Lord Jesus Christ; heed our plea! Together, we can carry the Cross to its greatest heights throughout the world.

"May God's mercy be forever with you.

"With Christian Love and Brotherhood;

"Signed: Alexius, Prelate of Constantinople, Emperor.

"Postscript: Our good Baron-General John Ducas and his aide, Capt. Bardas Anatol, are our chosen envoys and bearers. Baron Ducas is an excellent soldier and is completely aware of the conditions of our distress. He can report and answer any of your questions or doubts. His armor is Truth; his shield is his love for Jesus; his sword is his Faith. In the Name of the Father, hear him out."

There was the chill and silence of the tomb when the reading was over and the silences became alive. Urban's head was bowed, his fingers pressed together forming an arch, his face impassive. Ducas was staring, his mind's eye seeing Alexius sitting alone in his gallery by the red Marmora, huddled, awaiting a reply. The cardinal-bishops sat like stone statues, and for a few moments the world hung in suspension.

Urban broke the spell. "Would Baron Ducas have anything to add?"

Ducas, startled out of his trance, nodded. "I wish to extend the blessings and good will of my party for your hospitality and benefaction. There is much detail, but perhaps specific questions would accomplish more. The horrors are great and their results are gruesome. Our need is overwhelming." He paused, seeking questions.

There were none; no one spoke nor whispered. Ducas bowed to Urban. "I know your love and affection reach out to us. Our Faith was born in the East, and the black robes of the pagan and infidel cannot be permitted to enshroud the bright Star of Bethlehem. If the strong arms of your fighting knights unite with ours, the heathen cannot prevail. But if we cannot secure that aid, we have sworn that we will fight to the death to prevent the Turk from rejoicing in a victory easily achieved."

The council was moved and nodded their heads in approval. Urban had not had enough time to mull over the new turn of events, but he felt that something propitious was happening and that he had to think of a way to turn it to his advantage. He must understand it.

He had demurred, at first, to agree to present Alexius' letter to the Synod, fearing it might divert the council from its main task—excommunication of Emperor Henry. But closer study of the letter brought Pope Gregory's old plan of uniting East and West into one Church again, and promoting one great pilgrimage to Holy Jerusalem. This could be the spark to fire the hearts of Christians everywhere. It could resolve many of the difficulties of the lay nobility by thinning the ranks of the quarrelsome knights, of the second and third and fourth sons who inherited little or nothing. It would also accomplish something for God and His Church. He decided to present the epistle.

"We give thanks for the safe journey of our eastern brothers, and we commend them for bringing this matter to our attention," he told the Synod. "Our hearts are wrung by the message from our Beloved Prelate of Constantinople. We weep with him at his tale of affliction and cruelty. With our mutual love in Our Lord, I am sure we will rally to extirpate the cause of his distress."

There was an outcry of assent. "True! True!"

But Urban needed time for planning. To the envoys, he said, "Tell Brother Alexius how just we view his cause. At the first opportune moment, when the season is ripe for the harvest, we shall do all we can to honor his needful request."

"Yes! Yes!" came from the cardinal-bishops. Few realized that Urban had postponed action until the autumn or later.

But Ducas knew exactly what had happened, and his disappointment was etched in his face. He had been dismissed with a vague, verbal assurance, no promise of a call for action. A mustering of fighting men would be delayed for months or, perhaps, forever. He motioned to his aide, who rose, and the two Byzantines bowed to Urban and the Synod and left the room after mouthing the usual ceremonial farewells. He held his head high and his step was firm as he left; his aide walked with the precision of an officer on military parade.

To Urban, commitment was impossible. The struggle with his kings came first. And, then, commitment to what? He was not sure.

If, he reasoned, his partisans in the West were drained off to the East, Henry's armies would be supreme in Germany and Italy; Philip's knights would hold France; and Cluny would be endangered. No. He could not strip himself of fighting men just yet. Byzantium would have to survive on its own.

He knew Alexius could buy many knights—not the powerful and the rich— but the others. With a victory over the heathen, the emperor could turn his armed strength against Rome, bribing the knights with the captured gold of the Moslems. Power and gold could breach the walls of the Church; many Christians were weak, human, and subject to evil and sin. The allure of gold was strong.

Then, again—Byzantium and Rome! A wondrous idea of unity! Faced with an alliance such as this, the evil of the anti-pope, Clement, would fade away. The knights of the West could level the walls of the Church's schisms and create one Church again. More, they could act as a Trojan horse, controlling Alexius and bringing the Eastern schism under the domination of Rome! A most appealing fancy!

What if he did nothing to aid Alexius? Would the fall of Constantinople to the Seljuk hordes threaten the West as Alexius implied? Would the Moslems sweep through Europe as they had once come through Africa, to Spain and Italy? It was a difficult decision. He would return to Cluny and pray for direction. There, Hugh could help him . . . and Count Raymond, and his other powerful friends. Alexius would have to wait.

He suddenly realized that the others were sitting and watching him. He said to them, "We bless our council and all who have participated in our deliberations. Let the Will of the Lord be done. Amen." His hand's edge made the sign of the Cross.

"Amen," intoned the others.

He reminded them. "We will meet again in mid-November in Clermont. It is most important that each of you be there, for I would appreciate your thoughts at that time concerning this request from Alexius. Also, think deeply about Philip. France cannot be allowed to be delinquent in its duties while Germany is punished. There being no further need of this Council, we are adjourned. A favorable trip home and may God go with you."

5

The road was dusty and Leo raised sprays of fanlike forms with his feet. When Parenti stepped behind a tree to relieve himself, the boy hoped they would stop to rest, but the monk moved on and Leo wearily followed, falling further and further back. Parenti became annoyed and finally decided that a short rest, with a bite of bread and cheese, would be nice. And the wine would be refreshing.

"You can spread the cloth over there," he said, pointing to a small oak tree at the roadside. "In the shade."

Leo was tired. Perhaps his decision to go with the monk had been wrong, he thought. His hands and back were sore from carrying the bundle, and the dust of the road was in his mouth. He felt dirty and itchy, and Parenti had not spoken to him since they left the Madonna. He was happy to stop.

Parenti was suddenly very cheerful and rubbed his hands together. "You have done well this morning," he chattered. "We have not talked because I have been busy thinking. It is a fine day, and we could reach our destination tonight if we walk fast."

The anticipation of food and rest acted like a tonic to Leo's spirits, and he spread the cloth deftly, sliced the bread and cheese with skill, and then unwrapped an entire broiled chicken.

"Chicken!" exclaimed the monk. "You have provided well!"

"I have wine, and a goblet, too." Leo brought out the glass.

"Good! Very, very good!" purred Parenti. "You have done well."

All of Leo's doubts vanished in the warm glow of praise. With the flair of an expert, he split the chicken, poured the wine, and handed the food to Parenti. He was proud to show his knowledge.

Parenti chatted as he ate. "We must begin your education at once. You must learn to read and write; it is important."

"The priest showed me a little. But it was hard."

The monk held up the wine glass and squinted at the light shining through. "It is hard, but it is necessary. We of the Church are the chosen, and through God's Blessed Symbols we can find the true form of the High Spirit. Because we can read and write, we can spread the True Words of Our Lord Jesus."

"Then I will learn." He almost felt like a martyr.

"You will also learn obedience and discipline, for nothing must be considered impossible by a neophyte. You must never question your superior's authority—never!—no matter what he tells you to do, for he has been chosen to teach you. You understand?''

"Yes, Brother." The boy's head bobbed in confirmation.

Parenti poured some more wine, and sipped. "Ah-h-h, that is good. You chose well." He wiped his lips. "To get back. If you are given a task beyond your strength, and you fail to perform it, explain your failure, but if your superior insists that you try again, do not dispute; bow to his knowledge and strain yourself to the utmost. Rely on God, to whom all things are known, and He will heed your prayers. Do you understand?''

"Someone is coming down the road, Brother," Leo said.

Parenti was immediately on the alert. Every wayfarer was in peril and a monk had no special protection. Bands of runaway serfs, turned thieves, prowled the highways seeking victims, and monks, who had silver crucifixes, were prizes. During the winter, their woolen habits were eagerly sought, and only the most hardy and the most foolish traveled alone. Many clerics, relying on God and prayer, became easy marks.

With his right hand pushed into his loosely fitted left sleeve, Parenti clutched a long, sharp stiletto. He was ready to fight for his silver Cross and the belt he carried encircling his middle. It was his expense coin, given to him by Clement and necessary if he was not to waste his time in begging. He husbanded it carefully; his usual practice was to leave an inn, after he had established his credit, without paying his final bill. He had done this with Favio; and he was not about to give it up without a struggle.

The approaching man appeared to be alone, but appearances could be deceiving. Comrades could be in the bushes, approaching from the sides, concealed so the quarry would not be frightened.

"Quickly," Parenti whispered to Leo. "Pack up the food."

"But . . . don't we share with brothers?" Leo was bewildered by the monk's rapid change of behavior.

"*Obey me, you fool!*" Parenti hissed. "*There are murderers on the highways. Quickly! Pack it up!*"

Leo rushed, pulling the corners of the cloth together into a knot. He corked the wine and threw it inside the bundle.

The newcomer was large, rotund, and burly, with a cherub face, a huge red nose, small glittery eyes, and totally devoid of hair on his head. He walked with an easy, swinging gait, almost a waddle, thrusting his feet forward from his full-length robe like two kittens suddenly peeking out of a burlap bag.

"May God's Mercy be forever upon you," he called as he approached and extended his hand, palm open, to show he was unarmed. But Parenti noted that the staff he held in his right hand was thick.

"May it please God, we are well met," he said, formally. "Where is your destination?" The fat man gasped as he leaned heavily upon his staff.

"Where God wills," Parenti said with a shrug. "And you?"

"I go to Genoa. May the Blessed Virgin see to it that I arrive safely."
He wiped the back of his neck. "The road is hot. Have you met any traveling
my way?"

"No one. And you?"

"None. The ways are empty." The fat man was watching Parenti closely.
"I hear," he said cautiously, "that Urban is in Piacenza, but I didn't see
him. Do you go there for him?"

Parenti tensed. Was this an Urban monk? "No-o . . . I had not heard,"
he said carefully. "What seeks he in that cesspool?"

"Souls, as usual." The man dismissed it. "Would you have a crust to
share for a morning's meal? I have not eaten since noon yesterday, and the
pickings on this road are slim. My stomach is large, but it needs constant
refilling."

"Unfortunately, I have nothing." He moved to pass. Leo's face wrinkled
at the barren lie.

The fat man's stare grew grim. "Not good enough, Brother." A large grin
stretched his mouth, but his eyes flashed. "I know you lie. The lad carries
bread . . . there is still a crust on your habit, and I smell the wine."

"The boy carries old clothes and we have just finished eating the alms we
received this morning. There is none left. I am sorry."

The man bowed his head. "Lord, forgive me what I am about to do,"
he prayed. His head came up. "On your head will be my sinning," he said
wearily. "Open the sack, boy. Let me see your old clothes."

Parenti's stiletto was out and with a wave of the weapon he motioned to
Leo to move behind him. He faced the fat man with caution, watching the
cudgel, as he moved from side to side, ready to jump to evade the heavy shaft.
"Touch what is ours and you will feel the steel," he hissed. "Leo!" he commanded. "Move up the road."

Leo, bewildered, was slow to start. With an agility belying his girth, and
with a bellow of glee, the fat monk leaped forward and seized the bundle from
Leo's hands. In the scramble, he dropped his staff.

Parenti shouted in triumph. He lunged forward, his arm stiff, the point
of the stiletto seeking the man's innards.

The monk spun on his left foot and came about in a complete circle, easily
evading the oncoming dagger. In his hand, seemingly from nowhere, appeared
a three-quarter sword, a saber, and he swung the bundle at Parenti's head.
Parenti stooped to avoid the big bag. He tried to dive beneath it, to reach
the big man, but he had been diverted and his stiletto entered the sack. He
fought to release it. A new roar of glee confused him, and he twisted his body
to avoid the close quarters he was in. The saber flashed before his eyes, striking
his stiletto. Something was wrong! Then he saw it! The monk had passed the
blade to his left hand.

"Hoo! Hoo! Hoo! Look what the little man has! A pickle sticker!" The fat monk
seemed to dance before him. "Hoo! Hoo! Hoo!" And the saber swung again.

Parenti's hand went numb momentarily. The steel rang and he could feel the keen edge as it cut into his fingers. With a cry he dropped his weapon and reeled back, raising his bloody hand before his face to ward off his certain death.

But the fat monk did not move to kill him. The saber whirled above his head like a toy, and there was a large grin on his face as he gasped for breath. "You . . . need more . . . than a needle . . . on this . . . road . . . Brother," he managed haltingly. He tried to breathe deeply, to control his gasping.

His eyes full of hatred, Parenti searched for a weapon—a stick—a stone— but found nothing. Even the cudgel was too far away.

The big monk watched him closely. "You don't know . . . how to . . . fight, Brother. Lucky for you, I only want food. Others could have killed you; no trouble at all." His face became quizzical. "Maybe I should kill you just for lying. You must be a Clement monk, and you made me sin; I had vows not to fight anymore." He turned to Leo. "Hear, boy, and listen closely. All monks are not like this one who refuses Christian charity. Remember it." He turned back to Parenti. "And I did ask you nicely." His saber was swinging in close arcs. "A Clement monk for sure!" He spat. "Like the devil father, so imp son, always ready to prick you with a hidden knife, but a simpleton in a fair fight."

It was obvious to Parenti that the fat man was trying to provoke him to make some threatening move so as to kill him. He glared back but stood still.

"You say you travel where God wills? I say you scurry after the Devil's rump! Begone! Blow with his fart!" He advanced toward Parenti who backed away slowly. "Go on; be off with you before I change my mind." He motioned with his sword. "I need my breakfast. Take the boy with you."

Parenti, relieved, continued to move back. They would not be harmed. He motioned Leo to come with him, and, stiffly, he walked down the road, Leo trailing. At a safe distance, he turned and shouted. "We shall meet again, *Brother!* What is your name?"

The fat monk had found the wine and he pulled the cork with his teeth. Spitting out the cork, he lifted the bottle, took a short drink, and raised it in a salute to Parenti. "A good year, Brother! Let me congratulate you on your taste!" He laughed uproariously as he waved the bottle. "Go on! Be off!"

"Your name," Parenti called, doggedly.

The monk laughed. "You will not forget what I look like, but . . . you want my name? Francis, Brother Francis! Scat! I would eat in peace. Too much argument gives me gas!"

"We will meet again, Francis," warned Parenti. He turned to Leo. "Come." Erect and stiff, his head high, his chin thrust forward, he strode off. Leo followed.

Parenti fought to control his rage. The fight had ended badly, and he had lost his weapon as well as his food, but, most of all, he had been demeaned and belittled before Leo. He would have to change Leo's image of the fight. The

slight bleeding of his hand had stopped—it was only one finger. He could blame
it on the wound. That was it! A lucky cut had deprived him of his weapon.

The fat monk must have once been a soldier, perhaps even a knight, for
he used the sword as an expert. He was a son of Satan, an Urban monk, and
with one stroke he had opened the doorway to . . .? Heaven? Hell? He wasn't
sure, and that was wrong! *He should be sure!* Was his faith failing? There was
a blank moment of nothingness for the one startling instant he faced death.
Not fear! Not joy! *Nothing!* Was it he did not care? *He needed to care!* He needed
prayer, much prayer! And he began to pray as he walked.

Leo, dispirited, walked up ahead, kicking at the dust and creating miniature
storms. His mood changed and he picked up stones and spiraled them down
the road. He was free of his bundle, a fact more important to him than the
loss of the food, and his mind was a blank. The struggle between the two monks
had been exciting while it lasted, although both, in his eyes, were Servants
of the Lord, and he did not try to resolve the paradox which led them to try
to kill each other. For the present, he was not hungry; the weather was good,
and God and Parenti would provide. He kicked at a stone and whistled.

The afternoon was late when Parenti realized that he would not reach
Piacenza by nightfall, and he decided to stop and rest. A dull, impotent anger
still burned within him, an anger he could not vent and release. *Revenge*, he
told himself. *Revenge*. He felt dirty of skin and spirit. Leo, too, must be tired;
the boy had dropped behind him. Ahead, he saw the wheel ruts where carts
had veered off the road to a watering place. He could wash in the pond.

When he turned to call the boy, he saw Leo picking and eating berries
from a roadside bush. A surge of horror went through him. "No! Leo! Wait!"
he shouted. Some of those plants were poisonous.

Leo's mood had changed. Much of the thoughtless gaiety which had bubbled
through him earlier had evaporated, and his dream of a great, new adventure
had become a dull and dirty journey along a dusty road. And he was hungry.
Parenti walked alone, and the few times he had spoken to him, he sounded
much like Mama, scolding him. The bright aura of holiness which had mantled
the cleric earlier had disappeared. And he was hungry.

He saw some clusters of black berries on a whortleberry bush, and he picked
and tasted a few. The sweet juice stirred his appetite, and he began to pull handfuls from the thin branches and stuff them into his mouth, the purplish-black-red
liquid staining his face. The clusters were full and his hunger was enormous.

"You must be careful when you eat wild plants," Parenti warned. "These
are all right, but next time show them to me first." The monk picked some
berries and ate them. "Come. There is a pond up ahead. We can wash and
have some water to drink."

"When are we going to eat?" Leo whined.

"The Lord has provided us with water—and the berries. Let us partake of His provisions. Question not His will. Come." He started back toward the pond without watching if Leo followed him.

But Leo would not leave the bush. He worked quickly, pulling at the clusters and jamming the whortleberries into his mouth, and as he walked slowly around the bush his eye suddenly caught a slight movement a few feet away. He froze. A snake? He hated them. He peered cautiously around a hummock and caught his breath. Sitting on its haunches, calmly chewing, was a rabbit, its ears twitching, but evidently unaware of him.

Leo stood still, as his father had trained him to do on their hunting trips. The rabbit did not move. Slowly, using extreme care, he moved a little forward . . . closer . . . closer . . . then, with a quick leap, he pounced! And caught one of the long ears as the rabbit twisted its head and leaped. With a quick snap of his wrist, Leo broke the rodent's neck and ran his hand down the twitching body. Finding the bladder, he pressed, emptying its contents on the grass. He let out a whoop and ran down the road.

"*BROTHER!*" he shouted excitedly. "*LOOK! LOOK! I caught it!*" When he reached Parenti, he was babbling. "*WE CAN EAT! I CAUGHT IT! WITH MY HANDS!*" He waved the carcass at the startled monk. "If you have a flint for a fire and a knife, I can cook it. My papa showed me how." He was dancing.

The monk touched the still-warm body. "How did you catch it?"

"By the ears. I can hunt with bow and arrows, too. Can we get a bow and some arrows? Maybe I can make one . . . my papa showed me."

"We are of the Church and we do not carry arms except for defense. It would not be seeming for you to carry an exposed weapon." He reached into his habit and brought out a small box. "Here is some flint." He threw a fold of his habit back and exposed his upper thigh. There, strapped, was a leather sheath, and he drew a knife with a cutting edge from it. "This should do." He handed it to Leo.

Leo gutted the animal quickly and hung it from a tree branch while he gathered some twigs and dry grass. Soon he had a fire. He handed the flint back to Parenti, and by the time he had finished skinning the animal, the flame had settled into a hot bed of coals. He quartered the body and skewered the pieces, and the odor of the roasting meat made Parenti salivate. While they waited, the monk talked.

"You did that very well," he praised Leo. "We will have to find a way for you to hunt small game while we are traveling. Have you ever caught partridge? It is a favorite of mine."

Leo glowed under the laudation. "Birds are harder, unless you use a bow, or a sling, or maybe a throwing knife."

"A throwing knife . . ." Parenti had a thought. "Can you do it?"

"A little. But I am better with the bow."

"You cannot carry a bow." Parenti was firm. But a throwing knife? Who would ever expect it from a boy? He trailed off, thinking. Suddenly he came to a conclusion. "I will get you two knives and you will practice. We will depend upon your hunting." He sniffed. "I think the rabbit is finished."

Gingerly, the monk took the hind part of the rabbit in the tree leaf and ate ravenously. He was surprised at his appetite. His mind, having solved his other problems, turned toward food. Later he wiped his hands on the grass and washed in the pond. "I miss my wine," he told the boy, "but let us thank the Lord for the water."

The darkness was spreading, and Leo added some wood to the fire. His stomach had stopped its growl, and he was sated and warm, and his thoughts were inconsequential.

Parenti, however, was engaged in a fantasy which brought him great pleasure. He was in a duel with the fat monk, Francis, and—whissst—the fat carcass would be lying on the road, and Leo would be drawing his throwing knife from the body. He chuckled. What a quick way to conclude an argument. The boy had a hunter's instinct for animals, but what about men? That might require cultivation. His father had been a soldier and had killed men. Leo knew this. Perhaps the father could serve as a model for the son? Why not? It would be a simple transfer of thought.

"Did your father ever tell you stories about the wars he fought in," he said offhand.

Leo was tired. The day had been long, and his emotional swings from despair to heady exhilaration had exhausted him. His belly was full; he wanted only sleep, and he was drifting off when Parenti's voice invaded his drifting mind. He mumbled and settled himself comfortably. Soon, he was fast asleep, dreamless.

Parenti stared at the dark form lit only by the small fire's flickering light. Tomorrow, they would be at the abbey and the monks there should not see the boy. He had no doubts that he could set the tongues of the monks wagging and find out about the couriers from Alexius and Urban. The abbey would be buzzing with information. The decision made, he prepared for sleep.

But sleep would not come. His mind percolated and thoughts crowded and jostled each other. A long serpentine form, like a living fog, was winding in and out of the shadows, penetrating, billowing, and seducing him with promises and tantalizing revelations. It obscured, half-exposed, revealed, and quickly covered itself, pulling on his imagination, winding itself in and out of his half-dream. In desperation he began to pray, but the wraith-figure beckoned coyly, sliding and slithering, weaving seductively before him. In despair he began to sing *The Stabat Mater* to himself.

"*The Mother was standing . . .*" Slowly, he enunciated all the sorrows of Mother Mary as she followed Jesus to the Crucifixion. Finished, he tried to make himself comfortable in the earth, but, immediately, the long, weaving mist returned and began to form itself into a hazy figure. Painfully, slowly, it gathered substance. His mind exploded! It was Leo!

The boy was wavy but clear. He was removing his clothing, standing naked—like he had done before the wayside Madonna early that morning. He held the habit Parenti had given him, but the monk could see through it as though it was clear as water. It waved and distorted the body, making the bare flesh undulate, and the monk's eyes were drawn irresistibly toward the boy's genitals, exaggerating them, making them live and move. Sweat gathered on Parenti's brow; his teeth began to grind as he twisted his head away from the sight he had seen many times before with pleasure. But a giant hand was turning his head back, mastering his will and his muscles. He could feel his groin tense and his growing erection.

"Lord," he prayed, his eyes tightly clenched, "why dost Thou tempt me? Am I being tested? It has been more than three years, and I have put all that behind me. Afflict me not again, I beg Thee. I know it is an abomination in Thy sight." He was panting. "If it be Lucifer who does this," he raised his Cross with trembling hand, "then . . . get thee behind me, Satan! I will have none of thee!"

The picture faded from his sight and he sighed in relief. "It must have been Satan," he consoled himself, "retreating from the Cross. He still follows me, but God is with me." Calmed, his muscles relaxed and he drifted off into a black void, unknowingly.

6

Mary and Andre waited until Papa Toon and Michael had left for Genoa before starting their own journey to Paris. Mary was in good spirits, but Andre, who carried the basket, plodded after her with the heavy step of a troubled man. Her attempts at conversation were answered in grunts of annoyance, or silence, and his sulkiness finally drained her. Each walked alone and not even their first rest changed his attitude. She could not break through his wall of sullen hostility.

When the sun became low, Mary insisted they stop. They found a stream, and she splashed the cold water on her face and cooled the nape of her neck under her black hair. He watched her from the bank and cursed the night he had gone to visit her. She was thin, nothing like the plump girls at Cannelli's; her breasts were like two pears, hanging free when she bent over; not like Jeanne's, full and firm, a delight to hold. And when she stood up, the wet chiton outlined them like two small protuberances, hardly more than a man's chest. She had destroyed him, forcing him to leave the farm. Somehow, she would live, he was sure; but what about him? His self-pity grew, and, as he wallowed in the depths of his dejection, he heard singing, a ringing of small bells, and women's laughter.

Mary had heard it, too, and she turned toward him in fear.

They were in a small dell which led through a coppice of dense trees and brush. Tall timbers fenced them in on both sides, hiding the pond from the road, and around the trees were thick growths of spiny bushes. The music came from somewhere beyond the grove.

Andre sniffed the air. "Meat," he announced. "Roasting meat."

Searching about, he discovered a path, and he carefully pushed the branches aside as he began to follow it. Mary grabbed the basket and quickly followed him.

A camp was in a small hollow near the stream, and three men were playing lutes for two dancing women who juggled tambourines and whirled around a fire. The carcass of a small roe was spitted across the flame, and ever so often one of the women would dart forward and give the spit a turn. On one of her turns she saw Andre. "Company! We have an audience!" she cried.

The playing halted abruptly, and one man drew a dagger as the other two picked up clubs; all three advanced on Andre.

"Who are you? What are you doing here?" The armed man held his weapon poised.

"We-we're just travelers," Andre sputtered. "We heard the music. We meant no harm."

"What's your name? Who's with you?"

"Andre, Andre Toon. And my sister, Mary Toon. We go to Paris. We'll leave right—"

"Come out, Mary Toon. Let us see you!" said the armed man, sternly, nodding to his comrades in understanding, and they steeled themselves for any emergency.

Mary emerged and cowered slightly behind Andre.

The three men glanced at each other and grinned. They concluded there was little to fear from these intruders. The armed man made one final effort. "I see no weapons," he said. "Where do you hide them?"

"I—er—carry none," blurted Andre. He felt foolish.

The man laughed; the others smiled. "You are either a great fool or a firm believer in the powers of prayer. Search him, Tom."

A quick search revealed that Andre spoke the truth, and the tense atmosphere changed quickly once there was no danger. The armed man welcomed them and insisted that the two join the group for dinner. "We have much more than we need, and we love company. Come," he added, "it is only right to share the meat with you."

He introduced himself and his two brothers. One of the girls was his wife, Celia, who smiled quickly at Andre, and the other was Alicia, wife of Pierre, his second brother. Tom was unwed. They were a group of jongleurs, he explained, who passed from town to town, sometimes from castle to castle, singing, making music, dancing, and telling stories. They would entertain anyone who desired their fun and gaiety. They were welcomed everywhere for their free and frolicsome ways. And they carried the news from village to village, from knight to noble, and for that they were well rewarded. With winter approaching, they were wending their way back toward their home, in Paris. If Andre and Mary wished to join them they were welcome. It would be easier than traveling alone, and there was place for another girl, and another man, in the group.

Andre was overjoyed at the effusiveness of their welcome. Of course, he told them, he and Mary would like to join the group. He had never been to Paris, and he would need guiding. Celia, Charles' wife, passed him a hot strip of the roasted doe, and he fingered it gingerly in his hands. "Isn't the penalty death for taking a knight's deer?" he asked nervously.

Charles laughed and stopped nibbling on his strip. "Nobody takes us seriously. We are madmen, buffoons, jesters. We are birdies, chirpers, twitters, and warblers. We have no sense of responsibility. We are like children—and we harm no one. We are mirthfully unreasonable—we have no reason in our laughter—and our women are pretty and accommodating, for our lord's chamber. The worst we ever had was a whipping, while the girls collected some gold and jewelry, and then we were escorted out of the lord's forests to his neighbor's fife." He laughed uproariously and the others grinned with him.

"Then we were given food and drink, and told the tale—in a song, of course—and the knight tested Celia that night." He leaned forward and whispered loudly. "And I experimented with his lady. She was a pleasant wench, too." He smirked. "Stay with us and I'll show you how to enjoy your life."

Andre was not that sure he could agree. He did not like the easy ways of his newfound friends. Everything was too haphazard and uncertain, and, as Charles and his brother, Pierre, explained it, they never knew where they would stay the next day, nor what the next day would provide. They lived from hand to mouth, from day to day, and while some days were filled with luxury, other days were lean. Anyway, he had other plans, a new one. He had found his way to escape.

Mary was entranced with the jongleurs. Tom hovered over her and she reacted coyly to his attentions. She, also, had become intrigued with the magical world she had discovered when she viewed the display of finger rings, bracelets, pendants, and earrings worn by the other girls. And the dresses! Never in her life had she seen such a display of jewelry and gowns with such wild colors; and they were all of fine cotton. She vowed that someday she would have all that and more.

"Where are you from?" The question interrupted her mood. It was Tom. "You're not a city girl."

"I live on a farm near Genoa. My father's a winemaker."

"A winemaker! How wonderful!" He clapped his hands. "I have a ditty about a winemaker. I'll sing it for you." With broad gestures, he sang:

"WHAT A WONDERFUL LIFE A WINEMAKER LIVES;
WHAT JOY AND WHAT BLISS HIS HANDIWORK GIVES;
WITH WINE AND A SONG AND A GIRL IN MY HAND
THE WORLD IS A HEAVEN WITH ME IN COMMAND."

"You're funny," she laughed. "But it's really hard work."

"When you drink the product, you forget the work. My product is to make you laugh, and I have succeeded; now my life is devoted to your happiness."

"Are you always like this?" She felt bubbly.

"Of course. I'm a jongleur! I make everyone happy."

"What do you do during the winter? You can't travel and sing when it's snowing."

"We go home, to Paris, in the winter. We attend parties. The rich burghers and the knights always give parties, and we entertain them. But in the spring! That is the time! We are as free as the birds, and we can go anywhere. The sun shines and warms us; the sky is blue, and we sing and dance. If it rains, we live in the wagon, or a barn, or in a farmhouse—always somewhere."

"But that's a hard life. You must be hungry a lot."

"Do I look hungry? When we entertain the knights we always eat the best in the kitchen. The cooks love us. On the road, we always have bread and cheese, sometimes a bird, a chicken—and meat, like today. God always provides for a man of music.''

"I don't think I could live like that."

"Of course you could. Just think; we are free, not vassals, not serfs. We don't dig the dirt, and most of the time we are our own masters. Who else but we can say that? We live under the stars, and we don't fight, like soldiers. And, best of all, what we do makes everyone happy. When we leave a village everyone is sad, but they are laughing through their tears. What could be better in this life? And when we die, we will go to Heaven and we can do the same thing there. The Lord will clap His hands to our singing. Can you imagine anything better?''"

She shrugged. "I don't know. Maybe it's all right for you, but me?" She changed the subject. "When we come to Paris, will you help me find my sister?"

He took her hand. "That is your wish so I will find her. I swear by the Virgin Mary. Does that convince you?"

"Yes." She beamed at him, and his answering smile took on an expression she had seen before on Andre's face. His candid stare of passion aroused her and her skin became alive. The nipples of her breasts were hardening and she could feel their stretch. Her lips parted as she began to breathe shallowly in anticipation, and her mouth was drying. Their eyes were locked together in a shining embrace, and a soft glow was spreading over her neck, rising to her cheeks. She moved to make herself more comfortable, not realizing she was displaying the subtle coyness of a sensual cat.

He was sure she felt the same as he although some of her words belied her actions. Sometimes she was a little girl, simple in her ignorance and very young in her knowledge. Her body, and the way she moved it . . . he could feel his blood heating and pulsating in his temples. She was no virgin, he concluded, but she was two people: a woman, enticing him; a child, not understanding her innocent seductiveness.

Andre suddenly loomed over them. "Can we talk alone, Mary?" Tom excused himself. "These people have agreed to help us get to Paris if we agree to help them," he told her. "Charles says if you will help the two girls—in their work, and they'll teach you how to dance with them—we can all travel together. Do you agree?"

She was delighted. Tom had talked, but it was obvious that Charles ran the troupe.

"I see that you and Tom find things agreeable," he said dryly.

"I didn't know you wanted me to fight with him," she answered curtly.

His face became ugly but he did not reply. He walked off.

That night they bedded down near the wagon. Charles and Celia were inside; the others, not too far away. Mary was in a light mood, and it did not take her long before she was sleeping calmly.

Andre could hear her steady breathing. The effects of the day had touched him deeply, and although he was tired, he was determined not to fall asleep. But he nodded off as the night sounds of the fields lulled him.

He awoke with a start of terror, almost with a scream. Was it time? Had he overslept? He cursed himself for dozing. The blackness around him was spotty, the moon casting a slight light, and the stillness comforted him. He calmed; there was still time. Carefully he raised his head and kept his eyes on the small bulk, Mary, beside him. Was she sleeping lightly? Would she hear him? Suppose the others heard? He would say he was going off to relieve himself.

Slowly, carefully, he began to rise, and as he came erect, his eyes growing accustomed to the dark, he could see the bulk of the wagon and the two horses nearby asleep. With a light step he moved toward the rear of the vehicle, keeping in its darkness. He heard no one stirring and he sighed with relief. Becoming bold, he advanced toward the bushes, tensely waiting at their edge to see if anyone had seen him. All was quiet. Quickly, he stepped into their shadows and soon found the dell and pond where he and Mary had been earlier. It was only a few more strides to the road, the road home. He didn't look back.

"Good-bye, little sister," he muttered. "Have a good time." For the first time in many weeks he felt free.

7

The next morning, Baron Ducas and his party left the abbey at Bobbio and headed back to their ship at Genoa while another messenger carrying a document embossed by the seal-ring of the pope left for Abbot Hugh at Cluny, in France.

After reading Urban's letter, Hugh thought deeply, then read and reread the document. His first excitement remained, and he quickly summoned some of the older monks. One by one, they read the epistle and each, in turn, became animated. There was no mistake; Hugh had read correctly even though there was doubt and some confusion in Urban's thinking. Clarification was necessary.

They discussed Urban's proposal feverishly and came to the conclusion that God, in His infinite wisdom, had pointed out the way to Urban, and Cluny would be the chosen instrument for His plan.

Hugh ordered that all of Urban's requests were to be fulfilled immediately. The scribes hurried to sharpen their quills. Parchments were unrolled, and the copiers worked far into the night by candlelight. In the morning, the first couriers were ready to travel.

All during the week, riders left the abbey and bore their secret documents to the dukes, the marquises, the counts, and all their vassals—the barons, the seigneurs, the bishops—and their vassals—the knights and the cavaliers. Riders went to the shops of the more enterprising burghers and tradesmen with a slightly different letter than that delivered to the nobles, and the monks who left the abbey on foot talked to the priests who spoke directly to their flocks: the peasant farmers, serfs, and free artisans. There was a summons from Papa Urban and all True Believers would heed.

There was to be a stir and bustle in the land, a fermentation, touching everyone, but none but the highest nobles knew the full reason for Urban's call for them to be present at Clermont town on 18 November. To almost all it was an ecclesiastical order, not lightly to be disobeyed, for the pope was God's vicar on earth, and the faithful were always ready to listen to God's surrogate.

Curiosity mounted a rising edginess. The more inventive said that Urban had received a special message from Jesus, just as Moses had received the Ten Commandments from God. Others went further, even claiming they knew what the message was. The world, they said, was to have ended A.D. 1000, and that had been the time chosen for the Second Coming. But Jesus Christ had

45

begged a boon from His Father. He told God that there had not been enough warnings to all the sinners, and, therefore, they had not had enough time for full repentance. In His all-forgiving mercy, God had granted His Son's request, extending the Second Coming for a hundred years, to A.D. 1100, and the pope was going to make the announcement so all sinners would be able to be ready on time.

The ignorant, the learned, the foolish, and the wise, all shook their heads in agreement at this most plausible explanation, and the sinful crowded into the confessionals.

8

Parenti did not sleep well that night. He tossed, wakened, and dozed continuously, and the morning found him tired and gaunt-eyed. His pseudo-dream, his temptation, lay heavily upon him. At the stream, he washed the nape of his neck with cold water, hoping that the temperature shock would divert him, and, to his relief, it cleared his mind. He shook Leo awake.

"We will eat in the town," he told the boy. "If we hurry, we can be there before the noon hour."

As they walked, six riders, galloping furiously, passed them. They were gone before Leo recognized them. "That was Skora and the gentlemen," he told Parenti excitedly. "They must be going back to their ship."

"Then we must hurry," said the monk.

They arrived at Bobbio in the late morning, and Parenti searched for an armorer who might have some throwing knives. After much bargaining with the smithy, the monk handed the knives to Leo. Later, he told the boy, "You will practice until you become an expert. You will be able to hunt for our food."

"Yes, Brother," said Leo, obediently. He sheathed the knives with awe; he was now a man with his own weapons, and he tried to imitate a soldier's swagger as he played with them.

"Leo!" The reprimand came quickly. "You are sworn to the Church, not to the army of some knight. You do not show these knives to anyone, and you do not draw them except when you are hunting . . . *or when I tell you!* *Do you understand?*" His face was stern.

"Sure," said Leo offhand.

Parenti searched his face. "I am not so sure you do, but we will work on it."

"I'm hungry. When are we going to eat?"

"We passed an inn. Wait here; I'll bring some bread and cheese; maybe some eggs."

They ate as they walked to the abbey. In a field before the main building, a short monk was working on the earth, tossing potatoes into a wicker basket. Parenti told Leo to wait, and lifting the hem of his habit, he climbed the laid-up stone fence and approached the man. Soon they were in deep conversation.

The monk was garrulous, happy to have someone to talk to after spending all morning digging for the potatoes. He went into every detail of Emperor Henry's triple excommunication and the upcoming excommunication of King Philip, and when Parenti asked about the men from the East, he was able to describe all the fine points of Alexius' letter. "Alexius wants mercenaries to fight the Turk invading Byzantium. He even says that maybe afterward Rome and Byzantium can discuss ways to reunite the Church."

"Ah," said Parenti. "Did Urban agree?"

"Not right off. He told the Synod that it would be discussed further when they met at Cluny in November."

Parenti was ecstatic; he had found the nexus, the link between the two prelates. But he would have to follow the pope to Cluny to know the final decision. "Thank you, Brother." He left.

The old monk stared after him with great annoyance. The abrupt departure was an open breach of etiquette, a discourtesy.

Parenti would have to send the news he had learned to Clement in a hurry if he were to receive the credit—and the gold. The contents of Alexius' letter would soon be known in every inn and would lend spice to the drinking, but Urban's answer was the greater news. He speculated on Urban's reply.

Leo, unconcerned, was busy throwing his knives at a tree, and he was surprised to find that they glided straight and true. Using a line on the tree's trunk as a target, he found he could come close to it most of the time, but as he increased the distance of the throw, his accuracy diminished, and at a far range he could not even hit the tree's trunk. Parenti stopped his practice and hurried him along. As they walked, the monk talked.

He began to relate all the reasons for the dispute between Urban and Clement, but Leo, despite the monk's sharp admonitions to remain attentive, was not listening. The contorted, labyrinthian maze of the papal conflict meant nothing. To him, the pope . . . was the Pope, with his ring and his staff, and whoever had the ring and the staff was the Pope. If an emperor made one bishop pope, and someone made another bishop the pope . . . well, he didn't know if it was right or wrong. But whoever had the ring and staff—he was *the Pope*. To him, it was as simple as all that.

In disgust, Parenti sent him hunting, and Leo was off like an unleashed puppy. A whoop, soon after, from the underbrush, told Parenti that the hunt was successful, and Leo burst from the brush on the run, swinging a rabbit by the ears.

"It was easy," he boasted. "They are good knives. I got him with the first throw . . . see! . . . right here!" He opened the bloodstained fur near the neck. "One throw and I had him! If you give me the flint, I'll make a fire and we'll eat."

Parenti passed the flint. "Keep it," he said. "From now on you will take care of the fires."

"All right." Nothing could diminish Leo's cheerfulness. He gathered the wood quickly, gutted and skinned the animal, and, in short order, had the meat roasting on the flame. His exuberance and glow of confidence permeated his being, and he reveled in the monk's praise. He felt he had proven himself. From now on he would carry his share by securing food and preparing it; he was a man in his own right, no longer a boy.

Parenti watched his novice at work and took note of the change in Leo's demeanor. In a few short days, Leo had changed. He pondered that change as he cracked a bone and sucked the marrow. They were on a small rise, the road dipping and running straight in both directions. Up ahead the trees thickened and became a dense wood.

"You will practice with the knives, Leo," he said idly.

"I do well enough."

"You will still need practice." The monk was offhand. "Remember what happened when we met that fat monk? You must be ready to help me if we run into thieves again. And for that you need practice. That fat dog was a thief, and from thieves we defend ourselves just as your father would if a thief came into his inn."

Leo nodded and started to kick dirt over the fire when he halted. Fifteen paces from them stood a small, slender man, leaning on a stout staff which was taller than he, his bald head resting on the wood, his face a skull. The sleeves of his habit were tattered and open, and the bare skin was brown and splotched. The bottom of his robe was shredded, individual threads hanging free and encrusted with mud. The ragged bottom swung like a pendulum as he swayed.

The torn front of the garment showed his knobby knees and the dirty skin, in shades of earth-brown, mud-streaked where the wet earth had dried. The fingers holding the staff were long and bony, and the backs of his hands were veined and corded, with gray warts with tufted white hairs. He had no eyebrows; his small eyes, metallic dark, glinted under his heavy-hanging lids. A slight, obscure smile hovered about his small mouth, and the skin on his face was ash-gray. An unwashed aroma hung about him as though he was wrapped in an untanned, unwashed hide of a fresh-slaughtered sheep.

Parenti, in mock humility, bowed his head. "I did not hear you approach, Brother, but we are well met."

The man nodded indifferently. "I had no wish to disturb you, nor to interrupt your meal, nor your discourse." The voice was thin with a hoarse crackle. "I want for nothing except some water. My throat is hot, with much of the road's dust, and I choke."

"I am sorry," said the monk, "but we have none."

The man nodded as if he had expected the answer. He gazed at Leo. "What are you called, my son?"

Leo had never seen a man such as this, and he stared, wide-eyed. "I'm Leo," he managed.

The sun was low, reddening the clouds, and the shadows were darkening. Parenti wished to move on. "We have far to go, Brother. God be with you. Come, Leo, we must be off."

The old man stayed him with a shaking hand. "There are few things in *this* world, Brother, that we *must* do. When someone says he has little time, he makes excuses for saying good-bye." He took a deep breath. "I am called Brother Perfect." His voice trembled. "Are you a Papist?"

Parenti reacted sharply. The question had revealed the man! "A Cathari!" he snarled. A spawn of Lucifer! A devil worshipper! A heretic! . . . Unclean!

The old man smiled. "I see you are a Papist," he said without rancor. "So be it; it is God's will." He chuckled. "I reach the end of my Endura with a Papist. Truly a whim of the Lord. But I am at peace." He stretched out his hand.

Parenti shrank back. "Away! You pig of Satan! Away!"

"In your own faith, Papist, you seek mercy. And your Jesus tells you to grant mercy and aid the needy. I need your aid."

"We will aid in your death, Cathari!" Parenti spat.

"That is exactly where I need you," said the old man mildly. "I die, and my body needs burial under some stones if it is to be withheld from the wild dogs. Near that tree would be nice." He pointed. His slight frame folded and wavered from side to side.

"We will do it, Father," said Leo before Parenti could speak.

"Leo!" snapped the monk. "As a novice you keep quiet. Your teacher will decide."

"Swear it," whispered the old man, ignoring Parenti.

"To you he swears nothing," snarled the monk. "Away, old man! We have nothing to do with those who defile the Lord. We have no pity for Satan's pups."

The Cathari turned slowly to stare at him. "A great pity. I die and have not the strength to show you the true road. Your apostle, Christ, said, 'Blessed are the meek in spirit.' I see you are a true disciple of his."

"Do not quote scripture to me, heretic!" hissed Parenti. "I can give you chapter and verse! To Saint Matthew, Our Lord said, 'Think not that I come to send peace on earth; I come not to send peace but a sword.' So shall our swords drive heretics out! Away!"

A benign smile opened the man's toothless mouth. "Peace . . . and polemics." He shook his head. "I thank the Lord I am ready to leave this earth-madness." His voice gained some strength. "My soul shall be carried to the heavens by God's workers, the Eons." He chuckled. "And your Christ may be one of them. Another whim." He turned to Leo. "Will you swear, boy?"

Leo stood aghast, turning from one man to the other. He knew not what to do. To help the elderly had been ingrained by his mother, and he felt a welling pity for the old man. But that was pitted against Parenti's insistence of discipline. The monk had called the old man "heretic." No one could be cursed with a viler name than that.

The old man saw his hesitation. "My son, do not listen to that man, for he is perverted, and he will delude you. His truth is nothing more than a lie and his belief is an insanity. His worship of Christ as the Lord is false, for Christ was no more than one of God's Eons, a lowly worker at best. There is only One God, One Lord, One, not two, or three, or four. Love the Lord, not the Eons."

An attack of coughing wracked him. When it was over, he continued. "My time runs out. Learn this. It is the Archangel Lucifer who is the true master of this earth; it is his domain, given to him by the Lord. He uses Papists—such as this one—to mislead innocent souls and foster mistrust in God. That is how God tests us. Only through the sacred Endura, through chastity, through fasting and the refusal to harm any man can you reach the kingdom of Heaven. Beware the man and what he calls his love! I warn you, he will sacrifice you to the Devil!''

His voice rose, taking on new vitality. "You must not harm any living thing! No man! No tree! No flower. The True Spirit lives within you and within all that live. When you deny Satan, the earth, your immortal soul returns to Heaven!'' He was breathing hard, holding his side in pain.

Parenti had walked down the road. "Leo!" he called. "I wait!"

"I come! I come!" Leo shouted, but he was like a small animal held in fascination by the gleam of the snake's eyes. He did not stir.

"Endur-a . . .'' the old man muttered. "The fast-ing . . . the purifying . . . of the soul . . . the ulti-mate lib-er-ation . . . the death . . . I come, my Lord . . .'' Slowly, he crumbled, sliding down his staff, which remained upright a moment, then fell across him.

Leo, suddenly freed from his spell, shook the old man's shoulder. The body, in a half-seated position, rolled over, the eyes wide and staring, sunken deep into the skull. Involuntarily he shuddered.

"He's dead," he called to Parenti who was walking back.

"Good riddance," snapped the monk. "Come; it becomes dark, and we must find a place to bed down for the night."

"Shouldn't we put him by the tree? Off the road?"

Parenti, annoyed, contemplated the body. "I cannot contaminate my hands with a Cathari. But you are an Innocent. Pull him off the road. It should be kept clean. And hurry.''

Leo dragged the body to the tree and rested it against the trunk. He was surprised at its lightness. The man seemed asleep.

Parenti waited impatiently. In the silence which followed after they left the spot, he noticed the effect on Leo. "What are you thinking, Leo?" he asked.

The old man's words had burned deeply into Leo's consciousness. "Couldn't we have buried him? It isn't right to leave him that way."

"The Lord works in His own ways, Leo. If He wished that man to be buried, He would have seen to it that he was. Believe me."

"Maybe . . . maybe the Lord was testing us?" He looked to Parenti.

"I will know if He does. You must learn that we are always ready to root out all evils against Our Lord. There are nonbelievers—pagans; and there are unbelievers like the Jew and the Moslem. They believe in God but deny Jesus Christ. Then there are the misbelievers and they are the worst. They are the heretics, those who know but deny Jesus His Godhead. They are worshipers of Satan. They are his incubi—imps formed like men—and they seduce and fornicate with our women, while other imps—succubi, formed like women,

and passionate and beautiful—weave their nests of lust around the men, seducing them away from Christ. Beware when you feel lust for a woman; it may
be a succubi from Lucifer.''

"How am I to know?''

"I will teach you. As my novice, you will learn, and about women there
is much for you to learn. But one thing at a time. Let us finish about that
Cathari. Our job is to save souls for Christ and that man works for Satan,
sending souls to hell for his master.''

"How did you know who he was?''

"By listening. You heard him call me a Papist? That told me immediately
that he was against Our Lord. Only devils call us Papists. You must study
and learn the scriptures so they cannot confuse you. They always attack the
Lord's Church. Remember that! *They always attack the Lord's Church!* They are
apostates and they seek to destroy the True Faith! That's how you can always
find them!'' He had worked himself into a frenzy. "They are *fiends*!''

"But he was such a little man. He didn't even want anything to eat.''

"That is their disguise. They say they practice Endura.'' He laughed and
added slyly, "But they must eat, mustn't they? Or they would all die, and
we would be rid of them. But, no. They all die old because Satan feeds them
brimstone. That's how they live, by eating devil's fire.''

Leo was mystified by the monk's explanation. Devil's fire, to him, was
very real; it came from the warships of the East; it burned the flesh—like his
father's arm. But the old man's story about Eons? And Christ was an Eon?
That made no sense either. He was the Son of God. How could God let Lucifer
rule the world? And if starvation—Endura—was the way to get to Heaven,
there must be many poor people there; yet rich people also prayed and were
granted forgiveness and went to Heaven. It made no sense at all.

Parenti saw Leo's perplexity. "It seems strange to you now, but you will
understand as you learn more. When you follow your teacher's word, you will
be guided by God just as Christ was my teacher. You will understand all of
these strange things later.''

Leo nodded. It must be so, he told himself, and he dismissed the thoughts
from his mind. He snuggled into the soft earth and the darkness enveloped
him. His mind dulled. Tired, he was soon in a deep sleep.

Parenti settled himself into a cuplike dimple next to the boy, and he could
feel the earth's coolness coming through his habit. His head was cradled on
his arm; his eyes were open; and he stared into the night. He lay quietly but
his inner muscles began their tensing, a living, tortured rhythm he struggled
to contain. He felt a strange exhilaration, an emotional turmoil which was
heightening his fantasies. Leo, on his side, was in easy reach, and the monk
clenched his teeth.

He was slipping into a new dream, but he did not try to drive it away.
Instead, he slowly rubbed his one thigh against the other, luxuriating in the
feel and pleasure. He moved closer to Leo, who was breathing quietly, and

slowly pushed him on his back. The boy, drugged in his sleep, did not awaken, and Parenti lay silently beside him, struggling and tortured. His faith and desires were competing, with his conscience and his longings for the soft flesh locked in combat. The pain was crawling over him, spreading its threads and pulling them tight like the closing filaments of a spider's web. For three years he had fought, but now he heard his mind shout: "Even Clement does not practice chastity. Why should you?" He groaned outwardly; his neck was sweaty, and a sudden chill made him shudder. He curled inward on himself and trembled.

Other remembrances, recollections, crowded in to taunt him, whispering seductively of past pleasures, and they flowed through him like soothing balm, a warm stream of sated desire.

His hand, trembling, reached out and slid under the fold of Leo's habit. He could feel the warm skin at his fingers' tips, and he moved them slowly upward toward the groin, tenderly running them through the soft, downy hair of the boy's loins. Leo stirred. Parenti's hand froze, but the boy's deep breathing resumed, and the monk began his ministrations. His excitement grew, firing his internal volcano, as he felt the tensing of the boy's muscles, and his breath came faster as Leo began to move slowly in rhythm to the pressures of his hand.

The tempo increased, became more deliberate, and Parenti could feel the blood pulsating in his head, pounding his temples. He was holding Leo's genitals, firmly yet softly, in the palm of his hand.

The moon had risen and some light came through the trees, throwing an eerie, spotty glow over the dark ground. With his free hand, the monk drew back the folded habit, exposing Leo's nakedness to the fuzzy light. The boy had a half-erection, and the monk moved his hand over the penis gently, beginning to work it with soft rubbings. He was gasping and his lips trembled as the phallus came erect. With a moan, he bent his face toward the boy's groin, making soft animal sounds.

9

Urban, while still young in the Church, had been a secretary to old Pope Gregory, and he had listened often to his mentor expound on a project close to his heart—a mass pilgrimage to the Holy Sepulchre in Jerusalem. Now, mulling Alexius' plea for mercenary knights from the West, he had a sudden flash of Gregory's old fixation.

There were many troublesome, feuding knights killing good Christians and plundering the land. A plea for a great pilgrimage could turn these warlike marauders eastward, especially with the lure of Byzantine gold and Moslem land. This, too, would help the Church by bringing peace to Europe. They could, also, help protect Christians seeking penance in Holy Jerusalem. Such were his letters to the powerful princes, the dukes, and the counts.

He sought their approval and help, for he knew that once they were forsworn, their vassals and knights would follow. His message to them was secret, and they had kept his confidence, but as he moved from fiefdom to fiefdom, an aura of an impending crisis was building around him, and the lesser knights, peasants, and serfs felt that his presence was the forerunner of the oncoming doom of Armageddon.

One evening, after a long talk, a heavy dinner, and wine, he sat by the fire and dozed. He entered a dream.

He was in a huge courtyard speaking to thousands of people, more than he had ever faced at one time before. They became hazy and faded, and he was alone with Gregory, who stood clear, stark, and grim in his presence. Gregory spoke:

"The Church will rule supreme if you demolish the kings who seek to control her. You must stand fast on principle! Cleanse the sinful, and drive out all who consort with Lucifer!"

Urban bowed his head and with hands clasped, agreed. Then Gregory unfolded a massive vista, an avenue as wide as the stars, running into the future. A mass of people were moving inexorably on the avenue—to the Holy Land; thousands, on the road to Jerusalem.

"All this," said Gregory, "you will accomplish, and more. But know, all this has great cost. Watch carefully."

And he saw disaster! There was war and endless fighting! Hunger was everywhere! Pestilence and Death! The most beautiful, the best, the fairest flowers of Christianity perished! Those who were not dead were hurt, blighted, befouled, and stricken. Men, boys . . . women and girls . . . toddlers and newborn . . . all. Bodies were strewn over an endless plain where the hot, glaring sun rotted and petrified the human flesh. Vultures and other carrion eaters feasted. There was a keening wail, a dirge of infinite sorrow, shriveling his ears, cutting into his soul, and vibrating his body. A stench of burning corpses, griseous and black, stifled him, and the mounds of flesh lay in city streets, cities he had never seen. He shuddered and covered his face with his hands.

"No more, dear God!" he cried. "No more!"

The scene suddenly shifted. Thousands of Christians were tearing Crosses from their necks and hurling the sacred image into the dirt, turning their backs on the Church of Christ and embracing the Moslem faith. Thousands more, overcome by greed, clutched handfuls of golden coins and reveled with wanton women. Carnality was everywhere, and the people jeered and laughed at him.

Then the land turned crimson, and the sun became a fireball in the heavens. The Bright Star of Bethlehem grew scarlet. There was a sea of surging, red blood, its waves breaking against the Cross of Christ at Calvary. And the blood was dripping from His wound, flowing over His legs, and mixing with the rising red sea.

Urban shrieked and the vision vanished. Terrified, he huddled in his chair, a painful fear contracting his heart. Was he unleashing a sea of blood? Was this the meaning of his dream? An omen? His motives, he told himself, were pure. The Church must rule, for that was the only road to salvation, to redemption. The Church, the Mother Church, must be saved, no matter at what cost. He would pray for guidance.

In France he turned south, to the castle of his staunch friend, the devout and warlike Raymond of St. Gilles, of Provence and Toulouse.

Raymond, age fifty-three, battle-scarred veteran of the Moorish campaign, blinded in one eye, had a wide reputation as a warrior and statesman, equally admired for his military leadership and diplomatic abilities. One of the wealthiest lords of southern France, he had steadily increased his estates by selective marriages, his latest being the bastard daughter of King Alfonso VI of Castile, the fair Elvira.

Elvira was young, proud, haughty, and high-spirited, and she was devoted to the Church and firm in her loyalty to Urban. A bride of one year, she prayed for a son, and she welcomed the arrival of Urban to her home as a favorable sign of the Virgin Mary.

After the amenities were over, Urban lost no time in relating his vision, and when he was done, his face was ash-gray in pain. His friends were horrified at his agony, and Raymond sought to appease him.

"All great events are born in pain and torment, my friend. We live in sin, but Our Savior suffered for our sins, and we will be saved only through His Church. Many will fall by the wayside, but they cannot be the reason for the rest of us to also fall."

His countess said it a different way. "The Church has many problems, Holy Father, and they lie heavily upon your heart. Many suffer and die by the answers given to us by Our Lord, and salvation cannot come without penance and cost. But we shall be saved."

"My lady is right," said Raymond. "Father Gregory preached a great pilgrimage for the greater Glory of God, and your vision may be the only way to achieve it. It is ordained."

"And what of the maimed and the dead? What of the souls lost to the Church?" Urban's face was ghastly. "I saw the pits of the damned. Could that be the voice of Lucifer? Can Satan tempt me?"

"*No!*" Elvira was vehement. "The Servant of God stands protected by the flaming sword of Saint Michael, and the Devil can never have power over him. God spoke to you, not Lucifer!"

"Elvira is right," agreed Raymond. "You are overwrought. Your vision comes from heaven and will stand to the glory of the Church throughout all eternity. Urban the Second will be remembered as the Father of Unity, he who united Christianity, East and West."

"You flatter me, my friend. Let us pray that I will not be cursed as the destroyer of our people. I have a thought. Would you summon Adhemar to our council? His advice would be invaluable."

Raymond readily agreed. "I will, in the morning."

Urban rose from his chair. "I am tired, my friends. We will speak more when Adhemar comes. Until then, sleep well."

In his private chamber, Urban lay upon his bed in restless melancholia, thoughts racing through his mind. What if I summoned the people to a pilgrimage and few came? What if only a few knights answer? I will appear a fool to the world; I will be powerless and Guibert will be considered the true pope. With him, the Church would become a cesspool of sin, a haven for Lucifer, unpious. The thought made him shudder. *I must not fail! I must find a way to enlist the fighting men! God will provide!* He began to pray, and mumbling to himself, he fell into a restless sleep.

Raymond and Elvira lay on their canopied bed and discussed the exciting event of the evening. He bubbled with a youthful energy he had not experienced for years. "A pilgrimage! Think of it! Armed and ready to do battle for the Holy Places. Our son can be raised where Christ walked. I will carve a kingdom for him from the lands held by the infidels. A kingdom! And you shall be my queen!"

"And we can reign in the Name of Our Lord." She was ecstatic. "A vision of splendor! We can live out our days in the Holy Land! O, my lord! We must go! It will become our destiny, the fulfillment of every wish we have ever held dear."

"I will talk to Adhemar before he sees Urban. The interpretation of Urban's vision can be crucial. He must be urged to proceed."

"You must be the leader," exclaimed Elvira. "Who but you has had more experience in fighting the Moor? Who can command more knights? You were born to lead this pilgrimage. It is your destiny!''

"Do not forget, my dear, that he who commands must also possess statesmanship to deal with Alexius. I hear he is very cunning and devious. But I can deal with him.'' His mind turned. "I can sell all my lands here, and all that gold could muster an invincible fighting force. We will have a victory in Jerusalem!''

"O, my husband!'' she exclaimed, and rolled across him, kissing him passionately. "It is a dream of Heaven!''

Their lovemaking that night reached ecstatic heights. He had the fervor and intensity of his youth, and it was not until dawn, when depleted, that they fell into an exhausted sleep.

He was awakened a few hours later by his squire, who carried a message from Urban, a reminder to summon Adhemar.

"Go,'' he waved the man away, then stopped. "No, wait. When the good bishop arrives see to it that he speaks with me before he sees the Holy Father.''

The man nodded and left; Raymond crawled back into bed.

Bishop Adhemar of Monteil, of Le Puy, scion of a knightly family, had been a knight in his youth. A vassal of Raymond and a very close friend of Urban, he was surprised to learn that the pope was in Provence. He rode to the castle of St. Gilles happily, soon to be ushered into a small room.

"I have good reason to see you alone, first,'' Raymond told him. "What would you think of a pilgrimage to the Holy Sepulchre?''

"For you?'' Adhemar asked after a moment's hesitation.

"Among others. Urban has been talking of a great pilgrimage: knights, noblemen, freemen, burghers, even peasants. Think of it! A pilgrimage of thousands of Christians at the same time!''

Adhemar thought quietly; finally shaking his head he said, "If hundreds of armored knights entered the Holy Land, the Moslem would consider it an invasion, not a pilgrimage. Has Urban told you that Emperor Alexius of Byzantium is seeking mercenaries to fight the Turk who is taking cities from him?''

"No-o . . . he said nothing of that.''

"At the Synod at Bobbio, two of Alexius' envoys brought a letter. Alexius fears an invasion of Constantinople. He asked Urban to help him find knights who would aid him.''

Raymond reacted. "A military alliance with Alexius? Fantastic! A holy war to reconquer the Holy Lands! With an army of knights and a mass of Christians, we can populate and hold the Holy Places for the Church. No need to beg the infidel for favors! This is not a pilgrimage—*THIS IS A CRUSADE FOR ALL CHRISTIANS TO UNITE! EAST AND WEST! TO DESTROY THE ENEMIES OF THE LORD; TO RETURN JERUSALEM TO JESUS CHRIST!*''

An explosion of joy shook him. He felt light, airy, and his mind and body were levitating! He stared at Adhemar, who was wide-eyed, as in a trance.

"*HALLELUJAH!*" burst from the cleric. "The Lord's will be done! This is a vision of greatness!"

"A wondrous vision!" Suddenly, Raymond caught Adhemar's arm. "Urban! He has had another vision. Listen," and he told the bishop of the horrors the pope had related. "He seeks your advice, your interpretation, not that he would have left without seeing you."

As a knight, Adhemar had fought in many battles, but he had never witnessed destruction such as Raymond recounted. He shook his head. "This is unimaginable. It is a vision of Hell come to earth and most unreal. It is a tale reciting the miseries of the human condition in Hell." He paused, thinking. "Urban's mind is fluctuating. We cannot allow this to distort his true vision, his soaring spirit. We will have to transcend the evil with our spirituality, and with the Lord's help, we shall prevail."

"Those are my sentiments, too," nodded Raymond. "But this vision brings doubts to Urban's mind."

"He is wandering in the wilderness of his enormous task, and he needs to know that his friends stand with him. I see this dream as a visitation of the Lord's will to clarify Urban's thoughts. So I will tell him. What greater call can there be than to ride as a warrior of the Lord?" His eyes sparkled. "A soldier to reconquer the Holy Land! For that I will don armor again! So will others."

"I, too, will ride to the East for that purpose. Come. Let us find him and tell him."

Urban was seated in an open veranda which overlooked the valley. He was still in his dark mood, although the day was bright with sun, but his attitude changed with a smile when he saw his old friend. They had little time to talk at Bobbio; there were too many meetings, too many private calls on Urban's time by the other cardinals, and Adhemar was busy advancing the pope's doctrine with the opposition. Adhemar could be considered Urban's right arm.

Weary in body and spirit, his mind's uncertainty having taken its toll of his usual vigor, Urban eagerly sought Adhemar's advice. With repugnance, he retold his dream in every detail, every horror. Finally exhausted, he lapsed into a profound silence.

"Your dream does not make a pleasing tale," said Adhemar, "but you must think of it only as a dream."

"It may also be an omen, a warning, a testing."

"It can be, also, nothing more than a result of your worries. You have been driving yourself without mercy since Bobbio. You are tired. You sleep poorly. It is no wonder you think of all the evils."

"So Elvira spoke," nodded Raymond.

"My friend, listen to me," Adhemar went on. "As I understand it, with your worries, with Alexius' plea in your mind, you found a linkage, a synthesis, an answer. Do you not see it?"

"No-o. Not very well. Tell me."

Adhemar sat back in his chair and clasped his hands. "I think you hesitate to send knights to Constantinople. Why?"

"There are many things to consider. If I ask, many may go; many may not. The ones that go . . . perhaps they should be the ones who stay here; yet if his gold lures them, perhaps the feuding will stop here. But the Church may be weakened."

"You are right, but there is another answer. Many would not wish to leave their fiefs unprotected and so would hesitate to go. Thus, Alexius may only hire the poorer knights, and the feuds of the wealthier knights go on. Our problems do not abate, and our struggle with Henry and Philip continues. But the Church still needs a cleansing. Alexius might be helped, but the Church is not, unless we find a way to help the Church, too. And that you have done."

Urban looked from one to the other. "Raymond just nodded his head; and he smiles. What have you two discovered that eludes me?"

"Your large pilgrimage. Do the knights go to protect the Christians or to join Alexius' army? Do you expect all the Christians to return? Or the knights? Many will remain in the Holy Land is what I think."

"Ye-es. The journey back may be difficult for some."

"Women will also go; children will be born; many will die; whole families may disintegrate; new families will be formed."

Urban was thoughtful. "I see I had not thought this through."

"Let us expand the scope of our thinking. If we turn the military ardor of our knights against the infidel; if we could appease their hunger for earthly possessions by allowing them to be sated with Moslem gold instead of their neighbors'; if we convince them that they defend the Cross from its degradation by the pagan, we achieve our purpose. They fight at home because of greed and boredom. The East can sate any Nero in riches and slaves. Where else can a poor knight gain so much so quickly? Where else could a baron become a duke, a duke a king, in one battle? Let them fight for the Cross; and let them become as rich as Croesus."

"A perfect plan," said Raymond, his eyes shining.

"But . . . but what of all the dead?" Urban was still troubled.

"They go to liberate the Holy Sepulchre, to free Jerusalem. Those who perish will be martyrs of the Crusade—for a Crusade it will be! Our faith was born in martyrdom; Christ died on the Cross for all our sins in martyrdom. In martyrdom, the Christians died in the Roman arenas. Martyrdom has built the Church, and the blood of its martyrs has been mixed with its mortar. The Lord's places cry out for purification from unclean hands. Shall we deny them?"

The three men sat in silence, Raymond and Adhemar waiting for Urban to speak. But Urban seemed far away, wrapped in himself. Raymond, finally, could not contain himself any longer.

"Which knight can refuse the pope's call to battle for the gentle Christ?" he urged on Urban. "All Christians will link arms in Christian brotherhood."

"Your call," said Adhemar, "will awaken a sleeping lion, and the Church needs this burst of spiritual strength, this fire for a new cause, to reawaken the frenzy and daring of the early zealots. It will inspire the imagination of thousands to return to the Lord." He paused. "All this you can do, Urban; it awaits but your word."

"You sound as though the hand of God has touched you," said Urban. "You speak like the prophets of old. Thank you, my friends. You have torn the veil of uncertainty from my eyes, and I see a brighter sun. I will think more of it. Do not fail me at Clermont."

"One boon, Urban," said Adhemar. "As Prelate of Rome, as Pope, you must remain here. I request that I be made Papal Legate, for I intend to go."

"You have my warmest blessings, my friend. It shall be you."

"A boon, also," said Raymond quickly. "I, too, have decided to fight the infidel. The crusade will need an experienced campaigner and leader. I offer myself."

"You both overwhelm me. I have been twice blessed with friends such as you. Thank you, St. Gilles. But we know not who will go or who will stay. I expect a knights' council will be formed, and when they pick a leader, it *should* be you, but you know no one can dictate a choice to them. Each may wish to travel alone."

"Patience, Raymond," said Adhemar. "Whatever influence can be brought to bear will be exerted, but there can be no choosing now."

Raymond had to be satisfied with that. They were right; he had to seek allies and supporters from the lords who decided to go. He knew his wealth would arm many knights, and his contingent would be an army in itself, and that should convince many that his leadership was necessary, for his veto power would be great. The full command would be a worthy pinnacle of his career, of his life, and he was resolved to achieve it.

Alone with his thoughts later, Urban considered his thinking. Adhemar was right. He had been urging a pilgrimage, but he was preaching a crusade. Would the knights be ready to march eastward as Knights of the Cross rather than as mercenaries of Alexius? Knights of the Cross! It had a wonderful ring! Each lord had his own gonfalon, his own ensign, around which his knights would rally during a battle. Would they all unite under the Sign of the Cross? If they did, Christianity, led by the Knights of the Cross, could march for a final victory for the Church of Christ. A marvelous dream!

Enraptured by his fantasy, Urban, during the dinner meal, spoke glowingly of his plans. They all shared his enthusiasm and drank many toasts for its victorious consummation. Elvira, cheeks flushed, her dark eyes sparkling in her excitement, could scarcely contain herself.

"Isn't it wonderful to be living in times like these?" she said rhetorically. She raised her cup. "To the total victory of the Church! It shall reign forever! May it continue to bless its friends and confound its enemies until the end of time." She drank and broke into a spate of giggling hiccups. Embarrassed, she excused herself and retired to her quarters, leaving the men to talk.

Raymond was involved with the logistics of finances, horses, wagons, armor, and military provisions. How many vassal knights? How many footsoldiers? And what about that new invention, the crossbow? Experts for that were difficult to find, and they were expensive to hire, but he would have a squad of them regardless of cost.

Urban and Adhemar were consulting on the Synod at Clermont. Alive and spirited again, Urban was willing to hold off on the excommunication of Philip. It could wait; the crusade took precedence. The Lord, speaking through Adhemar, Urban insisted, had shown him the way; the rest was in his hands.

Urban arrived at Cluny and went into immediate seclusion with Abbot Hugh. Hugh was enthusiastic, and they spent most of the night discussing the prelate's proposal in detail.

"It is a vision from the Lord!" Hugh exlaimed over and over again. "It will unite the Church and root out her evil ministers! The Faithful will have the means to salvation, and in glory they will be able to save the Church and return to her the ownership of the Holy Places. It is a miracle!"

The other monks, called to conference, nodded and repeated in unison, "It is a miracle!"

Questions were posed and answers were formulated. There was much searching and probing until, at last, Urban was satisfied that all the preparations were meticulously completed. The knights were urged to be at Clermont by 18 November and be ready to answer to the greatest demand ever made upon their Christian faith. Then Hugh prepared Cluny for the coming Synod.

Expecting the pope's demand for the excommunication of King Philip, many cardinals did not come, and those present sat in sullen dejection as Urban railed at them. He lashed out at the evils he had seen during his journey; he spoke of the concubines of the clerics, of the hoarding of wealth by the lay-appointed bishops, of the buying and selling of church offices, of excessive taxing and tithing by the monasteries. He decried the squeezing of the laity and the serfs by greedy churchmen, of the neglect of worship in high places. He flayed the monasteries who did no work in their communities but shut themselves off, obsessed in their own salvation.

"The Church must be cleansed!" he cried again and again. But it was a cry of anguish, for there was no response from the assembly. They had heard all this before.

Urban glanced at Adhemar, who had seated himself in a far corner, sitting quietly, taking no part in any of the discussion. The bishop nodded to him in encouragement, and Urban decided it was time to begin his important announcement. His mouth dried as he waited for silence in the hall. He set his face into a stern visage and fixed his eyes upon a far wall as he waited. The silence lengthened. The cardinals began to squirm in their seats, wondering.

He began quietly, so softly that even those near the podium had to strain to hear his words. "There is a heartfelt need in the Church which flows from the highest thrones of the kings to the cottages of the lowliest serfs, from the prelate, here, myself, to the lowest curate novice in any monastery. It is a void felt everywhere. It is a need for a new affirmation in Our Savior, Jesus Christ.

"We are sinking into a morass of sin and damnation, and all the depravities and abominations spawned by Satan are receiving help, *help from our own churchmen!* We cry out to the Lord: *When will it stop?* But we receive no answer!" He glanced around the room and shook his head. His innards were tightly balled. *They are not listening!* Cotton-fluff dried his mouth and he coughed to clear the spittle. Adhemar nodded for him to go on.

"Father Gregory dreamed to unite the armed powers of Christendom and have them march on a special pilgrimage to Jerusalem, to the Holy Sepulchre. Some went, but his dream lay barren and unfulfilled." He paused to pray, *Do not falter now!* "I would have this Synod proclaim a crusade, a crusade of all good Christians to challenge the might of the Moslems, to liberate the Holy Sepulchre from their unclean hands, to restore it to our Mother Church. A crusade to bring Holy Jerusalem back to Christian hands, where it rightfully belongs!"

He paused to watch the effect of his words. Some cardinals shifted uneasily in their seats, taking little note. With others there was a sudden brightening of interest, a delayed disquietude. Then one sought the face of another . . . a look into the eye . . . questioning . . . a knitting of brows. One sprang to his feet.

"God be blessed! Did I hear aright?" he shouted. "*A CRUSADE?*"

"Yes!" Urban shot back. "A crusade to free the Holy Sepulchre! Thousands of our fighting men! Knights from all of Christendom! Believers from all our lands to redeem the Holy Places, to liberate Holy Jerusalem." His voice rose. "*HEAR ME, MEN OF THE CHURCH! LET US CALL UPON CHRISTIANS TO ACT IN GOD'S NAME!*"

A wind of excitement rushed through the room, a hurricane which stirred the waters and threw up massive waves; the cardinals twisted and turned like cockleboats running a torrent in a storm. "*LET US SOUND THE TRUMPETS FOR CHRIST!*" he shouted. "*LET US GIVE TONGUE AND HERALD THE DAWN OF A RESURRECTED CHRISTENDOM—A CRUSADE WILL FERTILIZE THE HOLY SOIL AND UNIFY ALL WHO ARE OF THE BODY AND THE BLOOD. AND THE CHILDREN OF GOD WILL RETURN TO THE FOLD, THE TRUE CHURCH!*"

Adhemar jumped to his feet. "*HEAR ME, MY BROTHERS! WE CAN GATHER THE KNIGHTS TO FIGHT FOR THE CROSS. THEY SHALL BEAR THE CROSS—CROSSBEARERS!*" His voice rang through the room like a sword striking a ringing shield and the walls reverberated.

A pulsation of life shook the body frames of the assemblage and penetrated their inner beings. A singsong of incoherent chants and discordant resonances, a hubbub of loudness, filled the room. Adhemar's voice rang above the din.

"Our Holy Father has been inspired by Saint Michael, captain of God's hosts! Let us acclaim this crusade as the command of the Lord!"

The deadly apathy had vanished, and the blanket of indifference which had enveloped the Synod was shredded like the early-morning mist. Suggestions and ideas poured from the enthusiastic cardinals like gushing fountains as they argued and debated every nuance, every possibility and consequence. Urban, they insisted, would be a new Moses, leading a Christian instead of a Hebrew exodus to the Promised Land.

Fired by the glory of their cause, inspired by the divinity of their purpose, called by a new demonstration of faith, they threw themselves into a feverish state of intoxication. The eighteenth of November was only two days away. Letters had to be written and delivered immediately. Never in their lifetime had they known such a revitalization, such a rebirth of faith and love for the Savior. They had been reawakened and reborn for Jesus!

10

There was a chill in the November day and the forests were growing damp. The roads were crowded with travelers; peasants trundling their two-wheeled carts, village folk riding in open wagons, townsmen in covered wagons. Some artisans walked with their tools strapped to their backs; others, like peddlers, carried all their worldly goods in sacks. Old people, young people, families with their children, groups of neighbors, and those who had become friendly on the way. All were headed to Clermont. The priests had told them that the Holy Father had called them, that he had something of importance to say to all the Faithful, and there had been a rush to obey Papa Urban's summons.

The merchant rode in his carriage, his fine guard of spearmen pushing the serf aside, his driver wielding the stout leather lash. The peasant drove his mule with a withy whip and herded his wandering children with his shouts. And the knight, with his meiny, galloped through all of them as they stood humbly aside to permit the coaches and carriages of the ladies, behind their curtained windows, to pass.

"Never," said Charles to Pierre, "have I ever seen the roadway so crowded."

The group had stood aside for a knight and his lady. Mary stared at the powerful horses, the bright chain-mail of the guards, the rich, fur-edged cloaks, the luxuriant gowns and jewelry of the ladies-in-waiting, laughing and happy in a coach all their own.

With Andre's disappearance, she had felt abandoned. The jongleurs had agreed to let her stay with them, but, except for Tom, the others, especially Alicia, treated her with condescension. She was given the menial tasks, and, as she was learning to dance, she was expected to beg constantly for coins while the others sang and performed. Internally proud, she found the constant pleading for coins degrading and she hated it. She turned to Tom for comfort and solace, and they soon became lovers.

Charles worked the troupe hard, stopping at every village and roadside camp as they moved toward Paris. Money collections were good, and their winter hoard was growing rapidly, to their delight. One evening, after their dinner, he announced, "With so many people heading for Clermont, we should too. It will be bigger than a fair."

There was immediate agreement, but later, when Mary was alone with Tom, her anger erupted. "You promised to take me to Paris! You said it would be

64

only a few weeks! If we go to Clermont it will take weeks longer! Why should we have to go?''

"We make more money," he explained wearily. "Sometimes, things are difficult in the city. We have competition from jugglers and acrobats—even old troubadours. Right now, money is easy. People are on a holiday and give freely. It won't be so long.''

"That's what you said a month ago," she retorted sullenly. "Charles stops everywhere.''

"Only a few more weeks, Mary. I promise. We will get to Paris before the winter.''

They lay together that night, but she was unappeased. "Your money does me little good," she cried bitterly. "Winter will come and Charles will stop somewhere else.''

"No matter what," he told her, "we always return to Paris. You'll like it there, especially our parties.''

"I have nothing to wear at parties," she said petulantly. "All I have now is what Celia and Alicia give me. I want my own.''

"I'll get you some clothes. We'll have the extra money we're earning now. Anything you'll like. I promise. Maybe there will be a lord at Clermont who will take you to his tent. If that happens, you'll get gold or jewelry." He put his arms around her.

"Is that what you want me to be?" she cried out. "*A whore?*" She pulled away from him.

"Why are you so excited? I told you how the girls get their jewels and clothes. You are always treated well—better sometimes than a lady—and the lords are generous.''

"I won't do it! I am not a harlot!" She was vehement.

"All right." He shrugged. "But that's how Celia and Alicia get all their fine clothes. And their rings and bracelets. If a knight likes you . . . well, you can ask for anything.''

"I won't do it!''

"Let me ask you. What if a knight sees you and asks you to go to his tent? What would you say? No?" He laughed cynically. "Maybe, he'll leave you alone, and maybe he won't. Maybe he'll have his squire just carry you in. Whom do you think will fight a knight for you?" He laughed again but there was no mirth in the sound.

She suddenly realized that she was helpless, completely and totally trapped, like a caged animal in the hands of a hunter. There was no one she could turn to, no one to trust, and like a wounded creature she turned on her tormentor. "You . . . you . . ." she could not find the words and she beat him with her fists.

He laughed at her and lifted her off her feet, holding her close. She tried to push him away, struggling and wriggling in his arms. His laughter grew louder. Suddenly, he kissed her, pressing her firmly against him, then with a quick squeeze, he pushed all the air out of her, and she gasped for breath and her struggling stopped. She lay passively in his embrace. He kissed her again and she did not move. "See," he said. "The wildness can be tamed."

She glared at him and he put her down. "You have to listen to reason. You may not like it, but there is no other way."

"I will not be a harlot."

He grinned evilly and reached for her again. Before she realized what was happening, he had her on the ground, reaching under her chiton. She cried out and struggled with him, but he was too strong and soon, exhausted, she lay limply in his arms. He did not attack her; instead, his kiss was lingering and tender. With soft, quick kisses, his lips moved over her eyes and cheeks. Her skin was heating to his touch and her lust came alive. She held him tightly, and when he entered her, she became wild with passion. Their short gasps mingled with the night sounds, and when it was over, he lay quietly beside her, looking up into the dark sky. Moments passed in silence, and when he turned toward her again, she was asleep.

The traveling was easy the next day, and the troupe covered the few miles from their camp to the field just outside Clermont's gates by early afternoon. There were campfires everywhere.

The men decided they would go into town and also explore the camping field while the women set up the camp and began to arrange the meal. When the men returned and they were eating, Charles said, "There should be a big celebration tonight and we should prepare for it. There's a talking stand near the chapel—it must be for Papa Urban—and that's where we saw the tents of the knights. People are everywhere . . . there are thousands . . . I never saw so many in one place . . . it's bigger than the fairs . . . and more keep coming. We can begin working right after we finish eating."

Tom was watching Mary, and he sighed when he saw that she was not listening. He had thought he had settled her mind, and he went to her, but after a few futile attempts to make her smile he left her to herself.

Charles had no intention of wasting any time, and when the meal was over, he rose. "Everyone done? Let's go, we have work to do." He turned to Tom. "Mary, too. She can help with the collection if she doesn't want to dance."

"Will you come?" Tom asked Mary.

She gave no answer. Instead, she rose and walked off. Tom spoke sheepishly to his brother. "She's angry."

"I know. What do you expect to do with her when we get to Paris?"

"I promised to help her find her sister. After that, well, I don't know. I had hoped that we . . . but now . . ." He shrugged.

"The girls don't want her, and Pierre and I agree with them. She's moody, and she won't help."

"Maybe she'll change after today . . . when we leave here."

"We don't want her in the troupe, Tom. We'll take her to the city, as we promised, but that's all."

"All right." He sighed and glanced where Mary stood near the wagon, watching the people close by, and he walked over and tried to place his arm around her waist, but she shrugged him off. He took her limp hand. She did not pull it away.

"We will start for Paris tomorrow, when this is all over," he said. "I promise you. Come with us now. The girls are going to dance."

She didn't answer him. Instead, she withdrew her hand from his and turned away.

He bit his lip and joined the watching others.

A great crowd was gathering, and, with the lighting of the campfires, the fumes of the cooking hovered over the field like a malodorous fog. There was a deafening din of barking dogs, screaming children, bellowing cattle, squealing pigs, and bleating goats and sheep. Young people, pulling carts, collected wood and cut juniper brush, and they were stacking it into a rising hill in the center of the field. Girls tied straw onto long staffs for torches they would light to dance with around the bonfire after dark.

Tom approached Charles and Pierre. "She says she's sick. We'll have to go without her."

"I think we can manage," said Charles ironically.

A juggler, leading a huge brown bear, came by, and the smelly animal, waddling on all fours and swinging its head from side to side in the search for food, brushed Tom.

He jumped. "Watch your bear!" he snarled at the sweaty juggler.

The bonfire blazed.

"Celia! Alicia! Hurry! It's starting!" shouted Charles. The men picked up their lutes and adjusted their clothing.

The girls scurried out of the wagon, fixing their dresses and hair. They started their dancing with the steady strumming and twirling of their tambourines, moving toward the large, flaming pyre which lit up half the campfield. Children collected around them, imitating their strutting walk, and followed them into the center of the ring formed by the crowd which gathered. Charles started a clapping song, the girls keeping the rhythm on their drums, and soon everyone was clapping the same beat.

Suddenly the tempo increased and many younger people jumped into the ring. With an easy transition, Charles changed to an old folk tune, a rigadoon, a dance distinguished by hopping of couples, and the young people were joined by their elders. The youths jumped about enthusiastically, and Celia and Alicia stepped back to allow the peasants to dance without them.

The tempo changed again. Faster and faster the couples twirled and hopped. The older dancers dropped out, exhausted. The dancing became wilder, and Celia and Alicia reentered the ring. They began to formalize their steps, moving together to make complex patterns. Other dancers dropped back to watch, and, as the music increased to arpeggio chords, the girls were soon alone, and they whirled in complete abandon.

With a wild cry, Tom dropped his lute and leaped into the ring. There was a frenzy of turnings and wild screams as he acted as a center pole as the girls swooped and pulled at him with a tameless, ebullient madness which infected and heightened the excitement of the watching crowd. At its height, with everyone clapping and screaming, there was a loud crash of the lutes' strings and the dance collapsed. The girls sank to the ground, exhausted. Tom stood between them, his head bowed, his chest heaving. There was loud applause and cheers, and coins began to fall into the upturned skirts of the kneeling girls.

Loud shoutings from the other side of the fire turned the audience away and it thinned rapidly. The girls counted their collections as Tom searched and gathered those coins which had missed the skirts.

"Not too bad," said Charles as the coins dropped into the money bag he carried. "I saw some of the knights' pavilions further back. Let's try there." He ran his fingers over the strings, beginning a walking song. Tom and Pierre picked up the accompaniment, and the girls walked in front of them, shaking their tambourines, begging coins of the passersby. They strolled, troubadour style.

The high flames of the fire had abated, and the women who had been making torches lit their staffs. The straw flamed; a single line formed, encircling the fire. The women chanted as they danced slowly around the receding flames. The blaze had settled into a large bed of hot coals and ashes.

With a whoop and yell, older boys began a game of jumping across the hot embers, proudly exhibiting their agility and bravery. Suddenly a girl screamed and came hurtling across holding a boy by the hand. Quickly, three lines of young people formed, a center line of girls, flanked on either side by lines of boys. With a yell, two boys, each holding the outstretched arm of a girl between them, ran as a trio toward the dying fire, and with a single leap, the three sailed over, landing and tumbling over the ground with a tangle of legs and high glee.

A second trio was on the way immediately; then a third; a fourth. The game stopped abruptly with the appearance of three acrobats who came charging toward the fire bed, whooping and ringing bells as they tumbled over each other. At the edge of the pit, they dropped their bells and began to hit each other with broad, flat paddles. As each was struck, he would scream and do a somersault or cartwheel, and they would contort and tumble, seeking to evade the paddle's slap. They created much jollity and merriment. Then they changed their tactics. Doffing their bright red hats to the crowd, they lined up and ran toward the fire's bed, completing an aerial somersault over the blackened embers.

There was a loud burst of cheering and thunderous applause. The acrobats doffed their hats again, bowed, and scuttled through the crowd begging for coins. As they received money they continued their antics: a large donation would be followed by an exaggerated display of humility and appreciation, while a refusal was pantomimed by astounded disbelief.

The crowd was happy and pleased. Loud hooting and whistling called everyone's attention to other entertainments. There were sutlers everywhere, peddling food, tokens, and images of saints. Pope Urban's likeness was a favorite choice. Men dispensed hot, spicy soup by the cupful, sliced roast pig and other meats, breads and cheese, spiced pig's head, beer, even mead. The night was one of high merriment, the greatest festival remembered.

The loudest and noisiest were the countless children underfoot everywhere. There was an endless parade of younger women who strutted about proudly, exhibiting their inflated abdomens as positive proof of their fertility. Babies reposed in the arms of their mothers or young sisters—except those infants busily suckling—and they all joined in a chorus of gurgling, hissing, caterwauling, and squealing. Toddlers stared wonder-eyed, or wailed, or screamed in endless dissonance, with or without reason, with or without clothing. Some chased each other, a dog, or nothing at all, but ran for the joy of it, or during a game, but never silently.

The knights pitched their pavilions on plots sized according to rank. Most had rugs at the entranceways, with cressets flanking the openings of the tents, and each plot was demarcated by stakes connected with ropes to prevent trespass. Before each tent door flew a gonfalon, the ensign showing the knight's claim. Those who had brought their wives with them had more luxurious rugs and furniture outside a broader veranda, and the women sat with their ladies-in-waiting, gossiping, embroidering, or weaving on small looms.

Here and there, a troubadour sang a love song to a lady who smiled at him and flirted because she was bored. Into this area, weaving their way between the stakes, Charles and the others walked, played, and sang, while the girls begged for coins from the ladies.

Mary lay across the bunk in the wagon, forlorn and disconsolate, unable to find a comfortable resting place. She heard the cheering and laughter and her spirits sank lower. She knew Tom did not believe her feigned sickness, but she did not care, for she knew that he only meant to exploit her, to use her, and she was determined that she would not let him do it. She felt bitter, for she could not leave him despite her unwillingness to remain with the troupe.

She twisted on the bunk, and on an impulse she rose and left the wagon. It was dark. Cold, she drew the woolen shawl tightly about her shoulders, stuffing the ends into the front of her dress. The stars were bright, but there was little light and the festivities were over. People were drifting back to their camps to retire for the night. She sat on the wagon's steps and looked up at the stars.

"Dear Mother Mary," she said aloud, "what am I to do?"

The stars twinkled back but did not send an answer, and she felt completely alone. Wrapped in her unhappiness, she began to rock, holding her knees in her locked hands. The camp was quiet; she could hear individual groups talking. Suddenly, there was laughter and the voices of men. Her head came up; it was Charles and the others returning. Impulsively, she ran, not knowing where she was heading . . . only to be away! Only to be alone! She could not face their knowing smiles, their verbal knives, their self-sufficient cheerfulness. Alone, she could heal herself, just as she had always done when she was small and hurting. There had been no one then, not Papa, not the boys, not Jeanne—only Ruth, but they had drifted apart, and when she needed Ruth most, Ruth had run away. Now, she had to find a hiding place, a place all her own where she could crawl into herself and be safe and comforting.

The field was dark and the campfires were blackened ashes. As she moved around the wagons and carts, the standing cattle, the sleeping people, a figure, hurrying to his own bed, would pass. She drifted to the more obscure areas, seeking seclusion. The walls of Clermont loomed, and in a dark niche, she huddled and cried herself to sleep.

11

The bells of the church had been clanging steadily since the early dawn, and there were few who slept soundly since then. People were stirring in the cold morning air, gathering around the campfires to warm their shivering bodies. Last night's holiday excitement lay buried in their dreams, and a hushed disquietude had wrapped itself around their stiffened joints as they rose from their earth beds.

New arrivals filled the spaces between the wagons constantly, pushing people closer together, and with so many gathering wood for fuel, the men had to scrounge farther afield. The smoke made the rising mist heavy, and the cooking scent of garlic and herbs combined with the pungent odors of the fresh animal droppings. Babies wailed, dogs barked, animals bellowed, and mothers called and scolded their high-spirited offspring. Thousands milled about—and more were coming.

Mary awakened with a start, stiff and cold. She could not remember that she had fallen asleep, and terror ran through her for she did not know where she was. Her anxiety settled quickly, however, when she recalled the events of the past evening, and she vowed that once she found Tom she would do anything he asked. A glance told her that the area was strange; she could not see the wagon; she was lost. People around her were busily preparing their breakfasts, setting up their camps, milking goats and cows, ignoring her entirely. She was all alone; her determination grew; she would find Tom and tell him; there was no other way for her.

Guessing where the wagon could be, she wormed her way through hordes of shouting children, moving toward the field's center. Last night, she remembered, the fire had not been far away; she could begin her search from there. As she pushed her way through the camps, she heard the girls singing and she ran toward the sounds. She saw Tom! She rushed to him and seized him, kissing him again and again.

He pushed her away. "Where have you been?" he demanded. "We spent half the night searching for you." He saw Charles watching.

"I was lost . . . it was dark . . . I couldn't find the wagon." She was breathless in her explanations—and fearful. "Oh, Tom, I'm so sorry. I'll do anything you say. I was so wrong. I thought about it and thought about it . . . all night."

He was still angry, torn between his desire for her and the knowledge that his brothers did not want her in the troupe. "All right," he said gruffly, "we'll talk later. We're ready to begin this morning's work. Clean up and join the girls." He walked to Charles. Maybe, he thought, if she changes enough, Charles will let her stay with us.

The morning wore on; people were still arriving. Four monks came from the abbey carrying rough-hewn lumber and erected a platform. They draped a gold-cloth canopy over it for a roof and a wide, white cloth, which had a bright-red cross painted on it, around the lower leg supports. Large poles were erected on either side, and from them they hung a royal-blue-and-white flag, the gonfalon of the de Lagary family, Urban's own.

The bells of the abbey were sounding steadily, and as the ringing swelled, people raised their heads in expectation, looking to the great door. Many were herding themselves toward the platform, and the tension grew although the mood was still jocular. But the noon hour passed and nothing happened, and the entertainers plied a vigorous trade, the crowd giving freely as the strain and anxiety heightened.

An hour after the noon sun, the side door of the abbey opened, and a group of monks in Capuchin habits, their pointed hoods bunched over their shoulders, their dark skullcaps on their heads, entered the crowd. They circulated and joked with the men, listened to the women, tickled the babies, scolded the children for being so wild, and healed the sick by the laying on of hands and offering prayers. They all had the same words to the same question: Patience. The Holy Father will soon come. Yes, he will deliver a message. No, we cannot tell you what it is. Patience. All in good time.

Never had anyone seen so many people gathered in one place before. Peasants and serfs from nearby fiefs came as if on a holiday; others were only a few days' journey away, but there were some who had traveled great distances. From the south—Gascony and sun-baked Provence; from the north—Flanders, Normandy, and Champagne. From Burgundy on the east; Brittany on the west; weavers from the far cities of Bruges and Antwerp; laymen and artisans; merchants and vagrants; peddlers and thieves; cutthroats from the cities: all were there. All of France, proud of their "Golden Pope," had obeyed the command and were present, but they were anxious and wondered at the significance of the call and feared the future.

The late afternoon sun was low over the field when the bells began to peal their most powerful alarms. Heads came up immediately, and a heavy sigh of relief rolled from the crowd. The huge mass of humans undulated as an ocean wave, as a field of wheat in a breeze. All eyes were fastened on the great front doors of the abbey.

Children stopped their play and ran to their parents, suddenly frightened by the ensuing quiet. Babies, as if they had knowledge of the importance of the event, stopped their wailing. A hush, heavy enough to be felt against the skin, settled in the air and fell like a mantle over the crowd. Everyone knew instinctively at once: It was time.

From a side door came a group of novices, in brown habits, holding pans of red hot coals, and they proceeded to light the torch stands and cressets which surrounded the dais. Although it was not evening, and there was sufficient sunlight to blot out the light of the flaming resin-dipped rags of the torches, the flickering flames infused an atmosphere of drama, highlighting the platform.

Then the two massive front doors parted, swinging slowly outward in stately equilibrium, and two lines of black-cowled monks, marching in slow, steady procession, chanting solemnly, moved out of the dark interior and lined themselves into a concave semicircular arc in front of the dais. Behind them, carrying two large red-painted wooden crosses, stepped two tall monks, all in white, their curled black hair lying like coiled worms against their white cowls, which had been fluffed against the back of their heads. Behind them, the gold of their chapes glittering against their brocaded purple gowns, came the bishops, followed closely by the archbishops and the red-gowned cardinals. The palliums worn by the archbishops were draped over each shoulder and extended downward to the hemline in front. The wool was pure white, and it sparkled each time it moved. Above each pallium was a red cross, and each man carried his crosier stiffly and straight. Their miters were fixed tightly on their heads, and they marched in a tightly held, firm, straight line. The crowd "o-oo-ed" and "a-ah-ah-ed" at the richness of the dress and the solemnity of the ecclesiastical procession.

At the end of the hierarchical cortege came Pope Urban, walking alone, erect as a soldier—which he had been—tall, straight, his miter higher than those of the cardinals preceding him, his fine, yellow beard combed and curled. He was robed entirely in white except for his pallium, which bore small red crosses in a line running across his shoulders and down in front. His face had a firm, grim set, yet he appeared at ease and composed, assured and determined.

He mounted the steps slowly and deliberately, and every eye was measuring every step with him. At the top he stepped forward, facing the thousands of upturned heads, and surveyed the mass of humans before him. His commanding presence brooked no sound, and not a murmur came from the vast multitude; a hushed awe radiated from every face, and an eerie silence settled over the thronged field. Not a baby cried; not an animal sounded; not a bird sang.

He took a deep breath and began so loud that his clarion voice could be heard almost to the rear of the deep field:

> *"YE MEN OF FRANKISH BLOOD, VALOROUS FOREVER,*
> *HARKEN UNTO ME!*
> *YOUR SINGING SAGAS SHAKE THE MIGHTY MOUNTAINS;*
> *DEEP IN MYTH AND STORY*
> *ROLL YOUR SURGING RIVERS ACROSS YOUR HAPPY LANDS.*
> *YE MEN TO WHOM OUR LORD HIMSELF*
> *HAS SHOWN HIS LOVE AND FAVOR,*
> *TO YOU I BRING MY PLEAS AND URGENT EXHORTATIONS."*

He raised both arms over his head and intoned:

> *"LET IT BE KNOWN, NOW AND FOREVER,*
> *CHRIST, HIMSELF, ORDAINS IT!"*

His voice took on a deep timbre, a vibrant sound which resounded from his large chest and shaded off into new colorations and emotional stresses as he spoke. He paused, taking another deep breath.

> *"WILDLY FROM THE EAST BLOWS AN EVIL TEMPEST;*
> *FROM CONSTANTINE'S OLD CITY, JERUSALEM THE HOLY;*
> *I TREMBLE AT THE HEARING OF ITS OMINOUS TIDINGS;*
> *OUR SWEET MADONNA WEEPS—*
> *HER TEARS FLOW IN THE HEAVENS."*

He paused and looked about. All eyes were riveted upon him. He raised his fist and brought it down upon the rail.

> *"A CURSED RACE OF MEN! PERSIANS! TURKS AND ARABS!*
> *WASTE THE HOLY PLACES WITH FIRE, SWORD, AND ARROW!*
> *MUTILATE THE EMPIRE OUR CONSTANTINE ERECTED—*
> *CHRIST'S HOLY, HOLY EMPIRE, SEVERED, TORN ASUNDER!*
> *ESTRANGED FROM GOD, THESE MEN*
> *BURN OUT THE LORD'S OWN CHURCHES;*
> *DROP HORSES' OFFAL IN THE CHRIST'S BAPTISMAL FONTS;*
> *POUR CHRISTIAN BLOOD, IN JEST, UPON THE ALTARS;*
> *WHILE OUR CHRISTIAN BROTHERS' CORPSES*
> *LIE IN DESECRATED HORROR*
> *IN THE BLOODY SOIL—*
> *UNSACTIFIED AND UNCONFESSED!"*

He dropped his head in silent prayer. A quiet sobbing had begun and swept through the crowd. His prayer finished, he gave absolution with the edge of his palm and said "amen." Dutifully, the crowd answered "amen." He went on.

> *"TURKS' DEMON ARROWS PIERCE THE HEARTS OF CHRISTIANS;*
> *ARAB SWORDS ROLL CHRISTIAN HEADS IN DITCHES;*
> *WITH SATAN'S KNIVES THE PERSIAN PEELS THE SKIN*
> *OF LIVING, CHRISTIAN BODIES.*
>
> *AND THE WOMEN! WHAT SHALL I SAY?*
> *VIOLATED!*
> *RAVISHED!*
> *AGAIN! AND AGAIN! AND ONCE MORE!*
> *FORCED TO BEAR THE CHILDREN OF THE PAGAN INFIDEL!"*

There was a loud gasp from the crowd and screams from some women.

"AND ALL ABOUT THEM BLEED THEIR DYING MEN!

> *AND THE CHILDREN—*
> *WEEP FOR THE CHILDREN—*
>   *ENSLAVED!*
>   *TORTURED!*
> *SENT TO THE MINES*
> *TO DIG THE BURNING SALT . . .*
>   *TORN FROM THEIR MOTHERS' BREASTS . . .*
> *TO BE RAISED AS CHRIST'S KILLERS!*
> *HOLY PILGRIMS PAY TOLL AND TRIBUTE TO PRAY IN HOLY PLACES;*
> *GOLD IS CLAIMED TO ENTER IN THE HOLY SEPULCHRE!*
> *IF POVERTY IS GREAT AND THERE IS NO RANSOM GOLD*
> *PILGRIMS' BOWELS ARE UPTURNED BY THE SWORD*
> *AND, PIG-LIKE, THE TURK WILL RUT THE CUD,*
> *SEEKING COIN HE BELIEVES THE PILGRIM SWALLOWED.*
>   *SUCH IS THEIR HEATHEN PERFIDY!*

> *WHO ELSE IS THERE BUT YE TO HEAR AVENGEMENT'S CALL?*
> *WHO ELSE BUT YE CAN DRY OUR SWEET MADONNA'S TEARS?"*

He paused. The quiet sobbing of the women had become an ever-increasing crescendo of wailing woe. The revulsion from the misery, from the horror, rose from the multitude, and the whimperings became moanings; lamentations became open sobbings. There was an outburst of plaintive crying, a requiem for the tortured souls.

The men were not immune but were crying silently, holding tightly to their neighbors in the forlorn grip of wretchedness and grief. Small children and babies soon joined the weeping chorus, lending their keening wails to the sorrowful din. Everyone sobbed unabashed, unashamed, and unrestrained.

Urban's eyes searched the crowd, and life coursed and tingled through his large frame as though lightning had surged through his body, leaving him unharmed but electrifying his nerve endings. He felt thousands and thousands of strings attached to his hands, and each string ending was attached to some person in the mass in front of him, a string of a joining. The strings vibrated in their excitation, like those of a lyre, and he and all the others pulsated and oscillated in a harmonic duality which melded and merged them into one unit, one unity. A fulfilling power surged back and forth through each string, and somehow he knew that each individual, though separate from him, was part of him, feeling all of his tremors and raptures. It was a strange linking, a rapport, an affinity he had never felt before with any living being. He was One with All.

Suddenly he felt an explosion of light. It blinded his eyes and overwhelmed all of his senses, and for a moment he was in Limbo, in nothingness; a conscience without form or structure.

The light starred and fragmented inside his head and traveled down his nerves, lighting each string as it met with it, and then coursed on to the people below him. He could see the glowing mesh!

Again and again, the light flashed! And all were of one mind! One body! One belief! One God! And over all the mesh flowed the Glory of the Cross, with the Celestial Light of the Lord! Beyond stood the Presence and the Power of the Almighty!

Now all things were possible. He raised his arms to the heavens. There was a hush. Effortlessly, his voice carried to the farthest corners of the field, and all who heard him, all who stood before him that day, swore forever that it was a voice coming out of the Heavens, in through Urban's body and from his mouth, which spoke.

> *"I CALL ON YOU, O MEN OF FRANKISH BLOOD!*
> *YE ARE THE GIRDED KNIGHTS! THE ARMS OF CHRIST!*
> *YOUR GLORY IS A THUNDER IN THE HEAVENS:*
> *YOUR LANCES SHINE; YOUR SWORDS FLASH FIRE;*
> *YOUR DESTRIERS SEEK SAVAGE SLAUGHTER OF YOUR FOES.*
>
> *LISTEN! AND HARK TO WHAT I HAVE TO SAY!*
> *WHAT I TELL YOU NOW MUST BE SAID TO YOU.*
>
> *TO SAVE YOUR SOULS GIVE UP YOUR WAYWARD FEUDS;*
> *TO RIDE TO BATTLE AGAINST ANOTHER CHRISTIAN*
> *IS NOT TO FIGHT FOR CHRIST!*
> *SERVICE TO OUR LORD REQUIRES A CHRISTIAN FOE!*
> *DEFEND YOUR LORD! WAR AGAINST THE INFIDEL!"*

A slow chant rose from the crowd, scattered at first, then finding adherents, a rising wave, "War against the Infidel!" With a peremptory wave of his hand Urban hushed it.

> *"SEEK A PILGRIMAGE AS KNIGHTS OF CHRIST;*
> *A PILGRIMAGE TO SAVE THE HOLY SEPULCHRE—*
> *TO WREST THE HOLY LANDS FROM EVIL HANDS—*
> *HALLOWED JERUSALEM—*
> *THE SACRED SANCTUARY OF THE LORD—*
> *CALVARY, WHERE HE DIED FOR US!—*
> *THE HOLY SEPULCHRE ITSELF—*
> *THERE HE WAS BURIED—*
> *THERE HE ROSE AGAIN—*
> *AND YEARLY DOES THE BLISSFUL MIRACLE REPEAT*
> *IN THE PASSION; IN THE DARKENED CHURCH*
> *THE LAMPS WILL BURN, UNLIT BY HUMAN HANDS.*
> *THAT LIGHT, DIVINE, IS OUR VENERATED LORD."*

His voice rose and thundered over their heads:

"SHALL UNWASHED CARNAL HANDS REFUSE US ENTRY
TO THE SACRED PLACES?
SHALL WE, THE FAVORED LAMBS OF GOD,
BE CONSTANTLY DENIED OUR SHEPHERD?

GOD WILLS IT NAY! AND THIS I SAY TO YOU—
DIVINE THESE HOLY REGIONS ARE,
DIVINE THEY MUST REMAIN!
 IN CHRISTIAN HANDS!
 THIS I SAY: GOD WILLS IT!"

He paused to catch his breath, his shouted words still ringing in his ears.
A cry went up, *"GOD WILLS IT!"* He raised his hands and a silence fell,
a quietness of tense expectation.

"WHO LIVES WHO WILL DENY THE WORD OF GOD?"

He waited for an answer and the litany came back, *"NONE LIVE!"*

"WHO LIVES WHO DARES FORSWEAR THE WORD OF CHRIST?"

The answering roar came, *"NONE DARE!"*

"GO FORWARD, HEROES OF THE CROSS, BE NOT AFRAID!
WHAT YOU OWN HERE WE'LL KEEP IN CHURCH-SAFE HANDS;
LET NOT YOUR PRIVATE LOVE OF RICHES STAY YOU HOME;
THE EAST IS RICHER FAR, IN GOLD, IN GEMS, IN LANDS;
ALL YOU TAKE FROM HEATHEN HANDS SHALL CLEAVE TO YOU.

IF YOU BE RICH, HELP THOSE WHO HAVE THE NEED
TO SHARPEN ARROWS, WIELD AN AXE, OR THRUST A SWORD.
THEY WILL FIND WEALTH AND REPAY A THOUSANDFOLD.

FROM THIS PILGRIMAGE LET NONE TURN YOU ASIDE;
NEITHER LOVE OF WIFE, NOR CHILD, NOR ELDER PARENT;
NOTHING SHALL STAND HIGHER THAN YOUR LOVE OF CHRIST;
NONE SHALL HAVE THE POWER TO DISSUADE YOU.
FOR JESUS DIED FOR LOVE OF YOU UPON THE CROSS
AND YOUR GREATEST LOVE MUST BE YOUR LOVE OF HIM.

THE ELDERLY, THE SICK, THE YOUNG, WHO CANNOT MARCH

 REMAIN WITH US FOR NEWS OF VICTORY.
 THEN THEY WILL SEEK THE HOLY LAND IN PEACE.

 IN THE COMING SPRING,
 WHEN RIVERS WASH THEIR ICE INTO THE SEAS,
 GATHER YOUR SUPPLIES, YOUR ARMS, YOUR NEEDS.
 WHEN THE RAINS ARE DONE, AND THE ROADS ARE DRY,
 GO FORWARD!"

Urban closed his eyes and rocked himself upon the dais. He raised both arms high above his head, stretching his fingers to the ends of their reach, giving a benediction:

> *"GOD HIMSELF WILL GUIDE YOU!*
> *GOD HIMSELF WILL BLESS YOU!*
> *GOD HIMSELF WILL LEAD YOU!*
> *DEIU LO VULT! GOD WILLS IT!"*

He stood as though frozen, stiff and erect, his head thrown back, his eyes tightly closed, his arms stretched to their extremities toward the sky, and his fingers pointed rigidly outward like steel spokes probing the heaven's mysteries. His state of ecstasy was transmitted to the thousands of people who stood transfixed before him. After a moment of unearthly silence a shout arose:

"God wills it! God wills it! GOD WILLS IT!"

Like a rising wind, it gained support, became a wild breeze, rapidly changing into a blowing wind and expanding into a hurricane, a raging sound which poured from the depths of the human souls and shrieked their defiance at the stars. The trees bowed to its fury, and the earth trembled at the stamping of thousands of feet.

"GOD WILLS IT! GOD WILLS IT! GOD . . . WILLS . . . IT!"

Again and again the tornado roared, wave after wave of frenetic sound, ready to wreck and destroy everything in its path.

Urban stood as stone, a rearing granite mountain, unmoved, as the fists of the sound-giants battered against him. Its fury spent, the roar finally subsided and he dropped his arms. Waiting until he could be heard, he went on:

> *"YE WHOSE SINS LIE DEEPLY CASED WITHIN YOUR SOULS,*
> *I OFFER ABSOLUTION;*
> *THERE IS NO SIN THAT GOD WILL NOT ABSOLVE*
> *FOR THOSE WHO FIGHT FOR HIM.*
>
> *FEAR NOT A DEATH BY LAND OR SEA,*
> *FOR CHRIST HAS DIED FOR YOU*
> *AND A DEATH WITHIN HIS CAUSE*
> *UNITES HIS DEATH WITH YOURS;*
> *ALL SINS ARE THEN REQUITED.*
>
> *ALL PARENTS, SISTERS, BROTHERS YOU FORSAKE*
> *FOR HIS NAME'S SAKE SHALL BE GLORIFIED;*
> *THEY SHALL RECEIVE A THOUSANDFOLD; AND*
> *AN EVERLASTING LIFE YOU WILL INHERIT.*
>
> *LET NO MAID GO UNLESS IT IS WITH HUSBAND;*
> *FEAR NOT THE THREAT OR ACT OF TORTURE;*
> *THAT WAY LIES THE ROAD TO MARTYRDOM;*
> *FOR THOSE WHO HOLD STEADFAST TO THE FAITH*
>
> *THERE ARE NO FEARS NOR DOUBTS.*
> *THE LORD PROVIDES.*

His voice changed again. No longer was he preaching precepts or rules of conduct. His spirit rose and soared.

"THE WAY IS SHORT;
THE STRUGGLE, BRIEF;
THE REWARD IS EVERLASTING!

VERILY I SPEAK THE VOICE OF THE PROPHET;
TAKE UP YOUR ARMS, O VALIANT ONES!
TAKE UP YOUR PIKES AND SWORDS!
SET OUT A MIGHTY ARMY—
CARRY TO THE EAST THE CROSS
AND DARKEN THE SUN WITH YOUR ARROWS!
SMITE THE INFIDEL WITH YOUR LANCES!
LET THE KEENNESS OF YOUR SWORDS PREVAIL!

ON YOUR GONFALONS SHALL BLAZE
THE RED SYMBOL OF OUR LORD,
AND EVERY HEATHEN MUST FALL BEFORE YOU!
AS DAVID SLEW GOLIATH—
AS SAMSON SMOTE THE PHILISTINE—
GO FORTH TO RESURRECTION!

AND I CAN SEE BEFORE YOU,
STRIDING STRONG WITH FLAMING SWORD!
LEADING YOU TO BATTLE!
URGING YOU TO VICTORY!
THE INVISIBLE STANDARD BEARER!
CHRIST HIMSELF!"

There was an eerie moment of silence, as though a gigantic streak of lightning had flashed across the sky, and everyone was waiting for the eruptive roll of explosive thunder. Everyone was reeling under the mighty image of Jesus leading His glorious hosts to battle, His flaming sword, borrowed from Saint Michael, the very one used to gain the victory over Lucifer, flashing in the heavens.

Then every human mouth opened, and a sound never heard before in all of Christendom burst forth, a roar which shook the mountains, created tidal waves upon the waters, echoed and reechoed into the deepest depths of Hell as well as to the Judgment Seat itself. It twisted like a live serpent, caught in the narrow confines of high rut walls, suddenly bursting forth to freedom. It was an explosion of a volcano blowing its hardened crust. Mouths of people were contorted, distended, and twisted in agonized pain as the air from their innermost beings was forced out of the farthest cavities of their writhing bodies.

There was a tumult everywhere, and some people were seized with a frenzy, whirling and devil-dervish dancing in disjointed, awkward thrashings of their arms and legs. Women fainted, slipping quietly to the ground or into the arms of their neighbors. Deformed, limbs akimbo, convulsed into a passion and grotesque, others rolled upon the ground as though possessed. Then a cry arose;

"GOD WILLS IT! GOD WILLS IT! GOD WILLS IT!"

It gathered adherents and swelled into a torrent.

"GOD WILLS IT! GOD WILLS IT! GOD WILLS IT!"

A burly figure, a bishop in all his vestments, forced his way to the front platform and fell on his knees. He lifted his right arm and shouted, "I swear to march to Jerusalem, a crusader of the Lord!" He rose and faced the crowd. "Who marches with me?" It was Adhemar.

A new roar went up. There was a rippling of the sea of bodies as from the tents of the knights on one side of the dais came the armored men, singly at first, then moving forward in a phalanx, the people parting before them and closing behind. They stood in a single line, arcing in front of the platform as no knight there would consider himself inferior to another and stand behind another. Their swords were drawn and extended fully with their arms, and they thrust upward as they, too, shouted:

"GOD WILLS IT! WE RIDE TO FREE THE HOLY LAND! WE SWEAR!"

Then they fell on one knee, as they did before their lord when they first received their knighthood, but this time they had their swords and they reversed them, holding them upward as crosses.

"We swear our swords to the cross! We swear to fight the Infidel! We swear to free the Holy Sepulchre! We swear to avenge Our Lord! On our lives, we swear!"

Adhemar, standing off to one side, threw up his hands and shouted, *"BLESSED ARE YE WHO TAKE THE CROSS! BLESSED ARE THE CRUSADERS!"*

More knights were coming forward, of lower rank, crowding the front area. They were in their hauberks, their cuirasses, breastplates, armlets, and gauntlets. Their chain-mail sparkled, and their spurs, whether gold or silver, glittered. They, too, knelt and swore.

Urban raised his hand and offered a prayer and blessing. As he prayed, a new disturbance arose near the center of the crowd. A large man, a giant of a man, broad in shoulder, huge and weighty, was resolutely pushing his way to the platform. He wore leather breeches and a leather japon cut at the waist, open, revealing a massive, hairy chest. The long muscles of his arms and shoulders were corded, but he moved smoothly, agilely, like a cat, working his way through knots of people and around groups, trying to disturb as few as possible. This was a man who worked hard and often.

Like a ship's prow, he was cutting his way to the platform, and all eyes were watching him for none knew what he was going to do. He looked up at Urban briefly and a flash of understanding flowed between them. The pope's head moved in an imperceptible nod and the giant fell to his knees.

"*Confiteor* . . ." he choked out hoarsely, "*confiteor* . . ."

People about him picked up the cry, and the call for confession ran like a riverlet in all directions through the crowd. The need for absolution was felt everywhere. People fell to their knees, weeping and whispering, babbling long recitals of their misdeeds. The catharsis of tears washed them clean and released their tensions.

Urban began a mass confession, repeated by the giant and the others. It was becoming dark and Urban was tired, depleted by his outpouring emotions. He moved the words quickly, as a catechism, and absolved them all with a hurried sign of the cross. Then he left the dais, his retinue of bishops and cardinals following.

Through the crowd passed the novices and monks, pinning two crossed pieces of red cloth on all who joined the crusade. Men milled around them, eagerly seeking the strips. The heat and the passion subsided slowly. People sought their families, babies resumed their caterwauling, the animals moved restlessly as the night was coming.

Small groups were everywhere, arguing, gesturing excitedly, disputing what the pope had said. A few things stood out that they could agree upon: they were to march to Jerusalem after the spring rains; they were all to become rich with the gold from the East; all their sins would be forgiven when they freed the Holy Sepulchre; and they would live forever in the Arms of the Lord if they died along the way. Lord Jesus Christ was going to lead them; and they would be free—no longer serfs bound to the land of a lord; no longer out of work and jobless, praying for work from a burgher or merchant; no longer a jobless artisan, searching for work and a crust of bread. The carpet and weaving factories would be emptied of their women and boys, for they would go with their men and fathers. Girls would seek husbands to go, for the pope had said, "No woman was to go unless she had a husband," and the men needed their women on a trip as long as this.

A great pilgrimage—a crusade—to the Holy Land! Everyone would be equal. Christ was to lead, not some noble, some duke or king. They would all be rich, and they teased the Jew peddler that they, too, would soon have untold wealth, much like his.

The Jew looked at his pack that he carried from village to village and wondered what they meant by the word *wealth*. He shook his head, for he knew that when the Christian and Moslem would fight, somehow during the battle both would turn and slaughter him.

The darkness moved quickly over the fields; the bells of the abbey had sounded the call to vespers and were now stilled. The torches had burned out but the people in the camps were still talking. Those who had taken the cross, the two strips of cloth, strutted and talked of their glory, much to the envy of those who still held back. Single girls admired the single men who wore the red pieces and hinted broadly they were ready, also, to go crusading.

A light burned from the embrasures of the abbey where Urban rested. He felt empty and exhausted as he lay upon his cot, his forearm over his forehead.

"Much was accomplished today," said Adhemar. "We have a good beginning."

"We have started a small fire," said Urban wearily. "So much more remains to be done."

"It is only a small fire today, Odo," said Adhemar, calling Urban by his given name, "yet it is greater than any seen through many centuries. You have struck a spark which will set the world afire beyond our imaginings. Pray God that those who are consumed in the conflagration die with the blessings of the Lord's final victory."

Urban closed his eyes. "Amen," he whispered.

12

To Jerusalem! Both Leo and Parenti heard the pope, but each in his own way. Leo hopped from foot to foot in his excitement, unable to contain himself, and his hands jerked as his feet jigged.

"We will go? We will go?" he begged. "Shall I get the ribbons? Look! There's a monk right over there."

Parenti did not hear him, so locked was he in his own thoughts. He was talking to himself. What now? Everyone will join him. Nobody can doubt it. Clement cannot deny a crusade to free the Holy Sepulchre. It would be insane. Everyone would leave him. Urban has produced a masterstroke. I should join him, too. Why not? What binds me to Clement at a time like this? A new Church is coming, a new world, and I will be part of it. Clement has lost. He snorted in contempt. He sits and does nothing! I will go with the spoils to the victor, he decided.

"Shall I get the red strips," Leo pleaded. "The monk's going away. He won't have any left."

Parenti stood up. "Yes, little brother. Get them. We will go—somehow."

Leo embraced him in joy and ran after the monk—and tumbled full against a large, rotund man who was striding by.

"Wo-o-o-offff!" The air exploded from the man's mouth.

Leo picked himself up. "I'm sorry," he shouted and ran off.

The fat man stood, arms akimbo, and watched the boy, then turned back to Parenti. "A nice state of affairs," he said, and his eyes widened in recognition. "By my saint's beard!" he exclaimed. "It's you! Brother? . . . er? . . . . Brother? What did you call yourself?" He was uncertain. The light was fading. "Devil take my memory! From the road to Genoa . . . that's it!" He was triumphant and laughed raucously. "How could I forget? I took your needle . . . and your food!" He laughed again. "But you faired well, I see."

Parenti turned away. He remembered too well, and it rankled him, but this was not the time for revenge although revenge, he promised himself, he would have.

"I'm Brother Francis . . . come, surely you must remember. The cheese and wine were delicious. What brings a Clement monk to listen to Father Urban?"

Leo, back with the red stripes in his hand, heard Francis.

"We are not Clement's monks," he retorted. Then he recognized the monk. "You stole our food!" His hand went to his sleeve.

"No! Leo!" exclaimed Parenti, restraining the boy. "We will not fight today. There will be other times."

"Why should we fight at all?" Francis was expansive. "We all love the same God," his tongue licked his lips, "although I may have some doubts about Clement." He was baiting Parenti. "And you?"

Parenti knew what Francis was doing. "As you were told, we are not Clement monks. Come, Leo." He turned away.

"Maybe not the boy, not yet, anyway, but I have small doubts about you. Why listen to Urban? Does Clement need an ear?" he guessed shrewdly.

"I follow where the Lord leads me," retorted Parenti, "and now he leads me to Jerusalem." He took two strips from Leo.

"Ah-ho!" exclaimed Francis. "A volunteer for the crusade? Who would have thought it? All the way to Jerusalem?"

"Come, Leo, we must go."

"No haste, Brother." Francis was solicitous. "It might sound incredulous, but I'm beginning to believe you. We should be friends, comrades, for I, too, have sworn today, and we will all march together."

"Except where I invite my friends, I go alone," said Parenti coldly. "We must go, Leo."

Francis stopped him. "Wait, wait. To forgive is to show love for Our Lord. Let us bear witness of your forgiveness."

"Let me pass. The Lord knows my heart."

Francis still held him. "I was mistaken in you. There, you have my apology. Who is your abbot?"

"I told you before; I go where the Lord leads me; I need no abbot. Now, will you step aside?"

"You cannot be a renegade. Come, come. I have apologized. I am no makebate, and I seek no quarrels. If you remember, you would not share that day. But we will travel together, and we will have enemies enough in the Moslem. Let me make it up to you. If you have no bed for the night, I can secure one for you at the abbey or the hospice."

Parenti just walked off and Leo followed him.

Francis, hands on his broad hips, watched them disappear. "A bitter Clement monk on an Urban crusade? He would bear watching."

"The Lord's ways are His own," said a voice behind him. "He turns men's hearts to Him regardless of their own reasons."

Francis turned. He did not know the old monk who spoke to him. "I did not see you, Brother, but you are right."

"I am called Peter the Hermit. I, too, shall go on an Urban crusade although I am not an Urban monk."

Francis peered at the thin face covered with a patriarchal beard. About the monk's emaciated body lay a gray-dirty woolen shirt, and the tattered robe hung about the knobby knees. Peter's feet were shod with twisted leather sandals whose thin soles were holed, revealing calluses dirtier than the leather. Next to him stood an old mule, patient and weary.

"You are not a Clement monk either, Brother," said Francis.

Peter nodded. "Neither Clement nor Urban. But I have seen a vision today that I had not seen in Jerusalem when I was there. At the Holy Sepulchre, the candles glowed as though they burned Heaven's own fire, and I could hear the angels singing. Urban's message is sending me back so I can hear them again."

"So shall it be for all of us. But I have work to do at the abbey. God speed you."

"And you, Brother. I will pray." He remained at prayer for a long time, then confident that the Lord had heard and listened, he walked to the side of his mule to mount. The animal shied sharply. "Son of an ass," he said without rancor. "Stand!" But the mule obstinately moved the second time. "I doubt you bear an omen," he scolded. "Stand still!" Again he tried, but the animal moved for the third time. "Would you prefer I walk?" he asked with irritation. "Stand, you heathen bastard of a horse!"

"Maybe he would ride you," laughed a deep voice.

Peter turned and scrutinized the big man who had kneeled before Urban. "Civility to your elders is the Lord's commandment. Respect the Lord's words," he said testily.

"Come, old man," said the giant. "I but jest with you. If you need aid I will help." He reached for the mule's bit.

Peter examined him. "You can help yourself more. Have you taken the cross?"

"Did you not see? Papa Urban himself heard my confession."

"I did not listen. Where are your red strips?"

"I do not see yours," the man countered.

"Mine will be there when I meet someone who can sew them on this old rag." He indicated his habit.

The man laughed, a deep rumble. "I have the same trouble. I am a blacksmith, not a seamstress, and I need a leather worker to put them on this." He indicated his japon.

"I am called Peter the Hermit. You are ready to leave your shop, your family, to go to the Holy Land?"

"I have no shop, nor a family," said the man gruffly. "I wander from village to village, seeking work, and, after a while, I go on."

"You carry no anvil on your back," said Peter shrewdly. "You are a runaway serf, no?"

"Papa Urban said those who go to Jerusalem will be free. I go."

"Come with me and you will be free of running."

"Why should I travel with you, old man? I do well by myself."

"Do you know the way?"

"No-o, but I can go with any knight. They can use a blacksmith."

"They take their own. A runaway serf loses his hand—and eyes."

The man pondered the words. "You know the way, old man?"

"I have been there before. And God will lead me again."

The man grunted. "If He leads you, why not me?"

"Because I walk in the ways of the Lord. Are you without sin?"

"I have been absolved. But I will sin again. The Lord has not given me the strength to be holy."

"Then come with me. Together, we shall find the Lord's way. Until the spring we shall seek others, and when the snows melt, together we shall all walk the road to Jerusalem."

The man studied the monk and suddenly nodded. "I will come."

"Good. Now, help me mount this ass's son." After he was firmly seated, he asked, "What are you called?"

"Chagon, the blacksmith."

"You have no wife? No children?"

"Not anymore." The voice was bitter. "But that is a matter between me and God. You are not my confessor."

A broad, bulky man edged forward. "Forgive me, Brother, but I have been listening. May I accompany you to Jerusalem?"

"We do not go until spring," said Peter. "You have no home where you can wait?"

"My home is where I lay my head. You will need help during the cold months. If you travel the roads, there is danger from animals as well as men. I can deal with both."

"I can protect the brother," said Chagon.

The man measured the blacksmith with his eyes. "Yes," he said, "in a fair fight, but what could you do against a trained sword? Have you ever fought with the steel?"

"I forge steel. If need be, I can fight with it."

The man smiled. "My name is Gautier. I have been a knight, but without wealth, without substance. Can you fight me?"

Chagon was awed. "A knight? I do not wish to argue with a knight, sire." He was subdued, humble.

"I grew sick of killing Christians when my son died beside me, spilling his blood in useless battle. I threw my sword away and sold my horse. I wander in penance, aiding those I can. Now, I have taken the cross, and I would give aid to you and those who will follow you to Jerusalem. They will need protection, and for that I am willing to pick up my sword again."

"This Gautier-without-wealth is right, Brother," said Chagon quickly. "A good sword is our best shield—next to God, of course."

"The Lord's will be done," said Peter. "You may come." He motioned Chagon to lead the mule on.

"A moment, Brother Peter. If you will."

Peter turned in his seat. "Who calls?"

Parenti stepped forward. "I. My new Brother Leo and I would go with you, also. He is but a novice in my care, but he learns quickly, and we can aid you in spiritual matters, with God's Grace."

"You are prepared to travel the roads in the winter?"

"If that is where you go, we shall follow," said Parenti.

"That is where I go," said Peter solemnly. He kicked his mule.

The strange group moved out of the field as dusk was turning into night. They bedded down on the roadside when Peter lifted his hand and called a halt. An old monk, a freedom-loving serf, a knight without sword, horse, or armor, a renegade monk with a runaway boy, all sworn to take the road to Jerusalem to free the Holy Sepulchre from the hands of the Infidel.

13

A week had passed since the jongleurs had left Clermont, and true to his word, Charles led them toward Paris. One night, Mary and Tom lay side by side under a large elm tree a short distance from the camp. There was no moon, but the night sky was clear, and the stars spangled the velvety blackness and flickered like candles in the wind. Their lovemaking had been passionate, and they lay close together, exhausted, in quiet lassitude.

"I'm cold," she whispered, burrowing under the blanket.

He laughed and put his arms around her, pulling her tightly against him. She pressed closer, wiggling her hips, rubbing against his nakedness.

"Whoa," he chuckled. "I need some rest, little rabbit. Let's talk." He became serious. "Do you think we should go on the crusade?"

"Whatever for?" she countered, not stopping her movements.

"Because Papa Urban asked us. Wait a minute! Stop!" He pushed her away. "I said talk. Don't you want to become rich? And have loads of jewelry and dresses? And in Jerusalem, all your sins will be forgiven."

"Well . . . I'd like to be rich; but I don't sin very much. I used to go to confession and make up all kinds of sins when I was a little girl. The priest would laugh at me, and once he said that just thinking about sinning was a sin. Imagine that. You can even sin by thinking, but I don't think sinful things anymore."

"If we don't listen to Papa Urban, we will be sinning."

"But we can't fight those . . . those . . . infidels. They are terrible, not even like people . . . they are animals. You heard what they do. No! I don't think we should go. Let the knights and soldiers go. They don't need us."

"But we're thinking of going," he said softly.

She pushed away from him. "You are think . . ." She had a sudden revelation. "*Charles* is thinking!" Her voice rose. "What about Paris? You promised we would soon be in Paris!"

He became impatient. "All I hear from you is Paris! We will be there in about two weeks. But in the spring . . . *in the spring*, we are heading for Jerusalem."

"Oh." She felt foolish. Papa Urban had said in the spring, she recalled. But her goal was simple: find Ruth. She liked Tom; he certainly made her more excited than Andre. But, Charles? No, she didn't like Charles. If Andre went with his brothers . . .? She would stay with Ruth. Let him go alone.

"Well, will you come with me? Papa Urban said that if women went they would have to be married. Remember?"

She was startled. "Married? You mean, we would be married?" She became excited.

"Wait . . . wait. There are problems. Charles says he isn't sure about you. There will be many knights and soldiers, and many of them won't have their wives and ladies with them."

She recoiled. "Do you mean you want me to become a soldier's whore?" She was aghast.

"No . . . not exactly . . . but Charles says . . ."

"I don't care what Charles says! I'm not going to be a whore for every soldier who . . . We can go without Charles. Just me and you. We don't need the others."

"But I do," he said softly. "I go with my brothers."

Her world teetered. "Then you don't want me," she whispered.

"Why are you always causing trouble?" he said desperately. "Nobody said you had to be a soldier's whore. Charles says that you have to be willing to . . ."

"I won't do it!" She jumped up, naked, and began to dress. "Just get me to Paris—as you promised. And when I find Ruth you can look for another wife—and harlot!"

"That's just what Charles said you would do. He said we would have trouble if you came along." He was angry.

"Some man you are!" She spat at him.

"I'm sorry, but you . . ."

"Yes, you're sorry! I am, too!"

A horse neighed and a woman screamed; there was a wild commotion from the camp; another scream—a man!

"*HELP! HELP! TOM! HELP!*" It was Charles.

Tom, naked, jumped to his feet and ran toward the wagon with Mary running after him. In the darkness, outlined against the sky, she could see the figure of a horseman, wheeling about, and another horse standing still beside the wagon. She hid herself.

"Get the men!" shouted the man on the horse. Turning, he slashed downward with his sword at Tom. Tom screamed, his body twisting as it fell.

A dark form lay across the doorsill of the wagon, another at the foot of the steps. In terror, Mary huddled on the ground.

A man emerged from the wagon carrying a box. "I found it!" he yelled to the horseman. "It's heavy."

"I got the third man," his companion shouted back. "Are you sure of the other two?"

"No problem. Two of the girls, too. Did you get the third?"

"No. She's still about. We ought to save her for some fun."

"Plenty of that later—in Paris. Let's go."

"She can't be far. Nobody's around. Let's find her first; but no knife until we're done." The horseman dismounted and started searching the bushes.

Mary cowered in terror, not daring to move lest the noise betray her. Her fear mounted as the man neared the thicket which hid her. Suddenly, he parted the branches and looked down at her crouching figure, a grin on his face. As she looked up at him, he raised his arm and struck her across the check with the back of his hand. She screamed in pain and panic.

Sprawled on the ground, looking up, to her his legs were massive tree trunks, rearing upward. He stood before her, a gigantic behemoth, his lips drawn in a snarl, his eyes burning like live coals. The fingers of his huge hands undulated like live snakes, coiling and lengthening as they reached for her. She shuddered convulsively, screaming in short gasps, trembling like a terrified animal as she scrambled backward, trying to escape. He grasped her hand, and she lashed out with her foot in wild abandon as he tried to pull her toward him. Her whipping foot caught him in the groin. He bellowed in pain, his hand seizing his crotch, freeing her. Instinctively, she kicked at him again and again, and he tried to catch her flailing feet. Roaring in pain, he dropped to his knees, cursing at her.

"SHE-DEVIL! BITCH OF A WOLF BASTARD! DEVIL BURN YOU!"

Mary's head suddenly cleared. Escape! Run! She was on her feet and darted deeper into the brush, gasping and crying in fear. The brambles caught at her, cutting her skin, drawing blood, but she ran on, unheeding, feeling none of it. And she ran full—into the other man!

The impact was hard enough to send both of them to the ground. A desperate cry escaped her. Terrified, she scrambled to her feet and scampered back into the bushes, numb with fright, her teeth chattering. *Run! Run! Run!* boiled through her head.

Twisting between the trees' shadowy trunks, her hands extended outward, she ran. Suddenly, the earth opened beneath her and she was falling! She screamed, clutching at branches which broke as she held them. She struck the earth soundly, her leg bent beneath her, and she could hear something snap. Pain engulfed her; her eyes rolled into the back of her lids, and the blackness of midnight overwhelmed her.

The second man found the first massaging his battered crotch. "I thought you had her when she screamed, but she knocked me over coming out of the bushes. What happened to you?"

"That bitch kicked me," snarled the first. "That's what happened. Devil take her!"

The other man laughed. "Let's go. We've wasted enough time."

"I'll find her first and give it to her, in the mouth."

"She'll bite it off. Come on, let it go. The wolves will take care of her. You'll get others in Paris." A horse neighed. The man jumped. "Someone's coming. Get moving! I left the chest with all the money back there."

They returned to the wagon, the first man still grumbling. "I should have given her my fist right away, right in the face."

They found the money box, mounted, and rode off.

Mary winced at the pain shooting through her leg when she returned to consciousness. She tried to move, but it was more than she could bear to straighten her limb. The gray light of dawn was in the sky, and she began to shiver, the biting morning air cutting through her torn dress and nipping at her blood-clotted welts. Her teeth were chattering, and she pulled her arms around herself to fight the cold.

She shifted the weight of her body, and her head rolled with the pain. Carefully, gritting her jaws, she moved. Her eyes widened in fear. The lower part of her leg was twice its normal size and turning blue. She touched it gingerly. Numb! It was broken, she knew, and she had to get back to the wagon. Tom! The immediate recollections of the dark forms on the ground, Tom's yell as he fell . . . they must be dead, and the men were murderers as well as thieves.

She writhed in sudden pain. What was she to do? Panic gripped her again. She was alone, with a broken leg, and there was no one she could turn to.

With grim determination she dragged herself out of the hole, her useless leg hampering every movement. She found a stick and used it to stand up and then as a cane to straggle her legs forward. Slowly, each step an ordeal, she moved toward the clearing where the wagon was standing.

There were voices, and she cringed in fear. The men? No, it was a woman and a boy.

The woman was old, her gray hair wild about her shoulders, and she wore a full-length, shabby frieze coat. A young boy, hunched forward, was pulling a body by the lower legs. Mary sucked in her breath in a spasmodic shudder. Celia! . . . her sleeping gown rolled up around her waist, exposing her nudity. The gown around her breasts was red and torn, the dried crust streaking her skin. Her head bounced from side to side as the boy pulled her alongside the other . . . bodies? Mary bit her hands to prevent her outcry. When he turned, she saw that he had a humped back. In a row, on the ground in front of him, lay the troupe—Charles, Pierre, and Tom . . . and Celia, and Alicia.

"That's the last one," the boy announced.

"Five. Hee-e-e-e," said the old woman. "An odd hand. There should be six. Hee-e-e-e," she wheezed heavily, sucking in air. "Three men; two women; it leaves one man out. Unless . . . hee-e-e. No; they would fight. Maybe number six ran away. Hee-e-e-e. Start digging. We'll look later. She can't be far. Hee-e-e."

Mary stood up. "Help me . . ." she pleaded and collapsed.

"There she is!" the boy shouted as he ran toward her. He helped her rise. She recoiled, shying away from his hunchback.

"It won't bite," he assured her. "It's safe. See!" He reached back and rubbed. "Rub a back that's got a hunch; you'll be sure to get a bunch. A bunch of luck! Luck!" He danced from foot to foot.

"Bring her here, Little John," the woman ordered.

With the boy's help, Mary moved to a stone and sat down. Her swollen leg made her cringe in agony.

"A bit of a problem, girlie? Hee-e-e." The woman bent over her and examined the leg by lifting the foot; Mary's head exploded in pain. The woman ignored her scream and probed with her fingers, each jab bringing a new outburst from Mary's lips. "Hold her by the shoulders, Little John," the woman ordered. "Hold hard."

The boy looked at her, puzzled.

"From the back. Hee-e-e. Put your arms around her and pull tight. That's it. Hee-e-e. Don't let go when she bucks, hear me?"

"What . . . are you . . . going . . . to do?" Mary gasped.

"You'll see. Hee-e-e." She probed gently and Mary winced. "Just like the goat," she muttered to herself. With great care, she raised the enlarged, puffed foot, holding it tenderly by the ankle. "When I tell you," she said to the boy, "grab her tight and hold. Hee-e. You understand me?" The boy nodded. "All right. Now!" she yelled. "Hee-e-e-e!" And she gave the foot a twisting pull.

The boy squeezed. A tornado of roiling, boiling, swelling pain erupted upward from Mary's leg. It swept over her like a huge tidal wave, drowning her, shredding her senses, vibrating her flesh in roaring pulsations, jabbing thousands of thorns into her brain. Her body heaved upward, arching into a bridge, and a hurricane of shrieks came from her writhing, distorted lips. Her mouth tore at the sides as it sought to distend wide enough to allow the sound to escape. Suddenly, the bridge collapsed, and her body folded in agony as she sank into blessed unconsciousness.

Hours later she opened her eyes; she lay exhausted, her lips parched, her mouth dry. There was a wet rag on her forehead, and she licked her arid lips. "Water," she croaked, "wa . . . ter."

A cooling wetness flowed immediately into her mouth, and she sucked eagerly. Her eyes focused, and she saw the concerned face of the boy looming over her. "More," she said, and the rag dripped with moisture. It ran down her face and dripped over her chin. She drank.

"Don't drown her with it. Hee-e-e. Give it to me."

Another face was above her, the old woman. She stared at the deep wrinkles around the mouth and eyes. The woman placed her arm around her and lifted her. She held a cup, and Mary drank eagerly. Surfeit, finally, she pushed the cup away and the woman let her rest.

Suddenly she remembered. "My leg! What happened to my leg?" She pulled the coverlet off and looked with dismay at her leg encased in a triangle of three sticks all bound tightly together.

"It was broken. Hee-e-e. But it will mend. Drink some more. It is good for the pain which will come."

"Will it be all right? I can't feel it."

"We will see. What's your name, girlie?"

"Mary, Mary Toon. I was going to Paris, to find my sister. Oh-h-h, my foot." She groaned as the pain returned.

"Here, drink this. Hee-e-e." The woman handed her the cup.

Mary drank. "What is this?" she asked. The liquid had an odd taste and it was gritty.

"Juice of the willow bark. Hee-e-e. It helps when things hurt."

"Why do you make that funny sound, that 'hee-e-e' noise?"

"It's in here." The old woman patted her chest. "Sometimes I can't breathe. Hee-e-e. It makes it easier."

"What happened to my friends?"

"Dead. Hee-e-e."

"All dead," the boy interjected. "I buried them." He was proud of his accomplishment.

"You were lucky," said the old woman. "There were no last rites, but I did manage . . . hee-e-e . . . a prayer for their souls. If they had caught you, you might have wished for a quick death, too. What were they after? Everything was a mess in the wagon . . . hee-e . . . but nothing seemed missing."

"The money . . . they took the box."

"Gold?" Little John broke in. "You had gold? Grandma, she says they had gold! Money!"

"I hear; I hear! We are very poor, and gold excites him although he has never seen any," she explained to Mary. "Hee-e-e-e."

Mary's face paled and she winced.

"The leg," said the woman. "Here, chew on this." She handed Mary a small twig. "Chew hard."

"What is it?"

"A withy branch; from the willow."

Mary chewed and the throbbing subsided.

"Well, girlie, are you going to stay here or do you know anyone?"

"Only my sister, in Paris." The pain was a dull pulsation.

"Then I guess you stay. Hee-ee. You won't be traveling until the spring. We can sell the horse and wagon—and the clothes and other things—I'll take them to market tomorrow. That will give us some money. What did your friends do, girlie? Hee-e-e."

"They were jongleurs," Mary whispered. "They tried to make people laugh . . . and be happy." She began to cry, sobbing at the pain and her loss.

14

WINTER—A PROLOGUE

There was a dark foreboding of disaster over the land, for the winter was harsh that year, ravishing the needy and creating desolation for the poor. Those who had hoarded the harvest carefully doled their supplies and watched them grimly as the winter months moved slowly by. The poor ate roots, tore bark from the trees for soup when they ran out of turnip rinds, and mixed clay with the bread flour. Famine touched every home and the weak wasted away, their bodies turning to skin over skeleton before they died.

The men had too much time to think. Those who had taken the cross looked down on the others who sulked because they were to stay at home. The crusaders had a hope and a purpose. Gone were their worries of plowing in the spring and repairing the damage to the stone walls. Gone was the back-breaking work of clearing fields of stones and hauling rock to shear up damaged marker walls. Gone were their duties to their lords, for they were to be free men—free to serve the Lord—and themselves, for the Holy Father, Papa Urban himself, had released them.

Jerusalem, the Celestial City! It sparkled in the clear, bright sunlight and lit up the skies! The roofs of its buildings were made of solid gold, and large jewels were imbedded in all the walls, shattering the sun's rays into rainbows. The paving stones were made of silver and gold in the walkways, and wine flowed in the fountains. There was never a dry throat in Jerusalem.

The deeply religious were excited by the ease they would have in ridding themselves of all their sins; the greedy talked of gold and how they would become wealthy, for Papa Urban had said they could take anything they wished from the Infidel without sin. They would all be free and rich in the Holy Land, like lords.

A farmer could harvest a crop every four months, for there was no winter, and the slaves would do the dirty work. All the houses were like small castles, built of marble, stone, and cedar wood, like King Solomon's temple. And they winked when they spoke of the women of the Moslem. Sloe-eyed, dark, mysterious, they lived in harems without men and would come to any bed eagerly. Brash and starved for love, they would dance naked, for they had no shame, and they bathed in oils and creams, making themselves sleek and pleasant to the touch. Their perfumes would drive a man mad, not like the women at home who stank like the goats.

In the great halls of the knights the fireplaces roared as the cold, wintry winds howled through the corridors, flapping the tapestries. The knights were gathering, their drunken tears flowing as the troubadours sang the "Song of Roland." They lifted their goblets in boastful toasts of the victories of the past and to those yet to come. They boasted of the loot they would take and how they would fashion the gold and silver into armor with golden scabbards and buckles. The Moslem harem girls would serve them at their bath and in their bedchambers, and the Moslem men would be their slaves. The mirth was high as the pages, bright-eyed and eager, rushed about filling the emptying goblets.

In the stables, the grooms combed the manes and tails of the big war horses, the destriers, and worked their muscles to keep them supple and relaxed. They mended and tested new harnesses and carved new saddles. The squires practiced their swordplay with enthusiasm and desperation, for this was the time to hasten to their knighthood and prove their mastery of the singing swords.

The ladies did their weaving and needlepoint in silence. Many feared the journey yet feared more to remain home impoverished, for their husbands, as vassals to their lords, were pledging their services and provisions: so many horses, so many lances, so many footsoldiers—provisioned and armed; axemen . . . bowmen . . . wagons and mules . . . grain . . . cattle, pigs, sheep, oxen—the list was endless. Marriages were made for convenience, a business contract between lords to maintain lands and wealth, to secure political dominance and extend holdings. Rarely was there an emotional attachment.

A youth did not inherit knighthood; he had to attain it. An heir could inherit a title as count or baron, but that did not automatically make him a knight. Being master of wealth—lands, serfs, gold—did not confer knighthood, and many a knight was poor, having little more than a horse, his armor, his sword, and perhaps some men-at-arms and a squire to attend him.

Urban's call to arms to rescue the Holy Sepulchre and his pronouncements of the wealth of the East made the poor knight's eyes suddenly glitter. It was a chance of a lifetime.

The knight of wealth and substance sat tall in his saddle, clad in his coat of mail, his long lance at his side, his sword—flat and wide-pointed—feared. He was judge, counselor, tax assessor, collector of tithes, and plunderer. His vassals secured what they could from their vassals who took what they could from their own vassals—and the serf and free man paid for it all. He feuded with other lords, raiding their granaries, taking their women, just as the others raided him. Ignorant, scarred, cruel, he lived by pure strength, gaining advantages only by another's death.

This was chivalry in Europe. That winter the raids of the lords became fierce.

The monks and priests walked the roads to every hamlet and village, carrying Urban's message and carrying the red strips for the volunteers. Men came forward by the thousands, eager to march after the spring rains were over, but the lords were not ready when the spring came, and Urban postponed the starting time to August. The pilgrim could throw what little he possessed on a wagon or cart, but the knights had to provision armies.

Only Peter the Hermit insisted he would march in the spring.

Urban knew he needed no more than five or six of the great knights, the strong and the wealthy, for then the lesser knights, the vassals of the dukes and the counts, would automatically follow; and their vassals would follow in turn. He spent the winter traveling and preaching his crusade, through Tours, Limoges, Bordeaux, Montpellier, and on to Toulouse where he visited again with his good friend, Count Raymond of St. Gilles. Raymond had pledged his entire wealth, and it was large enough to create an army by itself. With Raymond, also, would march many of his serfs and free men of Provence.

15

Sir Raymond of Toulouse sat by the fire and dully watched the blaze of the large logs. A hunting dog lay at his feet, and he idly scratched its head. It was late March and it was not cold, but the rains had made everything damp, and he needed the heat to drive the chillness out of his bones.

Fifty-three winters, he told himself, and again I gird for battle. It will be my last, a proper finish for my aging years. The journey would be wearisome for Elvira, his young wife, and he must, at all costs, protect his son-to-be-born. That was paramount, for he intended to establish a great fiefdom from the lands he would win from the Moslem, and his son would carry on the lineage.

"Why does milord brood?" asked Elvira from her needlepoint. "Do not the preparations go well?"

"Very well," he answered with no enthusiasm, burying his head deeper into his broad shoulders. "I have heard from your father. He has received my message that you are with child, and he offers three hundred knights to join us to protect his grandson."

She laughed gaily. "Both he and you are sure it will be a boy. What if the Good Lord gives us a daughter?"

His eyes sparkled at her mirth; her laughter was infectious. "No true princess denies her lord his just due. You are hereby ordered to produce a son."

She teased him. "Do you not fear that the Lord might deny you your arrogance?"

"I have no doubts that the Lord will favor us. After all, we go to Jerusalem to rescue the Holy Sepulchre, and we shall remain there to protect it until He sees fit to summon me. For all that I am sure He will grant us a son, to be with me on the journey and in the Holy Land."

"That will be very difficult without me," she bantered.

His face became tender. "I would not do any of this without you. You are my life, and you carry my life within you." His voice became anxious. "Are you sure you will be able to travel by August? Adhemar says Urban has named that month for us to start."

"You worry too much," she assured him. "Take care of your army and let female affairs be conducted by females. August will be fine. How is Adhemar? He does not visit."

"He is well—and very busy." He chuckled. "He frets and complains that his hand itches for the sword again instead of the bishop's crook. He swears he will ride with the men, not the women."

"Poor Adhemar," she said with sympathy. "He is a true warrior of Our Lord and he thirsts for battle."

"So he chose. However, he is Urban's legate and will wield full church power. That will be work enough."

She heard his burdened tone. "I know how disappointed you are not to be named as the leader of the crusade, but that will come. When the knights' council meets, who but you has had the experience of fighting the Moslem? You have fought so many battles in Spain, you know the infidel well."

He shook his head soberly. "Adhemar tells me that Duke Godfrey and his brothers are preparing. They are good men and strong fighters."

"But they will not stand in your way, especially Godfrey, and his brothers listen to him."

"There are others. Hugh of Vermandois, King Philip's brother; and there is Stephen, count of Blois. Philip has ordered many knights to go with Hugh."

"Hugh is a dandy and more interested in the courtly intrigues than in battles. Philip sends him to get rid of him. And Stephen!" She laughed derisively. "His only passion is the hunt."

"You forget, my little one, that he is married to Adele, and she never forgets that she is the daughter of King William of England. And she has enough warrior blood for both of them. He took the cross because she insisted, and she will have him stand for commander."

"And the others will follow him into battle? A man who fears to disobey his wife?" She laughed merrily. "No, my husband. Who will vote for a woman to lead the crusade?"

"Nevertheless, she will urge him on." He paused to think. "Robert of Normandy also comes."

Her laughter was loud and contemptuous. "Robert! Oh my sides . . . Robert! I . . . have . . . a stitch . . . Robert . . . it sticks." She gasped for breath and wiped the tears from her eyes. "Urban receives all the prodigals and rapscallions." She broke into another fit of laughter. "Husband, you will abort me with your jokes. How can you hold them as equal contenders with you? Robert of Normandy!" She was holding her sides again.

He found he had to smile, then laugh with her. "Short Breeches will have many vassals with him," he protested, "and you know the Normans are great fighters."

"When they fight. He could not defend his castles from his own brother. Short Breeches?" She let out a peal of laughter which ended in a coughing fit.

He rose and hovered over, worried. "Do not take on so."

She waved him away. "I will . . . be . . . all right," she gasped. She breathed deeply, then burst out again, "Short Breeches! I never heard him called that."

"His father said he was too short for his breeches—the name stuck. You know how these Normans are. King William, especially."

"Named Short Breeches by King William, truly a man for a leader. But I hear he is a jest, a folly, a womanizer, an emptier of cups, a gorger of boar's meat. His lusts and vices are the butt of every court. He is so simpleminded that even the pages laugh and trick him. Who would be so addle-minded as to choose him?"

"He lacks not for friends, and he is a stubborn fighter when aroused," said Raymond soberly. "Sometimes a commander is chosen because the others do not want a strong leader; they can bend a weaker man to their side. Politics creates alliances of the instant, and those who lead are not necessarily the best, nor the bravest, but the one with the greatest compromising ability. Such is Robert."

"Phafft!" she exploded. "His friends slop his wine and wash his women, but those are not men who wield strong swords. The crusade will not be a mild tournament. Who will vote for a wine-sotted brain and a frolicking chaser of sin? Who will trust their lives and fortunes to a drunken, gluttonous fornicator? No, no, my husband . . . commander? Robert of Normandy?" She burst into laughter again. "I—I am sorry . . . my Gilles . . . oh, my sides!"

"Do not take on so, my lovely," he said smiling, despite himself. "I do admit you make all your reasons sound admirable."

"Let us not talk of them," she answered, regaining her composure. "Tell me about the preparations. That will sober me."

"Well," he began, "Adhemar has finished the distribution of our land grants to the monasteries, and the tax monies from the cities come in, but slowly, and that is holding up the purchasing of supplies. But we will manage. The collectors have orders to be firm. We will have a large host of knights, soldiers, and bowmen—even a contingent of crossbowmen—and all will be well armed. Many peasants and serfs will go with us, to seek their own salvation in the Holy Land."

"I am glad," she said, "but if things go so well, why do you brood?"

"I don't know. Perhaps it is a foreboding."

"Perhaps it is an impatience," she said, soothing him. "The crusade comes too slowly for you, and you are discontented because of the delay."

"Perhaps, my love." He was unwilling to argue the point. "We could never have been ready by this spring. It is well Urban postponed it to August."

He buried his head deeper into his shoulders. The dog yawned and stretched, and Raymond's hand sought the animal's ear. He thought of his battle-scarred years and wondered. Never had he felt so old.

16

He was Lord Godfrey of Bouillon, duke of Lorraine, and he sat with his booted feet outstretched, the heels resting on the edge of the table, drinking morosely. He toyed with the empty goblet as he waited impatiently for the arrival of his brothers, Eustace, the oldest, and Baldwin, the youngest. Behind him hung the banner of the Church of Lorraine, a bright violet field interwoven with the images of the saints, an apt wall cover, for the duke was very religious.

He pondered his decision, urged upon him by his brothers. Many of his serfs had already vanished down the roads, following a barefoot monk called Peter the Hermit. The price of Urban's crusade was becoming enormous. Hard-coin money had practically disappeared, much of it into the coffers of the Church, and the scarcity of the metal was enough to frustrate a saint. It was easier to carry gold than drive herds of cattle and sheep, and the value of the land, buildings, horses, cattle, and sheep had dropped far because of the large amounts the crusading knights were willing to sell.

Prodded by his brothers, he had sent Lord Brennen, a lesser lord and a vassal, along with Baldwin, to Clermont to listen to Urban, and the two knights, caught up in the fiery enthusiasm, had taken the cross. Although their personal motives were different, both had urged Godfrey to sew the red strips on his shoulder, too. Brother Eustace had been convinced earlier and became another ardent persuader.

Eustace, as the oldest, had inherited the vast estates of their father, and although a knight, he was no equal to Godfrey's fighting abilities. He pushed his brother to join, promising to act as a vassal if Godfrey took the cross.

Baldwin, the youngest, owned nothing. Expected by his mother to become a member of the clergy, possibly a bishop, she had left him none of her estates. But with a temperament suited for contention, and a worldly lust for good living and women, he soon found himself in the snares of a questing lady who made him her husband. Children, three, came in rapid succession, and his mother refused to buy him a church position. With no fief of his own, he lived on the largesse of his in-laws and brothers.

Urban had promised vast lands, slaves—Moslem, of course—wealth, pomp, and gold—all for the use of his fighting arm, and in his mind, he could make his fortune and serve God, too. He would be an ardent crusader, one of the best.

But Godfrey was the key to the family decision. Young, strong, broad of shoulder, lean of loin, gray-eyed, with reddish-blond hair cascading around his shoulders, erect and tall, he was the epitome of knighthood. A vassal of King Henry of Germany, he was but sixteen when he had received his knight's sword, and he marched with Henry to Rome to drive old Pope Gregory into exile. With his horse and sword covered with the blood of the fighting monks defending the pope, he had driven Rudolf of Swabia, a defender of Gregory, into the Lateran and there killed him. For that, Henry rewarded him with the gift of the dukedom of Lorraine, but since then he had felt accursed, eternally damned for raising his sword against the Church. He suffered a continual fever and attacks to his head. He grew weary of swordplay and jousts, spending much time in his private chapel in prayer. Yet, he was the warrior of the family, and decisions involving the family were deferred to him.

Mild mannered, an even temperament, pious, and considerate to his peasants and serfs, he tried to rule as he believed God would have him rule: with peace, honor, love, and charity. In a world surrounded with brutality, greed, and cruelty, he was an innocent among the lords. He had expanded his mother's small inheritance into the dukedom of Lorraine and Rhineland, and his sword protected his fief from raiding knights and covetous bishops. He even fought his emperor, Henry, when Urban excommunicated the German king as a "delinquent Christian."

But the fever would not leave him. It sapped his energy and sucked his vitality, leaving him listless and fatigued. Urban's call for a fighting crusade did not interest him; but the idea of a pilgrimage to the Holy Sepulchre, to find absolution, filled him.

The constant dunnings of his brothers to don his armor took hold, and he agreed to become a Knight of the Cross, absorbing himself in the planning for the campaign. He breathed in the hope that it would be a sufficient penance for his crime, and his spirits rose as he came to the belief that he would be forgiven of all his sins.

The snows were melting and the freshets were running full in spring. He waited all morning and into the early afternoon with impatience. Irritated, he ordered wine, and, as he drank, his thoughts grew blacker. Finally, a small tantara from the tower heralded the arrival of his brothers. When they walked in, he did not rise to greet them, but his booted feet dropped to the floor.

"What kept you?" he asked Eustace.

A page boy scurried in with more goblets, anticipating a need.

Baldwin poured the wine. "The saddle is hot, and the roads are dusty. We have just come from Brennen."

"Do we have the gold, or do we need more?" Godfrey eyed Eustace.

"Maybe," answered Eustace. "I drink to an early departure."

"Just think," said Baldwin, wiping his mouth. "Constantinople! The City of Light! Charlemagne's own!" He poured more wine and glanced at Godfrey. "He *is* our ancestor, you know. Here's to Constantinople! May we be there soon!" He drank.

"It's managed all this time without us," said Godfrey drily. "Our goal is Jerusalem. But neither of you has answered my question. Do we finally have enough gold?"

The brothers glanced at one another. "There is a problem," began Eustace. "Much has been demanded by the Church."

Godfrey clenched his teeth and his face froze in a spasm. His lips drew back from his teeth and he trembled; then he recovered and drew a deep breath.

"Not enough!" he said finally. "Good Jesus, I have prayed for guidance, yet I suffer." His eyes glazed; in prayer, he murmured, "Do not prod me, Lord, when I falter. I have vowed and I am coming." He took another breath and turned savagely on his brothers, "Tell me, where are we to collect more gold?"

"Easy, my brother," said Eustace. "We know the fever wracks you, but you should not let your blood boil. Calm yourself."

With great effort, Godfrey controlled his grimacing face. "Lord, defend me from diplomatic tongues. Why do you aid the devil with this uncertainty? Where do we turn for gold?"

"We will talk of gold, but relax," urged Eustace. "Let your hot blood cool. Drink some wine. We will talk of . . ."

"You are a cunctator! Why must you add to my pain by dallying? What did Brennen say?"

"Brennen reported some attacks by Henry's soldiers, and we took some time to survey the damages," said Baldwin. "It was not very extensive. The Lady Benicia and her daughters send you their love." He was watching Godfrey closely.

Godfrey's lip curled. "Anne must be quite a lady by this time, ready to be wedded and bedded."

"Ask Baldwin." Eustace grinned. "She was very taken with him. He spent much time with her at Clermont, and her approval was marked at this visit." He glanced, with a wink, at Baldwin. "Careful, brother, Godehilde can turn jealous." He chortled.

"My wife has no cause," retorted Baldwin jocularly. "She has three good reasons to be content. By the way, all three children send you their greetings. And if you must know," he turned to Eustace, "Anne spoke very highly— and often—of you, as well as Godfrey. She knows where to set her cap."

"How old is she now?" asked Godfrey.

"Fifteen, sixteen." Baldwin shrugged. "It is old enough, but there will be no bedding without the priest's blessing. Lady Benicia has taught her fledglings well." He grinned at Godfrey. "There is no mistaking, though, whom she prefers, and she would ask outright, if she dared."

"For the benefit of her cubs, Lady Benicia will dare anything," said Eustace. "Brennen told me she insists on coming on the crusade; the girls, too."

"Why not?" shrugged Godfrey. "Baldwin takes Godehilde and his three."

"But Baldwin proposes to remain in the Holy Lands; Brennen will come home. He is opposed to taking her, especially for the girls' sakes, and he asks that you forbid it, Godfrey."

Godfrey grinned his denial. "There is little I will refuse Brennen, but this is one of them. Can you imagine Lady Benicia standing before me and demanding to know why I refuse her a place in Heaven? How can I answer a charge like that? No, Brennen will have to assert his manliness, or . . ." he grinned, "acknowledge his own defeat."

"I talked with her," said Baldwin, "and Anne about the journey. They say most eligible knights will be going; and there will be kingdoms won in the East. They wish to be part of it."

"Enough of all this chatter," growled Godfrey. "Brennen can care for his own. What of the gold?"

"We need more," said Eustace somberly. "Even the one hundred thousand crowns you received for Metz is gone. We tried to exchange land and animals for supplies, but the armorers and wagonmakers insist on gold. Most of the knights have already exhausted their coffers, with prices so high."

"What of the lands we sold to the bishop? Has he paid?"

"Yes, but it still isn't enough. We are outfitting thousands."

"What's left? We can't sell the castle. I promised it to the Church as an offering for prayers in our behalf."

Eustace hesitated and glanced at Baldwin, who turned away. "There . . . there is always Bouillon."

"No!" exploded Godfrey. "Bouillon remains!"

"The bishop of Liege offers three thousand silver marks and four thousand gold."

"No! No! It is worth five times that! Never! It is not for sale! There must be other ways!"

"Wait, Godfrey," said Baldwin. "He offers it for pawn. When we take that much from the infidel, we can redeem it. Eustace has stripped himself. All has been ventured on this crusade, and with God's help, we will not be left empty-handed."

"Think, Godfrey," urged Eustace. "It is but a temporary measure. There is only one other alternative I know of."

Godfrey turned on him savagely. "What? Tell me? Why do you hold it back?"

"It is not a course you would like to take; I know it. I have ordered it in my cities, especially Bologna. I have brought some of the gold back with me now, and much more can be collected . . ."

"*Why all this mystery!*" shouted Godfrey. "*What are you hiding?*"

"All right," said Eustace. He clapped his hands, and two pages entered carrying a large chest between them. They placed it at Godfrey's feet and withdrew. Perplexed, Godfrey shook his head. Eustace said to him, "With all your illness, and the time you have been spending in your chapel, you have heard little of the news. There is great enthusiasm for the crusade, and there have been many attacks on the Jews in the cities. My collectors have gone out, and for the promise of their safety, the Jews have been willing to pay extra taxes . . .'' He grinned. ''Some have paid very well.''

Godfrey suddenly understood. ''And you propose I levy the same taxes on my Jews.''

''Why not?'' said Baldwin cynically. ''The genealogy of Christ is Jewish; they were instrumental in His death; let them aid in the liberation of His tomb.''

''There have been burnings of synagogues and killings of Jews in many places, and the men doing it all wore Urban's cross,'' said Eustace. ''The Jews cry out for protection; we can give it. We can stop the looting of their quarters; we can protect their homes and families. We have done this, but we have insisted on payment. Your Jews know what is happening. Collections have already started in your cities. You have but to give the word.''

Baldwin refilled his goblet. ''There is enough gold in the Jewish Quarter to furnish our needs. We have but to mine it.''

''What of those who have no gold for payment?'' asked Godfrey.

''Let the others ransom them,'' said Eustace. ''They have jewelry and artifacts of silver. Baldwin is right. They can give us enough to arm our knights.''

Baldwin, with a major effort, had placed the chest upon the table. He opened it. ''Look, Godfrey. This is the first installment from Eustace's Jews. We haven't even counted it yet.'' He dumped it upon the table. ''We can get more of these easily.''

Godfrey looked from one brother to the other. Suddenly, he made up his mind. ''All right, I will give the order. But you count the money.'' And he strode out of the room.

Eustace and Baldwin began to pile the coins in rows.

17

His skin was dark as a Moor's and he was thin, for he did not eat any meat, only fish and vegetables. He said that the spirit of Saint Peter, the Big Fisherman, was in him, and, like his namesake, he, too, would fish for souls. But where was Peter the Hermit to find fish during the winter? Where, indeed, but that God provided for him, and there was no doubt in anyone but that Peter had been chosen and that God had put fire on his tongue.

Chagon walked in front, leading Peter's mule, and Walter walked to one side of the animal, his long hair flowing, his sword strapped to his side. Parenti, holding aloft a large wooden cross, walked on the other side, and after them came a long line of carts and wagons, with many pilgrims walking on foot. The line grew longer daily as families joined them.

They would camp by the village cemetery, and the people would gather to listen, for Peter had visions. He stood straight, a majestic figure with a long, white beard and a shock of white hair, his cross upraised, his face lifted to the sky, and he would pray aloud. Finished, he would bless all those who heard him, pause as his burning eyes searched his listeners' souls, and begin:

"I have a message for you from Our Lord Jesus Christ, and He has appointed me to deliver it. Hear me, O Christians! So sayeth your Lord! He has told me to tell you my vision!

"I was walking in a dense forest when suddenly I came to a clearing where the sun was shining. My heart was heavy, for I had heard how the Christians were suffering in the Holy Land, and I did not know how to help them. The evil Infidel ruled there, in an alliance with Satan, and Christians were forced into degeneracies. *Satan ruled supreme in the Holy Land!* And what could I do? I sank to my knees and prayed, 'Guide me, O Lord,' I cried out. 'Give me a sign so I will know Thy Will.'

"Dark clouds gathered, blotting out the sun, and the entire heavens were overcast. Thunder rumbled, filling all the world with its clash, until with a thunderous explosion—the heavens split! A long shaft of yellow light descended into the clearing where I knelt, forming a bright sun spot.

"It began to move over the ground, a swirling motion, raising the dust off the earth; then, faster and faster. The leaves spun and lifted! Then, the branches of the trees! Then, the trees tore themselves out of the earth! I stood transfixed, like rock, but a large mass was gyrating all around me until it became so huge that it blotted out the light. I was in darkness, and I trembled in fear.

" 'Lord! Save me!' I cried.

"Suddenly, there was a sucking sound and everything rose skyward. With an explosion, it split into two, and from its center a great white light pierced through to where I stood. In the center of the light, blazing and spinning slowly, flaming and glowing in glory as it increased its circle of spin, was a two-edged sword. It cut everything out of its path, and with swift strokes, it sliced the black clouds apart. There! Standing revealed! There was Saint Michael! Astride a pure white horse! Behind him, in battle formation, stood his warrior angels, mounted and armed!

"The sword flew to his hand, and he raised it up above his head. Lightning flashed, brighter than the sun at noonday, blinding me, and the thunder beat upon me.

"Then, the light of the sword exploded and the darkness ran before it, and another host stood revealed. Satan! And his imps! Thousands and thousands of demons, all dressed as infidel Moslems, astride char-black chargers, lined up for battle.

"Saint Michael pointed his sword of light toward this Devil host and his angels and cherubim charged. When the two hosts met, the heavens rang with the clash of iron, and the thunder and lightning made the infinities vibrate and echo. God's host fought the Devil's!

"Suddenly, Saint Michael's sword split into thousands of shafts of light-swords, glittering and penetrating the darkness of the struggle. They drove the demons of Satan before them, each slaying the demon it chased, and then it descended to the earth. Satan was vanquished! The black clouds were gone! The sun shone brightly!

"Listen now to the words of your Lord! You are those shafts of light, those thousands of swords! You are the dust, the trees, the stones that ascended to Heaven! Take the cross with me and become a flaming sword of the Lord in the Holy Land, destroying the demon infidels! Follow me to Jerusalem, and together we shall free the Holy Sepulchre!''

They listened in a trance, and by the thousands they pinned the two strips of the Cross on their shoulders. The line behind Peter grew longer and longer, and many huts stood empty after he passed through a village or hamlet.

18

Sir Walter practiced with the big sword daily, and Leo, watching him, was awed by the knight's ferocity, so different from his usual gentleness and even temper. When the knight stopped to rest, he asked, "Is the sword heavy?"

Walter hefted it with contempt. "A knight's sword is, but this one must have been made for a young squire not yet in his manhood. Try it." He handed it to Leo, a smile on his face.

Leo found he could handle it easily. "Can I try?"

Walter nodded. "Balance it in your hand. No, no, like you do with your knives before you throw." He shook his head as Leo tried to follow his instruction. "No, no. Feel its weight. That's better. Up and down . . . easy . . . that's it . . . now, swing!"

Leo swung and threw himself off balance.

Walter laughed. "Brace yourself when you do that. Use your whole body for the backstroke. Slowly, at first, then work up speed . . . that's better . . . faster . . . faster! Good! No. No! Too fast. Your feet must be firm. Do it again. Right, left . . . faster . . . again . . . again. Faster! There! You have it!"

"That's heavy," said Leo panting.

Walter chortled. "For you. You need more meat on your bones. Maybe a lance or a short spear would be better for you."

"I eat enough, but I don't get fat."

"I'm not talking about fat." He pinched his side. "That's what I've got; you need muscle." He considered Leo thoughtfully. "I don't think you were made to be a knight; you're not big enough. You move fast, but a big, quick man is best. Maybe you could be my squire, and I would teach you how to fight with all the weapons. You have good hands and you handle your knives well."

Leo glowed under the praise. "I practice a lot."

"Let me ask you. Suppose you threw your knives at a man, and that didn't stop him from coming at you. What would you do?"

"I—er—don't know. I . . . would run."

"You see, you need more than a knife. They are tricky, a surprise weapon, but a warrior fights openly, not with something he hides. You need a sword or a spear."

"But I'm to be a monk, not a fighter. I have taken vows."

"Suppose someone attacked me? Or Brother Peter? What would you do?" The thought was new. "I would use my knives." Leo was hesitant.

"Good, and after you threw them? What then? You would run?"

There was an awakened realization in Leo's mind. "I'd need a sword . . . or something for my hand." He shook his head, perplexed. "But I'm not supposed to fight. I'm to be a monk, a man of peace."

"We live in a strange world, Leo. The times are unsettled, and the road to peace lies through death and destruction of the forces of evil. We fight to destroy Satan."

"I suppose—so," said Leo thoughtfully. "Have you ever heard of a Cath . . . Cathari?" he asked suddenly.

"Yes," said Walter. "They are heretics. How do you know them?"

"I met one. He was dying. Brother Parenti wouldn't let me bury him. He called Christ an Eon, and he said Satan ruled the world and that we all work for Satan unless we starve. Can that be?"

"Of course not. That is what made him a heretic. We do Our Lord's work. Get rid of all such thoughts; they are from the devil."

"That's what Brother Parenti says, too. But we do such strange things. Maybe the devil is getting me." He was frightened.

"What are the strange things you do?"

"Like, we fight, but Christ did not fight. We kill, and the Bible says we shouldn't. Even you took an oath not to kill anymore. But Brother Peter says to kill the infidel is doing God's work. Even Papa Urban said that. Then there is Brother Parenti. He says . . ." He suddenly became very quiet.

"What about Parenti?" asked Walter.

Leo hesitated, unwilling to speak, but finally overcame his reluctance. "He bought me knives, and he says sometimes I would have to use them—on Christians—when he tells me." He became uncomfortable again.

Walter let the silence drag. He saw that Leo was caught up in an internal struggle which would surface sooner or later. He waited.

Leo fidgeted. Suddenly the words tumbled out. "Do you think that would be right? I don't want to kill Christians. And then . . ." He lapsed into silence again. Walter waited. "Can I really talk to you? You won't tell him?"

"Whatever you tell me, Leo, is only between us. What is it?"

"He says I'm not to tell anyone, not even to talk about it; it is part of Church secrets, secrets between him and me because I am his novice, and I don't even talk about it to a priest. Will you promise not to tell anyone else?"

"I promise you that as a knight, and you know a knight does not break his vows."

"Well . . . you promised never to fight again, and . . ."

"In God's cause any vow may be broken and God will forgive you because it is done for Him. But this vow I make for you. Whatever you say to me will never be revealed unless you release me from this oath, and I must keep it until the day I die."

Leo nodded. "I believe you. Well . . . Brother Parenti . . . well . . . he does things to me . . . and he wants me to do them to him. But I can't . . . and he says I must learn . . . but I . . ." He squirmed.

"What does he do?" asked Walter softly.

"He—he says monks must be celibate. They must not use women, he says, so they must help each other . . . they have urges . . . but they can't go to women . . . so they help . . ." He was lost.

"Tell me." Walter was gentle. "What does he want you to do?"

Leo was silent, struggling with himself.

"All right," said Walter, "let me ask you. Have you ever been with a woman, I mean as a man. Do you understand me?"

Leo's head bobbed. "I know what you mean. At the inn, the girls . . . once Nicholas showed me, on a sheep. And he used to take Lydia to the hayloft."

"Did you ever try—with girls?"

"Once Angie—one of Papa's girls—took me into a room and undressed me. But Mama came in and she was angry. She threw Angie over the bannister and hurt her. Mama gave me a lecture. I wasn't supposed to do that, she said, until I was married."

Walter laughed. "And you never tried again?"

Leo shrugged. "I wasn't married."

Walter laughed again. "But you saw men and women, who were not married, together all the time at the inn."

"But I can't! I've taken vows. I must be celibate."

"Do you want to be? Parenti didn't put you in a monastery or attach you to any Order. Your vows . . . we'll talk to Brother Peter. But tell me, what does Parenti ask you to do?"

Leo took a deep breath. "Well . . . he puts his mouth here . . ." He indicated his groin. "And he . . . I . . . well, I can't . . . I get all worked up . . . it spits. I feel funny . . . all sorts of things . . ." He lapsed into silence. Walter waited. "Then he wanted me to do the same for him. I tried . . . but I don't feel right. He says I must do it because we can't go to women. We have to help each other. I don't . . ." He became quiet in his misery.

"Don't you know," said Walter gravely, "that what he does is an abomination in the eyes of the Lord? You must never do it!"

"But he is a man of God, a holy man."

"He is a heathen! Even if he wears a monk's habit and a cross. Listen to me, Leo. God made Adam and gave him a wife. A man and a woman. Together. Not a man and a man. Disobey God and He will cast your soul into Hell!"

Leo was terrified. "No! No! I won't do it!"

"Leave him, Leo, leave him. If you wish, you can come with me. I need a squire. I can train you to be a fighter for the Lord. *You* will decide if you want to fight, not he. When the time comes you will be fighting for Christ, not burning in Hell for a wayward monk."

Leo rocked in terror. "Tell me, what shall I do?"

"Here, take this sword." He gave it to Leo. "Come with me, and I will teach you how to fight like a knight." He put his arm over Leo's shoulder. "Together we will make a strong team."

"I will! I will!" Leo nodded emphatically.

"Good. Then it's all settled. Pick up the sword and take the position. We will start the training right now."

Parenti faced Walter, and the monk's face was livid in anger. "You dare to interfere with the Lord's work?" he snarled. "You are corrupting a churchman! You know the penalty for that!"

Walter smiled. "I know the penalty for what you do, monk. Do not preach to me. Better look to the salvation of your own soul."

"The Lord knows my work," sneered Parenti. "How much Christian blood, by your own admission, have you spilled? How many women have you raped? How many churches have you plundered?"

"He who is without sin shall cast the first stone." Walter was grim and wished to stop the argument. "Your foulness stinks of the devil. If I told Peter you would be denounced."

"Push me not, knight," Parenti warned.

"Then lean back, monk, and take some of your own advice. We all go to Jerusalem to be forgiven. Let your penance start early."

"I need no counsel from you," said Parenti through clenched teeth. "Leo is my ward and my responsibility."

"I think not. As *you* know, he is a man and responsible to himself." He waved a hand. "But enough of this monkish debate. He asks to train with me and he shall . . ."—his face broke into a sly grin—"unless you wish to test yourself against me with steel. But I would not advise it." The grin came back. "But I would cherish it. What say you?"

"Sir Walter! Brother Parenti!" It was Chagon calling. He was hurrying toward them as they stood glaring at each other.

"We are not finished, knight," snarled Parenti, turning away.

"Brother Peter wants both of you right away," huffed Chagon. "At his tent. He has company from the city. Strange men."

Parenti hurried off. Chagon and Walter followed.

Peter, seated on a small keg, was waiting for them. A few men stood about him, listening to him converse with one of them.

Peter spoke to Parenti. "I have decided we will not enter Paris. It is too large. Instead, these men who come from the city say it will be better if we meet at the big cemetery. This man . . ."—he indicated the one to whom he had been speaking—"is called Tafur, and he says he is 'King of the Ribalds,' these others." He indicated the other men.

They were a motley group, strangely dressed in mismatched clothing, much of it torn and badly mended. There were patches of variegated cloth, oddly placed, some in a pattern. Their plumed hats were pushed back from their absurd, smiling faces at a rakish angle, and they were all grinning broadly.

"My people will spread the news everywhere," said Tafur, "and you will have a big crowd to talk to. Many, like us, have already put on the red strips. See." He pushed his forward.

"King Tafur," said Peter, "already has a large group, with wagons and carts full of provisions and supplies."

"If he brings his money to the common coffers, he is welcome," said Walter. "Can you bring me a knight's sword from the city?" he asked the little man.

"Perhaps," Tafur answered evasively. "We have no knights in our group, but it may be possible."

Parenti laughed sarcastically. "Who would expect knights among ribalds. Fallen women, murderers, defrocked monks, thieves . . ."

"Hymn chanters, cripples, and beggars, too," added Tafur. "All the common people Our Lord loved so well. Do you try to take us away from our chances to be with Christ, monk?"

"Cripples might be a problem . . ." began Peter.

"They all ride," said Tafur hastily. "In their own carts or on mules. We will take care of them."

"Father Urban said no women shall go unless they be wedded," said Parenti. "Our people are good and decent. They do not know such as these, whose sins and temptations will flow over them like a wave of vice and wickedness. They should not be with us."

"You judge harshly," said Peter. "Your holiness should be able to convert their sinfulness. They seek the Lord; they shall come."

Walter chuckled; Parenti choked on his anger.

"It is agreed," said Peter to Tafur. "Tomorrow, we meet at the cemetery, and your people will guide those in the city."

"We will be ready," said Tafur. "We live in the streets, and the wet and the cold are not strangers to us. We will be there."

"If you can bring a sword—and some chain-mail—it will be welcome," said Walter.

Tafur pursed his lips and glanced at his companions. One nodded imperceptibly. "For you, perhaps it can be arranged."

19

Mary leaned heavily upon a stick as she watched Little John pour the water out of the wooden bucket into the tub. "I'll need two more," she said, "and heat them longer. The water is cold."

"It takes too long," he whined, "and then it's too hot to carry."

"Too bad." She was sarcastic. "When Grandma takes off these sticks, she said she wanted my foot to be warm."

"She won't take them off now. She's gonna wait for a full moon. She doesn't do anything without a full moon."

"Stop arguing and get the water."

He did as he was told, moving quickly, for despite their bickering he was happy she was there. Her coming had changed his dreary life, and he feared to be alone with his grandma since the night she had yelled him awake and had coughed until the blood had come dribbling from her mouth. She had clutched him convulsively, trying to talk, but because of her coughing he could understand little. Somehow, he knew Mary would know what to do if Grandma had another fit.

Mary was nervous and irritated. She had not washed for a month, and she felt dirty and itchy. The leg had healed slowly, and Grandma had not permitted her to stand on it. Finally, she agreed to let Mary wash.

Mary, lying despondently on her straw mattress, had had much time to think, and, much to her surprise, she found that she did not mourn the loss of Tom so much anymore. Grandma and Little John attended her assiduously, catering to every whim and need, and, if her leg was well, she would be able to leave them. But where was she to go? Grandma had told her that they were living close to Paris, but the old woman would not take her into the city, and she advised Mary not to try to go there by herself.

Wheezing and clucking, the old woman came into the room from the back shed. She carried a crutch she had fashioned from a tree branch, and a pail of fresh goat's milk. She snickered as she placed the pail on the table. "Is your ladyship's bath ready?"

"Almost." Mary looked at the crutch with dismay. "You don't expect me to hobble about with that, do you? My foot feels fine."

"We'll see." She shuffled over to the tub and put her hand into the water. "Warm enough; get in." She pulled a three-legged stool to her and sat on it. Little John entered with a pail of hot, steaming water. He stood there, uncertain. "All right! Pour it in. Hee-e-e. We have to help our ladyship with her bath."

He emptied the pail, and she tested the water again and grunted, "Fit for a queen." She waved at Mary and stood up. "Here, sit here. Before we do anything, girlie, let me look at the leg. Hee-e-e."

With the boy's help, Mary seated herself.

The old woman raised it carefully and unwrapped the rags, unbinding the sticks. With a slight pressure, she rubbed the skin and probed it with her long, bony fingers. Finally convinced, she slapped it gently. "All ready for the washing, but take care. Come, Little John, she can climb up between us."

Holding fast to both, Mary slowly entered the tub, pulling her skirt up on her thighs. She grasped the folds of the cloth with both hands tightly and stared at Little John "Go to the manger," she ordered him. "I'm going to take off my dress."

Grandma laughed. "No need to be shy, girlie. He's seen all you've got when he helped me with your leg. You're no different than any of the others he's looked at."

"But I feel different. Please," she pleaded, "tell him to go."

It was the first time she had asked for something with any politeness, and her plea touched a chord somewhere deep inside the old woman. She stared at Mary with understanding and said to Little John, "Go on, get into the shed. Hee-e. Rub down the horse."

"Aw." He was annoyed. "Do I have to? I washed him yesterday. If she's so scared I'll see something, I won't even look."

"Go!" said the old woman, and with a grimace of exasperation he left. "All right, girlie, get busy. No need to put the sticks back, but you better be careful. Hee-e-e. For a week. After that you can go dancing. There's going to be some big doings over by the big cemetery later, so if you hurry, we can go. Something about Papa Urban's big crusade for all us sinners." She chuckled and almost choked as she gagged. "Hee-e-e-e-e!" she said, catching her breath. "That was a bad one. Guess I better listen with both ears, with all the sinning I've done. You too. And Little John. Hee-e."

Mary stopped her washing. "Papa Urban didn't say everyone had to go on the crusade—only those who wanted to."

"And didn't he have all that brimstone and 'Devil will get you if you don't' after he asked politely?"

"No, not what I heard. He said the men should go—as good Christians to defend the other Christians."

"That's not what I hear. They say he stood upon his throne and told everyone to go on this crusade to free their souls from sin and to take the Holy Sepulchre away from the heathens. Hee-e. That's what some around here expect to do. Hee-e-e-e." She was breathless.

"But I was there, Grandma. I heard him."

The old woman thought for a moment. "Just proves that people hear what they want. Around here, they've got sin on their minds, and that's what they're going to get rid of. Sin and transgression. Hee-e-e. We could all stand to get rid of some of that. Hurry up."

"I want to find my sister. If we are near the city, maybe we could look for her."

"Time enough for that later. Paris is a big place. We'll hear that Peter monk first. Preaches up a storm, they say. Hee-e. Best thing for your soul."

Mary became alert. "You mean you'll let me walk today?"

Grandma nodded. "If you keep the leg warm. Won't be more than a couple of hours in that cemetery. Like I said, it's good for the soul."

"I'll hurry. Anything to be up and about."

"No ups and about for you, girlie. Just out to the cart, and you stay in it until we get back home. All you're going to exercise is your ears. Hee-e-e-e."

Mary stood up. "I'm finished; can I have something for a towel?"

The old woman handed her a large rag.

Sir Walter, at the head of the procession, rode a horse that he and Leo had found in an open field, and it had taken little effort to capture the placid animal. Peter had remonstrated with the knight for not seeking the rightful owner, but Walter said it was a gift from Heaven, and promised to perform extra penance.

Behind Walter, in the procession, walked Chagon, leading Peter's mule, and on Peter's right, Parenti, carrying a large cross, followed by Leo with another cross. Behind them, riding in two-wheeled carts, in wagons, in drays, walking, or pulling wains like some animals, came the volunteers of the crusade. Mary could not see the end of the line.

"Find out if they go to the cemetery," Grandma told Little John.

The boy jumped out of the cart and climbed the embankment. He approached a man with a pack on his back. "Is the monk up front called Peter?"

"Yes, he's the Holy One," the man nodded. "He takes us to Jerusalem. It's far away."

"Can anyone go?" The boy fell into step. "Me, too?"

The man looked down on the boy. He nodded. "You should go. Christ can make your back straight in the Holy Land."

Little John became excited. "Can He do that? Even if He's dead?"

"He has risen, and the spirit of the Lord can heal anyone. If your papa takes the cross and brings you to the Holy Sepulchre, you will be healed. That's how the Lord works."

"But I don't have a papa."

The man looked down at the boy. "Then you have a problem. Without a papa you can't go. Tell your mama to find a man. Tell her the waters of the Jordan will heal you and wash all her sins away, and God will straighten your back."

Little John was crestfallen. "Can Peter make miracles?"

"He's a holy man, and God shows him the way to Jerusalem so he can lead us there. That's all I know."

Little John had heard enough. He bounded away, running back to the cart, his eyes shining, wild, and full of excitement. "It's Peter!" he screamed as he approached. "He gives crosses for the Holy Land. The man says he can heal my back! He can!"

"Peter?" Grandma was dubious. "You are sure?"

"I don't know! He says when we go . . . ." Suddenly he remembered. "He said I . . . need a . . . papa." He turned his saddened face to his grandmother. "Do you know where my papa is, Grandma?"

"No, Little John. Hee-e-e. I think he's dead. Climb in." The boy got into the wagon. "We will go anyway. We will listen to what Peter says. Maybe, we'll just follow the other sinners."

20

Three women rode in the covered wagon: an old woman, who held the reins of the two horses; Nina; and Ruth. The old woman, Ruth's bawd, had found Nina, a girl of seventeen, in the streets of Paris. She had been beaten, and the bawd had brought her home.

After a bath and some food, she told her story. Taken from a farm by a rampaging knight during a raid, she became his bed partner for more than two years. The knight had replaced her with a younger girl, and she was passed along to the knight's squire. When he tired of her, she became the plaything for the pages, and finally, to earn her keep, she had been sent to the kitchen as a scullery maid where she worked for almost a year.

Her departure from the kitchen came abruptly when the head cook had administered a brutal beating because some of the pots were dirty, and she walked the road all night to the walls of Paris. In the morning, when the gates had been opened, she wandered aimlessly through the streets. A gang of young boys had found her and took her to a cellar. When they were finished with her, they beat her and threw her back onto the streets. Ruth's bawd had been able to see her pert beauty through the grime and blood, and Nina was ready to go with anyone and do anything.

Despite her brutal experiences, Nina's spirit was full of zest, and she enjoyed her life as a harlot. Ruth accepted her readily as a friend and was happy to have her youthful company, and the two girls would giggle together as they related the foibles of the men who came to visit with them.

Ruth had stocked the wagon for the trip to the Holy Land with sacks of provisions and chests of clothes. Built into the chests were secret compartments to hold her gold and jewelry, all her wealth, for she did not expect to return to Paris. When Tafur had first told her that he was assembling a group to take the cross, she was not willing to go, but without his protection in Paris, she feared she would become easy prey to other bullies. And when he outlined all the wealth which could come her way in Jerusalem, she took the cross with enthusiasm. Nina, of course, went wherever Ruth went.

Tafur rode to meet Peter on a magnificent black-and-white stallion. His long coat had patches of red-and-green cloth, and its sleeves were orange and green. He wore a hat with a large red plume, interspersed with yellow feathers, and sewn to his right shoulder was a large red cross on a field of yellow. He waved a long baton ceremoniously as behind him was a walking group of men playing bandores and singing softly. Behind them were stretched his people: in wagons, in carts, with horses, mules, donkeys, and large dogs pulling the vehicles. Cripples sat in boxes, fastened to an axle, with a dog or a mule providing locomotion. All were dressed in garish garments, as if on a holiday.

When he reached the cemetery, Tafur raised his baton, held it upright, and waited for a moment. The long line behind halted; the singers stopped playing. Everyone waited.

Walter walked out to meet the ribald and the knight gaped at the horse. He patted its strong flanks and walked around it.

"We are early, Sir Knight. Where shall my people camp?"

"I will show you," said Walter, but his eyes and hands did not leave the fine animal. Finally, he took the bridle and led the stallion to an open area. Tafur twirled his baton and bowed from his seat at the stupefied crowd who watched him perform. Reaching the area, he turned in his saddle, gave his baton a few rapid turns, ascribed a series of circles in the air above his head, and punctuated each circle with a stab skyward.

"We camp here!" he shouted to his rear, and the baton swept the area in a broad arc. "Pass the word!" He slid off the saddle, landing in Walter's arms, losing his hat, but without any loss of his brash aplomb. He said, "Take me to Holy Peter. I would tell him I have arrived." And he fixed his hat firmly on his head.

Peter, seated at his tent, had seen Tafur's arrival scene and wondered what forces moved such a creature to the Lord. The ribald, meeting him, doffed his hat and bowed gracefully, somehow exaggerating the courtesy of a courtier.

"I have come, O Holy One, with more than one hundred carts and wagons. My people ask for nothing but your prayers."

"You are welcome, my son," said Peter. "Here we share everything with everybody because all that we have comes from the Lord. We call upon you to share with us."

Tafur nodded. "We are ready to offer what Sir Knight called our donation to the common coffers. Two pieces of gold for every person in my camp and one piece for every animal. Is it enough?"

"I say it is very generous," said Peter. "It will help, but we might need more before our journey is ended."

"We will settle our accounts with Moslem gold. If some is needed before then, we will find it. We have some very lucky people with us, lucky in finding, lucky in winning games." He turned to Walter. "What think you of the horse I ride, Sir Knight?"

"He is more than a horse," said Walter with awe. "He is a destrier fit for a famous knight. Would that I had one such as he."

"He is yours."

Walter gaped in astonishment. "But . . . what!"

"I have no need of him. I also bring in my wagon some chain-mail, a knight's sword, and what I was told are all the other accoutrements of a knight.

I had to guess at your size." He looked up and down Walter's height. "You are a big man."

Peter interrupted. "Do you say you stole . . . you attacked a knight to secure this?"

"Attacked? No! No!" Tafur was hurt. "We merely played a game—with the dice—and we were willing to take these things for bets—as collateral, I think you call it."

"It is inconceivable that a knight would part with these, especially his destrier and his sword," said Walter.

"In Paris," said Tafur drily, "all things are conceivable. For the right price, you can obtain everything, with gold, or by other ways."

Parenti had arrived and heard the last statement. "I hope you have decided to leave those other ways in Paris. They will not do here."

Tafur's eyes narrowed as he examined the man before him. "Monk, you have a hungry look about the mouth. The Lord tells us to love our neighbor, but I don't like you, so I suggest you do not become my neighbor."

"Let us understand each other," said Peter, to defuse the charged atmosphere. "There will be no quarreling between us. Our journey is long and hazardous, and we have much to forgive in each other. Our quarrel is with the infidel."

Tafur nodded, but his eyes still glittered. "Advise this brother, Holy Peter, to look to his own soul and worry me not." He turned to Walter. "Come, Sir Knight. Let me introduce you to your iron clothing. If it doesn't fit, there is some work to do." The men left together.

"Do you know the type of women he has brought with him?" asked Parenti of Peter. "Whores! Gutter she-goats!"

"How would you know so soon?" asked Peter. "Do they wear frilly gowns to expose themselves? Do they lure the men? Or you?"

"They wear sackcloth and cotton shifts, but that doesn't hide their bold eyes and suggestive ways," snarled Parenti. "They measure the men, waving at them and moving their shoulders salaciously. They bend forward to let their breasts hang out to draw on the men's ruttish desires. They swing their hips . . ."

"Enough," Peter stopped him. "You have seen all that? Strange. I saw the wagons enter and saw none of it."

"You will see it, Brother Peter. Yes, you will. They will seduce the men into gambling and fighting, and breed all the evil that men find in themselves."

"Yet, they, too, are God's creatures," said Peter, "and necessary for men. Lechery is a temptation of Satan and is difficult to exorcise, but God will prevail. I fear not."

He was a rock and a mountain, and he had been chosen by God to lead His people to the Promised Land. He was a reborn Moses, and God would not allow any diversion—by man or woman.

*   *   *

The sun was down, and the dusk was like a dull, velvet gown draped over the crosses and headstones of the old burial ground. The torches' rags, soaked in lard and goose fat, had been lit, and their smoking flames were throwing a flickering, sooty light. The cemetery was filled with people standing between the graves because of the outpouring from the city and the countryside.

Peter made his way to the center of the grounds and mounted a grassy mound. He pointed the large wooden cross to the heavens and cried out, "Hear me, O Lord! Your children stand before Thee, and they come to listen to the tale of woe which has befallen Thy Holy City. Stir their hearts and souls! Let them receive Thy Spirit, and they will know what to do for they will know Thy Will."

He dropped his head on his chest and prayed silently, and the quietness of hushed expectation mounted and tensed. Finally, his hands fell, and he gazed over the sea of flame-lit faces.

"Listen to me, children of God, for I speak the truth! God has shown me visions in the skies. Praised be the Lord and Our Beloved Savior!"

There was a murmuring from the watchers.

"When Papa Urban called on all of you to take the cross and march to Jerusalem, where were you? Those who follow me shall be redeemed, for I am guided by the Light of the Lord, day and night; but where are you?

"When that wonderful day comes in Jerusalem, and we free the Holy Sepulchre, all will be summoned to the Valley of Jehoshaphat, for Judgment Day will be at hand, and all your evils and misdeeds will be weighed and judged. Will you be able to say to Our Lord: 'I marched with Peter to Jerusalem and fought the Infidel?'

"It is written that after the Holy Land is free, Our Lord shall reign supreme, and we shall live in peace and plenty. In Jerusalem, you can harvest five crops a year; the olive trees bow their heavy-laden branches to the ground; the vines are heavy with sweet grapes; the wheat has seventy grains, and the barley stalks break with the grain. This is the land of milk and honey, Jerusalem, and there is no hunger or thirst in the Holy City!

"You who have not taken the cross, do so now! Load your carts and wagons; take your horses and oxen; your house goods; and, if you have none of these, walk the road with other good Christians at your side. Sell what you cannot carry, and give the money to me for the common coffers, to buy provisions along the way.

"I will lead you through the valleys and over the mountains, through the dark forests, and across the wide rivers.

"Ye who are the poorest are the most beloved of Christ, and He has not forgotten you. The knights seek gold and glory; they want fiefs. We sing of Our Lord and our love for Christ. Come with me, all who are meek and humble. Ye are the fruit of the earth, and He will gather ye all to His bosom."

He talked on, relating the stories of the massacres of the Christians by the infidels; the forced copulation of the women; the children raised as heathens; the Christian slaves in the salt mines.

The people wept and moaned in anguish at every gruesome tale, and with tears dropping from their eyes, they vowed to free the children from the bestial Moslems who consorted with Satan's imps, ate their meat on Fridays, and treated Christian women like beasts in the field. They gasped when they heard how the Madonnas were constantly weeping; how the wound on Christ's side, made by the lance of a Roman soldier, dripped real blood from every crucifix in the Holy Land. The Lord was suffering again.

Mary, like the others about her, wept bitterly. The wet faces glistened in the torchlight, and eyes shone from the wetness. And with fanatical hatred. They would take revenge! For God! For Christ! For the little children! For all the souls made to suffer by the demon infidels! They would rescue the Holy Sepulchre! They would kill the heathen!

And they all, including Mary, reached for the red strips of cloth.

Grandma and Little John spent most of the next day packing the wagon, and when Peter came by, Grandma steered the vehicle into line with the others.

Mary was dejected and filled with remorse. They had been so close to Paris, to Ruth. Could she walk back? Alone? Would her leg permit it? How would she find Ruth? Each bounce of the wheels took her further away. Suddenly, her eyes lit up. The ribalds! Their "king"! He would know! At the cemetery, everyone said he knew everyone in Paris. She would ask him!

Late that afternoon they stopped to make camp, and after they had eaten Grandma checked Mary's leg. She pressed the flesh and probed the bone area. Finally satisfied, she slapped the leg and announced, "Stand up, girlie, stand up. Make it work. Hee-e."

Gingerly, Mary put her full weight down . . . testing . . . and the leg held! There was no pain! She stamped—lightly . . . with greater force. Nothing! It was healed! She wanted to fly like a bird; to jump like a cat; to prance and strut! She was free! In her delight, she threw her arms around Grandma and kissed her.

The old woman was taken aback. "Time for that later," she grumbled. "For now, remember, no jumping, no running, no dancing. Not for a week yet. Hee-e-e. If you forget, you'll be hobbling again, maybe forever."

"I'll remember. Can I go for a walk now?"

The old woman thought. "It'll be dark soon. Don't go far. Take Little John with you. If you get tired, sit."

She started out eagerly, her mind set on the ribald camp. Little John walked at her side and complained. "You walk too fast." She ignored him; her head was full of questions she would ask the "king" when she found him. And there was only an hour before dark. What would she do if he could tell her where to find Ruth? Would she start back to the city? She didn't know the answer.

Little John became agitated as they approached the camp. "That's the ribalds over there and they don't like strangers. The monk says to keep away from them. They're bad."

She wasn't listening; her eyes jumped from wagon to wagon, seeking some way to distinguish Tafur's from the others. She had seen it earlier, but now she wasn't sure what it was like. On the side stood a large one with a shiny cloth, and a man, sitting on the ground with his back to one of the rear wheels, was diligently working on some leather. He raised his head as she approached.

"Hello, boy," he said gruffly. "Where'd you get that hump?"

Mary, taken by surprise, snapped, "Where can I find Tafur?"

He lifted an eyebrow. "You want the king? He's about." To Little John, he said, "Turn around, boy. Let me see it better."

"I will not!" Little John was angry.

"Feisty, ain't you?" The man smiled.

"Where is Tafur about?" Mary was annoyed.

The man shrugged, grinning. "How should I know? Look. God gave you eyes." He rose, and Little John and Mary were startled. There was a hump on his back, too. He ignored Mary. "How would you like to see mine?" he addressed the boy and chuckled. "That's right, just like you. Two peas in a pod! You and me! I could be your papa, but I ain't." He laughed. "But you just wait! When we get to Jerusalem, we're going to straighten out just like that." He snapped his fingers and leaned forward so far he was nose to nose with the boy. "We'll go right up to the Holy Sepulchre and tell Jesus Christ our trouble." He looked to the boy for confirmation. "Well, ain't we?"

Little John, intimidated and fascinated, nodded.

"And then," continued the man with relish, "He's going to heal us! Just like that!" He snapped his fingers again. "Do you know what we're going to do after that?" The boy shook his head, questioning. "We're going to find a few of them black-eyed harem girls. And we're going to bed for a week. That's right, a week! Night and day. We're going to guzzle wine, eat pomegranates, figs, melons, and we're going make us some sons. Lots and lots of sons! With long, straight backs. Day and night." He winked. "Those beauties know just how to do it. It's their best secret." He winked again. "Just you wait 'til we get to Jerusalem."

"Can't you please tell me where Tafur is?" Mary pleaded.

He wiped his nose with his finger and stared at her. "Well, there's a way to talk when you want something, girlie, and you should know it by now. Tell me what you're after."

Mary realized she would get nothing more from him unless she did as he wanted. "My sister lives in Paris and I thought if I went there I could find her if Tafur . . . maybe he knows her."

"If you're going to Paris, you're going the wrong way." He grinned sardonically. "That was in case you didn't know. What's her name, and what does she do?"

"Ruth . . . Ruth Toon. I don't know what she does."

"Ruth!" He burst out in raucous laughter. "She your sister?" In laughter, he examined Mary boldly. "Can't see the resemblance."

"You know her?" She was overjoyed. "Where does she live?"

He snorted. "Can't say I *know* her—not that way. But she ain't in Paris no more. She's here. With us. With a cross on her shoulder and her back in her bed, like the good girlie she is."

"Here? Where?"

"Straight down the way. Can't miss her. Three—four wagons. You'll see her bawd. Old hag." He picked up his leather and looked at Little John. "You and me got some talking, boy."

She grabbed the boy's hand. "Come, Little John. Thanks," she threw at the hunchback and hurried off.

The woman squatting on the mat, mixing the cooking pot on the tripod, was ancient. Her robe, piled around her haunches as she crouched, was soiled, and her uncombed hair, sharp nose, and pointed chin gave her the appearance of a witch brewing her magic.

Mary approached timidly. "Mother, I am looking for my sister, Ruth Toon. She is in one of these wagons. Would you know which?"

The woman scanned her and Little John suspiciously. "Who are you?"

Mary stammered, "Her sister. I just told you."

"Sister. Hrrumph-ph. Who is he? Her brother?"

"A friend. Do you know her?"

"What's your name?"

"Mary . . . Toon," she added.

The old woman tasted her brew. "Needs salt," she mumbled and produced a small packet from under her cloak. She jerked her head toward the wagon's rear. "She's in there. Resting. She worked hard yesterday."

Mary suddenly felt her heart in the grip of a giant hand. Her mouth was gritty, full of sand, and dry. *Ruth was here!* Maybe she wouldn't welcome her, even turn her away. She approached the wagon's rear apprehensively. A dark-haired girl sat there, sewing and singing softly to herself, and she smiled, a questioning smile which lit up her dark eyes and mouth.

"Hello?" The voice was friendly and pleasant. She cocked her head to one side. "My name's Nina. Who are you?"

"Mary Toon. Can I see Ruth? I'm her sister."

"Oh." The eyes became bewildered. "I . . . I don't know. She's been sleeping." She rose. "I'll see." She ran up the steps, which led to the inside, and disappeared.

Mary clenched Little John's hand so tightly the boy cried out. "Ow! That hurts!" He pulled his hand away.

"I'm sorry, Little John, I didn't mean to."

Ruth, her blonde hair messed, her eyes half-closed, stood in the doorway. "Mary?" she said. "Little Mary?" She reached out.

Mary ran up the steps and took her hand. They stood transfixed, holding hands, mouths open, hardly breathing, neither having a word to say. Ruth looked much older than Mary remembered. She saw a thin, pouchy face, relaxed from sleeping but struggling to come alive with surprise. The white skin was blotched, with small red spots, and the sleeping gown was dirty and wrinkled. But, in Mary's eyes, Ruth looked beautiful.

"Come in! Come in! Imagine! Mary! Nina! Look, this is my little sister! How ever did you find me?" She drew Mary into the interior of the wagon.

There were bundles, chests, baskets, and bedding everywhere, in disarray. Ruth fell upon a pallet with a mattress, and she pulled Mary down beside her.

"Tell me! Tell me everything! What are you doing here? Are the boys here, too? How is Papa? Is he still alive? Tell me . . . ."

"Wait, wait." She tried to stop the torrent of questions. "I don't know. I ran away from the farm, just like you."

"You ran away? Whatever for?"

"The same as you. Papa wanted to put me in a nunnery, so I ran. I was coming to Paris—to find you—but things . . . happened."

"You ran away? Alone? How?" Her voice trailed off.

"With Andre." She saw Ruth's face light up. "But he left me with some jongleurs and went back home. It's a long story. So many things happened. But now I've found you." Her face lit up. "We can go to Jerusalem together. Who would have thought it?"

"Mary, wait. You are here, alone?"

"Yes, in a way. But now I'm with you. I can leave Grandma."

"Grandma?"

Mary realized she would have to explain. "The jongleurs Andre left me with . . ." she began. "They were killed by thieves. I was the only one they couldn't catch, but I broke my leg when I ran away. Grandma and Little John—the boy outside—found me and she fixed my leg. Last night we heard Brother Peter and we joined. The ribalds came from Paris, and I thought Tafur would know about you so I came over."

"You saw Tafur?"

"No. I talked with an awful man, a hunchback. He told me where you were, so I came here."

"Guizio told you? I'm surprised. Did you give him any money?"

"No. He didn't ask for any, and I couldn't give him any even if he asked. I don't have any money."

Ruth's face was clouded. "You expect to stay here . . . with me?"

"Of course." Mary suddenly realized something was wrong. She reached out. "You do . . . want me to, don't you?"

"Oh, my little Mary." Ruth bit her lip.

Mary's world collapsed. A sickening pit opened in her stomach, a hollow emptiness which engulfed her. She read the refusal in her sister's face, and her eyes squeezed together as she fought her tears.

"There's no room. Nina and I work, sometimes in the day, sometimes in the night. Sometimes day and night . . . all hours. You could always visit . . . when we're not busy."

She was numb. Ruth meant safety, security; she was the mother Mary never had known. But Ruth was turning her away. Maybe Papa was right; she should have gone to the nunnery.

"Is Papa well? The boys? Jeanne?"

Mary nodded. "Yes. Everything's all the same."

Ruth took her hand. "It isn't easy to be away from home and by yourself, Mary. I know. Don't feel bad. We'll work out something. It takes a long time to get to Jerusalem."

"Why can't I stay with you?" she pleaded. "I can work, too."

"You don't know what you are saying. No, I couldn't. There's no room. It's better you stay where you are."

"Then you really don't want me." Mary stood up. "I'll go."

Ruth pulled her down. "Don't be silly. Of course . . ." She lapsed into an uneasy silence. "When Andre left you with those jongleurs, and they were coming to Paris, how did you expect to live in the city? What would you do?"

"I—I didn't think about that. When I found you . . . oh, I don't know. It sounds silly. I better go. Grandma's waiting and it is getting dark."

"Stop acting like a child!" Ruth snapped. "Andre should have known better. How could he . . ."

Mary broke into tears. "Oh, Ruth, please let me stay. I don't need much room, just a little corner. I'll do anything you say."

"You don't understand," said Ruth wearily. "How old are you now? Thirteen? Fourteen?"

"Fourteen."

Ruth stared at her, reliving her fourteenth year, so different from Mary's. Suddenly her eyes hardened. "Listen, Mary, Nina and I make our money by staying with men, sometimes during the day, but mostly in the night. The bawd who took me to Paris trained me for that. She offered Papa money for me, but he said that he had promised me to the priest, so I ran away with her. Didn't Papa tell you?"

"No," whispered Mary, "but Jeanne did."

"Did she tell you what I do?" Mary didn't answer, but her face said what she was thinking. "Have you been with a man yet?" Mary dropped her head. "Much?" Mary nodded, not looking up. "I see. More than one?" The nodding continued. "Then you know what we do. Maybe something can be worked out. You will need training, but Ellia, my bawd, can do that." She was becoming enthusiastic. "You could join Nina and me."

Something inside retreated. "I—I'm not—sure . . ."

Ruth didn't hear her. "We could rearrange schedules . . . and the beds . . . no! Not enough room! We need a bigger wagon, big enough for the three of us!" She saw something large and luxurious. "Guizio can get it for us in Cologne." She giggled in relief; the problem had been solved.

"I—can't, Ruth, I . . . can't."

Ruth stared at her in perplexity until realization came. "Of course you can. Every woman can; all of us; almost all the time. It's only in your head; you'll see; Ellia will show you. It's easy."

"But with *anyone*? Any man who wants to? Even if you don't know him?"

"You get acquainted quickly in bed," Ruth said drily. "When you close your eyes, they're all alike. You have no feelings for them; they're just there. Ellia will show you."

"But I always have feelings . . ."

"It's better when you don't. Believe me, Mary. I know. Do you know how many rich burghers follow Peter? Their fat wives waddle around like geese. Do you have any idea how much they are willing to pay for a girl like me or Nina? Or like you? Just listen to me, Mary. We are going to be on the road to Jerusalem for a long time, maybe years, and we can make our fortune between here and the Holy City. All our sins will be forgiven at the Holy Sepulchre. Peter says so. We can be rich, with a fine house, and servants. Like the ladies and the lords."

"But Peter took all of Grandma's money. Didn't he take yours?"

Ruth laughed. "Peter takes whatever people give him, but only fools—and believers—give him all they have. Those who know better pay as little as possible and hide the rest."

Nina came in. "Are you girls through? Little John's impatient, and it's becoming dark."

Mary jumped up. "I have to go. I'll see you tomorrow."

Little John whined as they walked back. "You stayed too long; look how dark it is. Grandma will worry."

"Don't be so upset," she appeased him. "Just think of all the new people you met. Isn't it exciting?"

"No." He was petulant, but she didn't care. Her spirits were high; she had found Ruth; somehow, it would all work out.

21

There was newborn freshening which hung in the warming air, and the earth was soft with the April rains. The multitude which followed Peter stretched for miles along the muddy road, and the trampling feet had churned the mud and the animals' droppings into a heavy brown plaster which glued itself to everything it touched.

Urban had postponed the departure to mid-August because the knights had found it impossible to be ready by the spring, but Peter had promised that he would leave for Jerusalem in mid-April, and he intended to keep his word.

"*Jerusalem, We Are Coming!*" was sung everywhere.

"Moslems are small, dark people with black hair and beards over their skinny faces, and their shiny, black eyes pierce right through you like knives. Their hands and feet are like sticks, but every one of them has the strength of five men, and they work together like the fingers of your hand. Each finger is the spirit of an ancestor, coming straight out of Hell, with fire and blood."

Walter nodded his head slowly, and his face was stern as he surveyed the terrorized children about him.

"They have special ways to cut the throat of a he-goat, and they catch all the blood that drains out. Satan then gives the blood special powers so when they dip their arrows into it, each arrow comes alive when it leaves the bow. Like a stinging snake, it seeks its prey, not resting until it finds its mark. If it misses, it twists and turns until it can strike and kill."

The children quivered in fear and crouched behind one another.

"What'll we do?" quavered a small voice.

"We hide, silly," said another, more brave. "I know a place where those arrows can never find me."

"In a church," said a third, knowingly. "Christ will protect me."

"I'll hide and pray, too," said a small girl, positively.

Leo, arriving, smiled. Walter delighted in telling these tales to the children, and although, he was sure, the infidels had all kinds of magic, they had no snake-arrows. "It is time for Tafur's squad," he said to the knight.

Walter stood up. "All right, children. That's all for today; I have work to do." He motioned them away.

Tafur had prevailed upon the knight to train the Parisians into a special squadron of soldiers whose main purpose, he said, would be to dispatch the wounded enemy after a battle. What he did not say was they would collect all jewels and valuables as they performed their duties.

Walter agreed, and he taught them hand-to-hand combat, pointing out the vital organs, and how to disarm and dispatch a wounded man quickly. They were familiar with street fighting—cut and run—and they were apt pupils under Walter's tutelage.

Tafur's tongue clicked in appreciation as he watched them work. He never tired of telling them how cutting a Moslem throat or cracking an infidel head was beneficial for them—and God. "A slit throat will gurgle, and mashed brains can't think. Make sure they are dead before you pluck them clean. You want no surprises."

One day Walter saw Ruth, and Tafur, quick to notice his reaction, suggested an introduction, saying she was available.

"She is one of the best, pleasant and agreeable. I recommend her highly, but she is expensive."

Walter was eager, but the number of coins in his pocket was meager. Tafur was willing to help by paying a small amount for the training of the squad, and Ruth, with the promise of future protection, if needed, was willing to shave her price. The friendship developed and Walter spent many afternoons with her, sending Leo back to the camp after the training period was over.

For days, Leo had been out of sorts, displaying fits of moody depression. He worked doggedly at his sword practice and with his knives, producing much sweat but a spiritless dejection. His knives were deadly. When his hand flashed, the knife appeared from nowhere and always found its target, even if it was moving. The constant exercise broadened his chest, made his arms muscular, and made him upright. Walter called him a soldier-knight, for he could fight with the broadsword or transform himself into a soldier, ignoring the knight's rules of combat. But Walter became disturbed with what he called Leo's "killer instinct."

"You always fight to kill," he remonstrated as he stopped Leo one day in his practice. "Remember, knights fight to overcome; we kill by accident or in self-defense. A live prisoner brings ransom; a corpse is only good for the carrion crow."

"That may be when we fight other knights, but do you expect to receive ransom from an infidel?"

"Why not? The Turk is rich and they know the gold is of no use to them when they are dead. A man will buy his life if he is given the chance. Wouldn't you?"

"But if you let the infidel live, he will fight you again."

"They are civilized men, with much medicine and art, and many are men of their word."

"But they are not Christians," Leo objected. "We must kill them."

"Look, Leo," said Walter patiently. "If we tried to kill everyone who wasn't a Christian in this world, we would never let up in the killing. And I don't think Our Lord Christ would favor that. We kill only when we must, and there will be much killing, but if an Arab will pay us gold for his life, so be it. We will take it and turn him loose with the promise that he will not fight us again. If he breaks his promise, and we capture him again, we will take more gold. Eventually, he will run out of gold.''

"What if he captures us? And I have no gold to pay."

"That would present a problem. But wouldn't it be nice to be able to give him back his gold so you could live?"

Leo shook his head. "But then I would have to promise not to fight for God. I wouldn't do that!"

Walter waved his hand. "That promise is no promise at all. It is a stratagem, a trick to defeat the enemy in time of war, and it is not binding."

"But if I don't keep my promise, and he doesn't keep his, what good is all this promising? Why should we demand it?"

"Because it is expected. The soldier on both sides has no money, so he is dispatched without a question. But a knight, or an emir, has gold—or is expected to have it. He pays you; you pay him; and you both live."

Leo was confounded. "But we do not go to play games, like at tournaments," he blurted. "We go to free the Holy Sepulchre, and the infidel will fight to kill as many of us as he possibly can. We will have to kill him!" He plunged his knife savagely into a nearby basket. His eyes gleamed in a deadly passion. "I want no prisoners and no gold." His teeth were clenched. "I go to kill."

Walter shook his head sadly. He recognized the blood-lust. "You heat your blood early, Leo. There will be much killing, but a true knight does not glory in wanton slaughter."

"I have heard stories about battles from my father, what it was like to be with men who are dying around you. There was no talk of glory—or gold—or ransom. Only kill; kill; kill! Or you died! What is it to kill a man? His skin is softer than a pig's hide. My knives are faster than any sword. I can throw them between the links of chain-mail, like an arrow. He will be dead before he can take his sword out of his scabbard. Or I can hit him in the throat. If he wears plate, my sword can break through that!" His eyes were on fire. "I do not want their gold; I want their lives!" He was panting.

Walter sighed. "Perhaps I have trained you too well; but do not exalt—you are not invincible. God did not make man to revel in the killing of his brothers. He branded Cain because Cain killed. Lord Jesus does not expect you to emulate Cain. You need relaxation, Leo, you work at death too hard."

"I relax when I can. I work the leather . . . I sharpen my knives . . . I groom the horses . . ." He trailed off.

"I know," said Walter, "but that is not what I mean." He dismissed the cataloging of chores. "Have you seen . . . has monk Parenti been about?"

Leo's face broke into an evil grin. "Three weeks ago he came to visit. I put a knife to his throat and he left quickly.'' He snickered. ''Maybe he found someone else.''

''What about you?''

''Me?'' Leo was perplexed. ''What about me?''

''Have you found someone else? There are many young girls around the camps. You feel no need?''

Leo was disturbed and did not answer.

''Shall we talk?'' Walter motioned Leo to a seat.

Leo nodded but sat in silence. Walter waited until he said, finally, ''Tell me what you feel.''

''It's a strange feeling,'' Leo began slowly. ''It's like I'm a wet log on a fire, and I suddenly explode inside. I'm throwing sparks everywhere—I feel like thorns pricking me. I feel a twisting in my belly, like cramps in my legs. My muscles become hard. And there is a bright fire behind my eyes, but I can't see it—but it's hot.'' He was almost whispering. ''It keeps me awake at night. Sometimes I dream . . .'' He shook himself. ''Bad dreams. Sometimes I think I'm going to explode, like that fire, and burn everything.'' He looked up at the older man. ''What am I to do? Tell me.''

Walter nodded. ''Have you been with a girl yet?''

Leo shook his head. ''No, I don't . . . no . . .'' He was silent.

''There is a way.'' Walter sat pensively. ''You have no money. Where would you get money? I will lend you some. Go. Wash and get dressed in your cleanest clothes, your finest tunic. We are going to Ruth's wagon. You have seen the girl called Nina?'' Leo nodded. ''She is just the one for you.''

Leo preened himself carefully and paced outside of Walter's tent, impatiently waiting for the knight to finish his toilette. His imagination was whetted by the tales he had heard of the easy morals of the ribald women, and he knew Nina.

Walter was in a jovial mood as they walked toward Ruth's wagon. He had enough deiners for Ruth, and he had found a few coppers extra for Nina. He didn't how much he would need, but he could always pay her later. He was brimming with advice.

''Don't be nervous, it is bad if you worry too much. Always be polite; show respect for her feelings, too. Nina is a wonderful girl, and she will help you.''

Arriving at the wagon, they found Nina talking to a stranger, another girl. It was Mary, and Nina introduced her. Walter took Nina aside and explained about Leo. He pressed a small bag of coins into her hand. ''I hope it will be enough, but if it isn't, I'll make it up to you next time.''

She dismissed his anxiety with a gay laugh. ''It will be enough this time. He is still virginal, you say? That should be fun.''

Leo, alone with Mary, felt embarrassed. Nina, he decided, was like the girls at his father's inn, laughing prettily because they wanted to please the man, but this girl seemed more natural, more herself. And she was pretty, too.

Mary was aware of his frank appraisal and she felt a twinge. He thinks I'm also a whore, she told herself. She liked his dark, curly hair, and his clean, chiseled features . . . so much like Tom's. Left alone with him, she started a conversation. "I hope it isn't going to rain."

His answer was quick. "I don't think so. Did you come from Paris with the rest of the ribalds? I've never been in a city that big. I come from Genoa."

"Genoa!" She was astounded. "I come from there, too."

"You? Genoa? But I thought . . . with Ruth? Did you ever hear of the Good Sailor's Inn? My father owns it."

"Of course." She laughed. "My father sold your father wine. I'm Mary Toon."

"Toon!" he became excited. "I know Master Toon. I know your brothers, too! They came . . ." He stopped. He should not talk of the peccadillos of the male Toons, not to a female of the family.

Mary understood what was on his mind. "Oh, everyone knew why they went there." She laughed. "It was no secret."

"Isn't it strange we never met?" What is really strange, he thought, was that she and her sister, who came from Genoa, were in the ribald camp from Paris. And Ruth was a whore. Was Mary, also?

"Many things just happen," she said. "Like I found my sister here, following Peter, although I joined Peter outside of Paris."

He felt uplifted. She wasn't with her sister. "I was with Peter from the beginning, at Clermont, where I listened to Papa Urban."

"I heard him, too." She didn't want to remember Tom again. It hurt too much. She changed the subject. "Were you always a squire?"

"No. Sir Walter is training me. Someday I will be a knight, maybe after the first battle. He has promised to make me a Knight of the Sword if he can."

"What is that?"

"When I do a brave deed during the battle—like killing many infidels—he can knight me right on the spot, or after the battle, in front of everyone."

Mary beamed at him. "Then I'll have to curtsy, like this." She spread her skirt with one hand, holding it out, and dipped.

Nina, approaching with Walter, asked, "Whatever are you doing?"

"Leo is to be a knight, so I'm practicing."

"Folderol!" snapped Nina. "Did you come on the crusade to be a knight and kill people?"

"Of course not!" He was indignant. "I go to free the Holy Sepulchre, just like anyone else. But we're going to have to kill the heathens to do it. You'll see."

Walter heard him and shook his head as he entered the wagon. Nina studied Leo. Suddenly, her mood changed and she smiled. "Enough of that," she said blithely. "We're all so far from home, we have to help each other all the time.'' She faced Leo directly. ''I think we ought to start right now, don't you?''

He was suddenly seized with panic. Somehow, with the ease of conversation he had experienced with Mary, he had lost sight of the original purpose of his visit. Nina's question knotted his tongue, and he could feel the blood rising to his face. He hesitated, resisting the pull of her hand.

''Don't be bashful,'' she said soothingly. ''It'll be all right.''

His mouth and lips were dry, and he stared from Nina, to Mary, to the wagon.

''Oh, come on.'' She was pulling him persistently. ''Let's have some fun.''

He allowed her to guide him up the few steps. In the doorway, he turned and looked back and caught a glimpse of Mary. She had turned away, and he had a fleeting wish that it was she who held his hand and was drawing him inside.

A candle burned in the semidark interior, throwing a flickering light, long shadows, and the burned odor of rendering fat. The wagon had been sectioned into a small front room by a rug hanging across its width as a wall, and a larger back room. A thick, rag-stuffed mattress lay on the floor to one side, with baskets piled together, perched precariously on top of each other. Leo could hear muffled sounds coming through the rug, thick as it was, and he knew it was Walter and Ruth; and the thought embarrassed him.

Nina kicked off her sabots, and the wooden shoes clattered as they bounced. She went to her knees on the mattress, smoothing its cover, and stretched herself across it, leaning her head on the palm of her hand. She patted the area beside her and motioned him to lie down. ''Here. Sit beside me,'' she said softly.

The candle's light glittered off the sheen of her eyes, and there was a saucy, pert smile on her lips.

He seated himself awkwardly, a slight distance from her, propping himself with a stiff arm as he sank into the soft rags. Despite his embarrassment, he watched her face intently, fascinated by her impish grin. The slight movement of her body was openly inviting when the fold fell away from her thighs.

Leo's obvious innocence amused her, and she felt a pleasurable delight in her ability to arouse him. She had a fleeting thought: he should be the aggressive lover, and she the innocent maid. She relished his shyness as she reached to caress him, and her first love embrace came back to her—and the shock and pain. This would be different for him.

''Do you have a sister?'' she asked.

''No . . .'' he fumbled, ''no sisters or brothers.''

''Then you are all alone, just like me. We are two orphans; no brothers, no sisters, all by ourselves.''

''Isn't Ruth? . . . Mary? . . . your sisters?''

''Not exactly,'' Nina laughed. Suddenly, she leaned forward and knocked his propping arm away, and he collapsed on the bed in surprise. She pinned him down. ''You forfeit ransom to get up, knight-squire,'' she laughed. ''Pay or you may never rise again.''

Leo lay in shock, confused by her sudden attack, uncertain what she meant. "What . . . do you want," he blurted.

"Well . . ." She pursed her lips in contemplation. "You could start with the usual ransom a defeated knight gives his lady—a kiss." She leaned forward and kissed him. "Not enough ransom. You didn't kiss me." She bent over him again, and her lips lingered on his. His arm crept around her, and one hand slid up her side and cupped her breast, pinching the nipple. She reared back, arching herself off his chest. "Where did you learn that?" she demanded.

"What?" He was confused.

"That business with your tongue . . . and your hand?" Her face came down close to his, their noses almost touching. "How many girls have you kissed and pinched?"

"Well, there were girls at the inn. They liked to kiss me that way. If you don't like it, I'll . . ."

"And the hand? The girls at the inn? What inn?"

"My father's . . . in Genoa. They always kissed me . . . until Mama found out."

She was quiet momentarily. "What else did they do with you?"

"Nothing. Just tickle me." She fought him off.

Recovering, she said, "Let's try again." She lay heavily against him, pressing him firmly against the mattress, and her kiss was soft. Her hands crawled under his tunic, and she moved against him, letting her hands move inside his trousers. He was fully aroused, and she could feel him, tense and trembling. "Take off your trousers," she murmured into his ear.

He worked eagerly, and she helped him strip his pants from his legs. They were laughing and tugging together until they fought the legs loose. Quickly, she kneeled, bunched her skirts upward against her breasts, and fell upon him. With a quick roll she slid beneath him, and he could feel her hands guiding him as he entered a soft, warm, moist place . . . and he was falling deeper, deeper. He held her tightly, his eyes clenched, and she was pulling and pushing at him, rolling from side to side. A sudden spasm gripped his groin, and he pressed himself down . . . there was an explosion behind his eyes . . . he shuddered convulsively . . . again . . . he was gasping . . . his face was twisted, and his teeth and jaw ached. Suddenly, he collapsed and he fought for breath. The tension was gone, oozing out of him, and his chest was rising and falling rapidly. He took a deep breath.

"My," she whispered in his ear. "You are fast."

He lay, all limp, upon her, breathing deeply until she shrugged him off. In a moment she was straightening her skirts. He felt naked and exposed and donned his trousers quickly. She rose from the bed.

"We'll have to do that again, very soon." She smiled. "Did you like it?"

There was an explosive burst of laughter from the rug-curtain, and Walter was in the room. Ruth just pushed the fold aside.

Leo was appalled. Had they been watching? he asked himself. There was a strange mixture of shame and bravado within him, but he did not know how to act. Walter nodded approvingly at Nina. "All done, I see," a broad grin on his face. To Leo, he said, "Let's go."

Leo suddenly remembered. "Wait. I didn't pay."

"It's all arranged," said Walter. "Come."

"No! I'll pay." He dug into his trousers and came up with a single copper. "This is all I have. Is it enough?"

Nina smiled as she took it. "This time it will be enough, but next time, it will be more. You will need . . ." she glanced at Walter, ". . . five."

He shook his head in agreement. As he and Walter left the wagon he took a deep breath, expanding his chest to its fullest. He felt exhilarated and alive. His eyes were searching for Mary, but she was not about and he was disappointed.

"When can we come again?" he asked eagerly.

"When we have enough money."

"Next time I would like that other girl, Mary."

"We'll work on it," promised the knight.

22

The Council of Cologne proclaimed a day of joyous celebration when the news came that Peter was one day's march from the city. Crossbearers had been gathering on the fields before the city's walls, and their camps had spread to the adjoining meadows. The burning campfires had formed a heavy pall of smoke which hung like a gray cloak, and the crosswinds had blown much of it into the homes of the inhabitants.

The city fathers had welcomed the early arrivals with generosity, giving food and gifts as acts of charity, but this had become a trickle as thousands arrived to wait for Peter. The council began to worry; the treasury was drained; the April rains had made the fields a morass of mud and filth. Children sniffled and elders coughed, and the council began to worry about sickness and plague.

The idle campers grew discordant and their tempers flared quickly. Many settled their disputes with knives. The priests labored to keep the peace and summoned the people to Masses, citing Urban's words often: Ye who fight other Christians do not serve Christ! Beware Satan! He sows discord! His imps ride the sunbeams like motes and scatter themselves like dust everywhere. The air is thick with them, and they infect and incite true believers. Beware! Do not fight with your neighbors!

Most prayed avidly and heeded the priests, fearing the Devil's Caldron, but others recalled Urban's other words: All sins will be pardoned if you take the cross. If pardon was automatic, why worry about any sin committed now? Christ will forgive.

Then, there were those who marched with Gottschalk, Volmar, and Emicho, who ravaged the countryside with pillage and rape, all in the name of Christ. In the cities like Worms and Speyer, they searched for food, gold, and women with torches and knives, first venting their rage against the Jews. Now, they were in Cologne.

"Kill the Jews!" they cried. "And revenge Christ! Take their gold and seed their women! Kill the Jews!"

The Jews huddled in their ghettos in dread, and the mobs descended upon them like locusts, stripping them clean. The bearded men were forced to their knees, and the blood spurted from their throats as the Crossbearers chanted, "Apostasy or death!" And the Jews died regardless of choice.

Church doctrine forbade forced baptism, but the churchmen fled for their lives, and Jews died by the thousands. The ghettos burned, and the mobs sought out the homes of the wealthy burghers, for the Jews did not have enough gold to satisfy the greed. The Christian burghers clamored to the council for protection, and the councilmen wrung their hands in anguish and fear.

It was a bright April morning, warm and full of sunshine, when the forward riders of Peter's escort were seen by the watchers on the city's battlements. Like a susurrus wind, word blew from mouth to mouth, gusted from camp to camp, and whistled down the narrow, turning streets of the city into the council's chamber. *Peter was here!* The council sighed in relief; the waiting was over. He must be hurried along and take his cohorts with him; the city could become normal again—and quiet.

They stood before Peter, tense and nervous. "We offer five thousand pounds of wheat and barley to feed the poor and needy. More will be available on the day you leave to help provide for the journey. Tell us how you wish to distribute it, and we will begin the delivery."

"We will take care of the distribution," said Parenti. "We can also use shoes."

"Shoes? Shoes?" The spokesman turned to his committee. "Have the cobblers been working?" A man nodded. "We will have shoes, brother. Is there anything else?"

"Good leather would be appreciated by some," emphasized the monk. "Have the boots sent to me. Some of us never ride."

"The finest leather, brother. I will see to it myself. Tell me when you wish to visit our cobblers, and I will make the arrangements. We have the finest workmanship."

"You are kind," the monk nodded. "I will call on you."

"For all this, we bless you in the name of Our Lord," said Peter. "We prepare our journey with a peaceful mind."

The committee took their leave with high hopes. It was to be costly, but they would rejoice when it was over.

Another group of men were waiting to see Peter: eight knights in chain-mail, their swords at their sides, their gold spurs on their shining boots. One stepped forward and bowed his head.

"Man of God, I speak for myself and these others behind me. We would go with you to Jerusalem. We have heard that Sir Walter—he who has been called 'the Penniless'—is with you and we would join with him. We have our swords, our horses, and our love for Jesus to offer."

"Sir Walter will thrive with your decision. I welcome you."

Walter was overjoyed. Talking with them, he told of the perils they faced, the mountains and rivers they would cross, the people—some Christian, some heathen—they would encounter before Constantinople would be reached.

"We have no fear," said the spokesman. "Our sword arms are strong and who does not respect that?"

"When we accepted knighthood, we swore to defend Christ," said another. "We are ready. And there are others who follow us."

Walter rejoiced and told them, "We will stay in Cologne only to mid-April. You will need tents for the march. I will see to that. If you have squires ready for knighthood, I suggest you give them the accolade as soon as possible. We will be a fine troop."

The knights agreed and Walter was jubilant. God had truly provided! He had a knightly escort. And he and Leo had trained others.

Each time Mary visited with Ruth, she took Little John with her, and the boy and Guizio had become fast friends. Tafur relied on Guizio to act as his bodyguard, aide, and surrogate, and the easiest way to reach the "king's" ear with success was to discuss a problem with the hunchback. Guizio always collected a fee for his "work"—shared, of course, with Tafur—and the two ribalds worked well together. Guizio spent much of his spare time teaching Little John the convoluted operations in which the "king" and he were engaged and was surprised at the boy's naivete.

"Haven't you learned anything?" he would say, dumbfounded. "What you need, you take for yourself, and you don't worry what people think. Just keep them off your back." He winked and cracked his knuckles knowingly.

The hunchback had never been close to another human being, not even to Tafur, but he opened his heart to Little John. In him, he saw himself, his lonely, early youth as a withdrawn outcast who repelled most people because of his deformity. The Paris gutter had been his school, and he could not understand the boy's lack of aggressiveness. Guizio had been running the streets since he was seven; his wits had been sharpened by street fighting; and he held the firm belief that whatever helped Guizio, helped the world. He honored only one code: his word.

Cynical in his youth, he permitted people to rub his hump for one copper; for two, he would remove his shirt. He promoted the idea that this would provide luck for any endeavor. As he became older, however, any suggestion to caress his back would provoke a growl. His temper was close to the surface, and his strong, large hands were feared by any who had the misfortune to be in their way. He was agile and quick, a survivor of many knife fights, and he had a delight to cut an antagonist's flesh. To many, he was called a butcher and a thief—but never to his face. This reputation brought him to Tafur's notice.

The "king" needed a bodyguard: a strong arm and a sharp knife, a man with street knowledge who could be trusted. Guizio agreed if Tafur would agree to two conditions: first, he would obey only those orders he agreed to carry out; second, he would be paid a gold piece each week. The price was exorbitant, but Tafur readily agreed—he had no difficulty acquiring gold. Both men found the arrangement satisfactory, but never became fast friends; they did not totally trust one another.

Despite his hardened shell, there lurked within the hunchback a longing for the touch of another human, and as he became older, the longing grew.

Little John was a copy of himself, someone whom he could understand and who could understand him, and someone he could mold in his own image. The boy reveled in his newfound world of excitement and fantasy, a paradise greater than his extravagant imagination could invent. This morning, however, when Mary left for Ruth's wagon, he stayed with Grandma.

She continuously complained—the smoke, the air, her wheezing, her coughing—and her spittle contained the dreaded flecks of blood. Under her direction, Mary had brewed an herbal tea, and the boy brought her some. Weak and bleary-eyed, she called him to her side. "Boy," she wheezed, "there is little more time. He-e-e. You are my daughter's son . . . I don't know your papa . . . hee-e. Your mama was such a little girl . . . and I never caught him . . . hee-e." She began to cough and had to stop talking. She lay back on her pillow to rest.

"There is the power of Christ and Mother Mary to help you . . . at the Holy Sepulchre . . . go. Hee-e-e-e . . . Mother Mary . . . will help . . . pray to Mother Mary . . ."

Her coughing was severe and the phlegm was pink. Little John held her hand when she stopped, the tears streaming down his cheeks.

"Pray . . . to Mother . . . Mary . . ." Suddenly, she collapsed.

"*Grandma! Grandma!*" he shrieked.

The old woman opened her lead-heavy eyes. "It's all right, Little John . . . I'm just tired . . . tired . . ." Her eyes closed again. Suddenly she sat straight up in the bed, and her coughing would not stop. "*Mary . . .*" she gasped. "*Get . . . Mary!*"

In stark terror, the boy ran out of the wagon toward the ribald camp.

Mary, flushed and inflamed with the excitement of her imagination, listened avidly to the stories Ruth and Nina told her of their "work." But she could not force herself to join them. She noticed that Nina was all smiles and laughter, becoming pert and playful when men were present, but would lapse into a dark, morose mood when the men left. She appeared to be two people.

She talked to Ruth, and Ruth said, "You grow up rapidly when you are with many men. You will see. Sometimes you *are* like two people, separate— one on the outside and one inside. When you are a child, you are the same outside and inside. That is you; you are still a child."

This sounded ominous to Mary. Meanwhile, Ruth's bawd gave her lessons in deportment. "Always look clean and neat. Smile, and when you laugh, laugh softly. When the men talk to you, be interested in what they say, even if it is boring. Sometimes ask silly questions so they can instruct you, even if you already know the answer. They will talk all the time about themselves, about their wives, their homes and troubles. Listen; but *never! never!* agree or disagree with them. Remain silent. They like to boast, so never disagree with their feelings. Do you understand?"

Meanwhile, Ruth decided to find a wagon large enough to include Mary. She sent Guizio into the city to find a wagon maker who could build what she wanted quickly, and after a short search, he found one, but he warned Ruth that it would be expensive. "One week," he said, "and it will need four horses."

She told him to get it, knowing it would take all her gold. As they spoke, Little John came running and screaming for Mary.

Mary, inside, thought she heard her name. She listened intently, no longer hearing what the bawd was saying. Little John! In panic, a black premonition seized her—Grandma! Grandma was dead! She rushed out.

Little John panted desperately as he ran. He could not talk when he reached her, but sank against the wagon's wheel, his chest heaving as he struggled to release the words. Around him stood Ruth, Nina, and Guizio.

Mary screamed one word at him, "*Grandma?*" He nodded, tried to rise, but sank back, his lungs bursting as he swallowed large drafts of air. Leaving him, she set off at a run.

Grandma was dead. The old woman had not died easily. Mary found her on the floor, her hand clutched to her throat as though she had tried to choke off her coughing. Her mouth was open; her eyes bulged; about her face and clothing were the regurgitated contents of her stomach. She had choked in her own cud.

She viewed the body in horror and fought the shudder of disgust that rose in her. With forced stoicism, she pulled the old woman back upon the mattress and closed the staring eyes. Carefully, she washed the wrinkled, gaunt face and combed the stiff, gray hair. After cleaning the floor, she sat down, exhausted.

Little John had not come back, but Ruth and Guizio were soon there, and Guizio took charge while Ruth walked Mary back to her wagon, trying to comfort the weeping girl.

The funeral arrangements came swiftly. Two ribald women cleaned and dressed the body; four men dug a grave next to the wagon; an old priest, who mumbled to himself while he clutched his Psalter, stood on one side and waved back and forth as the body was lowered into the ground. Little John burst into tears and clutched at Guizio, while Mary, also weeping, hung on Nina and Ruth. A few spectators gathered to watch, but the scene was becoming common, and they did not stay to mourn after the grave was closed.

The next day, Guizio had Mary and Little John remove what they wanted from the wagon and disposed of it. A neighbor bought the horse. Without any discussion, Little John went with Guizio, and Mary moved her few belongings into Ruth's new wagon.

Walter and Leo came to visit, and Ruth put them off. "There is too much to do. And Nina and I are busy tonight."

"You need some relaxation," he cajoled her. "We won't stay long." Walter could be very persuasive.

But Ruth was brusque. "Come back in a few days."

"A few days may be too late," he said enigmatically.

His tone made her stare at him. "What is happening in a few days?"

He brushed the question aside; he was all smiles. "Say. What about your sister, Mary? Nina and Mary would be fine."

"Not Mary." She was firm. "What's happening in a few days?"

"What's wrong with Mary? Leo likes her."

"Not Mary. Not yet," she added. "If you don't answer me, nothing at all will happen here."

Walter hesitated. Few knew of the plans he and the knights had been discussing, but everyone would soon know. He decided to tell her; maybe it would help.

"We could be leaving in a few days. It will be settled tonight."

"Oh?" She stared at him. "Nina's in the old wagon. Tell her I sent you."

When he was gone, she hurried to Tafur and, if not him, to Guizio.

Leo, talking to Mary, immediately saw that something was amiss. She told him what had happened with Grandma, adding, "Maybe if I had stayed I could have helped her." She was tearful.

"Nobody could have helped her," he said, comforting her. "It was her time, and God had so decreed. Her spirit will be at the head of our procession. Do not cry."

She sniffled. "That's true. Thanks for reminding me, but I can't help weeping just the same."

"I have some news," he said, hoping to divert her. "Sir Walter says that the knights may soon leave Cologne to start the pilgrimage. If they go, I will go, too."

There was a burst of laughter as Nina and Walter came out of the old wagon and walked toward the new one. Leo's eyes followed them as Mary searched his face, seeing his passion rise. She felt the sudden vibration of a major chord tingling inside her and a yearning to be with someone, to be held and comforted. Impulsively, she reached out to him, moving closer, and her body yielded to the pressure of his encircling arm. There was a moment of serenity; then she suddenly became rigid and moved away.

"Nina will be waiting for you." There was venom in her tone.

"I don't want Nina." His face was flushed. "I'd rather be with you."

"You may have to wait a long time," she said contritely, "and you say you are leaving soon."

"Not all of us. Maybe I'll stay. Someone has to help Peter." He turned her averted face back toward him. "From now on, it's only going to be you." His eyes held hers under a steady gaze and hers dropped. "I'll wait for you as long as I have to. Will you wait for me? Or go with Ruth?"

Her lips were trembling. "I . . . I don't know . . ."

"Since the first time I saw you, I've wanted you. More than anything else. I know you like me."

She was locked in a bewildering amalgam of emotional storms. His flushed face swam before her. Suddenly, she burst into tears.

Uncertain, Leo stood stiffly. As of one mind, he opened his arms and she came to him, sobbing against his chest as he caressed her hair.

23

The meeting was over quickly as few of the knights had anything more to say, and the topic had been privately discussed between them for days. The vote was predictable: they would start in two days for Constantinople. There would be no carts, no wagons, no women—only knights and their squires. Peter, they agreed, was procrastinating, and there was no need for them to stay.

Walter was unhappy with the decision, and he tried to have the departure date postponed for at least one week, but the others would not hear of it, and, in the end, he reluctantly agreed to go with them. He had been with Peter from the beginning, and he felt he had a duty to the old monk—but he did agree with the knights: Peter was delaying his departure. But he had a solution in mind.

He called Leo to his tent the next morning, indicated a seat, and came right to the point. "You know how we voted last night. When we leave, we will set the trail and the host will follow, but Peter's guard will remain."

Leo nodded, but half of his thoughts were turning on his own feelings. What could he tell Mary? Although the decision was not a surprise to him, he had never faced the thought of a painful departure from her.

Walter's voice broke through. "Peter must be protected, and the guard has many good axemen, bowmen, good soldiers, but they need someone to command them, to lead them, a trained fighter."

Was Walter saying he was not going to leave? A sudden hope flared in Leo's mind. "If you stay," he blurted, "I'll stay, too."

"No, Leo, I obey the vote." He watched Leo's exuberance collapse. "What would you say if I told you to stay?"

Leo's head jerked upward. "If you? . . . you don't want me?"

"You have a duty to do as you are commanded as long as you remain my squire. What if I ordered you to stay and guard Peter?"

Leo absorbed this silently. Finally, he said, "You promised to make me a Knight of the Sword. If you go, and I stay . . ." He paused, and his eyes lit up. "Can you do it now?"

Walter shook his head. "No, not now. But we will meet in Constantinople, for we have to wait for the great knights. Without them, we cannot go to Jerusalem; we cannot fight the Moslems alone. Stay; protect Peter. I will make you commander of the guard."

"Wha—at?" Leo was astounded. "Me?"

"Yes, you. You are a man well respected in the guard. And after the knights leave, who is there who can fight as well as you? Who can train others as well as you? The guard is two hundred strong, and you can easily raise it to five hundred. What squire could ever boast of commanding an army like that? Who could ever object when I give you the accolade after you have led an army like that to Constantinople through the heathen countries? Think of it."

Leo felt his head swim. Command! And Mary, too! If he left with Walter the joy of Mary would be gone from his life. What would she do? Go to Ruth and . . . a vivandiere. Something inside him shriveled. No! Not Mary! If he stayed, he could prevent it; they could be married! Married! The sun was suddenly shining again.

"I'll do it!" he said with vehemence. "I'll stay!"

Walter was relieved. "Good. I'll tell Peter." He smiled.

Leo was off, racing to Ruth's wagon, to Mary. The news filled his whole being, and he would burst if he didn't tell her. He leaped the few steps and pounded on the door. "*OPEN UP! MARY!*"

Ruth's bawd slipped the bolt and peered through the narrow slit. "Go away," she complained. "Everybody's busy."

"Busy?" The implication hit him suddenly. Gritting his teeth, he yelled, "*I WANT MARY! IT'S ME, LEO! GET HER!*"

"She is busy, squire," the crone mumbled. "Come back tomorrow." She pushed the door shut, sliding the bolt into place.

"Mary!" he screamed. He drew his sword and banged heavily on the door. "*OPEN UP, YOU OLD WITCH! OPEN, OR I'LL BREAK IT DOWN!*" His blows began to splinter the wood.

The door opened a crack, and he gripped the edge, swinging it out. Mary stood there, held upright by the bawd. She wore her chiton, her dark hair falling freely over her shoulders, her head limp.

He clutched her arm and pulled her toward him. The door slammed, and as he held her limp body, he could hear the bolt slide. Her head bobbed from side to side as he carried her down the steps, a passive, warm body, without life. He sat her down and she fell over; he took her hand.

"Mary? What have they done to you?" Drugged? He had seen his father mix something for unruly sailors, and they had become limp, just like Mary was now. He held her head between his hands, but her eyes remained closed, and she lay flaccidly in his arms. With a quick decision, he swung her over his shoulder and started for his tent.

He sat beside her as she lay on his pallet in a coma; he was frustrated and angry, sweating in anger and fear because of his uselessness. In final desperation and defeat, he stretched out beside her and held her hand. It was late when he fell asleep.

The dark sky was gray when he awoke; it was the dark-dawn, neither day nor night, and he was stiff and chilled. Mary's hand still lay near his, and he rubbed it because it felt so cold. She had not moved, but she was alive and breathing quietly, and he sighed in relief, for he had had a premonition of her death. He washed his face, then bathed hers, and she opened her eyes.

"Thank you, Lord Jesus," he prayed. He grasped her hand.

Her eyes jumped in terror—a rabbit seeking escape. She pulled her hand free and recoiled from him. With sudden recognition, she cried out, "Leo!" and collapsed toward him. "Leo! Oh, Leo!" and he took her in his arms. She broke into tears.

He stroked her head. "What happened? Are you sick?"

"I—I don't know. I was talking to Ruth. Her bawd brought me something. 'Drink this,' she said, and I drank. I remember I started to laugh. I couldn't control myself. I laughed and laughed; I felt so light, like I was floating . . . so happy." Her face changed. "There was a man . . . he pulled me down . . . I don't . . . remem—ber." She looked about. "How did I come here?"

"I brought you. I was going to kill that old witch. I thought you were dead." Suddenly, he remembered. "I'm not going away with the knights; I'm staying. Sir Walter is making me commander of the guard! He told me! He'll make me a knight when we reach the East! Just think! Me, a knight!" He gloried in the word. "I'll lead the guard to Constantinople! We can be married!" He clutched her by the shoulders. "Do you hear? We can be married!"

She was too bewildered to understand him. "Married?" she repeated. "Married?"

He shook his head vigorously and shouted, "Yes! Married! Are you ready!"

"Yes, oh, yes! Right away! Can we? I don't have a wedding gown. Or a dowry."

"We'll find something," he assured her. "Peter will marry us." His eyes twinkled. "I'll take you just as you are."

She embraced him passionately.

Leo bubbled with excitement as he told Walter what had happened to Mary and that they wanted to be married. He was surprised, then hurt, when the knight turned skeptic.

"You're sure you want to marry her? Why?"

Leo did not see the knight's knitted brows. "Why? We love each other. Do I need other reasons?"

"More than a new command? More than knighthood? More than the salvation of your soul?"

Leo hesitated. "These questions . . . they are not fair," he fumbled. "Papa Urban promised salvation to everybody: you, me, and Mary, too. What is so wrong . . .?" Words failed him.

Walter was grave. "You know what Ruth is; Mary lives with her; you have been with Nina; if you want Mary . . ." He stopped as he saw that Leo was becoming angry. "All right, look at it this way. You want to become a knight. There is much plunder in the East and you will receive your share. Would you want Mary as your lady, knowing how many others had been with her?'' He felt like a father advising a son. ''Marriage to Mary may be a grave mistake.''

Leo floundered. He had never expected Walter would be opposed, and the knight's reasoning left him bewildered.

Relentlessly, Walter went on. ''You are young and the blood is hot. I once denied myself women as a penance and I suffered. You will find many Moslem women in the East. There will be Christian noblewomen, some widowed, some virginal, who are on the crusade who will seek husbands. Many will have fair estates at home. Marriage to a knight is a bargaining affair. Do not make my mistake and marry cheaply. What does Mary bring to the altar but a tarnished name?''

The ground under Leo's feet had become slippery mud, and he reached out desperately for anchorage. ''We love each other,'' he said simply. ''We want to be together now.''

''You can have that for five coppers. Marriage is serious.''

''There is more than a bed . . .'' Leo fumbled. Walter raised an eyebrow. ''I don't want a whore; I want a wife. Is it so wrong to marry for love instead of for gold and land?'' He was in despair. ''Only the Lord Jesus knows if I will live or die. We want each other now; later, it may be too late.''

Walter sighed. ''I know what you feel, Leo, and there is no blame to what you say. Women hold up half the sky. They can make rich men poor, and poor men rich. They give us life just as they take it from us in agony. I have no cause to chide you; you are no longer a boy. I have given you my best thoughts, but accept my apology if I have hurt you. You have my blessings, if that is what you want, and anything else I can give you.''

A sweet rain of relief washed over Leo. ''Thank you, Sir Walter; I ask another boon. Will you stand for my father? I would like Peter to do the wedding. Can you ask him?''

Walter nodded. ''My service to you; I shall be honored. I must tell Peter that I ride with the knights tomorrow, and he may find the news unsettling. I go to see him later this afternoon so have Mary ready. We shall have the ceremony first.''

''Thank you, for everything, Sir Walter.''

The knight nodded thoughtfully. ''I will miss you, squire.''

Mary was dreaming with open, staring eyes. It was not right, she told herself, to be married in an old chiton; she should have a white brocaded gown from Bruges, or a one from byssus, smooth, like linen. There should be a train of guipure, not too long or the heavy lace would sweep the dirty floor, and she would need a page to hold it. Her feet should be encased in dainty leather shoes, finely stitched, with silver buckles, and she would wear bracelets of gold, with gems embedded in the metal. A long necklace of firestones would be around her neck, not the dull ones which sparked when struck, but the red, green, and white ones which flash when the rays of the sun shine on them. And upon her black hair would be the greatest prize of all, a tiara of bright silver whose peaks had colored gems flashing each time she moved her head as she walked down the aisle with Leo.

The wedding would be held in an open arbor, and many people would be there to watch. Trained birds would be singing with the choir, the throaty wren and the red-breast thrush with their clear songs. And all the people would stare and say how pretty she was.

Should she ask Ruth to come? Ruth was family, but Ruth . . . Was Ruth angry with her? She pondered the question and finally made up her mind: Ruth must come, and Nina, too. Maybe Ruth could lend her a dress—and some pretty jewelry. Yes, Ruth must come; she would tell Leo.

Leo decided that his bride would have a fine wedding gown, and as there was no time for fittings and sewings, he went to Guizio for help. Guizio listened and grinned. "No need to worry, squire," he chortled. "I knew she was different from Ruth the first time I glimed her, but a little advice from one who knows—watch your bed." He winked and raised two fingers behind his head.

Leo frowned. "Can you get a white one?"

"White . . . uhmmm . . . have you asked Ruth? She has a chest full of dresses. Nina, too."

"I—I can't go there," Leo said lamely.

Guizio raised an eyebrow. "Something happened?" Leo was quiet, uncomfortable. "Better say," Guizio went on. "Sooner or later I hear, so it's better I hear from you. Tafur has interests in Ruth's wagon, so let me hear."

Reluctantly, Leo told him what had happened the night before.

Guizio grunted and shook his head. "Tafur should know, especially if there are only two working instead of three. All right, Squire Leo, I'll find you a dress, but it will cost. Little John will bring it to Mary. Another word of advice. For a wedding there should be family; Ruth will come; maybe Nina, too."

"I don't think . . ." began Leo. He did not want Ruth there.

Guizio stopped him. "Don't think; just listen, and take my advice. Blood is blood—and it would be easier to get the dress. I say Ruth will be there. I'll do the asking, so there's no need for you to be involved."

"Can I come, too?" asked Little John eagerly.

"Of course," said Guizio before Leo could reply. "You're almost family; just like me."

To Leo, this was becoming complicated. "Mary will need it soon," he warned Guizio. "Sir Walter and I will see Peter just before sundown."

"No worry. We'll be there, and I'll bring the wine as a gift, some of Tafur's best." His eyes were twinkling. "Always good for the bride—makes them relax." He winked.

24

Chagon was naked to the waist, and his red, sweaty face glistened as he swung his hammer at the glowing iron. The hammer recoiled off the metal, then tatoo-ed like a drum's roll on the anvil. He sighted his work along its edge, grunted his satisfaction, and poked it deep into the hot coals. The forced draft of the leather bellows made the charcoal glow white, and he lifted his bass voice in a song-shouted tune, for he was jubilant.

> *"THIS WE GIVE THE TURBANED TURK*
> *WHO COMES ACROSS OUR WAY;*
> *OUR THIRSTY SWORD WILL FLAY HIS SKIN;*
> *AND DRINK HIS BLOOD ALL DAY.*
>
> *"WE STRIKE THE HEATHEN INFIDEL*
> *WITH SHARP AND CUNNING KNIVES;*
> *THE PAGAN IMP AND ARAB FIEND*
> *WILL RUE THEIR GODLESS LIVES.*
>
> *" 'AVENGE ME!' CRIES LORD JESUS CHRIST;*
> *'AVENGE ME, CHRISTIANS BRAVE!'*
> *WE'LL ROLL TEN THOUSAND MOSLEM HEADS*
> *ACROSS OUR SAVIOR'S GRAVE!"*

He withdrew the iron, spat on it, and watched the spittle dance on the red steel. As the reddish glow dimmed, he plunged the sword into a tub of water standing at the anvil's foot and leaned over to sniff the rising steam. A calm, sensuous sublimity suffused his face as he smelled the acrid odor. His spirit was exaltant. The bliss of feeling the heat and drinking the running, salt sweat as he shaped and bent the iron to his will was almost unbearable to him. He had missed it for more than a year.

All winter he had led Peter's mule and helped the old man mount and dismount, and his strong muscles ached for heavier work. Walter had secured the forge from the city, and he pushed the shoeing of the horses and mules onto the city's blacksmiths while he returned to his real love—fashioning swords. He was a master artisan in weaponry, and the knights delighted in his work. They brought him their weapons and marveled at his artistry.

When he withdrew the sword he was making for Leo from the water tub, he rang it against the anvil to feel its harmonic vibrations, and he clucked in satisfaction when it rang true. Back it went into the fire. The coals smoked and hissed as the water steamed. He thrust the sword deeper and worked the bellows as he raised his voice again.

Leo approached and listened appreciatively. "I come to see my sword, Chagon, and I see you are happy."

"Ah, Leo. It is a beautiful day, and the sword goes well. Yes, I am happy. If I am not interrupted, you will be able to test the steel tonight. It is good for a knight to see his sword made; it will fit his hand better. You should give it a good name so when it drinks its first blood, it can be praised with glory."

A high scream and the loud laughter and jeering of a crowd startled them.

"*Papa! Don't! Don't!*" A weeping, stumbling girl cried out as she cringed and jumped to avoid the withy whip of a man who roared at her and struck again and again at her evasive figure.

"Stand still, you hell-cat!" The fat peasant moved clumsily and she dodged to avoid the whip. "I'll teach you to go whoring!" he screamed, lashing wildly.

The crowd followed them, urging him on. The peasant struck out furiously, stung by the comments and laughter. He shouted imprecations, driving himself into a frenzy as he moved after the girl who was agile and escaped most of his blows, but not all.

She was young, no more than fourteen, already blossoming into womanhood. She was fair-haired, with a round, dirty face smeared with blood mixed with tears and mud. Her short dress was stretched tightly about her plump body, and it was two years old, for she had grown out of it, and where it was torn the round flesh appeared. The cloth had been shredded on her back, revealing welts on her skin.

"She won't eat your gruel long!" a man yelled with laughter.

"She'll bring you a bastard!" called another.

"Let her be!" screamed a woman.

Family fighting and feuding had become commonplace, and every day the host waited increased the disorder. It was two weeks since Peter had arrived; food was short and being rationed to the poor, although those with money had no problem. No one knew why Peter procrastinated, but he insisted on waiting, and tempers grew.

Chagon turned back to his anvil. "Priest's work," he mumbled.

With an ear-splitting roar, the man caught the screaming girl by the hair and forced her to her knees, twisting her head. His face, contorted with rage, was fiendish, and he struck her with his fist. She shrieked and tried to escape his grip, but he hit her again and again.

Chagon, his head lifted by the upsurge of noise, left the forge and strode up to the peasant. He stopped the man's swinging arm. "It is enough," he said. "She bleeds."

The man cursed and tore his arm free. "She is mine and I do as I wish!" he yelled. And he swung at the girl again.

Chagon caught his descending arm and with a twist sent the man stumbling away to the ground. The crowd cheered. A fight!

Chagon bent over to lift the weeping girl when, with a roar of hate, the peasant came off the ground with a knife in his hand, and he rushed at the blacksmith's back.

Suddenly, he stumbled! The knife fell from his hand as he clawed at his throat; his scream ended abruptly. His body folded, curled over and inward, and he fell head first toward the ground. Chagon, like a cat, pivoted to face the charging man only to see him fall. The crowd gasped in astonishment at the unexpected turn of events and did not know what had happened.

The man was on his knees, and a pool of blood was forming around the spot where his head rested on the ground. Leo walked to him and pushed him over, using his foot. He was dead; his eyes were wide open; his mouth was still twisted by his silenced scream. Leo withdrew his knife from the man's throat and wiped the blade on the jacket arm of the corpse. He resheathed it as the stunned crowd watched.

Chagon suddenly realized what had happened. The girl was on her knees before the body of her father, tears streaming down her bloodied face. A woman pushed forward from the crowd and spoke quietly to the crying girl. She helped her rise, and they disappeared into the hushed crowd which opened to let them pass.

Leo looked about. "Do any of you know this man? If you do, get a priest and see to the burial."

Two men came forward. "We are from his town," said one. "We will take him, Squire Leo."

Leo cocked his head. "You know me?"

The man nodded. "Everyone knows Squire Leo and Sir Walter. You did what was right. That one," he indicated the corpse, "beat his wife to death three weeks ago; then he started on the girl." He spat. "Although I should not speak ill of the dead, good riddance."

"In your hands then," said Leo and turned away.

Chagon had returned to his forge worried about the sword. He drew it from its fiery bed carefully and tapped it with his hammer, examining how the metal densed under the blow. If it flaked, there would be trouble with its final temper, and it might not keep its edge. After a moment's work, he sighed in relief and pushed it back into the coals. Leo watched.

"No damage," said the blacksmith. "I expect it to be a great sword." He worked the bellows. "I owe you my life, my friend. You were quick—and straight to the mark." He shook his head in wonderment. "Not many could hit so small a target, and it was moving quickly, too."

"Would that I was as good with the sword," Leo sighed. "You would do the same for me, friend Chagon." The tension was gone, and he was embarrassed by the blacksmith's praise.

Chagon stirred the sword. "This one will be like the extension of your arm," he said. "It will be delicately balanced, and its temper will be so true that its edge will cut armor and will slice an overripe fig after it has chopped through an iron helmet."

"Thank you, my friend. Better that I do not keep you from your task. I will come back later." He left the forge feeling very much the soldier tested in battle and had been valiant. But he sobered almost immediately. The battle had not been his; the peasant had not injured him; and his knife had been used in a surprise attack, not as a soldier's weapon. He knew he had only the satisfaction that his aim had been good; the knife had done his bidding.

Peter would demand an explanation, for killings had increased and the monk sat in judgment when the killers were brought before him. The usual decision was expulsion, and the guard policed the decision, but the killers had formed a small group of their own, and they camped at a distance. They said they were not to be denied their chance of salvation even if Peter had cast them out.

Later, Chagon began the long, tedious task of polishing the new blade and giving it its final edge. Deeply enmeshed, he pumped the whetstone with a slow, steady rhythm as he moved the sword across the face of the revolving stone, concentrating on the even pressure of his hand. It was critical that he be right. Its edge had been tapped flat to a smooth finish, but its keenness would be determined by the straightness of the sharpening.

He whistled his song softly between his teeth as he guided the steel across the whetstone. When he reached the end, he lifted it and his eye caught a movement behind some barrels. He twisted himself sharply and called out, "Who's there?" There was no answer. He gripped the sword tightly and moved in front of the barrels.

"Come out!" he ordered. "I know you're there."

Out came the young girl of the morning, still wearing her tattered dress. Her face, red, swollen, and battered, had been washed clean, and she had tried to comb her hair.

"What are you doing here?" Chagon was puzzled. When she did not answer him, but remained staring down at her feet, he said, "If you can't talk, leave . . . go away." He was annoyed.

"Miriam sent me," she whispered.

"Miriam?"

"The lady who helped me; she's Mama's friend." She burst into tears. "When my mama was here." She wiped her nose with her hand. "Now, Papa's dead, like Mama. Squire Leo killed him," she wailed.

"I know," said Chagon irritated. "He tried to kill me, maybe you, too. But what do you want here?"

"Miriam says . . . maybe you . . . should take care of me," she finished in a rush. "She says you don't have a woman, and I could help . . . I could clean . . . and cook."

"Wh—at?" He was speechless. "Go back! Go away!" In his amazement, he brandished the sword and she jumped behind the barrels. He stood in front of them, his feet spread, the sword gripped firmly in his hand, but his bewildered face belied his apparent ferocity.

"Come out, come out," he said finally. "I won't hurt you." He retreated from the barrels. She edged out. "What's your name?"

"Inda."

"Look, Inda. Go back and tell Miriam I don't need you. Stay with her. Just go away."

She began to sob. "I can't. She has four of her own and Elvram says they can't feed another. And there's no room." She sobbed.

Chagon, in confusion, sat down at the wheel. "Stop bawling," he said in exasperation. "Let me think." She quieted. "Why was he beating you?"

She hung her head, embarrassed, and pulled on her torn rags. "We were very poor," she muttered so quietly that he strained to hear her. "Sometimes, when we were hungry, Mama sent me to some rich man's wagon to beg, and sometimes I . . . I . . . stayed there for a little while to get the bread and cheese. Sometimes, Mama went, and she would bring a lot to eat back. Was that so bad?"

"Oh," said Chagon shaking his head knowledgeably. "Did your papa know what you and your mama were doing?"

"He knew," she said bitterly. "Only he made believe he didn't know. When Mama used to come back with lots of things, he would take the best for himself, even hiding them from us."

"Then? Why was he so angry?"

"Papa's friends called me and Mama whores, and it made him angry. Mama brought back some wine, and he drank it all . . . and then he started to beat her, and beat her. I couldn't make him stop," she sobbed. "She . . . she died. I couldn't make him stop."

He waited until she gained control of herself again.

"After that, he kept after me all the time and beat me when I didn't bring enough back. I was always so hungry . . . and yesterday . . . I went to . . . to . . . beg again, and he wanted everything. But I didn't have anything," she sobbed. "I ate it all. He started to whip me." She wailed. "Now, he's dead."

Chagon began to rub his face in consternation. "All right, all right. But you can't stay with me. Go back to that . . . Miriam. I'll talk to Brother Peter. Maybe he'll have some answer. Go now."

She was looking at his basket where he kept some bread, and his eyes followed hers. "Have you eaten today?" She shook her head no. "You can take something from the basket—some bread and cheese. Take it and go."

She opened the basket and attacked the food ravenously. He began to turn the whetstone, deep in thought, but he was not concentrating on the sword. After a few moments, he rose and began to pace the room as Inda's large, dark eyes followed him while she chewed. She huddled against the barrels. All this, he concluded, was too much for him. Peter would have to solve it.

For one fleeting moment he had recalled his own children . . . and now this. Peter was his only hope.

Leo decided to find Walter and tell him about the death of the peasant. He had condemned an unconfessed Christian to Purgatory, and what would Peter say? He felt that his appointment as commander of the guard hung in the balance, for Peter had warned him about using his knives too quickly, and Walter had cautioned him about it, too. When Walter did not chastise him after hearing what had happened, he was very surprised.

"Not many men could have been so accurate with a moving target," the knight said, "but you took a large chance. Your decision was right. If you had hit him in the arm, perhaps he would have dropped the knife, perhaps not; Chagon would have been cut or killed. A man can do much damage even with a knife in his arm."

"Will you help me explain this to Peter?"

"Of course. Chagon should be grateful that your aim was good. It proves that you are ready and think fast in a crisis. And that is good. Do not condemn yourself. It was right. I am pleased."

"Thank you for all you have done for me, Sir Walter."

"You are still my squire, Leo, and I am responsible for everything you do. Do not worry about Peter, but Parenti . . ." He shrugged. "He, I suspect, will seek mischief."

"Parenti!" Leo had forgotten about the monk. He would have words to say to Peter about Mary, Ruth's sister, who had stayed with Ruth and Nina in Ruth's wagon. They were a particular target of the monk, who complained bitterly about the morals of the camp. "What will he say about the wedding?" he asked Walter.

"I don't know," said the knight thoughtfully. Then, he grinned. "How can he object to a woman taking a husband for her journey to Jerusalem after Papa Urban decreed that no woman should go alone? Peter will understand that."

Leo nodded. But he was worried.

25

Peter listened as Chagon related the events which led to the death of the peasant. Then he questioned Inda. She told how her mother had died and how her father had taken the whip to her. Parenti interrupted.

"Did you ever tell this to your priest?"

"Yes," she whispered, "at confession. He talked to Papa, but he said I shamed him, so he beat me, and he said if I ever did that again, he would whip me to death." She sniffled. "Then, he made me do those things again."

"Do you not know, girl, that you must honor your father?" Parenti's voice was cold. "He is dead. Do not besmirch his name."

"Ye—es. But he . . ."

"Silence!" roared the monk. "We have heard enough!"

"All this has nothing to do with Leo," said Walter impatiently.

"It has everything to do with Leo." Parenti was caustic. "If Leo had restrained his knife, the man would not be dead."

"But Chagon might," retorted Walter. "He was defending a child."

"He was meddling with a father chastising his daughter," shouted Parenti. "He had no right to interfere."

"But she was bleeding," objected Chagon. "And he was beating her with his fist. Should I have let him kill her?"

"You still had no right," insisted Parenti. "A child must obey her father, and it is the duty of the father to punish her if she doesn't. You do not spare the rod. Laxity is a crime."

Walter snorted. "Killing a child is a crime, monk. You read the wrong parts of the Good Book."

"There are no 'wrong' parts, knight. You skirt damnation when you say that."

"Do not talk damnation to me, monk. Leo protected his friend from an insidious attack from behind; Chagon tried to stop a madman from beating his child to death. Both should be commended."

"A man died without confession," Parenti went on determined. "He could have been disarmed. We all know Chagon's strength. But Leo . . ." His lip thinned and curled. "Leo has been trained to kill, and it did not matter who was the victim."

"May the Lord preserve us," Walter threw up his hands. "When the righteous rule, the people weep."

"At the Second Coming," retorted Parenti, his voice cold as ice, "the sinful will truly weep, but in vain."

"Peace, brothers, peace," said Peter. "My head rings with all this rhetoric. The dead man's soul will reach Our Lord, as Urban has said." He turned to the girl. "Weep no more, my child; your father's sins will be forgiven. I will hear confession for Chagon and Leo and will proscribe penance. Let the matter rest."

"But, Brother Peter," said a worried Chagon, "what of the girl? She comes to me, and I do not know what to do."

"She cannot stay with you," said Peter. "But she can help you in such matters as washing and cooking, and in exchange for her work, you can help in her keep. She can stay with another family. What think you of this solution?"

"Verily a judgment of a Solomon," said Chagon relieved. "I will do this most willingly."

"Then it is settled." He did not ask Inda but turned to Parenti. "Can you find a good family to take her under those conditions? Chagon will help in her keep."

"I will try. It may not be difficult."

Peter sighed. "Please take the girl out, Chagon. We have something else to discuss with Sir Walter."

There was a sneer on Parenti's face as he watched Chagon and Inda leave. "He will be more than a father to her before this is done. I predict it."

Peter's face was strained. "You think too much of the frailty of women, Brother Parenti."

Walter sniggered; Parenti glared at him. "Woman has been the base of man's fall from grace," he said stiffly. "They league themselves with the devil and turn men from worship."

"One would think them all candidates for hell," jested Walter.

"They are! They are!" Parenti was vehement. "Beneath a woman's fair face lies the leering grin of a demon. Woe unto him who succumbs. She will drive him to her Master—Satan."

"Enough, Brother!" Peter was annoyed. "I would talk to Sir Walter. Tell me," he asked Walter, "is it true what Brother Parenti says? You and your knights are to leave us and begin your own march to Jerusalem?"

Parenti, always Parenti! Walter gritted his teeth. Only Tafur's camp was free from the prying eyes of his monkish network, and who could trust Tafur? He took a deep breath.

"Yes, Peter. But we go only to Constantinople. We will await you there. The knights see no reason to remain here any longer."

"And you go with them?"

Walter bowed his head. "I go with them." Suddenly, he lifted his head. "Tell me, Peter, why do you wait? There is no need. In the winter, we said we would wait until spring. Spring is here."

"We wait for those we called all winter," said Peter wearily. "Many still walk the roads, and we said we would leave by mid-April. We must hold for five more days to let all those on the road catch up, and for us to keep our promise.''

"Tomorrow is the fifteenth of April—mid-month,'' Walter pointed out. "We already number in the tens of thousands, and we travel slowly. Small groups can catch us easily, and those who do not can reach us in Byzantium where we will have to wait for the great knights.''

"You commit the sin of Pride,'' snapped Parenti. "You would lead your own armed men like the great knights.''

"I tire of your contentiousness,'' said Walter. "My tongue is not a sword to parry thrusts with yours, but my sword is ready to cut your tongue out if you persist.''

"The truth is the greatest sword of all,'' retorted the monk. "I fear you not. We must wait. The larger our host, the more souls we bring to salvation, to Our Lord.''

Walter laughed with sarcasm. "Ah-ho! See, O Lord, who holds the sin of Pride! You fathom yourself a second Aaron, with Peter as your Moses, leading a host to the Promised Land? The numbers you would lead pervert your senses.'' He turned on Peter. "Is this the reason you refuse to start? Do you not know that there will always be others who come later? The knights leave tomorrow. If you follow within five days, you should have no trouble finding our trail, but if you wait longer . . .'' He did not finish. Instead, he grinned. "Follow soon, Peter, and designate him . . .''—he pointed to Parenti— "to remain behind and await the latecomers. They will need a leader, too.''

"My faith shields me from the bitterness of your tongue,'' growled the monk. "Peter will do what is right.''

"I have no arguments left for him who seeks his own damnation,'' said Walter. "I predict, monk, you will die by the sword.'' As an afterthought, he added, "Unconfessed.''

Peter raised his hand. "Brothers, I have heard enough. We have been close companions throughout a cruel winter, and our mission is more important than all this bickering.'' He held his hands as in prayer. "To you, Sir Walter, I say may the Lord bless and keep you. Ride not too far ahead of us, for we pass through savage lands where pagans and heathens roam the roads between towns, and they fear not the Lord. Many of the host may suffer if they are not protected.''

"I leave, but most of the guard remains, Peter. The fitting commander is Leo, who also stays behind. He is well trained and I have appointed him as your personal bodyguard.''

Leo came forward. "I have been sworn by Sir Walter to protect the poor and needy, and I will take his place at your side.''

"A worthy oath,'' murmured Peter, "but the Lord protects me.''

Walter grinned. "So you told me a year ago. Let me answer. Leo's arms will only be another aid to the Lord's.''

Peter smiled back at him. "May the Lord protect all of us." He made the sign of the cross with his hand.

"Amen," said Walter. The two men gazed at each other with affection. Then, Walter said, "I have one last boon to ask of you, Peter. It is for Squire Leo. He seeks marriage and he would have you perform it."

"Leo!" There was surprise in Peter's voice.

"Leo!" said Parenti, and he turned to look at the squire.

"He has found a girl he wishes to join before God, Jesus, and Mother Mary. He chooses to remain with her rather than leave with me. Will you do the ceremony now, before I have gone?"

"Yes, of course. Who is she?"

"I doubt if you know her. She is called Mary and she joined us before Paris."

"Mary?" Peter paused. "A good sign. She carries the name of Our Virgin Mother."

"From what camp?" asked Parenti.

Walter ignored him. "She and her family and friends wait outside. Shall I call them in?"

Peter nodded. Leo brought Mary in and the others followed. Mary wore a simple white gown; Ruth and Nina were dressed more gaily; and even Guizio and Little John were washed and neat.

There was a sibilation, a hissing wind, and Parenti backed away. "Fallen women! Gutter females! You dare come here?"

With an overt gesture of chivalry, Walter bowed to Mary. "You look beautiful, my dear," he said graciously. "Let me be the first to congratulate you and Leo." To Leo, he said, "You have chosen well. Who stands for the bride?"

Guizio, carrying a flask of wine, waved it. "I do, and the girls are bridesmaids. We have everything ready." He beamed at Peter.

The ceremony was brief and Walter hurried the wedding party out. He saw that Peter was angry, and he thought he knew the reason.

Peter glared at Parenti. "Did you know of this?"

"Of course not." The monk was waspish and sullen. "Why did you do it? Fornicating whores! All of them!"

"Walter took advantage of me." Peter was bitter.

"Do you think it wise to grant Leo the command of the guard? He is young and married; he might make some grave decisions."

"Do I have a choice? Is there someone else you would suggest?"

"Leo should not command. He will be ruled by that ribald."

Peter was pensive. "I will summon him tomorrow for confession. We cannot cast him out; there is no one else who can lead the guard or whom the guard will accept as their leader. He has helped train all of them. It is now in God's hands; His will be done." He turned away. "I am tired. I would sleep."

Dismissed, Parenti talked to himself. "The rock crumbles."

*　　　　　*　　　　　*

Mary removed her white wedding gown carefully and folded it with caressing hands. It was Nina's, and Ruth had said that Nina wanted Mary to keep it as a wedding gift. Leo, she thought, would have to get her a chest for her clothes.

Standing in the semidarkness of the tent, she removed the hair combs, a gift from Ruth, and allowed her long hair to settle over her shoulders. She had sent Leo out of the tent, protesting shyness to undress before him on their wedding night. "It's bad luck," she insisted, pushing him out.

"Not for me," he insisted good-naturedly, but he went.

She felt a subdued excitement. Gone was the wild, uncontrollable lust which had maddened her and sent her burning with impudicity to Andre. With Tom, she had had the sensuous, throbbing convulsions so necessary for her fulfillment. She had delighted in his lovemaking and the tricks he had played with her body. A mist formed over her eyes as she thought of him, and her desire for love heightened. Leo was still a boy compared to Tom, but she would teach him what Tom had taught her. And she would love him, too, for he was considerate and kind, not much like Andre, or Tom either, for that matter. She and Leo would have a good marriage. And when Leo became a knight, he would be proud to call her his lady.

Undressed and naked, she slipped under the sheet Ruth had given her for her marriage bed. She must remember, she told herself, to change the straw of Leo's pallet for a rag mattress. "Leo," she called, "I'm ready."

Leo was inside the tent immediately. The small oil lamp's light was sufficient for him to see Mary's black hair spread upon a field of white, and her beautiful, soft-lit face was set like an ivory cameo in the center of a small pillow. She smiled at him, and his hands trembled as he unbuckled his boots and stripped his clothes.

"Put out the lamp," she said. "We won't need it."

He crept into bed beside her, and her skin was smooth and cool to his feverish hands. Without a word, she moved toward him, and he gathered her in his arms, pressing her tightly to him. He could feel the hardened, extended nipples of her breasts, and there was a sweet field smell, like clover, and other wild flowers pervading his senses. He rolled to lie over her, kissing her at the same time. Her lips were soft and yielding, and, as he tensed his legs against her, he could feel her hands forcing their way between them, seeking and finding his manhood, cupping and guiding it into her wet area.

He opened his eyes, and her face was a picture of rapture; a mystic, hallowed trance enveloped her as though she was being transported somewhere into her own dream world, hearing her own songs of delight. She was making little sounds as she moved her hands, pressing and releasing, and her moving excitement flowed into him. He dug his fingers into the soft flesh of her buttocks and pulled her savagely to him . . . ever closer . . . ever deeper. Soon, he was lost as he surged back and forth, and she moved against him . . . swelling, ebbing, rolling, breaking . . . awash in an undertow . . . twisting in a whirlpool . . . suddenly, he shuddered with a tidal disembogue that shattered his mind and exploded his senses. He was in oblivion, and lightning was everywhere.

Recovered, he found himself limply lying upon her, and his breath became more orderly.

"Don't move yet," she whispered and he obeyed her, lying still. When she released him, he rolled off and lay on his side, facing her.

Her eyes were closed and she lay in a passive languor. He reached out to move some stray hair which had crawled across her face, and feeling his hand, she opened her eyes. A beautified smile hovered about her mouth. Her hand wandered tenderly over his face. "Hello, my husband," she whispered.

He smiled back at her, took her hand, and kissed it. "Hello, my wife," he replied.

The next morning, at dawn, thirty knights in full armor, followed by their squires, also horsed, rode out of Peter's encampment at Cologne. More than one hundred pikemen, axemen, lancers, and bowmen walked behind them. They were to follow the river on the first leg of their journey to Constantinople. The poor had begun Urban's crusade.

It was April 15, in the year of Our Lord, 1096.

26

The sky was gray and overcast, and driblets of rain fell intermittently. A sullen, dreary mood pervaded the camps, feeding a rising chorus of discontent. Many said had they known of the knights' plans they would have followed immediately. The peasants called meetings of their committees and followed their spokesmen en masse to Peter's tent to urge him to depart.

And the cold rain beat unmercifully upon the host for three days. The people huddled in their tents and wagons; the fields became a vast bog of heavy sludge and muck. The spring sickness was everywhere, the coughing and the trembling with a cold sweat. Graves were opened beside the wagons, and the mud and water covered the sheet-wrapped corpses in the shallow graves, for it was impossible to dig deeply; the mud walls collapsed on the diggers. Misery seized the people, and they complained bitterly, believing the Lord was wrathful because of the procrastination.

Finally, Peter called Leo and said, "We will leave as soon as the rains stop. See to it that you are ready with the guard." When Leo began to tell him of his preparations, he stopped the squire. "I have no need to know the details. Just be ready."

"Yes . . . of course . . ." Leo left the tent hurriedly.

The rumors percolated through the taverns, and the city's councilmen rushed to Peter to confirm the truth of the whispers. They spoke of the drain on the city's treasury, but if a date had been set, they said, they would empty the storage bins for the host's provisions for the journey. Parenti, with a sneer of contempt, thanked them for their charity; Peter blessed them in the Lord's name and urged them to join the pilgrims.

At a special mass, Peter told the eager host: Prepare yourselves to leave when the rain stops. The first day we see the sun, we will begin our pilgrimage to Jerusalem.

Excitement seized the camps, for many had established themselves in semipermanent homes and had erected small communities patterned after their home regions. It became an arduous task to re-collect their goods and roving animals. Articles lent had to be repossessed; the bracing and buckling of carts and wagons, the tying of chests and sacks became a frenzy. But goodwill and gaiety pervaded the encampment; they were marching to salvation; and with the breaking of the clouds and the reappearance of the sun, they sang joyfully: *"LORD JESUS, WE ARE COMING; THE INFIDEL SHALL WEEP . . ."*

Leo issued his orders to his men: No one is permitted to wander off the main road; no one is permitted to forage for food without permission: no one is to take cattle or sheep which is not his own. Peter has given his word, and the city council has promised grains and salt fish in exchange for keeping the peace. "We are responsible," he told them. "If we lose the goodwill of the city, they will not help us. So keep the peace; restrain all disputes. We want no fighting."

He found an elation in his role as commander, and he had difficulty in suppressing it. He would prove—·to Peter, to Parenti, to everyone—how well he could lead the guard, and in his head he turned over plans to enlarge it to five hundred men.

The dawn was gray; the black clouds which had hung black and ominous the day before had broken before sunset, but a fog lay like a damp cloth over the encampment when the host started, nine days after the departure of the knights. Ghostly figures bustled around the shadowy wagons; smoky fires burned for a warming soup; and the din grew with the baa-ing of the sheep and the lowing of the cattle. The wagons creaked and swayed in their deep settlings before they were torn from the sucking mud. The host was on the move, and slowly, like some gigantic, uncoiling snake, it formed a living, weaving line which wandered out of the plain before Cologne's walls and headed south along the Rhine River.

Thousands and thousands of pilgrims: from the north and east of France; from the western Germanic provinces and the Rhineland; from Swabia—the forestmen had come north and now marched south through their homelands. They moved along the upper river valleys, and more Swabians shouldered their axes and left their villages, and the line lengthened as it lumbered along.

Turning east, it crawled through the Bavarian mountain passes, into the fertile valleys where the burly farmers, with their wagons loaded, awaited them. Into the forests, where they found Walter's trail, and, finally, to the headwaters of the Danube, which would guide them east.

These were the days of goodwill and cheer, although most knew not where they were—nor cared. Their faith in Peter was supreme, and every order he issued after the evening mass was obeyed unquestionably. Leo rode at the head of the procession, in Walter's old place, and the guard followed every command he issued and trusted him implicitly.

The Crossbearers heeded the orders of the armed men, and when Leo began to train more for the guard, he found no dearth of volunteers. He organized them into various groups according to their special skills—the Swabians became axemen; artisans became mace-men and lancers; hunters became bowmen; and the most agile and quick he gathered around himself as swordsmen although none could master the big sword. He sent roving scouts along the byways to explore for Walter's trail and to seek food.

The Swabians, tired of walking, felled big trees and lashed the stripped logs together. In languor, they drifted on their rafts along with the currents, poled through the shallows, and sometimes rowed just to break the monotony. In whimsy and jest, they catcalled and cheered the walkers each time the procession wound close to the river, and, as evening fell, they would beach their rafts and light their fires. Never had life been so good; truly the Lord provided.

The days of May were fair and warm, with little rain, and the pilgrims rejoiced at the sun and gentle breezes. The land was greening; the earth smells were good; and the peasant farmers and serfs felt a nostalgia creep over them. There was always a cow or sheep in a nearby field when meat was wanted, and the natives blamed the loss of every animal on the passing host.

They met strange men who spoke in unknown tongues, were dressed in smelly sheepskin hides and strange square hats of fur, their gray cotton shirts brightly colored with oddly designed embroidery. Their boots were of fine leather and looked at with covetous eyes, and their beautiful horses were admired and envied. They would appear suddenly and watch the host and the rafts impassively, not speak nor answer any questions nor shouts. Those in the fields, mostly women, would lift their heads, then quietly return to their work.

Where Leo's scouts found a speaker they could understand, they learned that these men knew nothing of Papa Urban's command to the Christians, and they were ignorant of the crusade and Jerusalem. But as they moved deeper into the land, they found natives who were less aloof and were willing to trade, despite the language difficulties. Leo's quick ear managed to catch a few words, and he was able to ask questions and act as a main trade-bargainer.

The news of the host's progress spread to the capital city, and King Caloman met with Peter at the old Roman-Magyar ruins at Buda-Pest, the twin towns cut by the river. The Hermit agreed to pay in gold for all supplies, and there was no lack of food, for the valleys were fertile. And the peace was kept.

Here the river turned south, and the host was in high spirits and began to sing and dance before the fires they built each evening. The host moved slowly, stopping early for cooking and for relaxing, and reveled in their journey. Each night, they raised their voices in the mass, in their many dialects, and, in spiritual contentment, sang their songs.

27

Chagon dozed; the heavy soup Inda had made for his supper, thick with fat-laced meat and vegetables, sat well in his stomach with the stale, but good, black bread. He burped, and his stomach rumbled as he slept. Black flies hovered about his head, and he brushed at them without waking.

Inda scoured the black iron pot with sand and banged it noisily with the hope of waking him, but he slept on. Her life had changed dramatically in the month since her father's death. Parenti had found a peasant, Anzgot, who agreed to have her under Peter's conditions. Parenti gave him further orders: she was not to remain with Chagon after dark; never was she to stay overnight. She was to cook, wash clothes, and mend; but the rest of her time was to be spent with Anzgot's family. Any disobedience of these rules was to be reported immediately.

Anzgot understood and agreed. His ailing wife could use a strong girl's help, especially with the five children, and the additional food provided by Chagon's payment was welcome.

Freed from the terror of beatings, and with frequent eating, Inda opened like a wild flower, and Anzgot eyed her furtively as she bustled about the cooking fire or played with the smaller children. She looked forward to her trips to the blacksmith, for though he spoke little with her, she could rest without feeling guilty of the sin of Idleness, the curse her father had often used for her idle moments. She liked to sit and watch Chagon beat the iron, awed by the display of his huge, rippling muscles under his brown, sweaty skin. "You must be the strongest man in the world," she said in open admiration.

"All blacksmiths are strong. It comes from pounding on the anvil."

"But you are the strongest," she said with admiration. "Everybody says so. You are also the bravest."

He laughed, pleased by her interest, and his hammer struck the iron a little harder and beat its usual tattoo, this time, just for her. "Best you go back," he said. "You've been here a long time."

She gathered her things and said good-bye, but all the way back, she brooded and thought. It was dark when she reached the wagon.

Anzgot chided her. "You are late. What kept you?"

"Chagon talked with me."

"Eh? What about?"

"Nothing. Just talk." She shrugged and went in.

Anzgot pondered her reply. A neighbor, who had been watching, called to him. "Heh. She's become a ripe plum, no? Juicy."

Anzgot did not answer, but his lips tensed and his brow furrowed. He knew her past, her visits to the other wagons when her father had lived—for food he had said. Heh. Anzgot knew better. She was no longer virginal, and it had been a long time since he had lain with his wife. Inda could be ready for him. A flash of fear shook him. Parenti! Or Chagon! He was not sure which he feared more. He licked his lips.

The next day Inda finished her work in Chagon's tent and told him she wanted to talk to him. Anzgot's wife had told her what to say.

"That was a good meal, Inda; you cook well." He rose and stretched his giant frame.

"I am happy you liked it." She bloomed under his praise. "I can cook lots of things. And bake, too, if you had flour."

"Maybe, someday. You want to talk? About what?"

She became shy and hesitant. But she had to . . . Anzgot's wife had told her that in a few months, her belly . . .

Chagon eyed her curiously. He had become accustomed to her shyness, and her reticence had pleased him, for he could not abide the endless chatter of women. He was able to see she was struggling with something of great importance, for she no longer feared him, and, much to his surprise, he had developed an affection for her. Since the death of his wife and two baby daughters by a rampaging knight, he had had little affection for anyone, except Leo. But he looked forward to Inda's visits. For the food, he told himself, at first. But then he admitted he liked her company even when nothing was said between them. She was an orphan, he said, and it was partly his fault . . . or maybe he was becoming lonely.

"Well?" he said. "Talk, but talk fast. Night comes, and you have to go back."

"Do I have to?" Her black eyes were imploring him, and her lips trembled.

He looked down at her pleading face, and for the first time in years he felt a stirring within him. "We promised Brother Peter." Her woeful face wrung him, and her eyes filled with tears. "Wait until tomorrow," he said gently. "We can talk long then."

She hesitated, then nodded. "All right, tomorrow. But I'd like you to think about it tonight." She was trembling again.

"What about?" He was mystified. "Has something happened?"

"Could you . . ." she sobbed. "Could you . . . marry me?"

He was dumbfounded; his large jaw dropped, and he looked upon her in amazement and stupefaction. Gaining his voice, he said, "Wha—at? What are you saying?" Her words rang in his head. He grabbed her by the shoulders and she winced under his hands. "Why are you saying things like that?"

Her words came in a rush. "I could stay here and take care of you . . . cook . . . and clean . . . everything. Please . . . he watches me every day . . . all the time. He keeps looking, and I know what he wants. And he keeps squeezing me and pinching me." She looked down. "I can't tell you where. All the time . . ." She shuddered. "Some night, he'll come to my pallet." She looked full into Chagon's astounded face. "What'll I do?" she wailed.

He had turned to stone, his mouth agape, his eyes staring. Finding his voice, he bellowed, "He wouldn't dare! I'll kill him!" He raised his fist to strike. A sudden thought shook him. "He hasn't tried, has he?"

She was frightened by the storm she had invoked. "No! No!"

"Good." His fist crashed on the table. "If he does anything more, you tell me, right away. Do you hear? Anything!"

"I will! I will! But I'm afraid." She turned around. "I better go. It's dark already."

"All right." He had recovered from his anger, but the fire still burned with him. "Remember. You tell me right away."

"I will," she promised. She slipped out of the tent and ran into the darkness. At the wagon, she was happy to see that Anzgot was not about. His wife was asleep, and even the children were quiet. She shook the woman awake. "I told him," she said breathlessly, but triumphant. "I told him!"

"Not about the child?"

"No; just what you said I should say. He became very angry, but he was quiet when I left. What will I do if he comes here?"

"He won't . . . unless you tell him something happened." She searched Inda's face. "I don't want trouble for my man."

"I told him nothing happened."

"That is right. Now, we wait, to let him think. You will have to find a way to get into his bed. That will seal it and he'll marry you for the child. He is a good man."

A painful yearning spread over Inda's face.

The dawn came early and Leo planned to scout the road ahead. He rode off with two of his men—Turgot, his second in command, and Burel, a good guardsman. As they rode through a small forest and mounted the crest of a rise, the road turned and they could see the walls of a town across a broad, flat meadow. There was a brightness, a shining from the battlements, and it puzzled them.

"What is it?" asked Turgot.

Leo shook his head wondering; then he had a sudden flash of recognition. "Armor! Knights' armor!"

The sun's sparkling reflections fascinated them, captivating their eyes as they rode toward the gates. Five children played there, and they ran off as soon as they saw the strangers.

The three riders walked their horses down a deserted, cobbled street. Each dwelling had an open plot of ground in front for grass and flowers, and the houses were not crowded one upon the other as they were in the cities. Some were two stories high. Behind, or along the side of each, were barns, with a goat or some chickens and geese walking about. All looked neat and well-kept, with their thatched roofs and indolent air.

The riders turned into a street which led directly to the town's square, and there before them they saw a group of men hastily assembling, with pikes, clubs, and axes.

They all stopped; then Leo moved his horse slowly forward and faced the men, a smile upon his lips, his right hand extended palm up in a friendly gesture.

Two men, their faces grim and determined, stepped forward, and Leo could sense their hostility. Their hands rested on the hilts of sheathed swords.

Something was wrong, and Leo flashed a warning glance to his companions. The host had had arguments with Hungarian natives as they moved through the land, but nothing serious had ever developed as King Caloman had sent riders along Peter's route with documents carrying his mark and seal, and ordered his subjects to treat the host well and to supply them with provisions. Everywhere, there had been a friendly reception and peaceful trade. Something had gone amiss; perhaps the king's riders had not reached this town.

With his right hand open and held shoulder high, to show he held no weapon, Leo addressed the natives. "I bring the greetings and prayers of Brother Peter and the Crossbearers who march with him through your great land." He pointed to the red cross sewn on the shoulder of his jacket. "We are Christians on a holy pilgrimage to Jerusalem, and King Caloman has granted us passage. We come in peace. We seek the trail of some knights who rode before us. Perhaps they have come this way. Have you seen them?"

There was an outcry from the crowd and a few men shook their fists in anger. The two men before him drew their swords.

"*Leo!*" Turgot hissed. "*Look to your right! His sword!*"

Leo glanced sharply—and saw! The sword had belonged to a knight of Walter's troop; Chagon had worked on it; he recognized the engravings on the hilt. The man held it awkwardly. A quick glance at the other men revealed that others carried knights' swords also, and some wore gauntlets. Walter had been here.

He walked his horse closer to the man who bore the sword in his hand. "That sword!" he called out, pointing. "The knights have been here!" He pointed to the battlements. "Armor of knights!"

The man grinned ferociously. He drew his finger across his throat; the meaning was obvious. There was contempt on his face, and he spat toward the horse's hoofs.

Leo studied him, then backed his horse off. "We leave here," he ordered Turgot and Burel. "Now!" He wheeled his horse about and galloped for the gate, the other two following him. The townsmen ran after them and jeered, raising their weapons and calling in derision after them.

When they were out of the main gate, Leo turned and glanced back at the armor. No knight would have parted with his armor unless he was dead, and he prayed Walter still lived.

The news of what had happened in the town ran through the encampment rapidly, and the story grew more foreboding in the retelling. Rumor said Walter was dead; his head was on a pike on the battlements with the heads of all the other knights and their armor; their bodies had been fed to the pigs; the townspeople were ghouls, demons in disguise; waiting to kill more Crossbearers, especially Peter, and to hang him alongside the armor as food for the crows. All true Christians were marked for death.

A rumbling surge of anger and a call for retribution ran through the camps. Peasants brought out their weapons and called on Leo to lead them in an attack on the town. But Leo urged caution, and after heated arguments, they disbanded, unsatisfied and angry. When they were all gone, Tafur, who had stood by Leo quietly, said, "They are right, you know. We must attack."

"We must keep the peace," insisted Leo stubbornly.

"Sir Walter was my friend," said Tafur, "and no one, fiend or demon, can feed him to the pigs and still live. They will bleed like any other men." He paused. "And there will be good plunder in that town," he added, his eyes narrowing.

Leo was surprised. "You think of plunder? What will Peter say?"

"Whatever he wishes." Tafur was nonchalant. "These pagans must be taught a lesson, a good Christian lesson."

Turgot listened closely and agreed. "We must go, Leo, otherwise we can expect them to raid us. We can't protect the whole marching line, and they can kill and plunder us anytime."

Tafur grimaced and pointed a finger at Turgot. "Listen to him, Leo. He is right. Word will spread that we don't protect ourselves, and you know what will happen then. Let the word be that he who harms a Crossbearer dies. That way we will save many lives—and with less fighting, too."

But Leo was stubborn still. "Peter gave his word to King Caloman: for supplies, we march in peace. He gave me strict orders: no fighting. If I disobey, he . . ." He did not finish, but he was thinking that Peter could take the command away from him. Yet these pagans had killed the knights, even Walter. That had broken the peace. When he had extended his hand in friendship, it was they who threatened him with a sword. Walter's blood cried out for vengeance. Turgot was right; Tafur was right. But how do you attack a town with walls and battlements?

"We cannot just march against a town," he blurted out. "They will close the gates. We cannot stay around in siege."

"So," said Tafur softly, "we cozen them."

"What? How?" Leo did not understand.

Tafur smirked mysteriously. "You worry too much, my friend." He rubbed his hands together. "You get the guard ready." He winked slyly. "Leave the rest to me—and my people.'' He laughed unpleasantly. ''Be ready on my signal.''

Turgot's eyes were bright. ''What will you do?''

Tafur smiled. ''Do not bedevil your head with questions.''

Leo hesitated. ''Maybe if I tell Peter . . .''

''Tell Peter and we do nothing,'' said Tafur quickly. ''What can he say?'' He shook his head. ''No! You don't tell Peter. You must show that you are the commander, that you make your own decisions when it comes to defending the host, the way Sir Walter would have done. We are attacked! We fight! God is with us!''

''He's right, Leo!'' said Turgot. ''We bear the cross!''

Leo still hesitated.

''Leo, listen to me!'' Tafur was stern, harsh. ''You cannot wag your tail on two streets at the same time; you cannot command by not commanding. We must go!''

Reluctantly, Leo shook his head in agreement. All the admonitions of Peter against fighting haunted him, but Tafur was right, too. He must avenge the knights who wore the cross or no one would respect him anymore; he must recover the knights' armor or it would become a testimonial for all to see the weakness of the host. He said to Turgot, ''Assemble the men in the forest behind the rise. Remember, we don't want to arouse Peter, and tell no priest nor monk, or Parenti will find out.''

Turgot scrambled away delighted. Tafur patted Leo on the shoulder. ''That is the way to think. I will get my people ready.''

By midafternoon the guard stood behind the rise, hidden from any watchful eyes on the battlements. Tafur told his simple plan to Leo: two ribalds, dressed as mendicant monks, would enter the main gate. They would create a disturbance in the town and lure the fighters out. Meanwhile, three other ribalds, dressed as traders, with a donkey loaded with pots and pans, would be at the gate to make sure it remained open when the guard charged in.

''And that will succeed?'' questioned Leo.

''Wait and see.''

Time passed slowly after the counterfeit ribalds had passed through the gates, and the guard waited impatiently. Finally, there was a burst of noise, so loud that it was heard by the watchers on the hillside, and the two ribald ''monks,'' their habits lifted over their knees not to impede their strides, raced out of the gates, followed by a group of men brandishing swords and screaming epithets at them. The spurious monks were fleet of foot—Tafur had chosen well—and they ran just fast enough to coax and lure the enraged townsmen to follow them with the hope of seizing them.

''Now!'' shouted Tafur to Leo. ''Charge to the gate. We'll take care of these fools!''

Leo nodded and all the horsemen began their gallop across the meadow. He could see his guardsmen surround the small group of natives, and he knew none of them would live. He reached the gate and Tafur's "traders" waved him and his men through. The "traders" climbed the battlements and dropped the armor to a few of the horsemen waiting below.

The townsmen responded quickly to the attack, but they had not expected the riders to be inside the town and the control of the gates to be in the hands of the enemy. They advanced on the horses with lances and swords in a close, tight formation and stopped just outside the reach of the lances of the riders. Suddenly, three of them stepped forward and began to whirl long chains with iron, weighted balls on the ends, cautiously approaching the horses.

Leo was mystified. What was this? With a quick movement, the three men darted forward, crouching low, the balls whistling around their heads, and the balls flew and entangled the chains in the front legs of the nearest animals. They reared and neighed wildly, trying to lash out, but were impeded by the chains, and they fell on their sides, screaming, throwing their riders.

Leo shouted. "Set lances and charge!" He aimed his lance at a man brandishing a knight's sword. Before his eyes flashed the straw dummies with whom he had spent so many practice hours when Walter was instructing him how to use the long lance. He felt the jarring impact of the strike—he had pinned the man fully in the chest—and he automatically wheeled his horse and flung the body free off the point. The dead man described a wide arc and struck a house on the other side of the street.

His kill-lust inflamed, he let out a gut-induced yell and searched for another victim, but he was surrounded and he dropped the lance and drew his sword. The natives were pressing him, reaching to pull him off his mount, and he turned his horse in circles, using its strength to clear his foes away. They broke and ran, or were knocked aside, or fell under the wide, swinging strokes of his weapon. The Crossbearers, he saw, had captured the center of the wide square, and he and some of the other horsemen were moving toward them when chain twirlers came out of the street and edged toward the animals. He pulled his knives and two of the twirlers died, but the others continued their advance. The horse next to him reared and fell, threshing and screaming.

"Charge them!" Leo yelled to his men and spurred forward, his sword swinging. He would show the way! He was the leader! He struck savagely at heads below him. Someone was shouting, "*Death to the Pagans!*" His men were pulled from their mounts! Chains and clubs beat them! His sword lopped off a head . . . struck a shoulder . . . an arm with a club . . . his head reeled . . . his eyes glazed . . . he fell from his horse.

A body broke his fall, a native who tried to move away, but they both rolled to the street. Instinctively, he reached for his knife, but it was not there. He did not need it; the man was dead. Leo's sword had penetrated his stomach when Leo had fallen on him.

He wiped the sword on the man's clothes and began the ground fight Walter had taught him—the knight's stand. His sword whirled and twirled before him rapidly as he moved against his enemies. He was a fighting machine, chopping pieces out of everything standing before him. Behind him came the shout: *"FORWARD FOR GOD! FOR JESUS!"*

The fighting spread from street to street and more townsmen entered the fray. Leo's guardsmen gave ground in a slow retreat. All the horsemen were down, fighting on foot, dead, or dying, and the stones of the street were slippery as the blood of both sides flowed and mingled. Leo's sword, like some demonic whirlwind, cleared an area in front of him, the natives fearing to come close. Arms, legs, torsos, necks—all felt the steel's sharp edge as he moved against them and left piles of bloody flesh and guts as he walked forward. His opponents retreated under the savagery of his frenzy. He stopped to catch his breath and noticed he was too far forward from the rest of his men. Suddenly Tafur and Guizio appeared at his side.

"Move back!" Tafur was motioning as he yelled, a sword in his hand. Guizio carried both knife and sword. His hair was wild and an evil grin was frozen across his lips. "Back! Back!" screamed Tafur, and the three of them moved backward.

The fight was going poorly for the guard. Outnumbered, they retreated steadily toward the main gates, leaving their dead and wounded where they had fallen. Leo realized that the attack had failed, although he had secured the hanging armor. He had no way of ordering a general retreat; he had no hornblowers or signals. He vowed to correct that. He shouted but could not be heard over the general din.

Guizio, standing next to him, growled, "We best get out. No point being killed in this stinking town."

Tafur, on his other side, motioned toward the gates with his sword, then began moving in their direction.

"No!" Leo shouted to him. "Stay with the men!"

Either the two ribalds did not hear him or had different ideas; they moved on toward the gates when there was a rising howl that swelled over the sounds of the battle. It drowned everything in its high-pitched dissonance—horns! Of every register and key! High and piercing! Low and bellyful. Keening like a high wind; bellowing like bulls in heat. The sounds penetrated every fighter's consciousness and slowed him in his struggle. The bloodied combatants stared at each other in puzzlement.

Word had reached the encampment that Leo and his men had attacked the town, and, in the joy of sweet revenge, in the thought of punishment for the demons for the death of the knights, the bolder men rushed for their pikes and axes. They would fight, too, side by side with the guard, for the Lord had decreed punishment.

Chagon, convinced that his friend would need help, seized his large hammer and joined the first group heading toward the town. He was in the forefront of the Crossbearers' charge through the gates, and hundreds of others followed him. With his giant hammer, he smashed heads and bones with glee, striking in wide swings. The Swabians behind him roared in joy as they waded in with their broad axes. Before this fresh onslaught, the natives gave way, and with a victory shout, the giant, bloodied blacksmith chased them down the street.

Close behind him came the howling crusaders, pouring through the gates by the hundreds . . . the thousands . . . carrying pikes, knives, swords, clubs, axes, pitchforks, hammers, mallets, flails, and cudgels . . . screeching like demons bent on slaughter. For God and Jesus! On they came! And they came! And they came! Like a stampeding herd, an irresistible wall of humanity shattered and destroyed everything in its path. They brushed Leo and his men aside in their search for the natives, and a red cross patch on a shoulder was enough identification to live. The rest died.

They flowed through the streets and into the houses, and the cries of the women and children mingled with the calls and moans of the wounded and dying. In less than an hour, it was all over. Corpses lay everywhere, and the stones were slippery with the blood and the excreta of the dead. Without orders, Leo's men, and others, separated their own dead and wounded from the body heaps and began a systematic killing of the wounded townsmen. A guardsman found Leo's knives and brought them to him.

The looting began quickly. Crossbearers broke into the barns and hitched horses to wagons and carriages and filled them with the goods they carried from the houses. They found wine and drank themselves into a boisterous, wild mob which bickered and fought among themselves over the pots and pans, the beds, the bedding, the furniture, and the clothing. Every native they found, the elderly, the sick, the children, the women, was butchered to the cheering laughter of the drunken onlookers. As they wended their way back to the camps, herding goats, chickens, and geese, they sang, for the wine was good and they were happy. Even the wounded smiled and waved as they were carried in, but the dead, and those who were weeping over them, were not seen.

Tafur and Guizio did not wait to see the end of the fighting before they rounded up the ribalds and sent them to the other side of the town where the battle had been minimal. There they invaded the houses, but with little interest in pots and pans. Their eyes searched for jewelry, candlesticks of silver, gold and silver icon frames, boxes made with precious metals, tapestries, and fine cloth, and, most of all, gold. They stripped rings and bracelets from the hands of the women, tortured them to reveal hiding places of gold, and slit their throats. They worked quickly, loading their wagons and moving on to the next house.

"We want all weapons," Leo told Turgot. "Organize the men into squads and bring all the wounded and our dead back to camp, but first bring all the able-bodied men together so we know how many of us are left."

The guard assembled before the gates; there were little more than a hundred still on their feet. "We have won a great victory," Leo said to them. "We have avenged Sir Walter and the knights, and no one will dare to meddle with us again."

The men cheered and went about their tasks.

Crossbearers were breaking into houses throughout the town. Chagon, using his great hammer, battered door after door, and the men tore through the rooms, seeking plunder. In one house, he wandered into a bedroom and saw a high chest in a corner and he thought to himself: I can use that. When he opened it, he gasped. Dresses! He took them out, one at a time, and the fine cloth caught on his rough hands. Inda! went through his mind immediately. She needed clothes! He lifted the heavy chest to his broad back, and, bent over, he carried it all the way to his tent. As he walked, he pictured her delighted face when he gave them to her. She would smile and laugh, be happy, and he would rejoice in her happiness.

The entire encampment was in a tumultuous uproar as the men straggled in with their plunder, and there was an immediate call for a celebration. Large piles of brush were gathered by the women, and the Rhinelanders and Swabians cut wood for the fires. The wounded were brought out and nursed; the dead were buried; and the priests and the monks hovered over the weeping women.

Selim had been swept clean of the living. Even the corpses had been robbed of their clothing, their boots, and their ornaments. That night, the carnivores prowled the streets and gorged themselves on the human flesh, and in a few days, the stench was so great that wayfarers passed it by when the battlements came in sight.

Peter, his face reddened with anger beneath his dirty beard, his eyes hard and blazing, pointed his finger at Leo and screamed, "You were to keep the peace! Do you realize what you've done?"

Leo, sullen and miserable, stood stiffly. "They had the armor and swords of Sir Walter and his knights. No knight would surrender those while he lived, not to a peasant. If they could kill the knights, they could kill us, too."

"You killed hundreds of Hungarians in that town!" screamed Peter. "We could have negotiated for the armor!"

"And what of Sir Walter and the others? Could we negotiate their lives back?" Leo was bitter.

"We don't know that they are dead," said Parenti.

"I know," Leo insisted. "They told me. We wanted to get the armor off the walls."

"And for that you wiped out the entire town?" Peter bellowed.

"My men didn't do that. Our Crossbearers did."

"There were women and children there. Did you fear them?" Parenti's voice was cold and stinging. "The blood-lust burns in you too much."

"You were the first to stir it," retorted Leo. "My men did not fight with women or children. We fought the men. Your priests and monks led the others," he threw at Parenti. "Your people! We fought only men."

Peter was beside himself in anguish. "My Good Lord, what have we done? An entire town. Can we be forgiven? Selim is gone."

"The news will travel to King Caloman," said Parenti, "and we better prepare ourselves for it. He will send his army for revenge."

"What can we say to him?" Peter was rocking back and forth, his hands clasped.

"What is done, is done," said Parenti grimly. "We are near a river. We should break camp and cross it as soon as possible."

"If we can cross, so can they," Leo pointed out. "We must organize a fighting force. The king cannot get a big army to march so soon, and we can train many pikemen and axemen."

"Whatever he sends will be trained knights and soldiers," said Parenti scornfully. "We have only fighting peasants. Can they stand up to knights? You make a fool of yourself." He turned to Peter. "We must outrun their vengeance; there is no other way."

"We will hold a daybreak mass tomorrow, and we will cross. Woe to those who lag behind. Let us pray they will be buried."

"There is a city across the river called Beograd," said Parenti. "I have been told it is part of Byzantium, and I am sure the Hungarians will not attack us there. It is Christian."

Peter nodded. "Christ can save us, if we hurry. Go. Do what has to be done." He was resigned and turned away. "I must pray. So many children . . ." he shook his head. "Lost souls from Christ . . . and hundreds of our own. They are golden spirits leading us. O Lord! Have I sinned?"

Parenti's eyes were sharp as gimlets, watching him.

"He suffers," said Leo.

"So do we all," said Parenti, "but we all do not weep."

Leo shrugged. "I am tired. I need to rest." He left.

28

Mary bubbled with impatience for Leo to return. She had watched the laden wagons of the Crossbearers as they came into camp, and she expected that Leo would have more than the others. When he arrived at the tent empty-handed, she became cross.

He tried to explain his feelings, his revulsion after all the killing, but she turned away.

"Everybody took things; why didn't you?" She was bitter. "What was the good of all that fighting if you got nothing?"

He tried to explain about the knights' armor, about the need to keep the host safe, but she did not understand. He became angry. "I could have been killed. Do you know that? And you ask me for pots and pans!" He unbuckled his sword. "I'm tired. I need rest."

"But you are the commander . . ." She was perplexed.

His shoulders sagged. "It was a big battle, Mary, and hundreds of people were killed . . . men, women . . . even children." He shuddered. "I don't know how many I killed. Have you no feelings?"

She drew back. "I'm sorry, Leo, but Turgot said . . . everyone went—all the men—and they came back with so much. There is going to be a big celebration tonight, a big bonfire."

"I'm too tired for that." He began to undress.

"But I can't go without you," she protested. "I'll help you clean up and we'll have a good time. Come on." She pulled at him.

His anger rekindled. "Maybe you didn't hear me; maybe you should have come with me! Here, have a knife!" He threw one of his knives on the table. "Take it! Go and kill someone! See if you can celebrate after that."

She recoiled. "You don't have to be angry with me. The other men were there, too. It wasn't only you. And they're having fun."

"Fun!" he shouted. "You talk of fun? I'll tell you about fun. We have to cross the river tomorrow—do you know why? The Hungarian army is after us. We can't fight an army; we'll all die if they catch us. Now, that's fun!" He was out of breath. He turned away from her and crawled into bed.

Mary was shocked. "When . . . when did that happen?" He didn't answer; instead he turned away from her. She had never seen him in such a mood, and she was flustered and fearful. An army? She could hardly believe it. All day she had waited and had built fantasies and dreams of how rich they were to be and what she would do with all the things he was going to bring to her.

The music was starting outside—she could hear it—and she had a sudden recollection of dancing with Celia and Alicia . . . and Tom was playing. Pain tightened her chest. She had loved Tom . . . but she loved Leo, too, she told herself. But it was different with Tom. Was there something wrong with her? Tom was dead, and she had nagged him, too. It had to be her. The music could wait. Tom was dead. Leo was important.

She fell on her knees, penitent, and reached for him. "I'm sorry, Leo. I should have known."

He turned to her and put his arm around her waist.

"Move over," she whispered. She slid in beside him and drew his head to her bosom. They lay close together and she soothed and kissed him gently. He held her tightly, and she was surprised to discover that he was sobbing.

Chagon removed the dresses from the chest as soon as he arrived at his tent. They were beautiful, and he pictured Inda's face when she saw them. But it was dusk, and Parenti had said she was not to be in his tent when it was dark. He had given his word and he struggled with himself. Why not? he wondered. What was the monk thinking when he made that rule? Was he, Chagon, untrustworthy? Let the devil take that skinny monk; he would bring Inda to his tent, dark or not, and he would show her what he had brought for her.

As he approached Anzgot's wagon, he heard a woman scream—in terror?— and a man's angry shoutings. With an oath, he kicked in the door and saw Anzgot holding a crying Inda, while his wife, screaming, beat at him with a pot. Inda squirmed in her futile attempts to free herself, while Anzgot, drunk, roared at his wife and fended her off. The children cowered in a corner.

The blacksmith acted quickly. His fist hit the drunken peasant on the side of his head and Anzgot dropped like a stone. Without a word, Chagon scooped Inda off her feet and carried her out of the wagon as she yelped and squirmed. He held the kicking girl tightly to stop her movements.

"It's me, Inda! It's me! Chagon! Chagon!"

With the realization that she was safe came her uncontrollable sobbing, and by the time he reached his tent, with Inda still in his arms, the tears had become sniffles and whimperings. In the tent, he put her on her feet, but she clung to him, and with one arm around her waist, his big other hand caressed her hair.

"It's all right," he comforted her. "You're safe. It's all right." But she was trembling violently as he led her to his pallet where he had laid out a few of the dresses. "Look what I've brought you, all for you; so stop crying. Just look."

Her sniffling stopped, and she opened her eyes in wide surprise. She wiped her wet cheeks. "These?"

"All for you," he nodded happily, a grin on his face.

She reached for one with hesitation. "Can I try it on?"

"Of course; it's yours." His face suddenly clouded. "He didn't hurt you, did he?"

"No, you came too fast." Her face was flushed as she touched one dress after the other; she held one against her body and smoothed it carefully. "This one," she said and looked up at him, "can I put it on?" He nodded. "Turn around, and don't look."

Dutifully, he turned. She dropped her rags and struggled into the pink and white dress, adjusting it to her, tying the bows at the short sleeves and pushing her breasts up to make her appear older. It fitted well and rounded out her emerging figure. She patted her hair and tried to push it into place; she smoothed the skirt and said, "You can look now." Her face filled with hopeful expectancy.

He turned, and she saw the immediate approval on his face.

"It's . . . very nice," he hesitated. "You look—good."

He watched as she preened before him. "Shall I try the others?" she asked. "Some are too big, but I can fix them with a needle and thread, if you have any."

"I can make a needle, but thread? Maybe some of the women . . ." His voice trailed off; he was too immersed in her youthful beauty. She had become a woman before his eyes. "Maybe Anzgot's woman . . ."

"I can't go back there," she protested. "He's there."

"Oh." He awakened as from a dream. "But . . . where are you going to stay if you . . ." He floundered. "No; you can't go back . . ."

"I'm so happy with this," she cried and threw herself against him. "They're wonderful! And I can wear them all the time for you." She kissed him suddenly. "I have never had so many dresses, and they're so elegant. Turn around! I want to try on another."

He turned, but his brow was knitted in thought. Where could he secure another place for her at this time of the night? The entire encampment was in turmoil. Everyone was celebrating. Peter? He couldn't talk to Peter; certainly not to Parenti. Leo? No. He couldn't bother Leo. His brow furrowed. He was in trouble.

"Turn around! Do you like this one? It's so big."

The dress was large and hung sacklike around her. Her breasts were half-exposed, and her bright eyes and flushed face brought back memories he thought he had forgotten. He found himself becoming alive, and he fought it as he looked at her.

She sensed the change in him and drew the garment around her by holding it tightly in the back. It molded her thighs and waist, and she became coy and moved closer to him. "I'm so happy you brought these," she said and suddenly threw her arms about him and began to kiss him. He stopped her but continued to hold her soft body in his arms. "I have nothing but that torn dress,'' she continued, with a bolder gaze, "and I was going about half-naked.'' She was standing against him, pushing hard, and he permitted it.

He didn't move, enjoying the thrust of her body, and he could feel his arousal. She looked up at him with her puppy eyes, dark with her passion and pleading for him to take her.

"Let me stay here, with you," she whispered. "There's no place I can go. You want me to stay; I can feel it. Please . . ." Her mouth was open and she licked her lips.

He was frozen in his indecision, and he could not resolve the struggle raging within him. She was embracing him ardently, and, despite himself, he tightened his arms.

"Please . . ." She was breathless.

The single word broke the dam, and he gathered her in his arms and carried her to the bed. With a wide sweep of his hand, he cleared it, the dresses falling to the floor, and he laid her gently upon the straw pallet. He was on his knees before her, and she still clung to him, her face flushed with expectancy and with a poignancy that aroused him fully. He broke away from her, unbuckled his trousers, pulled off his boots, and stretched out beside her. His hands fumbled beneath the dress and he gathered it up. She moved, with delight, into his strong arms.

The next morning, Parenti sent his monks through the encampment and woke the men from the stupor of their celebration. They were ordered to attend Peter's mass, where they writhed under the lash of the Hermit's fury. They cringed when he talked of what he called the murder of Selim's inhabitants; he warned them of the wrath of God and predicted that King Caloman would send an army of vengeance; and they became terror-stricken. There was only one way they could be saved—run to the river and cross. They were to break camp immediately—the river was only a half day's march—and pray that the Hungarian army would remain on this side. Woe to anyone who dawdled.

"Pick ten men," Leo told Turgot, "and keep them in the rear to stay with Tafur's men, and they can give us warning."

Leo counted off ten more. "These are for you, Burel. Ride to the river and search for boats—any kind. We'll use them to ferry people across. Send two men up river and two down river to look for shallows for the carts and wagons." When Burel and his men were gone, he told the rest of the guard, "Spread out the line of the march and push everyone along. I will ride the line, if you need me." The men hurried off.

He wheeled his horse and made for the Swabian camp. Soon he was in conference with their leaders, and the Swabians and Rhinelanders, with their axes, headed for a small forest. They singsang to each other as they felled the trees, stripped the branches, and carried the logs to the riverbanks. The logs were lashed into rafts and were soon put to use hauling Crossbearers over the river. Burel found a large ferry-raft, and the small carts were run up on it and moved across; the larger vehicles were sent to the shallows further up river.

The waters ran swiftly and deep, and the current spun the swimming horses and oxen about as they struggled with the wagons, capsizing many, and the vehicles broke up as they smashed against each other. The flotsam spun in the eddies and floated in the pools.

Leo rode through the hubbub and checked on his men as they directed the traffic. He found Ruth's wagon mired in the churning mud. The old bawd was whipping the straining horses and shouting curses at them in her rage. The animals foamed at the mouth and twisted their muscles, but the wagon remained mired.

Leo yelled at the bawd, "Stop beating the horses; you'll kill them!" He rode alongside. "Where's Ruth?"

"Can't you help us?" Nina screamed at him.

"I'll get some men. Leave the horses alone." He galloped off.

He suddenly remembered Mary. She was alone, somewhere in the pushing crowd, and he kicked his horse as he began his search for her, forgetting Ruth's problem.

He finally found her as she sat with the wagon near the river's bank, desolately watching the churning waters. The wagon suddenly lurched forward. "*DON'T!*" he screamed. "*MARY!* " He fought his way through the crowd, praying he could reach her before she drove the horse into the water.

Unexplainably, she heard him and stood up to find him in the mad, chaotic crowd. "*LEO! WHERE ARE YOU!*"

He managed to get through to her. "Why didn't you wait for me?" he chided her.

"Where were you?" There was relief and accusation in her voice. "I waited and waited. Everyone was leaving. I had to go, too."

He was off the horse and holding her close, and she was trembling with anxiety and fear.

"Stay here and don't try to move the wagon," he ordered her. "I'll put you on one of the big rafts. I'll be right back."

She nodded. "Don't be long." There was a tremor in her tone.

He came back with four of his men; he could not find an immediate spot for her on a raft, and he was going to try to ford the river. As he approached, the horse reared and headed for the water, the wagon bouncing behind it.

With a yell, Leo was after it, his men following, and he pulled himself into the driver's seat. Mary, frightened, had hung onto the side. Before Leo could seize the reins, the vehicle was sliding down the muddy bank, pushing the horse into the water. The animal floundered and tried to swim, but it was caught in its tracks, and the current captured the wagon and turned it lazily about, pulling the struggling animal with it. The wagon began a slow, continuous spin as it moved downstream. But Leo, holding Mary, had managed to jump free of it at the water's edge.

"All our things," Mary wailed.

"Why did the horse take off that way?" demanded Leo.

"I don't know," she wailed. "What are we going to do? All our things."

"We'll get others," he snapped. "Right now, I have to get you on a raft." He suddenly remembered. "Ruth! Come on; I'll take you to her. You'll all go together."

The large rafts built by the axemen were already in service, and the crusaders were moving across the river with the aid of teams of swimming animals and men poling at the sides. The Swabians worked frantically, building the rafts as thousands of Crossbearers needed to be ferried. Ruth stopped a gang carrying new-cut logs.

"Build me a raft to carry my wagon and I will pay you in gold."

The leader of the group appraised her wagon. "It is too large. We need the wood."

"You can do it," she insisted. "Ten pieces of gold for all of you." He shook his head. "Fifteen," she said desperately.

He laughed. "It's too big. Leave it here. Buy another one on the other side."

"No!" she said wildly. "It must go across! Twenty! Gold!"

The man shrugged. "Keep your gold." He ordered his men off, wiggling his buttocks suggestively at her. They all laughed and moved on, jabbering at her offer.

"Buffoon! Vulture!" The bawd shrieked at him. "May your man's staff weaken and bend! The Lord will smite you!"

Nina had seen Leo and screamed at him. "Where have you been? No one wants to help us!"

Ruth, her hair wild, her clothes spattered with mud, cursed at the wagon when Mary turned to her and wailed, "We lost everything. It's all in the river."

"Aw, shut up!" Ruth snapped, her eyes fired in her anger.

Leo ordered his men to hitch their horses to the rear axle, and slowly the wagon was freed from its bed. He stopped a gang of axemen and spoke with their leader, and the Swabians, after a moment of talking, nodded their heads and began the task of making a special raft. The logs were cut slightly longer than the vehicle; the horses were taken out of their shafts, and the shaft was tied high against the driver's seat. Then the logs were lashed under the frame and around the large wheels. Ruth provided the sheets for the lashings.

The Swabians were building an ark, using the wagon itself as a housing. When it was finished, the entire structure was pulled and dragged across the mud and launched into the river. The swimming animals pulled; the men steered and poled. Finally, it reached the other side and mired itself into the mud.

The men jumped into the waist-high water and cut the logs loose. They pushed, grunted, and swore as they dragged the wagon clear, aided by the animals, and after the horses were hitched up, the wagon rolled clear from the river's edge. Ruth and the others, waiting and watching from the other shore, called out in joy and danced together. Later, they boarded a raft and were ferried across.

The crossing of the thousands of Crossbearers took a long time, and as it proceeded in chaotic and disordered anarchy, a detachment of King Caloman's army was rumored to be engaged in a battle with Tafur's men in the rear. Panic seized those who were still waiting for the rafts. The rider who had brought the news to Leo had shouted it out, but the people around him had heard only one part of what he had said and that part spread widely. True, the Hungarians had sent a patrol; true, Tafur had attacked it; but untrue that there was a battle.

"Tafur killed every one of them," he reported to Leo. "He stretched a rope across the road, and when the patrol galloped up, the ribalds pulled the rope taut, tripping the horses." He laughed, remembering. "We fell upon the riders and . . . whiff . . . it was over."

There was a sudden loud cry from the crusaders on the rafts as the guardsmen spoke. "*SOLDIERS! ON THE RIVER!*"

A flotilla of five boats had appeared. Each had six rowers and ten soldiers with conical helmets and shields of iron-studded leather. Their chests were covered with iron breastplates over heavy leather foundations, and they carried short bows and a full quiver of arrows on their shoulders. Short swords were strapped to their sides. As they neared the first raft, a soldier at the bow of the first boat drew his sword and began shouting and waving his sword, indicating the bank of the river the host was leaving. The rowers feathered their oars, and the other soldiers stood up and placed arrows in their small, ram's-horn bows, on the ready.

The soldier-captain shouted again and again in a strange tongue, but no one understood him, and he became more and more exasperated and angry. Finally, he barked an order to his men. Like a small swarm of bees, the arrows flew over the heads of the crusaders on the nearest raft. He waved his sword rapidly and jabbed it emphatically toward the Hungarian shore, but with a shrug, the Crossbearers proceeded on their way.

Suddenly, the arrows were whirring, and they found marks in the men poling the raft. With cries of pain, men were falling and bloodying the water, and a wail of despair went up from the Crossbearers. The attack went on and more men fell.

Riding the river's current and pushed on by husky Rhinelanders, two rafts turned and headed toward the flotilla. The oarsmen rowed furiously to prevent a crash, but the Rhinelanders were bent upon a collision and counter-maneuvered. The soldiers of the other boats sent barrage after barrage of arrows against the attacking crusaders, and men fell, but the rafts did not alter their course.

Two more rafts, guided by Swabians, their axes gripped firmly, set out from the Hungarian shore. The first boat was rammed, the soldiers and rowers dumped into the river, and, as they floundered, the Swabians came alongside them. The axes rose and fell; each time an axe descended a man would disappear, and the water around would turn red. Some soldiers managed to break away and swim toward shore, but only one staggered out safely.

As the rafts approached the boats, the crusaders leaped into the bouncing craft and their axes flailed. The archers could not use their bows, and their small swords were swept aside as though they were thin sticks. The rowers were easy game; those who did not leap into the water were killed and their bodies hurled overboard. As each boat was captured, it was cleared and rowed to shore.

Of all the men who had tried to swim to safety, only two were successful. They were captured and brought before Peter. The monk, angry and vengeful, his patriarchal beard shaking, shouted at the captives. *"WE ARE CHRISTIANS! WE WEAR THE CROSS!"* He jabbed at the red strips sewn onto the shoulder of his cloak. *"ARE YOU HEATHENS?"* His eyes were bulged in his anger.

One soldier cowered in fear, but the other carefully placed two fingers against the cloth cross, pressed it, and withdrew them to kiss them.

"Ah . . ." said Peter. "You are Christian?"

The man's face lit up; his eyes widened in understanding and eagerness. He tapped his chest. "Christian," he repeated, beaming.

"God tests us in many ways," said Peter. "Why did you kill us?"

The man shook his head; he understood nothing. He spoke rapidly in a foreign tongue, pointed to himself, his comrade, the river, then uttered the one word he knew. "Christian."

Parenti, who stood next to Peter, snarled, "He is pretending so we will not kill him. He recognizes the cross and plays on our sympathies. We should kill them both for spilling Christian blood."

"Kill them! Kill them!" The cry went up from those who had crowded around. Peter tried to quiet them, but they would not be stilled.

Parenti's voice came through the din, "They have sinned before God! They must die!" And the others echoed his words.

Two Rhinelanders, standing next to Peter, wielded their axes in delight and felled the men with single strokes. The blood spurted on Peter and Parenti before they could get out of the way.

"Stop!" Peter yelled, but it was too late. He stood in shock as he stared at his stained cloak, then whispered harshly, "We drown ourselves in Christian blood." His face was gray as stone. "It shall not wash easily from our souls," he said with melancholy. He began the whispering of the last rites; the crowd hushed but raised their heads as they heard the gallop of horsemen.

Leo and another mounted man drew up. A glance told the squire what had happened. "Why did you kill them?" he shouted. "These are not Hungarians!"

"They were demons masquerading as Christians," retorted Parenti. "Meddle not in affairs beyond your ken."

"You fool! They are mercenaries of Emperor Alexius of Byzantium! You have killed Christians!"

"That is how they hide!" Parenti was wild.

Leo was off his horse. "Here!" he said to Peter. "Talk to this man. He speaks Greek and Frankish; he is an officer; we caught him when he came out of the river."

"Is this true?" demanded Peter. "You are from Byzantium?"

"Yes." He stood straight and military. "I am Captain Bayenko. I am the officer in charge of the river patrol which guards the boundary between King Caloman's land and Byzantium."

"And you kill Christians who cross here?"

"My orders are to permit no one to cross until they are examined on the other side. We were coming to talk to you when we found you already on the river and across it. I tried to wave your rafts back, but your people disobeyed me."

"We could not understand you," Leo interjected:

"I speak five different tongues. I called out in all of them."

"You are Turks . . ." began Parenti.

"Yes, Betchenaks. We fight for the Basileus. We guard the frontiers."

"Turks are Moslem—Infidels!" Parenti was triumphant. "You kill Christians!" He fingered his cross.

The officer stared at him. "Some of us are Moslem; some are Christian. I am Christian."

"How did you know we were here?" asked Peter.

"We found broken wagons, dead horses and animals, even people, below the falls. We have heard about Selim. We feared that there was blood-vengeance in you, so we came in force to inspect you. But we did not expect a battle."

"If you are Turks, how is it you speak our language?" asked Leo.

"I have served with others from your country," replied the captain. "We have much time on the frontiers, and we teach each other the different tongues. If we are not fighting, there is little to do."

Peter took a deep breath. They were safe; Byzantium meant they were in Christian lands; the Hungarians would not cross the river; Emperor Alexius, the Basileus, would help them.

"Can we secure supplies in Beograd? Are there many soldiers there?" Leo had his mind set on his two problems: he needed a new wagon for Mary, and the guard.

"There are supplies," said the captain, "but I don't know who is there now. General Ducas moves us to suit his needs."

Ducas? General Ducas? The name nagged at Leo; he had heard it somewhere before. He tried but could not remember.

"The crossing is almost finished," he said to Peter. "I will leave the captain with you; I think we will need a camping area."

Peter nodded. "Yes, we will have to dry out. Many have not had a good crossing. I will talk more with Captain Bayenko."

Leo rode off, his mind on his problem of a wagon. He did not care for the idea that Mary was staying with Ruth, but there was no other place until the host reached Beograd. He would have to ask Peter for the money . . . although Ruth had gold and he had saved her wagon . . . perhaps he would ask her.

29

Beograd (Belgrade)—outer edge of Byzantium; invaded by the Celts, the Romans, the Goths, the Franks, the Bulgars, and now in the hands of the Byzantines; trade center and fulcrum for the east-west caravans; where the wind blows two ways and the Danube turns east.

There was a strange stillness over the fertile plain as the crusaders plodded the dusty road toward the city. No animals grazed in the fields, and no women worked the small gardens near the farmhouses, picture-neat in the simmering heat. Chickens, ducks, and geese wandered the yards, but no children ran to watch the Crossbearers' column wend its way past their homes. Dogs barked, but no one came to see the reason. Where was everyone? became the question on every mind. Always there had been onlookers. Why not before Beograd?

"Maybe you shouldn't bother. I'll stay with Ruth," said Mary cuttingly. "You're hurting me." And she pulled her arm free from Leo's gripping hand.

"I'm sorry," he said, but he did not act grievous. They had argued all morning in a roundelay of stubbornness that brooked no opposition. He was irritated, put out by Mary's unwillingness to be reasonable. "I'll get a wagon in the city, Peter will give me the money. You'll see."

"Peter doesn't give money," she said scornfully. "He takes it. You could have brought what we needed from Selim, if you wanted to," she threw at him. "Look what Chagon got for Inda."

"We would have lost it in the river, anyhow," he said wearily. But they did need a wagon, he thought, and everything else. They had nothing but what they were wearing and his horse and saddle. Everything had been lost; he would have to change the situation.

"In two days, we'll be in Beograd. We can get everything we need. I'll buy you the prettiest dress in the whole world, I promise you."

"With what?" The bitterness remained, but the edge of her anger dulled. She knew she should not act this way, but she could not stop herself. "You never have money for anything we need. Peter gives you just enough to keep us alive. Everyone else makes extra coppers—even silver—but not you." She was contrite, buried in her accusations.

"Just wait," he said, tight-lipped. "When we reach the infidel lands I'll bring you all the riches you ever dreamed about. You'll have the finest dresses of lace and satins, not wool and burlap. There will be rings for your fingers and a silver—no, gold—necklace for your neck. And I'll find bracelets with rubies and diamonds for your hands." His arms encircled her waist and she yielded reluctantly. "We'll have a beautiful house with Moslem servants to do your bidding, and we'll walk in our garden of beautiful flowers and fig trees." He kissed her on the neck, nuzzling her, and she laughed, pleasured. His pressing hands caressed her, and she awoke to his ardent touch, her lips responding to his.

"I didn't want to be so mean," she whispered.

"I know," he whispered back. "We've just had our first set-to."

"We did?" She leaned back in his arms, acting surprised.

"We did," he said firmly. His hand slid along her side and cupped her breast. "We shouldn't argue anymore; we'll find a way."

"I know we will." She wiggled her pelvis against his. "I don't want to stay with Ruth anyway; there's too much traffic." Her eyes became mischievous. "We can't do anything."

"You have something in mind?" he asked innocently.

"Ummm." Her eyes shone. "If we fight, we have to make up."

"What about the traffic?"

"There won't be any for a while."

Later, he rode sleepily in his saddle as his horse trudged monotonously beside Ruth's wagon. His mind was blurry; first thing he needed was a wagon . . . and everything else . . . pots . . . bed . . . clothes . . . everything. Traffic with Ruth . . . Peter would give money . . . Guizio would help him . . .

Turgot woke him with disturbing news: Tafur was raiding the deserted farmhouses, searching for loot—building supplies, he called it. Turgot had tried to stop him but left when the "king" had threatened open violence; and now the looting was spreading; the men of the other camps had joined the ribalds.

Leo became angrier by the moment. He ordered Turgot to remain on guard at Ruth's wagon and set off for the ribald camp. He found Little John driving the "king's" wagon and Guizio riding alongside the boy, drunk and singing loudly.

"Where's Tafur?" he demanded.

Guizio peered at him with watery eyes. "Izzat you, Leo?" He hiccuped, and his head bobbed from side to side as he tried to focus on the blurry horseman. "Shtand shtill, Leo, sho I can shee you," he demanded. "You—you mo-ove tooo-o mush." He chortled.

"Where's Tafur?"

"Itch Leo," Guizio told Little John. "Shay h'lo to Leo."

"Tafur isn't here, Squire Leo," said Little John.

"Heish out!" Guizio exclaimed triumphantly. "Heish alwaysh out . . .

alwaysh . . . gone . . .'' He waved his arm broadly. "Away, tcho bring mo'
wine." He shook his head knowingly and picked up his singing again:

> *"OH-HO-O-O-O-O . . .*
> *DE GOL' ISH GOO-OD*
> *AN' DE SHIL-VAH ISH FINE*
> *AN' DE WIMMEN ISH ROU' . . .''*

Leo wheeled his horse and galloped to the head of the procession to Peter.
"Our people are looting again," he told the monk. "I think we should camp
and you should talk to them."

"We are close to Beograd," said Parenti. "It can wait." He looked toward
the captured Betchenak for confirmation.

"Prince Nichita rules these lands; he is Bulgar," said the captain. "He
has pledged loyalty to Emperor Alexius, but he will not stand idly by while
his people are being plundered. If you don't stop your crusaders, he will send
his militia against you."

"How soon to the city?" asked Leo.

"Not far. Maybe an hour's march."

Peter considered. "We will stop at the city walls."

A ribald contingent were the first to enter the open gates of Beograd, and
they wandered through the empty, silent streets with the puzzled realization
that the city was deserted. They heard only their own voices, and Tafur, fearing
an ambush, ordered his men to move cautiously. They advanced slowly, from
door to door; but there was no one.

The "king" scratched his head. "Maybe they're waiting for us in one of
the squares, like in Selim. Let's try a house."

The door was locked so they broke in. There were signs of hasty packing,
broken dishes on the floor, clothes scattered, empty places on shelves and
cupboards.

"Into the rooms," Tafur ordered. "Find someone."

They found no one. But they found a trapdoor into a root cellar, and they
found wine.

"*Tafur!*" Someone called from the street. The ribald came out of the house
and found three of his men, swords drawn, standing over a cowering, terrified
native.

"Where is everyone?" Tafur demanded of him.

The man squeaked a rapid answer which was incomprehensible. A ribald
raised his sword, and the native cried out, raised his forearm to shield himself,
and cringed further in the dust. He motioned frantically with his free hand.

Tafur, brows knit, said, "He's pointing toward the gates. Take him there
and if you can't get anything else out of him, kill him." To his other men,

he said, "Try some more houses. Spread out and see what you can find. We'll get some wagons."

They found the doors barred and they broke them down. But they found no people, and they began their search for gold.

After establishing their camps, the Crossbearers entered the city and wandered the barren streets. Word spread quickly that Beograd was deserted and there were goods in the houses. The crusaders drove empty carts through the gates, ready for plunder and spoil. There were some natives—those too old and sick to run—and they killed them. Although Peter ranted and raved at them, there was no halting their avaricious greed, and for two days they searched through the houses and picked them clean. Their avidity carried them into the cellars, and they broke into the walls as they searched for secret hiding places. Looters filled their carts, rushed back to the encampment to dump their findings, and hurried back to the stricken city to reload again. Every house was despoiled.

Leo rode through the gate alone on the first day, determined to find a wagon and household goods. He had not talked to Peter about money, for Tafur had told him he didn't need any—everything was there for the taking. On a side street, in a yard, he found a covered vehicle—the first he had seen—and decided it would have to do. There was a harness in the barn, but no horse, so he hitched his own between the wagon's shafts.

The house was small, but well-kept, with a flower garden on one side and some low bushes in front. The door was unlatched. The room he entered was clean, with pretty decorations, and there were shiny copper pots and oily, black-iron pans in the kitchen. Everything was neat and in place, as though the owners had merely stepped out for a short while.

He gathered everything from the kitchen, including the clean, clay dishes and brightly polished knives and spoons, and put them into the wagon. In the bedroom was a large bed with a rag-and-down mattress, soft as warm butter, and he took it out. In a standing chest were hanging coats, heavy winter garments lined with sheepskin, and other coarse, wool overcoats. He threw the heavy coats out, keeping the lighter wear, and took the chest to the wagon. There were three other chests to search.

The first had a large, down-feather quilt and down pillows. Beneath these were folded some wool blankets. When he opened the second chest, he gasped in disbelief. It was full of women's clothes: petticoats, coverings, stockings, shoes, cotton underwear, and other things he had never seen before. All were folded, clean, and neatly stacked. But it was the third chest which took his breath away. Dresses! Skirts and embroidered blouses! He could picture Mary's incredulous face when he placed all this before her. In high glee, he carried everything to the wagon.

When he was finished, he walked through the house again and debated with himself whether to take this or that, when he noticed an odd piece of finely tooled leather, soft to the touch, flush with the wall. It appeared to have no purpose; it was behind the spot where the headboard of the bed had been. He pried it out with his knife and found a casket behind it. Anticipating something precious, his hands trembled as he opened the carved, wooden cover.

Gold! And jewelry! Precious stones which glittered and sparkled like colored, heavenly stars. He touched them reverently, then snapped the cover down quickly and glanced furtively about, as though he suspected he was being watched.

He giggled at his fear and, with an air of bravado, pushed the box under his arm and sauntered out. He mounted the wagon and drove rapidly away, guilt, fear, and happiness churning within him.

No one, he told himself, was to know about the gems and the gold, not even Mary. People would see the wagon and Mary's new things, but the precious jewels would have to remain hidden. Maybe, he reconsidered, he could give Mary one piece—the necklace. He stopped the wagon and took the piece out of the box, quickly hiding the casket again. As he whipped the horse, he fantasized.

He would conduct Mary on a tour of the wagon and she would "ooh" and "ahh." The pots would shine and sparkle, and she would be appreciative of the fine bed—she hated his straw pallet—and fine wool blankets and embroidered coverlets. He knew she would seat herself on the bed to test it, and her face would be all smiles. Then he would open the first chest and show her the outer garments he had found. That would not be so impressive, for it was warm and there was no need of them during the summer. But wait until he opened the other chests!

He could hear her gasp in surprise, and he could see her flushed excitement on her cheeks as she picked through the clothes. He would have to sit quietly by and be very patient as she tried on the dresses and preened herself before him. He would have to tell her how beautiful she looked in everything. But when he handed her the necklace! He could not imagine her delight.

Jewelry was always an easy way to her heart. She would be ecstatic and dance for joy. He was sure of it.

He found her sitting by Ruth's wagon mending an old dress. She looked up as he approached and jumped to her feet. "You've found a wagon!" she exclaimed, but her face puckered immediately. "It's so *small*. Weren't there any larger ones?"

"This was the best of the lot," he told her with a grin. "What did you expect—one like Ruth's?" He climbed down. "But there are a number of good things about it, especially if you look inside."

Inside, there was an offhand air of disapproval as she peered about. She was cursory with the kitchenware and only slightly more fulsome over the bed and covers, and she said, "Is that all you managed to get?" She threw the blankets aside. "These are hot."

He experienced a twinge of anger but suppressed it quickly. Piqued, he opened the chests. Her mouth dropped and her hands flew to cover it. Her eyes became orbital stars, and she became petrified after she let out a squeal. She sank to her knees and buried her arms in the fabric.

"Leo! Where did you ever? Mother of God! Look at this!" She pulled a dress out and examined it. "Leo! How . . . I could kiss you forever!" She threw herself at him.

After enduring her kisses, he pushed her away. "Wait. I have something more." But she did not hear him, delighting in the examination of each thing she pulled from the chest.

"Look at this! And this one!" She pulled them from the chest one after the other and held them against herself. She threw them at him and picked up another, each one better than the one before. Suddenly, she stopped. "Look . . . at . . . this . . . one!" It took her breath away.

Lacy and frilly, with a sheen, satin undergarment of pure white, it was the perfect bridal gown. "You must have raided a castle," she said breathlessly. "This is for a lady . . ." The thought excited her. "I'm your lady and you're my knight!" she announced. And she held the dress closely and tried to curtsy.

Leo took her extended arm and bowed at the waist. He raised her. "Wait, my lady, I have something more for you, but first a kiss." She complied quickly.

"What else?" she said quickly. When he didn't reply, she stamped her foot, "Leo! Tell me!"

"Another kiss?"

"Even a thousand." She flew at him.

"Enough, enough!" he protested and pushed her back. "Would you smother me?"

"I will if you don't tell me right away."

He dangled the necklace before her.

She was speechless again. When her breath returned, she reached for it slowly. "Oh, my dear Jesus . . . my dear Mother of God . . . where did you get this? It must have been a count's castle . . ." Her joy was turning to fear as she turned a quizzical face toward him. "It must belong to some baron's lady." Her eyes swept everything. "All of this. He'll come after it."

"Where will he look?" He was cocky. "There are thousands of wagons. But don't worry; it wasn't a lord—or anything—only a small cottage."

"Only a duke could own these things, even if it was a cottage. Who else? He'll recognize the wagon. He'll send soldiers."

Her comments made him pause. What if she were right? he thought. "We'll change the wagon and he'll never find us. We'll be leaving Beograd soon; he'll never catch us." He dismissed it. "Here, let me put it on and see you in it."

She held her breath as he closed the catch behind her neck, and her hand raised the end of the loop. The light reflected from the large, center ruby and she gaped at it. She turned a serious and frightened face to Leo. "I'd . . . I'd be afraid to wear it. It's so beautiful . . . so shiny . . ."

"We'll put it away and wear it only on special occasions," he whispered. "We'll put most of this away."

She nodded and soberly gathered the garments off the floor. Carefully, she packed everything back into the chests, her hands fondling the cloth. Finally done, she closed the chests and looked at him. "Oh, Leo!" She was in his arms; she clung to him, her face buried in his chest.

"Shall we try our new bed?" he whispered. She nodded. He reached down and carried her to their new, soft mattress.

For four days, the host reveled in their newfound riches, celebrating with huge sheep and pig roasts, and wine. The city was denuded; every house had been entered and everything within it which anyone wanted, taken. The storage bins of the city's food traders had been full, and the provisions were distributed to every cart and wagon. Well fed and content, the Crossbearers broke camp and turned south along the banks of a tributary of the Danube, for the big river had veered northeast. The Byzantine captain had become their reluctant guide.

Inda glanced covertly at Chagon as he drove his covered cart in silence. Ever since the day he had made love to her, his unhappiness had increased and she didn't know why; she had tried so hard to show him that she knew how to act as a woman should, but he had not touched her since. Everyone treated her with respect, but she knew they feared his wrath, and they took for granted that she had become his woman.

The life within her was stirring, and she was troubled because she had no one to confide in. Last night, Chagon had watched her closely, not the usual casual glances he gave her, and he had remarked that she was filling out—as a young girl should, he had said—but there was something knowing in his voice. If he didn't lay with her again, would just one time convince him? Anzgot's wife had said once would be enough; Chagon would marry her. She pondered the problem anxiously. Would he believe her if she told him the child was his? What if he didn't?

Mary! Maybe she could talk to Mary. She was married and she should know, even though she wasn't with child herself. But what if Mary talked to Squire Leo . . . and he talked to Chagon? No. There were too many complexities for her mind to absorb, and she listened to the plodding of the horse as it walked slowly in the heat. She could feel the weight of Chagon's silence.

Chagon's inner turmoil asserted itself in an infrequent spasm. Inda's newly acquired plumpness, he knew, had not come from food, she ate so little, pecking at her meal with indifference. She delighted more in watching him eat and waited impatiently for his compliments on her cooking. Yet, there was a rounding of her belly, and he could swear that the area around the nipples of her breasts had darkened. The more he thought of it, the greater became his certainty: she was with child, his child. But could it have happened so soon? Surprisingly, the thought excited him. He would have a son! He would marry her!

He smacked his lips and cleared his throat, signaling he wanted to talk. "I have been thinking of something, Inda." Moments passed and Inda thought she would die before he spoke again. "I think . . ." He faltered. "Perhaps, it would be a good thing . . . if we were married." Inda's heart leaped. "You could live with me. I'll talk to Brother Peter."

"You will ma—marry me?" she stammered.

He nodded solemnly. "Tonight. After we make camp."

He did not ask what she thought, but she did not care. With her, a thousand angels sang, and she had become alive. She snuggled happily under his arm.

He looked down at her and smiled.

30

Emperor Alexius dismissed the courier with an imperious wave of his hand, and when the soldier was gone, he nodded to the two men who stood before him.

"Well, John? Symeon?" He did not wait for an answer. "Urban has sent us his offal. They sacked Selim, and now they have plundered Beograd. Tens of thousands of mendicants, all wearing the cross of Jesus, say they are marching to Jerusalem to free the Holy Sepulchre with their prayers. A monk called Peter leads them. The rest you heard." His brows knitted. "We have a problem."

"They have had a taste of spoil," said John. "Unless we prevent it, they will loot every town and hamlet along the way. We must deal with them promptly."

"They certainly cannot be allowed into the city," said Symeon. "We do not have enough soldiers to contain them."

"My sentiments, too, gentlemen," said Alexius. "But we have more than this rabble to contemplate. Duke Godfrey of Lorraine and his two brothers bring thousands of knights and soldiers on his march to our Imperial City. With him are his clods and louts."

He turned his face to the Marmora where the fishing fleet rode the soft, undulating waves with peaceful serenity. "We asked for a few fighting men, and Urban is drowning us with his starry-eyed believers and the dregs and vermin of his city streets. With his knights come the caitiffs and boors of the countryside." He faced the two men. "I would appreciate your thoughts."

"We could funnel them across the straits as they arrive . . ." began Symeon.

"We cannot be so offhand with the great barons," interrupted John. "More diplomacy is necessary. But with this mendicant monk, we can shuffle him and his peasants to the citadel where we sent those few knights who told us about him. How much time do we have before they reach the city?"

"Three weeks—a month at most, according to the information," said Alexius. "Prince Nichita has sent word that he will not tolerate the looting of Beograd, and he is preparing to attack the looters and recover their spoil. If we allow it, we will have a massacre on our hands."

He turned his head to gaze over the Imperial City, his city. The white walls and stone-covered flat roofs of the buildings were blinding in the bright sunlight, and he pinched his eyebrows to see the water, the dancing, sparkling waters of the Marmora. He had asked for an army but he was receiving an invasion. With sudden decision, he made up his mind.

"Symeon, I believe you should meet with Nichita and stay his hand. Duke Godfrey marches the same route as this Peter, and if something happened to the monk and his rabble, Godfrey may interpret it as a signal that he is unwelcome. A wrong attitude might develop as a result. We will suffer the bad to receive the good, in this case."

"Nichita will want something for changing his mind," said Symeon.

"We can offer to strip the plunder from the peasants, but without a battle," John suggested.

Alexius smiled. "Not a bad idea, if we can accomplish that, but Nichita might be seeking revenge also."

"He cannot handle so large a host without our help; his militia is not strong enough," said John. "We can point out that we can guarantee a peaceful passage through his lands. This host could devastate it if left unfettered. He will bargain."

"That sounds reasonable," said Alexius thoughtfully. "Symeon, offer him peace, with our guarantee to provision these beggars to prevent further looting. Of course, strip them of what they plundered at Beograd."

Symeon bowed his head. "That will be done. I will need to deploy at least two regiments and a contingent of bowmen. Using Nichita's militia, we can herd the crusaders here, and once they arrive, we can ferry them across the straits."

"So be it," Alexius confirmed. "Take what you need; the supply arrangements will be made. Let Nichita strip them, and if he is still dissatisfied, tell him we will make it up to him some other way. Go with God."

Symeon bowed. "Thank you, sire. It will be done."

"Tens of thousands . . . peasants . . . marching across Europe . . . for the sake of the Lord . . ." Alexius shook his head in wonder. "Truly, the Lord works in mysterious ways. We ask for knights and he sends us these . . . rabble. We have tens of thousands of our own; wherefore need we more?" He was locked into his own world.

"Perhaps, sire," said John quietly, "he tests our patience."

"Perhaps," Alexius nodded, "and I hope it is not more than that."

31

Horsemen! Soldiers! Bowmen, with arrows nocked in their bowstrings! On the right riverbank; in a concaved arc curled over the left side of the road; up over the rising hill. Peter's forward guard halted in consternation. Bayenko rose in his stirrups and uttered one word when he saw them: "Bulgars!"

In the middle of the road, astride his black horse, was an armored knight, his sword across his knees. Behind him, on a dappled mare, was a gentleman in a reddish-purple cape-coat trimmed with white fur around the collar and down in front. A head lappet of the same color, with a short string of pearls in front, was on his head, and his black, oiled boots shone in the sunlight. Beside him, on a huge, brown stallion, was a huge soldier whose long, blond hair blossomed out beneath his conical helmet, and the helm sported a plume of stringy horsehair. His ring-mail shirt was bright as starlight, and he wore long and short swords at his sides. He sat erect, his eyes narrow slits, as he watched Peter's guardsmen closely.

Leo had been riding behind Peter, and he spurred his horse forward to discover the reason for the sudden halt. He viewed the scene in dismay. The host was in a trap, with no possible escape except into the river.

He stared at the men in the road: the knight, the gentleman, the soldier . . . The large soldier? He sucked in his breath; his mouth opened in sudden recognition; he gasped! Skora? he questioned himself. "Skora," he shouted aloud. He was certain! "*SKORA!*" he screamed and spurred his horse. "*SKORA!*" he screamed again and rode pell-mell at the mercenary.

The mercenary moved forward immediately, his sword drawn and raised, and he called out, "No further! Halt!"

Leo reined his horse up sharply. "Skora!" he shouted. "It's me! Leo! Leo Cannelli! From Genoa!"

"Cannelli?" the deep voice questioned. Skora hesitated for the eternity of a moment, then boomed out, "Stay where you are!" He spurred his horse forward and met Leo face to face, but he showed no recognition. "I know a Cannelli from Genoa, but who are you?"

"I'm Leo, Favio Cannelli's son. I led you to the inn. Don't you remember? I brought you horses . . ."

"The boy . . ." Skora exploded. His lowered brows rose in sudden recognition. "The boy! But you are a man! What are you doing here?"

"I'm a Crossbearer; leader of the guardsmen," the words spilled out in his excitement. "We go to Jerusalem to free the Holy Sepulchre. What are all these soldiers?"

Skora ignored the question. "Come with me," he ordered.

They rode back to the two men in the road, and Skora addressed the gentleman. "Honorable General, I know this man. He is the son of my former comrade. He can give you much information."

General Symeon Phoacus stared at Leo. "Further on this road is a large plain. Have your people make their camps there." He turned to the knight. "Do you agree, milord?"

"Yes, Honorable General," said Prince Nichita, tilting his head.

Phoacus returned to Skora. "Tell your acquaintance to take a message to the monk called Peter. Inform him where his people are to camp; that there is to be no divergence from the road by any wagon, for any reason; and that after he is settled, I will call on him. Your men will lead them, captain."

"Yes, Honorable," snapped Skora, his voice flat and cold. He translated the general's words quickly to Leo, then added his own admonition. "Have your people do exactly as the general ordered. He will not tolerate disobedience. No mistakes. Now, go."

Leo nodded and hurried to Peter. The monk listened and sighed in relief. "The Lord has saved us. Send your guardsmen through the procession, and see to it that everyone understands the order. These men are our friends."

There were deep horns calling from the back hills, and they signaled that the Bulgar lancers had closed in the rear of the Crossbearers' line. The slow procession, watched closely by the armed bowmen, moved on and into the large field to camp.

General Phoacus and his staff came to see Peter, and the general stared at the emaciated figure of the monk huddled in his chair. Truly, he thought, the Lord moves in wondrous ways. Here was little elegance and no bright, burning spiritual light; no aura of divine majesty; nor did any glimmer of holiness emanate from the dirty, half-dressed, tired old man slumped in his seat. He decided to be formal and told himself: Men such as these understand and obey direct orders best.

Phoacus addressed himself to his task. "These are the commands of Emperor Alexius, First Prelate of the Apostles of God . . ." and he carefully explained what he expected Peter to do.

Peter had no reservations. "The Lord has said, 'Thou shalt not steal,' " he proclaimed, "and all stolen goods must be returned. Further, we shall pray for the souls of all those who have been seduced by Satan. We welcome your aid and protection, and we extend our greetings to your illustrious emperor."

Parenti compressed his lips in disdain of what he considered Peter's groveling. He was more sensitive to the schism existing between the East Church and the West Church, and as soon as Skora had finished translating Peter's words, he addressed himself to Phoacus in Greek.

"I will speak directly to make sure that there will be no blurring of my meaning by faulty translation. We come as Christ's swords, and as Christ's avengers we will spill the blood of the infidel wherever he stands in our path. It grieves us to see your emperor aligned with them and protecting them. Your soldiers are Turks and other pagans."

Symeon smiled at the thin monk. "Our alliances are military, not spiritual," he said mildly. "But let me add, we have no need of spiritual correction from any western cleric."

"Your diplomacy creates strange friendships," Parenti continued, ignoring the jibe. "Fortunately, however, we do not have to deal in such cynical ways. Your military alliances are your own."

"So they are, monk. We find narrow minds breed high walls of ignorance, and for such as you we have monastery cells. Isolation inhibits agitation and allows a tormented soul the calmness of a meditated peace."

"Our stay in Constantinople will be brief," countered Parenti.

"In that we agree," said Phoacus smiling. He turned to Skora. "Tell the Hermit that the emperor, in his benevolence, will supply all the necessary food for the Crossbearers, and that you will be in command of the divestiture of all stolen property. We have a report that Captain Bayenko has been held captive. He is to report to you for assignment."

Skora translated rapidly; he added his own commands. "Your people will be asked to pass through checkpoints established by my men, and they will dispose of all goods not rightfully theirs. Soldiers will enter vehicles as they wish and conduct searches. We expect full cooperation."

"And you will have it," said Peter emphatically.

"Captain Bayenko is with you. Please send him to me."

"It shall be done."

Later, after a full report to General Phoacus, Skora said, "A mob of this size could become dangerous if provoked. Shall we be prepared for battle?"

"You are right, captain," nodded Phoacus. "The other monk is a fanatic and dangerous. These people have bloodied their axes at Selim and, if aroused, could do so again. Keep a watch on that man. Isolate him, if necessary."

Skora bowed. "Yes, sire."

That evening, Peter preached a sermon of appeasement and railed against the sin of Theft. Everyone knew of the Byzantine plans for the next morning, and the anger and resentment against the Turkish and Bulgar soldiers ran hot. Around the campfires, the arguments and curses were mixed, and many pulled steel blades to show their displeasure and boast of their resistance.

Leo and his men circulated the camps and tried to reason with those who became intense. They pointed to the futility of fighting, and slowly the bitterness turned to resignation: Let the pagans have their goods—for the present, but the time will come when the true believers would receive their due. Meanwhile, they would accept the Byzantine's bread.

Skora invited Leo to his tent, and the squire talked freely of his adventures since he had left home with Parenti to follow the Greek gentlemen. He told of the speech of Pope Urban at Clermont. Skora listened but was more impressed by the changes he saw in Leo. "Blood will always tell," he remarked. "I knew Favio could not father a litter runt. He would be proud of you."

Leo beamed with pleasure. "Sir Walter trained me as a squire," he said proudly, "and he promised to make me a Knight of the Sword."

"I would not want to discourage you, Leo, but it isn't that easy." The Viking shook his head. "Others must agree to the knighting, and your Sir Walter has no standing with the great lords who are coming. I warn you, this march to Jerusalem will not be easy; the Turk is a savage fighter. Stay with me and enlist in the emperor's forces. I will be your sponsor and there will be easy advancement. Alexius offers good pay and there is no place on earth like the Imperial City. You can have a good life here."

"I have vowed to fight for the Lord and I will keep my promise."

"That is honorable, but think of what I say. What will you do after the fighting is over and if you do capture Jerusalem?"

Leo shrugged. "I hadn't thought about it. Perhaps, I could enlist with you then."

The big man shook his head. "It will be too late; the time is now, before the others come, and before all the fighting begins. You have vowed but you have been blinded by just one sun of faith, and your youth and inexperience hold you in fetters. In the East you will find a different world. Sooner or later you will ask which is the One and True God: the God of Jesus or the God of Mohammed? Perhaps He is the same God—the God of the Jews."

Leo was shocked. "How can a Christian ask a question like that? There is only one God and Jesus is His Son."

Skora smiled as though humoring a child. "You do not understand. The Moslem worships the One and Only God, too. He says the words of Mohammed are God's words, and no Christian is more pious or more spiritual than a pious Moslem when he pleads for salvation. He seeks Heaven just as you do."

"But he does not know Christ," exclaimed Leo, "so he cannot be saved; he cannot go to Heaven."

"And the Christian does not know Mohammed so *he* cannot find his way to Paradise," said Skora mildly. "Each is sure that his way is the *only* way to Eternal Bliss. Is it possible that both can arrive at the same destination by following different roads?"

"Without Christ there can be no salvation," insisted Leo. "We are Christ's flame, His swords, His defenders! Tell me, Skora, why have you changed? Have you lost your faith?"

Skora chuckled. "I have my own way to my own Heaven. I still worship my pagan gods, beginning with Odin, so I can spill Moslem or Christian blood without a conscience. But just think of this: A Moslem slaughters a Christian in a *jihad*—a holy war—and believes that the act will assure his entrance to the

Seventh Paradise, and he is willing to die to get there; and the Christian kills the Infidel in a holy crusade and believes he will reach Heaven because of his action, for he is ready to die to liberate the Holy Sepulchre from profane hands. With both sides having such perfect belief, each kills the other in perfect happiness, certain of God's blessing, but it is difficult for one such as me to be so sure of your God's will.'' There was mockery in his voice.

"I have no difficulty at all," said Leo firmly.

Skora's massive head bobbed affirmatively. "Neither has any Moslem. It is always the believers who are so sure of your God's messages who have no difficulties, and it is they who add to all the earth's woes." He was grinning. "Odin does not speak to me so I never know His will. But enough of priest-talk; we have business. Tomorrow, I must relieve your people of their Beograd goods, and I expect your men will help me. Do they know this?"

"We will abide by Peter's word." His conviction was not as confident as his words. How was he to tell Mary that all was lost again? Suddenly, he had an idea. "How will you know what to take? We had goods before we came to Beograd."

"There lies my problem," sighed Skora. "You also have what you took from Selim. Some Bulgar property will be identifiable, but much will be missed—and there lies the point of argument. We do not wish to spill blood, so tell your people that our decisions will be final but just, whether they think so or not. And let them accept them as 'God's will' although . . ."—and he grinned—"it will be our will, working, of course, as 'God's instruments.' "

Leo's nod was solemn and he shifted uncomfortably in his chair. "We will keep the peace, but you will be taking what people need." He squirmed unhappily.

Skora contemplated Leo's gloom and he could read guilt on the young man's face. "Do I detect a personal problem?" he asked softly. Leo could not meet his eyes. "Is it important that you keep what you have?" he asked finally.

Leo, tortured by transgression and necessity, nodded. He felt like a small boy caught in a net of sin by his mother.

"How important?" Skora was insistent.

Leo tightened his clasped hands. "It . . . it would be . . . ." He paused, embarrassed and tongue-tied. "Things . . . there are clothes, for my wife . . . bedding . . . we lost everything in the river . . ." He twisted in his chair. "Even . . . even the wagon . . . It's impossible without the wagon . . ." He trailed off and stared into the distance, not daring to gaze at the Viking.

Skora absorbed the information quietly. "That is difficult," he finally said. "Have you changed the wagon?"

"Some of the cover . . . some paint . . ." he wandered off, into silence again, into an internal horizon.

"That may be enough to make it pass," said Skora slowly.

Leo's head came up quickly. Was the big man offering to help him? "We could return some clothes, some chests," he ventured.

"What is your camp section?"

"Toward the rear. I am with the Rhinelanders. They are good fighters, and they guard my wagon when I am away."

"I will set up a checkpoint there and take your wagon first. Drop the chest out. I will sign your wagon with my special mark."

"But there are people who know . . ."

"They, too, will have things to hide." Skora leaned back. "It will become a game. We will find enough to appease Prince Nichita and it will be over. But the general wants no incidents, and if there is fighting, he will spare no one, so we will be stern. We can overlook much if everything goes smoothly; keep that in mind."

Leo rose. "I . . . how can I thank you?"

Skora smiled. "Think over what I have told you, Leo Cannelli, about the emperor's service. It is a good offer."

"I will, and thank you." As he rode back to Mary, he had to admit Skora's offer drew him—but there was an immediate revolt in his mind. No! He would become a knight; he would keep his vow; his destination was Jerusalem. He was a Christian, not a pagan!

He would have to persuade Mary to part with one chest; she would want to pick and choose. It was good fortune that Skora was willing to help him. He recalled the Viking's question: What will you do after Jerusalem? He hadn't thought closely about that at all. Would he be able to capture enough wealth to live like a lord? Everyone thought so, but was it true? Should he think of going back home to Genoa, or, maybe, he could open an inn in Jerusalem? Many pilgrims would be coming and they would need food and rooms.

He arrived at the wagon to find Mary tearful. "What is it? What's happened?"

She sniffled. "Inda says . . . she says . . . I'm going to have a baby. I am the same as she . . ."

"B-a-by?" he stuttered incredulously.

She nodded tearfully. "I was telling her . . . I didn't bleed last month . . . what are we going to do?"

"When?" His mouth was dry. Other people could have children, but they had too much to do before raising a family. "When?"

"I'm not sure. Inda says maybe in seven months. I didn't bleed. She says that's a sure sign. What will we do?" She knew he didn't want a child before they were settled in Jerusalem. She had taken the precautions Ruth's bawd had taught her, even the herbs Nina had given her.

Leo stared at her. "I don't know—nothing. It is God's will."

Suddenly she was in his arms, crying, and he was comforting her. The chest would have to wait; there was time until tomorrow.

32

Captain Bayenko knew of Tafur's raids on the countryside and the large collection of valuables the "king" had taken from Belgrade. He informed Skora and the Viking ordered him to conduct a search of all the ribald wagons.

"Take a twenty-man squad and do the job thoroughly. Prince Nichita will welcome valuables and gold; and it will set an example."

The Betchenak waited until Peter finished the early mass before he ordered his horsemen into the Ribald camp. The ribalds gathered into a group and followed him as he approached Tafur's wagon.

"They come," Guizio whispered sharply into the interior of the wagon.

"Tell Tafur I would see him," Bayenko said curtly.

"He's out." Guizio spat at the horse's hoofs. "And I don't know when he's going to be back."

Bayenko studied the hunchback. "You know my orders," he said finally. "The checkpoint for this camp is right here. Tell your people to get into line. All wagons will be searched."

Guizio's lower lip protruded as his forehead wrinkled. "Nobody orders a ribald to do anything," he said flatly, as though providing information.

Bayenko hesitated a moment. "All right. I'll begin my search with Tafur's wagon. Maybe he'll be back before I'm done." He faced the growing crowd and shouted, "Hitch your wagons and bring them through here in a single line. They are to be searched."

Guizio spat again; the crowd was growling. "Best wait for Tafur. He wouldn't like strangers poking into his things."

The ribalds pressed forward and the horsemen's mounts were stepping nervously. Guizio slouched nonchalantly in the wagon seat ignoring the rising tension.

"I have no time to waste," snarled Bayenko and barked an order. His soldiers wheeled into a line, their backs to Tafur's wagon and their heads toward the crowd. An ominous growl arose.

"Better wait for Tafur," advised Guizio.

Bayenko cursed. "Draw swords!" he shouted and the weapons appeared in the hands of his men. "Fold!" he barked, and the tightly gripped blades were laid across the horsemen's knees.

"Captain Bayenko!" Tafur's high-pitched call came over the din. As he walked forward, the ribalds opened a path but closed it immediately after his passage. "I am Tafur. You want me?" He gazed arrogantly at the Betchenak.

Bayenko looked down at the small figure from the height of his horse. "You know my orders, and Peter has promised cooperation. I am requesting the same from you. Have your people form their wagons into a line for a search.''

"Your men have naked swords, captain. House them.''

"Disperse your people and have them form a line.''

Tafur's thin lips smiled. "I understand we are to *deliver* all goods taken from Belgrade.'' Bayenko inclined his head. "I do not recall any mention of searchings.''

"The manner and method are our choice.''

"Well, we have little to offer you.'' He faced his people. "Does anyone here have anything taken from Belgrade?''

"No!'' roared the crowd.

Tafur turned back to Bayenko and spread his hands with an "ergo.'' "You see; there is nothing. I know this must be a disappointment, captain, but . . .'' He shrugged. "What can I say?''

"I will say that they are lying,'' said Bayenko through his clenched teeth. "All wagons will be searched. I'll start with yours.''

"I don't think you understood. We have nothing.''

"We will see. Stand back.'' He barked an order, and two men dismounted and made for Guizio, who rose from his seat and drew a knife. The crowd surged forward.

"Captain!'' Tafur shouted. "I would not recommend force.''

Bayenko barked another order, and the two men turned and advanced on Tafur. "You are under military arrest,'' Bayenko hissed. "Order your people to stand back. If any of them start anything, my orders are for my men to kill you instantly.''

Tafur stared at the Betchenak, then his gaze wandered off toward Guizio and he shook his head. Guizio understood and slid back into his seat, and the crowd eased off, wondering what the "king'' was going to do. He had just said "no'' to fighting.

"Kill me,'' his high-pitched voice carried over the crowd, "and my people will tear all of your men limb from limb, starting with you.'' For the first time his face became grim. "Peter and your general agreed to no fighting. Even now, I advise you to leave. My people grow restless when they think I will be harmed, and I may not be able to restrain them.''

There was a rising growl as the crowd moved forward again, and from his height, Bayenko could see whirling lengths of weighted chains. He knew what they were and what they could do. He spoke sharply to his men, and they backed away from Tafur and quickly mounted their horses.

"I will be back,'' said the enraged soldier.

Tafur bowed his head slightly in acknowledgment. "I will expect you.''

Another order from Bayenko, and his men sheathed their swords and followed him off, trying to be deaf to the catcalls of the ribalds.

The soldiers gone, the crowd turned to Tafur. They knew him, and they knew he had something in mind, for the soldiers, in greater force, were sure to return.

"When they come back," Tafur shouted, "what will they find?"

"What? Tell us!" they shouted back.

"We need little graves, all marked with little headstones; restful graves; graves for deliverance. Dig deeply."

An understanding cheer went up. Tafur had said: Bury your loot and mark it with stones. Then the Betchenak could search! Tafur had played for time. They hurried off to perform the funerals.

There was chaos at the checkpoints; Byzantine soldiers had been posted in each camp, and the wains and wagons were passing through in orderly fashion and dropping their spoils into mounds. At intervals, soldiers entered the larger wagons or poked through a smaller cart. The crusaders cursed while their women wept as something was taken, and the air was filled with hatred.

Skora entered the Rhinelander camp, and Leo, as first in line, dutifully placed a chest on the ground before the mercenary. Their eyes met for an instant.

"Is there anymore?" asked Skora loudly.

"No," said Leo softly and wondered if anyone heard the tremor.

"Pass on," said Skora and daubed the wagon's side with his mark in red paint.

The man next in line was heartened, but he felt cheated when Skora ordered two soldiers to search his vehicle. When they disgorged two extra chests, after he had given one, he shouted at them. "Thieves! Robbers! Those are mine! You did not search him!"

"More noise, old man," said Skora dryly, "and I'll send my men back to find what they overlooked."

In sullen anger, the Rhinelander curbed his tongue as he drove off.

The morning wore on and Leo circulated the encampment to check on his guardsmen, while Mary remained with the wagon. She sat outside, bored, when Little John ran up. Happy to see him, she was still surprised. "What are you doing here?" she asked.

"Guizio sent me to get you." He was agitated. "Come, you must come quickly to Ruth's wagon! There's going to be a fight."

"A fight? With whom? What are you talking about?"

"The soldiers. They're taking everything away. They're digging up the gold. Guizio says that Tafur is going to fight."

"There can't be, Little John. Leo's made all the arrangements. Nobody is going to fight." She tried to calm him.

"Not with Tafur, he hasn't. He's mad. All the ribalds are mad. There's going to be a fight. Let's go—right away!"

Why not go? Mary thought. Of course, there won't be any battle, but it was some time since she had seen Ruth and Nina, and she had news—her pregnancy—and she had nothing to do anyway; Leo was busy. "All right," she said, "I'll go. But stop jumping."

*   *   *

Leo rode through the camps and found that the earlier tensions between the soldiers and the crusaders had dissipated. The Crossbearers shrugged their shoulders in resignation and helplessness as the Bulgars removed their spoils, and verbal arguments were quickly settled when it became apparent that the searches were casual. The soldiers joked with the men and teased the women over bits of clothing and kitchen utensils, provoking as much laughter as debate, and Leo was relieved. It boded well for the march later. The rumbling soundings of the deep horns jolted him out of his serenity.

All activity around the checkpoint he was watching came to a halt momentarily. The Bulgar captain was suddenly galvanized. With a curse, he bellowed at his men and made a mad dash for his horse. The footsoldiers, who had been lounging about, fell into squads on military alert as they seized their bows and quivers of arrows. More horns were picking up the refrain and the calls became persistent.

The pale, overcast sky turned pink—fire!—and a black column of smoke rose from the rear of the encampment. Dense and broad at its base, it dissolved into wisps of murkish, feathery puffs of gray cotton at its height.

A man riding hard and waving his arm frantically as he called approached Leo. It was Geoffrey Burel, one of the guardsmen.

"Leo! Come quickly! The ribalds are attacked! Bulgars!"

The camp was a chaotic battlefield and the fighting was spreading. Carts and wagons were afire and blazing fiercely. Ribald men and women, dead, with protruding arrows and sword cuts, were sprawled about amid dead horses, their throats cut, soaking in their blood. Some had dead soldiers still in their saddles, their wide-eyed stares of fright and death caught in a final agony.

The horns of the Bulgars were insistent, calling more men into the battle, and the fighting had spread to the adjacent camps as more and more of the Crossbearers picked up their weapons and charged the invading soldiers with hatred.

The Byzantine Betchenak cavalry came with its trumpets singing, and a wild, exuberant shout rose from the fighting Bulgars. The horse bowmen loosed their arrows into the milling crusaders, and the barbs flew like a swarm of bees into the Crossbearers' ranks. There was an unholy screaming which built into an ear-shattering din as the men fell before the stinging arrows, drowning out the war cries of the Bulgars. But the horns never let up, and their deep reverberations echoed in gut-tremor vibrations in the chests of the embattled fighters.

As Leo and Geoffrey arrived, a squadron of bowmen on foot stood to one side and fired volley after volley into the oncoming Rhinelanders and Swabians. Geoffrey drew his sword and screamed to Leo, "Come on!" and hurled himself into the ranks of the bowmen. He was soon lost in the swirling mass.

"Wait!" shouted Leo, but he was too late; Burel was down. On the small hillock, Leo could see over the heads of the combatants. More squads of soldiers were coming at a jogging trot; cavalry were strung in a line alongside them, riding hard to the scene. Behind the battle area was his camp area. . . . Mary! His eyes widened in horror. The cavalry was attacking the Rhinelander camp. He kicked his horse savagely. Mary was *there!*

He could not find her. The horse was dead; the wagon lay on its side, its contents spilled and burning. The roof had collapsed inward. "Mary!" tore from his throat in anguish, but he could not approach the hot fire.

His blood boiled into his eyes and he drew his sword. "Kill!" he screamed and jabbed his spurs into his horse's flanks as he raced into the battle. "Kill!" The heavy blade lopped heads with each swing, and he cared not whether it struck Bulgar or crusader. He was the keen edge of the tornado, the rampaging wave of the wild river, and the hurricane's irresistible force. His horse battered and bulled a wide swath, and everything gave way before him.

There was a sharp blow to his chest, and he glanced down and contemplated dumbly the arrow protruding there. Another blow to his left shoulder—another arrow. He clawed at the shaft in his chest; it broke, and he felt the sticky wetness of the blood. The noise of the battle had disappeared, and the shapes and forms before him became fuzzy. He rocked in his saddle; everything merged and blended; his eyes glazed and he toppled from his horse into darkness.

Skora galloped in a black rage to the battle area. He gave an order, and soon the Byzantine horns were keening over the din, and the disciplined horsemen of the Betchenak Turks formed wide lines, bowmen in front, their arrows nocked and ready, then lancers and swordsmen. Shower after shower of arrows were unleashed into the ranks of the fighters, disregarding crusader or Bulgar. At a trumpet signal, the bowmen wheeled out of the front line, and the lancers and swordsmen ranged themselves into position. Another cry from the horns, and their horses were streaking into a charge, directly into the milling combatants, riding through them, piercing and chopping at unguarded heads, whooping and screaming their blood-lust as they vented their frustrations in the battle.

More crusaders were pouring into the field, but the discipline of the Turks began to exert its weight. The squads of footsoldiers formed and re-formed like the ancient squares of the Roman legions, and they cut their way through the churning mass of leaderless Crossbearers. The cavalry rode back and forth with no difficulty, trampling the fallen and wounded, the lancers using their points at will. The Bulgars' discipline slowly returned, and they joined the Betchenaks and an organized slaughter. Finally, the crusaders broke and began to run from the field.

The retreating undertow became a wave, and soon hundreds were scrambling for safety in the hills and the surrounding forests, pursued by the footsoldiers and horsed swordsmen. As the fighting subsided, the horns took on a different tune, calling the pursuers back to take care of the wounded.

The rout was complete and the soldiers re-formed their squads, the horsemen their lines, and the captains set their work details to righting the overturned wagons, collecting scattered goods, and separating the wounded from the dead. The priests reappeared to comfort and tend them, to murmur the last rites to the dying, and to close the eyes of the dead.

Peter, Parenti, and Chagon arrived on the hill where Leo and Geoffrey had stood overlooking the battle area. Peter viewed the destruction and clutched at his cloak in despair. Lifting his arms and head to the heavens he cried out, "Lord: just as King David of old called out to Thee, heed my plea. I speak his words:

> "DELIVER ME FROM MY ENEMIES, O MY GOD;
> DEFEND ME FROM THOSE WHO RISE UP AGAINST ME.
> DELIVER ME FROM THE WORKERS OF INIQUITY,
> AND SAVE ME FROM THE BLOODY MEN . . . "

Chagon, head bowed, intoned, "Amen."

Parenti, his face pale and drawn, clenched his teeth, then muttered, "Those who live by the sword shall perish by the sword, but the Christians who died here defending the Lord shall march forever with the angel hosts in Heaven."

Far to the west the armies of the knights were gathering. Hundreds of knights, thousands of soldiers, and tens of thousands of freed serfs, peasants, artisans, and burghers emptied many of the villages and hamlets—the west was moving east, east to Constantinople. One of the most magnificent armies was that led by Duke Godfrey, lord of Lorraine.

33

In Lorraine, the last days of July were blistering hot, and, while Eustace and Baldwin worked hard in the preparation for the march to the East, Lord Godfrey sat by himself. He prayed often in his little chapel, fretted at the delays, and agonized every time Eustace came to inform him of the need for more gold. Finally, early in August, they were ready, and the blue gonfalons assembled under the walls of Metz, a city Godfrey had sold to its burghers to raise money.

The ear-piercing notes of the assembly horns sounded at dawn and drowned the rising songs of the morning birds. Godfrey gave the order to march and the standards were raised.

They were three young men in their full strength and glory, their gray eyes aglow, who rode in a triangular pattern at the head of the army. They were large men, strong in bone and sinew. Each carried above his heart, across his leather cuirass, a red cross. Cradled in the crook of their left elbows, freeing their red-gold hair to hang loosely about their broad shoulders, were their plumed helmets. Godfrey rode first; a horse length behind him, each off to a side, were his two brothers. The blue standards flew as far as the eye could see. More than thirty thousand men—from the Rhinelands, from the Netherlands, from Lorraine—the vassals and soldiers of Count Eustace and Duke Godfrey.

They rode the roads which Peter and his crusaders had walked: out of Metz, through Ratisbon, then Vienna, to the Danube, on to Belgrade. At Beograd they were met by the armed patrols of Alexius, but the Betchenaks found that these men with the red cross had a different mettle from those who had come before, and they could not be herded nor bullied. The soldiers were stunned by the savagery of the instant reprisal to every harassment of a blue standard. Godfrey's soldiers would kill every wounded Betchenak after every foray, and the Betchenak patrols learned that the lines of Lorraine were not to be tested. They were willing to march peacefully if they were left alone.

The duke paid the natives in gold and silver for all provisions taken, and the villagers were eager to deal with him. But when some villagers attacked his wagons, their homes burned and many of them died. The word spread quickly: Better to trade with these men and let them pass.

At Belgrade, Baron Ducas welcomed the three knights with pomp and display. He was struck by their youth. Boys! he said to himself. The feared knights from Lorraine were overgrown boys! Incredible! And he bowed, his face revealing nothing.

"My dear duke . . . count . . . lord . . ." he said as he bent at the waist to each brother. "It is a great honor to meet all of you. Your fame as warriors precedes you, even to our far shores."

"My brothers and I greet you, Baron Ducas." Godfrey was stiff and formal. "We have heard that as a soldier and diplomat there are few your peer. Our guides tell us that we are but a few months' march from the Imperial City. Is that so?"

"Yes, depending upon the rate of your travel. But welcome to Byzantium. Emperor Alexius extends his joyous greetings and dearest felicitations. He commends you on your journey and salutes the discipline of your knights and soldiers. He suggests further that you hasten to meet with him before your army's arrival at the Imperial City. You will need winter quarters; the year's end is cold and rainy in our country."

"We thank the emperor for his concern," said Godfrey coldly. "We hold any suggestion from him in our highest esteem, but there is no need for me to hasten. We intend to quarter before the gates of the Imperial City."

Ducas' eyes flickered momentarily. He smiled. "The emperor has nothing but your interests at heart. Your army is cumbersome and large. It will require a great deal of room and that compels adequate planning. Other princes follow you and to house such large numbers is a mammoth logistical problem. His Most High Basileus believes mutual planning will aid everyone."

Godfrey searched the baron's face but found it free of guile. "The moment we arrive we shall lose no time to greet the emperor," he said coolly. "And with the knowledge that he awaits, we will hasten—with our forces. As for a camping site, he should be made aware, if he does not know as yet, that the princes who come have agreed to meet *before* Constantinople. We shall quarter there and await them."

The two men measured each other silently, their eyes locked in an understanding of mutual hostility. Baron Ducas scarcely inclined his head. "It shall be as you wish, Lord Godfrey," he murmured. "I shall convey your suggestions to the emperor. It was a pleasure to be of service to you." He bowed, turned toward Eustace and bowed. "And to you, Count Eustace, and Sir Baldwin."

Each nodded in turn.

"We shall meet in Constantinople," the Byzantine ended wryly, a faint smile upon his lips. Then he turned and left.

"Did you see intrigue in his offer?" Eustace asked his brother.

"Hostages, perhaps? To ask us to ride in alone? To behead the army?" mused Baldwin. "If so, he mistakes the temper of our knights."

"We have done little to make him fear us," said Godfrey, "yet . . . we have heard that Alexius is devious. We know how he treated Peter the Hermit and his people. Can it be that he fears the coming of too many Christians?"

Eustace protested. "How can you compare Peter's rabble with us? No, brother. There is no balance to your question."

"But there was good Christian blood in that rabble, many pious and God-fearing men."

"There were also thieves, murderers, cutthroats, and whores," said Baldwin. "Eustace is right. How can you compare?"

"Think, brothers," said Godfrey. "Urban warned us not to shed Christian blood. Alexius, who calls himself pope too, has no compunction to bleed Christians. We have vowed to seek the Lord's mercy, not to spill the blood of His servants; and to me, those who spill it needlessly honor not the will of the Lord."

Baldwin smiled. "Mother made a large mistake. She should have sent you to the Church instead of me. But, as usual, you are right. We must be wary of the gifts of Greeks. Homer taught us that."

Count Raymond, from his vantage point near the Garonne River, watched with pride as his army entered the city for its honors. No king's army was more magnificent, nor better armed.

The balconies of the city's houses were draped with brilliant, multicolored silks striped in gold, red, and black, and they pitched with gusto in the hot August winds. The church towers were vibrating under the constant clamor of the bells, and the priests in the doorways lifted their silver crosses and blessed the riders as they passed. Many were sprinkling holy water. From the upper casements came the gay laughter of the women who leaned forward and dropped kerchiefs on the knights. Cut grasses and dried leaves, wetted and spread upon the cobbles, diffused a clean fragrance which was tempered by the strong odor of the fresh horse droppings.

The knights had been ahorse all day, but still they rode at ease, buoyed by their welcome. Their march through Raymond's fief had become a triumphal procession. Each section—the stalwart, dark-skinned mountaineers of the Pyrenees; the smaller, goateed dons from Catalonia and Valencia (sent by the father of Countess Elvira); the robust, redheaded men from Gascony, and the gay, quarrelsome men from Provence, known for their love of battle.

Each section rode with elan and smiled at the flushed faces of the girls, the admiration of the boys, and the cheers of the men and women who greeted them in every hamlet, town, and city.

The knights rode on new saddles, bright with brocade, made of soft, crimson Cordoba leather. Glittering discs of silver and gold jangled and gleamed from their reins. Behind them, led by their mounted squires, were the destriers, their tails and manes braided. The animals, excited by all the din, tossed their heads and strutted, their nostrils flaring. Hundreds and hundreds of knights, the vassals—and their vassals—of the lord of St. Edigius, the one called St. Gilles, Raymond, Count of Toulouse, and he was full of pride and arrogance.

Behind the knights' squires came the footsoldiers, led by the elite crossbowmen. These swaggered as they carried their elegantly curved bows in their extended arms, for they were the highest paid professional soldiers anywhere. Behind them were the regular bowmen; and behind them marched the thousands of footsoldiers with their lances, pikes, and axes.

Oxen-pulled wagons trundled after the walking men, an endless line stretched far over the flat plain; and heading these wagons were the troupes of jongleurs, gittern-playing troubadours, acrobats, and jugglers. Forty-five thousand fighting men, and thousands more of traveling serfs and peasants, stretched in a line, followed Raymond, and vowed to remain in Jerusalem for the rest of their lives.

The Crossbearers sang of the Promised Land and carried a glorious vision of a land which would free them from hunger, from back-breaking toil, and from their sins. Forever, they would rest in the Bosom of the Lord. Their priests had told them so.

In the rear came the sutlers and their large wagons. They peddled all kinds of merchandise. Did the lady need a love potion? A poison to kill a rival? A scarf? Honey to sweeten her food? Or did the gentleman desire a lady for the evening, young, winsome, and amorous? Everything was available—for a price.

Raymond took his army across France, through the high mountain passes of the Alps, and on to Venice. There he called a halt, for he needed provisions. His large force moved slowly and winter was coming and he counseled his next move with Bishop Adhemar.

"We cannot camp before Venice all winter," he told the bishop. "We would lose too much time, and to feed this force during idle months would be costly."

"I will add other reasons: your Provencals are too fun-loving. My priests would have much work with their broken heads and cut skins if they had empty hours. Have you talked to the shipowners?"

Raymond grimaced. "They are afraid of the winter storms, and they have set their fees high enough to buy another ship if theirs sank. They tell me to prepare for many losses if I wish to sail this time of the year. Count Hugh of Vermandois would not heed them and lost every vessel but his own."

"Then we have to march the roads. We cannot remain here."

Raymond sighed and shook his head. "That, too, gives us problems. The northern roads are blocked with snow and ice."

"There is another way," said Adhemar. "We can move down the eastern coastline to Durazzo. The sea will guide us until we reach the old fortress, and from there we can march south over the old Roman road, the Via Egnatia, to Constantinople."

"We have no maps. And the natives tell me that it is all rugged mountains and high peaks with few passes, and the natives are not friendly. I have discussed it as an alternative, but I have been told that without maps we will be lost." He sighed again.

"We will find guides, fear not. Where there are people, we can find or buy cooperation. Trust in the Lord."

Raymond was pessimistic but, with no choices left, gave his army their marching orders. Slowly, they crawled down the eastern coastline of the Adriatic Sea. The lands were barren and the mountains were everywhere. The winds howled through the sparse passes, and the horses floundered in the deep snows, tipping many wagons into the deep abysses. The natives discovered the invader and preyed upon him, and Adhemar was wrong; gold could not buy guides; gold could buy nothing, for the natives spurned the yellow metal, finding it useless.

Raymond struggled on, guided by the stars at night and the sun by day. Provisions ran low; the sick and elderly died; and the soldiers foraged for food and stripped any farm they found. The natives retaliated with nightly attacks, but the army crept relentlessly southward into the warmer climate.

34

The passing days were a blur in Leo's memory. He lived close to pain and remembered only the dryness, the wetness, the darkness, and the soothing relief of cooling hands. Vague forms floated in his consciousness, and there were times when the grayness of a shrouding blanket lay over him. One morning he awoke with clear eyes and an empty hollowness in his stomach.

He was alive! And he could hear a woman singing. He licked his rough, dry, scaly lips with a furred tongue. Lying on his back, he could see a large chest with female clothing tossed over its open lid, a few chairs, and a makeshift table. Alongside him was another pallet, with two closed chests over near the tent's wall.

The singing became a humming which entered the tent. His eyelids flickered. "Mary?" It was a hoarse whisper.

Then, he could see her; the tent flap was open and the bright sunlight was behind her. Her chiton was translucent in the brightness and outlined her thin figure.

"Leo!" she cried in surprise. "You're awake!" She hurried and knelt at his side, her cool hand seeking his neck. "The fever's gone." Her pronouncement stirred him with its happiness. "You're going to be well!"

"Where are we? What's happened?"

"So many things." She rose quickly. "Rest. We'll talk later. I have to call Dalmus."

"Dalmus?"

"Skora sent a healer—his own—to take care of you, a Greek; he's been healing you since Sofia."

"Sofia?"

"Where we had the battle. I'll tell you later. I better go."

"Wait!" He held out an arm to stop her. "The battle? The wagon . . . it was burning . . . I thought you were dead . . . the arrow . . ." He rubbed his chest. "What happened?"

"Later," she soothed him. "Are you hungry? Dalmus said you would be hungry."

The question stirred his hunger and he nodded. "Yes, I suppose so." He struggled to raise himself on his elbow and followed her with his eyes. She was haggard; there was no sign of the baby. How long had he been sick?

"The baby . . . ?" he croaked. "Are you all right?"

She propped him into a semisitting position with pillows. "I'm fine; the baby, too. Rest. I'll be back soon."

"Wait!" he called again, insistent. "Where are we?"

"I'll tell you this and then I'm going," she said firmly. "We are at Civitot, across the waters from Constantinople. When we came to the Imperial City, there was a lot of stealing and fighting, and the emperor put us on boats and put us here. His boats come every five days and bring food and other things, but we trade for what we want with the sailors. Now, I must get Dalmus; we'll talk later." She rushed out of the tent.

Civitot—what kind of a place was it? He must have been sick a long time, yet it did not show on Mary. Her belly was not big. Skora . . . his mind wandered. Skora had saved him; he owed him his life, maybe more; he had to thank him for the healer.

He ran his hand over his wound. Where the arrow had entered the skin was flaccid and wrinkled under his fingers. He pressed, but it did not hurt and a deep breath brought no pain. He was healed. He rolled his shoulder. No pain. Dalmus knew his trade.

His thoughts wandered. How had they lived with the wagon gone? He had seen it burn. The gold hidden in it was gone. Where did Mary get the tent? . . . and the other things? Skora? Maybe Ruth? No, Ruth would not part with the money—if she had any left after the battle. What had happened to her?

So many questions. The heat oppressed him; his mind dulled; his eyes rolled up in sleep.

"Leo!" Someone was calling and he felt a shaking. His eyes snapped open. A strange face was close to his; an old face with a high, brown-wrinkled forehead, a large, bulbous nose, and small, dark eyes set deeply into the skull. Below the red, full lips was a brown beard flecked with white hair and neatly clipped into an oval hedge around a squarish chin. The ends of the mouth were turned upward into a pleasant smile.

"You . . . wake?" The voice was guttural, the singsong of a foreigner. Strong fingers were kneading the healed area of his chest and probing the rib section. "Hurt? No? Yes?"

"No," Leo shook his head, "not from the wound." This must be Dalmus. He winced as the fingers pushed against the bone.

The healer was watching him closely. "Breathe!" he commanded and inhaled and exhaled vigorously in demonstration. He placed his ear against Leo's chest and motioned with his hand. "Breathe! More! More!"

Leo inhaled deeply and let his chest collapse slowly.

"Good! Good!" Dalmus nodded, leaned back, and beamed in satisfaction. "Good. All finished!" He clapped his hand on Leo's shoulder, and his fingers dug into the flesh as his thumb moved under the collarbone. "Hurt?" Leo shook his head although he felt the probe. "Good!" There was another beaming smile. He rose from his seated position and turned his palms upward and pumped his hands.

"Up!" He was not a tall man, and his round figure was visible under the gown which fell to his ankles. "Up!" he commanded again, his face owlish with his round eyes.

Leo struggled to rise and found it difficult.

Dalmus stretched his arm in support, and the squire pulled himself to his feet although he weaved and wambled despite the steadiness of the healer's bracing aid.

"Walk!" Leo tried but found it was impossible to lift his feet. Dalmus leaned over and pushed his thigh forward, and Leo almost collapsed, his knees like running water, spilling in all directions. But Dalmus was demanding and forced him to slide his feet forward again and again. Mary watched them anxiously. Leo's forehead was wet with effort and desperation, and she remembered her broken leg. "Walk!" Dalmus commanded. And Leo walked.

"Good! Now, lay . . ." and the healer allowed Leo to sink down upon the pallet. He turned to the worried girl with a round-eyed grin. "He ver-r-ry good. He need food, and walk. You do like I said. You remember?" She nodded quickly. "Good. Now, I go." They watched him bustle out, clucking contentedly to himself.

"That was Dalmus?" Leo asked although he knew the answer.

"Yes. He says you have to walk and eat to get your strength back. Now that you're healed, he's going back to the city and leaving you to me."

"But you saw! I can't walk yet," he protested.

"You will," she assured him. "He said so. I know what to do."

The next few days were eating, sleeping, walking, and Mary's tales of what had happened after he had been wounded. He had lost eighteen days. The news of his recovery spread and Turgot came to visit. From his lieutenant, Leo received the details of the battle. Thousands of crusaders had been killed; more thousands had run off into the hills and forests, and despite the callings of the big horns not too many had returned. There were whispers that the Turks and Bulgars had hunted them down and murdered them.

Turgot spoke of revenge, but the host had marched under the swords of Skora's Betchenaks and Prince Nichita's Bulgars. Two full battalions of Betchenaks had met them at Sofia, the nearby city, and Skora had interspersed squads of the Turks in the host's line, and they kept order and the marching cadence. Food was provided, and the Byzantine general had told them: Obey orders and we will feed you. Disobey and you die. And many had died for slight infringements of Skora's commands.

Peter's wagon, with all the gold and money, had been lost. The guardsmen protecting it had been killed, and it was gutted and burned. Some accused the Turks; some the Bulgars; but others whispered that it was Tafur. All the ribalds had disappeared, but when the host neared the Imperial City, they suddenly came back—only thirty-eight starved, raggedy men and ten women like scarecrows. If it had been they who had stolen Peter's gold, they had none of it when they had returned.

"Tafur? Guizio?"

"Alive. And Geoffrey was slightly wounded. He and Rainald are important men now. He was elected leader of the Rhinelanders and the Bavarians. Rainald leads the Upper Normans and some from Lorraine. I stayed with the guardsmen."

"Who is this Rainald? Do I know him?"

"He was a wild one, from my squad, a troublemaker. And we're going to have more trouble with him now, especially because the Normans follow him and they are good fighters."

Leo studied Turgot. "You sound gloomy."

Turgot nodded. "Everything has changed. Peter no longer leads. People listen to him pray, but nobody obeys him anymore. Parenti says the emperor uses him to keep us quiet until the great lords and their armies arrive. We get food but just enough to keep us alive. We complain, but nobody listens.

"Rainald and his men raid the Turkish villages not far from here for food and women, and Geoffrey has begun to do it, too. They boast that they are doing God's work—and Parenti urges them on—but they rape the women and sow Christian seeds in Moslem nests and the Turks become angry. There will be fighting. Everyone curses that dragon's bastard Skora for our troubles."

Leo's head came up. "Speak no ill of Skora. He is my friend and he saved my life."

"After his Betchenaks almost took it," Turgot pointed out. "He killed thousands of our host and burned our wagons. Your friend is no friend of ours." He was bitter.

"He did not want anyone killed," said Leo, tight-lipped. "No one did, but he is a soldier and follows his orders. If we are not to fight, speak no evil of him to me." He shifted in his bed in anger. "Tell me of other things. Is Peter here?"

"No. He stays mostly in the palace with the emperor. He says he does it to get us food, but Parenti says the emperor uses Peter. He and Sir Walter are arriving today . . ."

"Sir Walter? Alive? Here?" Leo was bolted upright. "Does he know about me?"

"Of course. He is waiting until you heal. That's why he is coming today."

"Tell him! Tell him I've started to practice! My sword! Every day, a little! Tell him! You say he is coming? Tell him!" He was beside himself. He must get up. He must practice. He grasped Turgot's hands. "Tell him to come right away."

"I'll tell him when the boat comes, later, this afternoon."

With that promise, Turgot left. Leo found it difficult to restrain himself. He must remind Walter of his promise; he must become proficient with the sword. Skora had said Sir Walter couldn't make him a knight easily because of the great lords. But they were coming, with all their knights. If he was to stand equal to them, he had to become a knight just like them. He had to fight; that would enable Walter to make him a Knight of the Sword. He would show those knights what he could do in a battle, then they would accept him. The sin of Ambition was evil, but, as Skora had said, this was the right time. God had saved him—and Sir Walter—to meet again. He was convinced he was right.

In winter, at Civitot, the winds blow from the cool sea, a welcome change from the heated blasts which had gusted all summer from the oven-heated interior of Asia. During October, the sun burned orange-red and became oppressive, but many of the Crossbearers remembered the bone-chilling winter mornings and the shivering nights at home, and they were grateful for the heat.

Peter came rarely to Civitot. He had locked himself into his own mystical world and quoted oblique scripture in his few sermons. Most of his time was spent in his suite of rooms at the palace, which Alexius thoughtfully provided, sunk in his morbid desire for luxury. He was plied with food, wine, and flattery, honored before the entire Byzantine court, and soothed with music and services. Parenti cynically lamented his absences from the camp and took over the religious needs of the host.

He told the monks at the camp, "Peter's sins of Omission multiply, and his eyes are blinded by the pleasures of the palace. Too many forget that it was he who allowed the Byzantine to take our goods at Sofia; that it was he who lost all our gold and money; that it was he who told us to remain peaceful in the face of the attacks of the Turks and Bulgars. He licks his fingers and drinks the wine of the murdering emperor. Go; spread the word that he has become a Philistine. Use the confessional. You are all knowledgeable in the technique."

And irritated and bitter, the host waited impatiently for the coming of the great lords who would free them from the shackles of the Byzantine.

Leo sat outside the tent and watched the rounded rump of Mary, bent over the fire, stirring the pot of stew. The smell made his mouth drool; they had had little food for the past three days; but somewhere she had found a piece of meat. When she rose, he could see the roundness of her belly and the emerging fullness of her small breasts. She had an inner glow which emerged when she smiled but hid in the small corners of her mouth when she was tired and irritated.

They ate their meal in silence. The Byzantine boats had arrived that morning and were discharging their cargoes, and Leo was to board one of them with Walter when it returned to the Imperial City. Few Crossbearers were allowed to visit.

He wiped his mouth with the back of his hand. "Would you like me to bring you something special? They have many pretty things."

"Where would you get the money?" She was disinterested.

He shrugged. "From Walter, or Peter. Maybe, the emperor." He teased her.

"And how would you pay them back? It is better not to have big eyes. Buy nothing."

"All who visit say the city is a place of wonder. If I want something, I will find a way."

"Leo, please, no fighting. There are many . . ."

"What kind of husband am I if I cannot bring my wife a present?"

"Leo . . ."

He buckled on his sheathed knives. "Don't worry, I'll be good. Sir Walter will see to that." He leaned forward and kissed her. "I better go. He'll be waiting."

"Be careful," she whispered before releasing him.

They came to the Imperial City from the sea, sailing into a winding, curved arm of a waterway which snaked into the land. Leo was dazzled by the sight before him. A hundred cities glowed in the bright sunlight, a casket of brilliant jewels: of gold and white, of rose and green verdure. An immense carpet had been flung from the hand of a genie and had come to rest across the soft hills.

There was an endless expanse of houses: of marble and stone, of brick and stucco. And they were painted white or had pictures painted upon their walls. There were towers and castles, houses piled upon other houses in stories or crowded together, sometimes showing a greenness of a garden between them. The city had been erected for the greater glory of God, but it now reflected the greater glory of man.

On both sides of the entrance rivers stood the rich grain fields, vineyards and orchards, pastures of cattle and sheep, and meadows of horses. And the farmhouses, seen beyond the fields, were white blotches of paint upon the green hills. The horizon was a straight, violet-blue line.

They passed through a great double wall which encircled the city like a huge belt. Between the walls was a moat, and a thousand towers, broader and higher towers, grander than any Leo had ever seen, angled from the massive stone foundations of the walls and rose toward the sky.

The double-door gates were sheathed in iron and opened on an entranceway so wide that two wagons could pass abreast without scraping; their archways were full of dangling chains and pulleys. Soldiers walked the walls over the archways and guards stood at the gates.

The guardians of the Golden Gates—the outer wall—were tall, large men picked for their strength and girth. They were mostly from the north countries: Leo's father, Favio, had been one. They were much like Skora: their hair curled from beneath their helmets, and horsehair plumes dangled from the helm's pointed top. Their ring-mail, worn over thick, leather foundations, was polished jewel-bright, and swords hung in artistically etched scabbards. They carried long, halberd-type axes which could be used as spears or as chopping blades. Their brightly polished, leather boots, stopping just below the knee, glistened in the light.

The soldiers who walked the inner wall were smaller men. Their tunics were embroidered with gay colors, and their caps and vests were of fur. They carried lighter swords than the Norsemen and held a round shield on their left arms or strung it over back shoulders. They were the mercenary Turks of the emperor.

Inside the city, Leo gaped at the large squares, the beautiful fountains with their jetting waters, and the facades of the buildings with their elegantly carved marble reliefs. The markets were on the narrow, curved streets which curled back from the squares. Criers hawked their goods and crippled beggars crowded the doorways. Never had Leo seen such a display of food and exotic ornaments.

He marveled at the stalls of ripe fruit, all exotic and new to him: dates, figs, persimmons, dried plums, apples which shone, carob sticks, sugared pastries, tarts covered with red cherries. There were all kinds of breads, in all shapes and sizes; some hard as boards, some downy as a pillow. The sweet and sour candies which melted in his mouth overwhelmed him. Never had he seen such meats, fish, and fowl, and Walter kept buying pieces of everything for him to taste. And odors, mixed with ordure, permeated everything.

In some stalls he saw rolls of cloth, in all colors and in beautiful patterns: silks which slithered from your hand; wonderful brocades, puffed and soft; fine cottons; and light spun wool which seemed weightless and fine as camel's hair. It was a place beyond his wildest imagination! It was a paradise!

Flowers were everywhere, in shapes, sizes, and types he could never dream of. Jewelers hawked their wares, and their slaves bent over their small tables and did intricate work on gold and silver before your eyes. There were designs which the buyer could choose from parchment papers and watch the slaves cut, bend, and solder tiny pieces together to make broach or earring, or necklace or ring, or bracelet. He watched, his mouth open in wonder.

Animals bayed, barked, brayed, cackled in confusion with the calls of the sellers. The beguiling music of Indian snake charmers floated over the din, and they watched the cobras sway hypnotically from their baskets. Leo swayed with them, and Walter laughingly pulled him out of the way of a trader leading a docile mule train through the streets in single file.

They paused for some cool slices of melon; they split boiled watermelon seeds and peeled the shells of roasted chestnuts; they sucked the juice of ripe pomegranates.

They stayed the longest at an armorer's tent. Leo fingered the knives and marveled at the intricate designs etched into the handles of the blades. The trader explained how the etching not only beautified the weapon but also prevented the slipping of a wet or bloody hand. He picked a curved scimitar for Walter and blew some fine wool into the air. The gently settling wool had enough weight to be sliced into two parts by the sword's keen edge. Then, he struck a steel bar, denting it, but the blade remained keen enough to repeat the wool cutting. He offered the blade to Walter, at a fine price, he said, and when the knight declined, the trader shouted his curses and ordered them away from his stall.

A palanquin, with heavily draped windows, stopped near them, and the slender hand of a woman emerged from behind the curtain. A singsong voice said something and pointed to a stall; the vendor hurried to bring two persimmons and accepted payment with rapid bows and full deference.

"A Moslem lady," explained Walter. "She cannot show her face or form in public before strangers."

"Why?" Leo asked, curious.

"She would be dishonored," chuckled Walter. "A man might desire her, and only her husband has that privilege. What a man does not see, he seeks, and the isolation actually makes her more desirable."

"But the Moslems see our women. Does that mean they desire them?"

"I would say yes. A yellow or redheaded woman brings a high price on their slave blocks."

They were approached by two Betchenak soldiers. One, an officer, said, "I seek two crusaders called Walter and Leo. May it please, do you know them?"

Walter nodded in surprise. "I am Sir Walter. What is it?"

"I am happy . . ."—the man had language difficulties—". . . to find. Please . . ." he indicated that they were to walk before him. "My captain, Captain Skora, he says to find, to talk. Es-pe-cially . . ."—he finished the word triumphantly—". . . with Leo."

"Skora is here? And wants to see me?" Leo was delighted.

"Please . . ." The Betchenak motioned with his hand again. "I will . . . take, no?"

He led them to another part of the city where the houses were surrounded by fences of mortared stone and iron latticework. Tall windows of multicolored glass and colored mosaics of birds, trees, and flowers were cemented into the walls. Effigies, artistically sculptured, adorned the fretted gates and depicted holy scenes or individual saints. The gardens had masses of flowers, and water jets sprayed into rose-colored marble basins.

They entered a gateway which opened upon a well-tendered garden of a small stone house. One Betchenak remained at the gate; the other ushered them onto a small veranda, asked them to wait, and disappeared into the house. He was soon back, following Skora.

The mercenary greeted them effusively and dismissed the soldier with a blunt, "Well done."

The Viking's eyes measured Walter as a fighting man. "We meet for the first time, Sir Walter, but I have heard a great deal about you from our good friend, Leo Cannelli. Welcome to my pitiful home."

"I have heard much about you, too, Captain Skora," responded Walter, "but I must take exception to your calling your home pitiful. Many of us would pray to have no less and certainly could ask for little more."

Skora nodded cordially, pleased. "As soldiers, we must agree that a bivouac in the field is a far cry from shelter in the city. And you, Leo Cannelli? You look well and healed. Any ill effects?"

"None that I know of," said Leo. "I owe you my life, Captain Skora, and I give you my thanks and prayers."

Skora brushed it aside. "We do what we can for our friends. Come. Let us sit and talk." He led them to an iron, marble-topped table surrounded by iron chairs. "Ali," he called to the house, "bring some wine and food for our guests."

A young, dark-skinned man was already in the doorway with a silver tray with a decanter of wine, glasses, and some sugared red figs, and pastries. He placed the tray upon the table, bowed, and left silently with the grace of a cat.

"A wonderful boy," said Skora. "He anticipates my every want."

"Isn't he a . . . Moslem?" asked Leo. "He is so dark."

"A Moslem," Skora nodded. "Half-Arab, half-African. His father was a black slave to an Arab family in Egypt. While traveling, the family was attacked and the black man could save only the young daughter. Ali was their son. When he was seven years old, his father sold him to feed the rest of the family. The young make the best slaves. Ali has turned out well."

"But a Moslem?" wondered Walter. "Why did you not make him a Christian?"

Skora laughed. "Our Basileus frowns on Christian slaves, especially if owned by an army officer who is not Christian. He allows us to worship as we wish, and it was no concern of mine if Ali chose Mohammed, Jesus, or for that matter, Odin. Come, let us drink."

Walter sipped his wine and eyed the big man curiously. "How did you know we were in the city?"

Skora grinned. "Little what you do, or where you go, escapes us. I have heard of your prowess as a fighter, Sir Walter. Our army has places for such men, if you are willing to accept our pay."

"You are kind," said Walter, reaching for a pastry, "but I go to Jerusalem."

"Did you not come to kill the Infidel?" asked Skora slyly.

"I came to redeem the Holy Sepulchre and seek salvation," replied Walter easily.

"No revenge for the Infidel's misdeeds? For his abominations?"

"Maybe others, but not I. Worry of my own soul is sufficient."

"And you, Leo Cannelli? Have you had enough time to think?"

Leo squirmed; he had given little thought to Skora's question. He diverted the answer. "Was it you who found me when I was wounded?"

"No. It was Captain Bayenko. He saw you fall and he knew we were friendly. When he saw that you still lived, he brought you to my healer, who cut out the arrows and notified me. He is more responsible for your living than I.''

"I will have to thank him. And Doctor Dalmus.''

"You have your father's lucky star, Leo Cannelli. Dalmus told me the arrow went between the ribs and approached the heart. It was difficult to extract. You see, our arrows have a large barb which, once imbedded, invariably kills. Dalmus prayed hard when he cut it out and when the death-fevers raged.''

"Then I have to thank Jesus for answering his prayers.''

"I do not know whether Christian or Moslem shot your particular arrow, but they tell me that Saint Sebastian is your angel of bowmen. I am only happy it stopped in time. But, to the point! Have you considered my proposal? I hold a place for you.''

Leo came to an immediate decision. "I must fulfill my vows. I hope there will be time later.''

"You chance it, Cannelli,'' warned Skora. "We have word that the great lords are on the roads to the Imperial City with thousands of knights. Many, you may be sure, will be willing to take the emperor's pay, but our places are numbered. The time is now; for that reason I sought you out.''

"The soothsayers tell us that many who come will die and march in Heaven,'' said Walter. "The great lords seek fiefdoms, and a good soldier can always find a place.''

"True,'' acknowledged Skora, "but none can match the emperor as benefactor. Think carefully, Cannelli. I seek nothing but your gain because of my friendship to your father, but I must warn you, time passes quickly and so will opportunity.''

"I will decide soon,'' promised Leo. "May I ask another boon?''

"What is it?''

"I thank you for your concern for me, but I cannot impose on your charity forever. I must find some way to pay my keep. Can you help me?''

"Perhaps . . .'' Skora was thoughtful. "But I do not understand what you mean by my charity. I have done nothing but send you my healer. I demand no payment for his work.''

"I was thinking of the use of your tent and other things.''

"Use . . . of my tent?'' Skora's brow wrinkled. "You have no tent of mine. I do not understand what you say.''

Leo's face was knotted. "The tent . . . the chests?''

Skora shook his head. "Not mine, Cannelli.''

"Then . . . whose?'' Leo turned to Walter.

"Look not at me,'' said the knight. "I only know that Mary had the tent when you came to Civitot. It is a Byzantine army tent.'' He glanced at Skora.

"You say Byzantine?'' Skora was speculative. "She could have bought it from a soldier, although it is forbidden to be sold.''

"We had no money,'' said Leo.

"It is an officer's tent," said Walter. "Could it not have been given to her?"

"Bayenko?" ventured Leo, looking from one to the other.

"He is not known for his generosity," said Skora thoughtfully. "And an officer can sell nothing either. It is a court-martial offense, not lightly committed."

"Maybe Ruth . . ." speculated Walter. "She has gold. Her wagon was not harmed. She would have had dealings with the Byzantines."

"Maybe . . ." said Leo slowly, but a terrible thought had formed in his mind. Mary had denied receiving anything from Ruth. Was she lying? Or . . . he pushed the thought away, but it would not go. Suddenly, he knew he had to return to Civitot immediately.

35

As he waited for the supply ships to Civitot to be loaded, Leo paced the deck impatiently. His enthusiasm to explore the wonders of the Imperial City had evaporated, and even the emperor's rich and wondrous palace did not fascinate him anymore. In his despondency, he had concluded that Walter and the entire camp knew of Mary's betrayal, and he was convinced that everyone was jeering at him behind his back.

When his ship reached harbor, he saw hundreds of women milling on the quays, bantering lightheartedly with the Greek sailors who unloaded the vessels. They held out objects they owned for trade with the seamen who smuggled special goods. He could not find Mary.

He hurried to the tent, a thundercloud forming in his mind. She was not there. His neighbors shrugged their shoulders at his questions: They do not watch the comings and goings of the women, they said.

"It's a game," he muttered angrily. "They know, but no one will tell the husband." In the tent, as he waited, he grew ever more bitter. He had a sudden thought: *The chests!* If she had any hidden money it would be there. He dumped the first. Nothing. The second. Nothing. On the bottom of the third was a small cloth bag. He seized it in triumph and poured its contents upon the table. Jewelry! He was surprised. He had expected gold.

"Byzantine," he scowled. He examined a piece; he had seen similar designs on the parchments of the jewelry makers in the street markets. He jumped in guilt when Geoffrey and Turgot entered.

"We heard you were back," said Burel. "We have to talk."

Leo had little use for Burel. "What about?" He was curt.

"I have a proposition for you." Burel ignored Leo's manner. He noticed the jewelry and picked up a piece. "I know where we can get a great deal of this. Did you bring these from the city?"

"Yes," Leo lied. He swept the pieces back into the bag. "Where else do they make them?"

Geoffrey smiled. "I know where I can get them . . . and gold, too, if you're man enough."

"You're talking of raiding the Turks," said Leo.

Burel grinned. "What better place is there? Papa Urban told us what we take from the infidel is ours without sin."

"Why do you need me? You've been doing well enough alone."

217

"We can do better," Burel admitted, "if you're willing to listen."

Leo stared at him but did not answer and Burel took the silence as consent. He became animated.

"Near that island city—Nicea—is a large town. It's too big just for my men, and Tafur is willing to join me in a raid, but he doesn't have many men, and he insists that he wants your sword at his side when he goes. Turgot says the guard will go if you do."

"Does Rainald go?"

"No." Burel stiffened. "He and I do not operate together."

"Have you talked to the knights?"

"The knights don't raid. You know that."

"If the town is large you will need all the men you can get."

Turgot leaned forward. "Just think a minute, Leo. It's a rich place with flocks of sheep and cattle. Lots of horses, too. The people are rich. If we had enough men we could take the whole town, everything, just like Selim." He nodded in emphasis. "It's like a chicken, just asking to be plucked, and . . ." he shook his head and balled his fists, "it's richer than Selim."

"How many men do you have?" Leo asked Burel.

"More than two hundred, and all of them are fighters."

"Then why do you need me? Go! Take it by yourself."

Burel shook his head. "Not enough. Then there's something else. Not far from the town is an old castle called Xerigordon. It used to guard the town but no one's there now. We could fix it and make it our headquarters and raid the whole valley from there. Or," he chuckled, "we could make the heathens pay us *not* to raid them; you know, tribute. We could take taxes, like the knights." He laughed at his joke.

"Think, Leo," said Turgot eagerly. "We could rule like kings."

"What about Jerusalem and the Holy Sepulchre? Have you forgotten already?" Leo asked him.

"It can wait until the great lords come," said Geoffrey carelessly. "If they ever come," he added.

"They come," said Leo. "I heard in the city."

"Then we'll decide when they get here." Burel was offhand. "They wouldn't want a place like this; it isn't rich enough. But for us . . ." He winked knowingly.

"You forget the Turk at Nicea and the emperor in the Imperial City," said Leo drily.

"The Turk does nothing." Burel was contemptuous. "Their emir—they call him the Red Lion." He laughed. "He's so busy fighting his brother he won't know what's happening. The garrison at Nicea never once has fought us since we began raiding. And the emperor," he blew wind from his mouth, "he just wants us out of his way. If he objects, we can take an oath of vassalage to him and pay him some gold. What more can he ask?"

Leo decided he had underestimated Geoffrey Burel. He had to admit that the plan sounded good, but something nagged at him. He was sure he was overlooking a vital point. A successful raid, he knew, would supply him with everything he needed—a wagon and everything else. He could still go with the great lords when they marched on to Jerusalem. If the raid failed? Well, he was gambling with his life anyway. And then, there was Mary.

Burel saw that he was wavering. "You can lead the guard—as one of my lieutenants. And you can have Tafur's men, too."

The two men locked eyes, and Leo could feel his gorge rise. "If I go," he said tightly, "we will need Rainald's men, or we risk defeat because of petty jealousy. Selim taught us that. And I go as my own commander, not as your lieutenant."

Burel's eye ticked. "All right, but not with Rainald. I share nothing with him. He can botch the entire operation. I know; I have tried to raid with him before."

"Then I remain here. And I tell the entire guard why."

Turgot turned on Burel. "What have we to fear with Rainald? Like you said, he'll go his own way. There'll be enough for all of us, and he fights. Leo is right; we need all the men we can get."

"How can you prevent him from marching on the town at the same time?" Leo asked. "Turgot says he has more men than you, at least three hundred. He can attack any time he wishes."

"Then he fights alone," Geoffrey insisted. "I do not go with him; I will not fight with him."

Leo smiled. "He will take his own shares, as will I. When do you go?"

"Tomorrow. At sunup."

"I will be there with the guard." Leo was grim.

The two men nodded and left, and Leo fingered the jewelry, his thoughts returning to Mary. From now on, he decided, the infidel would supply all his needs. He would never have to beg anyone for anything again. But Mary had to answer for these. He put them back in the bag and waited.

Mary, a bundle on her arm, entered the tent and drew back in surprise, her humming ceasing.

"Where have you been?" A dark cloud hovered over him.

"I . . . I didn't expect you back until the next sailing." She tried to be cheerful. "Is something wrong?"

"I didn't say I would be away that long. Where were you?"

"No, but Walter said . . . I thought you would be with him."

"Where were you?" His anger was rising.

"Trading with the sailors," she said lightly. "We all do when the ships come in." She put her bundle on the table. "Did you like the city? Did you buy anything?"

"What do you trade? We have nothing."

"Oh . . . I wash some clothes for them . . . a little sewing . . ."

"You hate washing and you sew even less. The sailors gave you all this . . ."—he indicated the tent—"for washing and sewing?"

"Well . . ." She began to fidget. "I did some for the soldiers."

"And they gave you this, too?" He dumped the bag's contents.

She was startled but caught herself. "You went to my chest," she said accusingly. "You had no right."

"*How did you get these?*" His lips were a thin line.

She became a cornered rabbit, terrified before his anger.

"*HOW?*" His voice rose. She shook her head and wept. "*HOW MANY MEN?*" he said between his teeth. He ripped the carved, leather belt from the bundle and dumped the clothes. He picked up a dress. "*HOW MUCH?*"

She huddled into herself, trembling and crying.

"*HOW MANY? HOW MANY TIMES?*"

"Not many," she whispered. "You were sick and needed things."

"Skora could help! Chagon would help! Peter would help! Even Ruth . . ."

"Nobody . . . nobody!" She was shaking her head. "I couldn't get near Skora; the soldiers wouldn't let me. But they offered me the tent . . . and other things. Chagon had only enough for himself; Peter quoted the Bible and wept. What was I to do? You were half-alive and half-dead. Should I have let you die?"

"Ruth's wagon wasn't burned. You could have gone to her."

Haltingly, she said, "I . . . went . . . to . . . Ruth."

He drew back. "She . . . she did this to you?" His hand went to his small sword.

"Please, Leo . . ." She reached out to touch him and he drew back. "Please, try to understand. Ruth had problems, too. Everyone came to Ruth, asking for her help."

"*BITCH!*" he shouted with venom and despair.

"Please, Leo . . ." She was reaching for him again. "We thought you were dying. You needed a place, inside . . . the soldiers wouldn't sell a tent. There was no other way . . . not even for Ruth's gold. I did it to save you, for you . . ."

"*FOR ME?*" he shouted. "*YOU BLAME YOUR WHORING ON ME? THIS? FOR ME?*" He grabbed a fistful of jewels and threw them at her. He ran to her chest and threw her garments into the air. "*THIS? FOR ME? AND THIS?*" He shook a dress at her. "*WHORE! SLUT! VIVANDIERE! GO TO YOUR SOLDIERS! BUT DON'T DO IT FOR ME!*"

"Please, Leo . . ." The tears rolled over her face as she reached for him again.

He leaned back and slapped her full across the cheek. She cried out in pain and surprise and fell away from him.

"*FORNICATOR!*" he spat at her and stalked out of the tent.

When Rainald learned of Burel's plan, he assembled his lieutenants. He was not to be outdone; he ordered his men to be ready to march to the castle Xerigordon before dawn and garrison it. Burel would find him in charge.

When the sun was up, his crusader flag, a red cross on a white field, flew from the castle's main tower, and his men were at work rebuilding the fallen stonework and ripping planking from the floor to reinforce the main gates. He would keep the castle, he told his men, even if they had to fight Burel.

The Crossbearers under Geoffrey, Tafur, and Leo marched carefree and noisily to the castle. They were surprised to see the flag on the turret. Rainald's men jeered at them. Infuriated and vindictive in his wrath, Burel refused to enter the gates and turned his men back to the road. He would camp outside. He met with Leo and announced he would not attack the town with Rainald. He would go his own way tomorrow morning.

Leo did not object; he had not intended to remain with Burel or Rainald. Tafur would go with him. The next morning, Rainald's men, from the walls, jeered and catcalled as the other Crossbearers marched away. But Tafur and Leo went in another direction than Burel.

Kilij Arslan, the Red Lion, Emir, whose capital was in Nicea, read the letter rapidly and listened carefully to the words of the courier. He made up his mind quickly; he must return to Nicea. The maggots from that camel's dung heap at Civitot had become a plague. Each day they had become bolder, raiding villages and killing true believers, shaming the women, and showing no pity for the children. It was time to drain their blood. In the Name of the Prophet, he would let their stinking carcasses rot in the sun for the carrion eaters.

He called his generals and ordered them to finish the campaign against his brother without him. He explained that he would return to the capital and dispatch the murderous rabble.

"My people stretch forth their hand and weep piteously for succor. They ask, 'By the next, next deep sleep under the brightest moon, let the Prophet send you back to us. O Ruler of the Faithful, O Beloved of Mohammed, we are accursed and wounded by these Christian dogs which growl and bite us. May Allah's blessing descend upon thee and hasten thy feet to our rescue. We bleed and die by Christian swords and knives.' " He lifted his head and sighed.

"Allah has bid me heed the cry of my people," he told the assembled warriors. His plan was simple. He would take two cavalry squadrons and ride hard to Nicea. That, and the garrison at the city, would be sufficient. He would return as soon as the unpleasant business was finished. The next morning, at sunup, the green standards of his cavalry flew as he rode the road to Nicea.

Leo and Tafur, their horses on a slight rise, looked down upon a peaceful village in a hollow below them.

"Like old times, eh, Leo?" said Tafur with a chuckle. "It always reminds me of Selim when we do this."

"That was a hundred years ago," said Leo. "We are not the same men anymore."

"Still the same, only older, wiser, and more wary. But still the same. Here it will be like taking the purse of a carpet-knight. I haven't seen a single fighting man down there. Have you?"

"Not yet."

"Let Burel run to the bigger towns and get himself killed. We can take these small prizes with much less trouble, and gold is gold wherever you find it. There are no defenders here."

"We should make sure," said Leo. "We want no surprises."

They kicked their horses to a walk and advanced close enough to see the details yet remain hidden. The village slept in the warm sunlight. Children and dogs competed with the flies. It was, as Tafur had said, a place without defenders, and Leo wondered.

The men were old; the women, busy; the children, noisy. He saw no male over the age of thirteen or fourteen.

"Where are the men?"

"Maybe in the emir's army," said Tafur. "They don't expect trouble in a place like this."

"There's nothing of value here," said Leo suddenly prescient. "We should not bother with them." He turned his horse to go.

As they rode side by side, Tafur said, "We have less than they. The men have no noonday meal. Here, with a little fire under their feet, we can find gold, certainly food. There are enough women," he said with a leer, "to satisfy everyone. Some are real dark, beauties. Didn't you notice?"

"My mind was on other things." He didn't want this to happen.

"At your age, your mind changes fast." Tafur chuckled. "I should be as young as you. I'd show them. A soft woman after a good meal is just right for a day like this."

The men needed food and they would not be talked out of this village, Leo knew, not after Tafur told them there were no defenders. Reluctantly, he agreed to the raid.

Tafur's men were sprinkled amid the disciplined guardsmen, over three hundred men on horse. They were split into three groups of equal numbers: two hundred to charge from different directions and one hundred to remain in reserve in the event something happened. Swords drawn, the men galloped into the streets shouting, "God Wills It!" and herded the frightened people toward the water pool in the center of the square.

Children and women screamed and ran in all directions seeking escape. Dogs barked and a few boys drew knives. They were cut down by the riders as easily as stalks of grain. The older men and women hobbled stoically before the horsemen to the square. They had seen raids before in their lifetime and knew what was in store, accepting their fate calmly. Christian or Arab, it made little difference.

The women and children grasped each other for comfort and safety. They all milled about, terrified by the strange fighting men, with their wild eyes and menacing swords. In the square, the horsemen formed a corral and penned them in like animals.

Leo glanced through the poor villagers. What could these poor peasants have that anyone would want? Food was important, but the raid was a mistake.

Two elder men stepped forward to address him. They smiled weakly, salaamed continuously, and spoke in a high-pitched squeal. He could not understand the words.

There was a tumult and screams from a house. The women in the crowd cried out in answer, and the elder men lunged forward in an attempt to grasp the horses' reins. Christian and Moslem alike knew what was happening. Rape!

With a whoop, Tafur slid from his horse, his knife appeared magically in his hand, and he quickly and deftly sliced at the two elders who stood before Leo. They fell, their red blood spurting from their throats, staining their gray beards. The rest of the ribalds, with shouts, followed his example as they dived into the crowd, seizing the men. And the guard was not far behind. The Moslem men and boys died quickly.

The mass of hysterical women broke through the mounted horsemen and ran, and the pursuit began with lustful shouts and laughter. Young girls and children were snatched into the saddle, and the Crossbearers rode off with their kicking, screaming prizes. Others dragged women into the houses and carried their women into the bedrooms. Some crazed men stripped women bare and coupled with them in the street. There were not enough females and even the small children were taken.

When it was over, every woman and girl-child had been violated, a few of them many times as the men waited in turns. Many were dead, knifed by the men who, as they lay upon them, sought a final thrill in their death agony. Few escaped and ran into the hills.

The men fell hungrily upon the food they found. They killed chickens and sheep, roasted the meat, and used the burning faggots to fire the houses. Others searched diligently for gold and jewels. Houses were stripped, their contents thrown into the streets and set ablaze. Finally, satiated in limb and stomach, they dozed in the noonday sun or traded loot with one another.

Leo was stunned by the savagery and felt a rising revulsion. He felt as cold as frozen stone in the midnight air of winter. He had no woman-lust and had even lost his avidness for gold. During the carnage, he wandered off. Skora's words rang in his head, "The Moslem worships God and covets Paradise just as much as the Christian."

"No!" he cried aloud. "There is no other way but through the love of Christ! Lord," he sobbed, "give me strength. Make me not like these men. Suffer me not to lose Thy princely virtue, Mercy."

36

Kilij Arslan sat on his golden throne in his palace in Nicea and listened as the trembling man finished his tale of woe. He had heard of the attack on the defenseless hamlet three times this morning, but this report was from a man who somehow had escaped alive. All the other men and boys had been killed; all the women had been ravished; all the houses had been plundered, and most of them had been burned.

"What else," he asked his chamberlain, "can we expect from these unclean pigs? They are not civilized people, and as mad dogs they must be exterminated."

He made plans. His scouts had studied the encampment at Civitot, and he knew of the occupation of Xerigordon. Those at the castle would be eliminated first. Seven days, he predicted, would be needed for their total surrender, for he knew what the Crossbearers did not: the water for the castle came from a spring outside its walls. He would divert it. "We will see those filthy maggots suck themselves dry on the camels' dung heap," he told his chamberlain.

When the man finished his tearful story, Kilij murmured some words of comfort. "Allah will give you justice," he told the abject figure. "The Christians will pay." He clapped his hands and a slave moved forward. "See to it that he is fed."

He rose from his tired seat. "I will hear no more today," he announced to the waiting petitioners. "My heart is wrung and my spirit cries in pity. After prayers, I need time to think. Allah will give me guidance and vengeance shall be ours."

His chamberlain followed him as the court bowed in reverence.

At sunrise, five thousand Turks stared at the walls of Xerigordon, out of range of the Christian archers. The holes in the stone had been filled, the breaches mended, and the gates and entranceways bolstered with planking and earth. The Turks settled into a comfortable encampment out of the sun's heat as the puzzled Christian defenders watched them. Jeers and useless arrows were ignored. Rainald was perplexed at the end of the second day.

On the third day he learned the reason for the Moslem complacency. As the water ran out, the Crossbearers mounted the ramparts and shouted their imprecations and curses. They shook their fists and fired arrows in their sputtering wrath. Eight nights and nine days the Turks waited calmly; then the gate opened and the gaunt-faced men staggered out, croaking hoarsely for water.

Kilij ordered his men into the castle and found a horror. Stinking, rotting corpses, beset with flies and maggots, lay about in the sun's heat. The flesh was white, the blood had been drained and drunk by the living. Men, dead, were buried to their necks in the sand in a futile attempt to escape the heat; their face-skin was parchment brittle, stretched over skeleton-bone skulls. There were no live animals, but there were piles of horse bones.

The living were given some water. Rainald was found and pushed to his knees in front of Kilij. The emir pondered the short scarecrow who knelt in the dirt, his head between his knobby legs.

"You, Rainald, have a choice," he said pitilessly. "If you renounce your Christ and embrace Mohammed, you can live." His hand toyed with his scimitar.

"My men?" Rainald croaked.

"They have the same choice, but you go first. I follow the Prophet's teachings—or I would kill all of you. You have until the sun sets." He turned away and ordered the crusader removed. Wine, although forbidden, washed the bad taste out of his mouth.

Thirty-seven of Rainald's men elected to live. The rest were tied to stakes and became target practice for the lancers.

Rainald led the living before Kilij. They fell on their knees and babbled in trembling voices, "*Allâhu akbar. La ilâha Alla*"—There is no power save God's. God is great," which was the battle call of the Moslems.

There was contempt on Kilij's lips. "The next time you try to pray, face south from here, toward Mecca." In disgust, he motioned for them to be led away.

The news that Xerigordon was besieged by the Turks came to the crusader camps on the day Rainald surrendered. Burel stalked into Walter's tent with Leo and asked bluntly if the knight was ready to march to Rainald's aid.

Walter's eyebrows came up in surprise. "You worry about Rainald? Since when?"

"I have a plan," said Burel. "If we attack Nicea now, we can easily take it. It is undefended and it is fabulously rich. It is the Red Lion's treasury. From there, we could march on the Turk's army and destroy it. Rainald can attack from behind, from the castle. But we need thousands of men, like Selim."

"We can muster more than five thousand," said Leo, "and we can win easily if we coordinate our attacks. For the city, more thousands will go. They all remember Selim and they ache for loot."

Walter stared from one to the other. "This is high diplomacy," he said with irony, "not just some battle with the Turks. Alexius could be opposed to a war. What would he think? If he wanted to capture Nicea, don't you think the Byzantine army could have done it? We wait."

"If we wait we are lost," said Geoffrey.

"You propose to fight about five thousand trained soldiers and cavalry," asked Walter. "These are not the stupid villagers of Selim. We don't have the armament. And we don't have the trained fighters."

"And you don't believe Jesus will lead us to victory," said Burel turning away.

Walter's short sword was in his hand as he sprung to his feet. "What was that you said, Burel?"

Leo was between them immediately. "We have enough problems without fighting among ourselves."

"Enough talking," said Burel. "I'm rounding up all the men I can get. Some of the knights said they would go," he threw at Walter. "What of you, Leo? Most of the guard is ready to join me."

Leo hesitated. Walter was right, he felt, but the wealth of Nicea tugged at him. He needed gold! He needed battle!. . . to prove himself. Taking a wealthy, Turkish city would be a prize. Maybe Alexius wouldn't let them keep it, but the fame? It had once belonged to Byzantium and was still full of Greeks. And they could not fight the emperor, or the Turks who would come to recover it. But it was rich . . .

Burel did not wait for an answer. "Bah!" he said in disgust and strode from the tent.

"Don't go, Leo," said Walter. "Burel thinks he is a general but he faces an experienced warrior. He is no match for Kilij, even with ten thousand men. Trust me."

"But what of Rainald?" Walter was right; Nicea was a juicy plum and he longed for battle. He struggled with himself.

Walter shrugged. "Rainald . . . and Burel will have to decide this for themselves."

Burel and thousands of Crossbearers who had joined his men marched the next morning. In the early afternoon, bloodied and beaten, men were streaming back into the encampment. Exhausted from running, they gasped the story: It had been a massacre! The Turks were everywhere! They had walked into an ambush! The horsemen were upon them before they knew what was happening! . . . Arrows came from all sides! . . . *The Turks were marching on the camp!* . . . *Everyone must fight!* . . . *For Jesus!*

The later stragglers gave the details of the emir's trap. He had ambushed them in a forest; he had surrounded them on all sides. Arrows, by the thousands, decimated the crusaders' ranks. The Turkish cavalry were demons riding on dragons, and when they charged, they slew the Crossbearers at will. They cast a spell over the Christians using the Devil's Curse: "*Tahwil! Tacbir!*"

Leo turned a puzzled face to Walter. "What are those words?"

"*Tahwil*: There is no might or power save God's," said the knight. "And *Tacbir*: God is great; there is none beside Him."

"That doesn't sound like magic."

"It isn't," said Walter in disgust. "Burel is no general."

The encampment was in turmoil, and Walter rounded up the knights while

Leo brought whatever remained of the guard together to organize for the defense. Everyone agreed: the Moslems meant to attack in the morning. Crossbearers feared for their lives and drifted off into the hills; Chagon sent Inda, heavy with child, to Ruth's wagon and told Ruth to take refuge in the old fort near the sea. Ruth did not wait. With Nina, Mary, Inda, and Little John—sent by Guizio—she hitched her horses and made for the fort with several hundred other wagons. Those who remained girded themselves for battle with the coming devils of Satan.

37

The sun was a blazing torch early in the October morning, and the armed crusaders began to sweat as they sat and waited. In the clear sky, the fire crawled higher and voices questioned the coming of the Turk. Perhaps he had gone home, satisfied with the punishment he had exacted from Rainald. And the tenseness eased.

But Walter and Leo were less certain; and they knew the armed men would not wait indefinitely. Their relief would grow and they would disband. Walter devised military exercises to keep the men busy.

The heat grew more oppressive toward noon, and the big assembly horns called the men to return to ranks. Walter told them the waiting was over; the enemy had not come, but they would not be fooled; they would march out and destroy him before he attacked the encampment. The men cheered.

It was a large army, numbering more than twelve thousand men at arms, and the priests, in their white garments, marched at its head and carried their large, wooden, red crosses, and chanted.

Walter led the knights and the cavalry. The mounted guard had been split, with Leo leading the right flank and Turgot on the left. Behind the horsemen were the Crossbearers with bows and arrows, axes, pikes, and lances.

In a special mass, the priests had blessed them, assured them that the Lord marched with them, for they were doing His work—avenging the blood of their brothers by spilling the blood of the heathen. They were the wrath of the Lord.

They moved on the large plain until they came to Dracon Pass where the road contracted and sank between the rearing cliffs. It would dilate again on the broad flats before the hamlet. The defile stretched for almost a mile, and the horsemen could ride only four abreast. The army thinned and stretched, bunched like a mass of wool passing through the eye of a needle.

There was a sudden rumble of snake drums and the whine and whir of thousands of bees. Hundreds of arrows were homing in on the horsemen. Huge boulders fell from the heights, bounced off the side walls, and crushed horsemen and footsoldiers. The drums increased their tempo as horses and men screamed in their death agonies. The arrows penetrated the spaces of the ring-mail armor, and the knights in the lead fell. Walter was one of the first, and Leo saw the arrows protruding from his chest and back. The knight's destrier reared and fell upon him.

Like swarms of angry hornets, the arrows droned into the Crossbearers' ranks. Then, new horns sounded and the Turk cavalry attacked from the rear.

Leo huddled in a narrow cleft at the turn of the pass, where he and his closest riders had found an overhang. Protected from the bowmen on either side, the turn of the road gave them shelter from the archers on the wall. As men crawled in, horses were turned out, only to fall victim to the wall of death. Men nearby called and cried, and Leo, who had been joined by Tafur and Turgot, ground his teeth in anger and despair. To leave the cleft was to invite immediate death.

The cavalry died and the bowmen still fired barb after barb into the corpses. The pass was choked with stones and bodies.

At the mouth of the pass, the infantry was broken into a milling, disorganized mob, terrorized out of their minds, and fleeing in all directions as they sought to escape the screaming Turkish horsemen. The panic was epidemic. From all sides came the terrible war cry, "*Tahwil! Tacbir!*"—and the war drums quickened their beat. Above it all, the Moslem horns shrilled their triumphant song of victory.

Stricken, confused, and hysterical, the crusaders ran helter-skelter in complete madness. But there was no place to hide. And the murderous, turbaned horsemen followed them everywhere.

Guizio crouched low to the ground to make himself inconspicuous. His eyes were filled with red hate, and he bared his teeth at the oncoming horseman. He needed that horse to escape the field of slaughter. He muttered an oath as the rider veered off and opened the back of his quarry from neck to buttocks. Then, the horseman wheeled and stopped to decide his next victim.

Guizio's snarling grin widened and he moved quickly. The Moslem's back was toward him, and with a shouted oath he was astride the horse with a leap. His knife plunged savagely into the Turk's back, and he twisted and carved with all the strength of his great hands. The man arched his back and screamed. Guizio cut off the wind to his mouth with his arm and, in a few seconds, threw the body away.

He grasped the mane of the plunging animal, kicked ferociously into its flanks, and headed for the far side of the field. His body was flattened against the horse's back; his face was buried in the coarse hair of its mane.

Chagon lay against the rumbling belly of a horse, bleeding to death with an arrow in its throat. The rider, dead, was still in the saddle, his skull crushed by the blacksmith's heavy hammer. He gasped in short breaths as he grimly worked the thin, polished shaft of an arrow protruding from his left side just below the ribs. He could feel his strength flowing out, and the large beads of perspiration stung his eyes. The blood made his hands slippery. His teeth locked into a grimace each time he twisted the barbed head, and he jerked with the lightning pain.

Suddenly, he expelled the air from his lungs with a great sigh and rested.

He pondered the question: Why take the arrow out? He would be a martyr in Heaven like all the others. He would watch the survivors march to Jerusalem. The Good Jesus would forgive him for running away from his wife and children, for all his sins. The others would take care of Inda—and the baby.

Inda! The thought roused him. The baby! He struggled desperately with the arrow, ignoring each twist of pain. He took a deep breath; he clenched his teeth, and he tore the barbed head from his bleeding flesh. He threw the arrow away and pressed his palm against the wound to stem the flow of blood. His eyes swam; all sounds faded; a graying darkness gathered. With a moan, he toppled over on his good side; and the blood welled between his grasping fingers.

The Turk cavalry was spearing the rabbit-running Christians, and the mounted bowmen hunted the refugees as game. They displayed their skill as they fired over their shoulders as their horses ran in the opposite direction of their quarry. Their nimble fingers nocked arrow after arrow as they aimed with a glance. The Christians, by the thousands, lay dead and dying. Hundreds more were pursued as they fled back to the encampment at Civitot. They were followed into the forest and underbrush by the relentless enemy. The slaughter continued all the way to the camp, where their high-sounding horns announced their arrival.

With the horns, Kilij Arslan recalled his disbursed cavalry. They set a line, and at his command they charged through the tents and wagons and butchered men, women, children, and animals without distinction. Tents were fired; wagons were overturned on the blaze. Running Crossbearers were decapitated. Priests stood, their eyes closed, their crosses raised, and mumbled their last rites. The horsemen made them particular objects of torture by cutting at the robe first, then methodically slicing the stupefied men to pieces.

Women were disemboweled by the scimitar's thrust and twist. Able-bodied men were cut apart and dragged by their entrails. The camp burned, and the black smoke rose like some giant thundercloud.

In one area, Kilij's personal guard had formed a corral of horses, and young boys and girls were herded into it to become objects for the slave blocks. A comely, yellow-haired girl or a strong youth could bring a high price, and Kilij extracted payment for everything.

By late afternoon it was all over. Thousands of corpses littered the camping grounds and stretched all the way to Dracon Pass. What animals still lived were herded into the camp. The hysterical children in the compound were examined for health, beauty, and strength. All who appeared weak, sickly, or overly thin were led out and killed. The rest would return to Nicea. Peter's peasant crusade had reached its martyrdom. But there were some who still lived.

The sounds of the battle had stilled when Leo led his small band of men out of the rock cleft. The dead were everywhere. The men wept at their impotence;

their fists flailed at the imaginary enemy; their hands beat the ground in their rage. They crawled among the corpses and sought the living. But no one could remove the barbed arrows, and the wounded bled to death.

Tafur urged them out of the pass, on to the forest where they could hide. "We should not be here when those devils come back. We can do nothing. There is a time to fight and a time to run. This time we run. But there will be another time."

Leo mournfully agreed, and they slipped out of the pass and lost themselves in the woods.

Ruth and the others had established themselves safely in the old fort by the time the Turks descended upon the encampment. They found the roofless buildings large enough to contain them, but the walls were broken, and the entranceways had lost their gates. Under the direction of the older men, they set to work. Planking was ripped from the floors, and heavy masonry stones were placed into their previous positions. The small entranceways were boarded up, and the main gateway was closed with stone, earth, and wood. The wagons were arranged in the open central area, and the Crossbearers settled in to await the fate of the battle.

The sun was low when the lookout from the fort's only tower shrieked, *"THEY'RE COMING! THEY'RE COMING!"*

The green standards of the Red Lion came at a slow trot; there was no need to hurry, and the animals and men were tired. It was a small troop, under two hundred men. Their orders were to take the fort and kill the Christians hiding in it. After they camped, the crusaders could hear their laughter and prayers.

In the compound, the women trembled and huddled, for theirs, they believed, would be a slow martyrdom. Weaponless, except for a few axes and knives, the men knew they could not hold off an attack once the Moslem devils succeeded in entering the walls. Parenti, who had fled the attack on the encampment, held a mass and preached a sermon.

"Fear not death," he intoned, "for that way we become One with the Lord. Jesus is gentle, but our God is a vengeful God, and by His wrath the Infidel will suffer. Lift up your heads and pray, and He will answer your prayers." He was commanding the Sword of Fire. After a silent moment, he said, "I will hear confessions in the small room on the left."

Mary prayed as she had never prayed before. She poured her heart and soul into a desperate plea for the life of her unborn child and, as an addendum, mentioned herself. Her words had never held such a deep meaning to her, and the intensity of her fears invaded her spirit. There was a sudden clarity of her mind. The turmoil of her life, an understanding of what she was, and what she had been, overwhelmed her. In the fervor of her prayers, she was washed and cleansed. She floated outside the confines of her body shell and could see the fleshed form, the substance called "Mary." And she watched, devoid of all feeling, the suffering of the human as it writhed and wept, as it groveled and moaned—while her spirit was light and disembodied. Then, within her, grew the insistent need to return and confess her transgressions.

Weeping, she returned to herself. She craved forgiveness: for herself, for Andre, for Tom, for Leo, for Jeanne, even for her father. Whatever she had done, she felt she had done out of necessity. She knew not the reasons, nor did she care. Only the forgiving, healing solace of Jesus could allay her fever.

She sat before Parenti's improvised curtain and after a while the words came. "Forgive me, Father, for I have sinned. I have sinned in the desires of the flesh; I have lusted and lain with my brother; I have been with men before I was wedded; I have lain with others after I took the sacred vows. I have committed adultery for money and coveted fine clothes and jewelry to decorate my body. I have been mean and wrathful, and I have not obeyed my husband. Forgive me, Father . . ." Her voice became a whisper. "I have need of Your love, for now I understand what it means to love another. I wish to give life to my unborn child and not die tomorrow when the Turk comes. Save me, Father . . . save my child . . ." She was weeping uncontrollably and could not go on.

Parenti, worn, tired, only half-listened. He had heard so many of the others, and there were more to come. The night would be long, and he had his own peace to make with the Lord. And there was no one to hear his confession.

The voice had stopped and he could hear the soft sobbing of the woman. "Repent," he said aloud, "and spend this night in prayer. God has listened to you, do not fear, and when death comes welcome it, for you will join all the angels in Heaven." He yawned.

Little John stood in the center of the circle and hopped excitedly from foot to foot. "It's a good boat," he insisted. "I found it in the rocks, and it has a sail and everything."

"It's too dangerous," repeated Ruth. "You'll drown. You don't know how to sail a boat."

"I could go with him," said one of the older men. "I can sail it, and what's the difference if we do drown? We stay here and we won't live through tomorrow. This is a chance."

"How will you know where to find the city?" asked another.

"It's just across the straits," said the first. "If the boat's seaworthy, I'll find it."

It was dark, but they had little trouble finding their way to the sea. The boat was heavy but manageable, and they were soon lost on the black, night waters.

The palace guard could not understand the strange duo who suddenly appeared before them, but they heard and knew the name Peter.

Peter wept when he heard what had befallen his people, and although it was late, he demanded an audience with the emperor.

Alexius listened impassively. He was not unhappy that Arslan had removed a troublesome rabble from his responsibility, but he could not remain indifferent to the plea for rescue without making himself an accessory to their sure fate. The ignominy of another massacre in the fort with his knowledge would dishonor him forever.

Admiral Butumites and General Phoacus were awakened and the war council was brief. There was little time, but by sunup a few warships with soldiers in full armor were sailing across the straits. They were to be a show of force and to warn Kilij that to hamper their rescue mission would invite a larger conflict. Arslan, Alexius was sure, would understand and would withhold his troops from the attack to allow the rescue to proceed.

During the night, Inda woke in a cold sweat and clutched her midsection. The pain doubled her over as another searing knife thrust went through her. She screamed.

Mary, lying beside her, jumped, scare-eyed. "Inda?" Her hand fumbled in the dark. "What is it? Are they here?" Her mind was on the Turk.

Inda was too frightened to answer. Another twisting pain left her breathless and she groped for Mary. "*IT'S COMING! . . . IT'S COM . . . ING! I . . . CAN FEEL . . . IT! . . . MARY! O MOTHER OF GOD! . . . MARIEE-E-E-E!*" She gasped for breath.

Mary jumped up. "*RUTH! NINA! INDA IS BIRTHING! RUTH!*" She struck the flint with trembling fingers until the spark caught the candle. "*RUTH!*" she screamed as the two girls came in.

Inda was writhing on her pallet. "*LORD . . . JESUS . . . MERCY . . .*" "*MARY? WHERE ARE YOU? MAR . . . IE-E-E!*"

"Get the others," Ruth ordered Nina. "They'll know if it's time." She knelt beside Inda. "Help me prop her up," she said to Mary. "And get some rags. She's sweating."

They worked together. A memory struck her. "Remember what it was like in the barn when the sheep lambed?" She giggled in fear.

"We could use Ellia," said Mary. In a few months her time would come and she was anxious.

"She's gone and good riddance," said Ruth. "The others will do just as well." Her old crone had disappeared one afternoon when the supply ships had sailed back to Constantinople. She had tried to convince Ruth and Nina to go with her, but they had refused.

"Fools," she had cackled in anger. "You sit here in the mud, and there is gold in the streets of the Imperial City." She had spat and hobbled away. They never saw her after that.

Inda screamed again and Mary turned to Ruth. Ruth shrugged her shoulders helplessly. "God said women would have pain." She was philosophical. "Momma died with you, remember?"

Two women bustled in, glanced about, and took charge. They shoo-ed the girls out, but they could still hear Inda's moans and cries. Finally, there was one shrill scream which ended in a sob, cut off as it subsided, and followed by the wail of a newborn infant. The three girls sighed in relief.

"Let's go see," said Mary and they reentered the room.

The two women were busily washing the blood from a mewing boy and Inda. The floor was wet and slippery where she lay, and she smiled weakly at them, exhausted and happy.

Chagon never knew.

At sunup, Kilij Arslan rode to the fort. Captain Ilkhan reported stiffly and they toured the area. Arslan smiled as he studied the hastily fortified buildings.

"Burn them out," he ordered. "If that fails, go in after them, but get it done today. I am returning to Nicea. You will report to me tomorrow morning."

"Yes, your Honorable," saluted the captain.

Kilij glanced at the fort and remarked idly, "I wonder what Alexius is thinking." He mounted his horse and turned to the captain. "Tomorrow morning; and if any of them are worth keeping, spare them. We could use more slaves."

Captain Ilkhan moved quickly to fulfill his orders. Cut brush was placed against the improvised gate. The fire was stirred to smoke, and the wind blew it directly into the fort. Fire arrows were shot over the walls, and the wagons were aflame, their smoke curling lazily into the sky. The cavalry waited for the soldiers to break through the planking and dirt of the gateway.

Admiral Butumites saw the rising smoke and ordered that the oarsmen's beat on the drums be increased. Little John paled. "They're on fire! The Moslems have attacked!" He yelled at the sun, at the sea, at the Byzantines. "Faster! Faster!" and stamped the deck of the ship.

There was a sudden shift in the wind and the smoke rolled toward the Turks. Parenti, on his knees, cried out, "*WE THANK THEE, LORD! WE SHALL BE SAVED! PRAY, CHRISTIANS, PRAY!*"

And Captain Ilkhan decided that the burning was a failure. He ordered two squads to prepare for a frontal attack. Lancers moved in and scattered the brush from the gateway using their iron-tipped lances as prods. When the fire was gone, men clambered over the earthen breastworks. There was an opening large enough for a man to squeeze through, and as they did, one at a time, they were seized and dispatched by the knife-wielding defenders. Ilkhan soon realized that he would have to make a frontal attack. He pulled his men back, had the stone and debris removed from the opened gateway, and lined his cavalry into a column.

The appearance of the Byzantine ships of war made him hesitate enough to count them. He had no orders to engage the Greeks and he pondered his problem. Kilij would not welcome another conflict while he was at war with his brother. He, Ilkhan, had orders to be at Nicea by tomorrow morning. He decided that discretion was better than any possible glory and a few slaves.

The Christian pigs had been adequately punished; the few that remained were of no consequences and were certainly not worth an engagement with the Greeks. He signaled that the horns blow assembly and ruefully he withdrew.

The survivors welcomed the disembarking troops with tears of delight and screams of joy. They streamed aboard the vessels and hugged and kissed the sailors. They sang the praises of the emperor and the Lord. They were allowed only few of their belongings, and Ruth was heartbroken as she left her wagon and many possessions, clutching only a few chests of jewels and gold to her bosom.

The fleet triumphantly set sail for the Eternal City. At the quay they were met by a weeping Peter. The monk was on his knees. His body rocked as he beat his breast in anguish. The wail came across the water.

"*Mea culpa! Mea culpa!* Forgive me, O Lord, for I have grievously sinned. Forgive me," he sobbed. "O my Savior! What have I wrought?" The tears coursed down his weather-beaten cheeks and disappeared in his gray beard.

38

As Peter wept, a small crusader army, a lean fighting force of knights and soldiers, with no women, no pilgrims, no sutlers, crossed the Adriatic Sea and toiled through the winter passes of the Pindus Mountains. It moved through ancient Epirus, across Macedonia, and met the Via Egnatia, the old Roman-built road to Constantinople, at the Vardar River. There it sacked a Bulgar pagan town and met Emperor Alexius' troops.

Lord Bohemund was the last of the great lords to leave, but not the last to arrive. Of all the knights, Alexius feared this lord of the rapacious Italian Normans the most—and with good reason. His name headed many thick folios in the Hall of Records of the Byzantine Ministry of War. He had been the scourge of Byzantium's western lands for twelve years. He had destroyed two Byzantine armies before Alexius, finally victorious, drove him back to Italy. A wary, mutual respect, laden with heavy suspicion, burdened both men. The Betchenak patrols were never far away as Bohemund moved toward the Imperial City, but they never engaged in combat. Bohemund controlled his knights.

"First things first," he told Lord Tancred, his youthful nephew and second in command. "We come to fight for Jerusalem—and pick up whatever else belongs to the Moslem. Alexius, for the moment, is an ally."

He had learned about the crusade late. The Duke of Apulia, Roger, his half-brother, had called the family together to help besiege the city of Amalfi. The burghers had revolted when Roger raised their taxes. The knights of the family had gathered to crush the rebellion. But the siege went poorly and Bohemund blamed Roger and fretted. This afternoon, the duke hosted a dinner and amusement for the knights and their ladies, but Bohemund was disgruntled and in a dark mood as he and Tancred walked.

Tancred spoke to change the atmosphere. "Have you heard what the monks are saying?"

"Who listens to monks?" Bohemund grunted. "They talk to God too much and always hear the same answers. Reiteration is boring."

"They say Papa Urban wants volunteers to fight for the freedom of Jerusalem from the Turk. That is something new."

Bohemund stopped his pace. "When did you hear this?"

"It happened, they say, November last, at Clermont. Your old friend Emperor Alexius wanted mercenaries, but Urban says we should fight for Jerusalem, not Constantinople."

"Who will pay? Urban or Alexius?"

"What do you mean, 'Who will pay?' Urban says it is a holy war."

"So? We always fight for God. That is what pays for our souls. But payment for our bodies comes from somewhere else. I thought that was one of your early lessons. Who pays?"

Tancred was outraged. "We fight for the Church! Remember your vows, uncle!"

Bohemund snorted. "For you, nephew, to remind me of my vows is an unpardonable sin. Remember that. Each time a pope opens his mouth he thinks he speaks for God. But we know better. He only speaks his beliefs. He may be God's vicar on Earth, but he is not God Himself. He can bless wars or curse them, but, holy or damned, wars make gold for someone. And if we fight, we will be paid—by someone, be he pope or devil."

"Uncle!" The young knight was horrified. "You blaspheme!"

"And what is wrong with Christ's pay, Lord Bohemund?" The voice came from behind, and both knights whirled to confront the intruder, their short swords in their hands immediately.

A broad figure stepped out of the shadows. He raised his hands, with palms open, to show he was unarmed. He wore a monk's habit and a wide, cherub's grin. "Do not fight with me," he chuckled. "I am on the Lord's business and I object to a punctured skin."

"Francis!" exploded Bohemund. "Never challenge me from the rear."

"Nor from the front," said the sweaty monk. "I know."

"Greetings, Brother Francis," said Tancred, putting up his sword. "What are you seeking in Amalfi?"

"You both. And the sun is warm here in winter." He raised a hand to stop Bohemund. "Eh, eh, Bohemund. I know." To Tancred, he said, "He never tires telling me that he knows of a good, warm place for me. But the truth is we are both no strangers to Satan's devices." He examined their clothes. "I see you seek his cunning ways tonight."

"You are well sent," said Bohemund, "but you have no percipience. My question was: Tancred tells me Papa Urban trumpets a crusade to Jerusalem. What do you know of it?"

"Everything. I came to enlist you in God's cause. And to answer your other question: God pays."

Bohemund paused. "My men must eat, my old friend. Sometimes, it is difficult to collect God's coin. Does Urban have gold?"

"No, but the Moslem has. I have inquired of Alexius in your behalf. He is willing to forgive an old enemy like you if you are willing to bury old desires for pieces of his empire. *Quid pro quo!*"

"A fair exchange. What are his terms?" The suspicion lurked. "And how much can he be trusted?"

"You remember him well." He turned to Tancred. "He almost had your uncle's head. Did he ever tell you the story?"

"Many times. Over and over. He surrendered to the Turk."

"Better the Turk than Alexius. But you blather like an old woman," said Bohemund. "This comes when a fighting man grows soft and joins the Church. He grows stomach muscles."

"Not so," protested Francis. "I may have laid down my swinging sword, but I still carry one I can use."

"The one at your inside belt? Or the one between your legs?"

"Both, Bohemund." Francis grinned back.

They had reached the pavilion. Knights, ladies, pages, serving girls, and others who tended to the wine and food crowded the tables.

"We can't talk here," said Francis as he eyed the area.

"Why not?" Bohemund gazed about. "No one will pay us any attention and I have many questions."

"You do not need me, uncle," interrupted Tancred. "Whatever course you choose, I will be there, too. My thirst is great." He turned to Francis. "We are well met, Brother Francis, but I need refreshment and company." He bowed and disappeared.

"The acorn has not fallen far from the tree." Francis watched Tancred go. "You have done well with him. Oh, to be young again and to seek refreshment in wine and women." He turned back to the tall knight. "But you are only forty or so. You still have years."

"Old enough to know. Yes, he has done well for himself. But his tongue is sharp."

"A family characteristic," said Francis dryly. "But must we miss all that good food and wine. We can talk and eat, too."

"Later. Tell me of Urban and Alexius. What terms?"

"Alexius expects you and the others to pledge vassalage. But once you are out of Byzantium . . ." He spread his hands.

"And trust? We will be surrounded by Moslems and his armies."

Francis' grin was cynical. "Whom do you trust, Bohemund? Roger? who would speak with God if God would only speak back? Tancred? who would lay down his life for you? Richard of the Principate? or any other of your vassals? Your trust is only in your sword."

"You blather again. I do not need an old crone."

"Perhaps, but we are old friends and we understand each other. Must I be a scribe and list all the riches of the East? You have been there and you know. Remove them from the infidel."

"And here? At home?"

"Urban cannot give you Apulia even though you helped your father win it. For political reasons, it stays with Roger. But the Church promises to keep Bari and Taranto safe for you. Just think! You could link those ports with whatever seaside city you conquer in the East . . . your own shipping lanes, with taxes at both ends." He grinned. "Christ pays well for service."

"Spare me your sarcasms," said Bohemund. "I fight well in the Lord's service. He will not allow me my prizes in Heaven."

"Nor in Hell either."

Bohemund grinned. "Read me not my last rites so quickly. What else does Urban offer?"

"A few extra jewels. Dissolution of all previous vows, even marital. Your knights may find that invigorating. All contracts and agreements voided for those who go." He nodded toward the pavilion. "What would your knights say if all vassalage vows were suddenly dissolved?"

Bohemund's eyes widened. "He cannot go that far! What else?"

"Minor things. All your sins are pardoned while you partake in the Lord's work; all debts are cleared; all prisoners in jails are free to go; all spoils you seize—lands, gold, slaves—are yours with God's blessings. Pay enough?"

"In good faith! Pay enough! By the God you love, Urban will hold to all this?"

"I swear it on the Madonna. I swear it on my Lord Jesus! I swear it on my immortal soul! Faith enough? More I cannot swear."

Bohemund studied the monk's face. Then, he held out his arm in the old Roman and knightly armlock. Francis took it and they stood momentarily face to face.

"Before God," said Bohemund, "I believe you. I volunteer."

"Good," exclaimed the monk. "Now can we have some wine and food?"

Under a large canopy, the tables sagged with overladen platters of food: fruits from the southern islands; newly hunted meats; gamebirds—grouse, pheasant; fish from the warm Mediterranean; wines from various regions. There were spices and sugar-dried exotic tidbits from the East. Roger had spared little expense.

Troubadours passed through the crowd or stationed themselves beside the ladies of their choice. They engaged in small talk or sang songs of love and endearment, seeking liaisons.

A knight's realm was hunting and fighting; the singers catered to the soft whims of the ladies. Few bothered with love; only the children were important. For a troubadour, the wedded woman knew the true meaning of love. She had shared a marriage bed and knew the higher ecstasies, unlike her maiden sister who had only her trembling, shallow desires for her experience. The unwed maids sighed in their yearnings and listened to the older women.

The news that Bohemund and Tancred had agreed to march to Jerusalem spread like a newborn forest fire. No one could find Tancred and few dared ask Bohemund directly. When word reached Duke Roger, he accosted his half-brother in anger.

"Is it true? You plan to leave before the city is taken?"

Bohemund smiled and nodded. "I think so, brother."

"You break your vow to *me*? You just . . . leave?"

"Softly, dear brother. I have had a gutful of your delays. The Church has called on the faithful and I have obeyed. I would advise you to speak little of broken vows." He was enjoying this.

The knights, grinning broadly, gathered close. They had wondered when Bohemund would reach his flash point of anger and explode. It would create a new excitement.

"What do you expect me to do?" Roger was boiling. "This campaign has cost me a fortune in gold."

"Go home, Roger. Give the burghers what they want, and they will pay your new taxes."

"Take the cross, Roger." Francis, a moonlike smile on his face, dangled two strips of red cloth. "Take the cross. It will bring balm to your soul."

All eyes watched the trio. Impulsively, Bohemund reached for the ribbons and, using his mantle brooch, pinned them to his shirt. Roger balked off and turned away. Bohemund, with a gesture of contempt, drew his sword and turned toward their audience.

"*I FIGHT FOR THE CROSS!*" he cried loudly. "*WHO FIGHTS WITH ME?*"

There was a loud cheer and the knights pressed forward.

"*FOR THE CROSS! GIVE US THE RIBBONS! GOD WILLS IT!*"

The clamor spread as others came. Bohemund ripped his red mantle from his shoulders and, while another held it firmly, hacked it into strips. Eager hands reached for the pieces. Pins came from the ladies, equally caught up in the excitement. Tancred appeared, a lady on his arm, and pushed to Bohemund's side.

Bohemund grinned. "We go to Jerusalem, nephew. I have saved these for you." He handed the young man two red strips.

Tancred's lady provided a pin. Arm in arm, the two knights, their swords drawn, shouted, "*TO JERUSALEM!*" Their faces were red in their ebullition.

With one voice, four hundred of the assembled knights took up the cry. Brother Francis, his cherub cheeks puffed in a satisfied smile, closed his eyes and settled his clasped hands over his rotund stomach. Then, he sighed.

39

The warm days of December faded and the winds became wet and cold. Lord Godfrey of Lorraine hurried his army toward Constantinople. Before Christ's Day, the guards on the Golden Gates stared in disbelief at the thousands of gleaming helmets shimmering in the sunlight. With grudging admiration, they watched the precision of the erection of the encampment.

Duke Godfrey's pavilion was set in the center of an ever-expanding ripple of concentric rings: the tents of the vassal lords—the lesser knights—each according to rank, and ending with the tents of the soldiers. The wagons followed the orbital pattern. Squires let out thousands of war horses and patroled the herds. Cooks lit their fires, and the savory odors of roasting meats made the watchers swallow their rising spittle.

Godfrey was supervising the placement of his knights' pavilions when Baldwin, his younger brother, galloped up.

"I have news," Baldwin shouted. "Some of Peter the Hermit's men are waiting at your tent. They tell a story of massacre and death. I think you should hear them immediately."

"Is Peter with them?"

"No. They say Alexius holds him prisoner. They say thousands of Crossbearers have been murdered by the emperor."

"Murdered?" Godfrey was dubious. "That is a strange charge. All right. I will hear them."

They were a motley, ragged group, old and bearded, and appeared starved. Godfrey threw his horse's reins to a squire and said, "Bring some food . . . and wine. They look scarecrow hungry." He faced them. "Who speaks for you?"

"I, Lord Godfrey." A monk stepped forward. It was Parenti.

"You know me?"

"Who has not heard of the Duke of Lorraine? I saw you in Rome when you rode into the Lateran. I, too, was with Clement then."

Godfrey winced at the memory, the cause of his illness. "Remind me not of things past," he said harshly. "What have you to tell?"

Page boys were bringing food, and the starved men fell upon it ravenously.

"We came to ask a boon. Can we march with you to Jerusalem?"

"All Christians can join the crusade. You may stay behind the soldiers with the other pilgrims. What else?" He was impatient and annoyed. "You told Lord Baldwin of a massacre?"

Parenti nodded. "Trust not this emperor. We marched with Peter, more than thirty thousand of us, and here . . ." he motioned with his arm, "except for a few hundred women, children, and sick ones, is all who remain. We had few troubles until we were attacked by the mercenary Moslems of this emperor at Nish." He spat. "May they roast in Hell for all eternity!" His eyes glared. "They murdered thousands of good Christians at Nish: men, women, even the children. When we came to his polyglot city, he put us across the water, into Asia. There, we were slaughtered by the Turks. They fired our camps and took our best children for slaves. Trust not this emperor! He fears Urban's crusaders."

Godfrey remembered the Betchenak patrols who harassed his men. His face was grim. "What else," he said curtly.

Parenti felt uneasy. "We came to join you and to warn," he repeated. His agile mind sought something else to offer this cold, stern nobleman. "Some of these men are good fighters," he said in desperation. "All they need are axes and spears."

Godfrey examined the monk. The information was of little use to him. Evidently, the cleric realized it. He wondered what had excited Baldwin. There was no trust in Alexius' promises. And if the massacre story was true, it merely confirmed other reports.

"What is your name, brother?" He threw at the monk, "From what Order?"

"Brother Parenti." The other question was ignored. "I was the right hand of Peter."

"Well, Brother Parenti, I thank you for your news and the warning. You and the others can stay in the rear with the other Crossbearers. I have no arms for the men, but they should have little trouble securing what they desire after the first battle. God be with you." He entered his tent.

Parenti faced the others. "We stay. In the rear. Take your food and let's go . . . now! Quickly! Before he changes his mind."

Alexius pondered his problems as he rested in his colonnaded gallery. His head was on his chest; his eyes were closed. Baron Ducas stood quietly beside him, his eyes fixed on the rippling waters lapping the marble stairs. He shifted a tired leg. Alexius had been quiet a long time. His thoughts wandered to Godfrey.

The duke was recalcitrant. He politely accepted all the embassies and gifts the emperor sent but steadfastly refused to permit the emperor to ferry him across the straits to the Asian shore. The barons, Godfrey insisted, had agreed to meet *before* the walls of the Imperial City. And he would wait for them there.

Christmas was gone, and the New Year had passed. Each new day was worrisome and bred new suspicions.

"What are you thinking, John?" Alexius had come out of his reverie to penetrate Ducas' thoughts.

"Alternatives," Ducas replied. "Perhaps we can impress upon this stubborn Westerner that our winters can be dreary. His tents are thin. We can offer him castles on the other side of the Golden Horn. If he won't cross the straits, perhaps he will be willing to leave the walls and cross the bridges to the outer districts."

"A good suggestion," Alexius nodded. "Try it."

To their delight, Godfrey agreed. The tents *were* cold, and the fires and warmth of the castles were agreeable. He led his army across the bridge to the open countryside and occupied the proffered castles and villas. The golden waters of the inlet separated him from the city proper, but Godfrey felt it was close enough. It was certainly more comfortable.

To secure the knight's agreement, Alexius offered to sell him all the provisions he would need at an extremely reasonable price. Godfrey was happy to strike the bargain. Alexius breathed in relief. Lord Bohemund had marched out of Durazzo, and he did not want the two knights to meet alone. He organized a plan.

"Watch him closely," he said to Ducas. "Send squadrons of cataphracts to guard all roads leading to the bridges across the horn. We will have trouble with him."

His prediction was accurate. Mutual distrust had sharpened the suspicions of the Heretia, the Imperial Guard. Their officers were hand-chosen mercenaries from all the corners of the world, and they guarded their prerogatives jealously. Elite, proud, and arrogant, they feared the crusader knights and sought ways to diminish their strength.

Godfrey sent his men foraging through the farmlands, and there had been clashes between the guard and the Crossbearers. When knights died in a Heretia trap, Baldwin ordered immediate reprisals. The captured guardsmen were put to death. The Heretia struck back in force and many crusaders died. Angered, Godfrey ordered his camp evacuated and burned. Baldwin was sent to secure the bridges, which he did despite the guards deadly attacks. Godfrey then marched his men back to the rolling plain before the city's walls.

Furious, Alexius directed raids on the crusader camp until Godfrey, in desperation, attacked the Golden Gate in force. But he was not prepared for the strength of the thick walls. The bowmen repulsed his cavalry by turning their arrows on the horses, and the knight was aghast as thousands of animals were slaughtered. Shaken by the wanton killing, Godfrey ordered a retreat.

Alexius, triumphant as the Westerners pondered their next move, cut all supplies to the encampment, and Godfrey countered by sending his men through the countryside to pillage. But it was late March and food was scarce in the farmlands. He called a council.

"Gentlemen," he said grimly, "we have two courses open to us. We can withdraw completely and live off the land, or we can come to an understanding with Alexius. Neither choice is welcome, but I see no other alternative."

Baldwin spoke first. "We could attack the villas outside of the city walls and provide so much ruin that Alexius would have to come to us."

There was a lifting of heads. They *could* lay waste the outer farmlands. They were proud and they were galled to go hat-in-hand to Alexius.

The Knight of the Blue Falcon demurred. "We came to fight the Moslem. To kill Christians is to become allies of the Devil. Let us make the best bargain we can with Alexius until the other barons arrive. Then, we can leave Byzantium."

Many agreed with his wisdom and even Godfrey, despite his anger, finally nodded. "It will be a negotiation from weakness," he said, "but we will not remain here long. We will talk."

Only Baldwin was unhappy. He remained in the encampment when Godfrey and his escort rode into the city.

Much to the knight's surprise, Alexius came to agreement rapidly, and his terms were reasonable. He would sell all supplies at very reasonable prices if . . . Godfrey would agree to move to Asia immediately, and if . . . Godfrey and his brothers would swear fealty to him. Further, he would supply the army as it marched along the coast toward Jerusalem by using his ships; he would send guides along; he would lend sea and land support with soldiers if . . . Godfrey agreed to return all cities and lands the Moslems had taken from Byzantium. Godfrey was amazed at his charm and friendliness.

Godfrey did not know that the empire had once extended almost to Jerusalem. He did not know that Alexius' great generosity was enhanced with the knowledge that Bohemund was only two weeks away from Constantinople. He did not know that the emperor had intercepted Bohemund's letter urging Godfrey to be wary and not make any separate agreements with the emperor.

Gratified, Godfrey knelt before Alexius and swore fealty.

Greatly relieved, Alexius showered gifts of gold, wine, and women upon the knights . . . and ferried them quickly over the Straits of St. George to the Asian shore.

Ruth could hardly wait for the boat to dock. She rushed from the ship to the old fort to see if her big wagon still stood in the compound. She took Little John with her. As they approached, they saw a thin column of smoke. A small herd of horses was grazing near the gate. The boy approached the gateway cautiously and peered inside. He saw no one. The wagons had been pushed against the walls to enlarge the central area where a makeshift fire pit smoked. He scurried through the gate and hid behind a wagon. Ruth nervously waited for him to return and tell her what he had discovered.

"*RUTH! RUTH! COME QUICK! RUTH!*"

His high-pitched, excited call spurred her into action. She ran into the compound with dread. Little John was dragging someone by the hand and screaming. Her mouth opened as she gasped.

"*GUIZIO!*" It was a shriek of delight. "*GUIZIO! HOW?*"

She threw herself into his long arms and kissed his dirty, bearded face.

When the excitement cooled, he related how he had escaped death. He hid in the forest while the Moslems were about. He lived by raiding the local farms at night. He had wandered into the fort one night; he knew nothing of the rescue and wondered what had happened to the Crossbearers' bodies he had expected to find. Actually, he was seeking Little John's body to bury it. He had continued to live at the fort, using Ruth's wagon as his home. He had caught some of the old horses wandering in the fields, and when he wasn't engaged in searching for food, he collected arms: swords, knives, daggers, spears, axes, bows and arrows. He had a large assortment stored in the wagons. He had even retrieved the knights' armor.

"Leo?" Ruth was fearful, but hopeful. "Is he dead?"

Guizio raised his shoulder with a shrug. "Gone, like the rest of them, I guess, but I didn't find his body—nor Tafur's. They all stank so much after a few days in the sun I had to leave. The carrion birds were everywhere. It was a big feast for them." He was bitter. "Nothing remains but bones."

Ruth shuddered and crossed herself. "Maybe they escaped."

"Maybe." But neither believed it. "I found Chagon." He was quiet. "He pulled an arrow from his side before he died."

Ruth shuddered again. "The knights are coming. They will avenge us. We came back with Duke Godfrey, with thousands of soldiers. The Moslem will die for what he has done!"

Her vehemence excited the boy. "We'll take their heads and roll them like balls! We'll grind their bones and make dice!" He simulated a throw.

Guizio scratched his beard. "Nina? Mary?" he asked. "Inda must be ready to drop her bundle."

"A few months ago, actually while we were still here. You should see how big her son is—like Chagon. Even if he wasn't nine full months," she added meaningfully.

Guizio snorted. "What difference does that make now?" He was matter-of-fact. "It's good to see you, Ruth. I missed our own kind." He turned to the boy. "Come on, Johnny. I'll need your help with the horses."

"Wait, Guizio." She stopped him. "I was thinking. I've lost my old crone. I'll be needing a driver—and protector. Would you work for me?"

His eyes lit up. "I'll stay as long as you'd want me, girlie. Don't worry about the money; we'll work something out."

She smiled at him. "Find an extra wagon and horses for Inda. She'll need her own." She had an afterthought. "Take the biggest one you can find. It will be handy."

40

Less than five hundred knights, their squires, and meinies came ashore near Durazzo with Bohemund that early December morning. Approximately two thousand soldiers were in the infantry. The city's governor, John Comnenus, the emperor's brother, welcomed them. He had direct orders to provision the hated Normans and provide them with any aid they sought. No incidents were to occur and, despite the governor's many temptations, none did.

Bohemund passed through the countryside and turned into the byroads of the mountains. The trails were well known to him. He had used them extensively during the years he had fought Alexius. A mild winter was upon them, and they moved stolidly through the open passes, followed cautiously by a troop of Byzantine horsemen grimly determined to watch every move. Brother John was taking little chances that Bohemund would keep the peace he had pledged.

But Bohemund did.

The blossoms of the Judas trees had fallen when his forces saw the gray walls of Constantinople. The knights dug their spurs into their horses' flanks, and the footsoldiers set up a cheer.

Later that afternoon, Baron Ducas presented himself at Bohemund's pavilion. The diplomat eyed the tall, slender man with interest. He noted the still-lean loins, the deep chest, the powerful arms.

"The years have been good to you, Lord Bohemund," he said in admiration. "Not even a tinge of gray among the red strands of your hair. The emperor and I bid you welcome."

Bohemund smiled wryly. "Baron, I greet you. But I have little use for whiskers. The years, I see, also sit well with you. May I present my nephew, Sir Tancred?" Tancred, beside the tall knight, bowed. "And Lord Richard of the Principate?" Another bow. "And Girard, bishop of Ariano?" The bishop bowed.

"Gentlemen," the baron was expansive, "the honor is mine. In the name of the emperor, welcome."

"With you here to greet me," said Bohemund, "I would surmise that Alexius has something to tell me. Or have things changed?"

"No." The baron was smiling. "We have only become older . . . and, I hope, wiser. Let the past be buried."

Bohemund nodded thoughtfully. "What does he propose?"

"May I speak freely?" Ducas was bland.

Bohemund settled back. "We are not in negotiations, baron."

Ducas raised an eyebrow. No talk with Bohemund had ever been socially easy. "I had not realized we had progressed that far," he said dryly. "Emperor Alexius invites you to the palace. Tomorrow, before the noon sun. He wishes to greet you and reminisce."

Bohemund smiled knowingly. "Tell the emperor I am honored. I will be there—with my escort, of course."

"Of course," murmured Ducas. There was a momentary pause.

"Is there something else?"

Baron Ducas nodded. "I sense . . ."—he searched for the word—"a wall of hostility. It is the emperor's explicit wish that I make clear that a close rela tionship and a mutual belief in our sacred honor should provide us with friendship and trust. His very words were, 'Let our hearts and souls combine to bring to all of us a higher love for Our Lord's work.' "

Bohemund examined the diplomat's face. He knew diplomacy well, and he knew Baron Ducas. "It is a noble desire, and I echo it," he said blandly. "But I, too, will speak freely. It is my knowledge that Duke Godfrey preceded me by a few months, and . . ."—he paused—"and he has had a number of differences with the emperor."

"The noble lord arrived before Christ's day, as you Westerners celebrate it," Ducas said smoothly. "There were some misunderstandings. But they have been clarified. Friendship and agreement now prevail. Duke Godfrey awaits your arrival, on the Asian shores, with some impatience."

Bohemund nodded thoughtfully. "Odd. We were to meet here, on the plain before the walls." His demeanor suddenly changed. "Tell Alexius we shall be delighted to see him again tomorrow."

Ducas bowed. "It shall be done. Until tomorrow then." He bowed to the others. "Gentlemen." He left.

Tancred broke the silence. "You have no doubts, uncle? Riding into the lion's den may be painful. Godfrey may have been bitten."

"True." Bohemund grinned. "But I am neither a Godfrey nor a Daniel. Further, I believe the lion sheathes his claws for the present. He needs our amity, not our displeasure. Too many of us come. He may fear we will take his city away from him."

Tancred's eyes lit up. "That would be spoil indeed."

"Calm yourself, nephew. That is not the game anymore. We will need Alexius if we are to function in a sea of Moslem sharks. Further, his ships can supply us when we fight. He can help our trade once we establish our own fiefdoms. All must be smiles and pleasantries. In this chess game we plan ahead."

"Then I should not let down my guard?". He was facetious.

Bohemund beamed. "Well said, nephew. You are learning. Alexius will offer us gold, wine, jewels, fine garments, women, and silver. After that, he will give us more wine and more women. There are high morals in Byzantium—and many low women. And the women are the most plentiful and the cheapest. If you are willing to be bought, the offerings will be bountiful. I see no reason to deny him his desire and our pleasure.''

"But what of Godfrey?'' asked Richard, who had been listening.

"I hear Godfrey has turned churchman and seeks his peace with Jesus,'' said Bohemund. ''He must have refused Alexius' offerings.''

"Then we must keep loose swords in our scabbards,'' said Richard.

"Always,'' smiled Bohemund. ''To trust the emperor's deceptions is to invite disaster. To let your hand stray too far from your sword may be your last mistake.''

Bohemund came to his appointment with Alexius with a small escort of ten knights. The two old enemies measured each other in small talk for a few hours. Each played his assigned role well: Alexius, the host; Bohemund, the guest. They chatted jovially about old times and recalled their battle strategies. After their idle, diplomatic sparring, the talk led to more serious matters.

Pointedly, Alexius said, ''Duke Godfrey has taken the oath of fealty to me and the empire. Will you do likewise?'' He was prepared for Bohemund's guarded diplomatic denial.

"I have been waiting for you to ask,'' said the tall knight. ''The answer is yes.''

Alexius, taken aback by the unexpected, recovered quickly and cupped his palms. Dutifully, Bohemund knelt and placed his closed fists into the emperor's hands. Fealty sworn, Alexius arose from his gilt chair and embraced his new vassal. They walked arm in arm to a small dining room. The emperor's entourage and the knight's escort followed. They dined exquisitely and the talk was light and gay. The knights were charmed by the wit and knowledge of the ladies, so unlike their own uneducated wives.

The emperor's daughter, Anna, attached herself to Bohemund, and he could not refuse a tour of the special galleries under her guiding hand.

"They said you have eyes like a hawk, but that they are blue instead of black,'' she said. ''And that's true. And that your hair is red and you are tall, taller than the giant Norsemen who guard the Golden Gate. And that's true, too.''

Bohemund laughed. ''But, princess, I *am* a Norseman—a Norman from the Italian lands. Did you also hear I was the Devil Incarnate?''

"No-o . . . oh, yes, in some ways! My father says you can be as terrible as the Devil or as charming as Pan.''

"Have no fears, princess. I play no pipes,'' he chuckled. ''I shall guard you with my life.'' He was gallant.

The slight girl cocked her head as she looked at him. ''I like that,'' she said flippantly. ''Pan is a frivolous devil. I may ask father for my own special guard of Norsemen. I'm old enough. I'm thirteen.''

Bohemund grinned. "To me, you look at least fourteen, my princess," he said cavalierly. "It is too bad that I have some unfinished business that will not wait. Otherwise I might volunteer."

Later, he was led to a sumptuous apartment prepared for him by the emperor himself. Alexius had been magnanimous. Rich garments, trimmed with rare furs, were piled on the chairs. Upon the tables were vessels of gold and silver. Jewels and jade sparkled from two small chests. And a large chest was filled with gold coins.

Bohemund, almost penniless, contemplated his new riches and took a deep breath. From an inner room came the sound of running water and the low singing of a female. He smiled to himself.

He gasped at her beauty when she came into the room. She was dark and her naked form could be seen through her flowing, sheen gown.

"Your bath is ready, my lord," she said. "Shall I bathe you?"

Alexius was pleased with the evening's success. "It has gone well, John," he said to Ducas. "I believe the wolf has been tamed. Bohemund has asked to be my legate since I told him I would not lead our army south with the others at this time. What are your thoughts?"

"The tame wolf can turn savage quickly," mused Ducas. "He never forgets the sweetness of the blood he finds at the lamb's throat."

"True," nodded Alexius, "but as long as he wears the wool of the lamb, he can serve us well. I will not choose him legate, but I can dangle it as bait. That will keep him in line. We will need him for the ceremony when the others swear their oath. We must arrange it within the week. Raymond of Toulouse will soon arrive."

Imperial heralds summoned the knights from Asia. Before the dinner, each knight received a gold-lettered parchment and a gift of gold bezants. Alexius sat in his courtroom, surrounded by the grand nobles of Byzantium dressed in their most resplendent robes. The famed Vanangian Guard, "The Tall Ones," in their bright silver breastplates, their gold helms, and their brilliant, scarlet mantles, stood in a tight semicircular arc behind the emperor's chair of inlaid gold. One step below the stagelike dais, on the right of the emperor, looking uncomfortable, was Duke Godfrey. Across from him, on Alexius' left, erect and head high, was Lord Bohemund.

One by one, the knights of the Western armies knelt before the emperor and took the oath of fealty previously taken by the two leaders. They pledged their swords and their lives; they promised to return to Byzantium all lands they would conquer if they had once belonged to the empire; they swore their loyalty to the emperor. When the long afternoon was over, the feasting and socializing began.

"My scouts have found a city almost surrounded by a lake," said Godfrey. "What is its name?"

"Nicea," sighed Alexius. "Taken from us by Kilij Arslan, whom they call the Red Lion. He keeps it as his capital. Many of my loyal subjects suffer there under his iron hand." He sighed again.

"We could attack it." Bohemund sensed Alexius' desire.

"And it could be a first victory," mused Alexius, as he hid his pleasure that the suggestion had come from the knight, not him. To emphasize it, he turned to Ducas. "What do you think, baron?"

"A persistent siege could bring victory," nodded the baron. "Kilij is away at war and the garrison is not strong. Boats could cut their supplies from over the water, if we linked forces."

"An attack on the walls and a blockade on the water. Good!" Alexius turned to Godfrey. "What do you say, Duke Godfrey? Lord Bohemund can act as liaison. When Count Raymond arrives, he can join us." He became warm with his vision. "Let us drink to the first victory of the cross."

He clapped his hands for wine, and the scantily dressed, dark, African slave girls hurried to serve the goblets.

Bohemund scented that Alexius had a special reason for designating him as liaison. He readily agreed. As liaison, he would have the emperor's ear for other schemes. Godfrey, tired of waiting in idleness, was happy to march, to battle the infidel. They all smiled in agreement and lifted their goblets in a toast.

While the knights drank, Tancred and Henry of the Principate, of Bohemund's forces, quietly left the palace and sailed out of the city. They had refused to take the oath of fealty, and Alexius had duly noted their absence. He mentioned it to Bohemund, who assured him that they meant no disrespect. He would take care of it.

Back in their camp, the two knights found a strange group of half-starved Crossbearers awaiting them.

Leo was a gaunt skeleton beneath his dirty rags. Tafur, his bulging eyes glistening fanatically from his skull-like face, was a body propped on two knobby rail-legs. Wet drool hung from the side of his mouth, and he was constantly wiping it with the back of his bony wrist.

"We know all the ways," he winked at the knights. "All the paths. Give us some food—and wine—and we can show you where foraging is the best. We know." He winked again.

"We haven't eaten for two days," said Leo. "The hunting has not been good."

"Where did you get that knight's sword?" Tancred asked him.

"There are plenty of swords at the pass," said Tafur. "If you need any, give us food and wine, and we'll lead you there."

Tancred ignored him. "Can you use it?" he asked Leo.

"I have learned," said Leo. "When I fight again, you will see."

"After you have eaten, we will see. That sword is only for a knight to wield."

"He who wishes it will have to fight me."

Tancred smiled. "So be it." The food had arrived. "Eat. Then we will play. I would see how you use it."

The starved men came alive as they seized the cold meats. They stuffed their mouths with bread, bit on the bones, and sloshed wine down their gullets.

"Can we join your camp?" Leo asked between bites.

"You were with Peter the Hermit?" asked Henry.

"All the way to the bitter end, from the beginning," said Leo. "They trapped us in the pass . . . burned our camp . . . killed everyone . . . all the women, the children . . . ." He shook his head. He stopped chewing and his eyes became glassy. "Everyone," he muttered.

"We made them pay . . . oh, yes, we did . . ." chuckled Tafur, as he wiped his greasy mouth. His eyes lit up. "We keep sending them to Hell." He drew his thumb across his throat. "Every night . . . we catch some and . . ." He made the gesture again. "We watch the blood spill out . . . every night." He took a savage bite on the bone he held. "Corpse for corpse . . . we took a pledge."

Tancred sent his squire for his sword. "If you are done," he said to Leo, "let me see how long you can keep that sword."

Leo rose reluctantly. "I would rather we didn't fight. I was hungry and you fed me. And I am no knight, as you are."

"Then give up the sword." Tancred was smiling.

"No! It is mine."

"Then prepare to defend it." He was a full head taller than Leo, and he rocked confidently on the balls of his heels. He had no intention of killing the dirty skeleton who stood before him, but he could not allow a knight's sword to remain in the hands of a peasant. He was surprised to see Leo assume a knight's stance before combat.

The squire swung the sword to loosen his muscles. His belly was full, and the good wine had made the blood flow with renewed vigor and energy. He cocked the two-handed weapon over his head.

"I am ready, Sir Knight," he said and crouched.

Tancred paused momentarily. It was obvious that the man had been trained. He glanced at Henry, who shrugged with a smile. He brought his sword up, and the two men half-circled each other.

Suddenly, Leo leaped in, and his sword rang twice against Tancred's parrying weapon.

"You jump well, scarecrow," laughed the knight. "Here. See what you can do against this." His sword flew waist high with a blow which could cut a man in half.

Leo did not try to stop it. Instead, he jumped and turned, bringing his sword in a wide arc down toward Tancred's arms. Tancred had to loop his swing upward, and the two shafts of steel rang and vibrated as the two fighters fell away from each other.

Leo was agile and quick. He could handle his sword with the ease which comes only with practice. But he was worn and haggard. His newfound energy disappeared quickly. His muscles tired. He had neither the training nor the expertise of his opponent. His breath was soon coming in short pants. Suddenly, his shoulders sagged, and he planted the tip of his sword in the ground at his feet.

"I cannot fight you, Sir Knight," he said bitterly. "You could have killed me many times."

Tancred grounded his sword as Leo's. "You fight well. Have you been a squire?"

"Yes, to Sir Walter. His bones lie in the pass. This is his sword. I swore to keep it as long as I live. Now, it is over."

Tancred handed his sword to a page. "You have done him honor, squire. His sword should avenge him. You may march with the footsoldiers—and keep the sword. If any other knight should ask, tell him it is my word."

Leo bowed his head. "Thank you, milord."

Late that night, Alexius spoke to old, wily Admiral Butumites. "I have special orders for you, admiral. Kilij comes not to Nicea." He handed him a paper. "Here is a list of our spies inside the city. Rumors should be spread that these Crossbearers are barbarians; that they will burn the city and rape the women. We do not wish that to happen. It will not, if the commander surrenders to me."

Butumites smiled and bowed. "It will be done, your eminence. What terms should I present to them?"

Alexius grinned. "The usual: my protection and security of the families of the officers; the ransom demand will fit their purse; Arslan's wives and children will be treated with due deference, and with no ransom demand for them."

"And if they reject us?"

"Then tell them that the Crossbearers will seek revenge for the dead in Dracon Pass. They will be savage and bloodthirsty in their pillage. The city will be destroyed. I will find it impossible to stop them once they enter the walls."

Butumites bowed. "It shall be done, my emperor."

"Make sure that any messenger they send over the waters to Kilij is allowed to escape. He will send an army to relieve the siege so we must act quickly."

Butumites bowed. "As you say, my lord." He left.

"I give it three months," Alexius said to himself half-aloud. He opened a door and spoke to someone inside. "Your hair looks lustrous, Alan."

A slim, youthful woman entered, in a long, silvery gown. "I have just combed it," she said. "Shall I let it grow longer?"

He looked at her and held out his hand. "It is not important. Come," he said gently. "I have need of your warmth tonight."

41

The armies of Godfrey and Bohemund spent four days in preparation for their march on Nicea. On the fourth afternoon, they assembled on the great field of Pelecanum, the special army camp of Byzantium in Asia. Peter came from the city to preach a sermon.

He was gaunt-eyed and hollow-cheeked; his old habit hung loosely on his thin frame; his feet were bare and dirty. He was deeply immersed in his self-imposed penance, and he began his sermon in a whisper, his shoulders bent forward and his eyes downcast. But as he spoke, he straightened his back. His voice deepened, and he was seized by the spirit of his own passion.

"The Lord has tested us," he thundered, "and we must prove that we are worthy. Look to your faith. Death is only the passing of the flesh, but the Spirit prevails. The dead and the living are like one—One in the great flame of God's mercy."

For the moment he had once again wrapped himself in the mantle of Urban's chief advocate.

"Many have already passed into Heaven. Their flesh was murdered by the Infidel, demons with men's faces. Fear not to kill these demons. They have no power over the cross. When the hour of battle comes, strike terror and vengeance with the mailed fist of Jesus. The Infidel will tremble; the devils will die!"

He was overcome by his own rapture and collapsed. The host gasped as he crumbled. Was it an omen?

"No! He is not dead!" The priests calmed the milling men. "The Lord has poured the heady Spirit of Faith into his frail body and it wearied him. He will rest and be well again."

Mary sat beside the wagon and strained to hear Peter's words. All but Guizio had gone to the field. She was large with child and wept easily and often in her anxiety. She brooded over Leo.

Guizio had refused to hear Peter. "Who wants to listen to that preacher of doom again?" he said snappishly. "He sucks his wine on the soft pillows of the palace while we wait. Who needs him?"

To divert her, he told her tales of the Paris streets. She laughed at his jokes. Suddenly, she grasped his hand and drew in her breath as she sat upright in her chair.

"What is it?" He was tense. "The baby?"

She shook her head. "A pain . . . nothing; it's gone." She doubled over in sudden agony, her hand gripping his arm.

"You should lie down!" He hovered over her. "Come!"

She was afraid to move. Like a knife cut, the pains ran through her sporadically. Inda had said they would be far apart at first . . . as a warning . . . but they came often and close together.

Guizio trembled in his fright. "Is . . . it beginning?" Afraid of nothing, childbirth terrified him.

She nodded. "I think so." She gulped for air. "*DON'T LEAVE ME!*" she cried as he started toward the wagon. "*IT'S COMING! I CAN FEEL IT!*" She had begun to sweat and her body was on fire.

Not sure what to do, Guizio lifted her and carried her into the wagon. He laid her gently on a pallet. "I'll be right back," he comforted her. "We need some women."

She lay in a circle of dread, her mouth dry, and she tried to curl herself into the darkness. "Leo," she moaned, "Leo." The blackness closed about her. A sharp, stabbing pain went through her groin and she bloodied her lip. Her abdominal muscles rippled with the contractions. She gasped; the air moved out of her in a blast. Her head swam. She moaned as she lost track of herself.

"*OPEN YOUR LEGS!*"

The order came through clearly. She could feel hands pulling her apart, exposing her. She fought, screaming! *She was being raped!* She tried to twist. She couldn't move.

"*YOU CAN'T HAVE THE BABY WITH CLOSED LEGS! OPEN THEM!*"

"Relax, we won't hurt you." It was the calm, soothing voice of a woman. She allowed herself to be pulled apart.

The pains grew and grew. She was twisting, and being held . . . the muscles knotted . . . her body trembled and shook. There was a probing . . . an overbearing pain. She screamed and screamed.

Hands . . . hands all over her . . . on her legs, her arms . . . even inside her . . . they were prying. She squirmed, screamed as flashes of lightning exploded and flared under her eyes. There was a sudden blackness; her muscles shuddered, relaxed, shuddered again. "*MOTHER OF GOD!*"

"Push!" It was an order. "Push! Hard! Push!"

Obediently, she contracted her stomach muscles and pushed. The pain swelled like a tidal wave. It rode higher and higher. The crest broke. And she screamed in agony. "*AIGHEE-EE-EE-E!*"

She fought to escape, to tear free of the restraints. The tide receded. Her wind came in short pants. Her mouth was sand. But she could not break free.

"*PUSH HARDER! MORE! MORE!*"

The voice came from a distance. The tide was rising again. Higher! And higher! It rolled over her! She was gasping for air! A searing, knot-twisting pain cut through her. It sliced her flesh . . . a heavy blow was delivered to her groin. She tried to double up . . . but couldn't! A scream left her sagging.

Water? It was rising! She panicked in terror . . . it was washing over her . . . drowning her! She screamed for air! Air!

Her body arched and she was held down. From her unhinged jaw came a nightmarish cry for succor. Her mind exploded—a thousand fragments of shimmering lights, flaring into darkness.

"IT'S ALMOST OUT! PUSH! PUSH! PUSH!"

Somehow the words came through. With the desperation of the damned, she contracted once more. Her body humped forward and upward. Her muscles stretched like the gut of an archer's bow. A hurricane of sound and wind burst free from her bloodied mouth. Her body thrashed as it sought to expel her innards. She felt blocked, her cavities jammed. Suddenly, her flesh ripped, and there was a blessed cooling relief of wetness, of oozing slickness, an unblockage of pressures.

"IT'S HERE! I HAVE IT! ONCE MORE! JUST LIKE BEFORE!"

She filled her lungs. More and more. Beyond reason. Beyond thinking. Beyond stretching.

"P-U-S-H!"

She expelled everything in one gigantic burst and collapsed. She became a limp corpse. She was freed from her tormented body. She was weightless, a floating specter. And she was rising . . . high . . . higher . . . swaying, to . . . and fro . . . her spirit felt no pain; the turmoil of her physical self was over.

The woman who pulled the baby from Mary's bleeding vagina straightened her weary back. A slimy length of umbilical cord trailed after the child. She pressed Mary's abdomen. Her hands rolled firmly downward until the placenta came out—yellow-pink, slimy. She lifted the bluish baby, pushed its small limbs out of their tight coil, and with the cord still trailing, she wiped the mucus from its mouth, its nostrils, and its eyes. Ruth handed her a string, and she tied it tightly around the cord. With a knife, she cut the umbilical cord close to the flesh. Then, she turned the baby over and rapped it sharply on the buttocks. From its throat came a mewing wail. She handed it to Ruth.

"Here," she said without feeling, her voice matter-of-fact, "wash her. God help her." To Nina, she said, "Get a bucket for the rest of this garbage. Take it outside and bury it deep, so the Devil won't get it." Nina rushed to obey.

Ruth washed the red-skinned infant in warmed water and wrapped it in some old cloth. She brought it to her sister. "Look, Mary. You have a daughter."

Out of the fleecy clouds, where she floated serenely as a disembodied angel, Mary's consciousness slowly descended. Light as a down feather, she circled back to earth. She squeezed her eyes to peer at the red head moving fuzzily before her. Her back ached; her groin throbbed and burned. She felt a cooling of the flesh; she sighed. The woman had packed her vagina with water-dripping herbs. Her eyes rolled upward and closed.

"She's asleep," said Nina surprised.

"She needs it," said the woman. "God is good to her."

Little John ran, his arms waving in his excitement. "I've seen him! I've found him!" he shouted. "He's here! He's coming!"

Guizio stopped him. "Who?" he demanded.

"Leo! Leo!" He hopped from foot to foot. "He's alive! Alive!"

Guizio grasped him by the shoulders, almost lifting him off the ground. "Where?" He shook the boy. "Where?"

"Here! Here!" Little John was insistent. "At the Mass! I saw him! He saw me. Was he surprised! He thought we were dead."

Ruth and Nina, who carried the baby, came out of the wagon.

"He's alive! He's coming!" Little John called to them.

They were bewildered. Guizio explained. "Leo's alive. Johnny saw him at the Mass. He's coming here." His eyes lit as the excitement finally penetrated him.

"Our prayers have been answered," said Ruth. "Who else did you see?" she demanded of the boy.

"Only him. But he said there were others."

"Tafur?" questioned Guizio. Little John shook his head affirmatively. "Are you sure?"

"That's what he said." He noticed the infant. "Is that Mary's baby?"

"Yes," said Nina.

"Is *he* going to be surprised."

They waited for Leo in contained excitement. Ruth held the child. They had not told Mary, who had wakened, nursed the baby, and had fallen asleep again.

"Hello, Ruth." He had come up so quietly behind her that she had not heard him.

"Oh!" She was startled. "Leo!" She stared at him.

Guizio clasped him by the arm. "You all right? Nothing hurt?"

"I'm fine . . . fine. Not even a scratch." He stared at the child. "Is it Inda's or . . ."

"It's yours, and Mary's!" Nina exclaimed. "Your new daughter!"

Leo nodded, too choked to say anything. He put out his hand to touch the child but drew back. "Is Mary . . ."

"She'll be well. She's asleep, resting," said Ruth.

"Where have you been all this time?" asked Guizio. "Tafur? He's with you?"

Leo nodded, but his eyes remained on the infant. "We escaped. We raid the villages to stay alive . . . It's a girl, you said?"

Ruth nodded. She saw the sadness about his eyes and his grim mouth. "The baby looks like you."

He lifted the hood from the sleeping child's head. "How can you tell? It's all wrinkled."

"Women know these things," she said loftily. "I'm glad you're here. Mary needs you."

"I can't stay. We march on Nicea tomorrow. Mary can stay here."

"You know she can't be with me. We can get another wagon—like Inda's. She has a son."

His face remained stony. "Chagon is dead," he said flatly.

"We know." She brushed it aside. "Why can't you stay?"

"I'm with Lord Tancred. No families follow him, only fighting soldiers. He said if I fight well he will make me a squire." His eyes lit up. "Maybe he'll even knight me if I do well in the battle."

"You are moon-crazed if you think you can become a knight. Royal blood stays with royal blood. You are an innkeeper's son."

"We are nothing but dirt to them," said Nina. "We know."

"I had one who called me 'sir,'" chuckled Guizio. "Imagine! Me. A sir! Of course, a knife at the throat made him amiable."

"You don't understand," said Leo. "I can become a Knight of the Sword if I am a squire. Many knights will die between here and Jerusalem. If the Lord spares me, I can win knighthood. The crusade is like a hurricane. It will turn everything upside down. It blows glory and riches, as well as death. You never saw so much gold and jewels as the emperor gave the knights at Constantinople. This land has all of it, and the squires and knights talk constantly of wealth and fiefdoms. I intend to get my share—with my sword."

"There are other ways . . ." began Ruth.

"I am not a woman. And Mary is my wife." His face darkened.

"I am not a woman either," said Guizio. "Nor a knight, but I will find plenty for me."

There was a brief silence. "We each can do it in our own way, then," said Leo. "My way is through the sword."

"You men!" snorted Nina. "Stubborn, thick-skulled, and stupid. "You kill for gold and glory—you say, only to throw it at some woman in your bed. How many have you killed already, Leo?"

He shrugged. "I've lost count of the dead. Does it matter? If I die before Jerusalem, I'll be with the heavenly hosts. If I live, I'll be a knight, with a castle and slaves. Tell Mary I love her and I'll see her after Nicea." He placed his hand gently on the hooded infant's head. "Good-bye, my little one. I will come to see you after the battle, if I live." He grasped Guizio's hand. "Will you stay here?"

"You said Tafur was with you. Do you see him?"

"He was, but now he roams at will. He leads a band. I see him sometimes."

"Tell him I stay here, with Ruth."

"Thank you, Guizio. You ease my fears."

"And what do you have for me?" asked Nina.

He took her hand. Impulsively, he bent forward and kissed her on the forehead. "I shall always remember you." Then, he was gone.

42

Under a morning May sky, the crusaders broke camp and moved to Nicea. They came to the Valley of the Martyrs and a giant hush fell over them. Even the birds were still; the world had settled into silence. The bleached, flesh-bare bones, whitened by the carrion birds, the dry winds, and the hot sun, lay everywhere. Skeletons whole, and skeleton parts, in clusters, and separate, filled the graveyard. A shudder went through the living as they plodded on the trail. The priests murmured prayers; the monks repeated Peter's words: Mourn not the dead, for only the flesh is gone. Their spirits lead us. Do not fear the infidel for Christ points the way to a glorious victory.

The song started faintly. Soon all the marchers were singing:

"LORD JESUS, WE ARE COMING;
THE INFIDEL WILL WEEP.
WE MARCH, IN GLORY, SINGING;
OUR VOWS TO YOU WE'LL KEEP.

"FOR THE DEAD WHO LIE AROUND US;
LET YOUR RADIANCE SHINE ON THEM.
LORD JESUS, WE ARE MARCHING
TO JERUSALEM."

It was the old marching song but it had a new verse.

The huge wagons of Duke Godfrey, high as houses, swayed as they followed the fighting men. Their gigantic wheels, big as millstones, gouged foot-deep ruts in the soft earth. The duke and his brothers rode first; Tancred and Richard followed. Bohemund had remained in Constantinople with the emperor.

The riding squires led the destriers. The war horses were muzzled and hobbled; their fine coats glistened with sweat; their huge muscles trembled. Behind them came the noble ladies of Lorraine, of Gascony, of the Rhineland. Their faces were flushed with the heat and excitement; their voices were raised in high-pitched chatter.

The air was filled with the creaking and rumbling of the wagons, the noises of the animals, the gay laughter of the women, and the singing of the soldiers. Thousands of people, all moving as though they were on a gala picnic.

The soldiers were herded into units from the countryside in which they had been born. Bohemund's soldiers marched together as a single unit. Behind them were the peasants, the pilgrims, from the villages, the towns, the cities. They, too, were songing, and they stepped lightly over the mounds of ordure, the droppings of the animals who plodded before them. Everything was churned into the soft earth, which became a yellow paste under the thousands of feet and wheels.

They marched three and a half days. Then, they saw the washed walls of Nicea, battlements which rose out of Lake Ascania like a large fairy castle. Built by the Romans, the walls ran more than four miles and girded the entire city. Three sides were on land; the fourth rose out of the shallows of the lake. More than two hundred gleaming towers soared skyward. They were broad-based and so turned that archers had complete command of every section.

The Westerners paused at the sight. Except for the walls of the Imperial City, never had they beheld such battlements. Never had they laid siege to a city so completely cinctured. The green banners of Kilij Arslan flew from the standards on the towers.

Lord Godfrey's horns sounded, and his army wheeled into an encampment on the north, out of the range of the bowmen. Richard and Tancred, in the name of Bohemund, camped on the eastern side. The south was left for Count Raymond; Bohemund had sent word that he was on his way.

The western wall was footed in the marshes of the lake, and the Moslems, at their will, came and left the city over the waters.

Count Raymond of Toulouse had arrived at the Imperial City in a calculating frame of mind, prepared to dicker with Alexius, but his mood soon turned bitter. He had come ahead with a small escort. At the city, messengers informed him of continual attacks of the emperor's Betchenak patrols after he had left the camp. Bishop Adhemar had been wounded.

"Many died," said the messenger, "but Bishop Adhemar managed, despite his wound, to drive them off."

"My lady? My son?"

"All safe, milord." The courier handed him two letters—one from the bishop, the other from Elvira. "Bishop Adhemar has things well in hand."

Relieved, he dismissed the man and turned to the epistles.

The bishop's letter related the details. It ended with an admonition: I have concern for your safety. Beware of possible treachery. This emperor has a pro-pensity for malice.

It was an indignant, pugnacious warrior who confronted Alexius the next morning. He demanded retribution and compensation for the deaths of his men and the losses of his property.

Alexius, his smile fixed, had received prior news from his couriers, and he struggled to check his temper. His commanders had gone further than ordered—he had not desired a battle—but there was no turning back now.

"My dear count," he said smoothly, "you must understand that bandits swarm the highways. My men try to sweep the roads clean of such vermin, but they succeed only partially. It must have been the brigands who did all this damage to your people."

"This was an attack in force, planned and executed by military commanders," stormed Raymond. His voice became brittle. "Do you take me for a fool, sir? I am no callow youth!"

Alexius bowed before the storm. "The fame and renown of the count of Toulouse is well known and highly respected even at this distance from your home. If my men have erred, if they have shown excessive zeal in their tasks, they shall be punished, and compensation will be granted with our expressed wishes for pardon."

Raymond was mollified.

Alexius pressed forward. "Surely, you are aware," he sighed, "that mistakes will happen. To be just and even-handed, errors occur on both sides of a conflict. I have word of raids on our villages, of many dead, of rapings, and burnings of homes. Our soldiers have orders to protect our own. Come, my friend, we are both soldiers of many campaigns. We know how difficult it is to control the passions of eager men in the heat of battle. Nonetheless, you have my firm promise of satisfaction. We are One with the Lord."

Raymond, a diplomat, realized that Alexius played a double game. He allowed the emperor to appease him further. "I have not come to fight with Christians, but I do not intend to be taken for some mendicant knight. I will remain in the Holy Land after we have conquered Jerusalem."

He, too, played at diplomacy. Sooner or later, he would have to come to terms with Byzantium.

Alexius understood his subtle hint. "If you are to remain in the Holy Land," he said smoothly, "it would be best for us to become fast friends. Duke Godfrey and Lord Bohemund have sworn fealty to me and the empire. Will you take the same oath?"

The question required further thought, postponement without offense. "I come to do the Lord's work and He is my only overlord. My oath to Him should be sufficient." There was room to maneuver in the word "should," and Alexius nodded slowly.

"I see," he murmured. "Let us think on it. I, of course, cannot leave here because of conditions in the empire, but leadership is important. Someone must be my legate." He stared at Raymond. It was almost an open offer of appointment.

The eyes of the two men met momentarily, in complete understanding, but it was Raymond who turned away first.

An hour later, he was visited by Bohemund. The tall knight came directly to the point. "You know my history as well as I know yours, Count Raymond." He was brusque. "We are both versed in diplomatic obfuscation, but I will speak plainly. Duke Godfrey and I have sworn fealty to Emperor Alexius. So have Robert of Normandy, Robert of Flanders, Stephen of Blois, Hugh of Vermandois, and every other count, duke, and baron. We believe that it is proper that you do likewise. The road to Jerusalem may be long. It is our opinion that we all be in agreement regarding our relationship to Byzantium. To be otherwise is to court discord between us and give the Infidel undue advantage. Think on it.''

Raymond stared at Bohemund with dislike. He knew of the past wars between Alexius and the lord of Bari. The new loyalty of the tall knight meant hidden promises and agreements.

''I have already informed the emperor that I would consider the matter,'' he said stiffly. ''I have not yet concluded my thinking.''

''Consider, then, our own relationships. If we are to march together, we should have the same objectives. If we march separately, only the Moslem prospers, or we may attack one another.''

''I will consider that, too, sir knight.'' The audience was over.

Bohemund bowed and withdrew, his face fixed.

Raymond speculated whether Alexius had sent the Italian Norman, or whether Bohemund was attempting to make crusader policy on his own. His forces were to arrive tomorrow. He would counsel with Adhemar.

The two men met in the bishop's pavilion in the area previously occupied by Duke Godfrey.

''Bohemund seeks privileges from Alexius,'' mused the count. ''He has been bought with gold or promises—or both. Alexius' arm will be felt everywhere we do battle even though he sends no army. His hands reach out for whatever spoil we seize. His claim is previous ownership by the empire.''

''The empire has not extended everywhere,'' said the bishop, ''and we fight in one small corner. The Moslem surrounds him. If we win, we break the enclosure, and he wins, too. If we fail, he is not the loser. He can still come to terms with the Infidel. We can be independent yet act in concert with him and the others.''

Raymond's glance at Adhemar revealed his incomprehension. ''I do not follow you.''

''The Church of Rome and the Church of the East can act together yet remain separate entities. We each require each other's aid *now*. Later, when the campaign is finished, we may still need his goodwill. Bohemund may have turned mercenary already—but his objective is the same as ours. He will seek his own spoils. Further antagonism with Alexius will bring us no reward.''

''I will take no oath of homage.'' Raymond was cold.

''No need. You could swear negatively. Swear *not* to threaten the life or rule of the empire, or of the emperor. But neither will your sword be engaged *to aid* either emperor or Byzantium.''

Raymond's face broke into a slow grin. ''You have a devious mind.''

''Sometimes I even surprise myself,'' Adhemar grinned back.

Alexius found he had to be content with Raymond's negative oath. He urged the count to cross to Asia to aid the others besieging Nicea. Raymond agreed, and the Byzantine fleet began the huge task of ferrying his large forces across the straits.

The days of the crossing were spent in wining and dining. Alexius sought ways to soften the suspicious knight. He gave rich gifts to the count's entourage; he instructed his women to pay particular attention to Elvira and her young son; but Raymond remained cold and aloof until the emperor strummed a harmonious chord by the mention of his distrust of Bohemund.

"I find the Norman highly avaricious," he remarked one day as the two men strolled about the garden. "He never declines anything offered while you . . ." His voice trailed off.

"Perhaps the reason lies in his circumstances. He never had much after he lost his patrimony."

"And he has been an enemy of Byzantium for a long time. Would you place your trust in such a man?"

There was meaning in the question. "That would depend." Raymond was cautious. Alexius was probing. Was it an offer? "A tiger's spots never wash out completely," he said casually. "But a hungry cat has its uses."

"My sentiments exactly," nodded Alexius. "Where wealth exists between equals, there is loyalty and friendship."

Raymond nodded in silence. But Alexius had prescience. He knew the seed had been planted and had found fertile soil. He was patient and Raymond's antagonism softened. He hinted of an appointment of a legate. Raymond took the bait.

"Do you expect to send much of a force with us?" he asked the emperor, knowing the answer in advance.

"Some . . . perhaps a battalion . . ." Alexius was vague. "But I cannot afford many men because of the border defenses. Of course, I will aid wherever possible."

"You will need a strong voice in the councils. Without an army, your legate's voice will be weak—unless you have a surrogate."

"That is a problem which bothers me." He glowed inside. I have him, he told himself. "The choice will be difficult," he said aloud. He would play this paragon like a fish.

"Perhaps . . . it may not be as difficult as it appears."

A momentary spark of agreement glittered between the two men. Each smiled to himself and to the other.

But Kilij Arslan, the Red Lion, emir of Nicea, was not smiling at that moment. He threw the letter from his hand contemptuously.

"What makes these Christian pigs on a new dung heap any different from those of Civitot?" he demanded from a messenger from Nicea. "They poison the earth and pray for the walls to fall. Do I have to show you how to exterminate such vermin?"

"O Sun of Heaven," the man whispered, his head touched the earth as he groveled. "They are fighting men. The others were pilgrims."

Arslan considered the man's words. The commander had sent a soldier, not a regular courier. "How many are there?"

"They are like the stars, countless. The sun lights up their helmets and spears and gleams on their bright armor. Their fires are everywhere. And, O Magnificent One, we hear of another army of thousands, just come to the walls of the Imperial City and already in the boats of the emperor and landing."

Arslan became thoughtful. Was Alexius contemplating war? But the emperor, despite all his wealth, could not pay for an army as this man described. A soldier's exaggeration? But something new *was* stirring. Witness the masses of pilgrims at Civitot. Their bones were bleaching at Dracon Pass, but . . . He made a decision.

"Return to Nicea. Tell them I am coming."

The man rubbed his forehead in the dirt. "May the Prophet's wisdom always shine through you, O Chosen One."

Arslan's jeweled hand waved dismissal. The Christians had become a nuisance. Was Alexius in league with them? He would have to contact the emperor. Meanwhile, he ordered two battalions to be ready to march on the sun's rise: one cavalry, one foot.

An advance patrol, led by Captain Ilkhan, halted at the top of the forested hill to survey Raymond's forces making camp below. It had the same disorder and nonmilitary discord he had seen at Civitot. "More pilgrims," he told his lieutenants.

Boys herded horses and sheep; jack-men were erecting tents and pavilions; women worked with the chefs and prepared the food tables. Everywhere, there were the running children, the barking dogs, the lowing of cattle. Men lounged in the sun and drank wine. The air was full of dust. He could hear the sounds of music and laughter. Civitot! flashed through his mind again. He would make up for his defeat at the fort and give his men some sport. A quick raid—and there would be fewer Christians.

The trumpeters sounded the charge, and his men kicked their mounts forward in high glee, their battle cry coming to their throats.

The Provencals raised their heads at the noise. They did not recognize the calls or the green standards. Before they could react, the Turk was upon them and into the camp.

But their response was instinctive: when attacked, fight! Without waiting for orders, without armor, the knights and soldiers seized any weapon handy. "*Toulouse!*" their call to battle, resounded throughout the encampment. Men vaulted onto stampeding horses without saddles. Their big horns were blasting.

With cheers of jubilation, the hardened fighters of the Pyrenees raced to the attack. At last! The Infidel! For this they had marched thousands of miles and had endured every hardship.

They crashed headlong into the astounded foe. The big destriers rode the smaller Moslem horses down. The long swords sliced through the thin links of the infidel's mail. Heavy maces crashed through the small shields and crushed Turkish skulls. The lancers picked the surprised enemy right out of the saddle and flung him away as though he was a rag doll. The Turk reeled back—and ran.

Never had this happened before to the cavalry of the Red Lion. The Christians were savage madmen who rose before them with deranged screams and berserk fury. Their ferocity was unimaginable; those that died screamed their rage. The Moslem could only run. Allah, they were sure, would understand.

The victory calls of the Provencals mingled with the bellows of the horns. They pursued the Moslems into the forest, but the horns called them back. Raymond would not fight among the shadows of the trees. The men swaggered back in pride. It had only been a skirmish, but they had met and defeated the Infidel. The Devil's spawn was no fighter, no match for them. Bishop Adhemar led the mass; the prayers were humble, but the hearts swelled in glory.

The other crusader camps heard the news and the lords held a war council. Was the Infidel finally appearing?

"Was this a patrol from the city or has the emir returned?" Tancred asked the question. No one knew the answer.

"They came from the hills," said Raymond. "It must be the Red Lion. His standards are green. We must prepare a plan."

Godfrey agreed; the crusaders made ready.

Captain Ilkhan rallied his men in the forest. His sorrow was consuming him. Allah had dealt him a terrible blow. Under his gray beard, his face was ashen, for he had lost a full half of his command. It stunned him. The Christians had not been easy victims, and he could not explain the skirmish without incurring the wrath of his master.

Arslan received the news and raged. "Dog!" he spat at Ilkhan who kneeled before him. "Who gave you permission to attack? You were only a scouting party! Now, they will be prepared!"

Ilkhan groveled. His life hung on a word. Kilij was a severe master and defeat made him ferocious. Fortunately, Arslan had other things on his mind. He had formulated an immediate plan.

The Moslem column was ordered into a quick march behind the fast-moving cavalry. The Christians, Kilij reasoned, would not expect an immediate attack. He stood where Ilkhan stood and surveyed the camp. He was right. He saw nothing unusual.

The drummers began a soft cadence, and the horsemen moved into lines behind the hill's crest. Then, the trumpets sang. Over the rise came line after line of the cavalry, their wild shouting, "*Tahwil! Tacbir!*" echoing from the heights. They stood in their saddles; their swords were waving over their heads. Behind them, also shrieking, came the running soldiers. The snare drums thundered.

They were halfway down the hill's side when the Provencal horns answered them. Out of the center of the encampment, riding headlong into the Moslem charge, led by Count Raymond on his big, bay stallion, came the fierce knights of Provence, of Gascony, of Castile. Fully armored, their long lances leveled, they swept through the oncoming horsemen as though they were stalks of wheat. Dead, and unhorsed wounded Turks, were strewn in a wide swath. The knights ignored the Moslem infantry, which scattered as they approached. They wheeled their mounts about and charged back, scattering the Infidel cavalry into small fragments. Then they drew their long swords and hand-to-hand fighting erupted between the mounted men.

The Moslem infantry tried to reorganize their broken lines, only to be overrun by waves of axe-wielding soldiers. Bowmen lined up on the flanks of the fighting men and picked off whoever sought to escape. With a wild shout of *"Toulouse!"* lancers and short swordsmen entered the melee. The hardened Turkish fighters reeled back under the savagery of the attack. They were overmatched by these wild, exuberant men, who sought battle with delight and cut and sliced with heated exaltation and gleeful energy.

Into the pandemonium of sound came the high-pitched horns of Bohemund. Then, the bullhorns of Godfrey reverberated through the ranks of the struggling men. The picked knights of the other camps moved at a gallop into the battle. Running hard behind them were squads of soldiers.

Under the impact of this new charge, Arslan's cavalry broke down completely. Their hasty retreat became a rout, and they raced for the forests on the heights. The Moslem footsoldiers panicked. Led by Raymond, Tancred, and Baldwin, the knights pursued the fleeing horsemen, leaving the infantry to deal with the foot fighters. These men, in desperate fear, threw themselves into the lake. Many drowned; the rest were killed as they struggled in the muck.

A wild shout of victory rose from the battlefield. The axemen were busily engaged finishing off the Moslem wounded; the Crossbearer women carried the bleeding crusaders back to the tents.

The knights returned from the hill. They lolled in their saddles; they sang and called to each other; they waved their arms. Those who still had their long lances, sported the decapitated heads of the Turks, the blood still dripping from the severed necks.

There was a shout, *"On to Nicea!"* The knights spurred their mounts into a gallop and rode up to the walls of the city, unmindful of the arrows. They flicked their lances in wide arcs and hurled the heads over the battlements. Some hit and stained the walls. As they rode back, they shouted, *"DEATH TO THE INFIDEL! DEATH TO THE SONS OF SATAN! GOD WILLS IT!"*

Leo, wet with perspiration and stained with blood, leaned wearily on his sword. He was exhausted and was having trouble keeping his gorge from rising. He averted his eyes from the body which lay at his feet. With sudden memory, he could hear the crack of the neckbone and see the blood spurting from the neck as his sword sliced off the head. The eyes popped from their sockets, and he shuddered. About him were the dead. The guts of the disemboweled hung like the innards of animals in a butchery. The dying were pleading for help.

He could not force himself to kill the injured Moslems. He put the sword on his shoulder and staggered off.

A knight rode toward him, a Moslem's head on his long lance. The blood still dripped. "Well done, Soldier Cannelli!" he shouted. "We have all done well today!" The battle fever was still within him and he laughed excitedly. It was Tancred!

He shook his lance and dropped the head. "Come see me tomorrow. I may need a new squire." He rode off.

Leo straightened his bent body with a deep breath. His weariness fell away like a discarded cloak. Tancred had noticed him! And offered to make him squire! His spirits soared; his feet barely touched the earth as he moved toward the encampment.

"Help . . . help me . . . please . . ." The hoarse whisper came from a grotesque pile of men scrambled in a heap. "Help . . ."

The man was wedged between two dead Moslems. He lay on his side, his body curled, his head pulled into his shoulders. His left arm crossed his chest and held his right shoulder. The blood welled between his fingers. "Help me . . ." he sobbed.

Leo examined the wound. The scimitar had slit the cloth and sliced the skin but had not cut deeply. The bleeding was minimal.

"Get up and walk," he said snappishly. "You're not hurt bad."

"I . . . can't," the man gasped. "My leg . . . a horse kicked me."

Leo saw the leg appeared awkward, skewed to one side. He tried to move it; the man screamed. He studied the situation, then pulled one of his knives and cut the cloth. The bone looked smashed.

"What camp are you from?"

"Count Raymond's," gasped the injured man. "Help me get up."

Leo nodded. With his arm around the man's waist, the man was able to raise himself on one leg. Painfully, they started a slow walk, stopping often. Each time they stopped, he examined the man's face. There was something familiar despite the dirt and blood.

"My name's Leo Cannelli, from Genoa. It's strange, but I think I've seen you somewhere."

The man straightened up with a surge of surprise. "Cannelli? From Genoa? You're the Cannelli boy? I'm Andre, Andre Toon! Of course you know me! I know you, too!"

"Andre Toon! Of course! I know you! And Michael! I married your sister! Mary!" He could hardly contain himself.

"Mary?" Andre's face whitened. "Is she here?"

Leo nodded. "And your sister Ruth, too!"

Andre gulped convulsively, the spittle rising from his stomach. He sagged, his fingers tightening on Leo's arm. Then, he began to tremble.

43

Arslan realized he had to face an agonizing conclusion—he had to abandon Nicea, his family, and treasury. He sent a message to Alexius requesting terms of surrender for the city.

The emperor was well pleased. Things had gone well. He sent for Ducas, and the baron found him in a jovial mood.

"We have won," he told the baron. "Kilij asks for terms."

"How long can we keep the news from our friends? The spoils of the city are a great temptation, and they have lost many men."

"They will lose many more." Alexius was cynical. "They have little knowledge of the Turk's power." He shifted his thought. "Hear me through. We must walk a tightrope. We are brothers of the Crossbearers, but we want no religious war with Islam."

"You have something specific in mind?" Ducas knew Alexius well.

The emperor smiled smugly. "As Aristotle told the great Alexander, 'Armies without goals are useless toys for the bloodthirsty.' I have a plan. We have promised Bohemund boats to seal the water gate of the city. They are ready. Order a full battalion of men to sail in them. They have a specific task."

"May I ask what that is?"

Alexius rubbed his hands in satisfaction. "To rumble the drums, to clang the cymbals, to blow their horns. And, of course, to sing, to shout, to scream—loud and often. And . . ."—he warned—"at the appropriate time." He glanced slyly at Ducas and chuckled as he viewed the baron's obvious puzzlement. "We play a game."

"It is dangerous, sire," said Ducas and frowned.

Alexius became serious and nodded. "We will advise an attack. I have sent Taticius and his missile throwers to Count Raymond. These knights have no experience in heavy siege warfare. They throw lives away in futile sorties on the walls. Taticius will use his missiles at Raymond's gate until it falls. The other knights will attack their sides as diversions. Raymond will have the dubious honor to enter the city first—when I tell him. This should make him amenable to my suggestions. And if all goes well with the negotiations with Kilij, the garrison will surrender the city in two days." He was pleased with himself.

"It is a complex plot, sire, with many variables. Why allow the surrender to the crusader? It will create problems."

"Aha!" cried Alexius. "I know it's good if you did not see through it! We only *tell* Raymond that he will receive the surrender. Kilij will have the option: The crusaders or me. Which do you think he will choose?"

Ducas shook his head. "You walk the razor's edge, sire. One slip . . . when the knights learn of the duplicity . . ."

"Whoever promised tranquillity to heads of state?" Alexius interrupted. "Kilij will see it our way. The greater difficulty will be convincing our guests. That is your task."

Ducas sighed. "May the Lord be with us; we will need Him."

Taticius had specific instructions. He moved his *ballistrae* and built his palisades to face the main tower at Raymond's gate. He assured the knights that his iron-headed missiles would pulverize the stone even if it was six feet thick and built by the Romans. The plan was, when the tower fell, Raymond and his knights would ride through the opening. The attacks on the other walls would prevent a massing of the Moslems at the broken gate, and the knights could easily enter.

Raymond was delighted and argued forcefully in support of the plan. The council, finally, accepted it.

The next morning, the crusaders swarmed to the attack. They made fruitless sallies as Taticius' missiles beat steadily at the tower. Casualties were heavy. Eventually, the stone masonry crumbled under the heavy pounding, and the tower leaned. The Turks fought back stubbornly and beat off charge after charge. Daylight faded; the tower was severely damaged but still stood.

"One more day," said Taticius. "Prepare," he told Raymond.

What Raymond did not know was that the tower could have been demolished in one day. The captain of the garrison knew it and wondered why so many of the missiles were misdirected; why there had been an unearthly clamor at the water gate; why all the useless sorties on the other walls had been undertaken.

During the night, under a flag of truce, Admiral Butumites was allowed to enter the water gate. He handed a scroll to the garrison's captain. The document carried the official terms of surrender of the city to the emperor's forces and was signed by Alexius and Arslan. The captain read the scroll twice, and the two men bowed to each other.

Through the night, the garrison, their families, and most of their possessions were ferried out of the city to a far shore. There they were met by a Byzantine troop, and all disappeared into the night. A battalion of Byzantines, the Turcoples, entered the city and became the sentries on the battlements. Alexius had won.

At daybreak, the crusaders rose to renew the attack. They were dumbfounded to see Byzantine flags on the towers instead of the green standards of Arslan. A great cheer went up. The Turcoples shouted from the walls, *"NICEA IS OURS!"*

The city had fallen. Somehow, during the night, the Byzantines had gained entry! The fighting was over! Nicea was ours!

The men pounded on the great gates and demanded entry. They were confused when the gates remained closed. They shouted to the soldiers on the walls. But the Turcoples ignored them. They milled about in confusion.

The great barons were handed messages to meet with Admiral Butumites and Baron Ducas in Arslan's palace. They were permitted to enter the gates, but the others, who pressed forward to join them, were turned away. The gates were rechained and bolted.

The admiral and baron met the knights with smiles and seated them at a great table. They were served delicacies and wine. Each was given a scroll from Alexius inscribed with flowery accolades and high praises for their bravery. It congratulated them on a splendid victory and invited them to a great feast and ball, to be held at the emperor's palace in the Imperial City. There, Ducas told them, the emperor would bestow the rewards of their victory upon each of them—their shares for the capture of Nicea. A huge celebration was being arranged for the return of Nicea to the empire.

Ducas took great pains to explain why the crusaders were being denied entry to the city. The Turks had turned the original churches into mosques, and the emperor feared that this would incite the Crossbearers, or, worse yet, ignorant of the fact, the Christians might despoil the buildings. All the churches were to be restored as Houses of God. Further, most of the population of the city were Christians, past subjects who had been turned into slaves by the Moslems. They might be tortured and killed by rampaging crusaders.

The knights nodded in understanding and agreed to collect their rewards in Constantinople at the ball. All except Raymond. He accused Ducas and the emperor of betrayal. With his knights, he stormed out of the hall.

Word spread swiftly to the Crossbearers that they would not be permitted to enter the city. Groups formed at the gates and protested as their disappointment and frustrations grew.

Parenti and his followers joined Tafur and his band. They circulated the milling men and incited anger. They preached vengeance for Peter's martyrs; they invoked oaths taken in the Valley of the Martyrs for compensation; they dangled visions of loot and spoils of the city.

The cries grew loud, *"GIVE US THE MOSLEM!"*

"WHERE IS THE EMIR'S GOLD?"

"WHERE ARE THE EMIR'S CHILDREN?"

The women screamed at the sentries, *"WE SHED THE BLOOD! WE DUG THE TUNNELS! WHERE IS THE MOSLEM GARRISON?"*

The ribalds chanted, *"LET THE BARONS HAVE THE HONOR! GIVE US THE CITY! GIVE US THE TURKS!"*

The demands became a whirlwind of fury. The nervous sentries readied themselves for an attack. Women and children collected brush and lit fires at the gates to burn the wooden bars.

There was a sudden sound of trumpets and a crescendo of cymbals. Great teams of horses appeared, with open vans filled with tuns and casks of wine and beer. Spigots were opened and the beverages flowed freely. Sheep carcasses were spitted and the tantalizing odors made people drool. Singers, jongleurs, acrobats, and clowns were mingling with the mob. They had appeared from nowhere. A festive air was being created.

Coppers were hurled from the walls, and the people scrambled to catch and collect them. Only the diehards refused to move.

"You are being seduced by the Devil!" Parenti screeched from the gate. "Take the city! You'll have ten times what you get here!"

"Open the gates!" raved Tafur. "Give us the city!"

But the cries were enfeebled as the soldiers turned to the food and drink. Priests and monks climbed the wagons and harangued the crowd to rejoice in the victory of the cross.

"Forget the city!" they cried. "Have you come for plunder or for Jesus? Do you want Moslem women? That is a deadly sin! Do not seek the Devil! Rejoice with the Lord! We are victorious!"

The people drank and ate. An orgy was in the making.

Leo left Andre at Raymond's camp and hurried to Tancred's pavilion. His head was full of hopes and fancies. He ignored the festivities. A page boy told him that the knight had not come back from the conference in the city. Leo decided to wait.

The hot afternoon passed slowly, and the sky was darkening when Tancred rode up. The knight was in short temper. Secretly, he agreed with Raymond: they had been betrayed by Alexius. He did not notice Leo but stormed into the tent.

"Uvos!" His page came running. "I'm to leave for Constantinople in the morning. Have everything ready for a special ball."

The boy bowed. "Yes, sire. Any special cloak?"

"The dark red. Here, help me out of this . . ." He fidgeted with his mail. "And bring me a drink. I die of thirst."

Leo had followed the knight in. "Sir Tancred, I came . . . ."

Tancred scowled at him. "Who? Oh." Recognition came. "See me tomorrow. I'm busy." He slapped the page's hands away. "What takes you so long?" he growled at the boy. "You're all fingers." A thought struck him. "You . . ." he called as Leo was leaving. "You! Here! You said you were a squire?"

Leo nodded. "For Sir Walter. He was killed."

"I have use for a squire. Mine are gone. You will come with me to the Imperial City. Take me out of this mail. Uvos, get the wine." The boy, glad to be free, ran.

Leo stripped the mail. Uvos returned with the wine, and Tancred took a long drink. "Uvos, show him Alavar's clothes. Maybe something will fit." He glanced at Leo. "You're a little short. Clean up. I will not tolerate dirty retainers. We go tomorrow after sunup. Take care of Tobi right away. Uvos will show you where everything is. I go to meet with Sir Richard." He strode out.

"Lord Tancred is very fussy," said Uvos. "I'm glad you're here."

"So am I. Who is Tobi?"

"Sir Tancred's favorite destrier. He needs grooming. Alavar was killed yesterday. He was the last squire. I've been trying to do everything myself, but it's hard."

"Lord Tancred had only one squire?" The idea was preposterous.

"He had five. Two were knighted. The rest were killed. Alavar was sixteen and was to receive his sword."

"Oh." Leo fell silent. He washed and groomed Tobi; he cleaned himself. He was high-pitched and elated as he worked. Tomorrow, he would go to Constantinople with Lord Tancred. He brushed out Alavar's clothes. They were oversized but comfortable.

As he worked, his mind went often to Mary and the baby. He felt he was being pulled in three ways. Glory and wealth depended upon his sword—if he became a knight he could have lands and riches. But for whom? Nina was right. It had to be shared, with a woman, with Mary and his daughter. She had sinned, but was it all her fault? She had worked to save him. He would save her. He would visit her . . . and his daughter. He would forgive and forget.

Emperor Alexius received the crusaders with a great show of affection and solicitude. The Byzantine women fawned on them and vied with the serving girls in plying them with delicacies and wine. No knight was left unattended. Only Count Raymond had not come.

The emperor presented everyone with opulent gifts; caskets of gold and silver coins, of jewels; ornaments in precious metals and master-crafted jewelry; rich mantles of beautifully dyed cloth; saddles inlaid with gems; exquisite statuary cast in gold and silver, with colored stones imbedded in the metal. The wealth appeared to be endless.

The knights were overcome. They had never seen an accumulation of such riches. The gifts were all a part of Kilij Arslan's treasury and the ransom of his nobles, but the crusaders did not know this. They kneeled and thanked the emperor for his generosity.

Alexius did not forget the squires. Leo received a small casket of coins and a few jewels with trembling hands. The jewelry, he knew, would delight Mary. It would be a reconciliation gift.

The emperor was not finished. He promised to build a great hospital for all the wounded, and when any knight was healed, he could choose to rejoin his liege lord or remain in Nicea as an officer in Admiral Butumites' garrison. The admiral had been appointed the new governor of the captured city.

Through all the gaiety, Tancred remained surly. He agreed with Raymond: they had been betrayed. As the gifts were distributed, he remarked acidly to Richard, "We could have had all this and ten times more if we had sacked the city."

"Take the oath," Richard urged, "and forget Nicea. There will be other cities. The emperor will honor you."

"I need not his honors," snapped the knight. "My oath to Bohemund is enough."

"But Lord Bohemund has taken the oath to the emperor," said a Byzantine grandee standing close by. "Where does that leave you?"

Tancred, with an oath, drew his small sword. "I will show you," he spat, "if you have the guts for it!"

Bohemund, who had been watching, stepped between them. "Put up your sword, nephew! It is not fitting for a kinsman of mine to draw his weapon in the house of my friends. Put it away!"

Tancred, peevishly, sheathed his sword. "Let the emperor fill this pavilion with gold," he threw at the grandee, "and I will take his oath."

Bohemund drew him aside. "Your tantrums still govern your thinking. Your brain is clouded. If I can swear fealty, so can you. Diplomacy requires it! Swear, I command it!"

The two tall men stood and glared at each other in anger. The noisy court quieted—and waited. But Tancred yielded. He walked stiffly to the dais and sank to one knee. Everyone strained to hear the knight's oath as he placed his clasped hands into the emperor's cupped hands.

Tancred swore and the emperor rose and embraced him. It was a pointed demonstration that the emperor bore no malice. He held the knight's arm as he called out the list of gifts for the recalcitrant warrior. Tancred remained stonily indifferent to the rich gifts being piled by the running black slaves. Inside, he seethed. When it was over, he left the pavilion.

The party grew boisterous, but Tancred and Leo sailed back to Asia. The young knight, in a sullen mood, watched the black waters. He had been humiliated; there would never be forgiveness in his heart for it.

Andre's shoulder healed quickly, but the Byzantine doctor, trained by the Moslems, told him that his kneecap was gone; he would limp for the rest of his life. He took the news stoically. He had no fighting instincts, and the knee would keep him out of combat. There were other things he could do. He decided to find Mary and Ruth.

It was not difficult to track down Ruth's big wagon. As he hobbled up to it, he saw Inda playing with her son. His eyes hovered over her cheerful, flushed face and her slim body. His loins tightened. Inda had become demure when she had seen the young man with a crutch watching her. To hide her confusion, she picked up the baby and hugged him zealously. Guizio came upon them.

"Looking for someone, soldier?" he asked.

Andre nodded. "Yes, I was . . ."

He did not finish. Mary, who was carrying a basket of wash, had come around the wagon's side. The basket fell as she screamed, "Andre!" She ran to him. "Andre!"

Her embrace drove the wind from him. "When? . . ." she chattered. "How? . . . Oh, Andre! It is so good to see you! You're wounded? How bad is it?" She could not stop her babbling excitement.

"Mary," he kept repeating to calm her. "Can I sit down? My leg is painful."

The realization finally stopped her. "Guizio! Quickly! A chair for my brother! He's wounded! Oh, Andre!"

Joined by Inda and, finally, Ruth, they all laughed animatedly together as they recounted their stories. Andre learned about the death of Tom and his brothers, about Mary's broken leg, how Mary had joined Peter, what had happened at the fort after the massacre at Civitot. He told them how Leo had found and helped him.

"How was he?" Mary was anxious.

"Fine, as far as I could see. Not a scratch. He killed many Moslems." He stopped. "Isn't he here?"

There was an awkward pause as Mary turned away. Ruth interjected, "How's Papa?"

Andre was sober. "He's dead. Michael got married. It was Jeanne," he blurted out bitterly.

The girls were dumbfounded, then Mary began to laugh.

"I didn't find it so funny," said Andre. "Jeanne! that old, worn-out crow. He could have had anyone. I tried to talk to him, but he wouldn't listen. She threw me out! Imagine that? She threw me off the farm, and he didn't even try to stop her." He spat. "May they both burn in Hell."

"Andre!" protested Ruth. "He's our brother."

"A lot that did for me. I wandered about until I joined Count Raymond." He stopped. "It got me this leg!" He slapped his thigh.

"What happened to Papa?" Mary tried to divert him.

Andre shrugged. "You know Papa. He can do everything best. Well, he went to stud a cow and got in the way of the bull. He was gored. Jeanne didn't even mourn him. She and Michael were married the next day. Everybody was surprised." His eyes wandered to Inda, who averted hers quickly. "Are you all neighbors?" he asked no one in particular.

"We have three wagons," said Ruth. "This is Inda. Her husband was killed in the Valley of the Martyrs. She stays with Little John." She indicated the boy. "Mary's alone—because Leo has to stay with Lord Tancred." A sudden thought struck her. "How bad is your leg?"

He grimaced. "Bad enough. It will heal, but I'll limp."

"Why don't you come and stay with us? We have room. You could drive Mary's wagon. We could be a family again."

"I don't know. The emperor says we can work in Nicea. We'll need money. I haven't anything."

"We'll manage," Ruth pressed. "We have some money, and Leo sends some to Mary. Guizio needs some help. Stay, Andre, stay."

He glanced at Mary, awaiting a sign. Nina and a soldier were coming out of the big wagon. She saw the group and hurried the man off so she could join the others. Andre took in the cool, dark beauty of the girl and smiled at her. He looked from her to Inda and back to Mary. "Stay," said Mary.

"All right." He was smiling, his eyes lingering on Nina. "I'll stay. We'll be a fine family, all together."

Guizio, who was watching, cocked his head.

44

The Crossbearers were on the road again, and their hearts were singing. The Lord had shown them His pleasure and had granted them the first victory. It was an omen: the Infidel was doomed.

The Byzantine Empire lay behind them; the last towers of Nicea had disappeared. Before them, said Taticius, their guide, was the road to Antioch, an old city, a wealthy city called the Pearl of the East, the sister city of Constantinople. Caesar had sat in its theatre, and Jesus had given it to Peter, the Big Fisherman, the Blessed Apostle. But now it was in the hands of the Infidel.

The provision-laden wagons and oxcarts creaked as they swayed and rumbled over the dusty roads. The airborne particles crept into the smallest crevices and coated everything. It mixed with the sweat and formed a thin, brown paste over the skin. Everything turned brown-gray. The marchers slowed to a plodding pace; the gonfalons and banners lay limp in the windless heat; the laughter had been baked out of the Crossbearers' bodies.

After a few days, the Knights' Council met in conference. They decided to split the huge host into two sections. Lord Bohemund, with his knights and soldiers, would form an advance guard; Duke Godfrey and Count Raymond would follow. A two days' march interval would be kept between the two armies. Water had become a great problem.

Bohemund came through the hills and before him lay a long plain, flat and endless. The June month was ending and the sun was burning hot. At the foot of the hills was a small river and a marsh. He decided to make camp.

Tancred, commanding the patrols, reported small groups of Moslems in the hills, but the plains were empty. His knights had discovered the ruins of an old Roman castle on the rocky crags, also empty. Everything appeared peaceful. The men were soon splashing in the river's water and some went upstream to fish. The wagons were wheeled into circles and the jack-men set the pavilions and tents. The horses were let out to graze and to rest. But Bohemund remained uneasy. He ordered some soldiers to stand ready at arms; he commanded Tancred to patrol the perimeters of the camp with his knights.

One morning, Leo was jarred by a rude shaking. A knight stood over him. "Waken .Lord Tancred immediately. Quickly!" came the order.

Leo found the knight awake. "What is the noise?" he asked, and the knight pushed past the squire.

"We have found the infidel camp," the knight reported. "Thousands of horses and wagons. They are here in great force, in the back hills."

"Their sentries?"

The man grinned. "They do their duty in Hell. They did not expect us and they slept right through it."

Tancred shook his head. "That was not clever. Now they will know that we have seen them."

"What difference does that make? They prepare to attack."

Tancred came erect. "You are sure?"

"No doubts at all. The horses are saddled and ready. At sunup."

"We must tell Bohemund. What time is it?"

"About an hour before dawn. Bohemund knows. He sends you orders to dispatch a courier to Godfrey and Raymond. We will engage the infidel on the plains. He asks you to hurry. The numbers of the enemy are great. We hope the gentlemen arrive soon."

Tancred nodded. "You heard, Leo. Saddle a horse and ride. Go now; Uvos will help me. Be wary of their patrols."

Leo scrambled into his clothes. It was still dark as he galloped the road back to the other army. His daggers were in their sheaths, his long sword at his side, and his eyes were furtive.

In the false dawn, the crusader patrols pulled closer to their camp. The eagerness for battle among the Christians grew as they prepared, and by early morning, many watched the hills as they muttered their morning prayers. The war horses were all saddled; all the foraging beasts had been brought back to camp and yoked to their vehicles. Tension mounted; the men fingered their weapons and licked their dried lips.

A message from Tancred said he had sighted a large formation of Turks moving out of the hills toward the plain. He was ordering his men back to the encampment as there was no doubt but that the Turk was massing for an attack. Word spread from mouth to mouth, and the excitement grew. It was the Turk with the green standards, they were told, the butchers of the martyrs. They were on their own until the others arrived. Bohemund rode his soldiers' line.

"Be ready! Stand shoulder to shoulder! The attack comes soon."

Arslan swore, by the Prophet's beard, he would drive this Christian scum out of his lands. They were creating festering ulcers of all his villages and towns, roiling the water, stripping them of food, polluting the land, and killing his people. His talks with Alexius had convinced him that the emperor was suppling only token aid; his spies had informed him that Taticius led only a small detachment of engineers and sappers to man the siege machinery. Alexius had sent no

Byzantine troops. While the emperor could not be indifferent to the crusader goal—Jerusalem—he was not a serious ally in the fighting for the capture of that city. This was not a war with Byzantium, he concluded.

He had followed the crusaders, awaiting the right terrain and opportunity. He had taken special note when they had split their forces at the old Roman bridge near the town of Lence. He smiled when their lines grew inordinately long. There was a two days' march between them, he calculated. Enough time for his plans.

He outflanked the leading Christian forces and brought his men into camp in a hidden valley near the end of the hills. "They will camp by the river," he said to his captains, "and we will catch them there." The plain faced the Roman town of Dorylaeum. He had his whole army: hard-riding cavalry and battle-hardened soldiers. He had concluded a hasty peace with his brothers. On that first day of July, he waited for the sun to rise and drive the mists off the face of the marshes which partially hid the Christian camp.

At a word, the eager line of Turkish horsemen moved forward. The sun gleamed on their bright armor; their white turbans were even whiter in the expanding light. Beneath their chalk-clean headdresses, their dark, swarthy faces were lean, the white of their eyes and teeth shining bright from their sun-baked skulls. They spurred into a gallop as the drums rolled and the cymbals crashed.

The Seljuk Turk was a warrior. On one shoulder he hung a small round shield; on the other, a short bow and a quiver full of arrows. In his raised hand was the dreaded, curved scimitar, a sword which could slice through a knight's armor-mail or pierce the links and split them with a twist of the wrist. The thunder of their galloping charge made the earth shake and vibrate. Above the unholy din came the high-shrieking challenge of battle:

"*ALLÂH-IL-ALLÂH! ALLÂH-IL-ALLAH!*"

The long line of crusaders who faced the hills firmed; their arms tensed; their horses strained at the reins. Bohemund waited until the Turks were stretched into a line on the plain.

"Lances down!" The order was crisp and the long lances moved into secure positions.

He raised his mailed fist. "*GOD WILLS IT!*" he shouted.

Echoing him, from the throats of the hundreds of his knights came the call, "*GOD WILLS IT!*"

His big horns bellowed their unearthly blare; the knights' line jumped as the eager destriers, unleashed, dug their massive hooves into the soft earth and hurtled forward.

"*TAHWIL! TACBIR! TAHWIL! TACBIR!*" the Turks screamed.

There was a buzzing in the air, becoming louder, building until the air seemed to split and sizzle. The light darkened. A cloud whirred, shimmered, floated, casting a shadow over the oncoming crusader line. Suddenly, it wavered and bent. The expertly trained destriers faltered, they reared, they plunged. They screamed as they fell, their riders thrown to the ground so forcefully, many were knocked unconscious or killed. But the rest came on. Nothing could stop them; they were the living mountains, too heavy and ponderous for the deadly, slender arrows. The Turk evaded the long lances, and the knights took to the long sword and the mace.

But the Turk would not stand and fight. They wheeled their agile, smaller mounts and scattered, reformed their lines, and shifted, constantly charging and retreating. Iron hooks cleated themselves in the chain-mail armor, and the knights were pulled from their saddles. Heavy axes crashed through their casques, driving the iron into their skulls. Sharp scimitars pierced and bloodied them while the wielders grouped, reformed, charged, and scattered before the slower war horses. The knights broke off, wheeled and turned back, making room for the next line of charging crusaders, not sure how to fight these elusive foemen.

The Turks scattered again before the new charge, firing arrows backward at the pursuing knights. They would twist and turn, cutting off any knight who outdistanced the others, using their arrows or swords to dispatch him, never still, never engaging in a stand-off fight. Their deadly arrows were killing the horses and toppling the men. The screams of the dying horses and men were raising a horrible din. Bohemund, Tancred, Richard, Robert of Paris, Billemes the Mighty charged desperately again and again at the makeshift line of the Turk, and the Moslems yielded and closed in around them, trying to absorb them and swallow their strength.

At a signal from Arslan's horns, some of the Turk cavalry drew back, reformed into a new line, and, screaming their cries and swinging their scimitars, attacked the lines of the crusader soldiers who had stood guard for the camp. The horses leaped directly at the men, bowling them over, tearing large gaps in the line through which others jumped. The soldiers fought desperately to repulse the foe. They stood shoulder to shoulder, so closely packed that the dead could not fall. Their bowmen had exhausted their quivers and fought with any weapons they could find, taking them from the dead hands of neighbors. A deadly hand-to-hand battle erupted.

Bohemund ordered some knights back to defend the soldiers' line, and he leaped from his saddle, wielding his sword at the Turk soldiers. Others followed suit and a pile of bodies built around them with mounds of raw, bleeding flesh. Knights, still mounted, rushed the Moslem cavalry who retreated; but the Infidel circled and came back to the attack, only to retreat again when the crusaders rushed them again.

Priests, wearing their white vestments and unmindful of the fighting and the deadly arrows, were administering the last sacraments to the dying. Wounded knights, bleeding raw, fell from their horses and crawled to the clerics to confess their sins with their last breaths. Many lay with their hands crossed over their chest in death, the priests closing their staring eyes.

The fury of the battle mounted as the sun rose higher in the sky, and knights stood back to back, working their long swords and calling encouragement to each other.

Exhausted, the armies disengaged and drew back for a respite. There was a mutual respect and admiration by the fighters of both sides. Never had the Seljuk Turk been repulsed with such resolve; never had a knights' charge been so easily and quickly evaded. The crusader line held and the Moslems, out of arrows, returned to their camp for fresh horses and full quivers. But they were not gone long.

With their drums and horns calling, the Turk came sweeping down the hillsides in waves, their scimitars raised, their terrible cries mixed with the drums' roll-rumble and the cymbals' clanging clash. They were bent on complete destruction. They were the "Invincibles," and Kilij had set his mind that he had to finish off these stubborn fighters before the day's end, for behind them was another army. Never had any opponent withstood his cavalry's suicidal charge and he had no doubts now. But the mounted crusaders, undaunted, rode to meet him. The battle became deafening and dogged as the sun burned hot.

From back in the hills came the lowing, bellowing challenge of the horns of Lorraine. The gut-gripping sound reverberated in the sweaty bodies of the fighting men, and all eyes turned to the heights. Around the bend on the road, over the breast of the hill, came a large group of crusaders. They spread into a line as they reached the plain; their long lances came down; and their war horses broke into a furious gallop as they came at full charge across the right flank of the Turkish horsemen. Led by Godfrey, they cut a swath through the astonished Moslems. The cheer *"GOD WILLS IT!"* came from the throats of the weary defenders and was echoed by the new fighters. Behind them were line after line of Godfrey's men, led by his brothers, Baldwin and Eustace. Their lily banners were stretched to the wind, and their chargers were covered with a brown, mudlike paste of dust and sweat.

Behind them, screaming *"TOULOUSE!"* were the knights of Provence led by Count Raymond, thousands after thousands more.

Riding with Godfrey's charging knights, his long sword swinging and whirling over his head, was Leo. His horse was exhausted, and blood dripped from his flanks where the spurs had cut. Leo stood half-upright in his saddle, his voice hoarse but still shrieking with the others.

Far to the rear, at a jogging pace increased by the excitement of having arrived at the battlefield, came the armed soldiers. Many of the armed men had been left with the host to protect the pilgrims against a surprise attack, but a thunderous cheer went up as the spearmen and axemen hurried down the hilly road.

Bishop Adhemar, a wily old campaigner, split five hundred of Raymond's knights from the main force and led them around the entire battle to the rear of the enemy. The Turks were surprised to hear the raised shout "GOD WILLS IT!" come from their rear, and before they could realize what was happening, Adhemar was upon them.

Arslan was caught on three sides.

*   *   *

Leo found himself in the midst of the hand-to-hand fighting on the ground when his horse, pierced by innumerable arrows, collapsed under him. Thrown from his saddle, he lost his long sword but was lucky to find a short one just as a mounted Turk galloped by and reached down to cut at him. Steel rang against steel as he parried the scimitar, and Leo stumbled back under the jarring force of the blow. The Turk leaned forward to thrust at him with the point, and Leo fell to the ground in a twisting motion to avoid the scimitar's needlelike nose. As he fell, he reached for his knife and with a quick toss threw it at his snarling enemy. The knife bit into the big arm muscle of the Moslem, and with a curse, the man dropped his sword. Leo's sword lay beside him and he threw it at the mounted man. The small sword entered the man's chest as would an arrow and the Turk toppled forward, his teeth clenched in sudden pain. His horse bolted, and the dying man was dragged by one foot caught in his twisted stirrup.

Leo searched desperately for a new weapon and finally found a knight's long sword. He clutched it eagerly and made his way toward a group of knights fighting on foot not too far away. It was Bohemund, fighting as though possessed by a thousand furies. He had lost his casque, and his short, red hair stood on end like a flaming prickly brush. Two other knights were with him. Leo joined them and the four men fought off attack after attack.

There was a wild scream as a horseman bore down on Bohemund from one side. Leo shrieked back as he leaped forward, and with a wild swing of his sword, he cut off the horse's front hoof at the fetlock joint. The horse screamed and fell forward, pitching the Turk from his saddle, right against Leo, and the two men, both stunned, lay together on the bloody ground. Their recovery was simultaneous, and they were both on their feet immediately, snarling at each other. The Turk still held his sword, but Leo had lost his. His eyes searched desperately. The Moslem lunged at him, and Leo slipped as he jumped away but remained on his feet. The Turk came after him, his arm raised, his sword ready to cut down the Christian.

Leo threw his last weapon, his second knife. It cut through the center of the Moslem's throat. The man gurgled. His eyes popped wide in surprise and his feet faltered. He took a few paces forward and then collapsed, clawing at his throat. His sword had dropped from his stiff fingers, and Leo pounced on it and with one swing lopped off the Moslem's head. The blood was still running when Leo withdrew his knife from the flabby skin of the man's throat.

"Well done, squire!" yelled Bohemund who had witnessed the short and quick encounter. "I will remember!"

The pressure of the repeated crusader attacks was too much for Arslan's cavalry, and when they broke and headed for the hills before their horns sounded retreat, Arslan had his trumpeters sound reassembly, hoping to stem a rout. But it was useless. The crusaders, sensing victory, raised a shout, and the cries of "GOD WILLS IT!" and "TOULOUSE!" resounded everywhere. The Turkish soldiers were running for their lives and the mounted knights chased them. Others took off after the fleeing Moslem horsemen, spurring their tired destriers into the hills and forest in pursuit. The magnificent horses were faltering. They had been running for hours and the strain was telling.

The late afternoon wore on as the knights, still battle-fired, trailed the Moslems, and it was becoming dark when the Christians stumbled upon the Turkish camp. They found it unguarded and full of loaded wagons—supplies of every kind. There were weapons; thousands of arrows, swords, lances, maces, shields, and armor. Herds of relay horses were in makeshift corrals. Within enclosures were sheep, pack asses, camels, and cattle. Amphoras of wine and bins of grain and delicacies were in a special enclosure. With them were carts of cloth and rich silks and brocades, precious gems and filigree works of metal— *GOLD!* The word ran like a howling wind through the trees. A great shout arose. They had found the treasury of Arslan.

The crusaders came down like a swarm of locusts upon the camp. They poured in from every corner and ransacked everything. Daylight was breaking when they wearily staggered back toward Bohemund's camp, loaded with their loot, singing drunkenly, and leaving the Turkish camp in flames. Arslan would never fight again.

The power of the Red Lion had been mortally injured and he withdrew, snarling and licking his wounds. The back of his army had been broken and his reserves were gone. He rounded up whatever of his men he could find and regrouped, ordering his men to march onward, ahead of the Christian forces. As he passed through his towns and villages, he set fire to the growing fields and laid waste the land.

"These misbegotten pigs will be sent back to the sewers from which they came," he told his people. "Woe be to any of you who sell them any food. We will starve them until their bellies touch their backbones, and we will bury them in the camels' dung."

But for the happy, cheering, drunk crusaders, on the bright morning of that beautiful day in July, the road to Antioch was open. And the host rested as they tended the wounded and buried the dead.

45

They spent four days in prayers, in mourning, in the burial of the dead, in the tending of the wounded, and in the division of the spoils. The graves of the knights covered a wide area; the bodies of the soldiers and Crossbearers were buried together; the stripped corpses of the Moslems were left for the carrion eaters.

Bohemund had not forgotten Leo. He came to Tancred's pavilion and presented the squire with many fine gifts, so much that Tancred objected.

"You spoil him, uncle. He will exaggerate his worth."

Leo was grateful but he had dreamed of another gift—knighthood. The gift of the sword had been given for far less than he had done. He explained this to Mary.

"He could have made me a Knight of the Sword," he said bitterly. "I saved his life."

"There will be other times," she tried to soothe him. "Be thankful for this." She fondled the fine cloth.

"Take all the gold; I won't need it. I don't know when I'll have anymore. Lord Tancred is not generous."

Later, when they were in bed, she sighed. "I miss you so much. Can't you come more often?"

He held her tightly. "I miss you, too," he whispered. "Sometimes I dream of you. When this is over, and we are in Jerusalem, we will always be together. Kila will grow up and be a lady. So will you. We will have everything a knight and a lady need. And the Lord will love us for what we have done."

"Won't you stay for the night?" She moved close to him. "I become so lonely."

"I can't." He shook his head. "There's too much to do. You have Kila for company. There is Inda . . . and your brother is here."

"Inda and Andre stay together. If you stay I can send Little John to Guizio for the night."

He shook his head. "I must go. Even now I'm late. Lord Tancred will be angry. We leave early tomorrow. We are to be the advance guard." He rose from the bed and began to dress. "Will Inda and Andre marry?"

"I don't think so."

"They should. They can help each other." He buckled on his small sword. "Andre will find some work. How do they manage?"

"Inda . . . sometimes . . . works—with Ruth."

He was startled. "What!"

"Andre still can't do much." She was defensive. "And Ruth can't keep on supporting everyone. Andre thinks it's all right."

His face darkened. "And you? Will it start again with you when I'm not here?"

"No, Leo! No. I promise!" She reached out to him. "Let's not fight. We have so little time together."

He stared at her, indecisively. "You have enough gold for a long time," he said meaningfully. "Somehow, I'll get more. Take good care of little Kila."

She embraced him and hung closely. "Be careful, Leo," she whispered. "You are all I have—you and Kila. Don't be angry."

His arms tightened around her. "Take good care, my lady," he said softly. "You will be my lady; I promise." He kissed her and left abruptly. She sighed and sagged as he disappeared.

The road to Antioch was clear of the Turk, but the fields where the Red Lion had passed were burned black, and the villages were empty. The land was arid and desolate. The water had dried in the river beds, and the village wells were contaminated. The old Roman cisterns had been destroyed.

The cattle and sheep were the first victims; the people hoarded what little they had. They found a trickle in the large waterways, and they learned how to carry it in skins and mete it out carefully. The weak, the sick, the very old and very young, the wounded wasted away and died first in the insufferable heat. The host plodded on.

Once-proud knights rode oxen and cattle as their horses dropped. People loaded their belongings on their backs or discarded them by the roadside as their mules collapsed. They trudged wearily, their heads bent, their eyelids scaled, their ever-diminishing possessions strapped to their backs. The heat broiled them.

Leo visited Mary often, smuggling food and water to her. Uvos told Lord Tancred of the missing provisions and Leo was warned. The knight needed him, or Leo would have found himself in the grip of knightly justice—death for stealing from a lord. But Leo became reckless. Tancred, he concluded, would never knight him; nor was the knight generous. The squire had Mary constantly on his mind, the dancing brightness of her dark eyes, her vivaciousness; and a gnawing uncertainty was building within him. If he could not give her what she needed, another would. He would have to leave the knight.

He sought advice from Guizio. The ribald shrugged and scratched his grizzled chin. "We had no such problems in the city. Here, it is different." He scratched his head. "What if we hid you? The knight's too busy to look too hard."

"No," Leo shook his head. "It would spoil everything later. When I got my sword, he would challenge it. I have to find a different way."

"Don't go back," Mary urged. "It will work out."

But Leo rejected the advice. "I have to leave him with honor. According to the Byzantine general, we will soon come to a place of water and food. Maybe things will change there."

Downcast and moody, he returned to Tancred's pavilion.

Taticius had told the knights of the city of Iconium, a city in a fertile valley, with streams and wondrous orchards of dates and fruit. The desperate knights spurred their horses onward. They were ready to enter Hell for the waters of the River Styx.

They found Iconium deserted; the Moslems had fled to the mountains. The crusaders settled in to rest and recuperate. For five days they sported their pleasures and recovered their strength. Duke Godfrey went bear hunting and was mauled; Raymond became deathly ill and his recovery was slow. The falcons wheeled in the blue sky, and the ladies shot at game with their short bows and played with laughter again. The larders and water skins were filled, and the priests held masses with prayers and songs.

In the council, Taticius told the knights, "There are two roads we can follow. To the southeast, through the Cilician Gate, lies Tarsus City. It is garrisoned by the Turk. It is the shortest route, but it crosses two mountain ranges with deep gorges. Some paths are so narrow that only two men can pass in file. One slip, and the fall is long and fatal. Wagons cannot get through."

"And the other way?" asked Godfrey.

"To the northeast. The Roman legions went that way. It is longer and avoids most, but not all, of the mountains. The large towns have Moslem garrisons, but the people are Christian. Greeks and Armenians. They herd sheep and goats in the hills."

"We lose time," said Tancred restlessly. "I am willing to try the shorter route with some fighting men."

"I will go, too," said Baldwin, Godfrey's brother. "If we find it too difficult, we will return."

The two men moved through the gorges and clefts rapidly. They took the city of Tarsus and quarreled over the spoil. Baldwin had many more knights than Tancred, and Tancred, vowing eternal enmity, moved on. He found the city of Mamistra deserted by the Turks, and he left a garrison of sixty of his knights. Then he headed back to the main army and Bohemund, who had marched northeast.

The crusaders marching the northeast route found the Armenian Christians, peasants who wore crosses on their bare chests and called themselves nobles. They tended their goats and sheep, wore rags and tatters, and spoke loftily of their lost palaces and riches. Their worship of the Lord was fierce, and they were full of avarice in their poverty. They charged outrageous prices for milk and cheese. They told stories of Antioch, a city of enormous riches and wonders. And their voices were hushed in the telling.

Finally, the last great barrier loomed before the host, the Greater Tauras

Mountains. The ranges were high and the gorges deep. The bare cliffs soared, and the living winds chased each other through the narrow defiles of the rock and sang eerie songs. The crusaders craned their necks at the heights, and their icy fingers clawed at the abutments. Their blood ran cold; their bodies shivered and trembled with pain and fear. Most of their clothing lay in the burning desert. They sickened with a coughing fever, and many of them died.

There was little wood for fires. The wagons wound their way like spiraling snakes on the rising stone. The air grew thin and the breath came in gasps. The numbers of the sick and dead increased each day, and the priests held funeral services at the afternoon rests. The dead were buried in cairns, for it was impossible to dig graves, and the prayers for the dead grew louder as the crosses over the stone piles stood higher.

There was first a humming of the old marching song, but it became a dirge with new verses as the host struggled on:

> *LORD JESUS, WE ARE COMING;*
> *OUR VOWS TO YOU WE KEEP.*
> *BLESS THE SOULS WE'RE LEAVING*
> *ON THIS MOUNTAIN STEEP.*
>
> *LET YOUR MOVING MERCY*
> *NEVER FADE AWAY;*
> *LET YOUR STRENGTH AND GLORY*
> *SHINE HERE FOR TODAY.*
>
> *WE LAY TO REST OUR BROTHERS;*
> *SEND YOUR SPIRIT FORTH TO THEM—*
> *THE INFIDEL WILL TREMBLE*
> *WHEN WE REACH JERUSALEM.*

Hunger stalked the long, winding line as the Crossbearers plodded wearily onward. Hundreds were dying; crosses marked every foot of the narrow road.

"Inda, we must go; the wagons are moving." Andre stood beside the girl and urged her toward the wagon. Across the flat pile of small stones she had laid out a cross, and she moved the stones fitfully, trying to embed them firmly.

"They'll fall away," she said anxiously, "and his grave will be unmarked." She burst into tears. "Lord, my son . . ."

Andre cradled her against his chest. "He is with God," he said softly, "and the Lord knows what's best. Come, it is time to go. The others have already started."

She allowed him to put her on the wagon seat. "But he was so little . . . God didn't need him as an angel . . ."

"He'll always be with us, leading us to Jerusalem."

She nodded absently. "I'll watch for him." And her eyes searched the pale-blue mountain sky.

The road began its descent and there was the promise of green, fertile valleys. The Crossbearers' pace increased with the hope that their trials were over. They could see glimpses of plowed fields and standing orchards of fruit trees as they wound their way down from the heights. There were running brooks and gardens, and fields of vegetables. They had reached Syria and before them, on the plain, in the distance was the wondrous city of Antioch.

It was the middle of October, and Bohemund, with Tancred and his advance guard, looked upon the battlements of the ancient city in dismay.

46

There was a burning in Bohemund's heart when he looked upon the garden city of Antioch, with its stone houses, large villas, and grand palaces. Justinian the Great had built its early fortifications, and its history antedated Jesus Christ by hundreds of years. Both Peter and Paul had preached there, and their converts had received the name "Christians" there.

On the north the walls rose out of the marshes of the river plain, but on the east and west sides, they climbed steeply up the sharp slopes of the mountain. To the south they ran along the summit of the ridge, across the deep chasm through which spilled the frenzied torrents of the Orontes River to the plains below. The wall culminated in a superb citadel a thousand feet above the city, and the deep ravines of the mountains beyond made the fortress impregnable.

The Gate of St. Paul, leading through the Iron Bridge, opened to the road to Aleppo, and Bohemund made his camp there. The roads from Lattakieh and the Lebanese Coast ran to the Gate of St. George, and there were not enough crusaders to close it nor to bar the Bridge Gate, which led to the ports of Alexandretta and St. Symeon. Raymond camped at the Gate of the Dog; Godfrey made his encampment on St. Gilles' right, opposite the Gate of the Duke.

The city was a garden, with fields of grain, pastures for sheep, large, cultivated gardens of vegetables and flowers, orchards, and singing fountains, and Bohemund would study it for hours and sigh. His eyes grew possessive and his heart greedy. For a city such as this he had crossed the sea, climbed the mountains, and marched across the burning deserts. For this city he was ready to fight to the death, for Antioch could be the fitting capital of his kingdom in Syria.

"There is no way," he had told the Knights' Council, "that this city can be captured except by treachery. The walls are as broad as a river and they stand thirty feet high. Their towers are a good sixty feet, built by the Romans, and hardened by the ages. It is invincible."

"The emperor can build large mangonels and bring them by ship," said Taticius, "but it will take time."

"And repeat what he did at Nicea?" Raymond was bitter.

"Nicea has always been Byzantium," the Byzantine said coldly, "but now we are in Syria. I suggest we wait."

"And I suggest we storm the walls immediately," said Raymond, locking eyes with Taticius. "If we wait, we fritter away our substance. The Lord shall give us another victory."

Godfrey, who had said nothing, turned to Adhemar. "Does the good bishop concur with Count Raymond?"

All eyes turned on Adhemar. He had the respect and admiration of all the knights for his wisdom and the power of his sword. Further, his voice was the voice of Urban.

"If we act in the true faith we can be successful." He chose his words carefully. "The walls are high and broad, and they girdle the city, but faith can move mountains."

"May I, your worships?" It was a new voice; Peter the Hermit stepped forward. He was unwashed and unkempt, and his habit was dirty, shabby, and torn, smelling of animals. As usual, he was barefoot. Alone, deserted almost by everyone, he had locked himself into a cell of self-pity and penance. Alexius had been glad to be rid of him.

Given permission to speak, he began in his usual haltering fashion. "Kind sirs, may I bring the thought to you that we have come, with the Lord's help, to this point. We have not come to capture Antioch but to free the Holy Sepulchre. We belong in the Holy City. The days of October grow short, and if we are forced to delay here through the winter, the Christ will weep. We have traveled the weary road long enough and I beg and implore you . . . bypass this city; march onward to Jerusalem."

The knights heard him out, ignored what he said, and turned back to the debate. Bohemund spoke.

"There are only two courses open to us. We cannot leave this fortress in Moslem hands as it sits astride the land passes to Byzantium—and we will need Byzantium once we conquer Jerusalem. We cannot live on an oasis in a Moslem desert; therefore we must take Antioch. The question is how?"

The barons nodded, especially Raymond, for he too had counted the wealth of Antioch and saw it as a fitting capital of a kingdom which he could pass on to his son. He scorned Bohemund because he divined the lust in that knight's heart; they would be competitors for the city, he knew, but now he agreed with the tall knight: Antioch must fall. But the city must fall to him.

"I cannot agree with the good count of St. Gilles," Bohemund went on. "If we attack now we will lose hundreds—nay, thousands—of our soldiers and good knights. We cannot demolish or scale these walls at this time. The only logical course is to lay siege, study the walls, study our foe, and plan an attack later."

Raymond was on his feet. "The longer we wait, good sirs, the more time we give the infidel to organize an attacking army. He will not sit idly by watching us. Meanwhile, we have problems of supply. Already we strip the countryside bare, and our foraging parties must move further and further to find food. We do not have the forces to close all the city's gates and stop the flow of supplies into the city; will we have more as our forces are diminished by those who will move onward to Jerusalem as we tarry here? If we attack now, by the Lord's help, we can be victorious.''

"If we attack now and do not penetrate these walls—and I can see no way we can do that—then our forces will certainly be diminished greatly. We must conserve our strength for a successful plan. Otherwise, we are doomed.'' Bohemund spoke darkly.

The knights admitted that Raymond had many valid points but they voted with Bohemund. The need for rest after the trip through the mountains and the sure death of thousands made them pause. They preferred to wait, and the host settled in for the siege.

Patrols foraged the countryside, and they found the valley full of cattle, sheep, and fowl. The trees were bowed to the ground with ripe fruit, and the bounty of the tilled fields was heavy. Many of the cottage farmhouses, villas, and palaces were deserted, the owners having fled to the city, but the larders were full and the granaries overflowed.

The crusaders reveled in food and honey, in breads and meats, and many new strange fruits. There were dark-eyed Armenian girls, heavy-breasted and broad-hipped, who brought wine to the feasting, and slender, sloe-eyed Syrian women, who were willowy and always accommodating. Crusader women were few, for many had not survived the hardships, and the men leered at the native girls and took them at will, no woman daring to refuse. The goal of the crusade faded; the men feasted, lusted, drank wine, plundered, and quarreled.

The children found sweet reeds in the marshes. The Syrians called them "sukkars" and showed the pilgrims how to press out the sweet juice. The river was full of fish and the falcons hunted again.

There were rumors of a fleet of Genoese ships coming to the port of St. Symeon, and Tancred's men rode the highways to the sea to keep them free of Moslems.

In November the rains started and the food supplies dwindled. Taticius said that the seas would be stormy during the winter months, and if the ships did not arrive soon there would be little replacements for the larders until March. The Syrian and Armenian traders, anticipating shortages, were raising prices, complaining that they had to haul their goods for greater distances as the crusaders had depleted the surrounding areas. Meanwhile, Yaghi Siyan, the Moslem commander inside the city, stared pensively at the sea of tents and concluded that the Christian dogs were not going to attack but had settled in for a siege.

He had full faith in his fortifications, but his garrison was too small to man every tower, and he prayed to Allah that the scum outside would not find which towers were empty. Meanwhile, he sent couriers out begging for reinforcements, and raiding parties attacked the crusader camps every night. His raids were successful, and his contempt for the Christians mounted with each small victory.

He arrested the Christian patriarch, put him in an iron cage, and hung it from a tower. Torches were tied to the bars at night for the Christians to view the praying, unfortunate man.

Spies were everywhere, the Syrian traders selling information, and Bohemund searched desperately for a traitor, an officer of Yaghi's garrison who was greedy enough, or angry enough, or frightened enough to open a gate to the crusader forces.

November passed and a small fleet of ships dropped anchor in St. Symeon harbor. The news was greeted with cheers, for the larders were low, and Tancred and his men guarded the unloading and were to escort the supplies back safely to camp.

Leo walked the beach and watched the undulation of the ships riding the waters offshore. There was a yearning within him: home—Genoa. When the sailors came ashore he would talk with them. Surely there was one who must have heard of the Good Sailor's Inn and could bring word back to his mama and papa that he was alive, that he was married, and that he had a little daughter. He smiled, picturing his mother's twittering hysteria and his father's slow pride in his son's prowess with the sword.

Five of the ships were Pisan; six were from Venice; only two were from Genoa; and he waited impatiently for the unloading of these.

Out of one of the long boats which ferried the cargoes to the quays stepped a young, dark youth, heavy-set, with a broad back and muscular arms.

"Pietro!" Leo screamed.

The youth turned, perplexed.

"Pietro! It's me! Leo!" He had him by the arm.

Pietro's jaw dropped. "Leo? Leo? LEO CANNELLI! It can't be! Leo!"

They were hugging and hammering at each other's back.

"We thought you were dead," exclaimed Pietro. "Your papa was sure that skinny monk killed you after he ran off without paying."

"No," laughed Leo. "I just ran away with him. We joined the Crossbearers." A thought struck him. "How about you joining too? It will be like old times and we can go to Jerusalem together."

"Me?" Pietro burst into raucous laughter. "I confess regularly, after every trip . . . then I'm clean again . . . to sin again . . . you know what I mean." He dismissed it. "I don't need Jerusalem."

"Jump to, sailor." It was a rough voice.

Pietro jumped. "I've got to work. See me here, after dark."

Leo nodded. "Right here."

The sun had finished bleeding through the dirty, gauzelike clouds, and the far hills had turned purple when Pietro appeared. They talked as the stars twinkled on the water.

Pietro saw Leo's unhappiness. "Why stay here?" he asked. "For a few pieces of gold I can get the captain to take you home."

Leo shook his head. "You don't understand. If I go home what will I be? A cook? An innkeeper? Here I can become a knight, with a villa of my own, and slaves. You should see all the loot we get . . . the gold and silver, the jewelry and horses. When we sack a town we take everything. You become rich quickly here."

"So why aren't you rich?" Pietro shrugged. "And you think you will become a knight? You fool yourself. Here you die quickly, without a priest, too. Here you starve, unless we bring you food. How many Crossbearers have died already?"

"Their spirits lead us to Jerusalem. They sing with the angels."

"You sound like a monk. When I go to confession it only costs me a few words. I say I've sinned and I'm sorry, and I promise never to do it again. Even the priest doesn't believe me." He shrugged. "Maybe I'll go to Hell, but who wants to sing all day with the angels?"

"Do you want to burn in the fiery pits forever? God knows your sins but He will not forsake you. Like the priest said, 'Turn thee to the Lord and He shall receive thee in Grace.' "

Pietro's eyes were wide. "You have become a monk."

"Do you want to be a sailor all your life?"

"What's wrong with that?" Pietro was defiant. "It's a good life."

"You'll end up as fish food."

"And the worms will eat your fat. Winter's coming and we don't sail in winter; we sit close up to the fire and eat and drink. What will you do? Without supplies the worms will have you sure."

"We'll take the city," said Leo grimly. "The emperor in Constantinople has promised to help us."

Pietro shook his head. "Nobody trusts him. You should hear the captains talk. We got good money for our goods from your barons because that emperor sent you nothing."

"We have a Byzantine general and a whole squadron of his men with us," said Leo. "He's not going to let them starve."

Pietro snorted. "A lot he cares. If I were you I wouldn't let my tongue hang out too long waiting for his food." His tone changed. "Are you sure you won't come back with me? I can talk to the captain and you could come aboard tonight. We are going to sail on the tide."

"I go to Jerusalem," said Leo stubbornly. "Tell my mama and papa."

Later, with the moon out and bright, he walked his horse alone. The beach was quiet, the water lapping the smooth sand like a thousand puppy tongues, and he could see the silhouettes of the ships sitting still in the water. He felt a dull pain in his chest . . . home.

The December rains came in fits and starts and the cold winds, blowing from their lairs in the mountains, had sharpened teeth. Food prices rose steeply and hunger stalked the tents; sickness was everywhere. The river overflowed its bed, making a lake of the marshes, and the muddy waters spread disease through the camps.

Twenty thousand men, led by Raymond and a sick Godfrey, combed the back hills for supplies, and what they found went mostly to the knights' pavilions, the men-at-arms, and the pilgrims scuffling over what remained. Christmas was coming and the knights badgered Taticius about the emperor's promised relief.

Spies brought word to Yaghi inside Antioch that the crusaders were desperate, and the knights were organizing a new force to make another sweep, looking for whatever they missed before. Yaghi grinned and sent a large, marauding force into the camps as soon as the knights disappeared into the hills. The Moslems poured out of the Bridge Gate directly into Raymond's camp, and the Provencals bravely rose to the attack.

Adhemar came off his sickbed ordering his armor and horse and rallied the remaining knights into a countercharge, driving the infidels back. The Turks regrouped and burst through the crusaders' lines, spreading out across the plain, and charged the other camps.

One Moslem picked Ruth's large wagon as an objective and was hacking his way toward it, bearing down on Guizio and Little John.

"Get out of my way!" screamed the boy to the hunchback. "I can shoot him!" He had an arrow nocked in his bow.

Guizio jumped. The arrow caught the Turk full in the chest and he tumbled from his horse. Guizio was astride him immediately. He sliced the Moslem's throat with one quick motion of his hand, and while the blood spurted, he hacked furiously at the thick neck, finally raising the man's head triumphantly by the hair.

Grinning fiercely, he said, "Your first, Johnny boy."

Little John seized the hair and, raising the head until he was face to face with the grimacing visage of the Turk, spat into the dead face.

Leo, his sword bloody, galloped up. "All right?" he screamed.

Guizio raised his sword and knife and shook them while Little John swung the head proudly. Leo nodded and rode off.

The women were huddled in the big wagon, listening to the shouts and calls of the combatants. Inda was examining a knife.

"Do you have one of these?" she asked Nina. "Andre says I have to . . . use it . . . if I'm captured, to kill myself."

Nina laughed. "The Moslems are only men, too, Inda. They'll use you the same way as our men do—or kill you—so you don't need that."

The battle sounds were fading and Ruth herded them out of the wagon, but Andre, near the doorway, pushed them back. "It isn't over!"

Mary cradled Kila in her arms. "I think she's sick," she said to Inda. "Can you tell?"

Inda took the baby and pressed it close, her face pinched in pain.

Nina yelled from the doorway. "Lord Tancred and his knights have come back. Guizio just saw Leo."

"They're moving back to the river!" said Andre in relief. "I can hear Bohemund's horns."

A cold, pelting rain had begun and by mutual decision the fighting was subsiding. The Moslems were returning to the city and the knights to their sodden tents. The mud became deeper and more fluid, and the rain was washing the blood into the soil. The Crossbearers sloshed through it, picking up their wounded and cutting the throats of all the infidels, whether living or dead, taking no chances that a body lying quietly was a corpse.

Leo rode to Ruth's wagon, wet and shivering. He had fought well but there was no pride in him. He found Mary distraught; Kila had taken the fever.

Adhemar, still with fever, sat with Raymond and stared at his empty goblet. The wine had warmed their bones, but Raymond was tired and discouraged, the long sweep through the countryside had yielded little rations, and the battle had been costly.

"We sit here, mired in the mud, while the enemy drains our substance," mused Raymond. "How much better it would have been had we attacked the walls."

"The Lord will watch over us and show us the way to deliverance," said Adhemar. "He did not mean it to happen your way."

"As I predicted," Raymond was not listening, "men are deserting, even turning to the Moslem and embracing Islam for a bread crust."

Adhemar's head came up. "Conversion? Knights or soldiers?"

At the bishop's sharp tone Raymond became awake. "It's everyone," he sighed. "Pilgrims, too; whole families. They wander the hills murdering and stealing—even praying to no God."

"The Turks will take care of them," said Adhemar, "and may the Lord have mercy on their souls, but I worry about apostasy."

Raymond lifted the flagon. "More wine?"

Adhemar shook his head. "My blood has enough heat for tonight." He was agitated. Desertion was bad enough but conversion was the work of the Devil. To desert was to weaken the crusaders, but to convert was to increase the powers of the devil infidels. He clasped his hands. "Excommunication," he said, "might be justified."

"Urban is not here. How can it be implemented?"

"I will think on it," said Adhemar struggling out of his chair. "For now, I must be off to bed. Give my respects to Elvira and tell her I miss her company." He swayed. "The wine is heady."

Raymond rose quickly. "Are you all right?"

Adhemar nodded. "Fine, fine. Just a little unsteadiness." He stood quietly. "Sleep well, my friend." He shuffled out.

Raymond's brow was knotted as he watched the bishop leave. He poured himself some more wine, changed his mind, and went to Elvira.

At that moment Tancred contemplated the two men standing before him; one a knight in full armor called William the Carpenter, the other the pathetic figure of Peter the Hermit.

"Where were you going in the black night?" he asked them.

Peter, a ravaged skeleton, hung his head and remained mute, and Leo, watching him, felt a rising pity.

"You, sir," said Tancred to the knight, "bring shame and dishonor upon all of us. Do you run from death? You have vowed to fight to the death for Christ." His face hardened, *"Or do you seek to betray us?"*

The knight was startled by the accusation. "My sword will answer that," he said between clenched teeth. "When you are ready, sir."

"I am happy to see some honor remains in you. Good! Why do you run?" Tancred ignored the challenge.

"I am answerable only to my Lord. He knows my heart."

"He comes to protect me," said Peter wearily. "He is in the service of the Lord and the Lord will judge him, none other."

Tancred placed them under guard and sent them to Bohemund in the morning. "Do not disturb me again tonight," he told Leo.

The next morning the two men stood before Bohemund. Peter's only explanation was that he wished to go on to Jerusalem.

"The direction was wrong," said the knight, "and Sir William knew that." He turned to the knight. "You, sir, will be tried before a court of your peers."

William was excused after he gave his solemn oath that he would remain in camp, but two days later he disappeared. Peter wandered all alone, a forlorn figure. Hopelessness stalked the camps.

"Therefore, I warn my brothers that the Infidel gathers a large relief army and will strike at you in the spring months. Sultan Kerbogha, who is a renown soldier, is uniting the Moslems under his banner."

Taticius was reading a letter he had received by courier from Alexius. He held secret from the Knights' Council that Alexius had sent a secret communication to him. Alexius had concluded that the crusaders had reached the zenith of their power, and their graves would be before the walls of Antioch, caught between Kerbogha's army and the city's garrison, and he advised Taticius that it was time to leave the crusader ranks.

The Byzantine commander had come to the same conclusion. Hundreds of knights lay ill with the fever, and the deaths of the pilgrims and Crossbearers were uncountable. Hunger and starvation were as deadly as the disease, and the cold rains of January had turned the camps into quagmires of death. The

Syrian and Armenian traders still sold food, but only the wealthy knights had gold enough to buy it daily, and the rest lived on the fringes of privation. Desertions had reached alarming proportions, making Adhemar's threat of excommunication a mockery. With the emperor's suggestion to leave firmly in his hand, Taticius made his preparations to return to the Imperial City.

Carefully, he explained to the knights that he would have to go to Constantinople to supervise the construction of the large mangonels to break through the strong walls. He would also arrange shipments of supplies and food. His presence was necessary, for he had to design the siege weapons, and he knew what supplies would be best. He intended to leave his servants and men and travel only with a small escort to make his journey rapid.

He left the next morning and never returned to the host.

Bohemund denounced the Byzantine bitterly and charged that as no representative of the emperor was with the crusader forces any longer, all knights were freed of their oaths and obligations to the empire; Antioch was an open prize.

Raymond demurred. Alexius would still be a necessary ally and could be a dangerous foe. All the knights had sworn to aid the empire, he pointed out. Only he had sworn not to harm her.

"We should not cut all our ties to Constantinople," he insisted. "We are not yet in Jerusalem and we can use Alexius' aid."

But Bohemund was not finished. "I am thinking," he purred, "of returning to my lands, which have been sorely neglected. My obligations are heavy and my wealth is limited. I have given much, and I am prepared to give more, if . . ." he stopped and stared about, calculating the shock of his words, ". . . if there is agreement here that Antioch will be mine when we take it."

The knights were thrown into consternation. The crusade, without Bohemund and Tancred, could become a death march.

Raymond was on his feet immediately. "I have poured more wealth, and my people have given more lives, than any baron here. I say we stand on the code! Whosoever plants his banners first over the city, to him the city belongs! I will not fight to secure a city for other lords! Pledge Antioch to anyone and I will withdraw!"

The council was in a deadlock. Both Bohemund and Raymond were necessary; the tradition of the code was firmly entrenched, but many recognized that Bohemund was their best leader and fighter.

"I am ready to go on," insisted Bohemund, "but I must have some guarantees of compensation for my losses."

"Shall it be written in the chronicles that Bohemund, denied a city, left the sacred crusade to free the Holy Sepulchre, breaking his vows?" It was Adhemar and he locked eyes with the big Norman.

Any other man would have been challenged to the field of honor, but before the bishop's steady gaze, Bohemund retreated. Agreement was reached on Raymond's terms: Whosoever raised his banners first over the city would have Antioch.

Later, Bohemund grumbled to Tancred, "Only half-done, nephew. I may have eliminated Alexius, but Raymond still watches like a vulture with extended claws. We must find a traitor to give us entry to the city. That will ensure my possession."

The hunger increased, and Tafur's new band of ribalds, trained by the remnants of the others, scurried through the countryside like rats, searching out the last grains of wheat and murdering for dried crusts of bread.

The ribald "King" sat before a fire, a grin carved in perpetuity upon his scarred, chancroid lips, sniffing hungrily at the soup of grasses and leather simmering in the pot. His body was a wasted frame of bone and dry skin, the ribcage standing clear as a skeleton's, and his knobby knees were red and chafed. His heavy, torn clothes hung into the mud at his feet, and mucus ran constantly from his reddened nose. He would pinch it off and flick-flick it aside, indifferent to its final resting place.

Haunched in a tight circle around him was his "pack," eight men and three women, all wild and emaciated. Their hunt this morning had been fruitless, and they sat swallowing their rising spittle impatiently waiting for some warming, thin broth.

"If I had an arrow I could have skewered that dog," said one of the men. "We could have had some meat and a bone."

Tafur scratched his prickly chin. "Maybe Lord Bohemund would have one to spare," he mused aloud. "I should ask him next time."

Bohemund was not sympathetic. "We need what we have for Moslems, not for dogs or rats. We lose too many; wait for the next attack. You should find many then."

"That is easy for you to say, sire," whined Tafur, "but we starve. Look at me. I am skin stretched on bone." He pinched his side. "Would you believe I ever had any fat here?"

Bohemund laughed. "Be thankful your bones are hard. If you want fat go find a Turk and cook him."

Tafur's eyes lit up. "I give you thanks, sire, for your suggestion." He talked with his "pack" and the men found the freshest burial places of the Turks. They worked with a will, exhuming a few corpses, and after much prodding they carted one off to their campfire. Like butchers, they hung the corpse by the feet, drew the entrails, and skinned the body. The caldrons were boiling, and they threw the cut limbs and sliced flesh into the steaming water.

The odor of cooking meat spread, and a large crowd gathered, only to recoil in horror when they saw what had been done. But the ribalds ate with relish, offering the stew to those who remained about, watching them. None, however, would eat.

Soon the ribalds made it a daily practice, and others, invited open-heartedly, began to join them. Bohemund, hearing of it, laughed, and sent Tafur a jar of his best wine. The message read, "Dine well and often, and drink a toast to all dead Moslems."

Tafur and his "pack" grew fat, but when Yaghi Siyan heard about it from the Syrian traders, his blood boiled and he grew inflamed. He ordered all of the male Christian slaves in the city to be slaughtered and their bodies tossed over the walls.

"Let them choke on their own Christian flesh," he raged. "These are ghouls; only the damned eat humans!"

Cries of bitterness rose from the crusader camps when the Christians, who had been taken captive in the raids of the Moslems, were flung from the battlements. Bohemund had fifteen Moslem bodies exhumed. They were spitted and slowly roasted over large fires while hidden men shrieked and moaned as though the Turks were alive. Then the knight turned the bodies over to the crowd.

The fury of Yaghi's wrath seared his vitals. He ordered his captains to seek out fifty captured Christian women, taken from the knights' tents. His carpenters built fifty crosses, and on the summit of the wall he had the women crucified, their heads pulled back by the hair and tied to a peg. Pegs were driven alongside the ears to prevent the heads from moving, and he ordered his men to cut off the exposed breasts of each woman and stuff the flesh into her open, screaming mouth.

Then the arms were spread wide, tied, and nailed to prevent them from tearing free. The feet were nailed together and forced upward, spreading the knees, and a board was placed between the kneecaps and roped tightly into place. This pushed the thighs apart, exposing the women's privates. One by one, a white, wooden stake was driven into the vagina and left protruding from the pubic hair.

There was a frenzied cry of disbelief, shame, and despair rising from the camps as they watched the abhorrent scene, and the feeling of helplessness made the crusaders writhe in fury and passion. They raged and stormed, screaming obscenities, and called on the Lord to wipe out the Sodom they saw from the face of the earth.

As each crucified woman was hung from the battlements, Bohemund gave orders to his bowmen to move close enough to the walls to shoot arrows of mercy so the pitiful victims would reach the end of their suffering quickly. He vowed personal vengeance upon the Moslem governor, exclaiming that if Yaghi Siyan ever fell into his hands, the Moslem would plead for death.

But Siyan's wrath was still unappeased. He sent his raiders into the camps night after night to create more terror and havoc and to take more prisoners. The infidels would appear like ghosts during the early morning hours, firing tents, killing those who slept, and herding men and women at sword's point into the night.

Bohemund, cursing, increased the night guards—and found many with cut throats after the raids. The tents burned and the knights and soldiers slept with swords at their sides.

The council finally decided that something had to be done. The siege had become a mockery, supplies flowing freely into the city through the Gate of St. George in the upper hill area near the citadel. The Syrian and Armenian traders were warned to stay away, and if their caravans were caught in that area, all supplies would be confiscated. The traders retaliated by cutting off supplies to the crusaders.

"The city must be starved," insisted Bohemund, "or we might as well go home." He prayed he would find a traitor.

"Give me a thousand knights," cried Tancred, "and a mouse will not enter those walls."

It was agreed; Tancred would have his thousand knights, recruited from Godfrey and Raymond, and he was to scour the hill region.

Early that evening the knight called for Leo. He was in good humor. "Tomorrow we ride the back hills again," he told his squire, "but tonight I feel like celebrating. Bring me some wine and find me a woman. I am sick of these flabby Armenians and these passive skinny Syrians. Find me an active one, young, and with firm flesh."

Leo, perplexed at first, thought of Ruth. She, or Nina, would be the one for Tancred. There had not been too much suffering in the big wagon. Under Guizio's guiding hands, the three girls had been busy, and even Andre acted as a procurer, showing a cleverness of ingratiating himself with the knights' squires. The squires called on him when their masters wanted a woman, and it all worked well; the girls earned gold, food, and even wine.

Mary listened to the stories they told and the temptation grew inside her. Her demands on Leo increased and they fought often as Leo had little money. He mounted his horse to ride to Ruth's wagon.

Kila was still ill, a strange sickness, for there were times when she appeared well. Mary claimed it was the poor food. Her small breasts, still enlarged and full, would feed the child, but there had to be something wrong with her milk, she insisted. Sometimes, the child would vomit it all out, even while nursing.

Leo knew Lord Tancred would be pushing hard to find the trails of the caravans, to make good his boasting. If the crusaders caught a large supply train, he would have more to give to Mary. He, too, knew of the gold and food the girls earned in the big wagon, and he had watched Mary's eyes shine as she examined the trinkets some of the knights would leave at times as payment. He was not sure she would not go to the wagon while he was away, and the bitterness bubbled within him. Would he have this uncertainty all his life?

Suddenly, a shadow moved! His head came about with a jerk. There! Near that tent! He stopped his horse and remained still. His eyes sought to pierce the darkness. There! It had moved again!

He slipped quietly from his horse. Slowly, he moved toward the tent and waited. Everything was quiet. He peered about. Nothing! Could he have been mistaken? No! It had been something. He stood as a stone statue, a marble column . . . listening . . . nothing. He turned around to find his horse . . . and a thousand lights exploded before his eyes. A black hood of darkness shrouded him, and his legs would not let him stand.

47

His head throbbed, but his eyes saw nothing although his senses were slowly sharpening. He could feel the heaviness of the blackness which enfolded and smothered him. He was standing against a cold, stone wall; his arms were outstretched and manacled at the wrists; there were shackles on his feet; and the floor was slippery. The air, fetid and dank, made his throat rasp. He licked his parched lips in his thirst.

What happened? formed in his mind. An image of bodies hurtling over the city's walls flashed before him. Was he a prisoner of the Turk? He squirmed at his impotence.

The minutes pulled the hours through the night and the silence became oppressive. He sagged and slept. His head fell forward; his body curled away from the wall. He hung from his wrists and ankles, semicrucified.

It was the sound of the slap, not the numbing pain of the blow across his face, which wakened him. He could feel the bony fingers against his cheek as another slap jarred him. His eyes bulged, crossed, and rearranged themselves as they came into focus. A small figure stood in the yellowish light of a smoking cresset. Beside the small figure was the tall, dark mass of a man. The light moved to one side.

"He is awake, Mussad." It was a boy's voice.

"I see." The man was dark-faced, with a black, pointed beard, a thin nose, and gleaming eyes. The boy was a thin replica without the beard. The Turk rattled in a foreign tongue. Leo did not understand him but the tone was unmistakable: he was not pleased.

Leo shook his head. His eyes darted about furtively. He was in a small, stone-walled room which had no windows: a cell, with an iron door on the opposite side.

The man tried again. "I thought all of you understood Latin," he mumbled. "You are a soldier?" There was disappointment in the question. He had switched languages.

Leo raised his head. "I am a squire to a knight."

"A squire . . . but not a knight." The man sighed. "Well, that is better than a soldier. Who is your emir?"

"Lord Tancred . . . but he won't pay ransom for me."

"Aha! Better and better! The Ferocious One. Well, squire to Lord Tancred, know me as Mussad. I have a brother in the city your emir fights so hard to enter. My brother is an important captain, and he wishes to speak to your emir—the red-haired one we call Maimoun—Bohemund. Can you arrange that?''

"I . . . I don't understand." Leo was at a loss.

"Speak! The truth!" Mussad's hand closed around Leo's cheeks, making them pout. "Speak! Talk! Say!"

Leo shook his mouth free. "What do you want?" He was bewildered. "What should I say?"

The Turk gritted his teeth. "*They* say a squire is clever, almost a knight. What has Allah sent me?" He raised his hands in disgust. "I will try again. May the Prophet be kind. Listen . . ." His hands unfolded before his mouth as his speech came slowly. "I want to arrange . . . communicate . . . with your emir, the one called Bohemund. He is your Grand Emir, your *malik*, is he not? Is it possible for you to arrange? . . . to tell him?"

Leo thought quickly and became sly. "If you let me go, I can do it."

Mussad seized him by the shirt and placed a dagger at his throat. "Do not become tricky with me," he snarled. "If I wanted you dead, you would have died before you came here. Now that you are here, if I want you dead . . ." His weapon missed Leo's throat and grated on the stone. "You only live so you can speak. Do you understand? Go to Malik Bohemund. Tell him that my brother is an important captain who guards many towers on the wall. He has a proposal. If the *malik* is interested, you are to return here in two hours. Only you. There should be no others! Understand that well. If anyone follows you, no one will be here." He raised the dagger again to Leo's throat. "It is easy for you to die."

Leo understood. "I can do it!" A Turk was ready to sell the city to Bohemund.

"Good!" The Moslem smiled, baring his teeth. "Forgive me my past anger. Allah has not made me a patient man." He removed the manacles and leg restraints. "Go! And may Allah go with you."

The boy led him to his horse; his weapons were at its feet. He showed him the direction of the camps and disappeared.

Bohemund clapped his hands in pleasure. "At last!" he shouted. "Tell this Mussad that I await his company impatiently. I will be happy to talk to his brother. Tell him I have much gold for favors."

"There is a problem, sire," said Leo. "I am to ride with Lord Tancred tomorrow to the hills. He does not know what happened to me."

Bohemund sent his squire, Tulla, to fetch Tancred. The two knights huddled in talk.

Tancred wanted Tulla in exchange for the loss of Leo's services. "I have but one squire. Take him, and I am lost."

· Bohemund grunted. "You pick my best. All right, if Tulla is to be the price of Antioch, so be it. Take him now. May he never know."

Tulla was not happy. Of the two knights, he preferred Bohemund.

Leo was unaware of the riders who trailed him back to the stone house in the hills. He found the villa empty and settled in next to the waterless fountain to wait. The shadows darkened as the sun fell behind the hill's breast, but the Moslem did not come. Disappointed, he rode back to Bohemund.

"Go back and wait," ordered the Norman. "Stay all night. Maybe he will come by morning."

Leo went back, but there were no riders trailing him this time. He lit a fire near the fountain. He was alone.

"Do not reach for your weapons." The hiss was in his ear. "Do not turn around! Do not move! The dagger is ready!"

Leo, sitting upright, clasped his hands and nodded.

"Rise slowly and stand still!"

He did as he was told. The boy suddenly faced him. He took Leo's knives and sword and disappeared in the darkness.

"Now, sit down by the fire."

He sat, and Mussad came into the fire's light and sat to face him.

"I was here earlier but you . . ."

"You had friends behind you," interrupted the Moslem. "I said you were to come alone. It bodes ill if your *malik* cannot be trusted."

"I did not know about the others," Leo said hastily. "Lord Bohemund is a knight of honor. He has much gold and he wishes to speak to your brother."

"What we plan here requires mutual trust. My brother cannot leave the city. I speak for him. The lives of many loved ones hang by the silver thread of my agreement. You will be the voice of your Bohemund."

"I? I cannot! You must talk to Lord Bohemund!"

"Do you expect me to ride into your camp?" Mussad laughed.

Leo pondered. The Turks were masters of guile and trickery. Was Mussad who he said he was? Was this an attempt to capture Bohemund? Or murder him? The knight would have to decide.

"I can take you to Bohemund's tent and no one will harm you," he told the Moslem. "You have my word."

Mussad laughed again. "You are a child," he said. "No, no, my sudden Christian friend. Tell him I will meet him—alone!—in the center of that field." He indicated a clearing. "His men are to remain in sight along the edge. I will come from the trees. There will be no point for his bowmen to shoot me. He can come in his armor, but with no weapons. Not even a dagger. Tomorrow. Noon. I swear by Allah and the Prophet: This is no trap. My son will go with you as hostage to prove my words." He rose. "You will find your weapons by your horse." He was gone. The boy was by the horse.

Bohemund brushed all considerations aside. At noon, he stood alone in the field's center. His escort, along the field's edge, nervously eyed the woods, and fingered their swords.

Mussad rode from the trees alone.

The deliberations did not take long; to Bohemund, price was no object. When it was finished, the two men bowed to each other. Mussad called, and his son ran from the knights. He leaped behind Mussad.

"*DO NOT STOP HIM!*" shouted Bohemund.

Father and son disappeared into the forest. Bohemund rode back to his escort. "Squire Leo! You are to remain here. You will be our courier."

Tancred's blockade of the city was complete. The Gate of St. George was tightly shut, and the food convoys could not get through. Although individuals slipped out and into the city at will, the sorties from the walls were halted. Tancred, and the Provencals, captured a huge consignment of supplies, a convoy syndicated by Syrians and Armenian traders, and the food eased a difficult situation in the crusader camp. From the merchants, Tancred learned of a new Moslem army led by Kerbogha, "the Terrible." "The Scourge" was gathering Moslem forces under his banner to march to the relief of Yaghi Siyan in the spring, and destroy the "Christian Pestilence."

Leo brought bad news to Bohemund: The Turkish captain had been caught hoarding grain and had been suspended from his command. Mussad assured Bohemund that it was only a temporary suspension, and the time could be compressed if Bohemund would advance ten gold pieces. Firouz, the captain, by placing the gold in the right hands, would have his command returned.

Bohemund gave Leo the gold and sent a message. "I will forget these gold pieces if Firouz hurries. I grow impatient."

"The setback is small," Mussad assured Leo. "My brother waits for the right time." The city, he said, was abuzz with the news of Kerbogha's army, expected in May.

With this information, Bohemund called a meeting of the Knights' Council. There was a clamor to appeal to Alexius. The emperor's ships could arrive in the spring with supplies and soldiers. Raymond especially was insistent and Godfrey echoed him. Bohemund agreed, yielding to the pressure.

Only Tancred knew of Bohemund's dealings with Mussad. He conferred with his nephew. "Alexius will have a claim to the city if he helps defeat Kerbogha. We must take Antioch *before* he can come. All but Raymond are ready to give the city to me."

At the Knights' Council, Raymond argued bitterly about the ownership of Antioch. To settle the dispute, the council forced a compromise. The city, they said, would belong to the knight whose troops first entered it. If Alexius came with troops, and they were first, it would go to the empire. If there were no Byzantine troops, the empire's claim was voided. Lord Godfrey disentailed himself from the decision; to him, peace between the warring crusader factions was primary. Meanwhile, Leo sat at the villa with Mussad and waited.

He had little to do but wait. Supplies came from Bohemund's larder and Mussad's wife. He even found time for a few hurried visits to Mary during the evening, and he brought her food and news. Kila was improving and Mary's mood had turned cheerful.

Kerbogha approached Antioch as May ended, and the terror in the crusader camps grew as tales about his army spread. His fighters, it was said, numbered in the tens of thousands; they were ferocious horsemen and murderous soldiers, scarred veterans of scores of battles. Only the young would be spared, the girls to be sold for the harems and kitchens, the boys to be worked as slaves and trained for abominations. All others would be put to the sword, their bones to remain unburied, an open graveyard like the Valley of the Martyrs. Fear became a festering boil; panic became tumescent and its distention became a magnified ulcer. Desertions from the crusader camps soared as fearful Christians fled into the back hills.

Count Stephen of Blois, husband of Adele, daughter of William the Conqueror, led a body of knights back into the Taurus Mountains. It was a gross folly, he proclaimed, to remain and be slaughtered. Many Crossbearers and men-at-arms went with him.

Bohemund fretted. Leo sat and talked with Mussad. "Your brother will have to do something soon. My lord questions your reasons for the delay, and hints of broken promises."

"By the Beard of the Prophet," swore Mussad, "my brother speaks the truth. His pay is small and the family is poor. We depend upon him for everything, and the gold Malik Bohemund promises will save us all. Your knight must be patient. It will be soon."

The talk spread to other things. "I do not understand your faith in this person-god Jesus, by whom you swear. Muhammad was Allah's prophet, but he was a man, like you and me. To believe that Allah, like a man, lusts after a woman . . ." He shook his head. "He created Adam from dust; woman from a rib; He can create anything—this whole world!" His arm swept the horizon. "He had to plant His seed in a woman for a Son? That is incomprehensible!"

"The ways of the Lord are His own. He does as He sees fit." Leo was uncomfortable and preferred not to examine his faith. He was still bothered by some of Skora's statements and his own doubts.

"But we are all sons of Allah—you, me, everyone. We are all born with Allah's Spirit. But our seed comes from our man-father. Your Christ, like our Muhammad, had God's Spirit, too, but to think the other way is not to think but to babble like a fool. Allah does not deal with women."

"If I'd listen to you I would burn eternally in Hell," said Leo. "The Devil has his tempters everywhere."

"Tell me of your Hell." Mussad was insensitive to Leo's feelings. "What is it like?"

"In Hell," Leo began pensively, "all men are naked and without names. They fall into the black waters of the abyss and sink to the level of their sins. Some are swallowed by monstrous fish, then vomited out and swallowed again, and again, and again, forever. Some have their flesh and bones gnawed by huge demon-dogs—forever. Some are tormented by serpents, by fire; starve while food and drink sits in front of them, for they cannot eat. There is no pity, no mercy. To live is to sin, and to die unconfessed and unabsolved is to travel the road of the damned. Only the Mother Church can bring us to Heaven and God's Mercy."

Mussad was impressed. "You have a hard road to Paradise, my friend, and you carry a great burden. Tell me, what is your Heaven like? It must be as wonderful as our Seventh Paradise."

Leo stared at the dark-faced man with the intent eyes. "I—don't know. It's . . . it's just wonderful to be in God's grace."

"You have no women? No delights? You are not entertained forever?"

Leo shook his head. "I . . . don't know."

Mussad slapped his thighs in disgust. "You condemn me and all of the Prophet's Faith to your everlasting Hell so you can go to your Heaven—and you don't know what it is? You come to our land and kill our people in the name of your Merciful Jesus? And then you pray for an unknown Heaven? Allah knows all your misdeeds. You should pray He does not send you to your Hell."

"This is the land of Jesus and we have come because you have denied us our holy places. You murder our people and despoil our churches. We come to redeem our Holy Sepulchre. Our men die; our women are taken and raped; our children become slaves."

"Our men die, too. Our women are raped; and our children have been put to the sword or sold as slaves. You say you come for your faith; we say you have come to take our land and gold."

Leo laughed. "You have no land, and you beg gold from Bohemund."

"But you will take it from our emirs, who take it from us. It is still ours. Tell me, have you come for gold or from faith?"

"For both," Leo admitted truthfully.

The boy came running. "Someone comes! I think it is Mafusta!"

"Who is Mafusta?" Leo asked.

"The son of my brother. If he has sent Mafusta he is ready."

The message of Captain Firouz was urgent. He was in command of the Tower of the Two Sisters and defended a section of the wall facing Tancred. He suggested that Bohemund come this night with scaling ladders, and to show his good faith, and if Bohemund agreed, Mafusta, his son, could be held as hostage.

Bohemund was overjoyed; his hour had come. He ordered his knights and men-at-arms to be ready to march immediately. To confuse the wall-watchers inside the city, the word was sent out—the spies would inform Siyan—that the crusaders were marching to attack Kerbogha. The crusaders wondered why Bohemund wished to leave in the late afternoon rather than in the morning. Leo was sent to Raymond and Godfrey to summon them for a hasty, important meeting in Bohemund's camp.

"Tonight," Bohemund told the two knights, "if God favors us, we will take Antioch." And he told the astonished men what had transpired with Captain Firouz.

Godfrey rejoiced; Raymond restrained his temper, for he realized that the crusaders needed the city if they were not to be annihilated by Kerbogha. He agreed to the plan with reluctance.

Siyan watched from the walls and ordered his captains to prepare to attack the Christian camps. He sighed in relief. Allah had been good to him and had mercifully spared the city. Kerbogha had arrived on time.

He told his captains that when the news of the battle arrived, they would sally forth to attack the crusaders. Even as he spoke, the horns of the Christians announced their march, and he called to them, "Announce yourselves, ye accursed and damned! Allah will judge ye for your misdeeds. Go! Malik Kerbogha will aid you in your journey to your Hell!"

Bohemund, however, did not hurry his men and rode casually. He ordered them to camp early, but told his men to be ready for a night march. Later, they grumbled as they assembled, but they became wide awake when he told them they were to construct ladders; they were marching back to the city—to the walls.

"It is all arranged," he said to them. "We have found a way in. Quickly, and don't argue! You must be quiet near the walls!"

They moved silently through the deep gorges and steep clefts along the west wall. The hours dragged; the tension mounted. They saw the lighted cressets of the sentries on the battlements, and they huddled in silence, afraid to make a sound in the quietude of the night.

Cramped and nervous, Bohemund edged his way along the wall; his hand searched every inch of its face. He was not sure which tower was the Tower of the Two Sisters. Suddenly, his hand touched a rope! Firouz had kept his word.

"Quickly!" the knight whispered to Faulk of Chartres, the man who stood behind him. "Up the ladder! But quietly."

Faulk climbed. Bohemund waited until he could just see the bulk of the knight above him, then ordered the next knight up. One by one, they climbed. Suddenly, the rope ladder was shaken violently and a dark bulk was descending. It was Herman of Cannae.

"We hold the tower, Bohemund, but this Turkish captain asks for you. He insists that you come up."

Bohemund made a quick decision. If it was a trap, it was too late now; he was committed. He turned to the knight behind him. "Keep sending the men up behind me. Pass the word along: if the rope falls, or if they hear the shout from the towers, they are to use the ladders immediately." Then, he went up.

He was helped through the narrow window and found the crusaders in charge of the tower. The Moslem guards were all dead, by Firouz's hand, and the captain was almost in a panic. Bohemund and the Turk conferred as more knights came through the window. With the information he secured from the Moslem, Bohemund sent squads along the walls.

Shoutings suddenly broke the quiet night. The rope ladder broke under the weight of too many knights pushing to climb. At the sound, the soldiers immediately stood their ladders up and began ascending in haste. Everything, success or failure, was suspended in the fragile vacuum of the next few seconds.

From the towers came the ringing call: *GOD WILLS IT!*

The soldiers cheered and crowded in frantic haste. On the battlements, they drew swords and ran along the summit in search of the guards. The false dawn threw a hazy light, and the few sentries were quickly slain. The postern doors below were opened, and the wildly excited knights and soldiers who could not climb poured through. One large contingent swarmed down the street, sweeping the slight opposition they faced aside, and ran toward the main gate.

Yaghi Siyan, and the rest of the city, was awakened by the blasting calls of Bohemund's horns, announcing to Raymond and Godfrey that he had successfully penetrated the walls. Their horns were answering in paeans of victory. The knights pounded through the open gateways and into the deserted streets. Moslem soldiers who ran to defend the gates were slaughtered. Others just fled.

Siyan called his personal guard. From his bedroom windows, in the clear morning's light, he could see the fighting in the streets. With a gut-wrenching gasp, he realized that the city had been taken—his garrison was no match for the invaders. He mounted his waiting horse and fled with his personal guards through a distant postern gate, leaving the city to the victorious crusaders.

The cheering Provencals, led by Raymond and Adhemar, the screaming Lorrainers and Rhinelanders, led by Godfrey and Eustace, poured through the walls' openings. Raymond, as he came through the Bridge Gate, lifted his head toward the citadel and could see the blood-crimson gonfalons of Bohemund on the towers near the fortress walls. They fluttered in the slight breeze, bearing witness to all that the Italian Norman was claiming the city as his. Raymond's fury and disappointment mounted. But he swallowed his pride and frustration and spurred his destrier into the street.

Bohemund remained in the upper city and attacked the citadel where a large contingent of Turks under the command of Shamms ad-Dula, Siyan's son, was entrenched. Attack after attack of the knights were thrown back. Bohemund took an arrow in his side. Leo, who fought near him, brought him into a nearby house, aided by some soldiers. The owner and his family were killed while Leo undertook the arduous task of removing the arrow. It was in the knight's fleshy midriff and had not penetrated deeply. Bohemund protested at the removal of his armor; the attacks on the citadel, he ordered, must go on.

The rampaging Crossbearers found ardent helpers in the Greek, Syrian, and Armenian Christian slaves of the city. These had been praying for deliverance and had secretly prepared clothes with red crosses sewn to their shoulders. Blessing their liberators, they joined the soldiers in the slaughter of their former masters. They became guides, leading the knights through the streets and byways. They sought out the hidden Moslems and exacted retribution and revenge for their years of oppression. Pitilessly, they struck down whole families—men, women; children, elders; the sick and infirm—while the Crossbearers, similarly engaged, cheered them on.

Bohemund sulked while Leo bound the wound with some material he had ripped from a dress. He had been able to remove the barb, using great care, while the knight gulped wine and urged him to hurry. Finished, Bohemund lay down while the squire searched the house. He had gold and jewels on his mind.

He was distracted when a knight called him from the doorway. An Armenian peasant and his son stood there with the crusader, and each carried a large sack. One dripped blood. The man pleaded that he had gifts of great value to give to Malik Bohemund and begged to see him.

"Lord Bohemund is resting," said Leo. "Give them to me."

"No! Only Malik Bohemund! This is special! For him!"

Reluctantly, Leo led him to the injured man.

The Armenian bowed before the knight. "O Magnificent One!" he proclaimed. "Your Worship! I have brought you a gift!" He opened the bag he carried, and the bloody head of a Turk rolled out. The mouth was frozen in a scream; the eyes protruded, wide in terror; the lips were drawn tightly across the teeth.

"This is Yaghi Siyan!" The man was proud. "We found him walking the road, without his horse, and all his protectors were gone. We killed him and brought you his head."

Bohemund grinned savagely and picked the dripping head up by the hair. "You have done well." He stared at the agonized face. "For this you will receive sixty bezants of gold, but, for your sake, it best be who you say it is, or your skin will be removed and dried in the sun." He glared at the Armenian.

The man clasped his hands under his beard. "It is as I say, O Magnificent One. It can be verified by many." He motioned the boy to come forward. "And, here, I have brought you his sword and girdle. As a gift—for you." He bowed again.

Bohemund reached for the weapon and examined it. "Another sixty bezants for these." He examined the gems in the scabbard. "Have you found enough gold to pay them, Leo?" he asked casually.

Leo had, but he had hoped to keep most of it for himself. He brought out a silver casket, inlaid with gems. "I have this, sire."

Bohemund counted out sixty pieces of gold, glanced at the greedy eyes of the Armenian, and counted out sixty more. There was little left. With an impulsive gesture, he said, "Here, you can take it all! For Siyan's head, nothing is too much!" He grinned. "A just price?"

The Armenian was on his knees, his head scraping the floor. "May the Lord's mercy stay with you forever! O Most Generous One! May He watch over you and keep you safe! I will sing your praises through all eternity; and the prayers of my family will sing in your name." He turned to the boy. "On your knees, my son! Pray and give thanks to our deliverer! He has enriched us for life!"

Bohemund waved them away. "Enough! Enough!"

Leo pulled them to their feet. "Lord Bohemund is tired. It is time for you to go."

Bowing and muttering praises, they backed out of the room.

"Leo. Take the head and mount it on a pike." There was a fiendish grin on Bohemund's face. "Put it in front of the house for all to see. Tell everyone." His eyes were gimlets of pleasure.

"This day shall be remembered," he said.

48

In the squares, bodies lay in heaps as the Crossbearers ravaged the city. Every house was invaded; the hiding owners were ferreted out and killed, their corpses thrown into the streets. Moslems were chased to the rooftops, killed there, or forced to jump to the howling mob below. Blood ran in the street gutters like the red waters of a rain pouring from the heavens. The knights invaded the mosques where many had run to hide and pray, and in one a large group of elderly Saracens huddled together on their prayer rugs. The crusaders sprang forward with a yell, their swords descending. The blood poured on the smoothly polished marble floor, and the Christians slipped and fell, to the guffawing of their peers. In a rage, the stained-glass windows were destroyed.

The bestialities grew. Every woman and girl child was violated before she was thrown into the flaming pyres. Adhemar had denounced any Christian who left his seed in a Moslem nest, and the crusaders were carefully avoiding that. The roar of the crowd reached a feverish pitch when a pregnant woman was found. She was cut open, the fetus ripped out, and the woman was dragged about by her entrails before she was thrown to the fires. Men's genitals were cut off and stuffed into the dying women's mouths.

Leo, hunting for food and gold, drove his short sword deeply into the Moslem's chest and twisted the blade as he pulled it out. The Turk grunted as the air rushed in; his body arched and folded into a fetal position as a convulsive shudder shook his frame. There was a sudden relaxation of the muscles and a rising odor of feces as his bowels emptied in death. His face sagged and the body rolled. He was a boy of fourteen.

Leo turned away, his eyes scanning the room.

With an unearthly scream, another youth jumped from somewhere above and landed in a crouch in front of the squire. One hand held a scimitar, the other a knife. Hate was spread over the venomous mouth and blazing eyes. A broad band of purple flesh angled downward from his neck, across his bare chest, and to the hip. The skin beneath his tattered shirt was serrated and raw, with broken surfaces and dried droplets of blood.

He circled Leo menacingly as he sought an opening for his sword or knife. His voice was hard and brittle. Suddenly, he switched languages and Leo could understand him.

"Your mother made you a bastard he-pup," he snarled, "and she dropped you from her pig's rump. I'll correct it for her. I'll make you a howling woman before I'm done." He lunged.

Leo jumped; the scimitar sliced the air. The fingers of his sword hand tightened on the hilt. His eyes grew cold; everything left his brain except the urge to kill. An icy coldness coursed his veins, and he circled the moving Moslem with great deliberation. His eyes were fixed on the scimitar; they moved to examine the face; his left hand released his knife on his hip.

The Turk leaped forward with another scream. The curved sword arced down with the swing of death. Steel rang on steel as Leo deflected the sharp blade with his sword. He stepped forward, under the outstretched arm of the Moslem, and his left hand was thrust forward and upward with the full strength of his shoulder. The man, slightly bent forward from the impetus of his blow, took the dagger in the chest. Leo moved back quickly, freeing the blade, and the blood oozed from the small, red wound.

The Turk's eyes faltered; like a diving swallow, they swiftly changed direction, swooped, turned back toward Leo, then glazed.

Leo thrust with his sword. The Turk collapsed to the floor. Inflamed and breathless, Leo watched him die.

Tafur sat in the large, gilded chair and rested his feet, shoeless and mud-stained, on the marble-topped table. He held a silver goblet of wine in his hand. The tattered remains of his breechcloth lay at the foot of his chair. With two fingers, he splashed some wine onto his dirty chest and rubbed the liquid into the hair. He was listening to a choir of five boys singing in the back of the large room, and from time to time, he would conduct the song, waving his wine-stained fingers in the air.

His ribalds combed the villa's rooms for loot, and they piled objects of exceptional value on the table before him. Only those of gold and silver interested him; all other things were discarded. He caressed and gloated over every piece he accepted, kissing it with a passion.

"In! In!" Two ribalds pushed two scantily clad girls into the room. They wore flowing, white-cotton chitons. "Tafur!" called one of the men. "Look what we found! They say they are Christians captured by the Turk."

Tafur sat up when he saw the women. His feet came off the table and he stood up—naked. "Time for a little sport, eh?" he cackled. The goblet came down and he stepped forward to confront the girls. He reached out and lifted the bowed head of the shorter one.

"Young! Good!" The other turned away from his outstretched hand. "Picky, aren't you?" He examined his hand. "I have just the place for this." He reached out and grabbed her shift in front of her breasts. With a brutish jerk, he ripped the cloth away.

She recoiled in surprise and shock.

He seized her by the arm and swung her against him, rubbing his naked chest against hers while he pressed her nude body to his.

She cried out and tried to push him away, but he was too strong for her, and he laughed as he bent her backward and kissed her. She freed a hand and scratched him, drawing blood. He released her.

"*WE ARE CHRISTIANS!*" screamed the other girl. "*IF YOU TOUCH US YOU WILL ANSWER TO LORD GODFREY!*"

Tafur laughed sardonically. "You learned to say that in a Turk's harem?" he sneered. "We will let you live if you can say 'The Lord is my Shepherd.' " He laughed again and reached for the garment on the second girl. "It's too hot in here. Let's see what you look like." He disrobed her and wiped the mucus dripping from his nose with the garment as he walked around the cringing girl.

"I like you," he told her with a leer. He turned to the two ribalds holding the other girl's arms. "Take her; this one's for me." He waved them away. She struggled and screamed at them as they dragged her from the room.

Tafur held his hand out to the remaining woman. "Come here, little one," he said suggestively. "Let's see what the Turk taught you."

She turned away, her tears flowing freely.

He seized her wrist and pulled her to him; one hand held her back, the other, her naked buttock. She trembled as he kissed her. He turned his head to the choir. The boys, fascinated, were watching him silently. "Sing!" he commanded. "I want music!" He threw some pillows on the floor.

The choir, haltingly, began its song again. Tafur turned toward them and led them with his free hand as his head bobbed in time. "Louder!" he demanded. "Louder!" He pulled at the girl with his other hand.

"Please, kind sir, please," she begged. "If you take us to Lord Godfrey, he will reward you. Our father was a knight."

"A touch of noble blood! A fitting consort for a king, King Tafur! Come, what's your name?"

"Celeste, daughter of Lord Brennen," she whispered.

He laughed and pulled her down on the pillows. "Sing!" he shouted at the faltering choir. With a grunt, he rolled the tearful girl beneath him.

Outside, the bells of the churches began to ring the victory.

Guizio, followed by Andre and Little John, had something very definite in mind as he moved through the streets of the city. He avoided the fighting and took no part in the celebrations and looting. He found an uncrowded street and searched for an appropriate villa or small palace. He finally found one with broken, fretted gates, a small orchard, and formal gardens. As they approached the front door, he drew his sword, and Little John pulled a knife.

"This is the perfect place," Guizio announced. "Somebody's already been here and we may have to fight to get it."

They moved inside carefully and searched the ground level, room by room. The place had been ransacked, but little had been destroyed. Some furniture was broken, some scattered. The rugs were stained, but intact. Pictures hung wryly; statues were broken and on the floor. The walls were unmarked.

"They must have found gold and jewels," said Andre.

Guizio nodded. "Let's try upstairs. They may still be here."

As they approached the top landing, they heard sobbing and froze. A high voice spoke peevishly.

"Oh, stop it, Celeste! We've been all through it before! You had only one; I had four of those beasts. And look what they did to those boys."

"That horrible man! Why didn't he kill me? It would have been better."

"Maybe you think so now; I don't! Look how Mother suffered when they crucified her. Father would have been proud of the way she stood up to them, those animals."

The sobbing became louder. "I can't understand you, Anne. I don't understand you at all. Father's dead. Mother . . . so horrible . . ." The voice trembled. "We've been raped . . . again and again . . . and you pretend nothing's happened. Don't you care?" The voice shrank to an astounded whisper. "Don't tell me you actually . . . liked it?" There was a sharp intake of breath.

"There were moments . . . Saud was kind—at times . . ." The voice turned bitter. "Have you thought what lies ahead of us? Father's wealth is gone. His vassals will not listen to us. Lord Godfrey is sick . . ." The bitterness increased. "Do you think he will care what happens to us? Who will protect us? What knight will want two Christian harem girls? We have nothing! Nothing!"

Guizio had heard enough. He kicked the door open and burst into a bedroom, lavishly furnished. His eyes darted about, seeking possible enemies, although the conversation he had overheard belied anyone's presence. At his entrance, the girls screamed and huddled.

"*WE ARE CHRISTIANS!*" shrieked Celeste. "*WE ARE CHRISTIANS!*"

Little John and Andre, who had followed Guizio, stared at the scantily dressed girls. Celeste's eyes were red and rheumy and wide in terror. Anne stood defiantly, light-haired, slender, and pretty. Despite their bruises and manhandling, there was an air of bravado about them.

"Why are you still here?" demanded Guizio. "Who are you?"

"We are the daughters of the Knight of the Blue Falcon," said Anne proudly, "Lord Brennen, vassal to Duke Godfrey."

"There was a Lord Brennen . . ." said Andre. "His squire . . . Pietro! Where's he?"

"Dead, all dead, in the raid," sobbed Celeste. "They took us . . . and mother . . ."

"Your father is dead?" Guizio was wary.

"And Mother, too. They crucified her . . . on the towers."

Guizio nodded. "So she was one of those." He dismissed it. "Is anyone in the house with you?"

Anne shrugged. "We don't know. Those that came before you took what they wanted and left." Her eyes flared as she saw the bent back of Guizio. She stared.

The hunchback recognized the reaction. "Don't worry about me, girlie," he chuckled. "You're not for me. But if I was you I wouldn't want to be in the streets today." He turned to Andre. "Better we search the rest of the house. Someone may be hiding. Johnny boy, you stay here."

Andre nodded.

Little John played with his knife, taking sly glances at the girls from time to time.

Anne watched the knife, her eyes veiled. Finally, she said, "I think we better go, Celeste."

"Guizio said the streets are bad," said the boy.

"We can't go now," Celeste said fearfully. "We should wait."

Anne tossed her blonde head. "Everyone will know we are Christians." She was defiant.

"What if you met some Turks?" Little John was concerned.

Anne paused. "All right," she conceded. "We'll stay a little longer." She went to the window and stared into the street.

There was a silence. "There's no one in the street," said Anne. "It's deserted."

"Was your father really a knight?" Little John asked Celeste.

She nodded and broke into tears.

"Oh, stop it, Celeste!" Anne remarked peevishly. "We've done with our crying. Come on, let's go." She started toward the door.

Celeste didn't move. "Where? We have no place. We're alone."

"We'll find a place," Anne said ferociously. "We can't remain here."

"Why not?" asked Little John. "There's plenty of room. This house is big. I was alone once, but now I stay with Guizio. Maybe you'll find someone later."

Celeste shook her head. "It's different with a girl. First, it was the Moslems . . . then those awful men!" She shuddered. "And they were Christians. They . . . they . . ." She shuddered again.

"Celeste! You talk too much!" Anne was angry.

The boy stared at her. "I know what happens to girls who are captured by the Turks. They do things to boys, too, Guizio says."

Anne bit her lip and turned away as Guizio, followed by Andre, entered. "Still here?" he threw at her sarcastically. He rubbed his hands with satisfaction and turned to the boy. "Well, Johnny, there's nobody in the house so it's all ours. When things quiet down, we'll move the girls in. Meanwhile, there's work to do." He grinned at Anne. "You can leave anytime."

"But we can't go," wailed Celeste. "We have no place."

"Anytime," reiterated the hunchback. "Unless you would like to stay here with us." He grinned evilly. "Maybe Duke Godfrey will pay us a visit." The grin became devilish.

Leo listened as Bohemund, propped on some small pillows, dealt with a group of nine Saracens who had come to see him. How they had managed to persuade the knight's guard, and still live, was a mystery—unless gold had eased the way. The Crossbearers still were rampaging through the streets, seeking victims, and the nine men, their families, and their baggage had ingratiated their way into the knight's presence.

"We are a small family, O Most Admirable of Emirs," toadied their spokesman, "but we scraped together all of our gold, our silver, and our gems of value so we could offer you three full chests for our safety. We are not Turkish fighters," he wheedled. "We are not fighters at all. We have been caught in this most unfortunate . . ."—the tips of his fingers pressed together—". . . circumstance," he finished lamely. "We are ready to give everything for our lives and for our women and children. Our deaths would serve you no purpose." He cringed obsequiously.

Bohemund's eyes were crafty. "You have three chests of gold? For nine families? A fourth might convince me."

The man was shattered. "But . . . Beloved of Allah . . . of Jesus," he corrected himself quickly, "it is everything! By the Beard of the Prophet, I swear! We have wrung ourselves dry. Wait!" he exclaimed triumphantly. "Here!" He pulled the rings from his fingers. "I have these miserable baubles." He turned to the others. "Quickly! Quickly!" He motioned for the others to follow his example. The men crowed forward, removing rings and other ornaments they wore, and placed them in a heap at Bohemund's feet.

"We have nothing left," pleaded the Saracen as he searched the knight's impassive face.

"Very well," purred Bohemund. "I will accept these and the chests." He looked to Leo. "Seek out Lord Tancred and tell him I need him here."

The two knights conferred alone while the Saracens watched anxiously from the other side of the room. Tancred nodded his head and soon rose and left. Bohemund summoned the spokesman.

"It is agreed," smiled the knight. "You have the chests?"

"They will be brought as soon as we are at the gate."

"Here! Now!" Bohemund was angry. "Or you die here!"

The man fell to his knees, his head scraping the floor. "O Kindest of Warriors, we feared to carry it with us. We could be robbed . . . the streets . . . it is hidden. We will tell you where when we stand at the gates."

"You will tell me now!" snarled Bohemund. "Or you will not leave this room alive. Do I have to kill you one by one?"

"It is hidden in the garden of the house at the end of the street," the man said quickly. "Under the large myrtle tree."

Bohemund motioned to Leo. "You heard. Take some soldiers and bring the chests to me. Take this weasel," his hand indicated the Saracen, "with you."

The chests were not buried deeply and when Leo returned, Tancred was waiting. Bohemund chuckled after biting into a piece. "I feel almost healed just looking at them," he said to Tancred. "Get rid of them," he told his nephew.

Tancred herded the families out.

"Tonight, we celebrate, Leo." Bohemund's mood had turned jovial. "Bring some wine and food, enough for many."

"Yes, sire." Leo bowed and left.

Tancred was back within an hour. "It is done, uncle. I found two more chests afterward in their baggage. There will be no need to share yours with me."

"The filthy liar!" exclaimed Bohemund. "And I believed him!" He laughed. "A good price for nine Saracen heads."

"Not counting twenty-two women and thirty-four children. We threw the bodies into the gully before the citadel for the defenders to contemplate."

"You should have kept the children. We will need slaves, and there will be few Moslems alive in the city after this is over."

"A point to remember. Next time."

"Tonight we celebrate." Bohemund rubbed his hands together. "It has been a profitable day. "I've sent Leo out for food and wine."

"Your wound?" began Tancred. "Are you up to it?"

"A trifle." The knight brushed it aside. "With enough wine, and the right female, I won't feel any pain at all." He laughed. "Tell Tulla. He used to know some wenches in camp."

"Leo knows some also."

"Leo?" Bohemund was surprised. "He told me he has a wife."

"He has, but . . ." Tancred shrugged.

"Leo!" called Bohemund. And Leo hurried in. "Lord Tancred tells me you know where we can find some good women of our own kind. Girls for a celebration."

"Maybe, sire, if nothing has happened to them."

"Find them. Have you enough wine?"

"Yes, sire. The Moslem is not supposed to drink, but he has much wine in storage."

"Good! This will be a day for your grandchildren to remember! You will be able to tell them how you helped Lord Bohemund and his knights capture Antioch! Could you find any women?"

"I only know three girls, sire, and if . . ."

"Get them! Get them! Tulla may know more!"

"Yes, sire." He left immediately, for he would have little time to waste if he was to find Guizio and Ruth. The hunchback must have brought the girls into the city by this time. Fighting still clogged the streets. Where should he look? A quiet place! That was it! Guizio would have found a safe, quiet place . . . a good house. He moved toward the outer section of the city. He was happy with the errand. When he found Guizio and Ruth, he would also find Mary and Kila. He prayed for their safety.

By nightfall, not a live Moslem could be found in all Antioch. They still garrisoned the citadel, but the streets and houses had been emptied of the living infidels. Those who had managed to escape through the postern gates stumbled into Kerbogha's patrols, already in the hills before the city, and told the horrible tales of the massacres and bestialities of the crusaders. The plains before the great walls were littered with the debris of the Crossbearers' camps—the tattered remains of the wagons, tents, and carts, left behind as the crusaders rushed behind the protection of the battlements.

Godfrey and Raymond ordered the clearing of the streets, but the task was gigantic; the dead were everywhere.

"Hercules could clean the Augean stables by diverting a river," mused Godfrey, "but our river won't run uphill."

"We will have to burn the corpses," said Raymond, "or suffer plague. Their souls are already in Hell, so their bodies might as well be consumed by the fire, too. A fitting end for the Moslem."

Trees were felled for the pyres and the Crossbearers hauled the Moslems to their fiery graves.

The church bells rang steadily and many crusaders were on their knees before the altars. Bishop Adhemar led the hymns of joy and praise to Lord Jesus. In the bliss of victory, the misery and starvation of the past year were forgotten. There was a prayer of mourning for the dead, and a song:

> *LORD JESUS, FOR YOUR BLESSINGS,*
> *WE SING THIS REQUIEM;*
> *THE INFIDEL WILL TREMBLE*
> *WHEN WE REACH JERUSALEM.*

Kerbogha was only twenty-four hours away, and the Knights' Council was deep in session.

It was the third of June, in the year of Our Lord, 1098.

49

There was no time for celebrating. Raymond and Godfrey came to Bohemund's villa to discuss the arrival of Kerbogha and the lack of supplies.

"We find the Moslem's larders almost empty," said Raymond. "Tancred's patrols were successful."

"It is ironic," muttered Godfrey. "We have changed places with Siyan. We are now the besieged."

"What of the ships at St. Symeon harbor?" asked Bohemund of Tancred. "Can't they help us?"

"They have enough provisions, but we didn't have enough gold to satisfy their captains." Tancred was bitter. "Their prices are outrageous."

"There is enough gold in Antioch to empty their holds, no matter what the price," Bohemund said vehemently. "Pay any price; we will negotiate later."

"They want gold in hand, not promises," growled Tancred. "We should take the cargoes and hang the captains by their tongues!"

"Then what other ships would come?" asked Bohemund. "Today, we will pay their price; tomorrow will be another day." He turned to the others. "Agreed? Tancred could ride out tonight."

They nodded and Tancred left as another knight hurried in.

"There is an attack from the citadel! Kerbogha's men! They are trying to cross the ravine! With horses!"

Bohemund struggled to his feet. "Uvos!" he shouted. "Get my mail and sword!"

"Wait!" cautioned Godfrey. "You are wounded. We'll go."

Bohemund ignored him. "*Uvos! You hear me? My sword!*"

Godfrey motioned to Raymond and the two knights left.

There was good reason behind Bohemund's insistence. If his men could cross the ravine and penetrate the citadel in a counterattack, his banners would fly from the fortess' towers. He was afraid without him, Raymond might accomplish the same thing, and the argument over the ownership of Antioch would be resolved only with arms.

From his balcony, he could hear the sounds and calls of the fighting men, and he paced his room in frustrated rage. Uvos did not come. The horns of Toulouse and Lorraine were sounding constantly and informed him that the knights had engaged the Moslems. He cursed at his impotence.

Two of his escort guards crowded into the room.

"Shall we stay here or go?" one asked.

Bohemund controlled himself. "The houses on the ridge crowd the fighting area," he told them. "If the infidels reach the top of the ravine, they can penetrate the city." His eyes glittered. "Get torches and burn those houses. Tell Godfrey and Raymond."

Hundreds of dwellings went up in flames and the fires spread. The entire city was engulfed in black smoke. The Moslem attack was beaten back. In turn, the sorties of Raymond and Godfrey were stopped in the ravine, and the citadel was safe for the Moslems. Hundreds of Moslems and Christians, the dead and the dying, lay in the gorge. Kerbogha's raid had cost him dearly, and he decided to besiege the city instead of trying to enter her through the citadel. After his men cleared and burned the debris left by the crusaders, his huge pavilion was erected on the plain before the walls.

Tancred and his knights had missed Kerbogha's sortie. He approached St. Symeon and saw the smoke from the burning ships before he reached the harbor. Straggling seamen told him of the Moslem's surprise attack. Only a few ships managed to reach the open sea; the rest burned.

Cursing their ill fate, Tancred and his knights turned back to Antioch. They had been riding all day and the news had stripped their hope. They rode in a bitter mood.

Leo followed Bohemund's orders and searched for Ruth. He roamed the side streets, avoiding the fighting and looting crowds. When he noticed the burning houses on the ridge, he paused. Could Mary and Kila . . . Fear gripped him and he ran toward the fires, only to be impressed with the other Crossbearers to help fight the flames before they spread to the rest of the city. Exhausted and despondent, he returned to Bohemund's villa only to find the knight in a raging temper.

"WHERE HAVE YOU BEEN?"

Smeared with soot, Leo appeared as dark as any Moslem. He tried to explain, but the knight raged on, ending his tirade with, "Clean yourself up and get out of my sight! I will see you tomorrow!"

Leo staggered out.

Desertions began almost immediately. The "rope-walkers," those who went down the walls by ropes at night, fell victim to Kerbogha's patrols, but the numbers increased nightly.

Food supplies dwindled daily and the horses of the knights disappeared. Fruits were stripped green from the trees; gardens were destroyed for their tubers and roots. People dropped from hunger in the streets, and even the poorer knights sank into stupors from starvation.

One small ray of hope existed. From the sailors who had escaped Kerbogha's raid on the ships came the news that Emperor Alexius had mustered an army and was marching to Antioch.

Bohemund met with the sick Godfrey and ailing Raymond.

"We do not know where the emperor is," he told them, "but if the information is correct, he should be near the Taurus Mountains. Sir Stephen has departed Alexandretta. Maybe he will be able to see Alexius and give him the impetus to hurry to our aid."

Daily, the eyes of the Crossbearers searched the hills and prayed for a glimpse of the gilded standards of Byzantium. One evening, a star, brighter than the sun, flamed over the city and the crusaders gawked in awe. The comet broke into three parts and disappeared behind the Moslem lines.

"It is an omen that the Lord is concerned with us," Adhemar explained from the pulpit. "He has shown us the Holy Trinity, the Three, United into One: the Father, the Son, and the Holy Ghost; each One, yet Three, thrusting His fire and anger upon the Infidel. Raise your spirits! Victory shall be ours! We have the Lord's promise!"

Across the Taurus, at Philomelium, Alexius met with Stephen of Blois and pondered the gloomy knight. Stephen did not know that the crusaders had taken Antioch. But Alexius knew, from other "rope-walkers," and he also knew the crusaders were starving. The deserters also said that Kerbogha was besieging the city and had, by this time, avenged Yaghi Siyan by killing all the crusaders.

Alexius had followed the crusaders' line of march and had seized the towns and cities abandoned by the Moslems afraid to fight the Crossbearers. He had left garrisons in command of these places. If he crossed the Taurus, he would be in Syria, the heartland of the infidels, and there lay the great power of Islam. His army, without the aid of the crusaders, was not strong enough to cope with the combined forces under Kerbogha's command. He could be defeated, with no avenue of escape. He came to a decision.

The knights had served his purposes: they had defeated the Red Lion; they had helped him regain the lost provinces of the empire; he would like Antioch, but he had enough for now. He ordered General Ducas to prepare to retreat and to lay waste the countryside to prevent pursuit.

In Antioch, the gaunt bodies of the Crossbearers were piled in the streets and the fever and dysentery spread. The crusaders were encased in a tightening web of slow death. Outside the walls, Kerbogha sat patiently and waited.

"We will need six girls," said Tulla. "Sir Tancred is having a party to relieve his boredom."

"He is bored?" Andre asked in astonishment.

Tulla shrugged. "He likes to fight and hunt. Now, he does neither, so he is restless. A party will relax him. You have six?"

"Maybe . . . I have three—maybe five." He suddenly smiled. "Perhaps, another one . . ." He grinned at Tulla. "I'll let you know. It will cost you ten bezants apiece this time."

"Ten bezants! You are mad! It's too much."

Andre shrugged. "Everything is high. The knights have gold."

"But, ten! Sir Tancred will object." He shook his head.

"He can try elsewhere. The Syrian girls are cheap."

"You know he wants Ruth. Maybe you can fill in with Armenians . . . or Syrians, and bring the price down?"

"I stay with my own. Ruth and Nina get twelve apiece, but I'm only asking ten for them, just like the others."

Tulla sighed. "All right, I'll tell him, but he'll be angry."

"He'll pay," said Andre confidently. "We'll take jewelry and precious stones if he doesn't have the gold."

Tulla nodded. Tancred will lose his temper again, he told himself. Oh, to be back with Lord Bohemund.

Andre went immediately to the little garden house behind the villa where Guizio had allowed Anne and Celeste to take up quarters. After a frightening experience on the streets, they had pleaded with him to allow them to remain. Andre had cultivated a friendship with them, and they lived on the fringe of starvation, on the charity that Guizio permitted and what Andre, with an eye to the future, could smuggle to them.

"You will earn ten bezants apiece," said Andre carefully to Anne, "but since you will each have to give me one, you will have nine left, and . . ." he added significantly, "you will have supper with a knight."

"Who is the knight?" asked Anne.

"I won't go," said Celeste stubbornly. "We aren't whores."

Anne ignored her. "Who is the knight?"

"Sir Tancred and his friends. The top leaders . . ."

"We'll go."

"Anne!" Celeste was shocked and dismayed. "We can't! What if Sir Godfrey came!"

"Sir Godfrey is ill," said Anne. "By this time you should know that the only woman he loves is Mother Mary. He doesn't even turn to boys."

"Mother would whip you for that!"

"Mother is in Heaven; and we're here. When shall we be ready?"

"In an hour," said Andre. "Are you sure about her?" He indicated Celeste. "I have to know."

"We will both be ready in an hour." Her jaw was set.

When he was gone Anne turned on her sister. "Not another word out of you! Where else can we earn eighteen bezants? When did you last eat a full dinner? We have been living on charity! Would you rather fornicate with a Moslem? Or those gutter Christians, if we're turned out into the street? At least these will be knights!''

"But, Anne," Celeste moaned, "we could marry . . . but if we . . .'' She burst into tears.

"Has anyone asked you recently?" Anne was bitter. "The knights run to the cheap Armenian and Syrian women. You forget, they, too, are Christians—of a sort—and they can bring in food from their relatives outside the walls. We have to live, too, so count your blessings.''

Celeste sniffled. "I . . . I just pray . . . we don't meet anyone we know, that's all.''

"It will make no difference," said Anne acidly. "Word will spread.''

"We need six," Andre told Ruth, "and we are only five and there is no one else, except Mary," he added. "We could use the extra gold, too. Leo hasn't brought us anything for more than a week.''

Ruth glanced at Guizio who nodded. She bit her lip. "I can't ask her," she said. "It's up to you.''

Andre glanced at Guizio, who shrugged, then back to Ruth. "All right, I'll ask her." He climbed the stairs to her room and knocked on her door before entering.

Mary sat near the window, looking out into the garden.

He walked to the small bed where Kila slept. "Is she any better?''

"She still has the fever," said Mary. "She hardly eats.''

"There's little enough food for any of us," he said pointedly.

She shrugged. "At least we're in a house instead of a wagon. Does Ruth want me?''

"No . . ." he hesitated. "I came to talk. Have you seen Leo?''

She glanced at him curiously. "You know he hasn't come for some time. You see him when he's here.''

"Things are difficult with his knight," he tried to soothe her. "I know, I talk to all the squires. But they have food . . . and gold.''

She stared at him. "What do you really want, Andre?''

"Well . . . there is a chance . . ." He suddenly plunged in. "You could earn ten bezants—gold—and a good supper, if you're willing.''

"Willing? For what?''

"Sir Tancred has a party tonight and he needs six girls. We have five— Anne and Celeste are going—but we're short one girl," he finished with a weak smile. "It will only be a few hours.''

She felt a rising fire burn within her but then it was suddenly quenched. Why not? she asked herself. Leo didn't seem to care anymore. He stayed away for days and when he did come it was only for a few hours. Also, he brought little. She had been living off of Ruth's earnings long enough, and it was time she helped herself.

"I'll go," she said abruptly. "When do you need me?"

Andre, surprised at her quick agreement, stuttered, "Soon . . . right away . . . it's becoming dark." He rushed downstairs to tell Ruth and Guizio.

"Something must have happened between them," said Ruth. "Don't ever tell Leo."

"Maybe she'll be one of us now," said Guizio.

"I doubt it," said Ruth.

Tulla led Mary to a room in Tancred's villa. "Wait here," he cautioned her, "someone will come to you. Later, we will all meet downstairs." He bustled out, not waiting for an answer.

She looked about. The room was a richly furnished bedroom with a large bed on one wall. The floor rug was thick and soft, in bright colors, and there were pictures on the walls. Some wine jugs were on a table, and she poured a drink from one into a goblet. It was acidy, and she made a face as she swallowed it.

The door opened and Lord Bohemund came in. He was the tallest of the knights, and she recognized his red hair and broad shoulders. He wore a white linen shirt, and his trousers, also white, were gartered with red leather straps. His red leather boots sparkled, and his tunic, crimson, was the same color as his gonfalons. The tunic was pinned to his shoulder with a garnet worked in gold, and his short sword was at his side. His hot eyes stripped her of her flimsy dress.

She made no movement of welcome, nor did he seem to expect any.

He moved to the wine table and splashed some wine into a goblet.

"It's not very good," she said.

"You are an expert on wines?" He seemed amused.

"This wine needs no expert," she countered as she walked away.

He followed her with his eyes, took a quaff, sputtered, and spit the liquid from his mouth.

She laughed and there was an answering smile from him as he wiped his mouth with the back of his large hand.

"You are right," he said and threw the goblet to the floor. "But we don't need it, do we?" His eyes smoldered.

His aggressive admiration and desire was arousing a response in her, and she could feel his animism trapping her soul. Her heart began to beat faster and her breath became shallow. She stood like a small animal before a weaving snake, watching him hypnotically as he slowly walked toward her, his hand outstretched.

With an effort she moved away from his huge hands. He appeared surprised and he moved toward her again, this time his hand reaching out and bunching her dress between the open neck and the short sleeve, slipping the flimsy cloth off her shoulder while his other arm enclosed her entire body. He bent over and kissed her. She gasped as she felt herself lifted off her feet and deposited on the soft bed. Everything was happening too fast; she was lost. His mouth covered hers, devouring her, and she escaped momentarily to catch her breath.

He ripped her dress down to the navel. She was wearing nothing underneath and he didn't seem surprised. "Take the rag off," he growled, and when she didn't move he ripped it apart, and she lay completely exposed to his flaming eyes. He reached over and took her in his arms. She found herself melting and clinging to him as he kissed her mouth, her neck, her breasts, and the torrents began to rage within her. She pulled him roughly to her. Suddenly he stood up and divested himself of his clothing, and she was panting in expectation as she followed each piece of clothing to the floor with her eyes. He took her roughly and she was wild in the lovemaking.

Later, when it was over, she moved away from him and rested against the soft bed pillows, drawing the wrinkled coverlet over her nakedness. He swung out of bed and paddled through the wreck of his clothing to the wine. Pouring a drink from a different bottle than he used before, he raised the goblet in a toast, saying, "To you, and I hope this is better than the other one." He was surprised that it was, and he poured some and brought it to her.

"What does my wine taster think of this?" he asked jocularly.

She tasted and nodded. They sipped the wine together without speaking. Each time she moved and touched him, after he had returned to the bed, she quickly moved away. At the third time, he stared at her.

Finishing the wine in a gulp he threw the goblet from him. "Drink up," he ordered and his eyes grew beady and hard. He waited for her to finish, took her goblet and threw it across the room, then he took her in his arms again. This time she did not respond, lying passively in his panting embrace. She was glad when it was over and he rolled away from her, his chest heaving.

He lay on his back, staring at the ceiling. "Are you one of Leo's girls that Lord Tancred always talks about?"

She nodded absently.

"I like you. Next time I'll tell Leo to bring you. What's your name?"

"No!" She sat up. "Not Leo!"

He was puzzled. "What's the problem?"

"Not Leo! Tell Andre!"

"Andre?"

"Lord Tancred's squire will know him."

"Tulla? Why not Leo?" Suddenly he had a suspicion. "Are you Mary?" She didn't answer. "He will be downstairs, you know."

She didn't move from the bed and he suddenly realized the reason. "You will need a dress." He was busily putting on his clothes.

"I could pin this one and run home."

"Here." He gave her his garnet and gold pin. "Keep it, but it's the only pin I can give you."

She put on her dress, pinning and holding it closed. "Do you know how I can leave without being seen?"

"Stay here. I'll find a way."

A stairwell led to the back garden and Mary left quickly. The knight watched her disappear into the night, a smile on his face, then he went down to join the others.

There was a surprise on everyone's face when Bohemund entered the large room alone, but the knight greeted everyone and helped himself to a small mouthful of fish, ignoring their wonder.

Leo, who stood with the other squires, glanced at Tulla who shrugged his ignorance. He did not know why the Norman was alone. Inside, Leo was fuming for he was certain, after seeing the other five women, that Mary was the sixth. But only five women sat and dined with the knights.

Adhemar kneeled before the crucified image of Christ and prayed: "Beloved Jesus, hear me. A dark curtain hovers over the city and I fear for the souls of my flock. The Devil's caldrons spew sin and debauchery, and too many of the wearers of Your cross have been listening to Satan's oily words. They have fallen on evil ways and we all wander without hope.

"We need a sign, a signal from Heaven. The road to Jerusalem is closed to us, the Moslem stands astride it, and I despair of ever seeing the hallowed waters of the Jordan, or of kneeling on the sacred rocks of the Mount.

"Fewer and fewer of Your believers come to Your house to hear Your sacred words. Those who enter the confessional plead that their sins are deeds of necessity. How can I chide them, O Lord, when I know they starve and have need of Thy mercy? They have come to this holy land to fight for Thy Blessed Son but they are sorely tried. Ye, who gave water to Moses from a rock, who dropped manna from Heaven to feed the starving Israelites in the desert, can You not find it in Your Heart to give us one small ray of hope, one omen?"

He wept at his impotence, the aging years weighing heavily on him. Finally he dried his eyes and rose ponderously. His squire was standing in the doorway, waiting for him to finish.

"Two men ask to see you, Your Worship. One is a monk who calls himself Parenti; the other is a youth called Peter Bartholomew. I explained that you were at prayer, but the monk said they would not leave until they spoke with you. The Lord, he said, had sent him."

"The Lord . . ." Adhemar smiled wryly. "No doubt He spoke with them in a vision. With all the hunger men are seeing strange things."

"Shall I send them away?"

The bishop sighed. "No. I will see them. It is important that I speak with all who speak with the Lord."

The squire ushered the two men in.

"Your Worship," began Parenti, kneeling and pulling the youth down, "it was good of you . . ."

Adhemar interrupted him. "It is not necessary to stand on ceremony. Come, come. What is it?"

"I am Monk Parenti. I followed Peter the Hermit."

"Not many lived after the massacre in the Valley of the Martyrs. Is this young man also a survivor?"

"No, Your Worship. He is a serf, from Provence. He follows his master who follows Count Raymond. His master has died, and he has come to me with an unusual story, worthy of your listening, I believe, for he may have been touched by the Finger of Our Lord."

Adhemar pursed his lips. "No doubt he has had a vision?" He turned to Bartholomew. "Well, young man, I am listening."

The bishop's squire coughed. "Your Worship," he called, "Count Raymond is here and inquires of your health."

"Good! Good!" exclaimed Adhemar. "Send him in. He, too, should hear this new 'vision.' "

Adhemar explained the presence of the two men to the count and they sat to listen. Timidly, in the presence of nobility, the serf began:

"I was lying on my pallet trying to sleep, but could not for I was very hungry, when a great fear seized me and I trembled and shook. Two men suddenly appeared before me, one old, with a gray beard and gray hair, and the other young, and tall, and beautiful, more beautiful than any son of man I have ever seen. I was terribly afraid, and finally I said, 'Who art thou?'

"The old man smiled and said, 'Do not fear me, Peter. I am the Apostle Andrew. Seek out the Bishop of Puy and the Count of St. Gilles, Raymond, and tell them what I say and what you shall see. Come with me and I shall show you the Lance of the Lord Jesus Christ, and I tell you that it shall be given to the count, for the Lord hath intended it for him since his birth.' "

Raymond's eyes opened wide, his lips parted in surprise, and an excitement seized him. "You are sure he told you that the Lance was intended for me?" he asked in awe.

Bartholomew glanced quickly at Parenti, who nodded imperceptively.

"That is what he said." Peter licked his lips, paused as though he wanted to add something, changed his mind, and looked at Parenti again. Then he fell still as though lost in reverie.

Adhemar stirred. "What else?" he asked dryly.

Bartholomew, startled, licked his lips again and went on.

"I was suddenly—I don't know how—in the city, and he led me to the Church of the Blessed Peter. Only two candles were burning in the church, but the light, as bright as midday, shone everywhere. Then Saint Andrew said to me, 'Wait here,' and he went down into the ground, through the floor next to the altar, and when he rose out of the floor he had a lance in his hand, and he gave it to me, and . . ."—the young man's voice suddenly deepened and took on an imperious quality—"and he said, '*Behold the Lance which pierced the side of Him who brought salvation throughout the world!*'

"I held it in my hand and wept. 'I will take it,' I said, 'to Count Raymond, as you have commanded.'

" 'No!' he said. 'Thou wilt come again with twelve men and thou wilt look for it here, for here shall I hide it again.'

"And he went down into the ground and hid it. Then I was brought back to my pallet, I know not how."

Raymond was sitting at the edge of his chair. "When did all this happen?" His excitement was difficult to contain.

"Before we drove the Moslem out of the city," said Parenti significantly. "He went into the city *before* we won it."

"And you waited," said Adhemar, his voice laced with sarcasm, "until now to tell us." He stared at Bartholomew.

Bartholomew turned to Parenti, his eyes pleading.

The monk coughed. "Forgive me, your holiness," he said meekly, "but it is my fault. Peter came to me in the confessional and told me of his vision, but I said he should wait. My reason was obvious . . . to you. With so many starving, visions are not unusual." He smiled weakly, and his hands opened outwardly, expressively.

Adhemar studied the dark monk, then turned to Peter. "Continue, my son," he said. "Did anything else happen?"

Bartholomew licked his dry lips. "It was later, many days, when I went seeking food . . . at a castle. I found little and I lay down to sleep, hungry and tired, and a great light filled the room. It was Saint Andrew—and the other one—again. He chided me for not telling you. I pleaded with him, saying I was unworthy; I was only a poor serf; and that no one believed me. And he answered me thus:

" 'God has chosen thee above all others because you have merit and favor. Go! and fear nought!' " Bartholomew hesitated. "But I did not come . . . because . . ."—his voice sank to a whisper—"because I was afraid."

Parenti said, "Your Worship, who would believe his words? It did not seem right for such words to be coming from a serf."

Again Adhemar studied the monk. "Did the vision repeat?" he asked Bartholomew, but his eyes remained on Parenti.

The youth nodded. "Twice more," he whispered hoarsely, "and Saint Andrew grew very angry and said I would be sent straight to Hell if I disobeyed him any longer. I was to do exactly what he had commanded or my soul was doomed." He wrung his hands fitfully. "I went straight to confession and asked what I should do." He looked at Parenti.

The monk nodded. "When the city was taken—and Saint Andrew, in the vision, said we would be victorious, although many of us doubted it—I knew we had to seek you out." He turned to the youth. "It is all right, Peter. You have fulfilled your duty."

Bartholomew licked his lips again. "I didn't want to roast in Hell," he said plaintively. "Papa Urban said if we died we would all be angels." He looked from one man to the other.

Adhemar observed him steadily. "You did well to come to me, Peter," he said finally. "Go and be in peace. The Lord understands."

Bartholomew, relieved, sat back. "I have done right?" A large smile creased his face.

Parenti rose from his chair. "His Holiness says it is all right, Peter, so it is. Now, we must leave." He took Peter's arm. "Thank you, Your Worship, and you, too, Sir Raymond, for listening."

The squire led them out.

Raymond turned eagerly to Adhemar. "What are your thoughts?" he cried, leaning forward, his face flushed, his eyes bright.

Adhemar shook his head slowly. "Do not excite yourself in your illness, my friend," he said reprovingly. "I think the youth has a vivid imagination, helped by that monk who has burned this 'vision' firmly into place. The youth is simple, and the dark spots can be brought into the light quite easily in the confessional." He chuckled. "Imagine his temerity. Saint Andrew, no less. Why not the better-known Saint Peter? It is his church. Imagine, a serf speaks to Saint Andrew, and he is told that he had more merit and favor than any other man here." He chuckled. "We will also hear more from that bright, beautiful young man who stood by Saint Andrew's side." He became serious. "Think, Raymond. Saint Andrew told him to address me and you, and he gives you a birthing present, the Lance of Our Lord. The youth does not know that the Lance in Constantinople has greater credibility and credence, and that Emperor Alexius would be much astounded to learn that it is a fraud, after the Church has sanctified it. No, my friend." He shook his head. "The youth believes what he saw, but I think that monk had a great deal to do with the version we heard."

Raymond's face fell. "Then you hold it has no truth?" He sat back disappointed. "It is a strange tale, a wondrous story." He sat pensively. "What harm would there be if we tested it and dug the ground at Saint Peter's?"

Adhemar searched the face of his friend. "You seek a sign, a signal. Every day I pray for a choosing, a sign, a ray of hope. My spirits rise and sink in disappointment. What if we dug and found nothing? How could the Lance have come to Antioch? Saint Longinus pierced Our Lord on the Cross. Did he give the Lance to Saint Peter, who then carried it to the city, here, and buried it? How can it, if it is found, be identified from any other Roman lance? And what of the Lance in Constantinople?" He shook his head and sighed. "No, my friend, we can only say that the Lord's ways are mysterious and cannot be questioned. Be certain, if He sent Peter Bartholomew to us He must have some good reason but I see it not. However, I can mull on it." He paused and his voice became more personal. "Let us talk of other matters. You are ill and should not be up from your bed. What was so important that I could not have come to you?"

"I came just to talk. At my place, Elvira hears our conversation and she suffers greatly for she sees only the gloom. Here, we have some privacy and I can think with less emotion."

They talked late into the evening, with many lapses of silence, for Raymond's mind kept slipping back to Peter's story. He tried to persuade Adhemar to see some spiritual guidance in the vision but failed, and he left the bishop's house determined to seek out the youth and listen to the tale once again.

Little John had no trouble finding Leo, after he found Bohemund's villa. "Guizio sent me," he told the squire urgently. "Come quickly. Mary acts moon-touched sometimes and Kila is dying."

Leo felt an unseen hand squeeze the air from his chest and he choked. Without a word to Uvos, who stood near, he left.

Mary stood over Kila's bed, crooning softly to the shrunken, emaciated body of the child. Guizio and Inda were with her, but drowned in the depths of her sorrow she did not feel their presence, nor did she look up when Leo came in. She had wrapped Kila in a fine byssus fabric she had found in the villa, and the small, thin body, with its deep-set, bluish eye sockets and tight, shiny face skin, was overwhelmed by the delicate, lacy patterns of the cloth.

He stood behind her, his face contorted in his misery, wanting to reach out and take her in his arms, to comfort her, when she suddenly turned on him, her teeth bared, her dark eyes fired, her hands and face contorted.

"YOU!" she screamed. "You let this happen! Away from me! From her!" She turned back to the bed. "My little precious . . . I will save you . . ." Her eyes became violent again. "Why?" she called viciously. "Why? God had no need of her! He had so many of the others!" She broke down and sobbed.

Inda pushed the speechless Leo aside and took Mary in her arms. They rocked together in their embrace, Mary sobbing, Inda trying to soothe her. Leo fell on his knees before the bed and reached out, hesitantly, and straightened out a wrinkle in the dress. He touched the thin hand. Suddenly he took a deep breath and rose, turning away from everyone, his face hard and grim.

Guizio touched him on the shoulder. "Best you leave them for now," he said. "Come, we have to talk."

In another room, from the depths of a great chair, the hunchback said somberly, "She will get over it; they all do, but we have a problem. We have many mouths to feed and the gold is almost all gone. There is not much work. It is the fever that killed Kila; she wouldn't eat."

"She was so little . . ." Leo was lost within himself.

"She is with God, with all the other Innocents, but listen to me, Leo. We must take care of the living. Within days we will have nothing. You stay with a great lord; you must provide for us."

Leo stared at the gray face of the hunchback. "I have brought what I can. Lord Bohemund is not very generous these days . . . except to the ladies," he added bitterly.

Guizio ignored the remark. "The great lords do not starve. They do not make soups with leather and roots. We will take care of Mary." He paused momentarily. "To die here . . ." his hand took in the surroundings, "to die here, after we have come this far, is to hear the Devil laughing at us. I wonder if Tafur hears him, too."

Leo nodded, but he was not listening.

In a new version of his vision, Bartholomew had told Raymond that Saint Andrew had said to wait five days, and on the fifth morning Raymond and eleven picked men stood before the altar at Saint Peter's church and began the digging. Word spread through the city and a crowd gathered, full of hope and expectation. The earth was hard-packed, but they broke through, and a large cavity was formed as the men labored through the day.

The crowd swelled and waited as the excavated mound piled higher. Ropes and buckets were being used to haul the dirt to the surface. Vespers came; the men were exhausted; others took their places; and the digging went on.

Finally Raymond, weary from the tension, feeling his weakness due to the fever, departed for his villa, ordering that the digging go on until darkness. The crowd, restless and frustrated, began to disperse, their hopes shattered, their anger rising against Bartholomew and Parenti for the falseness of the vision. The mutterings began.

Parenti took Peter aside and spoke earnestly with the youth. Peter was troubled and kept shaking his head; the monk, insistent. As the last digger was raised from the dark hole, Bartholomew announced that he would go down into the hole alone and, if necessary, would dig all night. "Saint Andrew," he insisted, "would not lie to me."

"Everyone pray!" called out Parenti. He handed the youth a lighted cresset. "Pray that Our Lord Jesus Christ will offer up His Lance as a sign for comfort and victory!"

Peter was lowered into the hole and his digging could be heard from the above. Suddenly it stopped. From the depths came the shout:

"I HAVE IT! I HAVE IT! SAINT ANDREW HAS GIVEN ME THE LANCE!"

There was an outcry as people pushed and leaned over the edge, attempting to see into the blackness. Deep down was the flicker of the cresset, throwing its yellowish beams over a shadowy Peter who held his arm aloft and was jumping and shouting.

"Pull him up!" yelled Parenti, and willing hands hauled the youth to the surface. The crowd was thrown into a paroxysm of excitement as he neared the top, convulsions seizing many, and a few toppled into the hole and screamed as they fell. There was a mighty shout of joy as Peter's outstretched arm appeared over the pile of dirt, and people pressed forward to see and, if possible, to touch the new relic.

"The Lord," Parenti shouted, "has worked His miracle! He has given us a sign! The Lance has been found! Victory is ours!"

The news burst upon the city like an incredible clap of thunder after a tremendous lightning flash. Processions organized and filed through the dark streets, which were soon lighted by thousands of flaming torches, and the walls of the houses vibrated with the sounds of the impassioned hymns shouted by thousands of throats.

The Knights' Council met immediately and placed, over Raymond's objection, Bohemund in complete command. Adhemar, his face drawn and weary, sat silently in a corner, and Raymond, his face flushed with fever, his body wrapped in a blanket, insisted that the Lance be given to him. It was his by birthright; so had said Saint Andrew to Peter Bartholomew. Godfrey, as usual, sat quietly and said nothing.

The pilgrims and Crossbearers took no heed of the arguments of the knights. Starved, their nerves tingling with elation, their spirits jubilant and exultant, they marched through the streets urging that they be led into battle. Kerbogha's doom, they cried, was sealed. They were invincible and death had no meaning any longer. They were all Heaven-bound, and the Lance would lead and protect them. The prophecy, preached by Papa Urban at Clermont, had come true. The Standard Bearer of the crusade would be Christ Himself! His Lance would lead the way!

In the council Bohemund argued that it would be suicidal to mount an attack against the vast army of the Moslems. Too many crusaders were sick; too many knights were weakened by fever and starvation; most of the horses were gone; many knights would have to fight on foot against the cavalry of the Infidel.

Raymond did not disagree with him but insisted that he be given the Lance. If they were all to die, he would do so clutching the sacred relic to his bosom. Godfrey only listened.

Many of the knights agreed with Bohemund, but there were some voices raised on the side of the Crossbearers. To sit and do nothing was to simply starve to death. The finding of the Lance must have some meaning—and they turned to Adhemar for an answer. He had none.

They could not avoid some conclusion, and they finally agreed to ask Kerbogha for his surrender terms. Not trusting each other, fearing a separate understanding with the enemy, and further fearing that the Moslem would not honor a flag of truce and slay any knight who came under his sword, they agreed to send Peter the Hermit and a man named Herlwin, as a translator.

Kerbogha listened patiently. He was not without mercy, and Allah had been good to him, delivering his enemy into his hands.

"We are humane," he said, "and we offer you your lives. The Prophet has said that it is wiser to win the hearts of your enemies than to needlessly seek their heads. Tell your lords that if they will surrender to me, I will spare them and welcome them to Islam. They need only cease to embrace this Jesus Christ as their God and worship the One and Only True God and his Prophet, Mohammed. I will then give them land and freedom. They shall be emirs and ride on horses, and they will have towns and cities to rule. If they do not accept my mercy, I shall put them to the sword and leave their bones to shine on the plains. Their wives and children will become our slaves, subject to our will and desire. We deal such with those who lift their swords against us."

Herlwin delivered the Moslem's terms word for word.

Adhemar, aroused from his lethargy, rose in all his wrath.

"We have traveled the road to the Holy Lands and many have suffered and died. Until now, the Lord has seen fit to give us victories and I say unto you, the issue here is still not decided. We are the Soldiers of the Cross, and for the cross we stand and fight. Better to die for Jesus Christ, as did the martyrs in the Roman coliseums, than to embrace a false faith. Draw your swords! We will drown this holy ground with the blood of the Infidel and, if God so wills it, with our blood as well. We do not consider apostasy!"

To a man the council rose to their feet and shouted with him:

"GOD WILLS IT! WE SWEAR UNTO THE DEATH!"

All night the church bells rang, summoning the faithful to the houses of prayer. People knelt before the altars and robed priests, and prayed. Confessions were heard and absolutions were granted. There was a celebration of the Mass as the people took Communion of the Body and the Blood of Christ. All night the leading knights gathered around Bohemund, for to him was given the task of organizing the battle, and they listened as the knight explained what he expected to do.

The dawn crept from the east in red. It was the twenty-eighth of June. As the red light streaked over the skies, the Bridge Gate opened and Raymond of Aguiles, chaplain of Count Raymond, came out. He was riding a destrier, both hands holding high the Lance. Behind him, on foot, marched a small group of white-vested priests. And behind them, riding his destrier, was Hugh of Vermandois, brother of the king of France, the highest knight in the ranks of the crusaders. Behind him were his knights, mixed with his soldiers. Some knights rode oxen, some rode asses, but most walked on foot.

The crusade came out, to give battle and die.

50

Kerbogha, "the Terrible," sat on his horse and watched, amused, as the crusaders emerged from the fortress walls of Antioch. His spies had reported the finding of the Lance and the hysterical resolve of these strange people from the west to do battle the next morning. His heralds had aroused his warriors and he was ready. Beside him was his Arab commander, Watthab ibn Hahmud, who urged an immediate attack on the outcoming Christians.

Kerbogha shook his head. "Not so." He smiled craftily. "If we strike too soon we destroy only the advance guard. Allah, in His Benevolence, sends them all to us, and we will wait until all of them are in our hands. Then . . ." he did not finish, but his teeth shone as his lips lengthened in a grin.

His confidence was great, for he had more than ten times the number of fighting men than were in the crusader ranks, and although there were quarrels among his allies he had no worries of their fighting abilities. Emir Duquq of Damascus was nervous of the report of the landing of an Egyptian army in Palestine, and he debated whether to remain with Kerbogha or to march south and fight the invaders. The emir of Homa disputed violently with the emir of Menbij, his cousin, and they kept their troops apart, refusing to fight side by side. Saracen Arabs scorned the crass fanaticism of the newly converted Turks who, in turn, curled their lips and deprecated the vapid religious performances of the Saracens.

But, Kerbogha consoled himself, they were all servants of the Prophet and would bring glory to Islam together, eliminating this scum, this pestilence of Christians.

There was laughter in the Moslem ranks as the crusaders filed out of the gate and crossed the bridge. Only three hundred knights were mounted on horses; others were riding asses and oxen; many walked, their armor dull, their clothes raggedy. Broken bidents were in the hands of the soldiers who surrounded the knights on foot, and everyone looked starved and haggard.

Kerbogha was prideful of his army's armor. Their scimitars were highly polished and newly sharpened. Their bows had new gut, and their quivers, full of new arrows, numbered in the thousands. Their shields were freshly painted with lustrous colors, and the nobles had helmets of burnished silver. All stabbing knives were sharp, and gems were inlaid in the handles, not cut glass. They would dispose of the Christian rabble in short order.

Amused, he watched the crusaders cross the river, and each group turned to the right and took a place in a building line which had the river to its back. As the line reached the bridge, the next group turned left, and the line continued to elongate until, finally, it reached the foothills on the left. The line was long and thin on the ends, heavy and bulging in the center. Casually, he gave the order that a cavalry troop be dispatched to each end to flank the line and attack from the rear. It was an elementary maneuver, and he wondered at the military simplicity of these fighters.

He had been warned of stern-faced, terrible Christian warriors, but these were mendicant soldiers, pathetic in dress and military knowledge. With the river at their back they had no place to retreat. Truly, they were mad and Allah had made him His instrument to cleanse the land of the vermin. With one stroke his cavalry would cut them to pieces. He decided he needed a little more room to herd them for the slaughter, and he ordered a slow withdrawal before the advancing line, luring his foe cautiously into a trap on the broad plain.

He grinned broadly as the crusaders moved forward. They were more stupid than he had first imagined. Who had ever heard of men on foot, outnumbered by the thousands, advancing against an army of cavalry? He closed his eyes in humbleness to Allah.

Bohemund had conceived a simple battle plan.

"In this struggle," he told the knights, "we either win, with God's help, or we all die. There is no place to run and hide. My ancestors—and many of yours—lay buried on every battlefield in the west, and if we are to die in Syria, so be it. When we cross the bridge we will make one battle line, extending from the river to the hills, and we will attack . . . and attack . . . and attack, until we are all dead or the Moslem flees. There can be no surrender. We cannot ransom our lives.

"Each of you is to be an army unto yourself. Each man and soldier will march under the banner of his choice, carrying his own weapons, or if he has none, seizing one from the hands of the dead, be it Christian or Moslem. Those who have an animal to ride will mount it; the rest of the knights will walk with the foot. What is most important: *Keep the line intact!* There will be no division between horse and foot, and *the line must move forward! Ever forward!*"

He paused and looked for Tancred.

"Lord Tancred and I will hold the left flank," he went on after finding Tancred's eyes. "Count Hugh will hold the river flank, and he will have Drogo of Nesle, Clarambald of Vendeuil, and Albert of Aix to help him. Lord Godfrey and Bishop Adhemar will mass in the center. As Count Raymond is ill, he will stay in the city with two hundred knights and soldiers to guard against an attack from the citadel. All the rest—knights, soldiers, pilgrims, women, and the children—will leave the city.

"Bishop Adhemar has given us the words: 'We are all Soldiers of the Cross, and we fight for Our Lord Jesus Christ unto victory . . . or death. God wills it!' ''

The last contingent of mounted men to leave the Bridge Gate was the Apulian knights of Tancred's small guard. Walking behind them were the Christian women, carrying their infants, bottles of water, piles of cloth ripped for dressings and bandages, and blankets for litters. Their daughters and small sons walked at their sides, also carting water and bandages. The older boys marched with the men.

"What is there left for us if the men die?" the women had asked Bohemund. "Our water will quench the thirst of the tired and wash the blood of those who bleed."

Tucked in each girdle was a knife, to kill the Moslem if there was an opportunity, to cut an embedded arrow from the wounded, or to use on their children and themselves if all was lost. Antioch, except for Raymond and his two hundred men and the Moslems in the citadel, was empty. Those who were too sick to rise from their beds had made their confessions and awaited the end. On the walls stood one hundred priests, in their white vestments, praying to the Lord.

Leo marched in the ranks of the Normans, Bohemund's men. He had no horse. His long sword was in his hands, his short sword at his side, and his knives strapped to his waist. During the long night he had gone to see Mary, to say good-bye, to comfort her if he could, and to make some arrangements with Guizio if the hunchback lived and he did not. But in her room he had seen Bohemund's garnet and gold pin on the dressing table, and his supicions as to who had been with the big Norman had been confirmed. He left abruptly. He was sure that he was going to die in the coming battle and now he no longer cared. His world on earth had ended and, as a soul in Heaven, he would find eternal peace. Yet his anger at Mary grew, and when he helped Bohemund into his armor he silently cursed the knight and wished him a horrible death.

When Bohemund was fully dressed he suddenly announced, "I have a boon for you, Leo. If we live through this and your limbs are uninjured, I will consider you for knighthood."

Leo felt a momentary flare of excitement, then the fire died. He was no longer tempted; the will and determination were gone.

"Thank you, sire," he said with a slight edge of sarcasm.

Bohemund's ear caught the tone and he turned and stared at the squire. "God is with us, Leo, and we shall conquer. Never doubt that. To fight without faith is to welcome defeat and no true knight seeks defeat. God will have mercy on both of us."

Leo nodded and turned away. He had had enough of his lord's optimism, and he wondered whether Bohemund believed everything he said.

Later, seated on his horse at the end of the long line of crusaders, Bohemund

watched the Moslem corps of cavalrymen sent by Kerbogha to outflank him.
Rainald, Count of Toul, was near and Bohemund shouted, "Ride to Tancred!"
He pointed to the Turks. "Tell him to engage them immediately!"

Rainald raised his hand in understanding and galloped off.

Leo watched him go and envied his horse.

Little John marched beside Guizio and Andre. The hunchback had chosen
to be with Bishop Adhemar's men.

"If you are about to die," he said to the boy, "it pays to be led by a
priest. The last rites come easier, and the Lord is more understanding when
you follow one of His Chosen."

Andre, pale and worried, had wished to remain in the city with Raymond,
pleading that his leg would be a handicap, but Guizio had threatened him if
he ran off. He wanted Andre to help protect Little John during the fighting,
and Andre, sensing the deadliness of Guizio's remarks, yielded quickly to the
hunchback's demand. He limped beside the other two, his sword in his sweating
hand, complaining of the pain in his leg.

Tafur and his ribalds, armed to the teeth, were with Godfrey. They had
constructed balls and chains to entangle the shanks of the Moslem horses and
gleefully showed others how to make the device.

"We'll break their legs," Tafur chuckled to his band, "and what a feast
we'll have afterwards. We'll pickle their tongues and roast the ribs, and the
hides will make strong shoes."

"The eyes," cackled one of his hags. "Save the eyes for me."

They scooted about the line, seeking advantageous positions and walking
forward confidently, twirling their anchored balls around their heads, crooning
softly to themselves.

Parenti had had a very busy night and he was exhausted. He had spent hours
with Bartholomew, convincing the serf that a new vision of victory was necessary.

"If we lose the battle no one will remember what you said; we will all
be dead and with the Heavenly Father. But if we win . . . *think of it!* Everyone
will know that you truly speak with Saint Andrew. Don't you understand?"

"But he has not come to me," the frightened serf kept insisting.

"That is not important right now." The monk swept every objection aside.
"He has come to you and he has revealed the Lance."

"But it was not the Lance you . . ."

"*NEVER SAY THAT!*" Parenti was furious. "*You* found the Lance, the
real Lance! Everyone was there and was a witness to it! Saint Andrew promised
that the Lance would lead us to victory. Didn't he?"

Peter shook his head affirmatively, flustered.

"Remember! You were told what is to be the only way. *And . . . you . . . know . . . the . . . way.*" He paused while Peter, bewildered, stared at him blankly. In a hoarse whisper as he moved his face forward toward the half-hypnotized serf, Parenti said, "*The Lord will send the warrior saints to help us! There will be Saint Mercury, and Saint George, and Saint Demetrius.* Even Saint Michael, himself, may come to lead us to a glorious victory. Do you understand?"

Finally, toward morning, Bartholomew announced that Saint Andrew had visited him again and told him not to fear the coming battle. The Lord, Saint Andrew had said, would aid His children when it was necessary. The fighting saints would be watching, and they would enter the battle at the right time.

After Peter's announcement Parenti hurried away, for there was little time before daybreak and he had to find three horsemen and white sheets among his fellow monks. The white vestments of the priests would do if he could convince three priests. The horses should be white also, but it would be difficult to find them. He was surprised when an Armenian Christian peasant led him to three white asses. He decided that they would have to do.

Later, alone with Peter, he relaxed. "We stay with Count Raymond's forces," he told the serf, "but far in the rear for it is important that we come to no harm. Saint Andrew comes only to you, you alone, even though his miracles sometimes need a little aid."

The crusader line advanced slowly over the plain, following the retreating Moslems until, finally, Kerbogha halted them and gave the word to attack. The archers fired first; then the mounted men loosened their bows and charged, firing as they came toward the line, wheeling and firing as they rode back, then wheeling and firing as they came into another charge. Their arrows, like bee swarms, hummed and buzzed in the warm air.

They were met by the deadly volleys of the Christian crossbowmen. The crossbow, as a weapon, had a far greater range and was much more accurate than the Turkish short bow, and Moslem horsemen and riders fell by the hundreds each time they approached the crusader line.

Christians, too, were falling everywhere, but the line pressed forward, the living stepping over the dying and the dead.

Kerbogha decided to make an end of the playing and ordered an all-out assault. The cavalry was to go in and destroy the living enemy, leaving nothing alive. One final clash would end it. His men lined the plain by the thousands, forming a huge arc many lines deep. The drums began their churning roll and the mounted men drew their scimitars. The horns shrilled! With a slow canter the first line moved forward. As the pace increased into an outstretched charge, the men rose from their saddles, their blades flashing in the sun, and from their throats came the keening cry: "*THERE IS NO GOD BUT ALLAH! TAHWIL! TACBIR! ALLAH IS ALMIGHTY!*"

Thousands of hooves ground the dry grasses into churning powder, raising a blinding tempest of dust. Line after line of horsemen dug their spurs into the trembling flanks of their horses, took up the cry, and headed forward at the center of the oncoming crusader forces.

Kerbogha gasped. On foot! *These madmen on foot were charging his attacking cavalry!*

A roar went up as Raymond's Provencals broke unto a run. *"TOULOUSE! TOULOUSE!"* And their horns began to sing. Soon came the answering horns of Godfrey and from his ranks came the battle call of the crusade: *"DEIU LO VULT! GOD WILLS IT!"* It was soon resounding all along the line, and underlying it was the gut-throbbing roar of Bohemund's horns from the left.

The battle was joined.

As the Moslems approached, the mounted knights of Raymond and Godfrey swept forward through the running soldiers. Bishop Adhemar, swinging his huge sword and calling on the Almighty, was in the lead, followed closely by Godfrey. There was a resounding clash of steel as the crusaders' swords met the scimitars and knocked the crescent-shaped steel from the Moslems' hands, numbing the arm to the shoulder. The big stallions, their eyes rolling, their teeth bared, bowled over the smaller Arabian and Turkish horses and stomped them. The singing swords emptied the Saracen saddles while the destriers bit at the riders' legs.

Leaping ahead of the running footsoldiers were Tafur's scrawny ribalds, the "King" in front. Their chained balls were whirling over their heads, mixing the high-whistling wind with the inhuman shrieks from their hoarse throats. The released balls were soon wrapping their chains around the forward horses' shanks, bringing them to their knees as they screamed. With victorious hoots, the ribalds were astride the falling Moslems, cutting their throats and stabbing at their bodies with abandon. Others sliced the throats of the thrashing animals and danced as the blood gushed.

Crossbearers tore at the mounted men. Reaching hands were sheared at the wrists and forearms, the blood spurting over the horses and riders. Soft flesh yielded to the sharp, curved yataghans, the pointed, stabbing knives of the Turk. Heads of Crossbearers rolled from their shoulders like bouncing balls as the scimitars flailed about. The horses, not trained to fight among milling men, stampeded in their terror, kicking and biting at the men, but they were being swallowed and absorbed in the quivering mass of humanity. The knights on foot cut off their legs, and knives, axes, and pikes tore their flesh. The blood and intestines of the animals mixed and was beaten into the dry ground with the blood and battered flesh of the humans. Above all was the roaring of the fighters and the screaming of the wounded and dying, and the inhuman keening of the horns.

Guizio drove his short sword into the back of the Turk as his strong left arm, under the neck, arched the man backward in the saddle. The horse had

thrashed and reared when the hunchback had leaped his croup and finally succeeded in throwing the two men. With a swift, acrobatic roll Guizio was up
again, his sword firmly in his hand, his wild eyes searching for the Turk. A
glance told him the Moslem was dead and he searched for another victim.

A horseman bore down on him, screaming. Guizio jumped just in time
to avoid the swinging scimitar, but slipped. With a wild cry the horseman
turned and came back. Guizio cursed, jumped, turning his head underneath
him, and came up on his feet as he rolled over his back. The rider was just
passing, and the Crossbearer hacked at the leg and knee with a savage blow.
The horse screamed and convulsively pitched the Infidel to the ground. Guizio
was atop him immediately, stabbing the body again and again. Berserk, his
muscles knotted, his eyes a fury, his face and hands covered with blood and
pasty dust, he sought another antagonist.

Little John, in a hollow, crouched close to the ground as the Moslem arrows
whistled by. He carried a thin sword and dagger, having discarded his bow
as useless. Andre crouched beside him. Most of the crusaders had moved on
and Andre felt safe hugging the ground.

After a few moments the boy stood up, wanting to move forward, but the
man pulled him back.

"Stay here! We will wait!"

"But Guizio said we must fight," Little John protested. "If you can't walk
I'll go myself." He ran out of the hollow before Andre could stop him.

Cursing, the man started out, stopped, thought a moment, and returned
to the safety of the depression. If the boy was killed, he thought, so be it. He
had done enough.

Leo took a deep breath and raised his head. The Turk lay dead. Covered
with the sweat and the blood of the dead man, he could see Bohemund, on
his destrier, fighting off two mounted Infidels. A third Moslem was approaching
the knight from the rear, moving in cautiously.

Leo screamed a warning at Bohemund but the knight did not hear. Fum-
bling for a knife as he ran closer to the wheeling horsemen, he took quick aim,
stopped, took a deep breath, held it, and threw as hard as he could at the
third Turk.

Bohemund instinctively wheeled his horse. He saw the Infidel, his scimitar
raised and ready to chop at him, rise up in his saddle, his mouth open, and
twist in surprise and agony. Then he fell forward, dropping his sword and
clutching at his horse's mane with twitching fingers. As the knight completed
his turn he caught a glimpse of Leo. He nodded and kicked his spurs savagely
into his horse's flanks. The destrier surged forward; the large sword whirled
and one Moslem was almost cut in two at the waist, still sitting on his mount. The

other pulled back, but the knight's stallion's broad chest struck the smaller steed and it staggered backward. Bohemund swung again, and the man's head bounced as it hit the croup of the horse and rolled off. The horse bolted.

Leo searched for his long sword. A wild scream made him turn just in time to see a Turk, on foot, charging him with a curved knife, a yataghan. He sidestepped and looked about desperately for a sword. The only weapon he had left was his second knife, and he drew it, but he knew if he threw it and missed, he was defenseless. He had a momentary surge of fear. For the first time he was questioning his skill; never before had his own life depended so much on his talent and dexterity.

Instinctively he crouched as the man charged. The Turk, grinning viciously, came in for the kill. Leo's hand flickered.

The Turk stumbled as the hilt of the knife suddenly appeared in his chest. He gasped and dropped his dagger. Seizing the handle of the knife he pulled it from his body and threw it back at Leo.

Leo, surprised, was frozen and the knife struck him in the face, cutting his cheek. Coming alive again, he screamed, grabbed the knife and dived at his enemy, bowling over the Turk and landing on top of him. Again and again, he drove the knife into the squirming body beneath him until it stopped moving. Panting heavily he rose and wiped his bloody, dirty hand across his red-smeared face. His blood-lust inflamed, he searched desperately for the Turk's dagger. As he reached for it he heard the gallop of hoofs and raised his head just in time to see the animal loom over him. He swung the dagger wildly, feeling it enter flesh. Then the horse struck him.

There was a tremendous shock and he could feel himself flying through the air . . . falling . . . falling . . . and then another shocking jar as he hit something hard and firm. Before his eyes everything was turning red . . . then black.

In the rear the women and children wove a haphazard pattern as they heeded the calls of the wounded. Ruth had insisted that the girls remain close together, and they had spontaneously paired off: Ruth staying with Nina, Inda with Mary, and Anne with Celeste. They walked in a tight group, remaining in the far rear.

The first Infidel barrage had a telling effect. Many of the Crossbearers had no shields and had not had the good sense to improvise any during the night, relying on the mercy of the Lord. Hundreds fell and the women were busy.

Inda watched Mary closely. Since the death of Kila a warm feeling of mutual affection had grown between them, but Mary did not recover from her self-reproach, insisting that the child's death was God's punishment for her many sins and transgressions. Her thoughts fluttered like a butterfly's, and at times she had no idea where she was, sometimes reverting to her childhood and squealing with delight over some fancied or remembered incident.

Now she appeared to be indifferent to the fighting, and she paid no heed to the crying and calling of the men. Her eyes swept over the battlefield and the wounded, staring blankly, unseeing. She would react to Inda's suggestions with an automatic response, without thinking or understanding as she stood close to the girl, wetting rags and passing them to her whenever asked.

Inda was kneeling beside a wounded Crossbearer, washing the raw flesh from which she had just cut an arrow.

"Give me the water jug, Mary."

Dutifully, indifferently, Mary handed her the jug. Suddenly she received a heavy blow to her chest. She staggered back, her head flying backward, stretching her neck, her mouth opening wide as she gasped for air. She tried to scream; there was no sound other than the roaring in her ears. There was no pain, but her legs were becoming liquidy, and she could not control them. She could feel her warm urine flowing down her thighs and she tried to stop it. She was floating in a blackening void . . . everything was swimming around her. Convulsively she clutched at the shaft of the arrow in her chest, holding it with both hands. She swayed . . . and became nothing.

Andre looked up at the grinning Turk in surprise and compulsively tightened his sweaty palm around the hilt of his sword. With a cry the Infidel leaped at him, swinging his scimitar for the death blow. Andre rolled over the ground and the sword flashed by him, embedding itself in the earth. From his lying position, he swung at the forward-leaning Turk and caught the Moslem's arm at the elbow, severing the forearm from the upper arm. With a scream the Turk straightened up, staring amazed at his severed hand still clutching his sword, and fascinated by the blood spurting from the raw stump.

Andre, in terror, swung again, at the man's legs. The Turk fell and Andre immediately straddled him, hacking away at his neck and head. The skull split open, the liquid mass splashing out. Parted at the neck, the split bone fell away. Shaking with relief, Andre collected the scimitar and yataghan and moved out of the hollow. He shuddered as he tried to avoid seeing the battered corpse.

The impossible was happening. Crossbearers clutched at bridles and would not let go, even when dragged to death. Knights on foot fought back to back, beating off the soldiers and even charges of the mounted men. Arab horses, venturing too close to the knights, had their bellies disemboweled or their legs amputated by the big swords. Dying crusaders passed weapons to those next to them, whispered their confessions as their blood poured into the dry ground.

But the line moved forward, ever forward, absorbing the repeated charges of the cavalry, surrounding and destroying the horses and their riders, dying and dragging their enemy to death with them. The living stumbled over the bodies, climbing upon and circling the piles of flesh, not hearing the cries of the wounded. For the first time, knights and soldiers had heeded a preconceived battle plan. Lord Bohemund had said, "Attack! Attack! Attack!" Bishop Adhemar had said, "Attack!" Peter Bartholomew had said, "Saint Andrew has promised us a victory. Follow the Lance and attack!"

"Unto the death, move forward! Ever forward! For Jesus Christ! For God! For the cross! For the Holy Sepulchre! Attack!" Adhemar said.

There was a rising, exalting scream from the left flank as Bohemund and Tancred led their knights in a wild charge against a wave of oncoming Turks. It rose above the horns and the din of the battle, drowning the uproar with the thunderous power of the tempest.

"THE WARRIOR SAINTS! THERE! ON THE HILL!"

Men turned to search for the vision. Like the whistling hurricane the cry passed from mouth to mouth, increasing the wild uproar.

"THE WARRIOR SAINTS! PETER'S VISION IS TRUE! THE LORD'S HOSTS ARE WITH US!"

There were those who swore they saw the white angels astride their white chargers, with white banners emblazoned with a red cross flying in the wind as the steeds rode down the hill into the battle.

"It was Saint Mercury!"

"With Saint George! And Saint Demetrius! Glory to God!"

"WE HAVE THE VICTORY! THE LORD HAS GIVEN US HIS SAINTS!"

The crusaders became frenzied madmen, fighting with heightened abandon, a joyous victory shout on their lips as they died, an ecstatic paean to God as they slew the Infidel.

Duquq of Damascus had had enough. His men, in the forefront with the Turks in the first cavalry charge, had died by the thousands. These Christians were mad and a true Moslem does not fight madmen. It was time for his forces to regroup and his drums beat the roll of retreat. He had no knowledge what was in the mind of Kerbogha, and he cared less. He had to save his cavalry, for the Egyptians were moving through Palestine. Bewildered, but dutiful, his mounted men disengaged and pulled back. Fear struck the ranks of the other Moslems as they saw the Saracens withdraw and they, too, fell back.

Alarmed, Kerbogha sought to stem the retreat, ordering the dry grass to be fired in front of the advancing crusader line. He hoped the flames would delay them long enough for him to restore order among his troops. But Soquam, emir of Homs, would not have his troops fight as long as Duquq kept his troops out of the line, and he abruptly ordered his men to retire just as Kerbogha ordered a new charge.

The Moslem panic spread as contradictory orders came through the horns and the drums. The blazing grass fire had not stopped the crusaders. In a sudden flash of revelation, Kerbogha saw it was all over and his horns joined in blowing the retreat. The entire Moslem army cracked, their line crumbled, and the cavalry broke in general panic, heading away from the battlefield.

Godfrey massed the weary knights, those who were still seated on destriers, and pointed with his sword toward the center of the Moslem camp. There stood the giant pavilion of Kerbogha, with its bright-colored banners stirring softly in the slight breeze. With a shout—"*GOD WILLS IT!*"—he led a charge against the numerically superior protective guard of the emir.

Other knights hearing Godfrey's call pressed forward and shouted in response. Soon the elated cry was picked up all along the crusader line, and it surged forward with new enthusiasm and determination. Frantic men were dragging each other as they reeled on; men clutched at body wounds, trying to stem the flow of blood, or held in their guts with an arm across their bellies, but moved forward; others, screaming and running, tried to keep up with the horses of the knights.

They broke through Kerbogha's crack guard, scattering the corps, and running them down individually to slaughter them. They had reached the heart of the enemy and they went truly mad.

Behind the riders came the footsoldiers, stumbling, shrieking, crying and hooting their wild jubilation as they invaded the tents.

"*THE INFIDEL RUNS!*" was the battle call. The horsemen began the hunt of the fugitives. Tancred's riders, ignoring the loot, chased the escaping Saracens, hoping to capture Kerbogha and bring his head back to Antioch. Bohemund's bass horns announced his horsemen coming through the milling Crossbearer ranks, his crimson gonfalons flying.

The knights stared in awe at the richness of their captured plunder. Brilliant rugs in geometric patterns; gold vessels and goblets, exquisitely filigreed and sculptured; chests of all sizes full of gold and silver coins; worked gold and silver jewelry, inlaid with magnificent gems: pearls, amethysts, rubies, emeralds, and a clear stone which shone and sparkled like glass but which could not be broken. There were pins with flashing heads, rings with crusted gems, statuary and multiple artifacts more beautiful than the westerners had ever dreamed. Kerbogha had brought his treasury with him.

There were herds of cattle, oxen and sheep for food; there were herds of horses, donkeys, and camels for beasts of burden, milling in large corrals; there were hundreds of huge wagons used as storage bins for barley, oats, and rice. There were candies made of dried figs, dates, and pomegranates. They found other fruits and vegetables they had never seen before; and there was *sukkar*, that ultrasweet kernel which they had first found near Nicea, and they had come to love its delicious flavor.

The armory wagons were full of arrows, scimitars, swords, daggers, armor helmets, shields, rich saddles, and silver buckles on the harness. They searched for wine but found none. There was no need for alcohol. They were already intoxicated in their elation, their excitement and ecstasy of victory.

The power of Islam had been broken—shattered! The road to Jerusalem was open! The Lance had led them to total victory, but the exhausted crusaders moved back to Antioch, holding and sharing each other's strength, weeping for joy with their senses befuddled, rejoicing in their loot, and ignoring the wounded and the dead all about them.

It was the women who moved through the bodies and corpses. Aided by the children they sought out those who still lived. The priests were there, too, intoning the last rites for the dying men, using whatever dry grass they could find for the last sacrament, and closing the eyes of the dead.

Bohemund sat tall in his saddle as he rode through the Bridge Gate, back to the city, *his* city, for he had been the one to capture it, and it had been his plan which had saved it. Although he was only a lesser knight, the great lords, the dukes, the counts, and even kinsmen of the kings, had followed and obeyed his commands. It was the day of his greatest triumph.

He glanced toward the towers and stopped his horse so suddenly that some of his knights rode by him before realizing that they were in front of him instead of behind. They turned toward him in surprise and he pointed. On one tower of the citadel, hanging in the soft wind, was a Provencal banner, a gonfalon of Count Raymond. With a curse, the knight kicked his horse and rode through the streets at a gallop to the ridge where Raymond had installed his headquarters. He burst into the villa and found the count in conference with a delegation of Arabs from the fortress.

Ignoring protocol he pushed through the standing men and faced Raymond. "What is the banner of Provence doing over the citadel?" he demanded of the older knight.

"This is a delegation of surrender," waved Raymond. "I gave them a banner to announce their surrender, to tell all that the citadel had been conquered."

"By whom?" Bohemund found it difficult to contain himself.

"Honorable knight . . . ." It was an Arab who touched Bohemund's arm. "You are Sir Bohemund, the Great One? The big one with red hair . . . I was told."

"I am Lord Bohemund." The voice was cold.

"Then it is to you that I offer our surrender." The man bowed. "By the order of our commander, Ahmed ibn Merwin." He bowed again. "If you will be kind to give us your banners, we will be most overjoyed to secure them from the top towers."

Appeased, Bohemund and Raymond negotiated the surrender. The Moslems would be allowed to march from the citadel unharmed and depart from the city, leaving all their weapons behind. Raymond's banner was to be returned and Bohemund would occupy the towers. Furious, Raymond ordered that he be carried to his own villa, the former palace of Yaghi Siyan.

Ahmed, the Moslem commander, was so impressed by the valor and determination of the Christians, their zeal and belief in their God, that he requested conversion. Bohemund was delighted and immediately offered him a place with his forces. The knight knew he could trust the Arab, for a traitor to the Prophet would be singled out by the fanatical Turks for immediate death.

Night crept out of the hidden corners, and the bells of the churches sang in joyous paeans of the victory, summoning those who could still stand to the holy places. Candles in their hands, the light glowing yellow and orange on their tired faces, their eyes still burning with their devotion and battle fervor, they prostrated themselves before the altars, singing the glories of the Lord. Antioch had been saved for Jesus Christ.

Early toward evening, Anne found Leo lying in a pool of his own blood, unconscious but alive. His breath was feeble and his mangled chest had difficulties maintaining the flow of air. Carefully, she washed his face, and with her sister's help she managed to drag him back to their small cottage.

Guizio found Little John, dirty, bloody, and terrified, huddled with some corpses. Too frightened to move, the boy cried out in joy and relief when he saw the hunchback searching for him. Guizio carried him back in his arms, walking silently by Andre who was seated on the steps of the veranda, refusing to listen to Andre's explanation of Little John's escape from his custody.

Andre had returned alone, smeared with earth and blood, and with a grimy cut on his right arm. He held the wound tightly with his other hand. Exhausted, he could not lift his crippled leg and had dragged it on the earth. He sat-lay on the front steps of the villa, crying softly to himself in pain and misery.

Ruth, Nina, and Inda brought the body of Mary to the villa and placed it on her bed in her room. When the two other women had left, Ruth sat at the edge of the bed contemplating her sister, her face etched in sorrow. She sat in deep silence but she could not cry. Finally she rose and took the limp hand tenderly.

"Good-bye, little sister," she murmured, pressing the hand firmly, and ran from the room.

51

They dug a grave in the garden near the large tamarack tree, and they wrapped Mary's body in a white damask sheet. Ruth turned her face away and clutched Nina's arm as the priest mumbled some prayers. But when the first clods of earth fell over the white cloth, she cried out and ran into the house. Only Inda wept.

Leo lay in a deathlike coma for two days. When his eyes opened, they were fixed and glazed. He stared blankly at the wall across from his bed. His face was a mass of purple and yellow swollen flesh; his eyes were two peepholes in the mass; his chest, red-skinned and blackened, had welts as though he had been whipped. He lay comatose for hours. Celeste fed him, nursed him, fussed over him, and cleaned him. She would bend over him to check whether he was breathing, or had died.

Andre found a doctor, an Armenian Christian, who twittered and mumbled constantly to himself like a small bird and dug into a large bag of herbs for poultices. He clucked in a strange tongue while Celeste hovered over him and harassed him with questions which he never answered. Once he surprised her by saying, "God and time will heal everything—or he will die. Pray, my child, and if He wills it, we shall know His decision." One day he nodded thoughtfully and said to no one in particular, "I think he will live."

In joy, Celeste prayed often and fervently, and Leo's battered body began to heal.

The crusaders nursed their wounded and prayed in the churches reconverted from the mosques. Many of the wounded died and the corpses rotted in the streets. Moslems, who had been thrown into cisterns, remained there; the dead, who had been thrown into the swamps along the banks of the river, rotted there. The poisoned waters spread disease and the pestilence crept into the city.

The children were the first to go, but the wounded, the weak, and the older followed quickly. The Knights' Council met in Saint Peter's church, but the disputes started early. Raymond was carried in on his litter; he was too weak to walk. His chaplain carried the Lance and placed it on the altar. All the knights, even Bohemund, bowed to it as a true relic, for it had brought a miraculous victory.

At the end, the knights could agree to only three things: they would leave the city during the summer heat and live on the countryside; they would not choose an overlord for the city until autumn; they would postpone, for the present, the march to Jerusalem. Only Raymond and Bohemund vied for the overlordship, and Raymond said he would fight if the Norman tried to take possession. Men's hands went to their swords until Godfrey stepped in to stop them.

"I personally endorse Bohemund's claim," said the duke, "but I will not fight over it. Nor should anyone else. If we shed Christian blood now, the Infidel has won. I suggest a compromise. We have agreed to disperse our armies until All Saints' Day. Let us give Alexius one more chance to claim the city. If he arrives with his army to join us by All Saints' Day, we will give the city to him. If he does not, then his claim is forfeit." He turned to Raymond. "We can decide in November who is overlord and then march on to Jerusalem. This will favor everyone."

The knights shouted their agreement in relief. Hugh of Vermandois, who was anxious to return home, agreed to carry the message to Alexius in Constantinople if Adhemar would grant him dispensation of his vows. Adhemar blessed him.

Walking from the church, Tancred berated Godfrey to Bohemund for resurrecting Alexius' claim on Antioch. Bohemund chided him.

"There are many ways to shear sheep, nephew. I have sworn fealty to Alexius; Raymond has not. Godfrey uttered my words. Alexius cannot be here by All Saints' Day. It is now late July; Hugh will dawdle, as he always does, and he has to fight the Moslem all the way back. Alexius has to equip his army, settle his affairs, secure supplies, and march across the same mountains and deserts that we did. No; I don't think he can be here by All Saints' Day."

"You take chances."

Bohemund shrugged. "Maybe, but all life is chance. Raymond is ill with the fever. Maybe he will die. If I am right, I have severed Raymond from Alexius and erased my vows, too."

Tancred, suddenly wise, shook his head. "You are too devious for me, uncle. I learn all the time."

With the heat, the fevers spread and yet life in the city quickened. Traders brought supplies, and the remaining knights systematically raided the farms, taking Moslems as slaves. The ships of Genoa hastened to St. Symeon. The captains signed contracts with Bohemund, recognizing him as lord against everyone but Raymond; against him they would remain neutral. They brought new knights and pilgrims who were eager to participate in the conquest of Jerusalem. On one ship came the monk Francis.

After a sumptuous meal and good wine, he and Bohemund talked.

"Urban needed me," said Francis, "and I could not come earlier. You have helped him and he no longer fears Emperor Henry, or Clement."

"Tell me the truth, you tub of lard," said Bohemund. "You came after you heard the fighting was over."

Francis lifted his glass. "That, too," he admitted. "You fight so well for the Lord, He has no need of my sword. Anyway, as you have noticed, I grow too old for acrobatics."

"Your tongue has become glib. Why come at all? We are not yet in Jerusalem."

Francis became sober. "Urban has word of your disputes with Count Raymond. It grieves him. I am to persuade you to desist. He wants peace between you, and that you move on to Jerusalem."

"Peace? That is simple. Who is to rule Antioch? Urban can accomplish peace by telling Raymond to leave me here—in peace."

"And what of your vows, my friend? Do you forget Jerusalem?"

"I will keep my vows . . . all at the appropriate time."

"Mmm-m-m-m," nodded the monk sipping his wine. "Exactly what I told Urban. I said, 'Bohemund always keeps his vows at the appropiate time.' My very words." He grinned at the big Norman.

Bohemund grinned back. "You know me well, my friend."

Andre heard that Genoese ships were in the harbor, and he went to St. Symeon to see what he could use in the cargo. When he returned to the villa, he had Leo's old friend, Pietro, in tow, and Leo was overjoyed to see him. Andre told Pietro the doctor said Leo would recover, but that his left hand and arm were twisted; he would not be able to use the sword again.

"Your mama and papa were glad to hear I had seen you," said Pietro. "How do you feel?"

"I will be well again."

"Your mama asked me to tell you to come home, and I have the gold for the passage money, enough for you and . . ." He hesitated. "Your papa thought you would come with Mary . . . but I heard . . ."

"Mary is dead." A grimace of pain shot across Leo's face.

Pietro nodded. "We sail in two days. Shall I tell my captain that you come?"

Leo did not answer and the silence grew. Celeste's hand stole across the bed's edge and around Leo's fingers.

"Kila is dead too." Leo's voice was a monotone.

"I heard." Pietro was very uncomfortable. "It was God's will."

"God's will." Leo echoed him unemotionally. He had thought his love for Mary had been burned out but he winced internally. Celeste could feel his tension and she tightened her hand. He squeezed hers and was thankful for it. He closed his eyes to fight the pain.

"I—er—can't stay too long," Pietro stammered. "We're loading the ship and my captain . . ." He shrugged. "I had to beg hard for him to let me come. What shall I tell your mama?"

Leo opened his eyes. "Tell her I've been hurt, but that I'll be well again . . . soon. Tell her . . .''—his voice trembled—''that Mary and Kila . . . Mary . . .''

''I will. And about coming home?''

There was a silence. Celeste's hand tightened again and her face became anxious.

''Tell her . . . I have my vows . . . Papa will understand . . . tell Mama to pray, and I will see them when this is all over, if not in Genoa, then in Heaven.''

The plague spread and Bishop Adhemar was the first knight to die from it, succumbing on the Kalends of August, the first of the month. His wisdom and charity were missed immediately, and when he was laid out before the altar in Saint Peter's, the people filed past his bier and wept.

Bohemund stood nearby and said to the deacon, ''Do not fasten the cover over his face too tightly. He vowed to visit the Holy Sepulchre and I will carry him there myself.''

The people heard and praised the Norman, but the cover was fastened tightly because of the fear of the plague.

Andre and Guizio scoured the city like scavengers, seeking work for the girls or other profitable activities. Leo remained bedridden, complaining of pains in his chest and arms, but the hunchback said Leo was pampering himself.

''You need exercise. Go back to work for Lord Bohemund. It will give us one less mouth to feed, and you will be able to help us from his larder.''

''He won't have me,'' said Leo, ''not like this.''

''We'll have to do something,'' said the hunchback. ''Prices are to the sky. A chicken cost me eight gold pieces today.''

''Leo can have part of my share,'' said Celeste boldly.

''We have to cut all shares,'' said Guizio.

''You *are* a fool, Celeste,'' said Anne contemptuously. ''He isn't worth it.''

''I have done everything you asked,'' Celeste told her sister, ''but this I will decide for myself.''

''You are a fool,'' said Anne and shrugged. ''But do not come running to me later.''

''I won't,'' said Celeste defiantly.

Anne ignored her. ''I would like to leave the cottage, Guizio, and move into the villa. It is too crowded with Leo there.''

Guizio grinned. ''I don't see why not. You can come.''

Anne smiled and glanced at Andre who smiled back, but Guizio, who saw everything, shook his head and later talked with Andre.

''Better let her be, Andre. She can be poison.''

Andre was startled. ''There is nothing . . .'' but he stopped as he saw Guizio's stare. He left the villa saying he was going for a walk.

An hour later he led a heavily cloaked figure to Leo's bedside. The stranger's face was hidden by a large cowl, and only the eyes, bright and feverish, could be seen from the cloth's depths.

"You are Leo Cannelli, from Genoa? Son of Maria Cannelli of the Good Sailor's Inn?"

Leo studied the huddled figure. "What do you want with me?"

The old man turned his head. "You have a chair? I am tired."

Celeste brought a chair.

"I come from Bethlehem to search for you. We heard that the Infidel had been driven from Antioch and then he was defeated on the plains before the city. The pilgrims who passed told many tales of the great knight Bohemund and his squire. You were his squire?"

"Yes, but what do you want with me?"

A shrunken white hand, splotched with raw-red ulcerated sores, came out of the black habit the man wore. In the hand, silk-wrapped, was a small package.

"I have something . . . a favor to ask and you will be well paid to grant me the boon. First tell me. Do you expect to remain in the Holy Lands or will you return to Genoa?"

"I . . . I do not know my true feeling yet. The Holy Sepulchre is not free and I have made vows . . . what concern is this of yours?"

"Will you be able to fight again?"

Leo set his jaw. "I will fight." Deep within himself he was not that sure. He felt that his body had been broken, but he was mending slowly. God had kept him alive and He must have had a purpose. His knives still worked with good accuracy; he could use the small sword; it was the broadsword which he could not whirl with the strength and freedom he needed.

"There is no need . . . there are others . . ."

"I will fight, old man. It is no concern of yours. I will use the broadsword again."

The man's eyes softened. "We dream, but there is a time when we must awake and return to the daylight of reality. It is God's will. The squires' talk is that you will never hold the big sword again."

"The squires blow much ill wind. They all wiggle for places among the knights. If I am not in contention then one of them can be chosen. Enough! What do *you* want of me?"

"I ask again, will you stay in the Holy Land?"

"Why concern yourself?"

"It is important . . . to me. If you remain, my mission to find you is ended. If you return home, I ask a boon for which you will be well paid." He held out the package. "It is this. I wish it to be delivered to my brother."

Leo reached out and the man, holding fast to the silk cloth, allowed the contents, a small box, to fall.

"I would not have you touch that which I have held in my hand. The disease travels by touch, from flesh to flesh. Open the box."

Leo, curious, lifted the lid and his eyes opened in surprise as he stared at a gold crucifix, jeweled with emeralds. It was priceless.

"You trust me with this?" He was dumbfounded.

"Open the back. It will come apart when you push the two jewels at the ends of the crossbar."

Leo grasped the gems between his fingers, and a piece of gold which was encased in the long shaft of the cross fell on the bed. He picked up the piece, wondering.

"Look closely. You will see engraving on the gold."

On the top of the bar was etched a coat of arms which he recognized immediately. It was the heraldic symbol of Count Fienzo of Genoa. Everyone in Genoa knew it. Below it, in miniature writing, were a series of characters and figures he could hardly see.

"You are looking at the small writing practiced by the Hebrew scribes on their scrolls. They use many kinds of figures, plants, and animal forms, which convey a message. When you return to your home, please take this cross to Count Fienzo, my brother. You know of him?"

Leo nodded. "All Genoa knows Count Fienzo."

"Tell him that the words can be deciphered by a Hebrew scribe in the city. He will reward you greatly for bringing him this message from me. My time is not long and I live in hopes of seeing the Holy Sepulchre. The Egyptian Fatimids have conquered Jerusalem while you were busy here in Antioch, and they have taken control of all the holy places. Perhaps I will live long enough to see the Holy Sepulchre freed, but I am not sure."

"But . . . I may never return to Genoa. You might do better to give this to a captain of one of the Genoese ships."

"NO! You are to take it!" The explosive words made the man breathe hard. "Swear to me on the cross which you hold in your hand. Swear that you will take it and give it to no other. You are my courier; it says so on the back—Leo Cannelli, possessor and courier. Swear!"

"You trust me with much, old man. What if I just keep it? It is worth a small fortune."

"It will be in payment. The Lord has told me to trust you and that you will not fail me. Swear!"

"All right. I will swear by the love I hold for Our Lord Jesus Christ that I will try to deliver this to your brother. But I cannot swear that I will return to Genoa."

"It is sufficient. The Lord will guide you. Keep in your memory that the words can be read by a Hebrew scribe."

Leo nodded. "And what if I am killed?"

The head of the man dropped. There was a silence. "My penance will then be greater than my sins. It will no longer matter on this earth; all will be finished." He lifted his head and the cowl fell away from his face.

"Look, Leo Cannelli. I die by the wasting of my flesh, for once I was only concerned with the pleasures of the flesh. My sins were great, but the Good Lord, in His mercy, will not confer the sins of the past on the hopes of the future. I have repented much, and I have studied much these last years, and in this last year of my life it is my prayer that I have cleansed my soul. You must not fail me.''

His face was long and thin, the face of a bird of prey, sharp-beaked and bony. He had no hair, his skull-skin glistened with sweat, and when he pulled back his thin lips in a sudden grimace of pain, what remained of his teeth were brown stubs of rotting tissue. His face was blotched with open, running sores, and in some places the ulcers had eaten to the skeleton bone.

Celeste shuddered. This was the face of a cadaver.

The man covered himself quickly. "It is time for me to leave. Remember your promise, Leo Cannelli. My soul and your future depend upon it.''

Celeste led him from the cottage.

The harvest that fall was poor. The fields had been burned and the farms lay fallow, unplanted. They had been despoiled even of their seed crop by the marauding knights, and then had been plucked clean by the hungry pilgrims.

Pilgrims, weak and exhausted from starvation and the fever, were tired of the perfidy of the knights who, they said, were more interested in disputing over the captured villages and towns in Syria than in following the pope's commandment to liberate the Holy Sepulchre.

The Genoese captains plied a two-way trade in passengers, bringing new zealots full of hope to Antioch, and returning the disappointed and weary Crossbearers to their homes in the west.

In November the Knights' Council met again, the great lords riding into the city from the countryside. They were returning to settle the overlordship of Antioch and discuss the march to Jerusalem. The people cheered when Godfrey's knights rode in. Atop each lance was perched a Moslem head, and many captives followed the horses. The wretches were chained by the legs, and each had a head of a dead man dangling from his neck as a necklace. Bohemund entered the gates last and waved to the gay crowds.

The disputations started early and grew more violent each day, leading finally to the drawing of swords when Raymond spoke against those who favored Bohemund.

He said bitterly, "You swore on the Cross of the Lord, on the Crown of Thomas, and by many holy relics, that you would not hold any city which had belonged to Byzantium. Now, you break your vows.''

Bohemund leaped to his feet. "We have given Byzantium its just due!'' he shouted. "Alexius has turned his back on us, on Antioch, and on the crusade to free the Holy City. All Saints' Day has come and gone! We kept our vows by our offer; he broke his by not joining us. I say all vows are null!''

There was a tumult but Godfrey managed to quiet the unruly men when

Peter the Hermit requested permission to address the council.

Rail-thin and raggedy, the Hermit stared at the assembly.

"I wandered far until I arrived here, where Saint Peter preached," he said, "and I have listened to all of you, you men of war, but let me say this unto you: The people cry out, 'Enough! Let us continue our journey. We came to free the Holy Sepulchre, but the knights have forgotten!'

"In the summer we had little water; in this winter we will have little food; but we have thirsted and hungered before, and many of us have died and are with the angel hosts. They watch and wonder why we dally here.

"The people cry out, 'If our leaders continue to haggle over Antioch, let them beware! We will raze the city to the ground; we will level its walls stone by stone; we will burn its palaces and villas one by one. We will rip up its gardens and it will become a wasteland. Then we will have done with the arguments. It will not need an overlord anymore.'

"The people carried the Holy Lance to victory in Antioch, and they will carry it again in exaltation to victory in Jerusalem. We will go on from here. Our prayers are that you lords lead us. But, I warn you, we will go on."

The knights listened and many shook their heads in agreement. Peter's words had touched them more than all the arguments they had heard from both sides. They forced a compromise: Bohemund was confirmed in his possession of the citadel and three-quarters of the city; Raymond was to keep the other quarter, the Iron Bridge, and Yaghi Siyan's palace; the total overlordship would be decided after they conquered Jerusalem. They settled in their chairs in relief when the two sides agreed to the terms.

Raymond jumped to his feet and announced that he would start the journey south that very month, and Tancred shouted that he would join the count. The knights cheered and turned toward Bohemund. His agreement came reluctantly; Godfrey's answer was known.

There was an immediate scrambling for carts and wagons, and Guizio and Andre used all their guile to secure the vehicles.

"We could certainly use the big wagon now," Guizio muttered to Leo. "There is so much to carry . . . we can't leave it all here." He drove everyone into a frenzy of packing. Even Leo worked hard, enjoying the use of his muscles, but Andre lagged.

Ruth scolded her brother and Andre surprised her by announcing, "I am not so happy about leaving. Actually, I was thinking of staying."

All eyes turned on him. "What keeps you here?" Ruth asked.

"I have made certain contacts . . . I just prefer it. I have come far enough."

"If Andre stays, so will I," Inda announced firmly.

"Celeste and I will remain, also," said Anne.

"Only if Leo stays," said Celeste.

Ruth looked from one to the other. "What is happening to us? Do you all think it will be better here?" She looked toward Andre.

"Well . . ." Andre fidgeted. "I think we can do well here. I know a great many people, and if the girls remain I can get them many good customers. The city becomes wealthy and the ships from Italy increase every month. Soon the ships of France and England will be coming, too. The trade grows and the burghers become rich. All the ships' captains tell me this will be a big trading center."

"Most of the knights go south," growled Guizio, "and all the leaders go. There will be much loot—gold and jewels—to be taken from the Infidel."

"Not all the knights," said Andre. "I have heard strange things said about Lord Bohemund. He counts this city his and he will not leave it to go far. Also, there is much danger to march south. The Egyptians hold Jerusalem, not the Arabs, and they are hard fighters. I have had my fill of battles; let the others fight."

"Pouf!" snorted Guizio. "We have danger everywhere, even in Paris, but a man lives but once while his soul lives forever. Do you want your soul to be called 'coward'? Not I. As for trade, Jerusalem will be where all men come on pilgrimage, not Antioch."

"Guizio is right," said Ruth. "Jerusalem will be the home of the pilgrims, even the kings and the lords. Once we are established there we will be settled for the rest of our lives."

Andre turned to Leo. "Do you burn to fight again?"

Leo took a deep breath. The argument had caught him by surprise, he had taken for granted that they would all go on to the Holy City.

"I vowed to free the Holy Sepulchre. I will go," he said.

"Then I will go with him," said Celeste quickly.

"Celeste!" Anne was upset. "You can't . . ."

"What makes you so holy?" Andre asked Leo caustically.

"You have your reasons," said Leo, "and I have mine."

"Then, it's settled," said Guizio. "You can keep the villa," he told Andre.

52

December came and the crusaders moved south as the great lords had promised, but they marched in three separate divisions. Food was scarce and water scarcer. Bohemund had been right.

Bands of Crossbearers foraged wide for supplies. More than half of the original knights who had taken the cross were dead or gone, and many of the squires who had received their swords on the battlefield held no firm loyalty to the knights who had bestowed the honor. The new knights heeded no one. They were penniless, and they shifted their allegiances quickly, following whichever lord would offer the most. The great lords husbanded their gold and kept a central core of fighting men as personal armies.

Tancred and his knights rode forward-scout once again, and one early December morning they stared on a stone-walled city which was much like a miniature Antioch. The towers were high and the battlements were thick. In the center of the enclosed area, on a hill which dominated the entire city below it, was a large mosque.

The sun was rising and its rays had set the clouds on fire, and like a huge flame flaring from a hearth, its arms reached out and seemed to kindle the rooftops. The deep-blue hills began to lighten, and the dark crevices appeared like ribbons. The rays caught the dome of the mosque and were reflected in brilliant gold.

Tancred sent a courier back to Raymond, "We have reached Maara."

Raymond's army, and the Crossbearers who followed him, camped around its forward walls. There was a deep gully before them, and many were reminded of the other city, with its river in front. Five times daily they could hear the muezzins' cry, summoning the faithful to worship. "*Allâhu ákbar! Lâ ilâha Allâh! Lâ ilâha illa'llâh!*"

Raymond had waited at Antioch, but not this time. He ordered scaling ladders built and sent his men forward in an attack on the walls. Repulsed again and again, with many casualties, he called off the attack and began the construction of a large siege tower. It was to be higher than the walls, with two levels for fighting men. The upper story was to be manned by archers and a catapult. The arrows and stones were to keep the Saracens off the battlements while the men on the level below, which was level with the wall, would mount the ramparts and sweep it clean of the enemy.

Meanwhile, crews of sappers were sent to dig under the wall, and five

355

Melgorien coins a day were offered to anyone who would bring stones to fill in the ditch.

Raymond paced and railed at each wasted hour, for this city was to be his, captured before the others arrived.

The siege tower rested on four wheels, and soldiers and pilgrims, shielded by planking and heavy cloth, labored to push it over the filled ditch until it was close enough for the drawbridge to fall on top of the wall. As it approached, stones the size of dogs began to fall around it, smashing into it, killing men in the structure as well as those laboring below at the wheels. The catapult on the tower, and others in the field, hurled stones back at the defenders. All day the battle raged, but the tower could not be moved close enough to accomplish its end.

Meanwhile, scaling ladders had been raised and the knights climbed to do battle. The Moslems used the dreaded Greek fire, poured burning hot oil and lime at the climbers' heads, threw bee hives, and attacked the men who reached the top with swords and lances.

One knight, Gouffier of Lastours, managed to keep his position atop the wall, sweeping away all attackers with his broadsword. He was joined immediately by those following him, and a small group was able to beat off attack after attack while slowly adding to their number. Soon twenty knights were on the wall and a shout of victory went up from the crusaders. The Saracens faltered and gave ground slowly before the growing numbers of their enemy.

The sun had already set and the hour of vespers had passed. Darkness was settling over the land when the Moslem defense was weakened, and the Saracens retreated from the area on the wall held by the crusaders. Although there was starlight, there was no moon, and the knights, resting on the battlements, made no attempt to broaden their holding, fearing a trap in the darkness.

Word of this small success had been sent to Raymond back in camp, meeting with Godfrey and Bohemund who had arrived at sundown. The lords all agreed to wait until morning for the final attack; meanwhile, soldiers were sent to man the posterns to prevent any of the Moslems from escaping. The assault was planned for dawn.

However, the pilgrims and soldiers, starved and smelling food and loot, were not prepared to wait. Quietly, around the area held by the knights, they raised scaling ladders and clambered over the wall. Led by many new knights, in small groups, then in ever-increasing numbers, they crept over the battlements and into the streets. They opened the postern gates and their comrades poured through. Soon the calls and shouts of the fighting were ringing through the streets and could be heard inside the crusaders' camps. But the knights still held back, not sure of the battlefield or of the foe.

The Crossbearers were less timid and began their looting immediately, and small centers of struggle erupted as the Saracens sought to protect themselves and their families. The Christians, holding even their own lives in contempt, killed indiscriminately the old, the young, the mother, the child, the man, the woman, the able, and the sick. The Moslems were extricated from cellars, flushed out of secret hiding places, followed to the roofs from which they either jumped or were hurled to the streets below. The night was full of the sounds of the fighting and the dying.

At dawn the knights entered with orders to take prisoners needed for the slave blocks in Antioch. They stopped the killing and were soon leading strings of captives to the mosques for safekeeping, but the plundering went on.

Guizio and Leo entered the city during the night looking for food and gold, but they found little. Toward dawn they moved into a deserted villa which miraculously had been overlooked by the marauding crusaders. They found some food in the larder and some silver artifacts.

"The filthy infidels cleaned out and ran," growled Guizio.

"This could be a good place for us to hold," said Leo peering about. "We could move the girls in, come the morning."

"Are you mad? The knights vow to march on."

"Not what I hear from the squires. Raymond and Bohemund fight again; who is to be overlord of Maara? We'll stay here for some time; you will see."

Guizio scratched his grizzled head. "Maybe we should have stayed in Antioch," he rumbled. "If they're going to fight over every town along the way, we'll be on the road another year."

"Maybe so," said Leo. "Let's check this place and make sure none of the Moslems are hiding."

They searched all the rooms, the cellar, and even checked the roof, but the place was empty. Guizio left for the camp while Leo stretched out in a bed, waiting for the hunchback to bring the others back to the villa.

Leo was right. Raymond was choleric when he found that Bohemund had ordered his men to occupy themselves with looting. The count demanded a meeting of the council and accused the Norman of shirking the battle. Bohemund stood ready to challenge St. Gilles to the field of honor, but Godfrey intervened. He pointed out that the soldiers and pilgrims had sacked the city before the knights entered, and it was they who had secured most of the treasures. Raymond and Bohemund were pacified, but Raymond stirred the argument again when he sought to spread his control.

"We have had a victory with God's help," he announced, "and we should dedicate this day and the city to Him. The bishop of Albara can consecrate it in the name of Our Lord."

"The good bishop is your vassal," said Bohemund pointedly. "You seek to rule here as well as in Antioch. If you want my consent, cede your towers and palace in Antioch to me."

All the old arguments flared again although some pleaded that the decision should be postponed—as had been done in Antioch—until the capture of Jerusalem, but Bohemund rebuffed them.

"It is my decision that this is not the time of the year to be traveling the roads. There is little food and less water. After Easter we can organize a true army without problems, and that is how I intend to concern myself. I will leave a garrison here, but I return to Antioch."

He stalked from the meeting. The council broke up.

The next morning the bishop of Albara preached a sermon, and he turned directly toward Raymond.

"Our people grow weary from disappointment. Wherefore shall we count our victories if we sit here instead of proceeding to Jerusalem? Let us fulfill our dreams. The Holy Sepulchre lies not too many more miles to the south. Shall we stand haltingly at the threshold, too contentious with each other, and not enter the Lord's domain. Lead us, dear sire, we beg of you."

People burst into tears and all eyes turned on Raymond. Knights rose to their feet and knelt before him, imploring him not to dishonor himself and them, but to lead them to the Lord's tomb. Did not Saint Andrew give him the Holy Lance for that very purpose? He had been chosen, and let him but rise and set his feet toward Jerusalem and all would follow.

Raymond sat with a torn heart. Prize after prize had been denied him. His lands in Provence were gone; his huge wealth was diminishing rapidly; he must provide a fiefdom for his young son and his beautiful Elvira, for he was growing old. He glanced at her, so young, so fair, so innocent. He saw the tears in her eyes.

Impulsively, he rose.

"My good comrades, give us but one month to rest and recover our strength, and then, I swear by the Lord, we will resume our march."

The Crossbearers cheered; it was finally settled.

There was a hasty scramble into the city for houses, and the wagons were unloaded and the loot was restored into new homes.

Guizio led the girls to Leo's villa. Leo stood by the gateway, a large grin on his face as he welcomed the hunchback in with an exaggerated bow. Later, Guizio growled at him.

"We don't have enough food in the larder for a month, and the money is running short. We'll have to forage."

Leo shrugged. "We'll find some." He was optimistic, but there was little in the city.

They rode for miles, Leo on horseback, Guizio driving a cart, but always discovered that others had been there before them and had left little gleanings.

Meanwhile, Leo spent much of his time hardening his muscles and practicing with the broadsword. He could swing it again, but he tired easily, and he was awkward, his left arm troubling him and throwing him off balance.

The limb was askew, he felt, but he was determined to overcome the handicap. It was difficult to bend and would not respond immediately to his will, and he felt crippled.

Guizio, watching him strain with the big sword, remarked, "Why don't you lighten the blade?"

Leo churned the idea over in his mind. Why not? Chagon would have known what to do. The giant blacksmith would have fashioned a sword which would have become part of Leo's arm. Perhaps he could find another smith who could help. He searched and found Raymond's armorer.

The man was busy but willing to listen to the problem. He scratched the back of his neck while he thought.

"You want a sword to do the work of a broadsword yet be light enough for you to handle easily? You take me in two directions. I could make it shorter—or longer, or thinner—but it would not be a broadsword when I'm done."

"Make it the same size, only thinner."

"How much weight?"

"Try, I will stay with you and we'll test as you work."

"Not for a fortnight at least. I have too much work."

"I will wait, but will you try?"

The man scratched his head again. He knew Leo had been Tancred's squire, and it was Leo who had helped Bohemund find the traitor in Antioch. He had little love for Bohemund's men, but looking at the squire's arm, his pleading face, his antipathy softened. After all, the man had not gone off with the Norman but had remained in Maara with Count Raymond. He nodded.

"I'll try. Maybe in a week; I'll let you know."

Leo had his sword in ten days, and he found he could do almost as much damage with it as with the big sword. Slowly the strength in his right arm increased and the control of the weapon became firm. Guizio, his practice partner, gave up one day.

"It's too dangerous," he protested, his chest heaving. "You could kill me by mistake."

"You, yes, but not a knight. It is not heavy enough."

"You expect to fight knights?"

Leo laughed. "You are right." He wiped his perspiration. "If it takes care of scimitars it will be enough."

Nightly, he dropped the bottom of the emerald cross from its nest and examined the small scratches under the crest.

"If I could find a Hebrew scribe I would know what the old man was saying to the count, his brother."

"Is it important for you to know?" asked Celeste. One day she added, "Guizio asked me to ask you to sell it. Our money is very low and food is high. There is little work. He thinks of butchering one of the horses, but the gold . . ."

"I swore on Jesus Christ to give it to Count Fienzo."

"What if you lost it? And Guizio found it?"

He stared at her. "Would you have me break my vow?"

She turned from his stare. "You men talk always about your vows and your honor. What of a woman's honor? I only know I must stay alive if the life within me is to be born."

He gasped at her in astonishment. "Celeste! No!"

She nodded, biting back the tears. "Yes, I'm sure."

"Whose? Whose is it?" He was whispering.

She faced him. "You want to know? If I told you it was yours would you believe me?" He did not answer. "I have been in bed with you more than any other man, so it must be yours."

"But . . . you don't . . . know . . ."

"No! I don't know! How can I? Can you say it is not yours?" She was bitter.

"Have you told Ruth? Guizio? They'll know what to do . . ." He was bewildered at the unexpected turn.

"I wasn't sure until last week . . . and I'm not going to let them do to me what they did to Inda. She almost died."

"But, Celeste, we'll be on the road; there will be fighting . . . tell Ruth . . ."

"Maybe we'll be in Jerusalem by that time. Other women have babies; this one is mine. I know how to make money and I will take care of it." She was fiercely defiant.

"Celeste . . ."

Sobbing, she ran from the room.

He found Guizio and Ruth in the garden. "Celeste is with child," he blurted out. "She just told me."

"Oh, no," said Ruth. She looked at Guizio.

"We'll have to get rid of it," he said. "We can't be loaded down with a baby again, not now."

"She wants to keep it."

"It's not for her to decide." Guizio was grim.

"She has already decided. I won't let you force her."

"Be reasonable, Leo." Ruth spoke quietly. "No one will force her; Nina and I will just talk to her. It will be all right."

Leo stared at her. He did not like what was happening and yet they were right; this was not the time. A thought struck him. This could be his son . . . no! They would not kill it; Celeste would have the baby, and he would marry her, if he remained alive after Jerusalem.

"Another thing, Leo," Guizio went on, "that cross . . ."

"I swore," Leo interrupted him, "and I keep my vows."

"We need the money. If we had it Celeste could keep the baby."

"I do not trade my vows. When I am dead you can have it."

"That may be quicker than you think."

"If so, it will be God's will." His eyes narrowed.

"Guizio only meant that there is little work," Ruth interjected quickly, breaking the tension which had suddenly flared between the two men. "If we had the money from the cross maybe Celeste would not have to work . . . and she could keep the baby."

Leo stopped. It was a thought! But his vow? He would be damned. He had sworn on the cross. Maybe . . . maybe they could cut some of the gold away? Maybe he could forage something? Maybe he could take Celeste back to Antioch, to Anne and Andre and Inda?

"I will think on it," was all he said aloud and left them.

That night Tafur's ribalds found something unusual in the guts of the cadaver they were cutting up to roast for their evening meal. Two gold pieces lay in the "King's" clawlike hand, and his eyes glittered in greed as he chortled in glee.

"Oho! So that's where they buried it! Tell no one. Tomorrow we will have a giant roasting."

His men labored all night, exhuming bodies of the buried Saracens while the women gathered wood for a large funeral pyre. They lit the fire at dawn, a large crowd gathering to see what was going on. It was afternoon before the fire had been quenched, and to save water the ribalds urinated on the embers, inviting the curious mob to participate. Then Tafur's men and women began to sift the ashes with great care.

The first finding—a gold coin—drew cries of astonishment, and with great screaming and pushing there was a rush to find more. Men and women groveled on their knees while the ribalds screamed and tried to fight them off. The disputes grew and blood was spilled, but there were too many for the ribalds, and muttering threats they withdrew.

Dead Saracens were eagerly sought and more gold was found. Many Crossbearers did not wait for the fire, but sliced open the rotting bodies and probed the entrails with anxious fingers, muttering prayers of hope as they worked. The desecrated corpses were thrown aside and left to rot until the stench became so unbearable that Raymond ordered the practice halted and the bodies burned. But it did not cease. It went on during the night by torchlight, and the bodies were exhumed for gold and to satisfy hunger.

The new year came and passed into January, and Raymond decided that the crusaders could not remain in Maara any longer. People were dying of starvation; many were returning to Antioch where ships were bringing supplies; many were deserting and marching off into Edessa, deeper into Syria. The situation was grave and the count was morose with worry.

One morning, when he arose, his agitation was great.

"I saw Adhemar last night," he told Elvira forlornly. "He railed and scolded me for delaying the journey to Jerusalem. I tried to explain but he would not listen." He stopped talking and shook his head. "He . . . he pointed his finger at me and said sternly, *'The Lord watches you carefully, Raymond, and your judgment hangs in the balance. I warn you as a friend, do not tarry! If you do, it will be your damnation!'* "

Elvira became agitated. "Adhemar was always a true friend and even in death his spirit remains faithful. You must prepare for the road to Jerusalem immediately."

"There are great problems, Elvira," he said despondently. "I have less than four hundred knights ready to fight, and there are only three thousand soldiers left. If Godfrey, Robert, and Tancred were to join me, we would have a respectable force, but they are not ready. If I march alone I will be leading our people to their doom."

"Or to their salvation. Adhemar would not be pushing you to your doom. He came to warn you. Place your faith in him and the Lord, and you will find a way. You must."

Raymond shook his head, his eyes staring off.

The next day, he called the Knights' Council, to be held at Chastel-Rouge on the fourth of January. The town was midway between Antioch and Maara and all the knights came, except Bohemund.

He told them of the starvation of the pilgrims, of the many desertions of the crusade, of the many who turned Moslem to allay their hunger, and, finally, of the possible failure of the entire crusade—its defeat and death. The Moslems, he warned, would rise against the starved and weakened host and murder them all. Extreme sacrifice was needed.

He stood ready to aid the knights. Ten thousand solidi—nine solidi to one piece of gold—to Godfrey and Robert of Normandy; six thousand to Robert of Flanders; five thousand to Tancred; and lesser amounts to others if they would march with him. His sacrifice would leave his treasury bare.

The great knights disapproved. Tancred considered it a bribe. "I am not for sale at any price," he remarked.

Godfrey, too, would not take the money. "It would make us liege to him," he told the others, and the others agreed with him.

Spurned, Raymond knew not where to turn, and the disputes were renewed with greater animosity than before.

Peter the Hermit, followed by Parenti, left the meeting in disgust. Peter had heard enough; nothing would come from the disputing lords; the Lord was calling upon him once more to show the erring knights the way.

Urged by Parenti, who knew well the Hermit's persuasive powers, the monk decided he would call on the people to carry out his previous threat. He soon had a crowd gathered about him on the street.

"I have just left the Knights' Council," he told them, "and the lords rage and tear at each other again. They fight for fiefdoms, not for Jesus. We, of the people, have been chosen by God to show them the true path to righteousness. If we do not, if we falter in the task God has given us, there will be quarrels each time we free a town from the bondage of the Infidel.''

The Crossbearers, despondent and bitter, crowded about him. Of all the crusaders, except for the great lords, he was the only leader they recognized. With Adhemar gone, Peter's voice was the true voice of God.

"Rise up from your beds on the morrow and arm yourselves with your pikes, your clubs, and your axes. We do not attack the Infidel; we attack his city! We will level his walls and burn his houses! Then there will be no city, no fiefdom, no need to garrison this place. We will leave only desolation.

"The disputes of the knights are caused by the hateful sin of greed. Destroy the city and you will destroy the greed! God Himself has revealed this to me and has ordered me to tell you. Go! Tomorrow we will break the chains that the Devil has used to bind our leaders. We will destroy his fetters of greed!''

"We will burn the city and destroy the walls!'' The message went out like a clarion call through the houses of the pilgrims. As Peter made his way through the streets, the words sizzled and hissed from mouth to mouth. This was God's answer to the Devil who had enslaved the knights by covering their eyes and diverting them from the path to the Holy Sepulchre. He had offered them the temptation of gold and slaves, and they had been blinded. The people would tear away the blindfold, and their leaders would once again see the Holy Flame.

At daybreak the pilgrims and soldiers rose from their pallets and beds of straw and, taking their tools, made their ways to the walls. They dug at the limed joints with their knives; they gouged the old limestone from seams and cracks and drove their axes as wedges into the grooves. The large top stones broke free easily and they were toppled over. Wooden framing was torn out and heaped for burning.

The women worked side by side with the sweating men, pouring water over their heads and shoulders. They fed them a weak gruel to sustain their energy. There was sliced meat in more than one pot, but no one asked from what animal it had been cut.

The bishop of Albara, being awakened by his deacons and told what was happening, hurried from place to place and pleaded with the men to desist. He threatened them with the Lord's vengeance, and the men bowed their heads, listened with respect, and left the walls, but as soon as he was gone they returned to their task.

Stone by stone, the great walls of Maara fell, were hauled from the base of the battlements by teams of oxen and horses, and were laid in the fields. There was a wild feeling of a cleansing elating the spirits of the toilers, and their weariness was stripped from their wasted bodies. They began to sing as they worked, first sporadically, then with a cadence and to the beat of their old marching song. The men swung the mallets, driving the axes deeply into the joints, and hammered the iron as though they were tearing down the walls of Hell. Each dropped stone became a victory for Jesus and they cheered as it fell, and they would attack the next one with renewed gusto. Behind them, the city was burning, and when they stopped to rest, their eyes reflected their own fires of joy.

Word reached the knights at the council meeting and they gasped in horror. It was unheard of. The offense for destroying anything belonging to a great knight was punishable by death, and Raymond hastened back to the burning city.

He stared at the ruined walls and the blazing houses. He stared at the haggard, scarecrow skeletons, who, in their rags, grinned up at him idiotically. They were watching him closely, for they knew well the punishment for the crime, and they pushed together, wiping their running sweat and dripping noses. They could read their death in Raymond's horrified, angry face, but suddenly he turned his horse and rode off. He gave no orders to his meinies, and they rode after him, mystified, not knowing his wishes.

Alone, with Elvira, he held his head. "God has judged me. He has turned my own people against me. There is nothing left. My dream was true; Adhemar was right."

"No, my husband, it is not yet done. Adhemar has given warning but there is still time. Do you not see? Maara was only an example, a trial but not a judgment. It was accursed and Adhemar has removed it. He is showing you there is no need to remain here."

"You see truth more clearly than I, my sweet wife." He gazed at her with love and wonder. "You are an angel, sent to help and guide me."

He called his knights together. Gone were the fears and despair; gone were the schemes and the deviousness; there was only one way, and he saw it with the clarity of a rebirth.

His decision was simple, he told them. He was taking the road to Jerusalem. He did not know if they wished to follow him, and he freed them from their vows to him if they did not, but he would dally no longer. To a man, his knights knelt before him and swore that he was their liege lord, and where he led they would follow, unto the death.

Heralds were sent to the soldiers and pilgrims: Within the week, by the thirteenth, the latest, Count Raymond was moving on to Jerusalem. Those who wished to join him were welcome.

Not all of the city's houses had been burned, but when the Crossbearers marched out all the standing houses were kindled, for Maara was to be completely sacrificed to the Lord. Peter had spoken the truth; he had created a wasteland.

When Tancred heard what was happening he quickly volunteered to join Raymond. Tired of all the arguing and seeking action, he told his knights, "We sit here and rot, and our vows become undone. I am tired of it. We swore to free the Holy Sepulchre; let us do it."

His fifty-five knights agreed with him and they told Raymond.

At sunup, the thirteenth of January, Raymond, barefoot and dressed in a pilgrim's garb as befitted the leader of a pilgrimage to the Holy Lands, walked the road to Jerusalem. He had sworn he would approach the Holy City on his knees. Behind him came his riding knights, and behind them his soldiers. Following were the long line of Crossbearers, their carts and wagons, but most were walking, carrying their few belongings on their backs. Their clothes were threadbare; many had rags tied to their feet; many were barefoot.

There was a singing, a lilting refrain of many joyful voices:

"LORD JESUS, WE ARE COMING . . .
THE INFIDEL WILL WEEP . . ."

53

It was three weeks before Godfrey and Robert of Flanders followed Raymond, but they elected to take the coastal route instead of marching after Raymond to the mountains.

Raymond found the Arab and Syrian villages halcyon, avid for peace, and eager to please him. The exploits of the invading Christians had grown more ferocious in the retelling, and the Arab chieftains anxiously feted the knights, provided food for the Crossbearers and pilgrims, gave everyone presents, and urged them on.

The land was pleasant; the breezes were cool; and from the blossoming orchards came the fragrance of the fruit trees. The animals wallowed in the lush meadows and shaded themselves in the sweet-smelling cedars and pines. The crimson-red sunsets filled the skies with glowing splendors.

Raymond moved out of the valleys, and the hills began to stand up, stretching themselves into soaring heights. The count heeded the advice of the shepherds whose flocks roamed the slopes and turned toward the coast to follow the sea. The paths through the mountains, he was told, were narrow and the ravines steep.

He moved along the sea line and marched at a leisurely pace. The land was fertile and quiet; the fishing villages were prosperous; the farms were productive; and the people were amiable and cheerful.

Ahead were the cities of Sidon, Tyre, and Tripoli, and envoys came to greet the crusaders, offering presents of fine cloths, horses, and gold as tribute. Timidly, they told the count that they wished to serve him, that they only wanted peace. They were willing to bow their heads, and if their presents were not enough, they would bring more. They were only traders, they insisted, not warriors, and they had no desires to engage in any conflict.

Raymond was impressed by their wealth and toyed with the idea of establishing a fiefdom, but he would have to leave knights and soldiers to garrison the cities. He had word that the Egyptian sultans had strengthened their forces in the Jerusalem countryside, and he worried that he would become too weak if he left any of his men behind. Still, the temptation was great and he weakened.

Tripoli was a port town, almost impossible to seize by siege, for food and reinforcements could be brought in by water. But Arkah, a beautiful little city not too far inland, controlled what came into Tripoli and what caravans could leave. Arkah, with its flowering gardens and busy artisan shops, would make a savory prize, and Raymond began to burn with a passion to become its overlord.

The reluctant Provencals hammered at Arkah's walls for almost two weeks with little success before Raymond realized that his dream was fading. Many of his knights and soldiers died in the futile attacks, and the Arab chieftains brought the "invincible" crusaders presents of lesser value and finally stopped altogether.

Leo, in his eagerness to prove his worth, had been in the forefront of many of the assaults but had escaped injury. His sword had proven itself to be an effective weapon. One day, Guizio presented him with a suit of armor and a war horse.

"Do not ask where I found this," he told the gaping squire, "but it should fit. The man was your size. You pine to play the knight; this should give you your chance."

"I will pay you back."

Guizio dismissed the promise with a wave of his hand. "No need. I but ask that your sword be ready to defend Ruth and the others in the time of battle."

"It shall be done; I will repay in full."

"Then the talk of returning to Antioch is finished?"

"Finished, if we understand each other that the child Celeste carries, my child, remains with her."

"So be it. We will find a different way."

It was one thing to acquire a knight's accoutrements and another to be knighted, and Leo sought an audience with Raymond. Much to his surprise the count knew of him.

"You served Lord Tancred and Lord Bohemund." It was a statement of accusation.

"Yes," said Leo, "but now I fight with you. Many squires have moved from knight to knight."

Raymond nodded. It had happened with many, he knew. "I have heard you use the broadsword well and are adept with throwing knives. Your arm?" He stared at Leo's left side. "Does it not impede you?"

"Not against the scimitar. I can demonstrate if you wish."

"But against the broadsword?"

"I do not intend to fight Christians."

Raymond nodded his approval. "A good answer." He studied Leo impassively. "I have no need for a squire at present; perhaps . . . later . . ." He would watch Leo, who had served with Bohemund and who had worked secretly with the traitor in Antioch. "Remain close."

"I request a boon, sire."

"What is it?"

"May I ride with my chain-mail the next time the Moslem attacks?"

"You may not!" came the quick retort. "You ride as a knight after you have been knighted, not before!"

"Yes, sire." Leo bowed his head. His sword and new armor, he swore to himself, would find him a place, or he would die.

The walls of Arkah would not yield, and a stalemate developed as Raymond did not have enough men to close all the gates. News traveled to Godfrey, marching along the coast, that Raymond was under attack, and he hastened to the rescue only to find the count lounging at his well-furnished, full-stocked pavilion.

Raymond immediately offered to share the spoils of the city and to feed and reclothe the hungry and impoverished crusaders if Godfrey and Robert would help him take the stubborn town.

The lords spurned him, saying that they would rest a while, but they intended to march on. Jerusalem was waiting.

Tancred, disgusted as the fighting grew desultory, announced that he would leave with Godfrey, and many of the pilgrims and soldiers were beginning to desert Raymond.

Guizio came to Leo. "We have decided to move to Godfrey's camp. You will come with us? Maybe you will have better luck with Godfrey."

Celeste had a thought. "Leo! Lord Godfrey knew my father well, and he knows me. If I went to him and asked . . ."

Leo's face was reddening and he was becoming angry. "I need no woman to plead for me to a lord," he stormed. "I want no favors—that way."

Celeste gasped at his implication. "I did not mean it *that way!*" she retorted. Then she giggled. "I don't think Lord Godfrey has been with a woman for years—nor a man either," she added as Guizio raised his eyebrows. "He is celibate. My mother used to say that he never recovered from his attack on the Lateran when he drove old Pope Gregory out of Rome."

"What happened?" asked Leo.

"Godfrey . . . he wasn't a duke then . . . rode his horse right into the pope's house and killed many of the fighting monks around the old man. Since then he has been praying for absolution. Father said he came on the crusade to cleanse his soul and do penance."

"I still don't want you to talk to him. I'll find my own way."

She became angry. "You know, Leo Cannelli, for an innkeeper's son you carry too much pride. If we were back home my father would have had you whipped for refusing an offer of mine."

"We are a long way from home," said Guizio, "but, Leo, what can it hurt?" He winked. "A little oil smooths things out."

"If swords were handed to men of valor easily you would have had yours a long time ago," said Celeste. "You have fought hard and well, and many squires who have done much less are walking about already armored. Your way is difficult without a sponsor." She spoke with an air of conviction and determination.

He knew she was right, but Mary . . . she had gone to the lords . . . now Celeste . . . she had gone to many beds, too. He drove it out of his mind with anger.

"No! It will be done my way! I will not have a woman beg for me!"

"Men!" she snorted and turned away. "Go! Try!"

She did not obey him and made her way to Godfrey's pavilion. The duke's page was reluctant to bother his knight, but she convinced him to carry her name to the duke, and he was surprised at his master's reaction.

"Celeste? Show her in immediately!"

The boy ran.

Godfrey came forward to meet her, his hands extended. "Little Celeste! I would have hardly known you! You have become a woman, and a pretty one, too. How long has it been? How is Anne? Is she here with you?" He laughed. "I ask a thousand questions."

Celeste laughed with him. "Anne preferred to remain in Antioch, but I came on. I had enough of Antioch."

He sobered. "It is understandable. Since the death of your father . . . and mother . . ." He stopped, seeing her wince. "Forgive me my rudeness." His voice softened. "My sincere regrets. Somehow I lost track of you during those miraculous days." He changed the topic. "You must be married to come with me to Jerusalem. How was it you didn't invite me? One of my knights . . . or Raymond's?"

"I am not married but I seek a boon."

"Ask anything. If it is in my power, you will have it. If not married, then . . . what?" He glanced shrewdly at her. "For whom?"

"He was squire to Sir Tancred, then to Lord Bohemund . . ."

"And he is here? Now? How is it I did not know?"

"He was hurt at Antioch. After that, we left with Count Raymond."

"I see. How can I help?"

"He wishes to see you, to request . . . can you take him on as a squire? His arm . . . he was hurt . . . it is . . . bent."

"Bent? He cannot swing the broadsword anymore?"

"It is difficult, but he had a special sword made, and he practices all the time. He fought daily here at Arkah, and fought well, and he is determined to become a knight."

"Without the broadsword?" He shook his head. "Which arm?"

"The left. He uses only one hand with his sword. I beg you, try him. He can do many things."

He studied her. "All right . . . for you, and in remembrance of your loyal father . . . and mother. Tell him to come and see me."

"But, sire, he is not to know I spoke with you."

He nodded. "I understand. If you chose to do this, Celeste, he must be worthy. What is his name?"

"Leo Cannelli, from Genoa."

"Cannelli? Cannelli . . . I have heard the name before. He is not of royal blood . . . he . . . wasn't he the squire of Bohemund, who found the traitor?''

"Yes, sire." Her head was bowed.

"And you would consort with one like that? What would your mother have said?"

"It is more important, my lord, what you will say."

He stared at her momentarily. "I will keep my promise."

Leo's meeting with Godfrey was short. He was admitted to the duke's presence as soon as the page heard his name, but the knight made him wait. Finally he called Leo to him.

"You are Leo Cannelli? Squire to Lord Bohemund; the one who helped find the traitor of Antioch?"

"Yes, sire." Leo kept his head high. "I am surprised that you have heard of me."

"We had heard that you died in the battle with Kerbogha. The surprise is that you live."

"The Lord was kind to me. I recovered from my wounds."

"I see . . . Your left arm is bent. Hm-m." He turned. "What seek you of me?"

"I hope to be a squire again. I am healed."

"With a bent arm? How do you expect to wield the sword?"

"There are many ways to fight, sire. Watch!"

Standing against a pole was a Saracen's wooden shield. With a quick movement of his hand Leo sent a knife flashing to its center. His left hand passed the other knife into his throwing hand, and the second knife vibrated against the first's hilt.

The movements were faster than the trained eye of the knight, and Godfrey was visibly impressed. "You did that very well. But when the knives are gone, what then?"

Leo drew his sword. "This is not as heavy as the broadsword, sire, but with it I can outfight any weapon—small sword, lance, or pike—and I am nimble enough to evade the mace." Once again he used Guizio's words. "I do not expect to fight knights. My vows were to help free the Holy Sepulchre from the Infidel, and with this sword I have no problems against the scimitar."

Godfrey pursed his lips. "You make sense . . . and have courage," he said slowly. "I have a place for one such as you, but if you expect to move to knighthood, there may be difficulties. Objections will rise for one who cannot use the broadsword, but, if you act in good faith, I will see what can be done."

Leo's eyes lit up in hope. It was more than he would ever believed could happen. "I shall not fail you, sire. Unto the death."

"We shall see." Godfrey's thoughts seemed to wander. "There will be . . . much . . . and then there is Jerusalem. We will all need to be received in the Body of God . . . and in a state of Grace.'' He waved Leo away. ''See me tomorrow at noon.''

Leo was elated when he told Celeste what had occurred. She nodded happily and said a silent prayer for the duke. ''Lord,'' she prayed, ''whatever it is that troubles Lord Godfrey's soul, let it be expiated for this kindness.'' Leo had been saved.

Still, Godfrey and Robert waited for Raymond at Arkah and the pilgrims grew weary and impatient. Many loaded their ox carts and wagons and took to the road, and the stream from the camps became a steady flow. Soon, soldiers and then knights joined them, saying, ''If the lords refuse to move we will go on alone, without them.''

The exodus increased, and finally Godfrey and Robert decided they had waited long enough and struck their pavilions. Raymond bitterly forgot his dream and ordered his knights to prepare to move after the other knights.

Eight weeks had been wasted. The Provencals caught up to the host at Beirut. Tancred and his knights were leading the way and Raymond fell in on the rear. The count was despondent, feeling the pangs of conscience and sure that he was being punished by the Lord for the sin of Greed.

They marched ever south, past the pine forests of Beirut, the ruins of the old Roman citadel of Sidon, and on until they saw the dark walls of Tyre looming in the blazing sunlight.

Each day followed the next; each sunset saw the shadows lengthen. To the east, the gray mountains turned black, their dark ravines becoming foreboding slashes of midnight, while their cliffs and spurs shone like the outstretched talons of the falcon diving into the sun.

The roads grew rougher, the terrain becoming desolate with stray carobs, and stunted, wild tamarack trees dotted the dreary landscape. There had been no rain and the earth was a hard rind, with sharp ridges and a shriveled skin.

Onward they marched, ever southward, the carts and wains rumbled through the passes of the hills, and the water grew short. The pools had disappeared, and men and animals licked their parched lips as they plodded the dusty dry coast of Galilee. They contoured the bay at Acre and walked the dried river bed which finally led them into the fertile plains of Sharon. There they turned inward, toward the cities of Ramle and Lydda.

The ancient people of Samaria, the natives of Lydda, greeted them as liberators—the Moslem overlords having fled—and lavished food upon them. They showed the crusaders where the deep, underground cisterns of cool water lay, and the Crossbearers settled in to rest and recuperate.

They were eighteen miles from Jerusalem.

Messengers arrived to tell them that the Moslems had fled the port of Jaffa, and Godfrey sent a contingent of ten knights and two hundred soldiers to garrison the city.

In Jaffa, Leo found a Hebrew scribe who could read the shaft of the emerald cross. The bearded man in the long black cloak and small skullcap pressed the gold close to his nose, squinting at the scratches. Haltingly, he began to read:

"My dear brother: I will be dead when you receive this. The bearer should be Leo Cannelli, the son I told you I had sired in my wayward youth with the girl Maria of the inn."

"NO!" shouted Leo. "That is wrong; you have read it wrong! Do it again!"

The old man raised his head. "I do not make up words. I only read what it says here."

"But you read it wrong," insisted Leo. "I am the bearer—that is right— but I am not his son. You read it wrong."

The man squinted closely at the metal and shook his head. "I read what it says," he repeated. "The bearer should be Leo Cannelli, the son I told you I had sired in my wayward youth with the girl Maria of the inn."

Leo stood in shock, his mouth open, his eyes wide.

The old man gazed at him sadly. "You did not know?"

Leo shook his head. "No . . ." A fever surged through him. "He can't be!" His voice faltered. "He can't . . ."

"Should I read on?"

Leo nodded in his bewilderment.

"I beg you treat him as your own, for he is one of our blood, and he fights for Our Lord. When he gives you this cross I trust you will also make full provision for him, as you vowed before I left on my pilgrimage.

"Pray for my soul, beloved brother, and forgive the pain I have visited upon you. I suffer much for my sins. Your weeping brother, Eurde."

The old man lifted his head and sighed. "That is the end." He extended the gold shaft, and Leo closed his fist about it as though he was in a dream.

"My son," the Hebrew said gently, "it would be best to think deeply before you do anything rash. The Lord has His Own purposes and this news has its own worth."

Numb, Leo nodded and stumbled out of the house into the bright sunlight. His head swam. He was the bastard son of the House of Fienzo! Papa was not his papa! Poor Mama . . . did Papa know?

Suddenly he remembered all the jokes of the sailors about his size. Even Skora had poked fun at Papa.

He brought the news back to Guizio, seeking advice, and the hunchback guffawed in delight. "So your blood is royal!" he crowed. He bowed, mockingly. "Yes, sire; anything you wish, sire." He turned to Little John. "Bow, Johnny, bow! You are before a lord!"

"Then you can be a knight right away," exclaimed the boy. "Can I be your page?"

Leo stared at Guizio. "He speaks truth. What could hold me back now?"

Guizio sobered. "You are not in Genoa. We stand a few miles from Jerusalem, and the Egyptian infidels guard the walls. Many things can happen before you reach home with that cross."

Gravely, Leo nodded in agreement. "I have to tell Celeste."

Celeste found her knees weak in surprise and she stared wide-eyed in disbelief.

"Are you sure the Hebrew read it correctly? It's unbelievable."

"That's what I said and I had him read it again. He said the words were written. I am his son . . . nephew to Count Fienzo." The enormity struck him again and he threw up his hands. "It's impossible!"

"It could be possible. Many sons are sired by lords who . . ."

"Then you're saying that my mama . . ." He stopped.

"Women do not have the same choices as men." Her voice was dry. "A girl at an inn . . ." She shrugged.

"If you saw my mama you'd know it couldn't happen."

"It happens to any young girl. Is the count rich?"

He nodded. "Very rich. He even owns ships."

"When we get back to Genoa maybe he could help me. My father may have left some lands with the Church for safekeeping."

"When . . . we . . . get back to . . . Genoa?" He stared at her. "Yes! Why not? We'll be married—today! Now! If anything happens to me you can take the cross to Genoa, to Count Fienzo, and tell him I died fighting for Jerusalem. Tell him my soul watches over you . . . and my son, my son who carries Fienzo blood."

She embraced him passionately. "You will not die! You cannot! Not now! God will watch over you for me!"

He held her tightly. "We are all, even the Infidel, in His Hands." He kissed her gently.

The host moved onward, to Emmaus, and the knights met in council. Envoys from the town of Bethlehem came to them.

"Sires," pleaded their spokesman, "we are from the Church of Our Lord's Nativity. Free us, we beg of you, from the Infidel. Send us your knights and he will flee in terror, and the Light of Our Lord will shine on you forever."

Tancred jumped to his feet. "Who rides with me to Our Lord's birthplace?"

A hundred young knights were on their feet, shouting their eagerness and within a few hours they were armed and riding.

They found no Moslems, only Christians dancing in the streets and shouting hosannas—the Infidel had fled. Tancred set his gonfalon over the church. Later, he climbed a hill a few miles out of the town and looked toward Jerusalem. He was standing on the Mount of Olives and below him was the Church of the Blessed Mary in the Garden of Gethsemane. Off, across the gorge, in the distance was part of the great wall built by King Solomon, and within the wall—at long last—he saw Jerusalem. He fell upon his knees, his head bowed, and he prayed.

"I thank Thee, Lord, for bringing me safely to the Holy City, and I swear unto Thee that my right arm shall not fail Thee when it carries the Sword of Retribution to Thine enemies."

Jerusalem, the Holy. The city was protected by the earth itself; the deep ravines lay at the feet of its great fortress walls on the east, the south and the west. The city was approachable only from one small corner on the southwest, where the walls cut across Mount Zion, and from the north.

Jerusalem. Here, the aged Jews wept beside their ancestral temple wall, remembering the ancient kings of Israel, the enthroned splendor of David and Solomon, and their own degradation. Here the churches of Constantine lay in ruins along with the praetorium of Pilate; and the mosques of Islam rose over the crumbled palaces.

Jerusalem, the old. It was the glory of the faith of millions; it was the fountainhead of Belief! Calvary was here; and also the Grotto of the Holy Sepulchre.

The host toiled its way up the last hill and by noon the Crossbearers were camped on the summit. A mosque squatted there over the burial place of Samuel the Prophet, and below was the city, with its domes and cupolas, its flat-topped houses, and its round-roofed bazaars. The crusaders, seized with an ecstasy, their eyes swimming with tears, prayed. They baptized the hill, calling it the Hill of Joy, and they were transfixed as they beheld, at last, the final haven of their long journey.

Called by the Moslems Al-Kuds, the Holy One, Jerusalem was ruled by Iftikhar ad-Daulah. The Fatimid commander had sworn he would never surrender the Holy One to the Christian dogs in beggars' clothes who wept on their knees outside the walls. The Holy Koran said: "Praise be to Allah who brought His Servant at night from the Holy Mosque to the Remote Mosque, the precincts of which we have blessed." He believed firmly that the Prophet had been miraculously transported from the mosque at Mecca to the mosque in Jerusalem, and then He had ascended to Heaven.

He sent his soldiers through the countryside, rounding up the flocks of geese and chickens, the herds of horses, asses, and camels, the sheep, and the cattle, and had them all driven behind the walls. All the watering places were poisoned, and the wells were filled with rock and stone and dirt. Only the great pool of Siloam was left untouched, for the waters flowed into the city through the caverns cut through the rock by the Romans.

The Christians were all driven out, to eliminate traitors, and their property was confiscated. Bags of hay and cotton were stacked against the towers, and the forges glowed day and night, fashioning spears and arrowheads. Oil and pitch were collected, to be heated and poured on the heads of the wall-climbers. The large, underground cisterns, built by the Romans, were filled to the brims.

The spirits of the Egyptian army were high, and Iftikhar was well pleased with his preparations. He knew that there were no more than a thousand fighting knights with ten thousand soldiers, and he was full of confidence.

It was the seventh day of June when he beheld the host which had come from the west. He watched them from the battlements as they moved in procession along the road and made camp. Many were barefoot; many approached on their knees; thousands carried large wooden crosses; and they were singing, chanting, wailing, weeping . . . moving in a slow dirge toward the forward walls, and groveling in the dust.

A silent blanket of awe fell over the strange sight. Then the massed Christians lifted their voices in a chanting song;

> *"O JERUSALEM! WE HAVE COME TO THEE!*
> *O BLESSED MOTHER MARY; O RADIANT SON;*
> *TURN US NOT AWAY; FOR WE ARE THINE;*
> *WE GIVE THEE THANKS; WE GIVE THEE THANKS.*

> *"WE HUNGERED FOR THEE THROUGH THE MOUNTAINS;*
> *AND YOU GAVE US FOOD;*
> *AND WHEN THE HEATED DESERT BURNED OUR TONGUES*
> *YOU SENT THE BLESSED WATERS.*

> *"BEHOLD OUR TEARS OF JOY! O JERUSALEM!*
> *WE SING TO THEE; AND TO THE FATHER;*
> *AND TO THE SON, JESUS THE CHRIST,*
> *OUR HEARTS FLOW OVER;*
> *O JERUSALEM. "*

54

The hot, summer sun seared the earth, and there was little shade to temper its blinding glare. The passion which had erupted when the host had arrived at the Holy City ran its course in four days, and while the pilgrims settled into their camps in a state of euphoria, the knights met to plan the siege.

Only the north wall was accessible for an attack, and Robert of Normandy set his camp at its east end, at the Gate of Flowers. Godfrey camped next to him, opposite the Gate of the Column; and Robert of Flanders, joined by Tancred, pitched his tents on the west end. The knights were strung all along the wall, closing the road to Damascus and the port of Jaffa.

Raymond turned the corner to the south wall, but he found the ravine in front of him too steep to be able to mount an offensive, and he moved to Mount Zion where the approach was slightly easier.

The crusaders found that the Egyptians had stripped the towns bare and all the waters had been poisoned. The nearest supplies were twenty miles away. Skins of animals were sewn hastily, many of the hides still containing bits of raw meat and hair, and the water which was hauled in them became contaminated. Animals and men became sick.

Raiding parties of Turks and Egyptians attacked the heavily laden water caravans of camels and oxen, slicing the leather bags, and hooting their derision as the precious liquid turned the road dust to mud. It was an impossible task to haul enough water to take care of the thousands of people and the animals.

The Knights' Council planned and argued. One day they took a pilgrimage to the Mount of Olives, and an old Anchorite reproached them severely for delaying the attack on the infidels. He brushed aside their excuses.

"Are ye men of so little faith that ye have no trust in the Lord? If you fight for God He will provide the victory."

Godfrey felt shamed and vowed to attack the next day despite the lack of scaling ladders, catapults, and siege towers. Not to be outdone, the two Roberts agreed to join the duke while Raymond, hesitantly, nodded.

Late into the night ladders from twisted, scrub olive trees and small tamarack shrubs were constructed. In the gray of the dawn, after a short Mass, the Crossbearers shouldered their axes and lances and waited for the horns. At the blasting sounds, with the zeal of the righteous, they ran to the attack.

The outer defense wall was low, and the mounted knights broke through it easily. Elated, they drove the Moslems back, inflicting heavy casualties, and they soon raised a victory shout. The Moslems retreated to the city gates and managed to close them in the faces of the oncoming knights. Those infidels unfortunate enough to be left outside were slaughtered by the oncoming, cheering Crossbearers.

All squires had been ordered to remain on foot with the soldiers, and Leo was in the forefront of the first charging line. The squires were to be the first to climb the ladders, and if any were successful in gaining the summit their trained swords could clear an area for the others.

Leo bent over as he ran toward the wall. The arrows and stones fell all about him. Around him were the ladder carriers, shouting exuberantly. Quickly, the ladders went up and he mounted nimbly, but the ladder rungs collapsed under his feet, tumbling him upon the man below, and both of them on the others who waited. It was the same everywhere; the climbers becoming entangled in the broken wood and one another's limbs.

Again and again the men tried to climb as the crusader bowmen unleashed barrages of arrows against the walls' defenders, but each time they had to retreat. Many died under the stones, the hot pitch, the Greek fire, and the arrows of the Moslems. Finally, the horns sounded retreat, and, sullenly, the Crossbearers picked up their wounded and retired to their camps.

The dregs of defeat were bitter, and a dark torment of pain hung over the camps. Many complained that they had failed the Lord, becoming contrite and contentious with their neighbors.

The scarcity of water made everyone irritable, and the parched herds of oxen and cattle surged and lowed constantly in their thirst. In a raid on a farm Tafur had found a large wooden tun, capable of holding many gallons of water, and after mounting it on a strong wagon, he drove it to Bethlehem. There he was able to fill it, and he brought the precious liquid back to Jerusalem, portioning it out for two coppers a cupful. Quarrels erupted, but when Godfrey saw the tun he ordered twenty more built and praised the ribald for his ingenuity.

The crusaders were cheered when a fleet of four English and two Genoese ships entered Jaffa harbor with cargoes of food, rope, nails, and other supplies which could be used to build siege weapons. The knights dispatched two columns of men to help the sailors unload and to protect the supplies on the road to Jerusalem.

Leo rode with ten knights and twenty soldiers from Godfrey's camp while about two miles ahead of them were Count Raymond's contingent: sixty knights and forty soldiers. As Leo's group turned about a hillock, a large raiding party of Turks suddenly attacked.

Greatly outnumbered, the knights formed a tight circle and sent Leo in haste down the road to bring back the other crusaders.

Leo dug his spurs into the flanks of his horse and streaked away. He caught up to the others quickly, and in short order the knights turned and were galloping back. Reaching the battle area, they lowered their lances and charged, shouting their battle cry, "God Wills It!"

The Turks were caught completely by surprise as they were totally unaware that there were other knights about, and they broke into a confused retreat. Unwittingly, they moved directly into the path of the oncoming knights who, because of the narrowness of the road, were attacking in rotation. Their scimitars could not parry the long lances nor deflect the broadswords' swinging weight, and they scattered, seeking safety.

Leo plunged into the fray with the first charge and made short shrift of the Turk who rode against him. His sword slashed the infidel across the face and throat before the astonished man could bring his raised weapon down, and the Moslem rolled from his horse with a shriek. Not waiting, Leo was already seeking another victim.

Nearby, two Turks were dueling with a knight on horse, and Leo, using his sword as a lance, thrust it through the back of one just as he rose in his stirrups to swing his scimitar. William of Sabron, one of Raymond's knights, cut the other Turk down and raised his gauntleted hand in salute, recognizing the squire's aid. He would not forget.

The Turks had had enough. Goading their horses, they scattered pell-mell into the fields and the hills. Many escaped as the knights would not chase them but stayed to finish off the wounded infidels. The soldiers collected all the dropped weapons and corralled the free-running horses of the dead Moslems.

Singing, they moved on to Jaffa only to discover, to their dismay, that an Egyptian fleet was standing off of the harbor, blockading it effectively. Night was falling. In council with the captains, they worked desperately in the darkness unloading the cargoes, and when the Moslems took the ships the next morning they found nothing but empty hulls.

It was a wild, drunken party of knights, soldiers, and sailors who staggered back to the crusader camps, singing hymns as they led strings of loaded captured horses carrying the cargoes.

William of Sabron reported Leo's help in glowing terms to Godfrey and thanked the squire publicly for his aid. Godfrey was pleased.

"You have done well, Squire Leo," he beamed, "and you shall be rewarded. Raymond's knights have high regard for you. When we conquer Jerusalem, and if the Lord allows us to live, I will grant you your sword."

The knight's last objections to knighting Leo had disappeared when Celeste had told him that Leo was the bastard nephew of Count Fienzo of Genoa. "Noble blood," he had told her, "is easy to reward."

Bursting with the news of Godfrey's promise, Leo ran to Celeste.

"I have his word," he bubbled with excitement. "And this time it will happen—after we take Jerusalem. I'm sure of it!"

Arguments in the Knights' Council persisted, and even Tancred was chastised for raising his banner over the Church of the Lord's Nativity in Bethlehem. Some viewed it as a declaration that he was the overlord of Christ's birthplace, and Tancred, in a towering rage, strode out of the meeting and sulked for days.

A faction pressed for an immediate election of a king of Jerusalem but the priests objected violently. No man, they said, should rule where Christ was crowned with thorns. Some, who had washed themselves in the waters of the Jordan River, announced that they had cleansed themselves of their sins and were returning home, leaving for Jaffa to await the arrival of ships. Most of the crusaders, however, pushed for the capture of the Holy City.

Spokesmen for the carpenters announced that it would be impossible to build siege towers and catapults unless they received better wood. The native Christians said there was no suitable wood closer than the forests of Samaria, thirty miles away, and the land was in the hands of the Moslems. Robert of Flanders, joined by Tancred, volunteered to go and protect the axemen, and a large contingent sallied from the camps to collect the timbers.

Slowly the wood traveled on specially built wagons to the camps and the siege towers grew. The hot simoom, laden with dust and sand, blew from the southeast for three days, and the men and animals blistered, burned, and died, but the catapults and mangonels were built. Stones were heaped and ropes, twisted from fibers and soft reeds found near the Jordan, were woven. There was little rest, for the Crossbearers had received word that a large Egyptian army was being assembled and was expected to reach Jerusalem within the month. Morale began to sink, for few believed the machines could be finished on time. Desertions increased and many wagons traveled the road to Jaffa, seeking ships.

Suddenly, the rumor of a new vision raced through the toiling men. A priest insisted that he had been visited by the spirit of Bishop Adhemar; Adhemar the Kind; Adhemar the Just . . . so he was remembered; and now, in the hour of their greatest need, he had come back to help them.

The priest said, "He spoke thusly to me: 'The Princes argue who shall be the king of Jerusalem, but that does not favor the Lord. This is the time for fasting and prayer. If the wearers of the Cross forgo food for three days and then walk three times around the city's walls in their bare feet, in true repentance, then in nine days the walls will fall and God's Children will enter the Holy Ground.' "

Godfrey immediately declared it to be a day of awakening. "It is now July three," he announced. "We will fast for three days, until July six, and we will have our March of Repentance."

At noon, three days later, the astonished Moslems witnessed the strange spectacle. It began with the blaring of trumpets—first thought by the Moslems to be the signal for an assault—then from the camps came the procession. White-vested priests, carrying huge, wooden crosses, approached the walls. Behind them, in their bare feet, in pilgrims' garb, came the knights, the squires, the soldiers, the pilgrims, and the procession ended with the women and children. They were all weeping and chanting a *te Deum laudamus*.

The Moslems laughed and hooted at them, tossing dirt and filth on their heads as they passed close to the wall, and mocked and aped the weeping Christians in derision. A few scantily dressed women appeared on the summits and began a lewd dance, offering themselves by calls and enticing gestures to the priests and knights. Their ridicule followed the procession.

As the crusaders passed each gate, the trumpets would raise an unholy din, seeking to emulate the horns of Joshua at Jericho. But the battlements of Jerusalem stood firm.

A barrage of stones and arrows struck the walkers on their third circuit. The ranks broke but regrouped at the calls from the knights. The wounded and dead were picked up by their neighbors. The vision had commanded three times around, and the appeals to the Lord rose higher as the deaths multiplied.

At the completion of the third round by the priests, the stones from the catapults were descending like the shattered remnants of a mountain slide. Crusaders lay where they fell.

Parenti, struck in the chest, felt his ribcage collapse, and a stream of blood choked him. Numbed, he crossed his arms over his crushed body to prepare for death. The blood frothed his lips as he repeated the words of the last rites. He felt strangely secure and well; his soul would be in Heaven. His glazing eyes were fixed on a bulk above him. The numbness was spreading and he felt afloat.

"Your spirit shall sing in Heaven." The words were far away. Was he being moved? . . . Pushed? . . . Dragged? . . . A weight fell across him. Someone called his name . . . it didn't matter . . .

His eyes focused momentarily. The bulk above him had arrows protruding from it . . . many arrows. It moved . . . talked. The shafts wavered in the light. Recognition came suddenly. It was that monk . . . Francis.

Brother Francis had his eyes closed, fighting his pain. Four arrows had pierced his chest, almost simultaneously, and he was having difficulty breathing. He had seen Parenti fall—struck by a stone—and he had hurried over to provide the last sacrament. The arrows had struck him like giant fists, twisting him around, and he had fallen alongside Parenti.

The eyes of the two monks met briefly in recognition.

"Go-od bye, bro-th . . ." Francis murmured and his eyes became fixed in death.

Parenti choked as he tried to say something. Suddenly his body tensed as all his muscles began to move at once. "Go-o-o . . ." he managed before there was a sudden relaxation, emptying his bowels, and the light whirled and darkened. He was dead.

The procession wound up the Mount of Olives, leaving their dead strung behind them. Peter the Hermit preached for the last time, and with their trials and repentance finished, the crusaders returned to the walls, to pick up their wounded and dead. The Moslems watched them silently, withholding their arrows and stones.

The next day the Crossbearers were back at work on the siege castles. Bishop Adhemar had said nine days after the procession, and not a day was to be wasted.

The towers were three stories high. The first story was a ceiling to cover those who labored at the wheels, pushing the tower into place. At Maara, the men who did this were unprotected and many had died. The ceiling, and a leather hanging, stretched as a curtain around the outside perimeter of the structure, would be their shield.

The second floor, where the fighting knights would stand, was slightly higher than the summit of the wall. A drawbridge screened the attackers from the stones and arrows of the defenders, and its height gave the knights a slight advantage.

A catapult and a pile of stones were placed on the top level. Archers would fire at the Moslems from that height, and it was hoped that their arrows would clear a place for the knights to stand once they stood successfully on the walls.

Everyone worked. The women sewed ox and camel hides; children dragged timbers to carpenters, who bored holes for bolts, and the children then dragged the wood to those who were assembling the machinery. Men worked on scaling ladders, and the excitement and intensity mounted each day.

By July ten, the towers were ready and Godfrey ordered his tower moved to face the north wall. Raymond set his castle across the ravine of Mount Zion, facing the southwest corner. The chasm in front of the tower had to be filled before the machine could approach the battlements, and everyone from the camps brought stones and dirt to the ditch. Arrows and burning faggots, wrapped in chains, were fired at them by the defenders and decimated the ranks.

On the afternoon of July thirteen, the tower rolled slowly toward the battlements. Raymond's attack was to be a feint to draw the Moslems away from the other side where Godfrey's castle faced the wall but remained immobile.

The Moslem bombardment began immediately. Arrows with flaming pitch-rags struck the wooden timbers, and sparks fell like volcanic ash; flaming wood, soaked in tow and with long nails protruding from them, embedded themselves into the beams; huge stones pounded against the structure, rocking it despite its huge bulk; and pots of Greek fire threw flames over its face. A great haze of dust and smoke arose and enveloped the castle, swirling around it like venegeful thunder clouds.

By darkness Raymond's horns signaled that his siege tower was in place.

The Egyptian governor, believing that Raymond would attack the next morning, took personal command of the defense of the wall in the count's sector. All night the Moslems labored to build the wall higher to prevent access from the drawbridge, and all night the crusaders labored to repair the much-damaged tower.

The sunrise rose red on the fourteenth of July, and Raymond's horns sounded to signal the Provencal attack on Jerusalem.

The crusader catapults bombarded the newly built addition on the walls, and, as Iftikhar did not have the time to provide stone, the wooden framework collapsed quickly. The drawbridge creaked as the whining ropes lowered it atop the burning, splintered wood. With a shout—"*Toulouse!*"—the knights charged.

The horns of St. Gilles were singing, and soon the oliphants of Godfrey were answering, announcing that he had begun his assault on the north wall.

Leo, barely suppressing his excitement, stood close to Godfrey. He kept repeating Godfrey's promise, "If we live this day, and if the Lord gives us the victory, I shall present you with your sword."

The drawbridge bounced on the stone summit of the battlement and the knights surged forward. "*God Wills It!*" burst from every throat, soon echoed by the shrill ululation of triumph rising from the Moslems, "*Allâh il allâhu!*"

The two forces clashed in the center of the bridge. Godfrey decapitated an infidel and turned, his eyes rising toward the Mount of Olives. His face blanched. He beheld a spectre, a figure in a white flowing sheet stained with a red cross, holding a flying gonfalon with a red cross on a white field, riding slowly down the hill.

"*DEIU LO VULT!*" he shouted. "*SAINT GEORGE IS HERE! ON HIS WHITE STALLION! THE SAINTS FIGHT FOR US! ADJURAT DEUS— GOD JUDGES!*"

A great cheer went up from the crusader knights and they surged forward, swinging their great swords. Godfrey became a machine of death to all who approached, screaming his new battle cry, "*ADJURAT DEUS!*"

Leo fought like a demon possessed, all caution thrown aside, and he found his sword was more effective at close quarters than his broadsword had been. No scimitar could withstand it, and he slew two Saracens in quick order. He pushed the bodies from the bridge and slipped on the blood. An infidel reared over him only to be sliced almost in half by a knight.

Gaining his balance, Leo ran his sword through the back of another Moslem. His eyes glaring, his sword red, he stood in a half-crouch, seeking another victim while all about him steel clashed on steel and men shouted themselves hoarse. He leapt forward, an unearthly scream rising from below his chest.

The battle see-sawed for hours, the knights moving forward, only to be pressed back as new Moslems charged. The crusaders were tiring, but the Moslems were able to bring up fresh fighters constantly, and Godfrey realized that they could capture the siege castle. He muttered a prayer and sprang forward, calling on his men to follow. They grouped around him and moved in a wave.

Leo passed his sword to his left hand and drew a knife. He felt that this might be the last charge, and his daggers might as well do their just bit before he died. A savage face with a toothy snarl behind a beard caught his eye and he hurled his knife. The Moslem never knew what happened; his scream died into a gurgle in his throat, and his knees buckled under him. Leo drew his other knife, and his frantic eyes sought another victim.

One was not far and Leo's hand flickered. Once again, the knife was buried to its hilt in a man's throat, and the Moslem died quickly. Leo passed his sword back to his right hand just as a scimitar flashed. He twisted his body sharply and jabbed viciously at the Turk. The man screamed as the sword entered his chest and Leo pulled it back.

Crusaders, led by Eustace from the third level of the tower, were reinforcing the knights, and the Moslems were slowly retreating. Suddenly an exultant shout was heard, like an echo above the din: "*WE HAVE IT! ADJURAT DEUS! WE HAVE IT!*"

Two knights, standing back to back, their broadswords whirling like windmills in a hurricane, had cleared an area on the summit and were calling on the others to join them.

With a shout, Godfrey exploded and began hacking his way toward the two. Behind and around him, screaming, came a handful of his knights. The Moslems paused before the sudden eruption of these swords of death and retreated. Eustace shouted to his brother and led another charge to join him. The crusader knights spread themselves along the top of the wall, clearing a broad area while their calls became cries of triumph.

The impatient crusader soldiers, under the protection of their wood and leather shields, were milling about the wall, and they decided they had waited long enough. Picking up the shouts coming from the summits they began clambering their scaling ladders, adding their call for victory. Moslems ran to repulse them, but more and more knights were moving along the summits, and the screams of the Crossbearers were the shrieks of the tempest. The horns of Lorraine began to blast the thunderous message, and they were soon joined by Tancred's oliphants, and then those of the two Roberts; for the knights had used scaling ladders, and their joyous horns meant they were on the summits with the others. The entire north wall was under the swords of the crusaders.

Tancred had waited at the Gate of St. Stephen, and when the Moslems of that sector had run to aid their comrades under attack by Godfrey's knights, Tancred ordered his men to climb. The crusaders met with little resistance, and they captured their section quickly. Robert of Normandy and Robert of Flanders then ordered their attacks, and they, too, had no great difficulties with the thinning lines of the infidels.

The main body of soldiers, almost ten thousand strong, still clamored outside the gates. Stones and arrows still fell among them; Greek fire seared them; hot pitch and oil blistered them; but the blood-lust burned within them, and they were screaming for the gates be be opened.

The siege castle was aflame, and smoke cloaked the fighters on the drawbridge and the wall. The Moslem mangonels were crushing the men waiting below, and the crusader knights began to waver under the concentrated attack of new Moslem forces.

"THE GATE!" Godfrey shouted to those standing beside him. "GET TO THE GATE!"

Leo heard him and swung off the wall fighting his way through the mass of men struggling there. He was soon in the clear street, racing toward the

Gate of the Column. A knight, one of Tancred's, was running beside him, on the same mission.

They found three infidels on guard at the Gate, and the knight leapt forward and decapitated one before the Moslems knew whom they faced. Leo cut the other through the chest and whirled to face the third, but the knight was there before him. Leo opened the Gate.

The screaming Crossbearers, brandishing their pikes and axes, poured through the opening and into the streets of Jerusalem.

The horns of Tancred were calling his knights to assembly, and he led them through the streets in pursuit of the faltering Moslems. The infidels rushed to the Noble Sanctuary, the octagonal-domed Kubbet es Sakha, built over the sacred rock: the Mosque of Omar.

Four and a half centuries earlier the Arab Omar, who called himself *"Khalifah, Vicar of the Apostle of God,"* had knelt in front of the Church of Constantine, refusing to allow his soldiers to enter and kill the Christians who had fled there for sanctuary.

The Moslems believed that sanctuary would be granted again and surrendered their weapons, pleading for their lives. Tancred herded them and raised his gonfalon over the mosque as a signal to all that they were under his protection.

The Soldiers of the Cross were in the streets, pushing the ever-retreating Moslems toward Raymond's sector. Iftikhar, the Fatimid, was still struggling there with St. Gilles, denying the Provencals access to the walls, but, as the struggle in the street reached his rear, he retreated with his men to the massive Tower of David next to the Jaffa Gate. Bleakly, he realized that the Christians had entered the city and had won the victory, and he offered to surrender to Raymond if he and his bodyguard would be allowed to leave in safety.

Raymond agreed, and the grim-faced Egyptians rode out of the Jaffa Gate. They were the only Moslems to escape the wrath of the crusaders.

With the Jaffa Gate opened, the Provencals, who were fuming in their impatience, poured into the city screaming *"Toulouse!"* They joined forces with the Rhinelanders and the men of Lorraine and they all went mad.

Spreading out in every direction, they sought the Moslem everywhere and everyone—man, woman, and child—went under their swords. They ignored Tancred's banner and invaded the Sanctuary, and they hacked and decapitated the defenseless Moslems as they knelt in prayer.

Raging on, they entered the houses, disemboweling the screaming women, cutting up the wailing children, and stabbing and chopping at the aged and sick in their beds. They chased the fleeing to cellars and roofs and dispatched them on the spot, hurling the dismembered bodies off the rooftops to the streets below.

The raping of every female began early: the aged, the young, even the child. Their broken and dismembered corpses were hurled down stairways, bloodying the white walls, staining the carpets, and smearing the bedsheets with their excrement and blood as each was disemboweled after the act.

The pilgrims entered the city, and the Crossbearer search for gold and precious stones became intense. Tafur led his ribalds from house to house, slaughtering every Moslem they found in their path, ripping the furniture apart in their searchings and lust for the yellow metal. Old men and women stood resignedly before them, their lips murmuring their prayers as the "King" screamed at them to reveal their hiding places of their jewels. Parents watched with welling eyes as their daughters and sons were raped, mutilated, and hacked to pieces. The breasts of the older females were cut off; the penises and testicles of the males were chopped free; noses and ears were sliced from faces. At the end came the turn of the aged parents.

Blood ran in foaming streams in the gutters and puddled around the piles of corpses growing in the streets. By the tens of thousands the Moslems were being slaughtered.

Hundreds of the infidels had gathered in the Temple of Solomon seeking sanctuary, but the knights who rode their destriers through the gates moved into the portico and began a methodical killing. Their broadswords cut through the massed bodies, and the blood and filth ran in rivulets along the polished marble floor, making it slippery for the axemen who had followed the knights. They hacked the bodies until their arms ached and they could no longer raise their weapons. The blood was deep enough to lap against the fetlocks of the horses who trod gingerly upon the human flesh.

It was the Hour of Retribution! It was the Hour of Death to the Infidel! It was the Hour of Expiation of all Sins! It was the Hour of Avengement for all the hunger!. . . all the thirst! . . . all the suffering! . . . all the death! . . . to liberate the Holy Sepulchre!

The skies were deep red in the sunset, and the ruby, sanguine orb flushed the clouds with its bloody rays, staining them the same scarlet as the city streets below. The white walls of the buildings glowed pink, and the earth was disgorging a crimson hue.

Blood sun in Jerusalem! Blood sun of garnet, cardinal, and rouge! The city was afloat on a sea of blood, and the dying sunset turned gray as the mantle of darkness slowly folded itself over the ghastly streets. Bonfires were lighted and they threw their yellowish-red flames into the dark places, reflecting grisly sights. Bodies were burned, and mutilated human parts were heaped near the fires and tossed idly into the flames.

It was nine days—as the vision had foretold—July fifteen.

Guizio, followed closely by Pietro and Little John, had found a beautiful villa whose interior had not been damaged too much by the plunderers, and Pietro went back into the streets seeking food. The men stayed awake all night, guarding the house, for they knew that although the killing for the day was finished, during the night, and all day tomorrow, the pillaging would go on.

Celeste lay in a soft bed, trembling in a half-sleep, waking frequently by nightmarish dreams. She had been praying all during the fighting that Leo still lived, but no word about him had come, and she had gone to bed fighting the intuition that he was dead.

55

The dawn was heated on Saturday, July sixteen, and the rising sun washed the whitish clouds in crimson-gold. The crusaders were awake early, hunting through the streets and houses, down every alley and yardway. The excitement of yesterday had turned into a gruesome determination to finish the task begun the day before, and they inflicted new carnage on the stricken survivors. Every house was carefully searched for hidden rooms, and the cellars' foundation walls were tapped for concealed hiding places.

A heavy pall of smoke and the acrid odor of burned flesh hung in the heated air, for no wind had come.

In the early afternoon Godfrey led a procession of his knights, all washed and combed, all dressed in clean, white mantles, through the bloody, dirty streets. They had laid aside all the accoutrements of war and were on their way to the Holy Sepulchre. Behind the knights came a cortege of soldiers, weeping for joy, and they were followed by a mass of pilgrims wailing their thanksgivings and pleas for forgiveness.

It was the Sabbath and the Jews of the city had gathered in terror in their main synagogue to pray, and they huddled in the building in the hope of safety. Their low chanting, sounding like the buzzing of bees, could be heard through the closed doors and Godfrey stopped to listen.

"Burn it!" came his crisp command, and he moved on.

The soldiers ran to obey. Bundles of pieces of wood were tied together to make faggots; the windows were broken and burning torches were thrown inside. Arrows were wrapped in oily rags and fired through the smashed windows.

The chanting stopped momentarily, then increased in its intensity. *"Sha'ma Yisroel . . . Hear, O Israel, the Lord is God; the Lord is One!"*

The screaming and jeering crusaders fired more and more fire arrows into the building, and the smoke of the blaze billowed. The entire interior was aglow, red-yellow-orange—the flames flickered like snake tongues through the broken windows. The chanting changed, growing somber.

"Yit-ga-dal v'yit ka-dash she-me-re-ba . . . magnified and sanctified, O my God." The prayer for the dead rose above the roar of the fire and the crackle of the wood.

The soldiers waited, their weapons gripped in their hands, ready to kill anyone who would try to escape but no one came out.

Godfrey and his knights proceeded to the Holy Sepulchre, carefully skirting the heaps of corpses still lying in the streets. They entered the church grotto on their knees and began their ritual of purification, kneeling at the Tomb of the Lord with tears and groans, pleading for Divine Mercy and the expiation of their sins. They repeated their early vows: to liberate the Holy Sepulchre from the hands of the Infidel; to wreak vengeance on the Infidel for their destruction of churches and Holy Places; to punish the Moslem for all the sufferings they had inflicted on True Believers; and to glorify the Christ and the Church of God. Purged and dry-eyed, they returned to the villas and palaces they had appropriated as their own and celebrated their victory.

Godfrey kept his promise to Leo. While the Crossbearers were still rampaging through the streets in their private celebrations, the knight decided that Leo should have his ceremony of knighthood on the day Jerusalem was taken. He searched out Celeste and had her brought to the grand garden of the palace he had seized. Much of the ritual was to be eliminated.

Leo advanced toward the seated duke, his sword hanging from his neck, and the knight's chaplain stepped forward and removed the weapon, blessed it, and rehung it.

"Do you solemnly swear to fulfill all the duties of a knight?" asked Godfrey sternly.

"Yes, my liege."

"For what purpose do you seek to enter the order? If it is to become wealthy, to take your ease, to be held in honor without doing honor, you are unworthy, and you shall be deemed dishonorable."

"I have no such intentions, sire. I seek to do only acts of mercy, to help all who need my help, to bring honor to my name and upon the Order, and, in the Name of Our Lord, to protect the Mother Church and obey its will."

"Then let those who bear witness, and vouchsafe for you, bring forth their vestments."

The first knight to step forward was William of Sabron. Others followed. They undressed the squire and reclothed him in knightly array. A cuirass of leather was drawn over his body, hanging to the thighs; over this was buckled a hauberk, a coat of long chain-mail which did not fit too well, for there had been no time to make one for him; and he was given armlets, a pair of gauntlets, and gold spurs.

"And you swear further . . . " prompted Godfrey.

"I swear I will always speak the truth; that I will protect the poor and see to it that they have bread; that I will seek and love peace wherever it is in my province; that I will pursue the Infidel to his death or mine."

"What is owing to thy liege lord?"

"To my liege lord I owe my arms, my life, and all that I own. I will follow where he leads without doubt, without asking reason, without fear, or selfish purpose. I owe him loyalty more binding than that of home, or parent, or wife, or child, and I shall guard him, and the chastity of his women, with my life."

"And to the Order?"

"I shall be a brother in arms; I shall not be contentious; I shall seek only courtesy and give aid wherever it is needed. I shall honor, respect, and be a guardian of their women and seek only their welfare."

Godfrey rose from his chair and removed the sword hanging from Leo's neck. Leo kneeled. The duke gave Leo three blows on his shoulder with the flat of the sword.

"I now give you the last affront you may receive without redress," said the duke, and he slapped Leo across the cheek. "Hereafter, he who affronts you, or affronts any other knight of the Order, must be under your sword."

Leo bowed his head in acknowledgment and rose.

"Then in the name of God, Saint Michael, and Saint George, I make you knight. Here is your sword. Make it your honor and keeper of your vows."

Leo took the sword in both hands and kneeled. "My liege, I am your man, and by this heart and hand I swear I shall give both in your honor and safety from this day forward to my death. I shall be thy champion in right or in wrong, without judgment, so long as I shall live with God's good grace." He rose and buckled on the sword.

Godfrey clapped his hands and a knight stepped forward and handed Leo a lance. Another presented him with a helmet, and a third led in a destrier, one of Godfrey's own.

"These, I give to you, Sir Leo of Genoa, and it is my advice that you seek a villa befitting of your station."

Leo nodded. He adjusted the helmet to his head, leapt into the saddle, and with a wave to Godfrey and the assemblage, he rode out of the pleasant garden into the bloody streets.

The days which followed were filled with feverish activities. Duke Godfrey ordered the clearing of the dead from the city, and over the next few days the corpses were hauled outside the Gates and burned. Makeshift hospitals were organized for the wounded crusaders, and committees were formed to oversee the collection of food.

Leo commanded a small contingent of soldiers engaged in the burnings, and he became sick at heart as he viewed the carnage.

"Lord," he asked himself in a whisper, "were all these dead necessary? Was this the only way?"

He had attended the Knights' Council, the first held in the captured city, and he had voted to elect Duke Godfrey Defender of the Holy Sepulchre and Baron of Jerusalem; the council decided that a kingship of Jerusalem was not appropriate.

The other great knights—Count Raymond, Robert of Flanders, Robert of Normandy, and Lord Tancred—had left the Holy City to seek fiefs elsewhere and Jerusalem was almost completely deserted. Many of the soldiers and pilgrims, having fulfilled their vows, had gone to Jaffa to await the ships from the west, complaining that the stench of the burnings lingered in their nostrils and made them ill.

Lord Godfrey had insisted that Leo's and Celeste's wedding was to be held in his palace and that he would serve as Celeste's surrogate father. All the knights remaining in the city were invited, and it had been a gala celebration, with food and wines collected from many of the surrounding cities. He had given the bride and groom permission to return to Genoa, for Leo had to deliver the emerald cross to Count Fienzo and establish his bloodline.

Celeste slowly became aware that Leo was brooding.

"What troubles you, Leo?"

"I have been thinking. Do you really want to live in Jerusalem, instead of home where we belong?"

"We have no home, Leo," she said sadly. "Wherever we are together, there is our home. Lord Godfrey expects us to live here."

"I know." He was quiet. "But I was thinking. Do you remember Sir Walter, the knight who gave me my first training?"

"Yes, you told me."

"He vowed never to fight again, but he took up his sword to kill the Infidel and fight for God. But the Infidel says that he, too, fights for God."

"But that is only the Devil talking."

"Are we sure? *'Tahwil!'* they call out: 'There is no power save God's!' And *'Tacbir!* God is Great; there is none beside Him!' Can those be words of the Devil?"

"The Devil will say anything and do anything to confuse the True Believer. You know that."

"That is true. I met an old man once who said, 'Christ is only an Eon, a worker for God, just like any other worker. The Devil rules this world and man does His will so everything we do is the work of the Devil.' The old man asked me to bury him when he died, but Brother Parenti wouldn't let me. Parenti said that he served Jesus Christ but the old man called him a Papist." He turned toward her. "Oh, Celeste! There are windmills in my head. I keep thinking of all the dead—the Moslems, the Christians, even the Jews. The knights say we killed so many infidels that Hell must be full."

"The killing is finished," she soothed him. "Jerusalem now belongs to us and we will live here in peace."

"No . . ." he shook his head. "There will never be peace as long as we keep on killing the infidel. They will fight to win back their homes and their mosques." He sighed. "They will kill us just as we kill them, and the killing will go on and on."

"Our Lord will not allow that to happen. You brood too much."

"Skora said, 'All men fight for God.' I have killed Moslems who shouted 'God is Great!' just as I was shouting 'God Wills It!' And we fought to kill each other. Is that what God wants?"

"But you fought for Jesus Christ; the others do not!"

"Christ, my mother told me, was good and kind. I cannot believe anymore that He wants us to kill other men in His Name." He turned to face her. "I will not kill anymore. Here we take the home of an infidel . . . "—his hand motioned through the room—"and we will go on fighting to keep it. There is no need to fight for God. He is All-Powerful and has no need of our puny strength. We need to live in peace. That is what Walter said, what Skora said, and what Christ said. I will kill no more."

"Men will not live in peace if they are not of the same blood."

"We covet what is not ours; we have the sin of Greed. God made us all and we can foil the Devil if we are just."

"Leo, you talk as if you would enter the church and preach a Mass." She attemped to be lighthearted. "Let us talk of what we are going to do. Pietro says a ship's captain has agreed to take us to Genoa."

He was quiet for a moment, deep in thought. Finally, he lifted his head. "I know. He has told me."

"Duke Godfrey sent us another wedding present—a paper that will grant me all of my father's lands that have not been sold or given directly to the church."

"Were there any such lands?"

"I don't know. Father had large holdings; so did Mother from her family, and there may be something. Of course, if Anne comes home she will have most of it. "

He took her hand. "To live as . . . you should . . . we will need lands, and that may mean fighting again. I am the son of an innkeeper . . . "

"No! You are a knight, Sir Leo of Genoa. Never forget that!"

He shook his head. "If we stay here in Jerusalem I am Sir Leo, but if we go back to Genoa . . . Will you be ready?"

She stiffened. "My mother did not want to come to Jerusalem but she went where her husband led. So, she trained me to do. In the Holy Lands I became . . . a . . . " She could not bear to say the words. "In Genoa I will be a lady and you will be a knight."

He kissed her. "I don't know what I would do without you."

They sailed on the morning tide in a ship crowded with pilgrims and soldiers: crusaders turning westward. That night Leo slept peacefully, but far away, in Rome, Pope Urban lay upon his sickbed, a fever raging through his wracked body.

He had been bled by his Greek doctor, but the man had left his patient's room shaking his head, his lips compressed into a tight line, and the only answer he would give to the cardinal-bishops who crowded around him was, "It is all now in God's Hands."

Urban did not know that Jerusalem had fallen to the Christians and that his crusade had been victorious. He was not aware that the Khalif of Cairo had declared a *jihad*, a Holy War, and that an Egyptian army was marching across the sands of Jifar, rousing the Syrian and Arab clansmen, and the remnants of the Turkish forces, to meet at Ascalon where an Egyptian fleet would supply them with all the needs for the *jihad*.

Toward morning Urban was in delirium, his mind roaming freely through the events of his life in fragmented and scattered dreams. As the life forces of his body sank lower, his mind glowed, opening into an unending vista, and he saw himself as a spectator watching the Lord's final passion and agony at Calvary.

There was a dripping of blood from Christ's wound, a dripping which, to his horror, became an outpouring . . . a streamlet, and larger . . . a runnel. It waved itself as it puddled on the ground, becoming larger and larger pools, which merged . . . becoming a stream, becoming a river! . . . a raging torrent!

There was debris—broken houses—burning . . . collapsing . . . crashing into a sea of blood! And there were bodies . . . with crosses on their chests . . . swarthy, bearded Moslems . . . corpses of men! women! children! There was a writhing and tearing of muscles and limbs as they were sweeping past him . . . and unheard screaming . . . reaching for him! begging him! crying at him! . . . as they drowned in the red, raging flood!

A guttural, half-strangled cry fought its way from his chest and he struggled to rise, but firm hands restrained him, pressing him backward, irresistibly backward. He tried to protest, to cry out, but his mouth would not work; his lips would not form the words. A prayer began to form in his consciousness.

Holy Father; God in Heaven! What do I see? Thy Son bleeds for all mankind, but why does His Blood act like the wrathful waters? Is it my punishment that I see this? Have I been that great a sinner?

A great cry was torn from his bowels. Forgive me, O Father! Forgive me! I am but a man and I carry my sins on my back like any other gibboned human! Forgive me . . . I pray Thee!

A great light blossomed in his mind and he understood a message. "I bleed for all; and all bleed for me! My blood is the blood of all my sons!" The light exploded into a glaring sun.

A flood of sea-blood was spreading over the land . . . engulfing whole villages—smashing houses, drowning herds of animals . . . staining everything deep crimson—the land, the trees, the stones . . . reaching into the skies with clawing fingers and clutching at the pink-eyed clouds . . . reaching upward to the sun! . . . and raking it with its talons until the sun dripped blood! . . .

The blood was reaching for him! . . . rising over his feet . . . over his knees . . . his waist! his chest! . . . touching his neck!

His mind screamed! *DEAR GOD! DROWN ME NOT IN THY BLOOD!* He sobbed, the words gurgling from his throat.

A bishop standing near nudged his neighbor. "What did he say? He must be speaking to God and we must catch every word."

There was a roaring fire-wind and timbers were crashing from seated joints

. . . there was a booming of the red surging seas against fortress walls . . . there was the ululating wail of children; a screaming of women; a moaning of men . . . and a great roll of thunder shook the world, deafening him . . .

The clouds were burning, and the heavens were encased in a global flame where lightning flashed constantly, blinding him . . .

His body writhed against the restraints.

"He is listening to the list of his sins," said a bishop wisely. "It is the final agony, how we all fail the Lord."

"Is he gone? I did not hear his last words."

"He still lives," said the doctor, "but it will not be long."

He was standing in the Divine Presence, and before him stood three shadows . . .

"*ODO*," came a ponderous voice, "*YOU STAND BEFORE THE THRONE TO WITNESS WHAT YOU HAVE WROUGHT. PLEADING FOR YOU ARE MOSES, THE GIVER OF THE LAW; CHRIST, THE GIVER OF MERCY; AND MOHAMMED, THE GIVER OF LIGHT. WATCH!*"

There was a haze, a wiggling of shadows, a formless waving of wraiths, thin as silk blowing in that wind of light . . . out of the diaphanous mist came the measured tread of thousands of pounding feet . . . people marching past him in array . . . the old, the young, the weak, the strong, the sick, the crippled . . . all marching to a measured cadence . . . their clothes were ripped and shredded, their flesh mangled and torn . . . and from the red, raw ulcers of their wounds flowed their life's blood . . . they passed in thousands to the steady rhythm of the rolling drums . . .

There were knights on destriers, driving people before them with lances, while behind them were priests declaiming the gospels . . . there were emirs on resplendent horses, herding dark Moslems before them, followed by mullahs expounding on the Koran . . . then, all in unison, they began to repeat the laws of Moses while hundreds of Jews, their clothes and beards aflame, their hands clutching burning scrolls, repeated the Talmud.

The chanting rose higher and higher, reaching a keening cry, mixing with a dull thunder rolling through the infinities . . .

"Enough, O Lord, enough," Urban whispered.

"*WATCH AND UNDERSTAND! THIS YOU SHOULD KNOW! THESE ARE ALL MY CHILDREN! I AM THE FATHER OF ALL, AND ALL ARE MINE!*"

"All are . . . mi-ne . . . Father . . . to . . . all . . . " Urban repeated aloud. "All my child . . . ren . . . "

"Did you hear? He calls to his flock even in death! He is magnificent and we shall never forget him!" The bishop was ecstatic.

"All . . . my . . . " The wasted frame of the pope gave a convulsive shudder and sagged into the bed. Urban was dead.

* * *

The sun was an emerging, glaring eye on the horizon as Duke Godfrey, Count Raymond, the two Roberts, and Tancred, with a thousand other knights and eight thousand crusader soldiers, fought the combined armies of the Egyptians and Arabs on the plains of Ascalon and vanquished them. The crusaders returned to Jerusalem in triumph, conquerors and rulers of the Holy City.

Leo stirred sleepily on his pallet and turned toward Celeste, his hand sliding over her raised hip and on about her rounded belly. She moved contentedly against him, and they lay curled together in their warmth and happiness. The ship moved silently through the pinkish-blue waters of the sea, toward Genoa, home.

It was the fifteenth of August, in the year of Our Lord, 1099.